Praise for *FIRE*

"[An] entertaining novel ... loyalties that defy cruelty, ...

—*Publishers Weekly*

"There's a lot to enjoy here. Donati keeps the plot moving at a terrific pace.... Her characters compel the reader's attention.... Donati's strong women characters are the heart of her books."

—*Seattle Times*

"Consuming... *Fire Along the Sky*... centers on Hannah's healing and the ways that women come to grips with the tragedies and triumphs of life, a universal theme that will appeal to 21st-century readers."

—*Romantic Times*

"Readers will enjoy... Donati's mix of historical fiction and romance."

—*Booklist*

Praise for *LAKE IN THE CLOUDS*

"As good as it gets... Donati writes eloquently about frontier life."

—*Tampa Tribune*

"If you enjoy historical romances like Diana Gabaldon's Outlander series, you'll love this."

—*Daily American*

"A sweeping, highly enjoyable historical adventure–love story."

—*Booklist*

Praise for

DAWN ON A DISTANT SHORE

"The likable protagonists, a multitude of amusing secondary characters and exciting escapades make this a compelling read."
—*Publishers Weekly*

"Donati's skillfully told and captivating romantic historical saga brings a tumultuous era and dashing characters to life in what promises to be a very popular and rewarding series."
—*Booklist*

"Sara Donati writes a story of epic proportions, akin to those wonderful wilderness classics by James Fenimore Cooper, but with the modern twist of a Diana Gabaldon."
—*Romantic Times*

By Sara Donati

INTO THE WILDERNESS

DAWN ON A DISTANT SHORE

LAKE IN THE CLOUDS

FIRE ALONG THE SKY

QUEEN OF SWORDS

THE ENDLESS FOREST

QUEEN
OF SWORDS

Sara Donati

BANTAM BOOKS

QUEEN OF SWORDS
A Bantam Book

PUBLISHING HISTORY
Bantam hardcover edition published November 2006
Bantam mass market edition / October 2007

Published by
Bantam Dell
A Division of Random House, Inc.
New York, New York

This is a work of fiction. Names, characters, places, and incidents either
are the product of the author's imagination or are used fictitiously.
Any resemblance to actual persons, living or dead, events,
or locales is entirely coincidental.

Cover illustration © 2006 Kazuhiko Sano
Frontmatter map by Laura Hartman Maestro

Library of Congress Catalog Card Number: 2006042995

Bantam Books and the rooster colophon are registered trademarks
of Random House, Inc.

ISBN 978-0-553-58278-9

Printed in the United States of America
Published simultaneously in Canada

www.bantamdell.com

OPM   20   19   18   17   16   15   14   13

Dedicated to
the good people of New Orleans

Queen of Swords

REINA DE ESPADAS

New Orle

Bassin

Congo Square

Father Petits Chapel

Rue de Rampart

Philippe

Charity Hospital

Baronne

Rue Carondelet

Rue St. Charles

Rue Camp

Rue Magasins

Rue de la Levee

Conti

St. Louis

Dauphine

St. Peter

St. Ann

Orleans

Rue

Dauphine

Bienville

Rue

Rue

Savard's Kine-Pox Clinic

Redbone Clinic

Jackson's Headquarters

Pitot

Livingston

Rue

Girot House

The Cabildo

Cathedral

Presbytere

Suckling Calf Tavern

Place d'Armes

Douane (customs)

Market

Mississippi

Bayou St. John

Lake Pontchartrain

Old Portage Road

New Orleans

Canal Carondelet

Illustrated by Laura Hartman Maestro ©2006

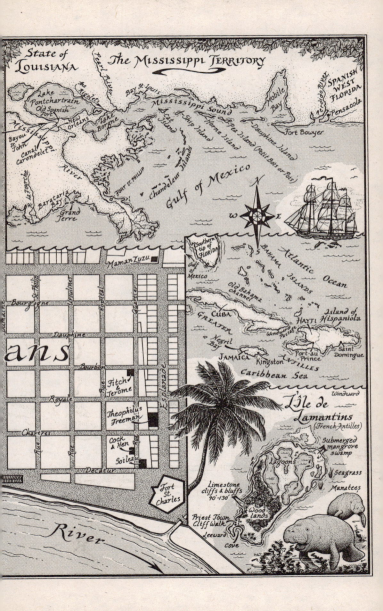

Primary Characters

The Bonners and their associates at sea

Hannah Bonner, also known as Hannah Scott, or called Walks-Ahead by the Mohawk, her mother's people, or Walking-Woman by the Seneca, her late husband's. Daughter of Nathaniel Bonner. A trained physician and surgeon

Lady Jennet Scott Huntar, originally of Carryck, Annandale, Scotland

Luke Scott, also called Luke Bonner, a merchant of Montreal, son of an early alliance between Nathaniel Bonner and Giselle Somerville

Major Christian Pelham Wyndham of the King's Rangers, of Quebec, on detached duty to Hispaniola and environs

The crew of the *Patience*

Piero Bardi, pirate, privateer out of Barataria Bay

L'Île de Lamantins (Manatee Island)

Anselme Dégre, criminal at large, based at Priest's Town on L'Île de Lamantins, French Antilles. Also known as Father Adam O'Neill Moore, an Irish privateer and defrocked priest

At Port-au-Prince, Saint-Domingue (Hayti)

Giselle Somerville Lacoeur and her husband, Gerard Lacoeur, merchant, D'Evereux Plantation

In Louisiana and Western Florida

The Savards and their associates

Paul de Guise Savard dit Saint-d'Uzet. Son of Jean-Baptiste Savard dit Saint-d'Uzet, a merchant and plantation owner, and his first wife, Catherine Trudeau

Julia Simon Livingston Savard, his wife, originally of Manhattan

Henry, aged 7, their son

Rachel Livingston, Julia's daughter by her first marriage, age 16

Jean-Benoît Savard, also called Ben, also called Waking-Bear by the Choctaw. Son of Jean-Baptiste Savard and Amélie Savard, FWC

Clémentine, FWC, housekeeper for the Savards

Maman Zuzu, FWC, Clémentine's mother, and a voudou mambo

Maman Antoinette, FWC, Zuzu's mother

Leo, FMC, young Choctaw who works for the Savards

Père Tomaso Delgado, a local priest and lifelong friend of Ben Savard

The Poiterins and their associates

Honoré Poiterin, son of Archange and Pauline Poiterin, both deceased; an adventurer and slave runner

Agnès Poiterin, a widow and Honoré's grandmother, of a wealthy banking family based in New Orleans and Pensacola

Mama Dounie, Honoré's childhood nurse

Jacinthe, a slave in the Poiterin household

Père Petit, Madame Poiterin's favored priest

Madame Noelle Soileau, an associate of Honoré's

The Livingstons

Edward Livingston, a lawyer, formerly of New York City, and his wife, Louisa D'Avezac Moreau Livingston, originally of the Sugar Islands

The Prestons

Andrew Preston, merchant, of Pensacola and New Orleans

Titine, FWC, his housekeeper, originally of New Orleans. Daughter of Archange Poiterin, a rich merchant, and Valerie Maurepas, FWC

Eugenie Preston, his elderly widowed sister-in-law, resident on the Bayou St. John outside New Orleans. Her servants Amazilie, FWC, and Tibère, FMC

The American military and militia

Andrew Jackson and his aides

Jean Lafitte and his men

Captain Pierre Juzan

Captain Aloysius Urquhart of the U.S. Army, liaison between the armed forces and the New Orleans Guard

General Villeré, New Orleans Creole and the commander of the first division of Louisiana militia

Major Gabriel Villeré, his son

QUEEN OF SWORDS

PROLOGUE

Queen of Swords: A woman possessed of keen logic and intuition. Forthright is she in manner, and well-armed.

QUEEN OF SWORDS

March 1814

In the mornings she went walking while the men slept. First away from the settlement and along the cliffs that looked over the cove, then down the rough stairs carved into stone. She moved slowly, one hand spread on the rock face like a starfish while the other held her skirts.

For a while she studied the world: turtles sunning themselves on the rocks, restless seabirds, fish dull and sun-bright, quick and darting, languid, sinuous. The constant of the sea, and the horizon. When she could look no more, she turned and began the climb, lizards skittering at the sweep of her skirts. She felt lazy eyes on her back.

The guards had been lulled by the regularity of her habits into complacence. And why not? She could have been no more tied down had they used ropes and chains.

The path she walked ran along the forest that made up the heart of the island. Shadowy cool in the heat, buzzing with insects. Mastic trees so big that it took four men to circle the trunk, arms outstretched; fragrant cedar; stands of mahogany so dense that walking among them was to twist constantly one way and then another. Tamarinds, wild mangoes, other things she could not name.

How her father would have loved this place. Orchids like birds in flight hanging over the frayed stump of a palm tree. Parrots everywhere, flickerings of scarlet and emerald and cobalt blue overhead. She thought of her father often, spoke to him in her thoughts as she made her plans. Imagined his reactions, and made changes accordingly.

The forest gave way to the wet side of the island, mangroves on stilt roots in swamps alive with crickets, flies, great armies of ants and termites. The stink of green things rotting, thick on the tongue. She picked her way carefully, skirts tied into a knot, back straight.

No one was following her now. She was never sure why, if it was simple laziness, or fear of where she was going, or the certainty that she would be back. The lagoons went on for miles, and then more swamps, and finally there would be the sea.

She had loved the sea, once, and dreamed of living on a ship. Now she spent as much time as she could in this particular place, where she could be free of the sound of waves breaking on the cliffs and the scream of gulls.

The lagoon spread out before her in the dim light. She held her breath and waited. A ripple, another. The surface of the water moved and broke.

Hello. She whispered the word while the bulbous body in the water rolled and rolled. Then another appeared beside it, smaller: her child. Water sliding off gray-green skin, a rounded hip, the long curved line of back.

She stepped out of her shoes and into the cool grasp of the water, thought of swimming out to them. To play among the selkies, and learn their language so that she might ask them for shelter and sanctuary. For herself and her child.

Her hands rested on the great curve of her own belly. The life inside it flexed and turned, another swimmer in a silent sea.

PART I

Ace of Wands: A new adventure that must be met with a bold spirit. A primal force released.

CHAPTER 1

L'ÎLE DE LAMANTINS
FRENCH ANTILLES
AUGUST 1814

The island, beautiful and treacherous, drew in the love-struck and rewarded them with razor-sharp coral reefs, murderous breakwaters, and cliffs that no sane man would attempt.

Kit Wyndham was sane. Out of his depth, perhaps, but Major Christian Pelham Wyndham of the King's Rangers was in command of all his senses, while Luke Scott was not.

"Major?"

The lieutenant hovered like a maiden aunt, stopping just short of wringing his hands. If given permission to speak, Hodge would say out loud what he had said too many times already: that they had no business here; that what Scott intended was madness.

Hodge was wrong about one thing: They did have business here, and crucial business at that. The only kind of business that could have forged this strange alliance between himself and the Scotts: They were after the same prey.

A fat moon hung in a clear night sky, sending the shadows of masts and rigging out to dance on the water. On the rail his own hands were drained of color, corpse gray.

He turned to assure his lieutenant that he would have no part in this night's insanity. Let Scott take his band of mercenaries and storm Priest's Town, and good luck to them one and all. Kit Wyndham had made a promise, and he would keep it: Now that their quarry was in sight, he would step back and let Scott lead.

Just behind Lieutenant Hodge stood Hannah Scott, dressed in men's breeches and a leather jerkin over a rough shirt, her person hung about with weapons: a rifle on her back, pistols, a knife in a beaded sheath on a broad belt. She could heal or kill; he had seen her conjure miracles and blasphemies with equal ease. No mortal woman, he had called her to her face, and she had not corrected him with words.

The moonlight was kind to her, as the sun was kind. In the year since they had made their uneasy alliance he had seen her every day, and still the sight of her was startling. By the standards of Wyndham's own kind, Luke Scott's Mohawk half sister could not be called beautiful. Her skin was too dark, her hair too black, her mouth too generous for pale English blood. Below deep-set eyes the bosses of her cheeks cast shadows. Most damning of all, the expression in those eyes was far and away too intelligent. If her skin were as pale as cream, her mind would have isolated her; Englishmen did not know what to do with such a woman.

Even at this moment she knew exactly what he was thinking, the excuses he had been ready to offer, the rationalizations. If he voiced them she would simply tilt her head and look at him. She would call him no names, but he would hear them anyway.

"Major?" Lieutenant Hodge's voice rose and wavered.

He said, "Fetch my weapons." And: "Miss Scott, please tell your brother I will be joining the rescue party."

All this, for a woman.

The men liked to speculate, when Luke Scott was out of their hearing, how much money had been spent on this year-long crusade, by the woman's kinfolk and the Crown. Scott wanted his wife back; none of the men doubted that for a minute. He wasn't the kind of man who would let himself be robbed, not Luke Scott. But it seemed that there was more at stake, something nobody was talking about. The fact that Wyndham had been sent after Dégre at the same time made that clear.

No expense had been spared. First there was the *Isis,* the great merchantman sitting idle in the waters off Kingston. She was too clumsy a ship for the kind of work they had to do in the islands, and so Scott had purchased the schooner *Patience* as thoughtlessly as another man might put down coin for bread and ale. The crew was well paid and the provisions—meat and biscuit and ale and rum—were generous. Beyond the material things, the Earl of Carryck and the Scotts had put down a fortune in pursuit of information.

Kit Wyndham stood back and watched the Scotts contrive. Their money was of less interest to him; he was born to wealth and had been raised among people who knew how to spend it. His family had been cultivating those skills for generations; his mother and sisters were experts. When Scott spent money he bought results. Fast ships, good men, names whispered in dark corners, maps drawn with a bit of charcoal on a tabletop.

Scott's men were expert soldiers, utterly silent, ruthless to a fault, loyal unto death. Part of that was generosity with coin, but not the biggest part. Kit had known men like these when he was in Spain under Wellington.

Now was not the time to think of Spain. He put those images out of his head and concentrated on the back of the man in front of him, called Dieppe. Scott's most important find: a small, quick, wiry man, his skin the deep true black of the enslaved African.

Just last month Scott had found Dieppe in St. Croix and

bought him for more than he was worth. Then he offered the African his freedom in return for one night's work. It was Dieppe who knew the reefs that built a fortress around this island. Without him they would need an army to take it, and no doubt the lady would die before they could get to her.

Night birds called, and their voices echoed off the water as the longboat wound its way through a swamp crowded by an army of mangrove trees. A sinuous tail as broad around as a man's waist flicked in the moonlight, and Wyndham touched the long knife at his side. He had seen an alligator twenty feet long rip the leg off a man with a jerk of his head.

Dieppe led them onto land so saturated with water that to stand still was to invite disaster. They followed one by one: Scott, his sister, then the others made a long coiling snake with Dieppe as the head. Dieppe and Scott and some of the other men carried machetes; Wyndham had his short sword.

For two hours they walked through the damp heat of the swamp in the wake of the swinging blades. Tiny gnats gathered at nostrils and the corners of lips and eyes, and Wyndham wiped them away with the back of his hand, thinking of the ointment he had been offered and turned down.

The lagoons, then, as they had been told: long commas of water silvered by the moonlight. The men broke into a trot until they came to the edge of the forest, where they stopped for five minutes while Dieppe and Scott spoke, heads bent together.

The swamps were bad, but these forests were worse. Wyndham concentrated on putting one foot in front of the other and not losing sight of the man in front of him. Something screamed, and the hairs on the back of his neck rose. This dark and fragrant place could hardly be more different from Spain's hot exposed plains and rocky hills, but his blood pounded here as it had there, and would spill the same bright color.

When they came out of the forest Wyndham touched his pistols and his sword lightly, and looking up, caught Hannah Scott's gaze on him. He had seen her kill, but she knew nothing of him in the field, except the stories told behind his back. Most of them were perfectly true.

The cove was small, well protected from the winds, and un-guarded. Looking down on it they saw two ships—Dégre's *Grasshopper,* and another unknown to them. If Scott had sailed the *Patience* into the cove and tried to walk up the path that had been cut into the cliff face, then perhaps one of the men sleeping with an empty bottle cradled between his legs might have woke to sound the alarm. As it was, they died quietly.

Scott sent half the men to deal with the ships, and the rest of them went into the settlement called Priest's Town. It turned out to be nothing more than a warren of shacks set up off the ground, most of them empty. Two old mulatto women lived in the smallest of them with their goats and swine. They seemed neither surprised to be roused by strange soldiers in the middle of the night, nor worried about their lives. That was another talent of Scott's: he could dispense calm as easily as coin. People trusted him, even when they should not. He could be kind, if it furthered his cause; but ruthlessness came to him just as easily. He would have gone far in the army.

The raiders turned their attention to the largest of the shacks. Directly in the middle, the largest room's outer wall was made of a series of doors, all open to the weather. A rail hung from the sagging porch like a broken arm. Lanterns swayed from blackened posts, some of them dead, others guttering and spewing black smoke. The inside of the house was crowded.

Scott's men moved like a company who had fought together in a dozen campaigns, silently, easily, joined by invisible threads just tense enough to keep them aware of each other. Kit tested the weight of his rifle, as familiar to him as any part of his body. The bayonet clicked into place. It caught what light there was and winked at him.

They waited for the guide, ten minutes, twenty, and then Dieppe came back, sweat covered, trembling. Scott asked him a question in rapid French, and got a nod in answer.

"A child? Did you see an infant?"

"Non." Sure of himself, of what he hadn't seen.

For the first time tonight, Wyndham saw Scott hesitate. No doubt he had been hoping to find the woman and her child together. If there was a child.

Again he felt Hannah Scott's gaze on him, as if she were reading his thoughts, and answering them.

It was an argument they had had too many times: whether or not the information they had about the woman's condition was to be trusted. Scott believed it was true; Wyndham was doubtful. The old woman who had told them that the lady they were after was heavy with child might simply have been looking for more coin.

In a few minutes they would know. Scott sent some of the men around to the back, and gave them orders to wait for his signal.

Wyndham saw the room for a split second before the battle started. Tables cluttered with dice and cards and cups, a long bar on the far wall, and men who had been enjoying themselves. A dozen of them, dirtier and rougher than many, but still just men burned by sun and wind and erratic fortune.

The one man who concerned them most sat at a large

table in the corner, his dark head thrown back in laughter. It had been more than a year since Wyndham had last seen the false priest, but he recognized Dégre. And on the other side of the room, sitting behind a small table with cards laid out before her, the woman. She was much changed, thinner and drawn and her eyes shadowed, burning with fever, or anger long held in check. Her belly was flat. If she had been with child, she was no longer.

It took less than a second to see all that, and then his rifle found its target and things happened very fast, and all at once.

There were very few things that Jennet Huntar could be sure of, but one of them was this: For as long as she lived, she would dream of palm trees. Spindle-fingered against topaz skies or storm clouds, dancing against bloody sunsets and bloodier sunrises, always beckoning: They would be with her forever. Right now she could look up and see them against the sky as the night leached away, if she just lifted her head.

But she was at work, and it was the work that kept her wits intact. She had a little table of her own, and two stools. On the table she dealt out her cards for anyone who could pay the price.

When there were few men interested in the cards she laid them out for herself.

The Hangman. The Tower. The Knave of Swords.

Tonight her steadiest, most devoted customer was drinking at the bar. He was called Moore, one of Thibodoux's men off the *Badger*. When the old Irishman was here, he spent half his coin on drink, and the other half he gave to hear her read him the cards. The other men spent money on the women in the back rooms, but Moore was content to sit and look at what he could not have.

Tonight he waited until the moon had set and he was so full of liquor that he would fall off his chair if Jennet leaned forward to prod him with one finger. And yet he was not so drunk that he forgot what he wanted from her.

He sat with filthy fingers laced into his long, tobacco-stained beard. The low forehead was remarkable for its deep reddish color, set off by a thick twisting white scar in the shape of a cross. His mouth made a perfectly round circle in the middle of his beard, and his tongue flickered when he talked, snakelike.

"Tell me, Lady Jennet, when will I get me a good wife?"

It was the question he always asked.

Moore was no better and no worse than the other men who drifted through this place. Always hungry: for drink and release and excitement, for sleep, and beyond all those things, for advantage. Hungry and not particularly worried about how he came by what he needed.

"Not tonight, Mr. Moore. But perhaps sometime soon. Let us look."

She took her time. Moore would not complain. It was mostly what he was paying for, the right to sit close enough to imagine the texture of the skin he could not see, would never see. She was the daughter and sister of an earl; surely her skin must be as soft and white as milk. Many of the men who came here would have delighted to quench their curiosity by taking her apart like a crab, cracking open what she tried to hold back. But she was Dégre's pet creature, and they must keep their distance unless it was to sit across a table and hand over coin.

As long as he came no closer and kept his hands to himself, Jennet was content to take Moore's money, and sometimes, when he had drunk enough, the one thing she really wanted from him.

"It's been a good while since you last came to see us, Mr.

Moore," she said as she shuffled the cards, slowly, carefully. "A long voyage, then?"

He looked about himself nervously, one eyelid fluttering. Fear cut through the drunken fog. "Aye. Long enough, missus. Long enough."

She had misjudged the timing, and put him on his guard. The Three of Swords. The Six of Cups. The Moon.

His gaze shifted to the table in the far corner, where men sat bent over their game. The one he feared was not looking in this direction, but that meant nothing at all.

He's got eyes in the back of his head, does Dégre.

She had heard men say such things too often to count. The man they called the Priest, or more rarely, Dégre—the man who owned this place and claimed the island itself—was a legend, a force as inevitable and ungovernable as the winds. None of the hard men who frequented L'Île de Lamantins would cross him.

Jennet had crossed him, and she lived still. Because in the year since she had begun traveling with him, she had come to understand the way his mind worked. She had planned very carefully, and moved fast when the time came, and she had succeeded. She was alive not because she had got the best of Dégre, but because he had plans for her that promised more satisfaction than a quick death dealt out in the anger of the moment.

The Priest was watching her now, as she turned over cards and talked about them. He might be thinking about nothing more than what he would eat for his supper, or of changing his shirt, or there could be something very different brewing there.

It worried Moore, but Jennet was beyond fear. Dégre had already robbed her of everything of value.

"The Moon," she said to Moore. "It shows itself often when you come to hear your cards read, sir. The moon is a guiding image for you, I think."

"Aye," he agreed, his small features bunched together in an attempt to convey sincerity. "And remind me then, Lady Jennet, what does it mean, the Moon card?"

"Inconstancy. Are you inconstant in your temperament, Mr. Moore?"

It was too much for him in his current state. He blinked at her owlishly, his mouth jerking at one corner as he tried to push himself up from the table, a puppet with tangled strings. Jennet gathered her cards together, waiting patiently for him to find his tongue and make it do his bidding. Later, it would be the expression on Moore's face she recalled first when she thought about this night.

As he opened his mouth, the sound of a dozen rifles firing together tore the world in two. Moore fell forward onto the table, blood gushing from his mouth.

Jennet dropped to her knees and then pressed her face to the floor. The room was filled with screams and gunsmoke and tumbling bodies, glass shattering and the wind, rising suddenly; she heard it howling and howling as the idea presented itself, very clearly: She was about to die, and she had brought it upon herself. The next volley would find her, and she would die here on this filthy floor in this hell-begotten place and she would never see him again, never in this life.

A man was standing over her. Dégre, his face lost in shadow and still she saw his eyes, wild with rage. Blood dripping from his scalp onto his shoulder, running down his arm. He held out a hand to her, and it simply . . . fell apart in a mist of blood and flesh.

He stood for a moment looking at the raw meat that was his hand, baffled, it seemed by his expression, at this turn of events.

And then Luke was there, pressing a pistol to Dégre's temple.

"Ah," the false priest said calmly. "Scott. Come to claim the leftovers, eh?"

• • •

To Kit Wyndham it looked as though Dégre smiled, even as Scott's pistol kicked and fired. The Priest's knees folded, and he fell.

Lady Jennet was falling, too, collapsing so slowly that when Scott caught her it looked as though they were practicing a new dance step. His head came up and turned, his gaze raking over the destruction they had wrought.

"Hannah," he said, holding out the woman. "Hannah, help me."

In less than an hour it was all sorted: a dozen dead men piled up and rolled from the porch like so much driftwood. The ones who had been in the rooms off to the side with the women, all prisoners now, had been divided into groups. Some of them were digging graves; the rest were marched down to the cove.

Overhead the early morning sky was darkening, and a rough breeze made the palms sway.

One of the women yawned. There was a splatter of blood on her skirt and her eyes were dull with weariness, but she raised her face to the sky and smiled. Another woman sat with her feet swinging, leaning toward one of Scott's men. His posture as he bent his head toward her was as obvious as a flag. Soldiers were as predictable as horses in their needs.

Kit rubbed the grit and gunpowder from his face and listened to what was going on in the corner where Scott crouched next to his half sister, the two of them a wall between the room and the woman.

Lady Jennet had come out of her faint and was weeping in Hannah's arms, weeping as a woman weeps when she has lost the thing she loves most in the world.

"Jennet," Hannah said, her tone firm but not harsh. "Jennet, calm yourself. You're safe now. You are safe."

Scott looked away. To Hannah he said, "I'll go search the other rooms."

"No," Jennet said. Her head came up with a jerk. "No, don't leave me. Luke, don't go."

What a gift that was to him. Scott couldn't hide his relief.

"We have to be away," he said to her, cupping her head in one hand. "Jennet, do you know where he kept the letters?"

She blinked, fresh tears coursing over her reddened face. "Letters?"

Hannah sent Scott a sidelong glance, one that told him to keep his silence. In a gentle voice she said, "The letters Dégre stole from you. The ones he threatened you with. We can't leave them where someone else might find them. Where are they, Jennet?"

"The letters," Jennet said. "Those letters. I burned them months ago."

Scott made a sound that came up from his gut, as if he had been punched.

Hannah said, "The letters are destroyed? You burned them?"

"Aye, and he beat me bloody for it." She might have been talking about a new hat, for all the emotion in her voice.

"He beat you." Scott's tone, so carefully modulated, took on a new tone, an underlying tremor. "Is that how the child died? He got a child on you and beat it out of you in a fury?"

She seemed to wake up at that, confusion giving way to understanding and then, more quickly, anger. A brightness came into her eyes, and Kit recognized her then as her father's daughter.

Wyndham had first met Lady Jennet at the dinner table

of the garrison commander at Île aux Noix, introduced to
him only as a missionary's widow working among the
wounded prisoners. Then he had not seen her for who she
was: a daughter of the fourth Earl of Carryck, and sister to
the fifth of the line. She had taken pains to hide her connections, but now her bloodlines were etched on her face. In
spite of all she had seen and done in this war, or maybe because of it.

She righted herself and looked at Scott, who was meant
to be her husband, who had spent a year looking for her.

She said, "Not his child, Luke. Yours. Our son. And he's
not dead. I know he's not."

Scott's face went very still as her voice came stronger.

"I gave birth to him right there, in that room. A month
ago he was smuggled away. I bribed them, and the captain
took him away, because he wasn't safe here. He wasn't safe."

All the color had drained out of Scott's face, all tension
out of his body; he swayed and bent forward over his knees,
his head hanging low.

"Oh, Christ," he said softly. "Oh, merciful Christ."
Spasms ran through him so that his shoulders jerked.
"Where?"

Jennet reached out a hand as if she thought he might
collapse under her touch.

"A town called Pensacola, in Spanish Florida." She
stroked his hair, and then he raised his face to her and he did
collapse and she opened her arms to catch him, arms that
circled closed.

Hannah had turned away, and Kit caught her gaze. She
walked out onto the porch, and he followed her.

She said, "He'll want to question the men who were taken
prisoner."

"I can do that." Kit rubbed his eyes. "I'll go do it now."

"Most of them are off the *Badger,*" she said. "They probably won't know anything about the boy."

"Probably not," Kit agreed. He didn't want to look at her. From her tone he knew what she was feeling, and he knew, too, how little she would welcome his intrusion. "But I'll find out for sure. You'll talk to the women?"

He turned to leave her and felt her hand on his wrist. Paused, and waited.

She said, "Thank you."

It was the most he would allow himself to expect.

There were injuries among the men. Not many, and none very serious, but enough to distract Hannah while Jennet and Luke talked.

She took off her weapons and put them aside, tried to clear her head of the last hour and the lingering stink of gunpowder. There were splinters to be drawn and burns that needed salving, and one of the men had taken a knife wound to the cheek.

When she let herself remember why they were here, she looked up to see that Luke and Jennet were gone, and the door to the room she had pointed out to him was closed.

The men had seen it, too. They got up, one by one, and wandered out toward the settlement.

Hannah thought of Wyndham, gone off to question prisoners. A man in search of a miracle. He would bring it back to offer to her on an outstretched hand, his quiet self-mockery held in front of him like a shield.

CHAPTER 2

To His Excellency Sir George Prevost
Quebec

I have the honour to transmit to Your Excellency the
news that Lady Jennet of Carryck is rescued this day.
The lady appears to be in good health and of sound
mind in spite of her long ordeal. In accordance with
your commands, I will see her transported safely to
Port-au-Prince, as quickly as unpredictable late
summer weather permits.

It is with less satisfaction that I report that I was
unable to fulfill the second charge entrusted to me
by Your Excellency. The criminal Anselme Dégre,
whom I was to return to Quebec to be tried for
grand theft, for abduction, and for the murder of
Colonel Caudebec and his men, was killed today
during the raid of his stronghold. A search of the
island has turned up no trace of the monies.
The only possession of any value was his ship,
the *Grasshopper,* which I have impounded and
which will be delivered to Kingston for
re-commissioning.

For my part, I will report to Negril Bay, where I
expect to receive my new orders. It is my hope that,

given the completion of my work here, I be allowed
to return to active duty with my own regiment in
Canada.

In anticipation of your commands,
I have the honour, etc.

Major Christian Pelham Wyndham
King's Rangers
on detached duty
L'Île de Lamantins
French Antilles
21st day of August 1814

The Honourable Miss Margaret Prevost
Quebec

My dear Margaret,

In your last letter you asked that I communicate to
you directly the completion of my assignment here.
By the same post I send to your father my final
report. I set out now for Negril Bay in Jamaica, where
I hope my request to be returned to King's Rangers
will be granted.

    Whether or not my commanding officers will see
fit to honour that request (and hence, whether or not
it is time for you to assemble your wedding clothes) is
entirely in their hands.

Your devoted,
Christian Pelham Wyndham
L'Île de Lamantins
French Antilles
21st day of August 1814

To the Earl of Carryck
Carryckcastle, Annandale, Scotland

Cousin,

Your sister is found and delivered from her abductors.
She bids me tell you and your lady mother that she is
in good health, and will write to you in her own
hand as soon as she may. I am to leave the telling of
the whole story to her, and trust you will understand
my need to grant her this wish.

Late summer weather in the Antilles is volatile, but
we hope to reach my stepfather's estate outside Port-
au-Prince within a few days, where everything will
be done to see to your sister's health and welfare. We
will be married there at the first opportunity.

As the *Isis* can have no role to play in the journey
we must undertake, I have instructed her captain to
return to the Solway Firth and report to you for
instructions. From this point on we travel on the
Patience, who has done us good service.

In all haste, I remain yours at command,

Luke Scott Bonner
21st day of August 1814

Madame Lily Ballentyne
Forbes & Sons
Montreal
Canada

Dearest Sister,

We have little word of how the war goes in the
north, and in any case no hope of getting a letter to

the family at Lake in the Clouds but that you will
take it upon yourself to deliver it with all possible
speed. They must be desperate for news.

Dégre is dead at Luke's hand and Jennet is
returned to us. Three months ago Jennet bore Luke a
healthy son. She named him Nathaniel. For his own
safety, and at considerable danger to herself, Jennet
arranged to have the boy smuggled away. Thus we set
out for Pensacola in Spanish Florida, to find the
family that has had the boy in their care and restore
him to his family.

Luke and Jennet will be married as soon as we
reach Port-au-Prince.

I wish that I could promise a swift return home
immediately after, but I cannot.

I know you will have many questions, but I beg
your patience a while longer. The weather bodes ill,
and Lieutenant Hodge must sail immediately if he is
to reach the next post packet out of Guadeloupe.

In haste,

Hannah, called Walks-Ahead by her mother's people,
or Walking-Woman by her husband's

CHAPTER 3

Hodge and a small crew raised the Union Jack on the *Grasshopper* and sailed her out of the cove, bound for Guadeloupe and then Kingston. Not six hours later a storm rose up with fists and let loose with screaming winds so fierce that the shack nearest the cliffs sailed off like an oversized gull.

They sat together in the main house, soldiers and sailors and the women from the town, listening to the winds, talking, playing cards by the light of a half dozen lanterns. For all its shabby appearance, the place was built to withstand storms. Hannah tried not to think of the *Grasshopper*, gone just a few hours now toward Guadeloupe. It would outrun the storm or it would not; there was nothing she could do for those men.

Luke came to her with a bit of rough bread and cold goat meat that was mostly gristle, crouched down beside her while she ate it.

He said, "She's sleeping."

Hannah looked at her brother, at the trembling of his hands. "She'll be doing a lot of that. You must let her heal."

"Florida." Luke put his head back. "Ah, Christ." There were streaks on his cheeks, as though he had been standing in a salt spray. As though he had been weeping.

"We've come this far," Hannah said. "We'll manage the rest."

It looked for a moment as if he would argue with her, list all the things that could go wrong. Between this place and where they must go, the sea was crowded with privateers and pirates and the British navy, massing for invasion. So far in this journey they had managed to keep clear of the war; as far as anyone knew, they were Canadians, under the protection of the Crown. The truth was far more complicated. It would cost them their allies, if not their lives.

And of course the boy might not be where Jennet believed they would find him. Hannah would not say those words aloud, but they were both thinking about it. The woman who had agreed to put him to the breast next to her own child could have sold the boy or simply dropped him overboard, once she was away from here. And if all had gone as Jennet insisted, there were other dangers. There was no protection for an infant from yellow fever or typhoid or any of the other diseases that ran rampant in that part of the world. The chances that they would find him alive and well were poor, but they must try.

Hannah's head ached, and she rubbed her temple with two fingers.

"You could go home, now," Luke said. He read her thoughts quite easily, or so he believed. "Go back to Paradise and take up your life. You have done enough, and more."

"No," Hannah said. "I will stay. For Jennet and for you."

The howling of the wind made her jerk in irritation. Luke glanced around himself, started to say something, and then stopped. "I must go back to her, in case she wakes."

"And sleep yourself," Hannah said. "The watch is in place, and no one will be sailing into the harbor in this weather."

"What about you?" he asked her, getting to his feet. His

face was lost in shadow, and she was glad. It was easier to lie to him that way.

She said, "Don't worry about me. I'll find a place to sleep easily enough."

Kit Wyndham had taken one of the smaller rooms for himself; it stank of sweat and cheap tobacco and men's leavings. He opened the shutters and let the wind and rain come in, glad of the cold on his face. Then he threw all but the best of the mats out, closed and latched the shutters, and took off his weapons.

The bones in his right arm throbbed with the weather, and always would; he had wanted no souvenirs of Spain but had them anyway. The rolled blanket from his rucksack went over the thin straw mattress and then he sat there while the whole building shivered like a wet dog. His stomach growled, but he was not hungry enough to go look for food.

The oil lantern he had taken from the main room stank, but it threw shadows on the rough walls that reminded him of lying abed as a boy, watching the fire.

She came to him when he had almost given up hope, slipping in and closing the door behind herself, any noise she might make lost in the tumult of the storm. Her weapons she piled carefully near the mat, and then she lay down beside him and let Kit fold the blanket around her.

They were quiet for a moment, and he wondered if she would talk to him this night, or if she would take what she wanted without words. It would not be the first time. She used him and he was glad of it; even in the light of day he couldn't dredge up any remorse or doubt.

Tonight Kit realized that he wanted the sound of her voice almost more than the pleasure and relief of her touch. Because the false priest was dead, and he would be going home to Canada.

She was breathing deeply, drawing in smells and holding them. Under the blanket their heat mingled. She sighed and stretched a little against him, as content as a cat, long and sleek and strong, her hands rough with work, demanding, knowing.

He said, "Do you worry about getting with child when you come to me?"

She turned her face up. Her eyes were so black that it seemed just now that she had no pupils. The question didn't seem to bother her, but then it was hard to tell how she felt about anything. He had never known a woman like her.

"No," she said. "I don't worry."

Kit lowered his head to hers and brushed her mouth with his own, an opening bid, an invitation.

She seemed to be considering it, and then her hands came up and settled on his shoulders, and she opened her mouth to his kiss.

Later, the memory of the things he was feeling would make him blush. He had never been a romantic; he had no ear for poetry and had never regretted that lack in himself. But kissing this woman—by whatever name she went— robbed him of the ability to express himself, and that felt like a loss.

She touched his tongue with her own and then pulled away suddenly, her mind made up. She might go now, and he could do nothing to stop her. Would do nothing to endanger the chance that she might come again.

Hannah shrugged out of her jerkin, lifted her shirt over her head. Kit looked up at her, black hair flowing down her back in a river, the glow of her skin in the light of the candle, the swollen mouth. For the rest of his life he would think of her like this. These nights together were about to come to an end.

She said, "Stop thinking." And then she showed him how.

Sometimes, afterwards, when they had tired each other out and she was floating in the mindless time before sleep, Hannah would tell Kit things about herself, stories from her childhood, of her family, of the husband who had been one of Tecumseh's warriors. She had borne a child, a son.

Always when she talked, Kit had the sense that she was holding back things she could not trust him with—or perhaps, he realized, she did not trust herself, and could not allow herself emotion of a particular kind. The only time he had ever seen her truly in danger of losing control of herself was the morning they had come across a report in a New-York newspaper, already three months old, of Tecumseh's death on the battlefield. What she might be thinking he would never know; she had turned away his questions and forbidden him the topic with a look.

Kit had first seen her when she was working among the wounded prisoners at Nut Island. In spite of her medical training, in spite of the fact that many of the prisoners owed their lives to her, none of the men would call her doctor; it went too much against the grain. In the garrison she had been known by her Mohawk name alone, Walks-Ahead. The garrison commander, the most prideful and pompous of men, had disdained to see her as anything but another squaw, and his officers had followed that example. They had paid dearly for their stupidity.

It had taken Wyndham too long to recognize his own blindness and begin to see the overeducated half-Mohawk woman for what she was. Much later, when they had been on board the *Isis* together for months, he realized first, that she was not Canadian, and, more, that she had never claimed to be. Her half brother was born and raised in Montreal; she let people draw their conclusions from that and did not bother to correct them. But the gaps in her stories began to knit themselves together in a particular shape, and soon enough Kit understood that she was American, or at least

that her father's family lived on that side of the border, in
the backwoods of Vermont or Maine, or the mountains of
New-York. Something she could not tell him, because their
two countries were at war.

Half asleep in his arms she flexed and turned. It was
enough to set his blood stirring again.

She said, "I'm afraid to go home."

He tried to hide his surprise, but she took his face between her hands and made it impossible.

"You don't like to think of me afraid."

"That's not it," he said. "I'm just wondering why you
have to go. You have a choice, don't you?" It sounded childish, now that he had said it.

"A choice," she echoed. She said the word as if it were
unfamiliar to her. "If I have a choice, so do you."

He would have liked to deny it, but he knew she would
like him less for the lie. "I want to go home. I miss it."

He didn't tell her the rest of the truth: that he didn't miss
everything, or everyone. If not for the miniature he packed
among his things he would have forgotten the face of the
lady he was engaged to marry. Certainly he had no memory
of her voice. But he would marry Margaret; he could not
imagine doing anything else.

Against her mouth he said, "What is it you want from
me, Hannah?"

"Just this," she said, and took it.

CHAPTER 4

"Luke," Jennet said. "Major Wyndham is in love with your sister, I hope you realize."

They stood at the rail of the schooner *Patience*. All around them the ship was in the turmoil that went with the last hour before sailing, a great rush of boxes and barrels and trunks marched up the causeway and into the bowels of the ship, like a calf being fatted for slaughter. The noise was such that Jennet had to raise her voice to be heard, but she kept her eyes on Kit Wyndham, who paced the wharf below them. He had given up leather jerkin and homespun for the dark green coat and silver lace of the King's Rangers; the sun glinted on his buttons and epaulettes and sparked the blue of his eyes. He was waiting for Hannah. They were all waiting for Hannah.

"I don't know if love is the issue, in this case." Luke covered her hand on the rail with his own. "Certainly he's infatuated."

In the full August sun Luke's own hair had worked almost white, while his skin had gone an even middle brown. There were deep lines at the corners of his eyes and mouth, but when he looked at her she still saw the seventeen-year-old boy he had been when he first came to Carryck, so many years ago.

"He's in love," Jennet said. "If he were not, he would be

on his way back to Canada at this very minute. I am sorry for them."

Luke made a noise that meant he was sorry, too, or would be, if other matters hadn't had such a hold on his attention. News of the war was everywhere, and while it had put the British who swarmed over these islands in a grand mood to hear that their army had burned Washington to the ground, the Bonners took it in with sober detachment. Now Luke watched sailors carrying a gunboat out of the warren of boat works, his expression severe and distant. He was wondering how much the war in the Gulf of Mexico would hinder their own journey.

Jennet touched his arm and watched him try to find the thread of the conversation: Wyndham, who was in love with his sister but must leave her. He said, "You mustn't forget that Kit isn't a free agent. And he has a fiancée at home in Canada."

"I'm not the one with the faulty memory," Jennet said. "Truth be told, he doesn't want to leave Hannah. No matter what noises he makes about having enough of detached duty."

Luke bent his head to her and spoke directly into the shell of her ear. "Why don't we go below where we can discuss this in private?"

At that, Jennet laughed. It sounded nervous to her own ear, as if she were a young girl unaccustomed to flirtation. Luke heard it, too; she saw that in the veiled expression just before he turned his face away.

Very soon they would have to put words to the things they had not yet had the courage to discuss, an idea that unsettled Jennet greatly.

"There's Hannah," Luke said. "I was starting to worry."

The wagon that stopped below them on the wharf was crowded with baskets and boxes. Hannah was involved in a discussion with the driver, a tall black man who seemed surprised at the number of coins she had put in his hand.

"More of her bits and pieces," Luke said. "I'll see that her things are stowed properly."

Wyndham had already started in that direction, but Jennet didn't try to stop Luke from leaving. She did try to stop her own sigh of relief, and failed.

From the privacy of Luke's cabin—her cabin, too, now that they were wed, and what a strange idea that was—Jennet watched Port-au-Prince grow smaller. From this distance the town looked like a magical place, sapphire and emerald, gold and blinding white where the sun touched thick whitewashed walls. Around it the fields stretched out—coffee, sugarcane, cotton, indigo—and above it rose mountain ridges that ran the length of the island.

Once she would have loved this place, and the idea of exploring all of it, mountains and hidden glens and savannahs. Now the *Patience*—how poorly named was this ship—could not move fast enough to suit Jennet.

Seven days they had spent here, seven wasted days when she must submit to doctors' examinations and interviews with the authorities, when all she really needed was to be moving west. But no one would hear of them rushing away, most especially not Luke's mother.

Giselle Somerville Lacoeur, once of Montreal, took charge of Jennet and no one—not her son, or her husband, or even the governor himself—dared to interfere. Age had not mellowed Luke's mother.

As a girl Jennet had loved Giselle and admired her, but now she found she had very little to say to this Mme. Lacoeur. For her part, Giselle did not seem to mind Jennet's impatience, nor was she swayed by her moods. Giselle was far too involved with making sure that the steady stream of seamstresses and milliners and mantua makers did their best work, and speedily. She would have her new daughter-in-law properly outfitted before she sailed. There was no excuse for sloppiness, she told Jennet. No matter how dire the situation.

The Lacoeur home was spacious and cool, standing as it did in a great sea of palm trees at the crest of a hill. The veranda that circled the house was wide and deeply shadowed, with comfortable chairs and chaise longues piled with pillows. Jennet spent most of her time dozing there, though she never put foot on the marble terraces that ran down to the sea.

On Jennet's third morning in Hayti, Giselle found her asleep when she should have been in her rooms, where the seamstresses were waiting.

"You may need to apply to the authorities anywhere from Pensacola to Mobile to New Orleans," Giselle said. "You may have to dine with governors and generals and bankers. The clothes you wear will speak more loudly of your resources and connections than any letter of introduction."

"I am so sleepy," Jennet said.

Giselle was unsympathetic. "No sane man would go into battle without the proper weapons, and neither must you. This is a war you are embarking on, Jennet, and the prize is your son. You must be ready for a long fight."

It was something they never spoke about directly, the fact that getting to Pensacola was only the beginning of the problems. They might not be able to get away again, if the war began in earnest along the Gulf coast—and Luke and all the rest of the male population of the island seemed to think that was exactly what was likely to happen. That would mean waiting, or traveling overland through territory that they didn't know and that might be hostile. They would need every advantage they could claim.

And so Jennet stood still while others draped her in the light silks and gauzes dictated by the climate; while the women talked about color and embroidery, hats and stockings and stacked heels. They discussed the fashions in Paris and London, and the peculiarities of Americans. Her own thoughts moved in a very different direction. While they gossiped, she made long lists of questions to ask Giselle's husband.

Anton Lacoeur was a sharp, doe-eyed man with a head for numbers and a talent for trade that had made him many fortunes. To Jennet's surprise, he had been the one who seemed to best understand what would make her time in Port-au-Prince bearable. He drew up lists of names, men who might be of help to them, others they should avoid at all costs; he wrote letters of introduction and drafts on banks; he brought them maps and charts.

When he came to the end of his own knowledge, he invited others to his home. Naval officers and army engineers, merchants and traders and others whose business practices were best left unexamined, but who knew the Gulf well enough to talk for hours of tides and treacherous marshes, swamps, bayous. They spoke of pirates and profiteers and smugglers, things that would have delighted Jennet as a girl—things that would have delighted her even a year ago—but now left her only vaguely uneasy. Luke took charge in these conversations, and Jennet was glad to leave it all to him.

It was Anton who brought Luke and the man called Bardi together. Bardi, who had lost his ship in mysterious circumstances and needed a way back to the Gulf through the British blockade. He was presented to them as untrustworthy, a man without morals or scruples but one who knew the area where they were going as well as any man alive. It was worth his own life to stay out of both American and British hands.

"Pay him well and never take your eyes off him," Anton had said. "And he'll get you to Pensacola or wherever else you need to be, and then be shut of him."

While Jennet's time was divided between Giselle and her husband, Hannah was free to seek out other women, dark-skinned women who watched and listened but rarely spoke to white people of what they knew. These were women who worked in the kitchens and laundries and nurseries, and from them she collected names whispered in throaty Creole French.

And then, finally, this morning Jennet found herself in front of a priest in a small Catholic church. He was an ancient Frenchman with a wobbling voice and kind eyes and he had married them and blessed them and wished them a speedy journey and quick recovery of their son.

In the few moments before they left to board the *Patience,* Giselle raised the subject of the boy. "Luke was taken from me at birth, remember," she said. "It was many years before I saw him again. You will be more fortunate." In a conspiratorial tone she added, "When you find the boy, bring him back here so I can see to his education."

But the truth was, Giselle didn't believe her grandson was alive; none of them did. It was so clearly written on their faces. *Poor Jennet has been through a great deal,* that look said. *Humor her, for the time being.*

It was uncharitable of her, but she could not help thinking such things, not even of Luke. He would do everything in his power, but in his heart, Jennet was sure, he had already given up on the boy. She held it against him, and didn't know how to stop.

Now they were married, and that was a good thing. The very best thing, something she had wanted for as long as she could remember, to have Luke as her husband. She had left Scotland not yet thirty years old, a widow of only a few months, to come looking for him.

Jennet pressed her trembling hands together, and wondered how long she could keep herself from weeping.

"Luke sent me down to see after you," Hannah said in the open hatchway, and just that simply the battle was lost. Jennet turned to her cousin with tears streaming down her face, and then collapsed into her outstretched arms.

They sat together on the edge of the bed for a long time while Jennet wept and Hannah waited, quiet and patient. Hannah was wearing the only gown she had allowed Giselle to order for her, figured Indian muslin over rose-colored silk. She had put it on for the wedding ceremony and left it on while she ran all her last-minute errands; there was a smudge of soot on her hem and a pulled thread in the lace at the neckline. She smelled of spices and something bittersweet, of sunlight and clean sweat, and under all that was another smell, salty and sharp; she smelled of Kit Wyndham. It was none of Jennet's business, not really, and it made her weep all the more, her tears wetting the bodice of celery green silk drugget with its elaborate embroidery. Her wedding gown.

Men's feet drummed on the deck in response to whistles and shouts, sails creaked and caught the wind so that the ship shivered and danced like an eager dog on a line. Jennet let herself be rocked.

Hannah had lost a son. She would never see him again in this life, and that thought brought Jennet up short. She pressed the back of her hands to her streaming eyes and tried to regain control of her voice.

"Not now," Hannah said. "Not unless you're ready."

"I am," Jennet said. "I think I am."

"Then tell me."

She couldn't tell, not everything. Not yet. But Jennet would start, and hope that half the story would be enough.

• • •

The words came slowly at first, forced up out of her throat
and mouth like bloody clots. She talked of the day Dégre
had taken her from Île aux Noix, the ship that had been
waiting, the men on the ship. How they circled around her,
delighted with the promise of diversion over the course of a
dull voyage south. The dissatisfaction when Dégre made it
clear that she was not to be marked. Lady Jennet was an as-
set first and foremost, and her value was not to be compromised.

Eventually prudence gave way to the sea and the monot-
ony of the wind and the rum, and the bolder of the men
began to approach her. There were many things they could
do to amuse themselves that would leave no mark, at least
none that others could see. They talked about this in her
hearing, as they might talk of slaughtering one of the pigs
that lived in a pen on deck while they rubbed knuckles over
its bristled skull.

It was too easy to imagine. She would be passed from
man to man, and each of them would use her in his own
way, casually or angrily or with a whispering kind of thankfulness.

Dégre, who never showed any interest in taking her,
watched and said nothing. Jennet understood that he was
leaving it up to her: She must find a way to save herself.

"Have you ever stabbed a man in the throat?" Her voice
was steady, but her hands trembled.

Hannah shook her head.

"It's like standing under a waterfall," Jennet said. "I was
covered with blood." And then: "I don't regret it. The others
left me alone after that."

Because I stank of blood, she might have said. *And it amused
Dégre to refuse me water to wash. As long as I live, I will dream of
the flies.*

Instead, Jennet told the story of the day she had given

birth, the long hours in a hot room where lizards clung to the walls and birds screamed in the trees.

"But he was perfect," Jennet said. "Perfect in form, and healthy, and so much like Luke, the shape of his eyes and his fingers and toes and the way his hair grows here." She touched the crown of her own head. "He was perfect. He is perfect, and he must be alive, or what was it all for?"

There it was, the question like a thorn struck through the heart. The question she had never dared put to Luke.

Hannah smoothed Jennet's hair away from her hot face. Her black eyes were without any expression that Jennet could read. She might say, *The boy is dead and you know it* or *The boy must be alive because we wish it so.*

She said, "Jennet, listen to me well. You and Luke must hold each other up. Don't turn away from him, not now, especially not now. You must trust that he can bear what you have to say. The things you cannot say to me, that you think you cannot say to anyone. Do you hear me?"

It was the best advice Hannah had to offer, and Jennet wanted no part of it. Her cousin must have seen that in her face, because her own expression sharpened.

Hannah said, "Do you know what I regret most? The things I didn't say to Strikes-the-Sky. The morning I saw him last, the things I should have said. Don't make the same mistake."

Jennet nodded, and shuddered, and nodded again. "Send him to me, would you?"

When Luke came a half hour later, there was a fine beading of sweat on his forehead. Jennet had a sudden picture in her mind of Hannah speaking to him, a finger raised in admonition. It made her smile. He smiled back at her.

In his hands he carried a tray with bread and fruit and cheese, and under his arm a bottle of wine. He put these things down on the small table under the porthole and then turned to her like a man awaiting sentencing. "It's not much, as wedding suppers go."

Jennet held out her hand. "It's not the food I care about. Come sit by me," she said. And then: "Do you remember the night you came to me with the pennyroyal ointment, when I went to sleep in the hay barn?"

"You were sulking, and so I seduced you into a better mood."

Jennet laughed, because he meant her to. "If you care to remember it that way."

He touched her face. "I remember the promises we made, under the waterfall."

She reached up and kissed him, felt his surprise and his delight and his caution, too, and so she kissed him again, putting her hands on his face and pulling him down to her.

He held back for a moment, and then he relaxed against her with a sound that came up from his belly. Jennet pressed her forehead against his and closed her eyes. She said, "I was never raped. I want you to know that."

She felt the words work on him, the way they dug into his mind and then, more slowly, moved through him, muscle by muscle. His arms went limp and then tightened so that she gasped.

"It wouldn't have mattered," he said. His gaze was steady, though his tone had coarsened a little.

"I might have been," Jennet said. "But I killed the first man who tried. I stabbed him, and after that the others left me alone." She would have gone on, but he pulled away to look in her face.

"But that's nothing to be ashamed of."

"I'm not ashamed of it," Jennet said.

"Were you punished?"

"No," Jennet said. "It amused Dégre, to—the whole episode amused him. I would do it again, and without hesitation."

"Of course you would," he said, his mouth touching hers. "I wouldn't expect anything less."

And then he kissed her, his mouth intent. And here was the surprise, that there were still such kisses to be had in the world, from a man like this one. Who could make her remember desire, and feel it again, that twist and pulse deep in the belly, the knowledge that it was there all along through all the months she had come to see herself as not an empty vessel, but a broken one. His voice was deep and rough and there was a trembling there, one that matched her own.

"Let me remind you," he said. "Let me show you."

It was ten days since he had come to Priest's Town to save her. He had slept beside her chastely, and held her when she wept, and comforted her as a brother comforts a grieving sister, and through all that Jennet had sensed him waiting and wanting, his body impatient for her but kept in check. She wondered how she could ever give him the things he deserved, the touch he wanted.

She turned to meet him, tasted salt on his skin and tears, and made herself a promise she wanted to keep, but could not be sure of, not yet.

CHAPTER 5

One day out of Port-au-Prince, Hannah sat on a pile of coiled rope with her daybook in her lap and considered the problem of the twenty-one men who made up the crew. Each of them had proved his trustworthiness over the course of the year, as sailors, as fighters, and, most of them, as companions. They had all hired onto this strange expedition knowing that she was a part of it. Luke had made his expectations clear.

The *Patience* had no other doctor, and so they had all come to her, sooner or later. She treated fevers and burns, bound bruised ribs, and lanced boils, and in time she had earned their respect and trust. With a few of them—the darker-skinned—she had struck up the beginnings of a friendship.

Now Piero Bardi had come on board the *Patience* to guide them through the Gulf waters, and Bardi's presence had upset the delicate balance Hannah had come to rely on. She could bear four more days of his sly comments and pointed looks and low laughter, but she could not force the others to ignore the man. She said as much to Luke, who had come to talk and crouched down beside her.

"I hope he gets us to Pensacola before somebody goes after him with a knife," she said.

Those who did not know Luke well thought him distant

and even disdainful. It was true that he was unshakable in most matters; but it was still in his sister's power to surprise and even to shock him, as she just had.

"I trust the crew," Luke said after a moment. "Unless he tries to lay hands on you—even then, they'd stop short of killing him." And: "But not too much short, I hope."

Luke could also surprise her, at times, and having Jennet back had softened him. Hannah was glad for him, and frightened, given the task before them.

A shout from the foredeck brought Luke to his feet. Hannah stayed where she was while he took the long-glass from the loop on his belt and studied the ship coming toward them at a fast clip.

Without looking at her he said, "Jennet will need assurance. Will you go to her? This won't take long."

Jennet was sitting at the small table in her cabin, bright patches of color on her cheeks and neck, and her eyes glittering as though she had had too much to drink.

"Pirates?" she asked as Hannah crossed the room.

"No. A British cutter. We knew this would happen, Jennet—you saw for yourself half the British fleet heading toward Jamaica. There's no cause for concern."

"They'll turn us away," Jennet said. "What if they turn us away?"

"Luke won't let anything come between us and the boy," Hannah said. "You know that."

Jennet blinked, and nodded, and some of her normal color came back into her face. "I am being childish."

"That's not the word I would have used," Hannah said. She looked at the table where Jennet had laid out the tarot cards. It was an old deck, hand-drawn and -painted, well thumbed. One of the cards turned faceup did not match the others. Hannah touched the rough edge.

"The Queen of Swords," Jennet said. "I left it behind, that day, for you to find. The Queen and the Seven both."

"Sometime you'll have to explain to me what message you meant to send."

Jennet hiccuped a laugh, but before she could answer the sound of Luke's voice raised in greeting came to them.

"They're coming alongside," she said, rising, wild-eyed, the pulse at the base of her throat fluttering. "They're going to board. Do you hear?"

There was a knock at the cabin door and it opened. Hannah expected one of the sailors with a message from Luke, but saw instead the strong, highly colored features of Piero Bardi.

To Jennet he said, "It is better if I keep out of sight. May I wait here with you, madame?"

Hannah was willing to concede one point to Bardi, and it wasn't a small one: He saw Jennet's distress, and spoke to it directly.

"The British don't interfere with their own mankind," he told her in his awkward English. "They have an eye on Spanish Florida, you see, just as they have their eye on New Orleans and everything else." He made a circle in the air to encompass the whole continent. "Cat Island is being made ready for the wives and families of the British officers. More arrive every week."

Jennet had been straining so hard to hear what was going on above them that Bardi might have been a pet bird chirping to itself, but the mention of the families caught her attention. "Children?"

"Of course. Last week they burned Washington, next week they expect to make short work the rest of the country. They think they can turn New Orleans into London." He lifted a shoulder and let it drop. "Bad news for the Americans, but it will make things easier for you. And do you hear? They aren't coming aboard. Your husband tells them what they wish to hear. You are Canadians, on your way to Pensacola on family business. The truth has its uses, on occasion."

Jennet focused on Bardi's face for the first time since he came into the cabin. "And you, Mr. Bardi? Where do you stand in this war?"

He touched a finger to his brow and gave a partial bow. "On the side of profit, madame."

A doubtful look passed over Jennet's face, and then her gaze fixed on his sleeve. She said, "You've got a wound."

For the first time he threw a glance Hannah's way. "An unfortunate misunderstanding with a tavern keeper in Port-au-Prince."

"Let me see." Jennet's tone had changed quite suddenly, shifting to one Hannah recognized: the laird's daughter, intent on getting her way. She would use honey rather than vinegar to begin with, but she would not be diverted. Hannah watched, amused, as Jennet prodded Bardi into rolling up the sleeve of his shirt and then unwrapping the bandage, which was streaked with bloody discharge.

"This is infected," Jennet said. She gave Bardi a sharp look. "What's this muck you've dressed it with?"

A single drop of sweat was making its muddy way through the bristle on Bardi's cheek, but his voice was steady. "Do not concern yourself, madame. There are doctors in Pensacola."

"Aye," said Jennet. "If you're fortunate you'll find one to take the arm off before the poison has got into the rest of ye." It was the worst of signs when Jennet's English began to slide toward Scots, though Bardi couldn't know this. He sent another nervous look Hannah's way.

Jennet scowled at him. "You'd rather chance losing an arm than put yourself in the power of a woman doctor, I see. Well, then, I suggest you say your prayers, and may the Almighty God have mercy on your bone-heided, kek-handed self."

Hannah was quite enjoying this confrontation, not so much because she liked to see Bardi in pain, but because it was a relief and a joy to see Jennet roused to anger. For his part Bardi seemed to realize that there was no escape, because he wiped his face with his free hand and then turned toward Hannah. "Will I lose the arm if I wait until Pensacola?" These were the first words he had ever addressed to her directly.

Jennet poked him in the shoulder. "If you want her help you'd best remember your manners. She has a name, you know."

He cleared his throat. "Miss—Miss—" He paused, clearly unable to recall her name, or perhaps to make himself say it.

"You may call her Walking-Woman," Jennet said. "It's the name given her by her husband's people, and a good honest name it is."

He managed to mumble his question, though he would not meet her eye.

"If you wait four days you won't keep the arm," Hannah answered, calmly. "If you want me to treat it, I can probably save it. If not your arm, then your life."

"Is that what you want, man?" Jennet asked. "Do ye fancy yersel a one-armed pirate, sailing the seas? Or will ye ask nicely?"

She had no mercy, and more than that, she was enjoying herself.

"I won't beg," Bardi said finally. "But I'll pay."

"Nobody's asking ye to beg," Jennet said. "All that's required is a wee bit of common courtesy. I'll go and get your kit, Hannah, and send for hot water."

He was a better patient than most. Hannah gave him nothing for the pain, but he stayed upright and made no noise while she cleaned out the deep gash that ran from his elbow to his wrist. If there was a story behind the wound, he did not offer to tell it and neither did Jennet or Hannah ask; they were not girls to be taken in by men's bragging.

"Bread and goat shit," Jennet said, her nose wrinkled in equal parts disgust and amazement. "Did you think that up yourself, Mr. Bardi?"

If Bardi wanted to compare opinions on the treatment of wounds, he was hampered by Hannah, who had taken up a scalpel to debride dead tissue.

"It's like being back on Nut Island," Jennet said cheerfully. "When I helped you with the surgeries, Hannah, do you recall? The selfsame stink. To think a body should go sentimental over such a thing."

While Hannah worked Jennet handed her what she needed and talked, for the first time, of the months they had spent together at the Canadian garrison, working among the prisoners, and tending to Hannah's younger brother, who had suffered wounds far worse than the one they worked over now.

There was something about Jennet's voice that reminded Hannah of a person waking from a long sleep. No doubt she would slide back into melancholy when she remembered the boy, but for the moment she was at ease and alert, and Hannah was glad of it.

Finally she said, "It's far too swollen to suture, but I'll pack the wound and dress it. It will seep. You must keep the dressing clean, do you understand? If there's any pain or discoloration or if it starts to stink of rot, you must come back to me."

Bardi's color had improved noticeably, but hard lines bracketed his mouth. Hannah could almost see the ideas forming in his mind, and when he asked the question he had been holding back, it came as no surprise.

"It is true, you're the captain's half sister?"

Hannah was wiping her instruments and didn't look at him. "Yes."

Jennet had gone very still, in surprise and gathering anger. Bardi didn't take note, or didn't care. His wide, pale-lipped mouth twitched. "I don't approve of the mixing of the races."

"She just saved your life," Jennet said. "Some gratitude would be in order, Mr. Bardi."

Bardi pushed himself away from the table with a jerk and then stood, not quite steady, before them. "I'll pay for services rendered. With coin."

"I have no use for your money," Hannah said easily.

"Or your sermons," said Jennet. "Be gone with you, man, before I let my temper get the best of me."

Jennet had been so weary for so long, but that afternoon she could hardly sit, so overwhelming was her anger at Bardi. Her mood lasted into the evening when Hannah had retired to her own small cabin. For all their history together, Luke and Jennet were still newlyweds and Hannah was mindful of their privacy, and her own.

Jennet told him the whole story over a simple supper of soup and bread. "And then," she finished, "he had the cheek to offer her money."

"So I heard," said Luke. "He tried to pay me instead—" He held up a hand to forestall Jennet's reaction. "I wouldn't take his coin, you know that. But he's not the kind of man who likes to be beholden."

Jennet hesitated, because this was sensible and also because it wasn't sense that she wanted at this moment.

He said, "So he talked, and I listened."

She snorted. "What did he have to tell that was worth his right arm?"

Luke leaned across the table to wipe a crumb from the corner of her mouth. "Wyndham hasn't gone back to Canada. They've sent him to Barataria."

He was waiting for her to make sense of those two statements on her own. Long ago, when he had tutored her in
philosophy and Latin, she had found these heavy pauses irritating, but more recently she had come to appreciate
them. He would not do her thinking for her. After a moment of studying her spoon she looked up sharply.

"They've turned him into a spy. Unless—" Jennet hesitated to say what she was thinking, because it was such a
disturbing idea. "Unless he's been spying all along?"

Luke rocked his head slowly from side to side, weighing
the idea. She saw doubt in his expression, and concern, but
whether this was for Wyndham's safety or some greater reason, she could not say. Which raised another question, one
that Jennet had not yet pursued for worry that the subject
would take her places she would rather not go.

She didn't know what Luke's own interests in the war
might be, and what he was doing to advance them. The last
time they had talked of such things was more than two years
ago, on the day he had told her he wanted to marry her but
could not, would not, until the war was over, out of concern
for her well-being. When trouble finally did come, it was
from a very different direction, and he hadn't been able to
protect her, after all.

Jennet could have put the question to him: *Are you spying, too?* And: *What might it cost us?* Perhaps he saw those
questions taking shape, because he reached over without
warning to grasp both her wrists and pull her out of her
chair. When she was settled on his lap with his arms around
her waist, he put his forehead against her temple.

"We haven't talked about where we're going, after," he
said. "Once we've got the boy. Have you thought of that,
where we should settle?"

He had always been good at distracting her; that's what
he meant to do now.

"Are we finished talking about Wyndham?"

"I see three possibilities, or four," he went on, implacable. "We could go back to Montreal, we could settle near my father and his family, or—"

"Carryck," Jennet supplied. "Would you want to go back to Carryck?" She found the idea odd and almost disturbing. The world had moved on, and she had gone with it.

"That's up to you," Luke said. "If you think we could make a life there. If you could be content, then so could I. Your mother wrote to say—"

She gave him a sharp look, but he went on without hitch or pause. "That your brother needs a new factor."

"Oh, no," Jennet said. "You might as well ask me to make time run backward. I couldn't take up that life again, not even for you."

His expression relaxed. "That's settled, then, and I'm glad of it."

He was holding on to her as if she were made of fine porcelain and might crack at the slightest touch, which was sweet, and irritating, too. Jennet leaned forward and nipped him on the jaw, hard.

He yelped and swung his head away. "Christ's bones, girl. What was that for?"

"If we can't solve the biggest problems this moment, there are still smaller ones to concern us. What about Wyndham?"

He rubbed his jaw. "There's nothing to say. Wyndham is on his way to Barataria, and it's not likely we'll run into him. And if we do—" He caught her head before she could nip again. His fingers threaded through her hair and he kissed her once, briefly. "We'll deal with it then."

"But we have to tell Hannah," Jennet said, drawing in a breath to explain why such a thing was necessary and then losing it unexpectedly. His hands tilted her head to his advantage and he kissed her until she lost track of the conversation, and then they moved down from her throat to her shoulders and then, insistently, lower. She had driven one set of thoughts from his mind and replaced it with others, quick and bright and hot. His intent was clear to read in the softening of his lips.

"What devilment are you up to now?" she asked, putting her hands over his.

"Ah," he said. "So I do have your attention."

"And I yours." She wiggled on his lap and he pulled in a hissing breath through his teeth.

"Think twice before you issue a challenge like that. If it's teasing you want, girl, I'll give it to you."

Tears came to her unexpectedly, unbidden, unwanted; he hushed her and kissed them away. "What's this, then? What's this?"

"I didn't think I could," Jennet said, the truth slipping away from her without warning. "I didn't think I could ever learn how to play again. Thank God you haven't forgot. I don't know how I'd live without this."

"You'll never have to," he said. "Not as long as I'm alive." His touch, clever and quick, made her draw in a sharp breath and hold it.

There was a fine humming urgency building between them, a quickening of her heart and his, and still Jennet was content to stay just as she was for the moment, wound up in kisses, long and soft. The fact of his hands lifting her, broad-palmed, spread-fingered, registered first as an interruption and then, quite quickly, something too long in coming.

Luke kept his eyes open and watched her face, the color rising up from her collarbones, the swelling of her lower lip; he counted her sharp breaths and made note of every murmur; to commit her to memory, to seal the promises he had made to her and himself, and to bind the woman who wept in his arms with joy and relief and gratitude to him yet again and forever.

CHAPTER 6

Major C.P. Wyndham
in care of Major General Keane
Negril Bay
Jamaica

My Dear Christian,

If you have arrived in Negril Bay before the end of this month, Major General Keane has delivered this letter to you by his own hand. At my direction, he has waited to do so until you received and read your new orders. Thus you are aware that if you have not yet been successful in your search for Anselm Dégre, you are now to desist in that pursuit. Effective immediately you have been reassigned to the Major General's staff as an Exploring Officer.

I expect that you were hoping to be sent back home to Canada, and that you are disappointed. It falls to me to share more unhappy news. God grant that it did not.

My beloved daughter Margaret passed on to her eternal reward three days ago, on the first of August. Her final illness was sudden and she suffered very little. Her sisters and I were with her at the last, when she asked to be remembered to you with great love and affection. The magnitude of our loss and grievous despair can hardly be put into words. You, who knew and loved her, will understand best.

Given this tragic event, I would like to believe that the change in orders will not be so very distressing. I might even hope that this opportunity to serve King and Country in a time of war will be a welcome distraction to you, as it is for me.

I continue to think of you as my dear Margaret's chosen partner, and thus as my own son. With that in mind, I take it upon myself to speak to another sensitive matter.

When you were invalided home from Spain I agreed to your request for transfer to the King's Own because I believed then, as I do now, that your exemplary service in the Peninsular Campaign deserved recognition and reward. Your strong wish to no longer serve as an Exploring Officer seemed to me a reasonable one given your experiences. Now, looking back, I am not so sure that it was a good decision on your part or a wise one on mine. The devils we run away from are the ones that pursue us most vigorously, and will only be defeated when you turn to face them down.

This you may still do, by taking on the role Major General Keane has devised for you. You speak Spanish and French fluently, you are familiar with our codes and methods, and you understand the importance of strategic information. I can think of no one more qualified to serve as Exploring Officer in the crucial battle for Louisiana and the Gulf. I know you will meet this challenge with all the strength of character

and body you can muster. For your own sake and in
memory of Margaret, who loved you with all her
heart.

Yours most sincerely,
G. Prevost
4 August 1814
Quebec

CHAPTER 7

No more than an hour out of Pensacola Bay, the storm the *Patience* had been dodging for a day caught up with her and put an abrupt end to the first part of Jennet's plan. And so she left the men to struggle with sails and went below to join Hannah who sat, feet and hands braced, in the near dark, tracking the course of the storm.

The ship pitched and rolled like a child in a tantrum, the keel slamming into one wave after another. Hannah felt the roar of the storm in her gut and wondered if she was to be seasick for the first time in her life. Jennet seemed to take no note at all. She sat next to Hannah on her narrow cot, and together they rocked with the motion of the ship. Something small slid across the floor and bumped into the far wall, paused, and slid back again.

She said, "Did you see?"

"Yes," Hannah said.

Just before the storm overtook the *Patience,* they had caught first sight of Pensacola Bay and found it to be crowded with ships of all kinds. Every single one of them, as far as Hannah could see, flew British colors.

Spanish Florida had declared herself neutral in the newest war between the United States and Britain, but there was nothing to see of that neutrality on this water. The Spanish king fed and housed and paid the salaries of the

men who armed the garrison, but all the trade here was
Scottish and English. The flag over the garrison was Spanish,
but the river of money that kept the city alive was English.

They had been warned about this in Saint-Domingue,
but Luke had seemed unconcerned. He would introduce
himself as the manager of Forbes & Sons of Montreal and
Carryck, here on a personal matter. The harbormaster, the
customs inspectors, the governor himself could raise no objection to such a truth, no more than they would turn away
a company with money to invest.

Hannah could tell Jennet these things she knew already,
and more. *We will get the boy and leave the same way we came,
and no one will try to stop us.*

But those words could not find their way past the fluttering in her breast, because something was not right. Jennet's
expression told her that much.

"If we set off walking," Jennet said. "If we set off today,
and made our way north, how far would it be to Paradise?"

Hannah tried to imagine that great distance over strange
territory, through forests like the ones she saw around
Pensacola, where a dozen kinds of trees she had never seen
before blocked out the sun. A richly damp, hot world full of
dangers she couldn't even imagine.

But they had money, and the names of powerful men,
and their own wits to get them through. What they didn't
have, what Jennet hadn't given them yet, was the whole
truth.

Jennet said, "There are things I need to tell you."

In the grip of the storm the ship groaned and howled
and thrashed. A flickering of lightning dashed through the
cabin. Jennet's voice was just as unsteady.

She grasped Hannah's upper arm and spoke directly into
her ear. She was groping for words as cautiously as a blind
woman would make her way through an unfamiliar house.
"I didn't know what else to do, you must understand."

Thunder filled the ship and set it to echoing, or so it seemed. Hannah waited until she could find her own words in that noise.

"Jennet," she said. "Whatever it is, we will find a way through."

Jennet's fingers pressed so hard that Hannah drew in a sharp breath.

"Listen," Jennet said. "The storm is passing."

The words were still hovering in the air when the lightning struck in a tripling pulse, white-hot and brilliant. The *Patience* shuddered and pitched so violently that the two women were thrown to the floor. There was a screaming, then, louder than anything that had come before. It took three heartbeats for Hannah to make sense of that familiar sound in this unfamiliar setting: the cry of a tree struck by lightning and rent to its core.

She managed to get back to her feet. Jennet was a pale shape on the floor, half hidden underneath the small table that was fixed to the boards. Her knees were drawn up to her chin and she was breathing rapidly, but her eyes were open.

"Did you strike your head?"

"No," Jennet said. "Not my head. Help me up."

As they fought their way up to the deck, an idea came to Hannah, an image so perfectly clear that it would remain etched in her memory forever: They would come out into the open and find themselves alone on the *Patience,* all the men gone, carried off by the wind and the sea.

Half on deck, clinging to the edge of the hatchway with Jennet beside her, Hannah was confronted with a very different picture from the one she expected. Lowry, whom Hannah had treated for a sore ear just last week and who played the penny-whistle, was caught against the rail in a web of tangled rigging, his limp head flopping forward and backward with the heaving of the ship. They had lost a mast and Lowry and perhaps others, but most of the crew were still scrambling over the deck, focused on putting things back in order. The storm was already passing.

Luke lurched his way toward them up the pitched deck.

"That was more excitement than I was hoping for," he said, his expression grim. He was looking at Lowry, and then he turned to Jennet, who had gone very pale. He put a hand on her head and rocked it forward to touch his brow to hers.

"We'll take the longboat in and leave this lot to see to repairs," he said. "No more delays."

The British had clearly claimed Pensacola as their own, and to make that clear, two armed sloops of war, a brig, and a dozen smaller ships were anchored in the bay. It was clear evidence that the war had arrived in the Gulf and could not be avoided.

When the longboat finally deposited them on land, Hannah found herself suddenly at the end of her energy, unable to make sense of the simplest tasks, or even contribute to the conversation when she had something to say. She stood silently next to Jennet and listened to Luke's conversation with the harbormaster and a British naval officer whose name she didn't catch, and didn't care to learn. Other men had gathered around their little party on the wharf, most of them in some kind of uniform, a few well-dressed merchants, a boy with a basket of seething crabs.

Luke was talking about the damage to the *Patience,* what materials the crew would need to make repairs, how best to get provisions to them. He turned and looked toward the point where the ship was anchored in the bay. Questions he did not want to answer he simply ignored or deflected by changing the subject. He made no mention of Bardi, though the harbormaster asked directly about passengers.

No doubt he had a good reason to withhold that information, but Hannah could not imagine what it might be.

Jennet had been calm through the hasty service for Lowry, and quiet during their evacuation from the *Patience* and the hour it took them to reach shore. Now she seemed almost to be walking in her sleep, no doubt at least in part because of the heat, which set the air to shimmering. The late afternoon sun, brutal enough on its own, reflected off the water and the metal buttons on the uniform coats and the spectacles perched on the long nose of the harbormaster, a Spanish gentleman with great pouched cheeks and a single eyebrow like a wing across his brow.

Hannah took Jennet's arm and realized that she was not trembling out of exhaustion or anxiety. Her skin was clammy to the touch.

"Jennet?"

She leaned forward, a hand to her belly and her face averted. That got Luke's attention. For a moment he looked more like a love-struck boy than the experienced merchant and soldier he was.

He said, "What is it?"

"Nothing," Jennet said sharply. "Don't fuss."

Hannah caught Luke's eye and shook her head. Things moved very quickly then, and within minutes the few cases they had brought from the *Patience* and the women themselves were secured in a borrowed carriage with Luke across from them.

Jennet leaned back against the cushions and closed her eyes. The flesh beneath her eyes looked bruised, and there was a sheen to her skin that spoke of pain or fever or both.

"What is it?" Luke asked again. Sweat stood out on his brow in great round drops, and in his face Hannah saw again, too soon, the desperation that had driven him through the last year.

"Indigestion," Jennet said. "All I need is a bit of privacy."

To that obvious lie, Hannah added nothing. There was nothing to be gained by telling Luke the things she was thinking, not just at this moment. The best she could do was to try to turn his attention elsewhere.

"How far is it to—Where are we going?" In the confusion of their departure from the wharf she had caught few of the details.

"I'll find out." He turned to speak to the driver.

Jennet pressed Hannah's hand and drew her close. "You must wait for me, do you understand? Don't go look for the boy without me."

"Preston's place is just here," Luke said. "There he is, he rode on ahead."

The driver had turned the horses up a broader lane lined with palm trees and substantial houses in good repair. Hannah caught sight of one of the merchants who had been on the wharf. He stood on the veranda of the biggest of the houses talking to a woman of mixed blood. From forty feet away Hannah met the woman's gaze. It felt like a physical touch, unexpected and oddly familiar and vaguely comforting.

"Preston will see to it you have everything you need," Luke said.

But Hannah placed her hopes in the woman, and found that her instincts had served her well.

The housekeeper was called Titine, a woman only five years older than Hannah and Jennet. She was efficient and quick-witted and she didn't ask unnecessary questions. Almost without discussion she and Hannah worked together in the large, breezy room where Jennet lay on a broad bed under swathes of mosquito netting. The things Hannah required—warm water and clean cloths, tea and broth and certain tisanes—seemed to appear before she could even call for them.

Deep in the night, when the worst was over and Jennet

was asleep, Titine sat down in the breeze from the veranda and wiped her face with her apron. She was a strongly built woman with a long chin and deep-set eyes the color of new spring leaves, the same color as Hannah's younger brother Daniel's. Hannah did not often suffer from homesickness, but Titine reminded her of the women who had raised her, and she felt the lack of them just now.

Her stepmother Elizabeth and Curiosity Freeman would know what to make of this strange situation, how best to proceed, what to say to Jennet when she woke. But they were not here and Hannah could not trust her worries and doubts to this stranger, no matter how much she wanted to, no matter how kind she had been.

Titine spread her apron out with her hands and drew in a sharp breath.

"I expect her husband is still waiting down in the parlor, but you'll want to talk to him your own self, you." She spoke an English heavily flavored with French and other languages unknown to Hannah.

"Yes," Hannah said. "I will speak to him."

"Mr. Preston is a fair man for the most part," Titine said in a conversational tone. "But one thing he don't tolerate is loose talk. What happens in this house stays right here, and as far as I'm concerned, the same is true for this chamber. Just so you know."

Hannah met the woman's gaze and managed a small smile. "Thank you. You see very clearly, I think."

Titine shrugged as she got up, working her shoulders. "I see some things, but I don't pretend to understand much at all. Servants' quarters are out back—" She gestured with her head. "If you need me, you send word by Koffee, he keep watch in the garden all night, him." She reached down to straighten the coverlet on the cot that had been made ready for Hannah. "You had best go to sleep, too."

Hannah should have gone straight to Luke, out onto the

veranda and down the stairs to the parlor where he was sitting with Mr. Preston, but the breeze that moved through the room felt fine on her damp skin and she could not think, for the moment, how to make her legs obey her. There was a crust of bread on a plate, and cold pork in a covered dish, and so she ate, first. To gather her strength and her thoughts as she looked out over the garden and beyond that, the glint of the bayou in the light of a half-moon. The air smelled of river water and the swampland beyond, rich and dank.

Jennet's voice came in the dark, not so much weak as weary. "I would have told you, but I wasn't sure."

Hannah got up. "That doesn't matter just now." She could not make out Jennet's face in the shadows. "What do you want me to tell Luke?"

"Tell him to stay close by," Jennet said. "Tell him I want him near. Tell him I love him, and no other. Or send him here so I can tell him myself."

Hannah hesitated, waiting for the rest of the words that Jennet was trying to spill. They came finally in a whisper.

"Did you ask about the Poiterins?"

This was only the second time Jennet had ever said the name of the family who were looking after her son. Hannah sat down on the stool beside the bed. Jennet's color was poor, but there was no fever and her pulse beat slow and steady.

She said, "Luke brought word a few hours ago, while you were sleeping. There's a Mme. Agnès Poiterin. She has a home down at the end of this lane."

Jennet stirred and tried to push herself up on her elbows, but Hannah made a warning sound and gently pushed her back. What she had to say was best said quickly.

"Mme. Poiterin left Pensacola when the news came of Washington burning."

Jennet frowned. "Go on."

"It's hard to separate fact from rumor, but it seems as though Mme. Poiterin fled in a panic."

"Where is she?"

"The old lady's gone to her other home, on the Bayou St. John, near New Orleans. She took her whole household with her."

"My son?" Jennet asked, her voice hoarse.

"There's a baby, yes. She calls him her great-grandson, and he's with her. Jennet, do you hear me? The boy is alive, and we know where he is. Luke is already making arrangements to travel as soon as you're well enough. He's written letters to our parents, and will send them off with the post-rider today."

Jennet turned her face toward Hannah. In the low light it looked like a mask molded from linen into a perfect oval, the eyes dark holes.

"I did what I did to save him."

"I know that. I understand that."

"But will Luke?"

Hannah could not say how her half brother would react to the news that Jennet had lost a baby she must have conceived when her son was less than three months old. Jennet had stood up in front of a priest and married Luke carrying another man's child. What Hannah could say, what she must say, might not provide Jennet with much comfort, but it was the truth.

She said, "Luke was prepared for the worst, when we found you."

Jennet gave a low hiccup of laughter that ended with a trembling sigh. It was a sound so desperate that the hair lifted on the back of Hannah's neck, as though someone unseen had blown warm breath across her skin.

When Jennet spoke again, her voice was almost normal in tone. "Did Luke have any other news of the Poiterins?"

"Not last I spoke to him," Hannah said.

"Ask him to come up, then," Jennet said. "I want to tell you both at the same time, and it can't wait any longer."

A single oil lamp hung from a hook lit the stairway, its flame reflected in a hurricane shade marbled by smoke. A moth bumped against the bars of light cast out through the jalousies as Hannah followed the steps down to the parlor. Poised at the door she heard a man's voice that she didn't recognize. She hesitated, thought of retreating, and then heard the outer door open and close again.

When she came into the room Luke was at the window, watching his visitor ride away. He was very pale, and he smelled of brandy and fear.

"You're breathing like you ran a mile," Hannah said. "What is it? Who was that man?"

Luke's expression was studiously blank. "Honoré Poiterin, of Pensacola and New Orleans. A merchant. M. Poiterin claims to be Jennet's husband, and the father of her son. Pardon me while I sit for a moment, will you? I have to gather my thoughts before I go up to her."

Jennet said, "It was not a legal marriage." And: "You must understand, it was never real. Moore was a defrocked priest, without any standing in the Church. And I only agreed to it because it was the price Poiterin put on taking our son away to safety."

Luke's gaze was fixed on the far wall and a muscle in his jaw shivered. Hannah could not remember ever seeing her brother quite like this, even in the days early in their search when it had all seemed hopeless.

"He tells a different story, I'm sure you can imagine." Luke's gaze shifted to Jennet, who had been propped up against bolsters. Her hands made fists on the covers.

"You believe him." Her voice wavered.

"No," Luke said. "I would never take his word over yours."

Hannah realized she had been holding her breath, because now she let it go in a rush.

Jennet lifted her face to them. "Every day Dégre took the baby away from me. Sometimes for a few minutes, sometimes for hours. I never knew if he would bring him back. I never knew what he would do. He pointed a gun at my son's head and I—I surrendered him."

Her tone was dull and almost without inflection, like a child reciting a poem it has learned by rote but doesn't really understand.

Luke started to speak, but she held up a hand to stop him. "Let me finish. I first met Poiterin on a day that Dégre didn't bring the boy back until he was screaming with hunger. Poiterin's ship had just come into the harbor. At that point I would have agreed to anything, and Poiterin seemed so reasonable, at first. He would take the boy back to his grandmother to be cared for, and then he would come and rescue me. He had a ship, and men, and his first mate had a woman who could nurse the baby. Most important, Dégre liked Poiterin and trusted him—" She hesitated. "Poiterin has a reputation, you'll hear about it if you ask."

"He's a pirate, a thief, and a slave runner," Luke said.

Jennet's eyes flashed, the first sign of anger she had shown during this confrontation.

"He is all that and worse," she said. "And he saved your son's life."

"And married you," Luke said.

"He did not," Jennet said. "There was no one there to marry us, I have told you. Dégre was never a priest, and Moore wasn't one anymore. Call Poiterin in here and see if he will deny it. He cannot."

Luke rubbed a hand over his face, drew a deep breath

and then another. "He can, Jennet, and he does. Poiterin claims the boy is his own."

She pushed herself forward. "I never saw the man until after I gave birth."

"He claims he was on the ship that brought you south from Canada."

"He is lying."

"No doubt," Luke said. "But who is there to deny it? It is your word against his."

"I would hope my word would count for more than that of Honoré Poiterin," Jennet said, her voice rising.

"With me, of course. But we are strangers here, and the Poiterin family is well established. He tells me that it's a small matter to get the marriage recognized by the church."

Color rose from Jennet's collarbones in a great rush. She pressed her hands to her mouth and then let them drop away.

Hannah put a firm hand on Luke's arm. "It's very late," she said. "And we won't settle this tonight. You both need your rest. There's a cot here; I think you should take it."

Luke hesitated, and then he nodded. Hannah left them and went to the next chamber, where she spent a sleepless night under a swathe of mosquito netting that looked like a shroud in the moonlight.

In the first light of day, Hannah and Luke went to speak to Mr. Preston over breakfast. It went against the grain and cost Luke a great deal to take a relative stranger into his confidence, but then Preston's name was on the list of potential allies that Lacoeur had provided, and beyond that small comfort, they had no choice. As it turned out, Andrew Preston could offer them little hope and only worse news. Honoré Poiterin was about to leave Pensacola for New Orleans, to join his grandmother. If he hadn't left already.

"How do you know?" It was the first question Hannah had ever asked him directly. He looked at her for a moment as if he were deliberating whether or not he cared to speak to her, and then he shrugged.

"The way all the news moves in this town, from slave to slave to servant to master."

His great pouched cheeks spread wide as he shoveled in another spoonful of porridge.

Luke said, "Is there anyone we could talk to who would give us more information about the Poiterins, anything that might be useful for us to know?"

From the direction of the bay there was a suddenly rolling *boom-boom-boom* of artillery fire, but Preston seemed unconcerned.

"The British navy is nothing if not well drilled," he said dryly. "That will go on for much of the morning." He brushed his mouth with a small triangle of linen and then put both hands down, one on each side of his plate.

"Agnès Poiterin—Honoré's grandmother, ye ken—is a formidable force in this town and in New Orleans, forbye. The Poiterins are a banking family. I canna afford to have her as an enemy, ye mun understand."

"Somebody will give us what we need," Luke said. "We're not without resources." He showed little concern for Preston's dilemma, most probably, Hannah guessed, because he took the man's protests for the opening gambit in a series of negotiations. Preston would help them, but at a price; he was a merchant, after all, and a successful one. She had learned a lot about the way white men of means traded from watching Luke for the last year.

Preston was fishing in a coat pocket, and came out with a tobacco tin enameled in Chinese red. He opened it and offered it to Luke, who shook his head.

"Aye, weel. There's Titine."

"Titine, your housekeeper?" Hannah leaned forward.

"My housekeeper, aye. She's been with me since she was seventeen, but she's a Poiterin born and raised. On the wrong side of the sheets, ye ken."

Preston paused while he produced three oddly dainty, tobacco-scented sneezes into a handkerchief the size of a small tablecloth. Then he blinked his watering eyes.

"Titine is the elder Poiterin's daughter by his mistress. Shall we leave it at that?" Preston pressed the tip of his nose with a knuckle, his eyes flickering in Hannah's direction. "It's no a topic for mixed company."

"Do go on," Hannah said. "There's little you can say that will surprise me and nothing that will shock me."

"Is that so?" The older man didn't look pleased by this admission. "Given your own family arrangements, I suppose I must take ye at your word. Weel. The way of it is simple enough. In New Orleans you'll find that some men of means—not sae many, mind, for it's mair trouble than it's worth, in my view of things—may have a second family. If a man isna satisfied with the young lady his family chooses to be his lawful wife, he may look elsewhere for comfort."

He cleared his throat; his face had taken on an unlikely rosy color. "I've traveled as far as China, and I've never seen the likes of New Orleans when it comes to matters of race. There's a whole city within the city, made up of free people of color, as they call themselves. Some of them far lighter of skin than I myself."

He observed the back of his own hand, burnished bronze by many years in the sun.

"You must realize that it's no the daughters of legislators and bankers and merchants who have earned New Orleans her reputation for female beauty."

Hannah was becoming more impatient with the old Scot's inability or unwillingness to come to the point, and so was Luke.

He said, "You're saying that rich white men take free women of color as mistresses."

"Aye," said Preston gruffly. "Sometimes it's no more than a passing alliance, and sometimes—though not so often—a rich man will buy a cottage for a quadroon mistress he wants to keep for himself. And as ye'd guess, bairns come of such long-term relationships."

"So you are telling us that Honoré Poiterin's father had children by his lawful wife, and by another woman," Hannah prompted.

"Poiterin and his wife are dead these five years, but his mistress is still alive. Her name is Valerie Maurepas," Preston said. "She had a daughter by Poiterin."

"Titine," Luke said.

Préston cocked his head. "Aye. Honoré is Archange Poiterin's legitimate son—his only surviving legitimate issue, and by his third wife, forbye. He lost the first to yellow fever and the second to childbed. Titine is Honoré's half sister."

Luke sat back in his chair. "She's unlikely to be of any help to us, then."

Preston was having trouble concentrating on anything but the filled plate before him, but now he put down his fork and his knife with a small huffing sound. "There's no love lost between Titine and Honoré Poiterin, sister and brother though they are. When their father died five years ago, Honoré turned Valerie Maurepas out of her cottage and stripped her of everything."

"Why would he do that?" Hannah asked.

"For the pure devilment of it," Preston said, picking up his fork. "And because his grand-mère wanted him to. Some say Agnès Poiterin outlived her son just to have the pleasure of seeing his mistress turned out into the street."

"Simple jealousy, or greed," Hannah said. Preston shrugged to indicate his lack of interest in the way a woman's mind might work.

"And what happened to Valerie Maurepas?" Luke asked.

"She came to work for me," Preston said. He pointed with his chin toward the rear of the house. "You'll understand that I had to take in Titine's mother if I wanted any peace. No doubt you'll find the whole gaggle of them out in the kitchen garden at this time of day."

When Preston had finished his breakfast and excused himself, Luke and Hannah sat in silence for a moment. The air was already gravid with heat at only ten in the morning.

Hannah said, "I'll go talk to Titine and her mother, but first you and I need to discuss something else."

"Not now."

She leaned forward and took her brother's hand where it lay fisted on the table. She felt him tense, and then she felt him fight to let his anger go, and fail. There were many things she could have said, but none of them were news to Luke, and none would help him now. He would learn to forgive Jennet, because he was a good man and he loved her, but it would not be a quick or easy thing for him to do. Hannah got up and pressed her brow to the crown of his head, and then she left him sitting there and went out to find Valerie Maurepas.

CHAPTER 8

Hannah heard Jennet's voice first, and realized that she had been outwitted. She picked up her skirts and trotted around the corner of the kitchen building into a small, well-kept garden alive with butterflies. In the middle of it, four women sat in the shade of an arbor heavy with flowering vines. Between Jennet and Titine sat an elderly woman with the bearing of a queen and the inquisitive, alert look of a girl of ten. She might be called a free woman of color by Preston and others like him, but to Hannah's eye she seemed white. Beside her sat another, older woman, this one far darker of complexion but no less alert. One of her eyes had gone the milky color of marble, and the hands in her lap were so swollen at the joints that they seemed hardly human.

Among these women Jennet's head of blond curls looked almost doll-like, but the stare she sent Hannah was pure defiance.

Hannah forced herself to smile as she approached. It was true that Jennet was pale, but the hands wrapped around the bowl of milk were steady, and the shadows under her eyes were no worse than Hannah's own. More than that, Hannah had the sense that these women were well aware of Jennet's condition and could be trusted to watch her closely.

"My sister-in-law Hannah," Jennet said. "I was wondering when you'd come to find me. Let me introduce you.

This lady is Mme. Valerie Maurepas, Titine's mother. And that is Gaetane, Madame's servant. They have a great deal to tell us."

It was clearly Gaetane's role to tell stories, and she was very good at it, though she allowed Titine and her mother to add the occasional comment or detail.

Hannah had the idea that it had always been this way, since the day Archange Poiterin had bought a cottage on the rue Dauphine and installed Valerie there with two slaves of her own to look after her, one of whom was a twenty-year-old Gaetane. Together they had been expelled from that same cottage, and together they had come to Pensacola to live with Valerie's only daughter.

Titine had not inherited her mother's legendary looks, and because her father had made no provisions for her in his will, she had accepted the position as Andrew Preston's housekeeper, and perhaps more. Hannah had the idea that Mr. Preston would require some kind of payment for taking in two old black women who could be of little practical use in his household.

Gaetane, it was very clear, disliked Pensacola and wanted nothing more than to go back to New Orleans, but she would not leave her mistress even if she had the means to do so. No doubt she would have escorted Valerie Maurepas to hell, if solely to make sure the devil showed her the courtesy she deserved. And Gaetane had quite a lot to say about Honoré Poiterin. Some of it was amusing, and all of it was alarming.

"Everybody know Michie Honoré, the same way everybody know the gator and the gar. I like the gator better, me, M. Caïmon. *Câlice!* We got one back there in the *ciprière* long as two men standing one on top of the other." She looked toward the tangle of green that started beyond a pasture where a few horses grazed in the shade of a stand of cypress trees. "Old M. Caïmon don't make no bones 'bout what he want, and don't pretend to be something he ain't."

Hannah thought for a moment. "What does Honoré Poiterin want?"

The three women looked briefly at one another, and then Mme. Valerie answered in an elegant, musical, and quite old-fashioned English. "Honoré cares about two things. The first is amusing himself. The second is pleasing his grand-mère Agnès, because she controls the money he requires to amuse himself."

Gaetane sniffed loudly. With one small, red-painted clog she crushed a yellow jacket crawling over the cobbles.

Hannah said, "Is it Agnès Poiterin's idea or her grandson's to try to claim my nephew as their own?"

Mme. Valerie crossed her hands on her lap. "That is a very good question, but there is no simple answer. My guess would be that once Agnès saw the boy, she decided she wanted to keep him, and Honoré went along with it."

"Mme. Agnès, she like pretties, her," Gaetane said. "And that boy of yours the prettiest child I ever seen in all my long years."

Jennet jerked and righted herself. "You've seen him? You've seen my son?"

"*Mais* yeah, we see your boy, your Nathaniel," said Gaetane. She pronounced it in the French way, *Nah-taan-i-el.* "See him just about every day. Jacinthe, she bring him by here and sit right there where you are, madame, with the boy in her lap while she pass the time with us. The boy got a smile like his papa's, like your man's."

Jennet stood, hands pressed to her mouth, and then sat again.

Titine said, "I would have told you, but you were so unwell when you arrived."

"Jacinthe is his nurse?" Hannah asked.

"*Mais* yeah." Gaetane rocked her whole body from side to side in approval. "She got sweet milk, Jacinthe, and a good heart. Deserve better than that devil Honoré, that for sure."

Titine said, "The boy is well taken care of with Jacinthe, Madame Scott."

Hannah saw the sharp look Titine's mother sent her. She said, "You disagree, madame?"

"I have no quarrel with Jacinthe, but it's not the girl who will have the raising of the boy. It's Honoré's grand-mère." She seemed to come to some conclusion, because she held up a hand to quiet Gaetane.

"Honoré might have turned out differently, if it hadn't been for the fact that Agnès raised him in her own image. I wouldn't put a good dog in her care, much less a boy. You had best go straight to New Orleans, and do what you must to get your son back. If you're fortunate Honoré will be away on business and you'll find a way around Agnès."

"And how do we do that? Can you tell me?" Jennet's voice was steady but she was trembling.

"If I knew how to get the best of Agnès Poiterin I would not be here," said the older woman. "I would be where I belong in my cottage on the rue Dauphine, in New Orleans—where you must go, without delay."

The hour in the garden had drained Jennet of the little strength she had, and she retired to her bed without argument. She allowed Hannah to wipe her face and throat with a cloth dipped in water sweetened with cloves and mint.

"Tomorrow," Jennet said.

Hannah hesitated, and then nodded. "Tomorrow, yes."

"You'll arrange it with Luke?"

"If you like. If I must." It was an invitation, but Jennet turned her face to the wall. Hannah was about to leave her when Jennet spoke again, her voice clogged with unshed tears.

"I can only fight one battle at a time," she said.

Hannah sat again. "You aren't at war with Luke."

"No." Each breath Jennet produced was short and harsh. "Of course not."

Jennet slept fitfully for much of the day, starting up out of dreams to find herself drenched in sweat. It was dim in the chamber and crossed by breezes that felt good against the dampness of her skin. Often someone was sitting beside the bed, Hannah or Titine or another young woman with skin the color of molasses who held a baby to her breast. The smell of her milk filled the air, and it made Jennet's own breasts ache.

She dreamed that her brother Simon was sitting beside her bed. He had died long ago as a young boy, but in her dream he was a man grown, with a shock of red hair and a deep voice he used to tell her news of home. *I watch over them,* he said. *I watch you all.* She dreamed of Honoré Poiterin, his laughing smile and the flash of an earring against black hair. A young man of some talents and many sins, who feared nothing and demanded everything. She dreamed of Moore's face across the table, his mouth forming the question *When will I get me a good wife?* While the white scar on his forehead twisted like a snake against red flushed skin. When he showed himself next he was reciting the marriage rites with the exaggerated care of a man who has drunk too deep.

Deus Israel conjungat vos in matrimonium et ipse sit vobiscum qui misertus est duobus unicis . . .

Jennet woke fully and finally in the last of the evening light at the sound of the door shutting and a step on the floorboards.

She said, "You needn't sit here with me all day."

"I've brought supper." Luke's voice, steady and calm, his tone unremarkable. Jennet opened her eyes and saw him sitting beside her. He had spent the day in the sun and his skin still glowed with it.

A beautiful boy, him, with a smile like his papa's, like your man's.

He helped her sit up and arranged the pillows for her back, sat by and watched her drink the tisane Hannah had sent up with the dinner tray, and smiled when she pulled a face at its bitterness. While she spooned soup Luke did the same, telling her between swallows about his day. The repairs to the *Patience* were moving along and she would be ready to sail tomorrow, if nothing else went wrong; he had hired a crew member to replace Bardi, a free man of color out of Mobile who could get them past the British and American navies to New Orleans by a back route.

"Bardi has left us?"

Luke told her the story, one with no real surprises: Bardi had taken off in the night. Jennet felt a vague relief.

"As long as we can leave here tomorrow," she said.

There was a small and uneasy silence, undercut by the sound of a man's voice raised in tuneless song to the rhythm of a scythe. The smell of fresh-cut grass came to them and Jennet was struck with an unexpected surge of homesickness for Scotland, green and damp, where her mother must be waiting for news. Jennet had yet to find the words to write the letter her mother must read.

"Do you feel strong enough to walk?" Luke's voice brought her out of her thoughts.

"Now?"

"It's cool out, and it's still light. You needn't worry about running into Poiterin. He sent a note saying he's away on business for a few days."

"Did he." Jennet summoned a smile. She wasn't ready yet to discuss Honoré Poiterin with Luke, and neither did he seem eager.

"Hannah thought it would be good for you to get out,"

Luke went on. "If you feel strong enough. And if you finish the tisane."

It was good to hear some of Luke's old teasing tone. She finished the dark, cold tea in two swallows and let him help her dress.

Where the dirt lane turned to run parallel to the harbor, an old woman sat in the window of a shack overgrown with a riot of flowers that glowed like a scattering of burning stars in the gloaming. She was an Indian of a tribe Jennet could not name, her hair hanging limp over rounded shoulders. The woman watched two naked children with skin like tarnished copper who looked up from their game and only blinked at Jennet's greeting. She felt their eyes following her. She would have liked to talk to them, but most likely they would have no language in common beyond her small bit of Spanish.

"I have seen some poor villages in the last year," Jennet said. "But I expected more of Pensacola."

Many of the cottages that lined the lane were abandoned or collapsing in on themselves. More pigs and goats roamed the lanes than people. Their owners had made themselves scarce, most probably because soldiers or sailors loitered on corners or lounged, half asleep, under trees. A few men greeted Luke, but most pulled caps down over their eyes and pretended not to take note.

"The Spanish can't manage this place," said Luke. His voice trailed away while his mind turned to trade, and to the concerns he had left in other men's hands in Canada. He was thinking about returning to Montreal, whereas Jennet could hardly imagine that such a world still existed. She tried to conjure up the house on the rue Bonsecours, to see herself at the dining table or her son playing in the garden, but the only picture she could manage was the rough shed she had lived in with Hannah in the garrison followers' camp on Île aux Noix.

Jennet tightened her grip on Luke's arm and slowed her pace. She kept her gaze on the bay, scattered with ships that rocked in a good wind. The sky had already faded into a colorless night. Beside her Luke went very still. Jennet had let go of his arm to wrap her shawl more closely around herself, but she imagined she could still hear the tension humming through him.

"What?" She followed his gaze out into the bay. "What?" Though some part of her understood already.

"She's gone? The *Patience*?" Jennet found she could not catch her breath.

"Bardi," said Luke. There was no particular emotion in his voice, not anger or surprise. "And here is the harbormaster, come to report the obvious."

They waited while the man rode up. Luke took Jennet's hand, and that simple act flooded her with courage as no words could have. The Spaniard slid to the ground, his expression so studiously serious that his jowls, blue-bristled, drew up in pleats all the way to his cheekbones.

"M. Scott." He bowed. "Madame. I come to report—"

"The sailing of the *Patience*," Luke finished for him. "We can see that ourselves, Señor Uribe."

The harbormaster blinked at them and then turned to look out into the bay. The rising moon cast a path across the water like a curl of silver ribbon.

"The *Patience* has sailed?"

Luke didn't try to hide his irritation. "Unless she sprouted wings and flew off like a bloody gull. You hadn't noticed?"

"I have been otherwise occupied." He bowed again, not so much out of politeness, it struck Jennet, as a way to hide an inappropriate half smile. He was a man who enjoyed delivering bad news, but knew enough to be ashamed of this in himself.

He said, "There is no kind way to relate this; forgive me. One of your men has been found behind the tavern with his throat cut."

Luke drew in a sharp breath. "Bardi," he said again. "This is his work."

A fluttering of muscle in Uribe's cheek. "No. Not this time."

"And how do you know that?"

"Because it is Bardi whose throat was cut. Whoever did this went a step further and took Bardi's head with him," said Uribe. "The rest of the corpse was dumped at the doorstep of a——" He paused in consideration, and then bowed from the shoulders. "Shall we say, a lady of flexible standards who knew him well enough to identify the remains. What is the expression in English? The chicken has come home to roost, is that correct? Bardi was a scoundrel, and not to be mourned. As to who took your ship——" He looked over his shoulder at the bay again as if he expected to see some answer written in the sky. "I don't know who's responsible."

I know. Jennet could not make herself say the words out loud, but there was no reason to; from Luke's face she saw that he was guessing already what she could have told him. Suddenly she felt light-headed and unsure on her feet. She pinched the flesh between thumb and forefinger until her vision cleared.

"But perhaps this will explain." The harbormaster was busy patting his chest in the way of a man with too many pockets and a poor memory. Finally he pulled out a square of folded paper with a large red seal and presented it to Jennet with a flourish and a bow.

"For you, madame?"

The letter was addressed to Lady Jennet in a strong, flowing hand. A hand she had never seen before, but recognized nonetheless: The great loops and grandiose swirls spoke the name of the writer as clearly as a signature. While she stared at the letter in her hands she only half heard the harbormaster's questions, all directed to Luke, about Bardi.

Finally he bowed again, this time so low that they had a view of the circle of nut brown skin at the crown of his head.

"I see no need to disturb you further about this crime," he said to his shoes. "But I would like to question your men, when they return with the *Patience*. If they return."

There was just enough light, and so Jennet cracked open the seal on the letter as soon as the harbormaster's horse had taken him out of hearing. A single page, covered with that bold hand.

Luke said, "Read it to yourself first," and he walked off three paces and stood looking out toward sea. It was that simple gesture of understanding, of faith and love, that gave Jennet the courage she must have to face whatever waited for her on the paper.

The sheet shook in her hands so that the words seemed to jump on the page. It was in French, a language she spoke fluently, but it might as well have been written in Arabic for all the sense it made to her.

She forced herself to take three deep breaths, and when her head had cleared, she read.

My dearest wife,

What a lamentable turn of events! You are new arrived and I must away without even a kiss. It is too cruel, after so long a separation. If only you had not found it necessary to bring a second husband with you. Whatever were you thinking, my dear? Had you been more patient, I would have come for you eventually. And now you must somehow rid yourself of—by what name does he go? Mr. Bonner? Mr.

Scott? I suppose that depends on whether he is passing himself off as Canadian or American, does it not?—before you join me in New Orleans. I wonder how you will do it.

As a dutiful husband responsible for your spiritual and moral health, I must admit that I am disappointed in you. My beloved grand-mère will think it far too generous of me to take you back, but a man in love is not always wise, and in the end I will persuade her, though I suspect she will make you dance to her tune before she allows you near the boy. Agnès Poiterin has many things in common with the Church and the law: all three are severe in their treatment of faithless wives, and is it not proper, so? I do hope that further separation from our son will not prove necessary.

I wonder if he will remember you? I fear not, but should you prove sufficiently penitent, you will have many years to atone.

Your disconsolate but devoted husband,
Honoré Poiterin

Postscript: To hasten my journey I have taken the liberty of borrowing the ship *Patience,* which, after all, belongs to my esteemed brother-in-law, the Earl of Carryck. As I prefer my own men to the rabble hired by the false husband, they have been dismissed. Your own possessions you will find in the abandoned cottage opposite the boat works at the eastern end of the wharves. I see that you have used your time well in at least one way. Such finery! We will make the perfect couple.

Jennet went to Luke and held out the letter, but he didn't take it. Instead he put his hands on her face and lifted

it to the light of the moon. Jennet could not bear the sadness in his expression, and so she covered his hands with her
own and went up on tiptoe to press her mouth to his. He
tasted of the meal they had shared, of salt and bread, of himself. For a moment she feared he would not respond, and
then a shudder went through him. With a groan he pulled
her close to bury his face in the crook of her neck.

"I swear to you. I swear to you that he means nothing to
me, and never could. I will kill him myself before I let him
come between us and our son. Now read this, so you know
the kind of man we are dealing with."

Luke took a deep breath, and finally he nodded, once.

They walked quickly to the next cottage, where a lantern
hung at the door. A woman came to greet him, no longer
young, scantily dressed. Her smile was broad and hopeful and
insincere, and Jennet did not need to hear her voice to know
what she was proposing. Luke sent her away with a few words
and a coin pressed into her hand.

When he had finished reading he folded the letter. "The
crew," he said, his voice hoarse.

The ship, the weapons, the stores—all those things he
could replace, and would, no doubt, before another day had
passed. But the crew was another matter entirely. Capable
men who had earned his respect and friendship, some of
them with families.

Jennet said, "Shall I come with you?"

That was the last thing Luke wanted, and he told her so.
From her expression it was plain to see that she was relieved. He wondered how much she knew about Poiterin's
methods, how much more she was holding back, and why.
While he walked her back to Preston's he managed to keep
his questions to himself, and once they arrived there was no
time. He stopped only long enough to borrow a horse and
gather the things he might need.

CHAPTER 9

When he came out of the house again, Hannah was there with her medical kit, and a second horse was being led around from the stables.

They rode through the night by the light of the moon alone. The wind was high and cool and pleasant after the heat of the day, but Luke found he was damp with sweat.

Beside him Hannah was silent, her gaze moving steadily back and forth, hearing everything, and seeing more than Luke could imagine. She had been raised in the backwoods, and her instincts were better than his own when it came to moving through unknown territory. It occurred to him now, as it had every day for the last year, that without his half sister he could not have come this far.

Once all he had hoped for was Jennet's safe return. Now he knew how childish he had been, like a boy who doesn't bother himself with thoughts of the marriage that will follow the wedding night. Jennet's safety, Jennet's health, Jennet's honor; those things had seemed simple, just a few weeks ago. She had been maimed or scarred, or she was whole. She had been forced to submit to another man, or she had somehow found a way to resist. She had borne a child. For those injuries or insults he would admit as possibilities, he had worked out a response, as if this were a chess

game he had been caught up in, and could win with wits
and foresight alone.

He hadn't spoken to Hannah of such things. Instead he
told her different stories, of the years he had spent at
Carryck. He dug deep for memories and spread them out
before his sister, an offering to prove his worthiness, his connection to Jennet, his sincerity.

Luke had been nineteen when he first came to Scotland,
when Jennet was a girl of eleven years. Small and slender, her
skirts always muddy, barefoot, wild, blazing with intelligence
and wit and warmth. She had thrown a bright cloak of words
out in welcome, questions and statements and complex explanations, all in broad Scots. When he was confused she
stopped to give him a lesson in that language, and then had
raced ahead to the next topic.

While Luke spent most of his time with the earl or his
men, Jennet took it upon herself to see to his tutoring in
subjects far more important, she seemed to think, than tenants and crops, trade and politics. It was Jennet who taught
him how to negotiate at market, how to respond to the
greetings of crofters and grandmothers without giving offense or making himself look foolish. She had tutored him
in the way to behave in the kirk, where he must attend
services with the rest of the earl's family, though in the privacy of the castle they called themselves Catholics. She had
shown him the hidden passageways and secret doors in the
towers, and the back lanes in the villages.

It was Jennet who saw when he was homesick for
Canada in the first months, and who drew that pain out of
him by asking about Montreal and his boyhood. To her he
had spoken for the first time of the way he had been raised,
by a grandmother, knowing he had a mother who could
not claim him and a father who didn't know he existed.
What it had been like to see Nathaniel Bonner for the first
time, and recognize his own features in a stranger's face.

How he had learned to accept the decisions his grand-mother had made to keep him safe, and that he wondered if he would ever be able to forgive her, or his mother.

Then Giselle—it had been a long time before he learned to call her *Mama,* as she wanted him to—came to Carryck, and it was Jennet who taught him to see her clearly and un-derstand her, as much as anyone would ever understand Giselle Somerville. Forgiveness had been longer in coming.

Before the events that had brought him face-to-face with his father and grandfather and eventually sent him to Scotland, Luke had been in danger of growing into a soli-tary man without room for affection or playfulness in his life. Carryck had changed that. Jennet had changed that.

Then, late and unexpectedly, the earl's lady had produced a son. Luke might have gone back to Canada, but the earl had grown to rely on him, and he found that he liked the freedom that came with his new role. He had never been able to see himself as an earl, and now he did not have to learn that trick. He had a place in the family, and responsi-bilities, and friends. But things could not remain the same; he had learned that when Jennet turned sixteen, and the first young men had begun to follow her with their eyes. Luke had found himself looking at her as something other than a friend or cousin.

For three months he had tried to school his thoughts and forswear his attachment, but Jennet hadn't allowed that. It was not in her to deny what she was feeling, or to tolerate such dishonesty in anyone else. By the time he had come to accept the inevitability of the connection between them, it was too late; Euan Huntar had offered for her. The earl was in his last illness and worried about his daughter's future. He did not see, or did not care to see, the bond that existed be-tween her and Luke, and he held the Huntars in high re-gard. He had agreed to the match over Jennet's objections.

In his hurt pride and anger, Luke had stepped back without

a fight. He left Jennet to a man she didn't love, and he left Carryck for Canada. Where she had come to him, ten years later, and he finally found the courage to admit to himself that he must have her.

"There," Hannah said.

Luke shook himself out of his daydream and saw where she was pointing. The wharves, deserted at this time of night, the boat works, and the abandoned cottage. A clutch of gulls huddled on the sagging roof, glowing in the moonlight. The windows were shuttered.

He said, "Does this feel right to you?"

"No." Hannah was checking the powder pan on her short-barreled musket. She had exchanged the workday dress she wore when they were in port for leggings and a wide linen shirt that reached to mid-thigh, cinched around the waist with a belt.

A boy slept in the doorway of the shack under the light of a smoking lantern. He didn't stir when they dismounted, or wake in response to any of the languages Luke used to address him. It took Hannah's less than gentle prodding to bring him leaping to his feet.

His gaze jerked back and forth between them, dark eyes perfectly round and glittering in the lamplight. Hannah was busy listening for noise from inside the shack, but some part of her mind was counting the boy's ribs. She wondered when he had last eaten.

Luke held out a coin, and the boy snatched at it with one hand while he flung a piece of paper toward them with the other. Then he was gone, without having spoken a word.

Hannah took the lantern from its hook and pushed open the door with her musket while Luke read. Then he kicked the door open with such fury that it cracked down the middle and tore from one of the hinges.

The crew was here, each man gagged and tied hand and foot. Lantern light caught the glitter of open eyes—at least some of them were alive—but Luke held Hannah back, made a signal that meant she must wait.

When he had checked the shadows for enemies, they made short work of freeing the men. Hannah found that her hands were trembling, out of anger and fear, but she forced herself to speak calmly to each man as she examined them. Most of the wounds were minor, blows to the face and head, shallow cuts.

The man who called himself Tangle, a sailor all his life and not given to idle talk, spit out his gag and coughed and spit and worked his mouth.

"Shit," he said. It seemed enough.

The promised trunks were in the middle of the room, and propped on one of them, at a jaunty angle, the severed head of Piero Bardi. Flies swarmed like a halo around it. The eyes had rolled up in their sockets in the moments before death, and so he seemed to be studying the roof over his head with an oddly pious expression.

"What now?" Hannah asked. "What next?"

"We go to war," Luke said. "And then we go home."

Hannah told Jennet what had happened in a few brief sentences.

"Luke discharged the crew?" Jennet frowned, as if she had trouble making sense of this idea.

"It seemed the right thing to do, as we are without a ship."

"How are we to get to New Orleans?"

"Luke is negotiating the details with Mr. Preston," Hannah said.

"Och, aye," Jennet said, leaning back against the pillows with the ghost of a smile. "Then there's naught to fear. Luke is a fearsome rival in negotiation."

Hannah was so pleased to see even this slightest glimmer

of Jennet's normal spirits that she sat down on the edge of the bed and grasped her hand.

"We will get the boy," she told Jennet. "I swear we will."

Jennet closed her eyes, and her smile faded away.

As was to be expected of the North American representative of Lockleer & Macomber of Edinburgh, Andrew Preston was an excellent merchant and a keen negotiator, but in this case he found that his talents were to go to waste. Luke Scott of Forbes & Sons was so amenable to the proposed trading arrangements that Preston simply forgot his concerns about offending the Poiterin family and agreed to help Scott in any way he could. After all, he was a countryman in distress, and—this much went without discussion—his superiors in Edinburgh would be well pleased with the trading concessions that would give them a footing in Montreal.

In excellent spirits, Preston set about making arrangements for Jennet's trip to New Orleans.

CHAPTER 10

Nathaniel Bonner
Paradise
on the west branch of the Sacandaga
New-York State

Father,

We are in Pensacola, where we believed we would
find a family by the name of Poiterin. These are the
people who have been caring for Jennet's and my son.

The Poiterins left this place a week ago when the
British navy took possession of the port and made it
clear that they will use this place as a point of
departure for marching on Mobile and other points
inland. They have gone to New Orleans, and thus so
must we, though it will take us deeper into the war.

In our short time here we have learned some
things about the Poiterins, who are Creole bankers
and merchants. Disturbing and unsettling things
that caused Jennet such extreme distress that I
worry not just for her health, but for her peace of
mind. She blames herself for putting the boy in the
power of such people, though she seems to

understand at the same time that she had no other choice, and that any reasonable person would have done the same.

Were my sister Hannah not here, I would be lost.

Because we are unsure of the Poiterins' interests and motivations, we must approach them with some caution. Our plan is to go to the city and have Jennet make first contact. Not until then will we have any sense of what must be done to get the boy back. With the added complication of the war in the Gulf, I must tell you that I have no clear idea of when we will be able to start for home, though I fear it will not be soon, and may be as long as a half year, if a legal battle becomes unavoidable.

I send two copies of this letter by different post routes in the hope that at least one of them will reach you. Should the postal service continue in spite of the war in this part of the country and you would like to chance a letter, please direct it to the care of Mrs. Eugenie Preston, Maison Verde, Bayou St. John, Louisiana. This is the widowed sister-in-law of a Scots merchant resident in Pensacola who has been helpful to us in return for business accommodations.

I send you fond good wishes from Jennet and Hannah both, as well as my own. I remain your devoted son,

Luke Scott Bonner
Pensacola, Spanish Florida
11 September 1814

PART II

The Tower: Sudden change in unsettled times, disruption, crisis, chaos.

CHAPTER 11

Jennet left early the next day in the company of Titine. With the two women were Preston's own armed couriers, who were to see the women safely to the home of his widowed sister-in-law on the Bayou St. John, just north of the city of New Orleans. Mrs. Preston was elderly and infirm, but the household ran smoothly and Jennet would be comfortable there. At Maison Verde—for so the house was called—she would receive visitors and begin negotiations with the Poiterins to have her son returned to her.

The post packet which was to take them most of the way made the trip along the Gulf coast with great regularity, in spite of the war and—thus far, at least—without incident. Therefore it was plain bad luck, the captain explained to Jennet at the end of that first day, that they had run into what looked to be the beginning of a full British assault on Fort Browyer.

"They're landing men and artillery, do you see." The captain was an Irishman of late middle age, florid of complexion and expansive. Perspiration soaked the collar of his shirt and his hairline.

Jennet closed her eyes for a moment. "Captain Lewis. You are saying that this Fort Browyer is between us and New Orleans?"

The captain's head bobbed so that his jowls wobbled.

"They'll be after capturing the fort there so they can sail up the bay to Mobile."

"An invasion force." Jennet's voice came reedy and high.

"Looks that way to me. And here was I wagering good money that it was New Orleans they'd go after first. Me brother had the right of it, and now he'll have me coin, too." He wagged his head from side to side in dismay.

"How very unfortunate," Jennet said. "But what interests me more, sir, is how we get to New Orleans, given this change in circumstances."

The captain's mouth pursed itself and then relaxed. "You'll pardon me, missus, but I suppose what I'm trying to tell you is, we don't. I can't sail through a battle, now can I?"

"Could you sail around it?" Jennet asked, struggling to control her tone.

"That way?" The captain peered south into the deeper waters of the Gulf as if dragons were lurking there. "Well, no. Even had I provisions enough, half the English navy is out there on the other side of Cat Island. Lord knows what devilment they're getting up to."

"You are saying you wish to turn back."

He looked pleased to have her speak the words herself. "We've no choice."

"*I* have a choice, sir," Jennet said. "You will put my party ashore here and we will journey overland."

He blinked at her in his surprise. "But, missus. Do you see—" He made a circle in the air with one arm. "They're after landing a thousand men on that shore. All bent on mayhem, and a good number of them Creek Indians. *Creek* Indians, missus. You have no idea—" He cleared his throat. "You can't mean it."

"I never say things I don't mean," Jennet said. "If you'll excuse me, I have to go speak to the rest of my party. We'll be ready in an hour."

• • •

Once on land again, Jennet understood that in spite of the dangers and difficulties of the journey, she had done the right thing. Titine saw the truth of it, too.

She said, "Sometimes a woman just has to keep moving or worry will beat her right down where she stands." And: "Miss Jennet, you had best pull that veiling down a little tighter if you don't want to be overrun by these flies."

Titine reminded Jennet of a younger version of her own mother, who had been housekeeper of Carryckcastle before she was the earl's lady. With little effort at all Titine seemed to make things happen. The mercenaries, first balking at this change of plans, lost their sullen expressions after five minutes with Titine and went off as she directed them, with coin in hand. Within a few hours they had returned from their canvassing of the farms in the area with horses and mules enough to undertake the next stage in the journey.

The captain of the mercenaries was a curt Frenchman no more than twenty-five with a chin beard like a puff of smoke, but he knew the lay of the land and planned a route that would keep them clear of the fighting. It also added many miles to the journey as they made a great circle around Mobile Bay, but they were moving, and for that Jennet was thankful.

The day passed in a dozy drone of flies and by afternoon they were out of earshot of the battle.

They spent that first night on a small plantation populated by a single woman, two small children, and a dozen slaves. The master of the house had gone to join the fighting, Titine explained later, and the lady, afraid that he would never come back, was glad of their company. Jennet excused herself as soon as she could from the younger woman's detailed descriptions of what might happen to a white woman

who fell into the hands of the Creek Indians, and went to a
solitary bed.

Sleep should have come to her immediately, but instead
she lay awake cataloguing the twitching of her muscles and
trying not to think about Luke and Hannah, whose whereabouts she could only guess. When she parted from them, it
had seemed safer that she should not know too much of
their exact plans, but now she could only find fault with
that idea. Cannon fire and war and hostile Indians could not
frighten her half so much as a simple and unavoidable fact:
She was alone again. For the boy's sake, they had agreed to
this most desperate of plans.

There was a hollowness in her that had nothing to do
with the child she had lost, a child she could not mourn,
and everything to do with Luke's absence. In the dark of the
small, strange chamber she pressed her palms to her eyes and
willed herself not to weep.

By horse and mule they made their way north and then
west and then south again. On the second day—or it might
have been the third, so dull were Jennet's senses—they came
to a small village on the edge of a swamp where they
boarded the flat-bottomed boats that would take them the
rest of the way to Bayou St. John by means of the minor
waterways.

Lulled by the steady rhythm of the pirogue, Jennet fell
asleep almost at once. Heat and exhaustion and the deep
slow meter of the songs of the mercenaries kept her in a
dream state for most of the day.

In the afternoon the heat woke her. The muslin traveling
gown she wore felt as heavy as double-cut velvet; sweat
trickled between her breasts and down her spine and along
her scalp. When the pirogue moved through a patch of sunlight, the canvas awning that had been erected over her head

turned the cramped space into an oven. It felt to Jennet as if the air itself had turned to water. She would have refused the bread and cheese and most certainly the lukewarm tea that Titine pressed on her, if the older woman had not insisted. She slept again, and woke almost relaxed, to watch the swamp glide by.

It was an odd world she found herself in, different from the island that had been her prison for so long, different from anything she had ever experienced. Here trees grew dense and green out of muddy water, branches trailing great veils of moss like tattered tapestries fluttering in a fitful breeze. Everywhere she looked crowds of odd, rounded trunks poked up out of the water, like the stumps of fingers bitten off at the knuckles.

The layered green canopy overhead was alive with beating wings, birds and insects and moths. A hundred, two hundred, a thousand parrots with boldly colored wings against the vibrant shimmering sky. A butterfly as large as a woman's hand settled on the netting pulled down over Jennet's face, its furred body the color of peat.

Titine, who had been an attentive and pleasant companion if a silent one, leaned toward Jennet.

She said, "You remember Gaetane talking about the gator in the ciprière?"

"The one as big as two men." Jennet worked a fan, though it did precious little good.

Titine pointed with her chin. "There's his daddy, there."

Jennet righted herself and studied the shape in the water, one she would have taken for nothing more than a floating log. Then she realized that she had been seeing such logs all day, and that most of them—like this one—tapered at one end into a tail.

"You got to tip your hat to that one." The youngest of the mercenaries looked back at her from the front of the pirogue and touched his own slouch cap. "He's an old king, him. You find him here whenever you come this way, lying in the sun. Don't do anything all day but eat and—"

A great eruption of water set the pirogue to rocking. Jennet would wonder later if she could trust her memory, because the alligator had not so much lunged toward his prey as simply flown up and forward as quick as a snake. In the same second his jaws closed on another alligator, a third his own size. The sound—it reminded Jennet of a great door slamming—seemed to still be echoing in the air when the waters settled again. Both gators were gone.

"—make babies." The mercenary laughed at the way Jennet craned her neck. "You won't see him no more, madame. *Le caïmon* busy with his dinner, him."

"We call him *Grand Nez*," called the captain from the other pirogue. "For the bump, here." He wrinkled his own quite considerable nose, and grinned. "You like our ciprière, madame?"

Nearby a hawk screamed, saving Jennet the discomfort of a response. The captain laughed, a little insolently. Titine snapped a few words at him, and he lowered his head before looking away.

"Never you mind about Grand Nez," she told Jennet. "Agnès Poiterin is enough to keep you wrapped up in worries as long as you care to stay around these parts."

"Tell me about her, then," Jennet said.

Titine shaded her eyes with one long hand. "My whole life I been afraid of that old woman," she said, finally. And that was all she said of Agnès Poiterin for the rest of the journey.

After the endless fluid heat of the ciprière, Lake Pontchartrain was a welcome sight. It was open and broad under a glassy blue September sky and while it was just as hot here, there was a breeze. Jennet found it odd that she had to come out of the swamp before she could understand how everything about it had oppressed her.

It was late afternoon when the men steered them toward a break in the shoreline. A small fort in questionable repair perched on the right, protecting the entrance to what seemed to Jennet a river, but which was, Titine told her, the Bayou St. John.

Jennet had come to the conclusion that a bayou really wasn't so much a river as a long stretch of water without the will to go anywhere in particular. This particular bayou was much the same as the others in all but one very important way. Jennet sat up, struck by how odd it was to see neat shell roads and stretches of tended lawn peeking out between the cypress and palm and live oak trees that lined the banks. In the golden light of late afternoon they passed two-story galleried houses in colors that would forever remind her of this part of the world: warm pale orange, pallid blue, milky yellow, the pink of a little girl's hair ribbon. Each was surrounded by gardens and outbuildings and fields. The properties all seemed to extend to the bayou. Wide railed platforms furnished with benches and canvas awnings spanned the drainage ditch that ran parallel to it, some of them bordered by cypress palisades.

A well-dressed young man rode by on a horse worth many years of a laborer's wages; a barouche followed him, sunlight catching the gilt molding on doors and wheel rims, only a little more bright in the sun than the hair of the woman who sat alone in a cocoon of velvet cushions, a watered-silk parasol over her head.

For every white person Jennet saw, there were six or eight people whose skin ranged from a deep blue-black to ocher and sienna and umber. Slaves were everywhere in evidence, most of them tending gardens or crops or animals, some washing windows or sweeping walkways or watching over children.

There were many questions Jennet would have liked to ask Titine, but from the older woman's expression, all anticipation and undisguised pleasure, she knew that it would be wrong to interrupt this homecoming.

The lake had disappeared behind them when Titine pointed to a spot farther down the bayou. "Do you see that bridge? Just beyond there is the start of the canal that goes directly into the city."

On either side of the arched bridge there was a small settlement of fine houses.

"There," Titine said gesturing to a smaller house. "Maison Verde."

Andrew Preston's house was a little smaller than some of the others that lined the bayou, but it was very handsome, from the pale green stucco walls and dark green shutters to the pots of flowers spilling color along the gallery balustrade.

"They got word," Titine said, almost to herself. "See, Miss Jennet, I told you they'd know. They heard we was coming."

In fact the walkway that led through the garden to the house was lined with people, all of them, from what Jennet could see, household servants. The women all wore white aprons and calico head wraps, and the men were in homespun breeches and vests over loose linen shirts. Nearest the bayou was a middle-aged, strongly built man with startling, deep-set gray eyes in a cinnamon-brown face, and beside him a woman in a starched white apron who must be Titine's aunt Amazilie, her mother's sister.

"My aunt," said Titine. "And her son, Tibère."

Jennet saw no sign of Amazilie's mistress, which worried her more than a little; if it turned out that the elderly Widow Preston wasn't ready to take in a houseguest with so little notice, all of their plans, so carefully worked out, would have to be adjusted.

Titine, at least, seemed unconcerned by the absence. She

stood in the pirogue as a boy caught the mooring rope tossed to him, and then she sprang like a colt onto the dock and into the arms of the woman waiting there, both of them talking so quickly in patois that Jennet had no chance of following the conversation, even if her attention hadn't been elsewhere.

The captain offered her his arm and she let herself be helped out of the pirogue, glad of the solid ground under her feet and aware of the start of an ache between her eyes, the result of too much sun and too many unanswered questions. Titine and her aunt seemed to remember Jennet just then, and drew her forward as they might have done for a shy girl, Amazilie clucking softly in distress or disapproval, talking of food and tea and rest not to Jennet, but to Titine.

"Is Mme. Preston at home?" Jennet asked.

"She is," said Amazilie. "But she don't move so well, you understand, and she like the cool of the house. But the other lady waiting on you in the parlor."

"What lady?" asked Titine, drawing up short.

A deep furrow appeared between Amazilie's brows. "Why, it's Mme. Poiterin herself, sitting there in the parlor, and Père Petit with her. And the *bébé—mais non*, your son, madame?"

It took some seconds for the words to order themselves into ideas in Jennet's head. She said, "My son is here?"

"He look like you, sure," said Amazilie with a quick smile. "But we keep him you don't want him, such a beautiful child."

Jennet picked up her skirts, and ran.

CHAPTER 12

She hesitated on the porch, unsure of where to go. The entire front of the house was lined with doors, all with jalousies tilted against the sun. A strange sound came from one of the rooms, a whispering followed by a click: *whoosh-whick, whoosh-whick*. With the sun still hot on her back and neck, Jennet tried to make sense of it, to calm herself, to breathe.

"Come in," said a woman's voice in French, creaking and whispery with old age. "Come in, madame, and take some tea."

A servant opened the doors in front of her, no more than a shadowy figure in the dim of the room. Jennet stood there, half in and half out as her eyes adjusted to the lack of light.

It was a large, square room with a great empty hearth on one wall and a table in its center. Over the table, a fan the size and shape of a sash window hung suspended on ropes. A young black boy was pulling the cord that worked the fan. *Whoosh-whick. Whoosh-whick.*

Sweat ran down her face and she shivered. "Madame Preston?" she said, her own voice sounding unsteady. "Madame Preston?"

And saw the old woman seated at the far end of the table in a deep winged chair.

"Mme. Preston has retired," said the vaguely slurred voice in French. The woman was small of stature, very old and very stout, with a face like a pale full moon with a ruffle of chins beneath it. She was wrapped in lace and watered silk, all black, like an insect in its shell.

"My son," Jennet said, her voice steadier now. "My son is with you?"

An arm ascended into the air, the index finger heavy with rings, and pointed to the opposite corner, where a cradle stood in the shadows.

"My great-grandson."

I am terrified. The thought came into Jennet's mind as she made her way around the table. *I am trembling; I must stop trembling*. And: *He won't know me*.

There was a canopy of fine netting, and behind it, the boy, asleep. She pressed a hand to her mouth to keep herself from crying out and found that her face was wet with tears. She wiped them away, drew a hitching breath, and carefully folded back the canopy. Jennet crouched down beside the cradle to look at her sleeping son.

He had come into the world on L'Île de Lamantins, and she had named him Nathaniel, and now here he was: flushed with the heat, his reddened cheeks working in his sleep as they had once worked at her breast. Another woman nursed him now. Jennet felt her watching from the shadows, as she felt the old woman, Honoré Poiterin's grandmother.

Very gently she touched the boy's face, the curve of his brow, the faint line of eyebrow, the feather of fair hair that showed at the edge of the embroidered linen cap. At that he opened his eyes, and looked at her.

He studied her, unafraid, unmoved, and Jennet wondered, as she had wondered every day since she put him into the arms of strangers, if he had any memory of her face, or if he saw her now as just another set of features. Even in the low light his eyes were strikingly blue, the same blue as her own eyes. If she could put his face to her breast, would he know her by her smell? For now her voice alone must suffice.

She spoke to him as she had done since she had first

known he was growing inside her, in Scots. Though she
tried to govern it, her voice trembled. "Did I nae tell ye that
I'd come?" And "What a fine lad ye are, Nathaniel, bonnie
and braw, and won't your faither be proud."

"His father is very proud," said Honoré Poiterin, behind
her. "How could I be anything less?"

It was the priest, a Frenchman of middle age, with bloodshot, slightly crossed eyes and a disturbing smile, who took
over this strange meeting. While servants brought coffee and
cakes and platters of meat and bread and cheese, he directed
each of them to chairs at the table. Jennet went willingly, the
boy in her arms, and did not look at Honoré, who sat opposite her, relaxed, smiling, one elbow hooked over the back of
his chair. His grandmother kept her place at the far end of
the table, and the priest, whose name was Père Petit, took
the other end. Through the jalousies Jennet could just make
out the shape of a woman she thought must be Titine.
Listening. She said a small and silent prayer of thanks and
put a hand, very gently, on the back of the boy's head.

First in her arms, her son had studied her with all the
solemnity that an infant of four months could muster, neither protesting nor welcoming, which was less than she had
hoped for but not as bad as she had feared. Now he sat in
her lap with his head on her breast, mouthing a fist. Beneath
a fortune in lace and fine linen he felt solid, well rounded,
warm. Alive. Jennet was trembling with emotion, with joy
most of all but with fear, too, that the woman at the end of
the table, that lumpy pudding of a woman, all pink powdered flesh inside her shell of black silk, would snap her fingers and the boy would simply disappear.

Behind Jennet's chair she could feel another presence,
the woman—the girl—who had the care of her son. No
one had introduced her—slaves were never introduced—

but she knew this to be Jacinthe from Titine's stories. She had met the girl's eyes only once, and from that brief encounter knew a few things. First, that she had real affection for the boy; and second, that she had only a few months to go before she brought her own child into the world.

Honoré was sitting at this table with perfect ease, as he sat at any table, at every table: as if he owned it and everyone around it; as if the old woman could give him the rest of the world, too, if he could be bothered to ask for it. When he directed his smile to his grandmother it was all fawning condescension, though the scar on his face was livid. She doubted if he heard the priest's dry, high voice droning on in a French that had its origins in Canada.

"... most irregular," he was saying. "But after consultation with my superiors, we have agreed to hear your confession. That will fall to me." The thin blade of his nose wrinkled at such a distasteful idea. "Should you prove penitent, this whole regrettable affair can be set aside. If not," he said, raising a finger, "forgotten."

It was very hard to pretend to listen, but she must. Jennet understood exactly the nature of this first examination, and the results if she failed: They would take the boy away from her—she had no way to stop them, after all—and hide him where she would never find him. She heard Luke's voice and Hannah's, reminding her of how carefully she must tread, but most clearly she heard Gaetane, who had warned her about the old woman at the end of the table. Agnès Poiterin was the force here. If Jennet showed any truculence, the smallest, weakest spark of defiance, the old woman would make sure that the boy disappeared. Then it might be possible, working through the courts, to get him back, but it would take long months, if not years.

"If it comes to that," Luke had said, "we will take him. But we have to know where he is, or an army wouldn't be enough to back us up. Don't give them any reason to hide the boy away."

Gaetane was more specific. She said, "What you got to do first is set the old spider's mind at ease. You be as soft and bendable as a willow twig, you mind me now. You bow your head and say *Oui, madame. Mais oui, madame. Merci bien, madame.* You don't look her in the eye, no matter what wicked things she got to say. She call you a slattern, a liar, you say, *Forgive me, madame.* If you can make yourself color up, you do that. You don't got a temper when it come to Grand-mère Poiterin, you don't got a thought in your head but what she put there. You got to think like a slave and act like one, because that the only way you put her off guard. If you got to go hide in the swamp later and scream out, you do that. But be sure first she a good mile away, or she hear you. She got a wide web, her."

While the priest talked Jennet listened to Gaetane and to Hannah, who had pressed her cheek with her own and said those words that she must repeat to herself again and again: *Do what you must.*

The priest paused, and Jennet raised her head just enough to meet his disapproving gaze. In her best French, she stated her sincere wish to atone for her many sins. She made public her gratitude to her husband Honoré Poiterin for his generosity and did not let the gall in her mouth be heard in her words. She thanked his grandmother for her willingness to entertain her apologies, and accept a daughter-in-law of compromised reputation into her family and home.

She sensed rather than saw the old woman's face turn toward her. There was a moment's heavy silence, during which not even Honoré ventured to smile. It was his expression, studiously blank, that made Jennet understand the wisdom of Gaetane's advice. Honoré Poiterin was afraid of his grand-mère, and so she must be. For the sake of the child asleep against her breast. For her son's sake, anything at all.

In her slightly rough voice, Agnès Poiterin said, "As to

that, you must prove yourself before you will be allowed to join my household. I will not have you at Larivière until I am satisfied that you are shriven, and the marriage has been acknowledged and blessed by the bishop. I must have my own doctors examine you. No doubt the men you have known were filthy, if not infected."

Honoré's mouth twitched at that, but he said nothing. Jennet felt herself flushing, which would please Gaetane; the urge to defend herself was almost irresistible, and yet must be resisted.

The old woman was watching her closely, and now she made a deep sound in her throat, neither pleasure nor anger but simple satisfaction.

"When you are clean of body and soul, and you have demonstrated to me your good manners and piety, then there will be time to say your vows again, in front of a priest of my choosing. After that I may allow you to join your husband under my roof. Until then—" She made a gesture with her hand, and Jacinthe was suddenly beside Jennet's chair, holding out her arms for the baby. "Until that time, you will reside here at Maison Verde, if Mme. Preston will have you. In her place, I would not, but she is a willful woman and not of the true faith. Honoré, you will not be alone with this woman you claim as your wife until I have decided she is worthy. She must also realize that were it not for her family connections, I would never have agreed even to this much."

Every muscle in Jennet's arms cramped, but she forced herself to give up her son to his nurse, who did not smile at her but instead closed her eyes briefly as if to say that she understood.

"Of course this is all the more difficult because of the war. The Americans have yet to send us the troops we require for our protection. If they wait much longer we may be overrun and burned by the English, as Washington was. You have shown very poor sense in traveling about the countryside in times like these. That must stop. You will never go out unaccompanied. In fact, you shall go out very little. Beyond daily Mass, that is."

"But not at the cathe—" the priest began, and she cut him off with a sharp look.

"Not at the cathedral," she said. "Père Antoine is far too lenient in his dealings with sinners. Nor will I inflict you on the Ursulines. There are too many impressionable young ladies of good family there, and you are as yet unproven. I think it best that you are looked after by Père Petit, who says Mass daily at the Chapel of the Sacred Heart, on the outskirts of the city. You will attend, and Père Petit will hear your confession immediately afterward.

"If Mme. Preston will not give you the use of a pirogue or a horse, you will walk. There is a path that follows the Canal Carondelet the whole way into the city. When you return here you may see the boy for an hour. Jacinthe will bring him, suitably guarded. If your behavior does not displease me, you may accompany her in the afternoon when she takes him for a walk along the bayou. You will attend me at Larivière when it is required of you.

"If you will not abide by my rules, madame, you should say so now, and you can be on your way. You are no longer young, but your family is wealthy. You may find a husband who is willing to overlook your disgraceful past for the right dowry. You may have more children. For all your serious faults you have produced a fine son, who is made in the very likeness of my own dear son, Honoré's father, Archange. May he rest in peace."

She crossed herself with one pudgy hand. Jennet bowed her head and did the same, hoping that her surprise could not be read from her face. When she raised her head the priest was holding out a miniature for her to examine, though she had the idea that if she were to try to touch it he would snatch it away. It was the likeness of a young man of some twenty years, fair-haired, blue-eyed, with a weak chin and a bored expression. Honoré's father, and Titine's.

"You see the likeness, of course."

Behind Jennet the baby was stirring, rousing himself from sleep with small sounds. He was hungry. Jennet felt the tug in her own breasts, though the trickle of milk she had left could not even begin to satisfy him. It was Jacinthe who would nurse him and sing to him and rock him. She made herself relax and fought to put a small smile on her face.

"Oui, madame."

The old woman was looking at her with narrowed eyes. "Jacinthe," she said finally. "Take my great-grandson home."

The door opened behind Jennet and closed again. There were tears on her face, but she did not dare wipe them away.

"I agree to this trial against my better judgment," said Madame Poiterin. "Because my grandson Honoré wants you. I tried to instill in him an appreciation for the importance of good breeding, but he fancies himself attached to you. An error in the way I had him educated, no doubt. But you have given me a fine great-grandson, and I expect, if all goes well, that you will give me more, if Honoré spends his time where he should—in your bed, and not in the Quadroon Quarter."

Her tone made it clear that she had come to the end of what she had to say, for which Jennet was thankful. She cleared her throat.

"I agree to your conditions, madame. With thanks." She heard in her own voice a slight wobble that would give away her rage to anyone who really knew her.

"Of course you agree," said the old woman. "Who would not, with my Honoré as the prize?"

Jennet could not help herself from looking at Honoré, who smiled at her. This man who claimed to be her husband and the father of her child, who had saved her son's life at this terrible price, smiled at her, and Jennet forced herself to smile back.

CHAPTER 13

Dearest Luke, my love,

He is here, he is well. He is beautiful.

We arrived three days ago, but it was only this morning that Madame P fulfilled her promise and allowed me to spend time with him. I can hardly write for agitation and joy and dread. Today he was mine for a while at least, but tomorrow is unknown.

I held him for an hour, in the shade of the veranda that overlooks the Bayou St. John. He is your son, from the shape of his toes to the way his hair grows in a whirl at the crown of his head. He looks at me so calmly, this son, this child you and I made. He looks at me as though he is trying to remember where he saw me last. He has not yet smiled at me, but then the young slave woman who cares for him, Jacinthe is her name, tells me that he has always been solemn and thoughtful for such a young infant. You see, in this he is your son as well. He will not take after his rash mother, whose reckless behavior has exacted so great a price.

I walked with him and talked as I would, in Scots, which I may not do when I might be overheard, for fear word will get back to Madame Poiterin.

The old lady is much as we were led to believe she would be. The small indignities she thinks up for me are bearable; anything, anything is bearable if it brings the day closer when I can leave here and put the boy in your arms.

She requires that I attend Mass and visit the confessional daily, at her own chapel. We owe Titine a great debt for accurately predicting this, because otherwise there would be no way for her to meet Hannah and you would never be reading this letter.

The priest who hears my confession daily is neither a good man nor a bad one, but he is certainly curious.

In the dim light of the confessional he wants most to hear those details that should interest him least. He asks questions about the island and the men there, what they might have done to me and to each other in my sight, if I dwell on such memories, if they cause me to sin. He asks me about you, whether I allowed you the privileges of the matrimonial bed, and if so, which ones, and how many times, all so (he tells me in a voice a little breathless and hoarse) he can decide a suitable penance. I can hardly imagine this going on every day until we are away, but I will do whatever is necessary.

Today already I was taken by the almost irresistible urge to describe for him exactly what it is that men and women do together. I don't know if he would be satisfied then, or if it would simply incite further questions. I do wonder, too, if he reports my confessions to Madame P in detail. It is a most disagreeable idea, and yet I would not be surprised, such is the hold she—and her money—have over him.

Madame P claims that when I have convinced her

and the Church that I am truly repentant she will allow me to join her household as her acknowledged granddaughter-in-law and H's wife. If it were not for the war that creeps closer every day, I should say that the best course for us would be to take the boy and run now, immediately. Holding Nathaniel this morning this idea seemed not only appealing, but obvious and necessary, far more reasonable than giving him back into another woman's arms without knowing if she will bring him again. Every day there is more talk of Jackson and his troops, where they are and what they are doing and when they will be here to fend off the British, who must surely strike at New Orleans very soon. The rumors tumble over each other: He is here already, in disguise; he has turned back for the north; he has fallen in battle. All I want is to be safe away, with you and Hannah and our son.

But you need not fear, I will not divert from the plans we made so carefully, though my heart will break anew every time I must give him up again.

You must know also that I have nothing to report about Honoré Poiterin, as his grandmother forbids him all contact with me until I am deemed free of sin and properly chastised. He did not seem at all put out by this restriction, and indeed it was a huge relief to me. I need not tell you, though, to watch for him. He is close by, so Titine and her aunt Amazilie tell me.

I see very little of Mr. Preston's sister, who is bedridden and so afraid of Madame P that she shakes at the mention of her name. I depend on Titine and Amazilie and on Amazilie's grown son Tibère, who have taken on our cause as their own. Because they are kind, good people, but also because they hope that the resolution of our troubles may also mean that

Titine's mother might return to her home in New Orleans, which H.P. has taken from her at his grandmother's urging. Titine will carry this letter with her every day until Hannah comes to the chapel. I hope that I have learned the code correctly and that you will be able to read this with less difficulty than I have had writing it.

I think of you hourly and with great love, my one true husband. Your devoted wife,

Jennet

CHAPTER 14

Hannah, who had spent many months in Manhattan and lesser amounts of time in Albany and Montreal, understood some unavoidable truths about cities, the most obvious being that they stank in the heat. They stank of people crowded together, of livestock in the streets, of spoiling meat, of those on the brink of death and others waiting to be buried, of waste. To all this, New Orleans added the heavy smells of the swamps that surrounded it, and the river.

She came into the city by back trails seldom traveled, making her way by virtue of the directions she had memorized. Her own clothing she had given up for worn homespun and a much-mended apron, bought from a farmer on the edge of the Faubourg Marigny. The man would have taken the clogs off his wife's feet for more of Hannah's coin, but she kept her moccasins and instead bought the woman's straw hat, broad-brimmed and low-crowned, sweat-stained and limp.

The farmer watched as Hannah opened her pack. She let him see her pistols with their well-worn grips while she got out the coin she owed him. Then she did something no Indian woman should do: She met his eye.

He might still follow in the hopes of robbing her, but he would do so at enough of a distance to give her the advantage.

She passed from the suburbs into the city proper in the early morning, walking along the levee, a high earthenwork bank that must be meant to hold back the river when the waters ran high, but that also served as a thoroughfare for all kinds of traffic. Hannah hardly knew where to look first.

She stood for a long time at a spot just opposite the central plaza that was the centerpiece of the old city. A cathedral flanked by two imposing buildings faced the river from the far side of the Place d'Armes; neighborhoods were laid on three sides of the plaza on a grid of narrow lanes as neat as a needlework sampler. The plaza itself was run-down and gave the appearance of a sawyer's yard. It seemed the building trade had claimed the whole Place d'Armes as a place to pile their bricks and boards and great heaps of charcoal, with dozens of slaves busy moving things from one place to another.

The wharves were just as crowded and frantic. Hannah worked her way along the levee through crowds of sailors and boatmen, merchants and slaves, oxen and horses and mules. A small black man passed her with a crate of chickens clutched in wiry arms, a dog trotting at his heels; another man, his skin a deep glossy black and a scarf tied around a shaved head, pulled a cart heaped with coils of rope. The two men greeted each other in Portuguese. Hannah heard Spanish and French, Scots and Dutch, a smattering of other languages she couldn't identify, and less often, English.

There were fewer soldiers and militia than she had expected, but there was no mistaking the fact that trade had been put to a stop by the war. There was a great wall of merchandise piled outside of every warehouse and in every corner: bales of cotton and barrels of sugar and rice, mountains of bundled furs, a mile of lumber. A fortune in hard goods left to cook in the sun.

There was still a lot of traffic on the Mississippi, a forest of masts, ferries, and barges. Hannah stopped a slave woman.

"I thought there was a trade embargo." She pointed with her chin to a great fleet of flatboats with dozens of slaves crawling over them, bearing the cargo away to waiting carts.

The woman looked, her dark eyes moving up the river. "Flatboats come down the river," she said. "All the way from Ohio, some of them."

This river could take her back to Ohio territory, where she had lived with her husband, where she had borne her son. Where she lost everything. If she began walking today and followed it, it would take her back through time to another life.

The woman was saying, "When the flatboats get down here they break them up for firewood or lumber. Some day soon, they say, we going to see one of them steamboats go upriver. But then folks will say just about anything. I'll believe it when I see it, me." She looked harder at Hannah. "Who you belong to, girl?"

Hannah had been warned about this question. "You are neither fish nor fowl," Giselle had said. "Not a slave, clearly Indian, but you are nothing like the Indians they know, in speech or bearing or dress. Some will assume you are a servant, others will assume you are some exotic African and ripe for plucking. In New Orleans you are a free woman of color, you must remember that. You wear a scarf over your hair whenever you are out on the street, or a hat. Pay me heed, Hannah, this is very important."

"I was born free," Hannah told the woman. "Up in New-York State."

"You got papers?" asked the woman. "You best got papers, 'cause if one of them freebooters stop you to ask and you can't show your papers, you find yourself on the auction block soon enough. Them freebooters ain't fussy about the difference between red and black, them. The only color they know is white, and that ain't you."

Hannah had papers, drawn up for her by Lacoeur and

sewn carefully into the lining of her shawl, carefully folded away in her satchel. She thanked the woman for her concern and continued on her way, feeling light-headed suddenly, her mouth sour and dry. The marketplace must be just ahead, where she could buy something to eat. With something in her belly she would feel better, she told herself. It sounded so reasonable, if only she could convince herself.

There had to be a hundred stalls in the long open building that served as the main market, and every one of them was filled to the brim. Leather raw and rough or finely cured, sewn into boots and shoes and harnesses, a tinker's cart laden with pots and pans, knives and forks that winked in the sun. A dozen kinds of fish, oysters, shrimp, sides of pork, and beef crawling with flies in spite of the young black children who had no work but to fan them away. A half dozen alligator tails in a pile, with a dog standing watch over them. Bushels of carrots, potatoes, kale, cabbage, melons, okra, beans, apples, peaches, pears, other crops that Hannah didn't recognize. In the last year she had made many meals out of foods she never knew the name of.

She paid a butcher a few coins and got in return a thick slab of bread spread with butter and piled high with crackling hot, salty pork sliced off the spit. There was a long row of men selling drinking water out of barrels, and Hannah took her place in a line that had no white people in it at all. She paid a penny for three dips of the tin beaker, the last one of which she poured over her face and neck. Finally she bought a ripe peach and ate it as she listened to the merchants hawking their goods: chickens, eggs, goat's milk, thread and needles, straw brooms, boots and slippers, fine muslin and huckaback, tinware, nails, baskets, candles, medicines sure to cure everything from ulcers to broken hearts.

She listened to well-dressed men talk of crops and rain

and the embargo, of funerals and baptisms, of bankruptcies and new buildings, in French and Spanish and English and German. Mostly she heard talk of the war.

Two Spanish men had been arrested as possible spies and were sitting in the Cabildo awaiting trial. The fort at English Turn was falling into the river. There were a hundred British warships in the Gulf and more on the way. The city could not stand up to a British invasion force. If Andrew Jackson did not come soon it would be too late; they must get their women and children out of the city. Andrew Jackson was only three miles away; Andrew Jackson had gone back to Tennessee. The only way to survive was to surrender immediately. No, the British had their eye on Mobile, and there would be time to flee once that city fell, and really, what difference did it make? New Orleans had been passed back and forth between Spain and France and the United States so many times, they could handle the British, if it came to that.

A young boy the color of living coal stood on the cusp of the levee and played dance tunes on an ancient violin. He played to the great gray-green river, which paid him no attention. Hannah dropped a penny in his cup and went on her way thinking of home.

Finally she turned from the levee and walked into the city itself, glad now of the shade in the narrow lanes so closely built that the sun was kept permanently at bay. The lanes were hard-packed dirt, the sewer lines of wood, and open to the air. A raised brick sidewalk ran down one side of the street, but Hannah knew better than to set foot on it.

She lowered her head and walked quickly: nothing more than another servant on an errand, taking note out of the corner of her eye of small, low-slung cottages, fine two-story buildings with fancy ironwork on the balconies, sheds and stables and smithies, shops small and large. All of the buildings, the simplest and the most elaborate, had casement windows shuttered by jalousies that had been tilted to let in breezes but keep the light out, and all were built up off the ground on an arrangement of wooden props. Water butts stood sentinel on every flat roof, whether for fear of fire or drought, Hannah could not tell.

New Orleans was a city of blinding white sun on plastered walls painted in pink and blue and green, the air as dense as seaweed. She was glad of her straw hat, especially now that she was away from the breeze that came off the Mississippi. She passed taverns and coffeehouses, every one of them doing brisk business. At a coffeehouse called Maspero's, a notice for a ball was tacked to the wall:

A ball will be given at Saturday next and commence at seven o'clock. Supper to be served at twelve o'clock. Nobody is permitted to dance in boots. The price of a subscription is twelve dollars.

And below that, a broadsheet:

The firing of guns and pistols in the streets is prohibited by a corporation law, under the penalty of a heavy fine—heretofore this law has not been rigidly enforced; in future it certainly will be and the citizens are cautioned against violation of it. The beating of a drum or drums and playing of fife or fifes through the streets after night is unmilitary, and it collects crowds of idle boys, servants, slaves, etc etc to the great annoyance of the citizens. The officers are requested to prevent a repetition of this disorderly inconsiderate practice, as they regard the peace, good order, and safety of the city. Signed: a Candidate for Alderman

The city was nothing like Albany, and exactly the same: grocers and dry-goods shops, blacksmiths and chandlers, ladies' fashions and men's haberdashers, booksellers, tea importers, a print shop papered with broadsheets. She could not help but stop and read for a moment, and then wished she had not, as every other notice seemed to deal with the slaves: getting them by auction, selling them, leasing them out, and pursuing the ones who ran away. It was no different from any of the islands they had visited in the last six months, but Hannah had not got used to it yet, and never would.

She turned down the rue Royale, where the buildings were larger and finer and, it seemed, deserted: The poor must stay in the city through the summer to twitch in the heat, but the rich had second homes on lakes and bayous. For the first time she let herself wonder what she would do if the man she was looking for was away.

She turned onto the rue des Ursulines. She passed a building as large and imposing as a palace but without ornamentation. A half dozen nuns working in the gardens announced that this was a convent, as did a simple sign that hung on the open gates. Hannah had been baptized by a Catholic priest as a very young child but she had never practiced the religion or even claimed it as her own. Now she would have been glad to sit in the shade by a small fountain for even a half hour, just enough time to catch her breath and quiet the pounding of her head.

She turned again, this time onto the rue de Bourbon. Beyond the houses she could see the startling green of theciprière, by which she understood that she had come to the outer edge of the city.

The house on the corner was relatively new, so that the paint on the sign suspended from the scrollwork arch was still clean and fresh: Fitch & Jerome, Textile Exchange. The business took up the ground floor of a substantial and well-maintained building. Elaborate ironwork balustrades fronted the balconies lined with French doors, all shuttered against the sun.

The American army hadn't arrived yet, but American merchants had begun their invasion as soon as the ink was dry on the papers that transferred the Louisiana territory into American hands. They had made substantial inroads into the business of the city, if not into its heart. She wondered if all the newly arrived American merchants chose to build, or were forced to by a less than enthusiastic reception from the more established families.

She shook off her curiosity—a luxury she could ill afford at this juncture—and prepared herself for an interview with Mr. Fitch, a stranger to her.

Hannah opened the door into the business office and stepped in, and saw right away that the woman behind the counter had been watching her. A white woman whose dress proclaimed her the mistress, and whose expression said very clearly what was going to happen next.

"Micah." She raised her voice only slightly. Two people came through the open doorway from another office, both of them black.

"Micah, call the constables. This—creature has intruded, no doubt bent on thievery." By her accent the woman was originally from Boston or somewhere near there. This was the first American woman Hannah had seen in almost a year.

Micah never stopped to look at Hannah; he just turned and disappeared back into the dark, and from there, Hannah supposed, through some other door out into the city.

She said, "Mrs. Fitch, I am no thief. I bring a letter for Mr. Fitch." And when the woman's posture and expression changed not at all: "From M. Lacoeur of Port-au-Prince."

The elderly slave woman who stood behind Mrs. Fitch rocked forward. In heavily accented English she said, "Madame, shall I get the letter from her?"

Hannah said, "No need," and put the letter on the counter.

Then she took five steps backward until she felt the door behind her. She was not annoyed or even angry but only weary.
It was not the first time she had come across a white woman
with a deep and unshakable hatred of Indians, and it would not
be the last.

"You go," said Mrs. Fitch. She wouldn't even look at the
letter. "Squaw go, now."

"The letter requires a reply," Hannah said. "I was told to
wait."

Hannah knew that her French was not perfect, but her
English was without flaw. She could, when she wished,
sound exactly like her stepmother, who was a well-bred
English lady of the first rank; she could also sound like her
father, who was a backwoods hunter and trapper, or a dozen
other white men and women of different backgrounds,
philosophies, and educations.

Out of pique she had used the most formal, the most educated English at her disposal, and saw now that she had
chosen badly. This rich merchant's wife was offended.
Hannah might launch into a perfectly composed discourse
on Plato or the current political situation in Europe and the
woman would not hear her, did not wish to hear her, not so
long as Hannah stood here in homespun and moccasins
with a dirty face and red skin.

"You go!" said the woman, her voice rising shrilly. "No
squaw here!"

Hannah said, "I will wait in the garden of the chapel at
the corner." She met the eyes of the black woman, and saw
that she, at least, understood what Hannah meant to say, no
matter how deaf her mistress chose to be. That must be
enough. Hannah left.

In an alleyway behind a locksmith she found a black man—
she thought he must be a free black man, to be roaming the

city selling goods from a pack on his back—willing to exchange a bruised orange for one of her coins. Then she went
to sit in the chapel garden and she ate while she waited. One
part of her mind wondered if Mr. Fitch would find her before the constables, or if maybe the priest would come out to
chase her away before either of those things could happen.

It was a vague worry, easily put aside because there were
other things, more puzzling things, to consider. The foremost of them was the fact that Hannah believed she must be
running a fever. She felt a heat that had nothing to do with
the sun, one that seemed to come from inside herself, pushing outward. Her head throbbed so that she had the odd idea
she could feel the shape of her own eyes, pressing in their
sockets.

She was cataloguing her own symptoms—headache, light-
headedness, fever, a twinge of nausea—when she looked up
and saw a man walking toward her.

There were a few more people in the lanes now, mostly
soldiers and servants and slaves; Fitch stood out in his fine
clothes and polished boots, as he was meant to. He saw her
and turned in her direction, his expression shifting from
preoccupied to resolute.

"Miss Bonner."

"Mr. Fitch."

"I apologize for the confusion. My wife—"

"No need for explanations," Hannah interrupted him.
His mouth tightened with displeasure.

"Very well. The letter from Lacoeur speaks of Luke Scott
of Montreal."

"My half brother," Hannah said, out of some irresistible
urge to make the man uncomfortable. It could have something to do with her headache, or simply with the fact that
the set of Fitch's mouth irritated her.

"So I understand. Where is he?"

"He has been detained in Pensacola," Hannah said. "I am

here alone." They had worked out their story very carefully, and she found it easy to supply the lies. If Fitch doubted her there was no sign of it on his face; apparently the introduction from Lacoeur did not extend so far as to allow him to meet her eye.

He studied the earth beneath his boots. Hannah remembered, quite suddenly and without warning, another pair of boots, of green Moroccan leather. The boots her stepmother had been wearing when Hannah first saw her. She wondered now what had become of those boots, if they had been lost in a fire or if they lay at the bottom of a trunk somewhere and would be dug out in a few years' time by a grandchild as yet unborn, who would love them as Hannah had loved them as a little girl.

She had money. She had more money than was really safe for her to carry on her person, alone in this city or anywhere else, but they had weighed the risk and decided that it was necessary. She could buy a dozen pair of boots, but in this city—in most cities—they would do her no good at all. She could dress herself impeccably and that, like her perfect English, would make no difference. Once that had prickled, but now it was only an inconvenience, another barrier between herself and the things she must accomplish.

"Mr. Fitch," she prompted. "If you cannot help me, please just say so."

"I cannot help you in the way you might want me to," he said, stiffly. "If your half brother were with you, perhaps. But as it is—" He paused, and then seemed to come to a conclusion.

"I am in Lacoeur's debt, and I will do for you what I can. I have already sent word to an acquaintance who will be able to give you lodging. The neighborhood is a little..." His voice trailed away.

"I understand," Hannah said. She brushed bread crumbs

from her skirt and stood. "Just give me the directions, if you please."

She lifted the pack and staggered, just a little, before she caught herself. Mr. Fitch tried to look concerned, but really it was more distress for himself, that she might do something to keep him here, to delay his retreat from this distasteful errand forced on him by a man to whom he owed a debt.

He said, "Are you unwell?"

"It's nothing," Hannah said. "I'm unused to the weight."

In fact, her pack weighed very little, but Hannah was as eager to be quit of Mr. Fitch as he was of her.

With her new set of directions memorized, Hannah set out. As she moved down the rue de Hôpital, the cottages grew smaller, the lane more crowded, and the stench enough to bring tears to the eyes, but still she felt more at ease, and was a little sorry that she had been so short with Fitch, who was one of the few contacts she could be sure of in New Orleans.

In this part of the city, at least, she would draw less attention to herself. There were few white faces to be seen, though every other color was in evidence, every shade of black, and many shades of red. She saw only a few Indians, none of whom showed any interest in her. The women of mixed blood watched her more openly, talking about her in loud voices she was meant to hear but in a patois she could only partially understand. Their voices, rough and full of laughter and pointed, seemed to echo in the narrow lanes.

In this part of the city there would be little or no chance that she might come across Jennet by accident, who had been at the Prestons' house on Bayou St. John for a full week. From the armed guard they had learned of her safe arrival; from Jennet herself there had been no word. That would change in the next day, but for the moment it did no good to worry. Jennet had withstood worse in the last year than a mean-spirited old woman. If she had been reunited with her son, she could put up with that, and much more.

"What you got in that poke there?" a man's voice said close behind her. "Let's have a look-see, shall we?"

That, Hannah told herself, was what came of daydreaming. She pulled her pack more firmly under her arm as strange hands tugged at it, and then she turned to face the three men who had been following her for—how long? A few minutes at least.

They were white and young and poor, the worst possible combination. All three of them looked at her with eyes brimming with what Curiosity Freeman would have called *plain mean*. One wore an overlarge hat that had slipped down to cover his eyebrows. He pushed it back up with the muzzle of a short-barreled musket. The other two, bigger than their friend by more than a head, were just as roughly dressed but fully armed. One had a knife that he tossed carelessly from his right hand to his left and back again. Sometime not so long ago somebody had knocked all his front teeth out, and it gave him the gleeful look of a boy of seven.

The crowded lane emptied, as it would do anywhere in the world but especially now, in this place, with war all around them. People had enough trouble served up to them day by day and needed none of hers.

"You be friendly now," said the gap-toothed one. There was something slightly cajoling in his tone, and beneath that, the flickering hope that she would fight.

"Open up," said the one with a knife, winking at her. He crooked a finger at her pack.

Hannah did as she was told, and pulled out a pistol. It was one she had used many times before, and it felt comfortable in her hand. Maybe they saw how easily she held it; maybe

they understood without having to be shown that she was
willing to use it. Certainly their faces changed.

"I can open up," she said. "If you really want me to."

They were gone around a corner in a flash, but Hannah
had the idea they wouldn't be far away. She set her mind to
finding the shack Mr. Fitch had told her about, before the
day got much older.

The woman was very old; she had a scattering of brown
teeth, earlobes that had been elongated by heavy brass rings,
and eyes as yellow as a cat's. The color of her skin was lost
under a coat of grime. At the mention of Mr. Fitch's name
she spit over her shoulder onto the dirt floor, but she
pointed with a lumpy, swollen hand to a corner of the shack
where a dirty blanket lay crumpled. Then she curled the fingers of her other hand in a gesture that needed no words.
Hannah put three coins in her palm and the hand disappeared into the open neck of the old woman's dress where
her breasts hung like empty sacks.

That was the beginning of her first night in New
Orleans, which brought her little sleep and no rest at all.

There were drums, not so far away, and voices raised in
chant, and a constant low thrumming, the sound of feet
pounding into the earth. Hannah had heard this kind of
music before, on the islands they had visited looking for
Jennet. Now she wondered sometimes if she was dreaming
but found her eyes were open and stinging. Sweat ran down
her face, but when she reached for her water skin she found
it empty. She could not remember ever being so thirsty, but
neither could she imagine going out into the night to find
water.

The old woman, who had no name she cared to share, sat
at the door of the shack on a low stool, a shawl around her
shoulders in spite of the heat. A torch sputtered and smoked

on the wall, and the stink of it filled the small space. Hannah
turned her face away but could not escape the sound of
voices. People came by and talked to the old woman, who
had a hoarse, whispery voice and a chortling laugh.

I have a fever, Hannah said to no one at all. *I have a fever,
and no medicines.* She spoke Kahnyen'kehàka, the language of
her mother's people, and the words hung about her head
and shimmered like dragonflies.

A man came, a white man who stood in the door and
spoke to the old woman in a tone that was unmistakable:
You are nothing, not worthy of the effort it would take to
crush you. He asked her questions and she answered, her
tone so different that Hannah understood even from the
depths of her fever that she was in fear of her life.

No English, she said. No British here. She lived for nothing more than to do laundry and bring the coins she earned
to her mistress. She had no interest in English promises of
freedom. Where would she go, if she were free? What would
she do?

To Hannah it sounded as if she meant what she said. The
white man believed her, too, because he went away.

In the morning her fever had broken. She felt light-headed
when she went in search of water, and then paid too much
for the privilege of drinking her fill. She paid more for a
bowl of it to wash her face and neck and hands. The glands
in her throat and armpits and in her groin were swollen and
hard, and she had the idea that the fever was not finished
with her yet.

She left the old woman's shack with all her belongings
and the intention of never going back, and found her way
to the little chapel that had been described to her near the
Turning Basin near where the Canal Carondelet ended.
Inside it was cool and dim, and Titine was kneeling in front

of a very old statue of the Virgin Mary carved out of dark-ened oak, riddled with woodworm.

Hannah touched her on the shoulder, and together they went outside to talk in the shade of a hanging oak.

Hannah said, "Jennet?"

"You just missed Miss Jennet, she went straight back after early Mass."

But she was alive, and well, and Hannah was satisfied to know that much. When Titine was done telling her the rest of it—none of it a surprise, and some room for guarded op-timism—the tone of Titine's voice changed.

"How long you been sick like this?"

The expression on her face told Hannah denials would do her no good. "Since yesterday afternoon."

"You about to fall on your face. Where you staying?"

She made a deep sound of disapproval when Hannah told her, bowing her upper body over her arms and shaking her head.

"Somebody looking out for you, that's for sure," she said. "Some angel keeping watch. It's a plain miracle nobody put a knife in you last night. What was the man thinking, send-ing you there?"

It wasn't a real question, and Hannah didn't try to an-swer it.

"We got to find you a safe place, and right now," Titine said. "Someplace they look after you when the fever come down again. Your brother here yet?"

"No," Hannah said. "Not yet."

Titine's mouth twitched in irritation or worry. "There's someplace that might just do, but it won't come cheap. I hope you ain't the kind who looks down on working women."

Much of the rest of the day was lost completely to Hannah, who let herself be led like a placid child through the back alleys of the city. It felt to her as though her skin were dissolving in the heat and wet of the air, as if she would soon float through the lanes, bumping against walls and trees. When Titine spoke to her it came in a slow echo, the words drawn out and wrapped up in gauze and unrecognizable. Very soon she gave up trying to understand; she gave up on language altogether.

When she woke again she thought it must be evening by the quality of the light on the walls around her, which otherwise told her nothing of the place where she found herself. A small square room with windows on two sides, a row of hooks on the wall, her clothes and shawl on one of them. A table, a stool, and the bed in which she found herself, made up neatly with linen that was rough but clean.

She had on a thin lawn nightdress she didn't recognize, and everything—sheets, pillow, nightdress—was soaked with her own sweat.

"I can't fall sick, not now." She whispered these words to the walls and was marginally comforted by the sound of her own voice, even when the things it said were clearly false. She could be sick. She was sick. If her head weren't aching so, she would be able to make sense of her symptoms and figure out what needed to be done.

As it was, she couldn't even reach for the pitcher of water on the table beside the bed. Her arms wouldn't obey her, nor would her legs. She stank of thin vomit, and sweat.

Hannah remembered Titine quite suddenly, Titine who had come from Pensacola with Jennet and had been visiting the chapel every day, waiting for Hannah to arrive. Titine had brought her to this place, and she must be nearby. She tried to raise her voice to call and succeeded in making only a very small sound. And yet the door opened, as if someone had been listening for exactly that.

It was not Titine who stood there or anyone Hannah had ever seen before, but a woman of middle age, painfully thin

and with a tiny pursed mouth. The red stones in the earrings that swung beside her neck worked brighter and bigger than her eyes, two small dull peas pushed into the hard
flesh of her face. Some part of Hannah's mind realized that
this woman who was looking at her with such distaste was
wearing a great deal of jewelry of substantial value.

Behind the woman, who had still not spoken, was a
smaller and much younger woman, plainly dressed. A far
prettier woman, though her skin was golden and her tilted
black eyes were cast down in the way of servants everywhere. Hannah had come across a few Chinese in the last
year, but all of them had been male.

"Girl," said the older woman in a clear, carefully modulated French. "You will see to it she drinks as much water
and broth as you can force down her throat. You will wash
her. You will see to it that she does not soil the bed. If she
dies in the night, fetch Tim and he will dispose of her body."

The Chinese girl bent her whole body in a nod. *"Oui,
madame."*

"Missus," Hannah said, her voice as steady as she could
make it. "Where am I?"

A thin lip curled. "I am Noelle Soileau, and you are in my
establishment. The mulatto who brought you here paid rent
on this room for a week, and hired the part-time help of
Girl."

"Where is she?" Hannah asked.

"If I thought you were contagious I would never have
allowed you in, and if you forget your station, I will cast you
out without hesitation."

Then she closed the door behind herself, and Hannah
was left with the young Chinese woman called Girl.

Hannah could already feel herself slipping away, down into
the boiling fever. She wanted to ask questions, but the girl was
lifting her head with one small, very strong hand while she
held a tin cup to her mouth with the other. The water was

clean and warm and tasted of metal. Hannah drank, and drank, and drank, and slipped away into sleep.

Hours passed, or days; she could be sure of very little except that she was still in the same room. Sometimes the Chinese girl was sitting next to her on the stool and sometimes she was alone. She roused at different tastes in her mouth: water, weak tea, salty beef broth.

This is swamp fever, she tried to say. *Call an apothecary.*

There was music in the night, a piano, a fiddle not so far away, the sound of women laughing. Doors opening and closing, a man crying out in pleasure or pain. There were gunshots, too, and artillery fire in the distance, the low coughing boom of cannon, but whether these things were real or part of her dreams she was never quite sure.

Nausea overwhelmed her so that even broth and water could only be taken by the spoonful, and still sometimes she brought them up. When the fever was at its worst she sometimes heard other voices, a jumble of languages, Mahican and Scots and English and Kahnyen'kehàka, the languages of her girlhood. Her father's voice, her dead husband's. Her stepmother's, reading from Shakespeare.

The Chinese girl went on with her work placidly, undisturbed by the universes tumbling through the room. Hannah woke once to find her sweat-caked skin being bathed in a solution of water and vinegar. Now and then Hannah heard her speaking to someone at the door. She spoke French in the same accents as the woman who owned this place, with no hint of any other language.

Finally the day came when Hannah could whisper a question and be understood.

"My friend?"

"The mulatto? She has not come back." The Chinese girl never smiled, but her face was an expressive one.

"How long have I been here?"

"Today is the first of October."

The room began to spin, slowly, grandly. Hannah closed her eyes and tried to make sense of the idea that she had been in this room for so long, and that Titine had never returned.

The girl had worries of her own, which she shared freely. If her mistress was not paid another week's rent tomorrow, Hannah would be put out, sick or not.

There had been money, money enough to rent this room for months, and more than that, there had been the letters. Her pack, guarded so carefully, was nowhere in the room that Hannah could see. She asked about it, her voice hoarse.

"The mulatto woman took it, for safekeeping."

By her tone Hannah understood. The girl believed that Titine had stolen Hannah's pack and run away. Hannah herself did not believe this, would not believe it, but that didn't matter. She fought back panic through the throbbing of her head, thinking through the things that must be said before the fever made talk impossible.

"You must go to an apothecary and get me some cinchona bark," she said. "I have swamp fever."

"With what money?"

She forced herself to breathe deeply. She said, "Is there an almshouse in the city, or a clinic where they would take me in?"

"There is no place for someone like you."

"And the negroes, where do they go when they're ill?" Hannah asked.

The girl shrugged. "The free colored have their own doctors and healers and midwives."

Hannah's head began to swim again, but she bit down on her lip to make herself focus. "Do you have another name besides Girl?"

"It is the only name Madame allows me. I was born in this house to one of her whores. I belong to her."

Hannah said, "If you can get me paper and pen, and if you can deliver a note successfully, I will buy you from Madame and give you your freedom. And you can choose your own name."

Girl looked at Hannah calmly. She said, "This is the only place I know."

"Do you want to be a whore for all your life?"

The girl blinked at her in surprise, as if Hannah had asked whether she was in the habit of breathing. She turned her head on its long stem of neck and looked out the window. "To be the servant of Redbone woman is less than I am now."

"You would be free," Hannah said.

There was a long moment's silence, filled in only faintly by the sound of a horse and carriage passing on the cobblestones outside.

Girl said, "I will try."

But the fever came roaring back, so that her fingers could not command the quill, and her head was too heavy to lift. The sickness dragged her off to the shadowlands where her grandmothers sat together, the ones she had known in life and others she knew only by the stories their daughters had told, all of them offering advice. The other world pushed at her now and then, voices she did not recognize, blurred faces the color of the earth, of the night sky, of whey. Arms lifted her and she flew through the air, her hair swinging around her head, wind on her face. A voice, low and murmuring.

She spoke to the dead. Long ago—months? years?—she had made peace with her husband and her son, and now they came to sit beside her, sometimes together, but most often it was just Strikes-the-Sky. She said, *It is very kind of you to sit with me while I die. I'm sorry I could not do the same for you.*

Sometimes her grandfather Hawkeye was with them.

I have missed you so, she said. And: *Did you find the death you were looking for?*

Other faces flickered around her like fireflies in the night. Men on battlefields, bleeding to death of wounds she could not staunch, children dead of fever, an old man whose name she could not recall in a river, red maple leaves caught in his hair.

Let me sleep, she told them all. *Let me sleep, I have done all I can.*

Sometimes Jennet was with her, as she had once been, bright and full of life and stories. Kit Wyndham came, too, and asked her questions in languages she did not recognize, the same question, it seemed, over and over, until he grew impatient and asked in English: *Are you content to be a whore for the rest of your life?*

She answered him in Kahnyen'kehàka: *I am who I am.*

CHAPTER 15

Strangers came most often. Dark-skinned women and others, milky pale, most of them of middle years but one quite young and beautiful.

Hannah said, *I don't believe in O'seronni angels, go away and let me sleep.* The young woman said, *Finish this broth and I will go, but let me assure you first I am no angel.* Then another face, this one immediately familiar though she had not seen the man in many years. Quick dark eyes underscored by shadows, strong nose and chin, hair cut unfashionably short, shot with gray.

She said, "Did you die of drink, Dr. Savard?"

He laughed, and that was when Hannah understood that she was awake, that she would live, and that she had failed Jennet completely.

At first the periods of wakefulness were short, but Hannah found that if she fought for more than her body was ready to give her, she paid in another lost day.

"Malaria," Dr. Savard told her. He must be forty now, and Hannah found that the ten years had mellowed him in some ways but not all: He was still plainspoken when it came to his medical opinions. "And pneumonia of both lungs on top of that. I thought more than once that we would lose you."

"Indians don't get malaria, I've been told," Hannah said.

"A hypothesis you have disproved."

He looked very healthy, which was a bit of a surprise. She told him as much.

"Things change," he told her with his old acerbity. "I no longer drink, and you, I see, are out of the habit of dining with senators."

His transformation was due, Hannah saw, to the attentions of the woman who nursed her, a Quaker by her dress, and Dr. Savard's wife. Julia Savard was of an age with her husband, a neat, pretty woman whose hands were red and rough with hard work, but whose way of speaking marked her for the daughter of a privileged family. She was also the mother of the beautiful young woman who came every day to feed Hannah broth and tea. The girl seemed pleased to see Hannah recovering, if for no other reason than she had one more person to talk to. Rachel was sixteen and in need of a confidant who was not her mother or her stepfather or, worst of all, her young brother.

While she was with Hannah, Rachel talked constantly in a light, easy way that was distracting and comforting both. She told Hannah the story of her life thus far, and more important, what lay ahead of her: courtship and marriage. It seemed that such things were much more complicated in New Orleans than they had been in Manhattan.

"It has been a lesson in humility," Rachel told Hannah. "And one my mother says was overdue. At home—in Manhattan—a daughter of the Livingston line was always sought after, but here—" She flicked her fingers toward the window. Her manner was studiously dismissive, but Hannah saw the confusion and unhappiness the girl did not really mean to hide.

"You are not Creole," Hannah said.

"I am not French." Rachel sniffed. "If it weren't for the fact that my uncle Livingston married a Creole lady, I would be received only by the wives of the American merchants and lawyers."

When Julia finally realized how Rachel was spending her time in the sickroom, she would have put an immediate stop to it, had Hannah not insisted.

"She does me a world of good," Hannah said. "I'm learning quite a bit about the way the city works, or fails to."

Hannah found it easy to talk to Julia, who understood without explanation what a disaster this illness had been for Hannah. Rachel needed to talk about fashion and the parties given by her aunt Livingston, and Hannah needed to talk about the fact that by falling ill she may have cost her cousin everything. And then the fever bore her away again.

In the next days she took note of very little beyond the constant struggle to breathe with lungs that seemed to be filled with hot water. She could make sense of nothing, least of all why there should always be someone forcing more liquid into her mouth. As if the world were not wet enough; as if she were not already in danger of floundering.

When her head began to clear and she realized that she was getting better, that she would survive, she began to worry again. And she came to understand how patients fell in love with their nurses, because the sight of Julia at her door filled her with a weepy gratitude. She was always calm and good-humored and endlessly understanding of what Hannah needed before she could even think how to ask; she brought cool water and sweet tea to drink, warm water and fine milled soap to wash away sweat and the stink of illness, and newspapers that she read out loud in her clear, precise way.

It was during one of these sessions that Hannah finally recognized Julia. She had tilted her head, which was wrapped with a wealth of dark blond braids that peeked out from under a neatly folded linen cap, and the sun struck her face in a certain way. At that moment Hannah made a connection she might have seen earlier if she had been well.

"You are Dr. Simon's daughter." It was at Valentine Simon's Manhattan clinic that Hannah had studied under Dr. Savard, the summer she had learned how to vaccinate against small-pox. "But I thought—" She stopped herself, suddenly unsure of her memory.

"You do remember," said Julia. "I wondered if you would, we met so briefly. Your uncle Spencer introduced us one day in the park that summer you spent in Manhattan. I was Mrs. Livingston then. My first husband—Rachel's father—died in the yellow fever epidemic of 1803."

She said all this as she straightened the bed coverings, and then she sat down on the chair beside it and folded her hands in her lap with the air of someone finishing a story she has told many times before.

"We came here when Paul's father started to decline, more than a year ago now."

"Dr. Savard's father lives nearby?"

"He did," Julia said. Her gaze shifted to her own hands, and Hannah had the idea that she might be praying, briefly. "Yellow fever, again. Both my father-in-law and his second wife."

"That is very hard," Hannah said.

Julia folded her hands together tightly. "There are important things to talk about, I think, now that you are stronger. I can see you are ready to leave us, or at least you think you are."

"You have saved my life," Hannah said. "But I must go. There are people who are waiting for me, who are depending on me. They will think I am dead."

This speech brought on a bout of coughing. When it had ended, Paul Savard was standing in the doorway. He said, "We will send word for you, but you're not going anywhere just now or all Julia's nursing will have been wasted. Your lungs are barely recovered, Hannah Bonner, you know yourself what that means."

"You don't understand," Hannah said. "My brother, his wife—"

Julia Savard exchanged a pointed glance with her husband, who came in to stand beside the bed.

"Then you must tell us," Julia Savard said. "Tell us exactly what it is you need, and we will do our best to help you."

"Best to wait," said Dr. Savard. "Until my brother can be found. He's more likely to be of help to you than I can be."

Hannah woke at the sound of voices at her door. Julia came in first, with a boy of about seven years close beside her. He had Paul Savard's dark hair and eyes and Julia's mouth and chin, though set in a much more resolute and willful line than his mother's.

"Papa thought you were going to die," said Henry Savard with all the tact of a young boy. "So just about everybody got to sit with you while they waited to see if you would. Except me, they wouldn't let me in."

"Henry," said Julia and Rachel together.

He looked a little abashed. "I'm glad you didn't die," he explained. "Now you can tell me stories about your family and the Indians and the Ohio territory. You were there, Papa said."

"I was," Hannah agreed. "I do have many stories to tell."

"Stories that will have to wait," said Paul Savard from the doorway. "If I may introduce you, Dr. Bonner—"

There were few men in the world who would give her that title, but Paul was one of them.

"—my brother, Jean-Benoît Savard."

Paul's brother ducked his head to clear the doorway and came into the light.

Jean-Benoît Savard was a man who made his living out-of-doors; his hands were rough with work, and his clothes rougher still. He might be a farmer or a woodsman or a hunter; he might be a soldier, out of uniform. His silence was not born of hesitation or good manners or even care for her fragile health, but because he was observing. In his expression she saw the same sharp intelligence that had propelled Paul through the most difficult medical education in the world, but a calm that was distinctive and his own.

Beyond those things, it was clear that the two men had not shared the same mother. Paul was white; his brother's skin was neither black nor white nor red, but all three, like iron-rich clay mixed with earth and then stirred into a great deal of pale sand. The two brothers looked nothing alike, except for the fact that they both had very dark hair shorn almost to the scalp. This made Paul's face seem narrow and sharp, but in Jean-Benoît's case it gave prominence to large, deep-set eyes with hooded lids, eyes the blue-green of Caribbean waters over a sandbar, or turquoise beads wrapped around the wrists of veiled women. Shocking eyes in that particular face, with its high flat cheekbones and a strong nose and a sharply defined mouth, too full for a man but still somehow severe.

"Ben has come to hear your story. He knows this city better than I ever will," said Paul.

"Uncle Ben knows everything," said Henry Savard. "He knows theciprière and the river and the swamps and the bayous and everybody who lives in a thousand miles. Uncle," he said pointedly, "never gets lost."

"Henry," said Julia Savard gently.

"And my sister Rachel knows what my uncle doesn't," Henry went on in all seriousness. "Except it's mostly about who bought a new hat and who's invited where and who's in love—"

"Henry," Rachel said, in strangled tones.

"And your mama?" Hannah asked, amused.

"Mama knows everything about everything," Henry said. "Without Mama, Papa couldn't have saved your life."

"Yes," Hannah said. "That's true."

"Now that we are clear on our various areas of expertise," said Paul, "perhaps we should get on with it. My brother and my stepdaughter are both here because between them, as Henry put it so astutely, they know everything about the city."

Jean-Benoît Savard said, "If you will tell me your story, I will do what I can." His voice was raw, as though he had once strained his vocal cords beyond endurance and they had never recovered. His language was just as unusual, English that was native in the way the words were strung together, but nevertheless had to find its way through a thicket of other languages, French first among them.

Julia said, "Run along now, Henry. Clémentine is waiting for you. Time for your bath and bed."

Henry launched himself at the uncle he so clearly adored. Jean-Benoît leaned over and put a hand on the back of the boy's head. He spoke to Henry but smiled at his sister-in-law.

"Henry, no good will ever come from disobeying a woman, especially your mother. She is always right."

When the boy was gone, it seemed as though he took some of the light and air from the room. Weariness washed over Hannah as the sound of his footsteps receded. Julia came to sit beside the bed and put a hand on her forehead, and Rachel poured water from a beaker into a glass and handed it to her.

"Her fever is coming up again," Rachel said to her stepfather.

"No, it is not," Hannah said. "I am recovered, and I must talk."

Because she had been so ill, because she was weary beyond reckoning, and most of all because it was not often Hannah allowed herself the luxury of memory, the words came from her reluctantly. She cast her mind back to the previous summer, to the garrison on Île aux Noix and the day Jennet had been abducted by the false priest. She told the Savards about Luke, about their uneasy alliance with the British Crown through Kit Wyndham, about their year-long pursuit of

Anselme Dégre, about the rescue at L'Île de Lamantins. By that time the story had taken on a life of its own and flowed through her like icy water.

Now and then one of the women drew in a sharp breath, but the men's expressions never changed from polite attentiveness, and would never change, no matter what they were feeling about the story she told. Very little could shock Paul Savard after his years in the hospital wards of the Manhattan almshouse; Jean-Benoît Savard was unknown to her, but Hannah had the idea that he was a man who never gave away what he might be thinking unless it suited him to do so.

There was a small silence when she finished. Then Dr. Savard made a deep sound in his throat, gruff acknowledgment and something of sympathy, but not too much, lest it distract them from their purpose. The sound a physician makes when unwrapping a festering wound.

"You've had a run of bad luck," he said. "Enough bad luck for a lifetime."

"And now Agnès Poiterin on top of all that," said Rachel. She shuddered.

"It's Jennet I'm worried about," Hannah said. "And the boy."

Jean-Benoît had listened without asking questions, but he spoke up now and got right to the heart of the matter. "Tell me the things you believe."

It was a strange formulation, but Hannah understood him. With some effort she calmed her thoughts, and then she began.

"I don't understand why Titine never came back to see to me. She knew I was ill. I fear she must be locked up someplace, or dead."

"Or worse," said Rachel. "Slave traders sometimes snatch up free people of color."

Hannah closed her eyes and let a wave of nausea pass through her.

"Or worse," she echoed.

"We mustn't assume the worst," said Julia.

"Go on," said Jean-Benoît, calmly.

"I believe that my pack and everything in it—the money, the letters of introduction, the letter Jennet wrote to Luke—is gone. Maybe Jennet has it. I hope she does. Otherwise thieves took it from Titine or the Poiterins intercepted it. If that is the case, Jennet has been in a difficult and possibly dangerous situation for two weeks. She must be frantic for some word of us, unless Luke has found some way to contact her. I know my brother will be searching for me, though he can only do so indirectly if our plan is to work. Unless he is dead, too."

Her head had begun to ache again, and she closed her eyes so she did not see, could not imagine Jean-Benoît's expression.

She heard him say, "Look for me tomorrow in the late afternoon. I will find out what there is to know, and then plans can be made."

Then a large, hard hand covered her own hands where they lay, fingers cramped together, on the covers. It was a fleeting touch, but firm and resolute and comforting.

When Jean-Benoît had gone, Rachel sat down beside Hannah. She said, "You can sleep peacefully now."

"Yes," said Julia. "Ben has made your concern his own, and you could not have hoped for more."

Hannah said, "He is a Quaker?" The surprise in her voice couldn't be hidden.

"He takes what he likes of my religion," said Julia. "And of any other he comes across." She sounded more resigned than anything else.

"Ben will do what he can," said Dr. Savard, more soberly.

There was some comfort in the idea that Hannah was no longer alone, but not enough to dispel the dread that lay on her tongue, its taste as bitter and distinct as cinchona bark.

CHAPTER 16

When Titine came to report on her first meeting with Hannah, Jennet had been so light-headed with relief that at first she had simply failed to comprehend the bad news: Hannah had arrived safely in New Orleans, but she was sick with swamp fever. How sick, Titine had refused to speculate; instead she had consulted with her aunt Amazilie, filled her apron pockets with herbs and medicines, and gone straight back to the city. And never returned.

By the second day it was clear to them all that Titine had been abducted, or was dead at the hands of common thieves. It was then that Jennet allowed herself to contemplate the full weight of the facts: Titine was gone for good, and Jennet was responsible for this. Add to that, news just as bad: Titine had disappeared before she had thought to tell anyone where Hannah was hidden in the city. Hannah was stranded someplace, ill unto death, without money or papers. In the pack that Titine had brought back to Maison Verde for safekeeping was the letter Jennet had written for Luke, in code.

Luke was missing, too, and there was no word of him. In short, all their plans had gone wrong.

Despite all this, Jennet had no choice but to present a calm and benign expression to the world in general, and to Mme. Poiterin in particular. Her daily routine did not change with

Titine's disappearance, except that Amazilie was now required to accompany her to Mass and confession every
morning, followed by Mme. Poiterin's men.

And so Jennet concentrated on her son. When Jacinthe
brought him, Jennet could put everything else away for that
short time. She set herself the goal of making him remember, if only by touch and voice, who his mother was.

It was Jacinthe who suggested, shyly, almost apologeti-
cally, that Jennet put her son to the breast.

"Let him suckle," Jacinthe had told her. "Let him pull hard,
the milk will come back."

"But . . ." Jennet, afraid to take Jacinthe at her word, had
hesitated and asked the more crucial question. "Surely
Madame will object?"

Jacinthe blinked at her and put a long hand on her own
high rounded belly. "Madame got another great-grandchild
coming," she said. "This one will need to suckle, too."

Jennet had the idea that Mme. Poiterin was not likely to
acknowledge Jacinthe's child as her own blood, but she did
not say so. Instead she put her son back to the breast and let
him draw. The pain, at first, was exquisite, but it was not
long before her milk came back, and in such abundance that
she was swollen with it when Jacinthe brought the boy later
than usual.

The joy of having her son back in this particular way was
enough to offset the unpleasant nature of her afternoon duties, when she was expected to arrive at Larivière at three
every day to take coffee. Or rather, she had been summoned
to read aloud while the old lady took coffee and ate a multitude of sugary little confections called pralines. Jennet
might have taken some satisfaction from the simple act of
reading well, if Madame had not interrupted constantly to
correct her French pronunciation or to lecture.

The old lady used the newspaper reports as a way to
launch into her daily catechism, which began with a biting

critique of everything having to do with Americans. She found them to be vulgar, brazen, uncouth, greedy; she deplored the garish houses they were building in the sprawling new suburbs that clung to the city like leeches, and most of all, she resented their insufferable interference in Creole business and society. Beyond all that, she disdained their inability or stubborn refusal to learn French, the only language that Mme. Poiterin cared to hear spoken around her. New Orleans would always be French, could be nothing less than Creole.

The reports of Commander Patterson's raids on Barataria and his routing of the Lafitte brothers made the old lady so angry that her plump hands shook. The Lafittes had offered their services to the Americans—why they should do such a thing she could not imagine—but instead of showing their gratitude that men of courage and wide experience were willing to assist them, the American navy had destroyed the village at Grand Terre, taken dozens of prisoners, and confiscated half a million dollars in property.

She had no doubt, Madame said darkly, that the milled soap and Belgian lace and embroidered fabrics she had ordered from France were now in the possession of an American woman with a loud voice and no sense of style. The only comfort was the fact that the Lafittes had eluded Patterson, and would soon be back in business.

"What would be best," she pronounced finally, "is if the British and Americans killed each other off entirely, and let us return to our own ways. What do you say to that, miss?"

Jennet sometimes wondered if her face might crack from the effort of hiding her feelings, and thought that Mme. Poiterin would actually like to see that happen. It seemed to be her goal.

The oddest thing of all, Jennet had decided quite soon, was that Madame seemed unable to take the threatened English invasion seriously. It mystified Jennet that a woman who prided herself on her political acuity and good business sense would refuse to entertain the idea that anyone might try to impose their will on her, or to take something she called her own. Jennet, who had been raised on a steady diet of Scottish history, could have told Madame something of the way the British treated the people they defeated, but she also understood that this was not a discussion, but a lesson. If she wanted to be accepted as a Poiterin she must take on the opinions and positions that were presented to her, and make them her own.

Jennet wondered if Honoré might be able to convince the old lady that she needed to make plans in case the worst should happen and the city was overrun, but she had seen Honoré very rarely since she came to Louisiana, and he was never present when she paid her long afternoon calls at Larivière. It was a surprise, and an unsettling one, to find him in the parlor a week after Titine's disappearance, his legs stretched out before him and a coffee cup balanced on the silk brocade vest over the flat plane of his stomach. He pretended surprise when she came in, and then played the concerned and loving husband, bringing her pillows she did not want and coffee she would not drink.

Madame was not taken in, either, and she pursed her small pale mouth in displeasure. Jennet could not tell if Honoré's purpose was to anger her, or if he simply didn't care about her mood. Another possibility presented itself, far more frightening: Honoré was here because of Titine's disappearance. Maybe he had learned something and was just waiting for the opportunity to give her bad news; perhaps he knew exactly what had happened to Titine, because he had made it happen. She thought of Piero Bardi's head sitting on top of her trunk in an abandoned shack, and she shuddered.

"Are you cold?" he asked her. "Can I get you a rug for your lap?"

His grandmother tsked at such a bold question, but Honoré

ignored her. He wanted to know how Jennet fared, if she was comfortable in her new home, whether she required anything from town that he could get for her.

"Have you had word from your family?" he asked, and a shower of gooseflesh rushed up Jennet's back at the expression on his face.

"Of course she has not," his grandmother said sharply. "You know there has been no post from Europe. It is most inconvenient, this embargo."

"I fear you must miss your brother and mother, my dear." Honoré persisted in speaking to Jennet directly, and his grandmother in answering for her.

Titine was dead, and Honoré had killed her; of that Jennet was suddenly quite sure. What she could not know was how much information had been forced from her before she died. Jennet pinched the flesh between her thumb and first finger until her vision cleared and she could control her breathing.

"Why should she?" Mme. Poiterin was saying. "She has her son. She has you, or will have you, if it turns out her good behavior is not a ruse. It is the way of civilized society: A young lady forsakes her mother for her husband's family." She sniffed delicately, as if remembering her own mother.

"Grand-mère," he said. "Has my dear Jennet not been tested enough? Surely it's time to acknowledge the marriage."

Jennet dropped her head in fear that her expression would give away too much, but Mme. Poiterin, who was just as surprised, turned all her attention in Honoré's direction. Her round cheeks flushed with color and her eyes narrowed.

"You talk of this matter as though it were nothing more than a dinner engagement," she said. "Shame on you, Honoré. If you had gone about this marriage properly to start with none of this would be necessary. As it is, you will wait until I am entirely satisfied that Lady Jennet will be a suitable wife and mother to your son."

Mme. Poiterin had started calling her Lady Jennet in a dismissive tone. Jennet might have objected, but she found her title much preferable to being called Honoré's wife.

The old lady was saying, "I will admit she has proved to be biddable, if perhaps a bit simpleminded. Père Petit reports that she is repentant, though sometimes I believe I still see a hint of rebellion in her expression. However, if things go on as they have, we will be able to have the banns read starting next month, and celebrate the wedding Mass early in the new year."

Honoré didn't try to hide his irritation. "You forget, Grand-mère, we are already married."

"So you say," said his grandmother. "But I have yet to see your marriage lines." She looked at Jennet when she said this, and Jennet returned her gaze evenly. It was an odd circumstance that Honoré had constructed for himself. He could not produce the marriage lines, because no such document had ever existed. She had wondered for some time why he didn't simply forge something to show his grandmother—it seemed like something he would do without hesitation—and then realized that he hadn't yet decided where the greater advantage might be, in a real marriage or a false one. No doubt it had to do with his claim on her family's money, and his grandmother's, both of which he would keep, if he could manage it. Her son was nothing more than a chip in this game of chance.

What he didn't know, what she would not tell him, was that she did have a set of marriage lines, these absolutely legal and binding in the eyes of both the Catholic Church and the law. She began every day by sewing that piece of paper into the hem of whatever gown she was to wear, but she wondered sometimes what would be worse: to lose it, or to have it be discovered by Mme. Poiterin. To declare herself the legal wife of another man would be to hand over her son to these people.

"It's all very silly," Honoré said. "But if you insist."

"I do," said the old lady. "And there is another matter I will insist upon."

Jennet was surprised to learn that Honoré had joined a militia troop, from which it followed that he needed money for the elaborate uniform and for new weapons; it was expected of him as a son of one of the first families. His grandmother, always sensitive to such claims on her reputation, got a wily look in her eye and commanded Honoré to write a letter asking to be excused.

"With the cane harvest coming so soon you're needed at the plantations," she said. "Especially now. I worry that the slaves at Grand Trianon will be seduced by the lies of the English, and as far as Amboise is concerned, I have lost faith in Cheveau. Others have extracted themselves this way. You can, too."

"You would have me branded a coward?"

She rapped her knuckles on the carved wooden arm of her chair, as large as a throne. "I would have you alive."

"You think there is going to be a real battle?" Honoré smiled. "The British have the Americans outnumbered and outgunned by a factor of ten. They will make short work of the navy on the Gulf and then march into the city without firing a shot. The legislature will strew rose petals before them if that means sparing the city, and their properties. They are already huddling together in corners, wondering about the best way to surrender."

"Then why bother?" said Madame. "Stay home out of the cold and rain."

"Because if New Orleans must fall to the British, our officers will be required to negotiate with their officers. The men who make up that party should be—"

"Creole," said his grandmother. "And of the first rank. It would put you in a good position—"

"To see that our interests are protected, once the fighting is done. And," he added with a smile, "who else could do the uniform justice?"

Jennet had begun to wonder how much more critical the situation might get when the heavens took some pity on her and struck Père Petit dead with an apoplexy. It happened while he sat at his supper table, and thus at Mass the next morning she had something to be thankful for. She was so busy with her own thoughts that it wasn't until Communion that it occurred to her that the new priest—a younger man of average looks and bearing—would be the one to hear her confession.

She hoped he would not be as invasive and curious as Père Petit had been. She hoped he would let her recite a list of small transgressions and be on her way. From the look of him at the altar she could tell nothing of his personality.

After Mass she went into the confessional to wait for him, closing the door so that the small space—it always made her think of a coffin set on its end—was almost completely dark. It smelled of cypress and tallow and incense and sweat, with a hundred other scents lingering just below the surface. Fear, regret, submission.

The door to the priest's cubicle opened and closed, and then the grillwork on the window that joined Jennet's space to his slid to one side. She could see nothing of the priest through the curtain; she was not meant to see him. She waited for the familiar prayers to begin and then, after a moment, raised her head.

"Père?"

"I am no priest." The voice was hoarse and very low, one she had never heard before.

Jennet's throat closed in fear and hope. She had to swallow hard before she could force words out of it.

"Do you bring me a message?"

He said, "I bring you news of your cousin Hannah."

Jennet closed her eyes. "Who are you?"

"My name is Jean-Benoît." And then: "She is at Dr. Savard's free clinic on the rue Dauphine. She has malaria and is not well enough yet to leave her bed. You must come to her so that together you can make plans."

"But I can't," Jennet whispered, her voice cracking under the strain. "I cannot risk my son's well-being. Do you have any idea what Mme. Poiterin would do if she found out?"

With utter calm he said, "If you cannot bring yourself to trust me, I cannot help you, your son, or your cousin."

Jennet pressed her handkerchief to her eyes. She wanted to believe the voice behind the screen, but she was terrified.

"I think Honoré is suspicious," she said.

"Then you have less time to act, not more."

At that moment it occurred to her that whatever information Honoré had forced from Titine, he could not know of Hannah's presence in New Orleans, or Hannah would be dead.

She said, "Tell me something about Hannah."

There was a small silence, and she had the sense that he was choosing his words carefully. "She is tall for a woman, taller than you. She is half Indian and half white and has the best features of both races. She speaks English like a schoolteacher and French with a British accent. She is a trained physician who studied for a time in Manhattan. Her worry for you and your son and for her brother is keeping her from a full recovery."

Jennet couldn't help herself; she sobbed out loud. "Yes," she said. "I believe you now. Do you have word of my husband?"

"Not yet," said Jean-Benoît.

Those two words filled Jennet with hope for the first time since Titine's disappearance. She forced her voice to steady.

"I will come to Hannah, if you can arrange it without arousing Mme. Poiterin's suspicions."

"When you go to read to her this afternoon she will suggest the trip herself," he said. "Be ready."

"Wait," she said. "What does the new priest know about all this? Have you bribed him to allow you to speak to me?"

"Not all priests are like Petit. Tomaso Delgado is a good man, and my friend. Does that satisfy you?"

It did not; it could not. She said, "I am struck by the coincidence that Père Petit should die just now, so suddenly. So conveniently for my cause."

After a moment Ben said, "Do you want my help?"

"Of course," said Jennet. "Of course I do."

CHAPTER 17

Amazilie waited outside while Jennet made her confession. She stood near the entrance of the graveyard talking to an old woman with a basket tied to her back, filled to the brim with fresh clams. Mme. Poiterin's men waited, too, slouched against a wall. If Jennet spoke to anyone, if she looked too long in a shop window or greeted a lady on the lane, they would report as much to their mistress.

And so she waited until she was sure the men were out of earshot, and then she waited a while longer before she asked Amazilie if Père Tomaso was known to her.

"Tomaso Delgado?" Amazilie looked over her shoulder at the chapel. "Sure I know Père Tomaso. Everybody know the Delgados, an old Creole family with a plantation on the Bayou Teche. Went to school in France, but he get along with everybody, him. Even with the Spanish priests."

There was a civil war going on in the local Catholic bishopric, one that Jennet knew about because it was only slightly less interesting to Mme. Poiterin than the latest outrages committed by the invading American business interests.

"The bishop won't send no priest to say Mass here without Mme. Poiterin like him," said Amazilie.

"What is the power that Madame holds over the bishop?" Jennet asked. It was a question she had held back for a long time, and could resist no longer.

Amazilie had beautiful eyes, light brown in color and so large and perfectly formed that Jennet was reminded of a painting that hung in the chapel at Carryckcastle, the Madonna with her child. Now Amazilie turned these eyes to Jennet and regarded her soberly, with a little sadness and some impatience, too.

"Money," she said. "Priest or pirate, it's always about money, *chère.*"

At Maison Verde, Jacinthe was waiting on the porch with the baby on her hip. When he caught sight of Jennet he broke into a great smile that showed his empty pink gums. Jennet put out her arms and he reached for her and she thought, *Anything. Anything to keep him safe.*

Jacinthe handed the baby over without hesitation, and promptly went to nap in a chair with her shawl wrapped around her while Jennet walked back and forth along the bayou, exactly as far as she was permitted, and no farther. She told her son stories and he listened, mouthing his fist and rumpling his forehead in a way that made him look just like his father studying account books. Later she took him back to her room and nursed him and then they fell asleep together. When she woke it was to his milky breath on her face.

At that moment she understood that it didn't matter how Père Petit had died. She could not let herself feel remorse for him, for anyone who tried to keep her son from her. If the worst had happened, if Luke was gone, she would do what she must do to get her son and Hannah home to Paradise. It would take more than the Poiterins to stop her.

When Jennet arrived to read to Mme. Poiterin that afternoon, she found that the man who called himself Jean-

Benoît had been right. Père Tomaso sat with the old lady in the good parlor, a paper-thin china cup balanced on his knee while he answered the questions put to him. He followed Madame's example and did not even raise his head to look at Jennet when she took a seat in the corner. As if she were invisible, which she must be, until Madame declared her otherwise.

It gave her a moment to study him, but there was little remarkable about the man. He could have been a baker or a schoolteacher or a planter; she might have passed him on the street a hundred times and never taken note. In fact, Jennet realized, she had sat through his Mass and could not remember anything of the sermon he had given, beyond the fact that it was short.

What she could say about this man was that he knew exactly how to talk to Mme. Poiterin. His tone of voice, the measured deference in every turn of phrase, his basic understanding of his place in her world, these things pleased Madame and made her complacent.

"But surely not," Madame was saying. "The bishop is such a prudent man, so very cautious. All the priests are to be vaccinated?"

"They are," said Tomaso Delgado. "I went yesterday." He touched his sleeve to indicate a particular spot on his upper arm. "It was a matter of moments, and the discomfort was fleeting and minimal." He described the clinic on rue Dauphine and the vaccination process in careful detail.

"Very well," she said finally. "You may tell this physician—what is his name?"

"Paul Savard."

"Savard!" snapped the old lady. "Why did you not say that to begin with?"

He inclined his head. "Pardon my oversight. Of course, you must know the family."

"Of course I know the family. Jean-Baptiste," said Madame,

drawing herself up, "was a favorite of my dear son's. He was the most elegant of young men, so well-spoken, a credit to the Savards, at least until—" She stopped herself, and for once Mme. Poiterin looked somewhat flustered. "Until his wife died and he moved to his plantation permanently. I was sorry to hear of his death."

There was a silence while the old lady was lost in her thoughts. Finally she said, "You must send Dr. Savard my regards and tell him I expect him here tomorrow at eleven to vaccinate my family."

"I'm afraid it is most likely he will be unable to accept your invitation," said the priest. "They are so busy with vaccinations that they make no calls at all. Everyone comes to the clinic. The legislature, the mayor, even Père Antoine went to them."

"To a free clinic?" Madame drew back her head like an affronted hen.

"And tomorrow," the priest continued. "Tomorrow I believe Mme. Tremé and Mme. Marigny are both expected."

Jennet had to avert her face lest her expression give away too much of what she was thinking, which was very simple: This humble priest was moving Mme. Poiterin around like a pawn on a chess board.

"Very well," said Madame. "Then it must be this afternoon."

"Now?" The priest sounded doubtful.

"Of course, now." She was reaching for the bell pull to summon the housekeeper when she caught sight of Jennet.

"Have you been vaccinated against the smallpox, girl?"

"No, madame," Jennet lied.

"Then you will come, too." To the priest she said, "I trust this unfortunate girl made a satisfactory confession this morning?"

Jennet dared not look away or even blink.

"Most satisfactory," said the priest.

"Hmmmm." Madame considered Jennet for a moment. "Well, it cannot be helped. Go ahead, Père Tomaso, and tell them to be ready. We shall be at the clinic by five."

Rachel said, "I know you are impatient to be up, but in this case I think my mother is right. Another few days in bed will only do you good. Would you like to hear what happened yesterday when Mme. Girot came face-to-face with my aunt Livingston in Mme. Villeré's parlor?"

Hannah, who understood too much of the value of redirection in the sickroom, was not taken in, and said so. In just a little while Jennet would be here. Ben Savard was going to make her appear, like a conjurer in a story, and what else could she think about, but that?

"My stepfather said you would be impossible to divert, but I should try." Rachel sat down abruptly and folded her hands on her knees. "But it is gossip of the first order, and I was there to see it."

Hannah had been ready to disavow all interest in the social life of the New Orleans élite, but Rachel had a story to tell and would not be slowed down.

"You would think," Rachel said in disapproving tones, "that by now—it has been ten years—the Creoles would forgive my aunt Livingston for marrying an American. Especially such an elegant and well-spoken American as Edward Livingston, who was—they all seem to overlook this—a member of Congress and mayor of New-York City, as well. But none of that matters to Mme. Girot."

Hannah, as tense as she was, found herself listening with growing curiosity to the story of Edward Livingston's marriage to Louisa D'Avezac de Castera Moreau. She had been nineteen to his forty-one; already a widow, and impoverished. Her family had lost everything in the Domingo rebellions, and so she had come to New Orleans and taken up work as a seamstress to support herself. Her life had changed again when Edward Livingston moved from Manhattan to New Orleans to open a law practice.

"Only a person with a heart of stone could be unmoved by such a romantic story," Rachel pronounced. "But then, Mme. Girot has a face like a gargoyle as well, and I can only think she is jealous of my aunt's beauty."

Hannah should have scolded Rachel, but instead she laughed.

"You will like Louisa," Rachel pronounced. "She is very intelligent and very observant and funny. And she will like you, because you are unusual. She collects unusual people."

"You talk about me as if I were a teapot," Hannah said. "To be put on a shelf."

Rachel blushed. "Mother says I am too flippant, and she is right. I apologize. But you will like my aunt Livingston, I am sure of it."

"You do have connections," Hannah said. "I see now why your stepfather thought you might be able to help me."

"All I have is information," said Rachel. "But that I will share gladly."

There was a short knock at the door and Paul stuck his head in. "She's here. Rachel, I need you." He sent Hannah a sharp look. "I won't send your cousin to you unless you get back into bed."

But she could not, simply could not lie still in the neatly made bed while Jennet was somewhere in the building. Hannah got up to walk the length of the room and tried to clear her mind. Instead she saw Luke, as he had been that day so many weeks ago when they parted, his eyes squinted against the sun as he looked down at her. Where he was now, whether he was alive, she needed and feared the answers to these questions in equal measure.

There was a knock at the door and then it opened and Jennet came in. Jennet, looking smaller and narrower than she had when they had last been together in Pensacola. She stood motionless for the space of three heartbeats and then came to put her arms around Hannah. She felt very slight, and she trembled.

"I have never been so frightened," she said. "I thought you were dead."

Hannah hugged her back and then stepped away to look at her more closely. She felt a little faint, and at the same time stronger. "How much time do we have?"

"A half hour at least. They put Madame and her lady's maid in a private examination room. With all the clothes she wears it will take ten minutes to bare the old bat's arm."

Hannah heard the slightest spark of the old Jennet in this story, and was glad of it.

"Then tell me about the boy," she said.

"He is well," Jennet said, her face brightening. "He is very well, and beautiful. But he was left behind with his nurse. The grandmother won't allow him into the city."

"Afraid of illness?"

"Or that I would run off with him," Jennet said. "As I surely would, if only I knew how. If you were well enough to travel. If I knew how to find Luke."

"If there were not war and swamp and water on all sides," Hannah finished. They were sitting now on the chairs by the window. She reached out to put a hand over Jennet's clenched fists. "Tell me the rest of it, tell me everything I need to know."

While Jennet talked, Hannah kept her face immobile, though she found she was still capable of anger as the details unfolded. She felt the illness in her blood pushing, and she pushed back. When Jennet was gone again she could sleep.

"So both Luke and Titine are missing," said Hannah.

Jennet was very pale. "I have no way to go looking for

them, and neither do you. It's a fine mess, aye?" Her voice trembled a little.

"But we have help, now," Hannah said. She told Jennet about the Savards, and her connection to Paul. Once reminded, Jennet began to remember some of the details from Hannah's letters the summer she had spent in Manhattan. The same summer her own father had died, and she had been forced to give up the man she loved for the one who had been chosen for her.

"But who was it who spoke to me in the confessional?" Jennet said. "Certainly it wasn't Dr. Savard?"

"No," Hannah said. "That was Paul's brother. I am supposed to send for him now. He is our best hope, if he will help us."

CHAPTER 18

Worry had dug its way into the nape of Jennet's neck so long ago that the perpetual itch of it was something she had learned to tolerate. But now all her muscles ached and her head throbbed and all because she would have to leave Hannah soon, and had no idea when she would be able to see her again. From the doctor's wife she had heard the details of her cousin's condition, things Hannah herself must know, as a physician, facts that meant she would not be able to travel at all—much less travel rough—for weeks to come.

Now they waited for a man who might be able to help them, but she could not bring herself to hope. Any son of a well-born New Orleans family would have dozens of allegiances in this small city that would be more important than the troubles of two stranded women, one of them red-skinned, no matter how well disposed he was toward them. And then there was the war. If she had begun to forget about that, this trip into the city had brought that single fact back into bright focus. The streets were filled with soldiers and militiamen, and the boys who hawked newspapers screamed out bad news in a half dozen languages.

Then he came in, and Jennet understood that there was some hope, after all. Because Jean-Benoît Savard was not a typical New Orleans gentleman, or any kind of gentleman at all. His skin was the wrong color for that. She could not put a name to it, beyond the obvious fact that he had had at least one grandparent who was Indian, and another who was part or all African.

"Mrs. Bonner," he said, bowing his shoulders gracefully.

Jennet stood and held out her hand, and she saw the first flicker of surprise in his eyes as he took it. She said, "We owe you a great deal, sir, and I hope we may yet owe you more. It was a great chance you took this morning."

"Not so great," he said. He stood in front of them in the simple clothes of a man who might be a tracker or a hunter. He had a number of weapons on his person and moccasins on his feet, but he could have been wearing the uniform of a general, so exact was his bearing.

Jennet said to him, "We have only two chairs. Will you bring another one, so we can talk more comfortably?"

When he was gone Hannah said, "You were staring."

"I know," Jennet said. "I'm sorry. You said he is Paul Savard's brother?"

"Half brother."

Before she could ask anything more, Ben was back. He sat down opposite them, put his hands on his knees, and leaned forward slightly.

"I have no news for you of your husband and brother—"

Jennet saw Hannah's shoulders collapse slightly, and felt her own breath leave her in a rush.

"—but there is still room for hope," he finished. "If he is alive, I will find him. If he is not, I will tell you that, too."

Without hesitation Hannah said, "There is no time to wait. Jennet and her son have to be taken to safety."

"Not without Luke," said Jennet, and to Hannah: "Not without you."

"And if your husband is dead?" Ben asked, before Hannah could object.

Her throat was tight, but Jennet forced out each word clearly. "I won't leave Hannah here alone."

"Let me understand," said Ben Savard in a voice so deep and dark that Jennet might have been afraid, if there had been even an inch of room for more fear inside her. "You want to escape Mme. Poiterin's control, but you won't go without your sister-in-law."

Jennet nodded.

"Who is too ill to travel."

She nodded again.

"You realize how dangerous the situation is. Poiterins have long arms, and fists filled with money."

Jennet felt like weeping, but she would not. "Yes."

"If there's nothing you can do for us, we must help ourselves," Hannah said, and his sharp gaze turned in her direction.

"There's a great deal I can do for you," said Ben to Hannah. "If you will trust me."

There was a scratching at the door. Ben Savard went to open it, and spoke a few words to whoever was standing there. When he closed the door and turned, Jennet saw that he held her sleeping son in the crook of his arm.

After the first shock of such a sudden reunion, Ben allowed them a few moments.

"I regret to say there is very little time," he told them. "This is a delicate business and I need your complete attention."

Jennet wiped her face with her free hand and nodded.

"Père Tomaso is waiting downstairs. He has a horse for you. You will leave the building and ride away with him toward the south, and make sure that people on the street see your face. With any luck they'll begin to search for you in that direction."

"And the boy?" Hannah asked.

"He stays here," said Ben. "It will be an hour at least before they even know he's gone. He was taken in a way that will make it look as though his abductor rode east on the Chef Menteur road, toward Fisherman's Village. When you come back here late tonight, the two of you will be entered into the clinic logs as an Irish widow and her infant daughter, and Paul will isolate you as possibly contagious. You will be confined to the family apartment in this house, but you will be safe."

He went to the window and scanned the lane. "You must go now," he said to Jennet. "There is no time to waste. You will be back here by midnight if all goes well."

Jennet leaned forward to press a kiss to Hannah's cheek, and then, more lightly, on the boy's forehead. She whispered, "Look after my son," and then she was gone.

Hannah said, "It is such a long time since I held a child this age." She said it mostly to herself, but Ben turned to look at her from his post by the window.

"Do you have children?" she asked, but he only averted his face as if he hadn't heard her.

If he were white Hannah might have thought she had offended him, but the silence between them was one she recognized: thoughtful, and resonant with possibility.

He said, "It's starting."

There were raised voices on the lane, first without agitation. Servants called to each other as they looked for Jennet. Then the tone changed and there were shouts and finally the whole house seemed to erupt. There was a drumming of footsteps on the stair. Hannah settled herself on the bed, put the sleeping baby beside her, and pulled the covers up to her chest with her knees raised just enough to disguise his shape.

The door flew open without warning and a stranger burst in, breathing heavily, his face flushed. He seemed to recognize Ben because he addressed him directly, in rapid French. He was looking for a blond lady in blue, had Ben seen such a person?

"Pas de tout." Even in her distracted state Hannah noted

how everything about Ben Savard had shifted. He was, at this moment, Jean-Benoît: a Creole of mixed blood, who spoke not a word of English nor cared to.

"Et elle?" A splayed thumb jerked in Hannah's direction.

Hannah shook her head. *"Non."* The man gave her a long, hard look and then turned to trot off. Ben crossed the room to close the door and turn the key, and then he stood there as they listened to the man going from room to room. From farther away came the outraged tones of a woman not accustomed to being denied.

"Mme. Poiterin," Hannah said, and Ben nodded.

He came to sit on the chair beside her. He put his hands on his knees and lowered his head as if to study them. They stayed just like that for fifteen minutes, Hannah afraid to move lest she wake the baby and his crying attract attention they could not afford: a white child, a child who could not be her child, or his. The whole while the house seemed to seethe as Poiterin's men searched for Jennet, and then, suddenly, gave up the search. There was the sound of coaches and horses in the lane and then the whole party was gone, racing south.

"She's already thinking about the boy," Hannah said. She had never met Mme. Poiterin, had never even seen her, but somehow she had a sense of the woman, her anger and her intent. "She already suspects."

Ben nodded. "And she doesn't like being bested."

Hannah peeked beneath the covers and saw that the baby was awake, wide-eyed and solemn. She smiled at him, this nephew who had drawn them a quarter way around the world, and drew him out into her arms.

"Whatever other sins you have to lay at Honoré Poiterin's door, the child has been well taken care of," said Ben. "He has never known an unkind word or a day of hunger."

It was true; the boy had the wide-eyed, curious way of healthy, well-settled infants.

"Sic a braw lad, the verra image o' your faither, young Nathaniel." Hannah spoke to the boy in Scots, a language she rarely used these days but one that came to her easily enough. She spoke to him in Scots because it was the language he had heard from his mother. Whether it was her tone or the language, the baby reached out with one plump hand and touched her face, and then he gave her a wide smile that showed pearly-pink gums.

"I had a son." Hannah wondered who she was talking to, and why. The noise in the house and lane had faded away. It seemed unusually quiet to her, as if everyone else had suddenly disappeared from the world.

Ben said, "Tell me how you lost your son, and your husband."

Hannah looked at him. His expression gave nothing away, and his tone was unremarkable. He might have been Paul Savard asking for her medical history, or a minor official asking to see her papers. And it was this tone, precisely, which allowed her to answer him.

Hannah raised her head and looked at Ben. "Among my mother's people a woman chooses her husband. A man may show interest in a woman, but it is for her to decide if she will have him. I chose a husband when I was very young, and we went west to join Tecumseh.

"I can't know what our lives would have been had we lived in peace among his people, or my mother's. As it was, it was good for a long while, and then things changed. He changed, and I changed, and the whole world changed. And then he died, and I was taking our son home to Lake in the Clouds so that he could be raised there, by my father and uncle and brothers. But the boy died, too, on that journey, and at that time I was myself as much as dead to the world."

She managed a small smile. "But my people would not let me go. My father and stepmother, my aunt and uncle and Curiosity, my brothers and sister. My Kahnyen'kehàka family is large. Many others."

"You are not alone in the world," Ben said. It was the thing she most wanted him to understand, what she had lost and what she still had, would always have.

She said, "They pulled me back into the world, against my will at first. It was a long and difficult birth."

The baby was mouthing his fist in an increasingly frantic way.

"He's hungry," Hannah said. "I can't give him what he needs."

"There is a woman," Ben said. "She's waiting downstairs." He held out his arms and she gave him the boy.

"You thought of everything."

He hesitated at the door. "I have no children," he said. "I have never been married. Until a few years ago I thought I never would marry at all."

There was a question he wanted her to ask, and so she did.

"Because," said Ben, looking at her directly. "Because I intended to take Holy Orders and become a priest."

Hannah blinked at him, and he smiled broadly at her expression.

"I've shocked you."

"Yes. What changed your mind?"

He jiggled the mewling boy thoughtfully, opened his mouth and shut it again. Finally he opened the door. "I opened my eyes."

Hannah said, "I'm glad that you did. I don't know how we can ever thank you."

"Wait until midnight," said Ben. "Wait until your cousin is here and safe, before you worry about ways to thank me."

CHAPTER 19

Louisiana Gazette

The editors appeal to the citizens of New Orleans and environs in the distressing case of the abduction of an infant, the son of Honoré Poiterin, one of the first of our brave young men to volunteer for the *Dragons à Pied,* Commander Henri de Ste-Gême's élite militia unit.

The child was taken by force from the home of his great-grandmother, Mme. Agnès Poiterin, on Bayou St. John. The abductors knocked the child's nurse unconscious. The Poiterins were in the city for the afternoon at the time.

The authorities speculate that the mother, who is by all reports a gentlewoman not in full possession of her faculties, given to erratic and hysterical behavior as well as delusions of persecution, may have conspired with others to abduct her own child and run away from those whose only concern is her well-being and eternal soul.

This lady, who is known as Lady Jennet, is the sister of the Earl of Carryck of Scotland. She is about thirty years old, some five foot three inches tall, with unfashionably short, curling blond hair and blue eyes. She was last seen on horseback, leaving the city in a southwardly direction. The lady is a danger to herself and her child, and the authorities encourage anyone with information on their whereabouts to come forward immediately. The Poiterin family will reward useful information with a liberal hand.

* * *

For sale. A strong, healthy, high pregnant mulatto female, twenty years old, trained to household but perhaps better suited for field work, as she has proved careless when given responsibilities beyond the manual tasks best suited to her race. Inquiries should be directed to Jean LeFlor, factor to Mme. Poiterin, Bayou St. John.

Hannah saw first, on coming into the small chamber they shared, that the newspaper in Jennet's hands was trembling.

"What is it?"

"Mme. Poiterin is selling Jacinthe," Jennet said. Her voice was calm, but a muscle twitched at the corner of her eye.

Hannah looked away, out over the gallery and into the inner courtyard, the cobblestones slick with cold rain. With deliberate movements she took off her cloak and hung it near the brazier Julia had sent to supplement the small hearth.

"Paul warned us this might happen."

Jennet folded the paper and put it aside, took in a deep breath and pushed it out. The baby, asleep in his cradle, stirred and then settled again.

There was nothing they could do for Jacinthe, who had nursed young Nathaniel and cared for him as her own, and now would be sold away from the home where she had been born, from her family and friends. From the man who had fathered the child she carried.

"As bad as Honoré can be, I find it hard to believe that he would allow such a thing," Jennet said fitfully.

Every day Jennet seemed more fragile. She did her best to hide what she was feeling, and she succeeded when others were present. But Hannah saw what Jennet meant to keep to herself: discouragement, anguish, growing panic. The lack of information about Luke was the worst of it, Hannah thought, but in many ways Jennet was more of a prisoner in this safe and comfortable place than she had been at Maison Verde, and she was suffering for it.

Jennet dared not leave the Savard family apartment on

the top floor of the clinic building. At any time she might come across a stranger—a boy delivering a letter, a servant come to visit in the kitchens, one of the merchants who supplied the household. Anyone could draw a connection between the new face at the clinic and the broadsheets the Poiterins had posted throughout the town advertising a large reward for Jennet's return to them. And so Jennet moved back and forth between the small chamber she shared with Hannah and the Savard family sitting and dining rooms, looking after her son, reading, and trying to keep her mind occupied by turning her hands to whatever work Julia sent her way. She mended shirts and darned and knitted and rolled great mountains of freshly laundered bandages. The household servants who had come with the Savards from Manhattan understood the ways of a household set up according to Quaker principles. The only other servant allowed abovestairs was Clémentine, the cook who had been with the Savard family since Paul and Jean-Benoît were young.

That Jennet should turn to the newspapers for distraction was to be expected, and still Hannah wished she could banish them all. The news seemed to grow worse and more alarming day by day, and Jennet read it all.

Now she said, "Is there no end to the misery I have caused?"

Her expression was calm, but her eyes, damp with tears, were filled with regret. She must have looked something like this on that long sea journey from Canada to Priest's Town, Hannah thought, in the days before she put a knife in a man's neck.

"There's barely a mention of Honoré," Jennet said, her eyes running down the column of newsprint. "I wonder what that means. I wonder if he objected to Jacinthe—" She broke off. "Maybe Jean-Benoît can tell us."

But more days went by and they saw nothing of Ben.

Hannah was not unhappy about his absence, mostly because she was embarrassed to remember their last conversation, and unsure of what had actually passed between them. She had told him about Strikes-the-Sky, and he had told her that he had once wanted to be a priest. Hannah could not think of a single statement that would have surprised her more. She resolved to put Jean-Benoît Savard out of her mind.

She and Jennet might have both been swamped by melancholy but for Rachel and Henry.

"I know why Ben is staying away," Rachel said by way of greeting on a cold and rainy afternoon. She put down the tray she had brought with a rattle and a thump. Jennet saw a flicker of something—irritation? discomfort?—move across Hannah's face and then disappear behind a wall of resolve.

"Hello, Rachel," Hannah said. "We were just reading the papers. There's a ball on Friday, I see. Are you going?"

"I will tell you why he is staying away, though you pretend you're not interested," Rachel said as she poured.

"To allay suspicion? To put Mme. Poiterin off the trail? To tend to his own business? No, wait," Jennet said, striking a playful tone.

Rachel held out a filled cup to Jennet. "Why are you teasing?"

"Because Hannah doesn't want to talk about your uncle Jean-Benoît," Jennet said, trying to smile kindly and falling just a little short.

"I have no objection to hearing what you have to say," Hannah told Rachel. "But I can't imagine what there is left to tell. We've heard the whole Savard family history. Jennet, your yarn is in a tangle. Let me sort it out for you."

Rachel was very young, painfully romantic in her sensibilities, and, in spite of a good heart, more than a little silly. Most of all she was stubborn, and almost impossible to distract when she had set herself a goal. One of her current projects, it had become clear as soon as Jennet came into the household, was to make Hannah see that Jean-Benoît Savard and she were meant for each other.

What Rachel believed to be true, others must also believe, if only she had time enough to make them see things her way. Thus she had spent a good part of Jennet's first week here telling stories of the family her mother had married into. All her stories led to the same place: Ben Savard. Jean-Benoît's colorful history was far more interesting to Rachel than her stepfather's, except where the two intersected.

Jennet realized that Rachel was looking at her with a hurt and impatient expression.

"Tell us, then, if you must," Jennet said. "Why is Jean-Benoît so long away?"

"Because," Rachel said pointedly, "he must have picked up your husband's trail."

Jennet let her knitting drop into her lap and she leaned forward to grasp Rachel's hand. "What a sweet thing ye are, Rachel. I hope you've the right of it."

"Yes," said Hannah. "Let's hope."

"Of course, the other reason is that he's half in love with Hannah and is afraid of falling the rest of the way."

Rachel sat back with a satisfied look, and Hannah laughed aloud. "You are the most stubborn person on the face of the earth," she said, not without some admiration.

Rachel grinned. "I have a present for you, Jennet. Look." And from a pocket she pulled a small square parcel wrapped in paper, which she unfolded carefully. When she had placed her offering in front of Jennet, Hannah saw that it was a tarot deck.

Jennet blinked in surprise. "How did you know?"

"I mentioned it," Hannah said, thinking how sorry she was to have been so impatient with Rachel. For all her silliness and youth, she had her mother's ability to comfort where it was most needed.

"Have I presumed too much?" Rachel asked.

"Oh, no," Jennet said. "Not at all." She smiled. "But where did you find such a thing?"

"I asked Clémentine," Rachel said. "Clémentine is the source of all real knowledge about New Orleans."

"I'll thank her directly," Jennet said. "Now, shall I lay out the cards for you, then? Should you like that, wee Rachel?"

And of course, that suited Rachel exactly.

When she left them an hour later, Henry came for his daily visit. He began, as he always did, with a mournful appraisal of young Nathaniel and the announcement that babies were useless when it came to really important things, like playing soldiers or raiding the larder. He jumped from topic to topic in the way of young boys, and Hannah and Jennet both enjoyed him tremendously. His stories usually revolved around family, but in his versions there was no underlying message, and a great deal of entertaining detail.

According to Henry, Ben Savard knew every path and waterway and tree for three hundred miles; he was a master of swamp and bayou and could live hidden and comfortable for a year, if he so chose. Best of all, Jean-Benoît's mother had been a Seminole princess, or sometimes, if the story demanded it, a Choctaw princess. Her background was varied enough to allow him to choose.

Henry had known Amélie Savard only a few months before her death, but she had made a lasting impression. People might come to his father's clinic to be vaccinated against the smallpox, but his grand-mère Amélie had known about charms against ghosts, and love potions, and how to deal out justice in the most satisfactory ways. And Grand-mère had owned a parrot who could recite prayers—and curses—in Spanish, Italian, and Portuguese. Henry had wanted this parrot for himself when his grandfather and grandmother died within a week of each other, but it was living still at the plantation at Grand Terre. Where Henry intended to live, when he was grown. The fact that it had all been sold meant nothing to the boy; he would simply buy it back, house and fields and parrot, too.

According to young Henry Savard, New Orleans had nothing to fear from the British. His uncle Ben would simply not allow them anywhere near his family, and thus they were all safe. And on top of that, the great Major General Andrew Jackson was coming. Really, the British should just turn back for home.

Hannah thought it was a good thing that the boy had such faith in his uncle.

"I heard M. Perdu speaking to his son," Henry told them. "When they were waiting to be vaccinated. M. Perdu believes the British will take New Orleans, and that his son is foolish to join the militia, he'll only get killed or taken prisoner, and then what good will a fancy uniform do him, except as a shroud. I think really M. Perdu didn't want to spend the money to outfit Phillip. Everybody says he is very mean with his money."

"And how did you overhear all this?" Jennet asked, trying to look censorious and failing.

"People don't notice me when they're waiting. Which is why I would make such a very good spy, if they would only ask me," he said wistfully.

"They hang spies," Hannah said.

"Only if they catch them," Henry said, and went off to find somebody to play with.

CHAPTER 20

The next morning, cool and wet and overcast, Hannah woke and realized that she was truly hungry for the first time in many weeks. It was an odd feeling, uncomfortable and reassuring both. She was recovered. For now, at least. Paul Savard had warned her of what she knew already: It should never take her so near death as it had this first time, but swamp fever would return, and she must be prepared for it.

Jennet was soundly asleep with the baby tucked into the curve of her body, one fist pressed against his cheek. Hannah washed quickly at the basin, in part because the water was icy cold, in part because she didn't want to wake her cousin, and dressed, sparing a moment, as she did now almost every day, to think of all the fine clothes that had been made for them at such expense by Luke's mother. Now it was all lost, and Hannah was secretly glad of it.

Jennet had come to the clinic with all her own funds as well as with the contents of Hannah's missing pack, and so Julia had taken the money they pressed on her and in short order she had assembled a serviceable wardrobe for both of them. Stockings and sturdy footwear, underskirts and skirts, dresses and shawls and cloaks, most of it Quaker gray, to Rachel's horror.

It was a color that Hannah liked, because it reminded

her of her stepmother's eyes. Over the course of the last year she had trained herself not to think much about Elizabeth or home, but now, in the relative safety of the Savards' protection, she found it far harder to avoid those thoughts, and she sometimes woke with tears on her face and a sense of dread.

Luke had sent a letter home to New-York State from Pensacola, but it was at least a thousand miles from the endless forests to the Gulf of Mexico, and the waterways and roads that joined them were clogged with the detritus of war. In Paradise, at least, it would be peaceful. No army would bother with such an out-of-the-way place of no strategic importance. Hannah thought of her family and willed them well, and safe, and free of worry for things they could not help or change.

Now her hunger for news could not be willed or reasoned away. She would like a letter in her stepmother's clear, fine handwriting, closely written with news of her brothers and sisters and the village where she had grown up. She dreamed sometimes of Curiosity Freeman, who was as much a grandmother to her as anyone of her own blood. For the first time since she had left Paradise with Luke to find Jennet, Hannah was homesick.

She admitted this to herself as she pulled on the fine knitted cotton stockings and shoes. Then she left the family apartment.

The clinic on the rue Dauphine was built something like a fort. Three wings and a separate kitchen and stables were grouped around a large internal courtyard where rain turned the cobblestones a rich red color and made dimples in the water of a fountain.

She went out onto the open gallery where staircases joined each floor to the next. The wind was high and cold and lashed with rain, and Hannah was glad of her shawl.

The middle floor had been turned into a series of hospital wards. Passing the windows Hannah had a glimpse of a row of cots, half of them filled, and an attendant ladling something hot into bowls. She found, to her surprise, that she was curious about the patients: whether Paul admitted surgical cases or restricted his practice to epidemic diseases; if there were patients who paid for his services or if this was exclusively an almshouse. She thought of the considerable cost of establishing and running a facility like this, and wondered whose money was behind it all.

Her mind, forced by fever into oblivion for too long, raced, thoughts and questions tumbling without rhythm or reason. It was a way to not think, for a while at least, about Luke.

On the ground floor she came into a small foyer where Henry Savard had set up a battle between tin soldiers on a battered wooden table. He had a smear of porridge on his chin and his hair stood up in spikes so that he looked like a smaller version of his father.

"I see you are hard at work," Hannah said. "Who is winning?"

"No one. Mama says no one ever really wins a war," Henry said with a small sigh. "Mama is a Quaker." Then he seemed to realize he was seeing Hannah in an unusual place.

"Did you ask permission to get out of bed?"

Hannah found herself smiling. "I am about to go and do that. Where will I find your father?"

Henry stood. "He's having his breakfast in his office. You could have some, too." And he started off down the hall at a trot. Then he stopped and turned toward her. "You used to have a little boy."

Hannah felt herself start. "I did."

"You talked about him when your fever was very high. Sometimes you talked about him in English and sometimes you talked in another language."

"I'm not surprised," Hannah said. "I miss him every day." But she found she was alarmed at the idea of the things she might have said, and to whom.

Henry nodded as if he had got some important business out of the way, and then took her to Paul Savard's office. He made a face at the door and put his hands behind his back.

"Uncle is here and they are talking about things I'm not supposed to know."

"Your uncle Ben?"

Henry nodded. "He came very late last night."

Hannah watched him trot back to his toys, and then she knocked.

Julia said, "Don't fuss at her, Paul. She is likely to die of boredom if she's not allowed out of bed and given something useful to do."

Hannah hid a smile in the teacup Julia pressed on her, looking over its rim at the two men who sat at the other end of the long table that served as a desk. No one would ever guess that Paul and Jean-Benoît Savard were half brothers, unless they happened to catch them like this, turning toward Julia with heads canted at exactly the same angle.

She focused on the plate before her, but still Hannah could feel Dr. Savard taking stock, appraising her color and looking for symptoms of fever.

". . . and you could use help in the apothecary, you know it's true," Julia finished.

"I'm not convinced," Dr. Savard said. "I think another day of rest would do her some good."

Hannah looked at Ben and managed a small smile. "Is he as bossy with you as he is with everyone else?"

"He is some better since he married," Ben said. "But even Julia can't perform miracles."

Paul raised his shoulders in a good-natured shrug.

"You see?" Julia said. "He doesn't even deny it any-more."

"My character flaws are a subject we've explored enough for one day. Hannah, do you want work?"

"Yes," Hannah said simply. "Jennet has the baby to occupy her and her tarot cards, but—" She stopped herself before she finished the sentence.

"—but all you've got is worries about your brother," Ben supplied.

Julia slid into the chair beside Hannah. "Go on, then," she said to her brother-in-law. "Don't make her ask for news."

"If my brother is dead, it would be best to just say so."

He was looking at her steadily, as she had seen her father and uncle and brother study a problem to be solved. A tree stump that would not be moved, a broken trap, a rifle that misfired. It was unsettling and comforting, too, to be the object of such attention. She had the sense that Jean-Benoît Savard did not turn away from a problem because it was difficult.

He said, "I have no news, good or bad."

His gaze moved away from her face to Julia's, and then back again. She was as much a stranger to him as he was to her, and he looked to his sister-in-law for direction. Hannah said, "I'd rather know the worst."

And so Ben told them what he knew in his rough, low voice and vaguely singsong English: Luke had set out from Pensacola on a schooner called the *Leopard* that belonged to a trader out of Mobile. The *Leopard* had been bound for Galveston, but it had never arrived there. There had been no storms and there was no clear reason to believe the ship had gone down, and in fact, Ben told her, he thought something very different had happened, though at this point he was only guessing.

"The British may have taken the ship and the whole crew," he said, "if the *Leopard* came within range of the British cutters. He is Canadian born, your half brother?"

"Yes." Hannah struggled to make sense of the idea. "You're saying he may have been pressed into the British navy?"

Ben nodded. "That is one possibility. They don't hesitate to take Canadians."

"They don't hesitate to take anybody able-bodied," said Julia. "If the Royal Navy hadn't got into the habit of snatching American sailors at every opportunity, we might not be in the middle of a war to start with."

Hannah sat back, her plate forgotten. She had imagined Luke dead in a dozen different ways, imprisoned, injured and unable to travel, but this idea shocked her. She said, "The other possibilities?"

Ben looked at her directly. "The Gulf is full of privateers and pirates of every stripe. Or the American navy may have picked him up, if he was very unlucky. He's a Canadian, and out of uniform."

"But with Americans he calls himself Luke Bonner, a native of New-York State," Hannah said. She thought of the newspaper reports and the constant alerts issued by the governor, who seemed convinced that British spies were busy fomenting rebellion among the slave population.

"If he's been pressed into service, there will be records," Julia said.

"No doubt," Ben agreed. "The problem is getting that kind of information in the middle of a war. It's a challenge, but not impossible."

There was a small silence while Paul and Julia exchanged glances.

"Let me point out that if you get yourself shot as a spy you'll spoil Henry's best stories," Paul said.

The two men regarded each other for a moment, Paul's

challenge hanging in the air. Ben spread a hand out on the table, long, strong fingers slightly curved.

He said, "I wouldn't want to cause Henry any trouble."

"Of course not," Julia said dryly. "So exactly how are you going to get this information, if I may ask?"

When Ben turned his face to Julia his expression had gone blank. He was not angry or irritated or amused; there was nothing there at all. It was the face of a man who knew how to keep his own counsel, one who would give nothing away until he was ready to do so. In that moment he reminded Hannah of her uncle Runs-from-Bears, who could turn his face to stone, and just that simply stop a conversation cold.

Julia said, "Jean-Benoît Savard, if you think I am so easily put off as that, you are sorely mistaken. I'll have a civil answer, and without delay."

Hannah let out a small hiccup of a laugh, and Paul grinned.

Ben said, "I apologize, sister, but I can't tell you what I don't know myself."

Julia made a small humming noise. "Is that so. I think you and I will continue this conversation later, without an audience."

After a moment Hannah said, "There's another favor I need to ask of you, Julia. It's about Jennet. She has nowhere to go with her anger. It might help if you had some work for her, something to make her feel as though she is contributing to the household."

"Of course," Julia said. "I should have thought."

"I would be glad of work, too. Where do you most need help?" Hannah said to Paul Savard.

"I need help everywhere." Paul got up and dropped his serviette on the table. "But I'm afraid the only place for you is the apothecary. It's a waste of your talents, but it's the best

I can do. Send Henry to find me when you're ready, and I'll get you started."

"I'd like to talk to your sister-in-law before I leave," Ben said to Hannah. "If you could take me to her."

One thing to be thankful for, Hannah told herself as they made their way up many flights of stairs, was that there was no sign of Rachel. She wondered, and not for the first time, if she had been badgering Ben with her attempts at match-making; the very thought made the blood rush to her face, and her fingers twitch with annoyance. Just now she wanted nothing to do with any man, Jean-Benoît Savard included.

But that was only a partial truth, Hannah had to admit to herself, because quite often in the last week she had found herself thinking about Kit Wyndham. Relieved of her worry about Jennet and the child, her mind had opened a door and Kit had come through it. Which was only reasonable, she told herself. They had traveled together for more than a year, and for much of that time Hannah had allowed him into her bed, where he had made her re-member what it was to have a woman's body, what kind of comfort and release a man could offer.

Kit was only the second man she had known. She had chosen him specifically because he was nothing like the husband she had lost; two men could hardly be less alike in looks or upbringing or worldview. She could not pinpoint the day she had made the decision, or recall the conversa-tion that had preceded his knock at her door. Hannah re-membered only that he had met her needs with his own, that he had neither coddled nor overwhelmed her, and that afterwards they had found a companionable silence and, eventually, a kind of talk that had grown important to her. Kit Wyndham had become, against all expectations, a friend, a man she liked and sometimes lusted after, one she admired for his self-discipline and sharp mind and his fearlessness. And yet she had let him go without regret, and had spared him very little thought, until just recently.

She realized that Ben had said something to her and she stopped and turned, one hand on the rail.

"I'm sorry, I was lost in my thoughts."

"I'll wait for Jennet in my brother's parlor," Ben said. "If you want to get to work I can speak to her alone."

Hannah had the uneasy feeling that Ben knew exactly what she had been thinking. She touched her forehead, felt the film of cool sweat there. Reached for something to say, and found herself empty of words.

CHAPTER 21

The clinic apothecary was immediately familiar and comforting. Hannah spent the entire morning there, making herself familiar with Dr. Savard's system and habits. She was thankful for work that required all her concentration. The walls were lined with shelves and glass-fronted cabinets, all filled with crockery and tins and great glass vials. The small space was perfectly organized, fully equipped, scrupulously clean.

Two thin metal hooks hung down from the ceiling over a standing desk. On the left hook Paul had threaded paper receipts waiting to be filled, perhaps a dozen of them. On the right hook completed receipts were kept for reference, and it was packed so tightly that it looked like an old-fashioned ruffled collar. There were leather aprons hanging on the wall, scuffed and stained. Hannah took one and was comforted by the familiar smells.

She had been trained by her uncle Todd, and while she had proved a good student in this as in everything else he ventured to teach her, she had never much liked this work. Uncle Todd preferred his laboratory to patients. There was no ambiguity in a reverberating oven, he told her once. A finely made scale never challenged its betters or claimed more for itself than was its due. He had been a demanding and irritable teacher, but he had taught her well, with no regard for her sex or skin color, and she had come to understand, with time, what a tremendous gift that had been.

Richard Todd left the villagers of Paradise with their scrapes and burns and broken bones and sore ears to Hannah, quizzed her on what she had seen and what she had done, corrected her without thought for her feelings, and only came to see cases where someone was dying, or he had some procedure to demonstrate. When she thought of him she saw him hunched over a microscope, the daybook filled with meticulous notes and equations and drawings, layered with his correspondence with other doctors and scientists.

Hannah thought about Richard Todd off and on for the rest of the morning as she measured and weighed and counted, stopping to record what she had done on a receipt or look something up in Paul Savard's collection of notes.

At noon, Hannah realized that she had been working without pause for four hours, and what had started as a small pain between her eyes was now a full-blown headache. She mixed the remedy and drank it where she stood, and knew that Paul Savard would scold her for pushing herself too far too fast, and he would be right. She was prepared, when his knock came at the door, to admit as much immediately in order to forestall the lecture.

But it was Jean-Benoît Savard, and Hannah found that she was glad to see him. He came in and closed the door behind himself.

"Julia sent me to call you to the dinner table," he said. "But I wanted to talk to you for a minute first, if I may." His English, always a little awkward, had taken on a formality, as though he were a schoolboy presenting a well-rehearsed answer to a difficult question.

Hannah backed up until she felt the cool of the wall between her shoulder blades.

"Of course," she said, and tried to look interested when

in fact she was contemplating escape. She could duck around him and be out the door before he spoke another word. The idea was schoolgirlish and silly and immensely appealing.

Ben lowered his head for a moment and then looked her directly in the eye. It was rude to look away, she knew, but she couldn't help herself. It took all her self-discipline to look back again.

He said, "I've got the idea that you're mad at me. I don't know why, exactly, but I can guess. Has Rachel been nosing around in your personal business?"

Hannah heard herself make a small strangled sound that was meant to be a response, one he could take any way he liked. As a denial, an acknowledgment, a plea for mercy.

He nodded. "I feared as much. You're her third run at finding me a wife. You look surprised."

"I am," Hannah agreed. "I had no idea."

"The first was her uncle Livingston's cook, a Métis by the name of Paulette, and then, just a few months ago, she got it in her head that I should fall in love with a lady's maid just in from France. The granddaughter of an African king, she told me."

"And you declined the royal invitation?" Hannah asked, warming to his playful tone.

"I'm a simple man," Ben said solemnly. He cleared his throat. "She's a good girl, but she's got a romantic turn of mind and she jumped to some conclusions. She didn't mean any harm, but I fear she's caused some anyway. So here's what I need to say. I know you don't have any interest in me, so you don't have to worry anymore and there's no call to be uneasy."

"Oh," said Hannah, wondering why her mind had gone suddenly to porridge and she could think of nothing reasonable to say; certainly she couldn't object or disagree, though there was something wrong, something quite wrong in this sincere speech, if only she could put her finger on it.

"And if we've got that straightened out," Ben went on, seemingly unaware that she hadn't explicitly agreed with him, "there's one more thing, about the work you're doing. Or not doing, better said."

Hannah shook herself. "Yes?"

"I don't suppose it comes as any shock to you that there are doctors in New Orleans, ones who trained in places like Paris and Rome, who aren't allowed to treat white people."

"Free men of color," Hannah said. "Yes, I know such men are here, though I haven't met any."

"I don't see that you will, unless you go looking for them," Ben said. "They've got business enough with their own kind and don't bother much with anybody else."

He rubbed the line of his jaw with a knuckle while he considered what he was going to say next.

"This city is cut up like a pie. About a third of the people here are white, and they've got their own doctors. French-trained, for the Creoles. The Americans who move here bring doctors with them from up north. Poor whites look after their own or go to the Charity Hospital, or they come here to Paul."

"And the other two thirds of the city?"

He glanced at her from under the shelf of his brow. "Mostly some shade of black. Half of those slave, the other half free. The free people of color, that's a world all of its own. The ones who have been here longest and have the most money send their sons to Paris to study music or philosophy or medicine. The poorer free blacks go to see Dufilho at his apothecary shop, but most of them go to one of the healers who came here from Saint-Domingue after the rebellion. And the slaves, they're looked after by the men who own them, or not at all."

"And where do you fit into all this?"

He hesitated for a moment. "I get the idea that where you come from, things are easy between Indians and colored."

"More than easy," Hannah said. "We get along very well." She thought of telling him about Curiosity Freeman and her family, and then put the idea aside for the time being. "That's not the case here?"

"No," Ben said. "Just the opposite. You know some free men of color own slaves?"

"I didn't know that," Hannah said.

"The Indians, too, but to the east. Around here what's left of the tribes is too poor to own much of anything. But they make some money going after runaways."

He looked her directly in the eye. "I guess you can see how things around here get complicated."

On the expanse of the worktable he drew her a map with a piece of charcoal, starting with water: the half-cup that made the Gulf of Mexico and the rivers: the Mississippi, the Tombigbee, the Tennessee. Then showed her the world as it had been: a sprinkling of salt along the coast of Florida for the Seminole, ovals of sand for the Apalachee, Yamasee, for the Natchez and Choctaw and Chickasaw, with dimples made by a fingertip for the main villages. Powdered alum, white as snow, for the White Sticks of the Lower Creek nation and tobacco from the pouch at his side for the Red Sticks, the Upper Creeks. He paused to ask her what she knew of the Red Sticks, who had accepted Tecumseh's call to take a stand against the whites.

He said, "You lived at Prophet's Town until Harrison burned it. Your husband and your uncle died fighting beside Tecumseh. You understand what I am saying."

To hear Tecumseh's name spoken always caused Hannah's whole body to flush with heat. Not out of love or hate, but simply because it brought with it a flood of memories that threatened to drown her. Hannah nodded. "I know what happened to the Red Sticks at Horseshoe Bend."

It was a story that had repeated itself so many times, one that Hannah had lived herself on the banks of the Wabash at Prophet's Town.

"You think the war is lost, as well as the battle?" She asked this question because it had to be clear between them, where they each stood.

"I know that it is, and so do you. To survive we must learn to fight a different kind of war."

He was intelligent, and clear-sighted, and he was right, and some part of Hannah resented his ability to say these things out loud. And so she turned her mind to the matter at hand.

"You spoke of slavery, and the relationship between Indian and colored."

He said, "You will come to think of me as a man who only brings bad news."

"Nevertheless," Hannah said. "You must tell me."

The story was simple enough, told as it was by means of his own family history. One of his great-grandmothers had been a child in an Apalachee village when it was wiped out by the Creeks, and all but a few of the most promising children had been sold to Carolina plantations. One great-grandfather had arrived in chains on a ship from the Guinea Coast, to be bought at auction by a Seminole chief. The African had children by one of the Seminole women, who were born full and free members of her tribe, though their father remained a slave until his death.

Another great-grandmother had been Ibo, who had been no more than fifteen when she was dragged into the New Orleans slave market, still defiant after months of beatings. She had run away from her owner, a free man of color, and been caught up by a pair of Seminole hunters. They would have returned her to her owner for the reward, had she not fought so well. She took an eye from one of them and bit the other's ankle to the bone, snapping a ligament so that he walked with a limp for the rest of his life. The Seminole took her back to their village, where she survived the hardest tests the women of the tribe could contrive.

The chief had been so impressed that he had given the Ibo girl the name Black Hawk Woman for her strength and cold fury and skin that soaked up all the light and gave none of it back. Black Hawk Woman was adopted into the tribe, and she lived among them all her life as a free woman, no longer African or Ibo or black, but Seminole. She bore the chief three sons, and adopted as daughters two young white girls taken in a raid. When she died she had four slaves of her own, two Africans and two Chickasaw, who worked in the fields tending corn and squash and beans, okra and indigo. One of her sons had been Ben's grandfather, called Crooked-River.

When Ben had finished, there was a long silence between them. The thoughts that came to Hannah were many and disjointed. What it was like to sit in Curiosity Freeman's lap when she was a little girl, how she smelled of soap and good things to eat, how she laughed, the sound of her voice, this woman who had been born a slave. Curiosity's son Almanzo, who fought beside Hannah's husband Strikes-the-Sky. The way people had looked at her that first day she came to New Orleans and walked along the levee. She had taken their stares for curiosity, but wondered now if she had been mistaken.

"That night I spent with the old black woman, my first day here—"

"It was the wrong place for you," Ben said.

Of course Mr. Fitch could not have known when he sent her there. An American merchant would know nothing, care to know nothing, of the animosity between Indians and Africans.

Ben said, "There is more. Over the last two months, five free people of color have been stolen off the street and sold into slavery."

"By Indians."

"So it is believed, though I have reason to doubt it."

She raised her head and looked at him. "Titine?"

He nodded. "Possible."

Hannah thought it through.

"Is there anything to be done? Can we find her, and buy her back?"

"It would be difficult in the best of times. Now—" He looked out into the courtyard as if he could see the next few months playing out there: the battles that would be fought, if things went badly, all around them.

Hannah had been standing during all of this, and now she sat down heavily. "Titine never showed me anything but kindness," she said.

"Not all Indians believe in keeping slaves."

"Are you speaking of your own beliefs?" Hannah asked, looking him directly in the eye.

"I think that together, black and red, we might have had a chance to make a place for ourselves here. The British understood how dangerous that alliance would have been to their own interests. They did everything in their power to drive a wedge between the two peoples. I have no interest in continuing that work for them."

Hannah considered the question she wanted to ask, and picked her words very carefully. "Where do you fit into this—unhappy situation?" She could have said: *What do you see when you look in the glass? A red man, or a black one?*

"I have strong ties on all sides. To the Choctaw and the Seminole, to the slaves and to the free people of color," Ben said. "That has to do partly with my mother. She wouldn't choose between them and I won't, either. So I don't much mind if somebody wants to call me Redbone. It can't make me feel low if I don't let it."

Hannah straightened her shoulders and pushed out a long breath. "But you want a clinic for Indians."

"For the Indians and for the ones like me," Ben said. "They've got no place to go."

"The colored doctors won't see to their needs?"

"Some might, if they thought they'd get paid. Most won't."

"They can't come here to your brother? He refuses them?"

"Paul can't turn away who doesn't come," Ben said. "And they aren't welcome at the Charity Hospital."

Hannah tried to remember the last time she had seen a darker face among the groups of people who moved through the clinic, and was surprised to realize she could not.

Jean-Benoît was saying, "If they did come, and Paul didn't turn them away, there would be consequences."

"The whites would stop coming to be vaccinated."

"Of course. So he has to go to them, if he can find them."

Hannah wiped her hands on a piece of sacking, and untied her apron. "What are you suggesting, exactly?"

"Just take a short walk with me this afternoon, and you'll see for yourself."

CHAPTER 22

"I think I could learn almost everything there is to know about this city just listening at the window," Jennet said to Hannah later that day. "Listen, here comes Mr. Occhiogrosso."

Hannah stood to look out the window. A small man was walking along the street, as laden as a donkey. There was a wooden frame on his back filled with panes of glass in all sizes that rattled with every step. He carried a long wooden ruler that he used as a sort of walking stick, clicking it against the cobblestones. He looked up at Hannah in the window and flashed a smile around the stem of his pipe, his teeth the color of tobacco.

"How do you know his name?"

"Henry has made a study of all the vendors and workers who come by. He's especially fond of the Italians because they stop to talk to him. Won't Jean-Benoît be waiting for you?"

"I wish you could come with me," Hannah said. "It's not good for you to be cooped up here constantly."

Jennet threw her a suspicious look. "Don't tell me you're afraid of Ben Savard. Not Hannah Bonner, who faced down the likes of Mac Stoker and Baldy O'Brien."

Hannah knew better than to respond when Jennet was in a mood like this: unable to voice her fears, and set on distracting herself and everyone else with the combination of wit and impudence that was all her own. She wondered, again, if she should have told Jennet this latest news about Titine.

She watched for a moment as Jennet turned over a card and considered it. Then she asked a question she had been holding back since the day they had come to the L'Île de Lamantins.

"You've never explained about the cards you left behind at Nut Island."

Jennet looked up. "The seven and the Queen of Swords, aye. I missed them. There was no paper on the island except for the navigation maps on the ships, so I had to make replacement cards out of palm fronds that I wove and cut to size."

Hannah said, "And who is the Queen of Swords? Is that you, or me?"

"It will have to be you," Jennet said. She tilted her head thoughtfully. Her expression said she was looking back to the day Dégre had taken her away, out of her life and into his, and set them on the path that had brought them to New Orleans. Hannah had seen many men talk of battles with the same expression: as closed and unwelcoming as a fist.

Jennet said, "I knew Luke would come after me, but I wanted you too. I wanted both of you."

"I needed no convincing," Hannah said. "There was no question but that we'd come after you." She bent over the baby on Jennet's lap and ran her fingers through the curls, feather soft and slightly damp, that fell over his brow. He looked up at Hannah with perfectly round and trusting eyes, her brother's son. Her missing brother.

"We never lost faith that we'd find you," Hannah said, and she saw a tremor move across Jennet's face. "We must do the same for Luke."

Then she kissed them both and left Jennet to her solitude.

With the coming of the late fall, New Orleans was filled with a new vigor, due, Hannah had no doubt, to the fact that the terrible draining heat of late summer was truly gone. Here the coming of winter was welcome, because with it came parties and dinners and long walks on the levee without fear of sunstroke. It all reminded Hannah how far she was from home.

At Lake in the Clouds there would be at least a foot of snow on the ground, and soon the ice on Half Moon Lake would be thick enough to support a man. Partridge would explode out of the underbrush in a shower of snow so white against a pale blue sky that it made the eyes water. But in New Orleans the breeze that came off the Mississippi was warm enough that she might have done without the shawl draped over her shoulders.

Standing in the courtyard while she waited for Ben Savard, the sun, even low on the sky, touched her face like a blessing. Tomorrow the cold rain would most likely return, but she could be thankful, just now, for this small respite, for the deep red of the damp cobblestones and the shadowy loggia with its arches and pillars. Even now there was a good deal of green about: a red clay pot of chives on a windowsill, fig and date and palm trees around the fountain in the middle of the courtyard, where water fell from the mouth of a mermaid to wash over alabaster breasts and pool around her tail.

Paul Savard bought this property from a French merchant who had gone bankrupt. Now the kine-pox clinic was on the ground floor with the general clinic immediately above it. The family apartment where Jennet was hidden away was on the topmost floor. From the courtyard

Hannah could see the window, but there was no sign of her cousin.

She caught movement to her right and turned to see Jean-Benoît coming down the stairs from the small apartment over the kitchen, in a building all its own.

"I didn't realize you lived here," she said, and then wished she had not, though he didn't seem to take offense.

"The *garçonnière* is here for me when I'm in the city," he said. He gestured with his chin. "It's that passageway we want, beside the stable. Clémentine, *bonjour*." He inclined his head and shoulders to the cook, who was watching them from the kitchen doorway, and Hannah did the same.

She followed him out of the courtyard through a narrow passageway that ended in a heavy wrought-iron gate. Jean-Benoît lifted the latch and it swung open silently into a smaller courtyard, partially cobbled and surrounded on three sides by low, one-story buildings with overhanging eaves. All of them seemed to be empty.

"When the American troops get here they'll requisition every square foot of space," Ben said. "I doubt they'd displace a clinic, though. So there's no time to lose."

Many questions came to mind, but she restricted herself to the problem at hand. "What exactly did you have in mind?"

He showed her a long building that had once been a carpenter's shop. It still smelled faintly of wood sap and grease and of men's labor. It was solidly built, with whitewashed walls and a sturdy plank floor, light-filled and airy, with a large hearth at one end and a Franklin stove at the other. There was plenty of furniture available, Ben told her, cots and tables and cabinets, and she would have full access to the apothecary where she had spent the morning.

"The space is adequate?"

Hannah raised her shoulders and let them drop. "I have looked after the sick in much worse places." She thought of the blood-soaked ground at Tippecanoe, of the garrison gaol where her brother Daniel had almost died, of a dozen different battles, and turned her mind away from those images. Then she turned her mind to the people here who needed care, and asked about them.

"We'll go meet some of them," Ben said.

Hannah hesitated. She thought of Jennet, hidden away from the Poiterins and waiting for word of her husband. She thought of Rachel, who would be coming soon to tell her daily stories and share the gossip. She felt her fingers twitching with the need to be doing something, anything, and she nodded.

Ben opened the door, and Hannah stepped out into the city.

"I hardly remember any of this," Hannah said a few minutes later. "Though I think I must have come this way, when I first got here."

The weather was fine and the breeze was welcome on her face, and Hannah felt truly well for the first time in so many weeks.

She said, "When I was very little I dreamed of adventures, but this morning I was thinking that I've had quite enough of them in my lifetime."

Ben glanced down at her. "The first lie you've told me." He grinned to take the sting out of the truth. "You aren't the kind to sit quiet by the fire, or you wouldn't be here in the first place."

"I could learn to be that kind of woman," Hannah said, feeling herself flushing a little. "It would be a relief."

"You want to sit by the fire and sew?" He shook his head. "I can't see it."

"Maybe you don't know me as well as you think you

do," Hannah said, irritated now. "Maybe you don't know me at all."

"I know enough," he said. "Paul told me about that summer. He told me about the riot, and what happened after. What you risked."

Hannah felt herself flush with embarrassment, though she couldn't say exactly what bothered her: that Paul Savard had been telling stories, or that he had told them to Ben.

She said, "He exaggerates."

"My brother?" Ben looked amused. "I know no man less inclined to exaggeration. He is far more likely to err in the other direction."

Because Hannah could not argue with that very true statement, she remained silent and was relieved when Ben let the subject go.

In a short time they had passed out of the neighborhood of large, well-maintained homes and businesses into an area that was populated by artisans and skilled laborers. Most of the houses were two-room cottages that were of a size with the cabins Hannah was familiar with. A space to sleep, and one for the business of living, a small garden. The spell of warmer weather had brought out washtubs and clotheslines, and women called to each other as they worked. It would be easy to imagine herself in some other country, because Hannah saw not a single white face.

It struck her for the first time how the community of free people of color made New Orleans into a city unlike any other. Nowhere else, not even in the states where slavery had been outlawed, did so many live, if not in perfect freedom, then at least with a good measure of self-government.

A ragman, his skin as wrinkled and dark as roasted hickory nuts, came toward them leading a donkey laden down with sagging panniers. He nodded to Ben and didn't look at Hannah, but at the faded blue cotton *tignon* she had taken from her pocket to wrap around her head. She was not any shade of black, but neither was she white, and thus the law applied to her as well. And yet she had the impression—fleeting, unsettling—that the old man would have snatched the cloth from her head, if Ben had not been beside her.

She said, "In Manhattan I only had to be wary of how whites looked at me."

Ben made a sound in his throat, one that she thought must be meant as acknowledgment.

They passed into another part of the city, far more run-down. Fewer of the children on the street were colored, and more of them called to each other in Spanish. The wooden gutters that lined the lanes in the rest of town were missing here or broken, and puddles of dirty water and waste and trash pockmarked the road. A half dozen piglets dug in a pile of refuse, curled tails working furiously and without pause, even when a window opened and a shower of slops rained down on them.

They passed a butcher and then skirted a great heap of headless, hollowed-out carcasses outside a tannery. The stink in the air was so thick that Hannah's eyes watered and her gorge rose sharply and it took all her concentration to make her stomach settle. Then Ben turned a corner.

Hannah stopped, in surprise and unease. It was as if a whole village—any of the Indian villages she had known at different times in her life—had been fit into the short lane of cottages. Women and older girls sat in doorways, grinding corn or tending pots hung over fires made in the open. A grandmother scraped a deer hide stretched on a makeshift frame, an infant with a lesion on its cheek looking over her shoulder. Children ran back and forth with sticks, chasing a ball made of a pig's bladder. Three old men, their faces folded with wrinkles, sat on a blanket on the ground, their hands open, palm up, in their laps. A water barrel stood just next to them, a tin dipper on a rawhide thong dangling from the rim.

From across the crowd one of the old men looked at Hannah with milky turquoise eyes, his face as impassive as a sleeping infant's.

She said, "These people don't belong in this city. What are they doing here?"

"Some of them are slaves," Ben said. He looked at her with eyes just the same color as the old man's, but his gaze was sharp and knowing and anything but passive. "Their masters put them into these cottages and hire them out as day labor. They don't run away because some of the children are kept on the plantation as surety. In the spring they'll be called back there for the planting."

"There are no young men."

"They've been lent to the planters who have cane fields. The harvest will start soon."

"All of them, slaves?" Her voice shook a little. She had understood what Ben told her earlier, but to see the truth of it was something very different. Some day she would be among the Kahnyen'kehàka again and she would tell them about this place, where the Real People were bought and sold and worked like mules.

Ben was looking at her with something like sympathy in his expression. He said, "Not all. What you see here is some of what Jackson left behind him after Horseshoe Bend."

Horseshoe Bend. Hannah shook her head, to rid it of the images.

Ben took her first to see a man who worked in a hut just large enough for himself and his cobbler's bench. He was bent over a boot with a loose heel. There were only three fingers on each hand, and one leg was gone below the knee, but otherwise he looked healthy, if not especially well fed.

He was dressed in rough work clothes, and his hair had been shorn.

The dark eyes met Hannah's first and then moved on to Ben, and he smiled and rose from his work. The language he spoke was completely unfamiliar to Hannah, but she did notice that beside her, Ben had stiffened, ever so slightly.

"What?" she asked him, when he had replied.

"Blue-Deer says he is glad to see that I have taken a wife, and that there will be wailing from Mobile to Galveston."

Hannah shot Ben a sharp look and got a calm one in return.

"And you corrected this misconception."

"I told him what he needs to know."

"What name did he call you?"

Ben inclined his head and smiled. "He calls me by my Choctaw name, Waking-Bear."

Then Ben turned back to the cobbler and took up the conversation again. Hannah watched Blue-Deer's expression shift and soften, and then he replied.

"He has a son who is going blind in one eye," Ben translated. "He would take him home to the healers in his village, but the village is gone."

"I will do what I can," Hannah said. "If he will come to see me at the clinic."

That easily her decision was made.

All the people she met had a few things in common. They were Indian, though many had had at least one African or white parent or grandparent. One in six or seven had eyes the same startling turquoise as Ben Savard. They were all poor, and they were all pleased to see Ben, and eager to talk to him. And once he had introduced Hannah, they were eager to talk to her, too. They told her about fevers and wounds, about cures they had tried, the ones that had worked and the ones that hadn't; about cousins and sisters and grandfathers who had died suddenly or slowly;

about children who wasted away even when food was plentiful; about rashes that came and went without explanation; ulcers and coughs and belly cramps.

For the next hour they worked their way from one family to another. Sometimes they could speak French, but mostly they spoke the local Creole or their own languages, and then Ben acted as translator.

An old woman who had the look of a clan mother asked her the question she had been waiting for. Hannah recited her lineage, and Ben translated.

I am Walks-Ahead, daughter of Sings-from-Books of the Kahnyen'kehàka, called the Mohawk by the O'seronni. We are the People of the Longhouse, Keepers of the Eastern Door, the Kahnyen'kehàka of the Six Nations of the Haudenosaunee People. We live far to the north of this place, in the Endless Forests. Where it is so cold in the winter that the birds flee to the south, and snow makes a blanket for Brother Bear that lasts until April.

I am the granddaughter of Falling-Day, who was a great healer. I am the great-granddaughter of Made-of-Bones, who was clan mother of the Wolf for five hundred moons. I am the great-great-granddaughter of Hawk-Woman, who killed an O'seronni chief with her own hands and fed his heart to her sons in the Hunger Moon, in the time when we were still many, and strong.

She wanted to tell these people about the other women who claimed her as their own, who had taught her well, women who did not look like the people around her now. The stories they wanted to hear had to do with other Indians, the tribes to the west and the battles they had fought.

And so Walking-Woman told them. As she spoke and Ben translated she noted how his tone shifted, and tensed, and grew strong with the flow of the story.

She spoke of the days she had been known as Walking-

Woman. She told them of her husband, Strikes-the-Sky of the Seneca, of her uncle Strong-Words and the rest of her family. She told them about Tecumseh, also called Panther-in-the-Sky, and his brother, The Prophet, who had been the undoing of all their hopes. She told the story of her years living among the Real People on the Wabash at Tippecanoe and the day Harrison's troops came and destroyed it all. She told how her uncle Strong-Words and his sons fought and died in that battle; she spoke of her own husband, who had been sent out to recruit other tribes to Tecumseh's vision of a nation of red-skinned men and women united in their determination to keep some of this continent for themselves. How Strikes-the-Sky had gone out on this sacred mission and never returned.

She knew as she told this story that she was being judged, and that many found her lacking. Her husband had been a Red Stick from the north. It was men like him who had roused the Upper Creeks to a war. A war that had been lost, once and for all, at Horseshoe Creek, at unimaginable cost not to the whites, but to the rest of the Creek nation, and to every other tribe. It was because of that war that they were here, where they did not belong and did not want to be.

Hannah, agitated and truly alive for the first time in so many weeks, found she was thankful for the opportunity to tell her own story to people who understood, because their stories were much like her own.

An older man asked through Ben what she knew about the future, and whether it was true that Jackson was coming to this place to drive the Real People into the sea.

To Ben Hannah said, "Tell them I know less than they do. You can answer their questions about this war better than I can."

"I can't tell them what they want to hear," Ben said, but he spoke for a long time anyway, and Hannah saw that the people liked and trusted and respected him. She understood almost nothing of what he said, but she knew, because it was all so familiar. Another O'seronni war, and the Indian tribes had to decide where they stood. Which side they would fight for, or if it might be possible, this time, to come away from another O'seronni war with the little they had intact.

In the dusk they walked back to the clinic on the rue Dauphine. Glad now of the shawl that she pulled close around her, Hannah walked with her head lowered. The past had come to claim her, and it would not be shaken off so easily.

"Was I wrong to take you there?"

Ben spoke French. Hannah wondered if he realized it, or if he meant to say something by that choice of language. *You are among my kind now,* or *You must put aside what you think you know.* Or maybe he was only tired, as she was. Tired but content, as she had felt after a day in the cornfield as a girl, cleansed by hard work and sweat, having earned her food and her rest.

"You know you were not," Hannah said. But she thought of the last woman she had examined, no more than forty years old though she looked sixty. The troubles she brought to Hannah were the kind that nothing in the clinic apothecary could cure. Ungrateful children, stolen opportunities, broken promises that left a burning in the gut.

"What do you have for that?" The woman had been jittery and eager, her black eyes too bright as she caressed the grinding bowl in her lap. The smell of corn and sour sweat and bitter words hovered around her like a shroud. "You got something to bring justice down on a bad heart?"

"No," Hannah had told her through Ben, glad for once that she did not speak the same language. "That's not the kind of medicine I know about." And she saw that she had said the right thing. She had passed some test set for her by Ben Savard, and earned his trust.

• • •

"While you've been out exploring," Jennet said, "I've been whispering in corners with Rachel. Don't grimace, cousin, it will give you wrinkles before your time."

Hannah held up the shoe she had just pulled off her foot. "I'd give a great deal for a pair of moccasins, or even the doeskin to make my own. So tell me about Rachel, before you burst."

"She's in love. She's really certain this time."

Hannah pushed out a great breath. "Mr. Bellamy?"

"Oh no, Mr. Bellamy was days ago. You must pay better mind, Hannah. Rachel has given her heart to a M. Reynaud. Who is, she assures me, the perfect gentleman. Half French, half English, tall and fair, and he dances like an angel."

"Does an angel dance?" Hannah asked, yawning.

"When he is not busy making his fortune, yes. He dances and pays court to a highly strung sixteen-year-old who takes great satisfaction in the drama."

Something in Jennet's tone caught Hannah's attention. She turned to look at her cousin.

"Pay me no mind," Jennet said, blushing a little. "Nathaniel was unsettled all afternoon and none of us could comfort him."

Hannah was across the room and leaning over the baby's cot while Jennet went on, her voice wobbling. "The general opinion is that he's got a tooth coming. Please don't wake him, Hannah. Dr. Savard came up earlier and pronounced him perfectly healthy."

"Hmmm," Hannah said, and Jennet gave a weak laugh, putting up both hands in a gesture that said she was done protesting. Instead she came to stand beside Hannah while she examined the sleeping boy, her touch quick and so gentle that he hardly stirred.

"Clémentine thinks something I ate spoiled my milk, and says that I'm to have nothing but boiled hominy for a day. I've come to the conclusion that cooks are the same wherever you go. Do you remember how we sat in the kitchen at Carryckcastle and listened to Cook lecture on the evils of eating the strange things my faither was growing in his greenhouse?"

"Food as both the cause and the cure for every human ailment," Hannah agreed. And then: "You are trembling, Jennet, but he's in perfect health, now that he's done such a fine job of worrying his mother and setting the household on its ear."

Jennet collapsed into the chair next to the cot. She said, "I don't know what I'd do if I lost him, too."

Hannah put a hand on her cousin's shoulder and pressed, and then she went back to stretch out on her bed. For a long time they were silent, and Hannah was about to drift off to sleep without eating dinner or washing or even changing out of her clothes, when Jennet spoke.

She said, "Is it settled then, about your clinic?"

Hannah turned on her side. "New Orleans is an odd place, Jennet."

Her cousin leaned forward to cross her arms on her knees to listen, and so Hannah told her what she had learned and seen, and she heard her voice trembling.

When she had finished Jennet said, "But you needn't, if you don't want to."

"I'm not sure I do," Hannah said. "But I think I must try."

CHAPTER 23

The best, most carefully laid, most elegant of plans could go wrong. It was one thing to know that; on the dull wet afternoon Luke Bonner came to New Orleans almost four months late, he learned what it really meant.

On that first day he forced himself to start with the smallest and simplest tasks. A mile south of the city he found a tavern that catered to the mule drivers and dockworkers. The men who worked the canal between the Mississippi and the bayous that led through one swamp after another, forty tortuous miles between New Orleans and the island of Grand Terre.

Luke bought bread and meat and ale and suffered the suspicious looks of the local men. The landlord, who cared only that there was money in his pocket, made sure that it went no further, and then congratulated himself on his foresight when Luke paid too much for a room without argument.

He paid more good coin for the use of a hip bath and the hot water to fill it. A young woman with a swelling stomach and no teeth on one side of her mouth came with a ratty towel, and stayed to offer her services, which she listed with all the poetry and vigor of a fishmonger.

"What I'm interested in," Luke told her, "is news from the city."

Her name was Nancy. Aside from her pregnant belly she was stringy-lean in the way of people who grow up hungry,

with dark hair and bloodshot brown eyes. Luke guessed her
to be no more than twenty and already near the end of her
best years as a whore. But she was quick-witted, and she had
his measure.

She said, "Talking and fucking cost the same. It's up to you."

So Luke asked questions while he sat in the hip bath and
scrubbed himself raw. Nancy answered them, perched on a
stool near the door. Only once she interrupted him, with a
question of her own.

"You came up from Barataria?"

Luke nodded.

"You're not a spy, are you? If you was to turn out a Tory spy
I'd have to report you, or end up at the end of a rope. I ask because you look to me like you've been at sea for a long time."

"I'm not a spy," Luke told her. "I've got no interest in the
war, one way or the other."

That made her laugh, and not in a pleasant way. "You stay
here, you won't have much choice. The war going to take an
interest in you, *chèr*."

The things Nancy had to tell were of little use to him.
Rumors that Jackson was on his way; the British were about
to invade, had already invaded, were at the gates. He heard
no familiar names, no descriptions of the people he was
most interested in. He provided no information that she
might have used against him, though when she repeated the
question he had ignored, he answered her.

"I've been at sea, pressed into service on the *Puma*."

"The *Puma*." She stopped where she was, all pretense of
disinterest gone. "I've never heard of anybody getting away
from the *Puma*. The stories I've heard of Ten-Pint—"

"Most probably true, every one," said Luke. "But here I
am, after four months at sea, to Cartagena and then to Brazil."

"Brazil," she said. "I'd like to see Brazil someday, but I
doubt I'll ever get the chance."

Luke snorted water. "You never know," he said. "You may

end up there someday when it's the last place in the world
you want to be."

He paid Nancy to run some errands for him. She came
back an hour later and dropped a bundle of newspapers at
his feet. "None older than four months, just like you said.
The one on the top is today's."

November 26th. Luke touched the inky print and tried
to make sense of it.

She said, "The clothes should fit you; I've got an eye for
that. The barber be here in a few minutes. You call me, you
need anything else," Nancy said as she tucked the coins into
her bodice.

"Any of the other girls tell you I'm away or busy, they're
lying."

With his belly full, clean for the first time since he left
Pensacola, freshly shaved, Luke settled down to read newspapers and kept at it until his eyes burned and the candles gut-
tered. The impulse to go into the city and ask for straight
answers was strong in him, but there was no knowing how
delicate the situation might be. If Jennet and Hannah were still
here and in hiding, he couldn't risk drawing attention to the
fact that he was looking for them, not if Poiterin was around.

Most of what he read didn't interest him, but he
skimmed it all, looking for specific names: Poiterin, Bonner,
Scott. He looked for death notices and for names of ships
that might have taken passengers. There were not many of
them, given the war, but too many at that.

His sister, his wife and son might have left. In four months
they could be anywhere at all. Back at home, in Montreal, in
New-York, in Scotland. In their graves. Because he had
got on the wrong ship, and that ship had been captured by

privateers, and the privateers had been short of crew members, and he was strong and well grown. Because it had been two months before he could get away, and another two to get back here. Because he had failed them.

In a paper dated October 15th, Luke came across the first mention of the Poiterin family. Mme. Poiterin had attended a funeral in the company of her grandson Honoré. After that it seemed the name was in every column of every paper. The Poiterins had things for sale: horses and crops, slaves and hay. No mention of a baby or great-grandchild, of a wife for Honoré, or of visitors from out of town, though such visits were recorded for other families.

He was about to put the papers aside and give in to the need to sleep when an article on the front page of the November 13th edition of the *Louisiana Gazette* caught his eye.

The editors appeal to the citizens of New Orleans and environs in the distressing case of the abduction of an infant, the son of Honoré Poiterin, one of the first of our brave young men to volunteer for the *Dragons à Pied,* Commander Henri de Ste-Gême's élite militia unit.

The child was taken by force from the home of his great-grandmother, Mme. Agnès Poiterin, on Bayou St. John. The abductors knocked the child's nurse unconscious. The Poiterins were in the city for the afternoon at the time.

The authorities speculate that the mother, who is by all reports a gentlewoman not in full possession of her faculties, given to erratic and hysterical behavior as well as delusions of persecution, may have conspired with others to abduct her own child and run away from those whose only concern is her well-being and eternal soul.

This lady, who is known as Lady Jennet, is the sister of the Earl of Carryck of Scotland. She is about thirty years old, some five foot three inches tall, with unfashionably short, curling blond hair and blue eyes. She was last seen on horseback, leaving the city in a southwardly direction. The lady is a danger to herself and her child, and the authorities encourage anyone with information on their whereabouts to come forward immediately. The Poiterin family will reward useful information with a liberal hand.

Luke was suddenly, absolutely awake. He tore through the remainders of the paper and saw no evidence that Jennet and the boy had been found. Just the opposite—in yesterday's paper he found a notice that Mme. Poiterin had raised the reward for the return of her great-grandson.

Today was the twenty-sixth day of November, which meant that it was two weeks since Jennet had run away from the Poiterins, taking the boy with her. Fourteen days ago they had both been alive, and free of Honoré Poiterin. And what of Hannah?

Outside his window, the river sparked with the reflected light of torches. Even this late there was traffic along the levee. Prostitutes with shawls folded over their heads against the cold drizzle. Men on their way home from a game of dice or cards, the watchmen who were paid to keep thieves away from warehouses filled with goods that would be sent to eager markets in England and Europe as soon as the war was over. Soldiers and militia in twos and threes, morose with drink or laughing wildly.

He had no way of knowing where his family might be, but Luke could find the Bayou St. John. He could talk to Andrew Preston's sister-in-law. Maybe Titine, who had come here with Jennet, was still in that household and could tell him what he needed to know. If all else failed, he could find Honoré Poiterin.

It took only two days to create a clinic out of nothing. Furniture appeared as if by magic; Clémentine descended with a half dozen servants to scrub every surface; and the new shelves and cabinets seemed to fill themselves. There were basins and ewers, linens and blankets, great stacks of muslin and gauze for bandages, all the instruments she might need to treat everything from wounds needing suturing to gangrenous limbs. Paul refused to discuss any of this, insisting that he was giving her only scalpels and needles and lancettes he did not need. Once she had had a beautiful surgeon's kit of her own, but that had been lost in the looting after Tippecanoe. She found that she was able to talk to Paul about that day calmly, because, she thought, she knew he would take the story she had to tell in the same way, and not burden her with his own reactions.

While they talked he arranged the small apothecary corner, though he made it clear to Hannah that she was not restricted to the basic supplies there.

"Send Leo to get what you need from the general stores," he told her. Leo was thirteen years old, as quick and bright as a new candle, and his only duties were to run errands for Hannah and assist her wherever she needed him. He had lived most of his life with his mother in a Choctaw followers' camp and spoke a half dozen Indian dialects, and Hannah had the idea that Leo would be more useful than any scalpel.

"Without counting cost." Hannah repeated what she had heard both Paul and Julia say many times already.

"You won't bankrupt us," Julia had assured her. "We have a generous benefactor, who approves of our mission."

Hannah, who was uncomfortable with the notion of any kind of mission at all, forced herself to raise a difficult topic.

"You realize," she said to them over dinner on the day she was to see her first patients, "that I may not be here for very much longer."

Ben was not at the table, which made it both easier and more difficult to say such a thing. But it turned out that she had been worrying for nothing.

"Philippe will be arriving as soon as it's safe to get passage from France," Julia said. And: "Have we not told you about the youngest of the Savard sons? He has been in Paris these last six years, studying medicine."

"No," Hannah said. "I didn't realize there was another doctor in the family."

Paul's mouth twitched in a way that made Hannah think there was more to the story of Philippe Savard than Julia had volunteered. No doubt Rachel would provide details at some point.

"There's enough work for the both of you, should you care to stay on," Paul said.

Julia sent him a severe look. "What my husband is trying to say is that we would welcome it should you decide to make your home here and continue in practice. There are funds enough for a salary, and we would find you lodgings of your own, of course."

Jennet did not bother to hide her surprise or her shock. She put down her fork with an uncharacteristic clatter to make her feelings clear. "But you want to go home," she told Hannah. "You want to go back to Lake in the Clouds. We will all go, together."

"Yes," Hannah said. "We will, Jennet, we will all go home together." To Paul and Julia she said, "I thank you for your kind offer, but I am glad to know there will be another doctor to take over when I leave here."

"I don't ever want to go back to New-York," Rachel said firmly. "I am happy here, though it is deadly hot in the summer. Of course one day I'd like to see Paris, and London." She blushed as she said this, and could not meet her mother's gaze. Paul was less easily put off by her maidenly posture.

"Have you had an offer from Reynaud?" Paul asked, in the blunt manner of any father with a sixteen-year-old daughter with a crush.

"No, Papa," Rachel said, with a great deal of dignity.

"Why would you want him to offer you anything?" Henry said with all the disdain he could muster. "M. Reynaud is twice as old as you are. I heard you telling Jennet so."

"I think that is quite enough of this very private subject," Julia said, putting a hand on her son's head. "We must trust

Rachel to let herself be led by what she knows is right, by her common sense and native intelligence."

Rachel did not raise her gaze from the untouched food on her plate, but her color rose another notch. The blush turned her from a pretty girl into a striking one.

"Life would be so much more pleasant if we could forbid children speech until they reached the age of reason," Paul said, but he winked at his stepdaughter, and his tone was kind.

After dinner Rachel followed Hannah out to the clinic. To help, she said, wherever Hannah might need it, but Hannah feared she had been singled out as Rachel's newest confessor.

"I have the oddest mother in the world, without a doubt." She worked as she talked, folding bandages neatly and quickly. "It comes in part from being raised as a Quaker, but I do wish sometimes she could be more like other mothers."

"My stepmother is a great deal like your mother," Hannah said. "If it's any comfort to you, she won't seem so odd as you get older."

Rachel's brows folded in on each other in silent disagreement. "She doesn't seem to care if I never get married."

"You are only sixteen," Hannah pointed out. "Why are you in such a hurry?"

"My aunt Livingston was married at sixteen," Rachel said.

"And widowed at seventeen," Hannah said.

"That was not her fault."

"Of course not," Hannah said. And, by way of comforting the girl: "Once your parents have met M. Reynaud they may be more sympathetic."

"When are they to meet him? They never go out socially," Rachel said. "They turn down all my aunt Livingston's invitations. They are too busy. They have no interest in dancing or parties. And M. Reynaud—" She stopped herself and went back to her work, silent for so long that Hannah believed she had decided to drop the subject.

"I am a silly girl, after all," she said. "And my parents are right. The truth is that M. Reynaud shows me no more favor than any of the other young ladies."

"But last night he asked you to dance?" Hannah wondered why she felt it necessary to encourage the girl, but it was too late to call the question back.

"Three times," Rachel said, with obvious pleasure. "That was a *great* compliment; everyone took note. But really all he wanted to do was ask me about Papa and the clinic. And he asked about you."

Hannah looked up sharply, but Rachel's attention was on the gauze in front of her. "There's a lot of talk about you now, the Indian woman at Savard's clinic. Uncle Livingston remembers when you were in Manhattan; there was a newspaper article about you. I asked Papa, and he recited bits of it for me—"

"Your father's memory for the printed word is not always such a blessing," Hannah said.

"But why should you mind?" Rachel said. "If someone were to write such complimentary things about me I shouldn't mind. And you must prepare yourself, because the local journalists will come around wanting to write about you, that I can almost guarantee. Just as soon as word gets out that you are seeing patients on a regular basis."

"I want no such notice," Hannah said. "And certainly it would be a bad idea to have strangers intruding here. For reasons you well know."

Rachel said, "No one need hear anything about Jennet. It's you they're interested in."

"You realize what might happen if the Poiterins should even suspect Jennet and her son are here?" Hannah's tone was purposefully sharp, but Rachel didn't flinch, though she took on an air of affronted dignity.

"Of course I do," she said. "And I would never do anything to put them in danger. I may be silly and vain in some things, but I am not careless."

Hannah said, "I'm glad to hear it."

That very afternoon Julia came to the door of the little clinic with three ladies who had called on her with the express wish to see the Mohawk woman who had been trained as a doctor. *As though I were a bear in a cage,* Hannah thought as she took off her leather apron. *Supposedly broken and admissible to polite company, but still enough of a risk to provide a thrill.*

Julia, apologetic, introduced her to Mrs. Louisa Livingston. "You have heard Rachel speak of her favorite aunt," she said. "Mrs. Livingston came here from Saint-Domingue after the rebellion."

Louisa Livingston was just as Rachel had described her: full of laughter and playful, young and very beautiful, physically fragile but radiating a personal strength and purpose. She took one of Hannah's hands between two spotless white silk gloves embroidered with lilies.

"I earned my living as a seamstress when first I came here, before I met Edward. I know what it is to work for my bread."

Hannah said something polite but inconsequential, which somehow managed to delight her visitors.

"*C'est incroyable,*" said Mrs. Livingston. "To hear you speak and not see your face, who would know you to be an Indian?"

It was meant as a compliment, one Hannah had heard so many times in her life that she no longer could be shocked.

Not that Mrs. Livingston would have noticed. She had already turned to her companions, chattering in French.

"What an excellent example you are for your people," she said, switching back to English. "Now tell me—"

Hannah saw Julia tense, and she herself tensed, expecting the question they had anticipated and talked about at so much length: *How is it you come to New Orleans?*

"Have you had any word from your family? Have they survived the war in the north thus far?"

"We have not had word in a very long time," Hannah said, and then realized her mistake.

"We?" said Mrs. Livingston. "You are here with companions, or"—she turned to Julia—"are you acquainted with the family, as well?"

"Yes," Julia said. "My husband is. We are all very concerned for their well-being."

Hannah had such a surge of affection and thankfulness for Julia at that moment that she felt the warmth of it in her face and hands.

"I will expect you all at four on Wednesday afternoon," Mrs. Livingston was saying. "I will not take no for an answer, Julia. It has been far too long since we sat together and talked at leisure."

"Perhaps you will get to meet M. Reynaud," Jennet said, when Hannah told her of the invitation. "Or even better, you could find a way to talk to Edward Livingston. Perhaps he could get us on Mr. Shreve's steamboat when he makes his maiden journey up the river."

Hannah made a sound in her throat that she hoped Jennet would take as agreement. In reality she doubted she would even see Edward Livingston, and a conversation with him—especially one about his monopoly of the steamboat concern and the litigation around it—was even less likely. It was one of those political matters that men never tired of discussing, in the paper every day and the subject of dozens of editorials. Sooner rather than later, somebody—Mr. Shreve, if he could circumvent Livingston's legal claims—would be the first to have a steamboat fight its way upriver all the way to St. Louis, and beyond, at a lofty three miles an hour.

"Three miles an hour is better than standing still," Jennet announced when that number was brought to her attention. "Imagine, Hannah. We could step on a steamboat right here, and step off again more than halfway home. We'd be back in Paradise in no time at all."

Hannah thought of the impossibility of the roads in the spring thaw. She thought of the long journey she had once made on foot, and the winter she had spent living by the shore of the hollow lake where her son had died.

She made herself breathe deeply and she smiled at her cousin. "We will get home, one road or the other. That is the important thing."

Just past dawn on the next morning, Leo opened the doors of the new clinic and Hannah saw that the word had spread far, and done its work. There was a crowd of people waiting, and all faces turned toward her. Impassive or hopeful or reluctant, they came forward and filled the long room, put down blankets, and sat to wait.

She treated a woman's ulcerated leg, her nostrils flaring at the high keen smell of putrefaction as she scraped and cut. She mixed ointment and folded herbs into a muslin bag to be steeped in hot water. Leo translated her instructions on how often the tea must be taken and when the woman should come back to be seen again. Finally she turned and cast a pinch of rough Indian tobacco into the open door of the stove where a cypress wood fire burned. As the bittersweet smoke rose she murmured a prayer in her mother's language and when she turned back, she saw a new expression on the woman's face. Surprise, and satisfaction.

All morning Hannah saw one patient after another. A young woman who was heavily pregnant with her fourth child, her ankles swollen to twice their size. A man who needed prayers and medicine to calm the pain in a hand he had lost to a mercifully clean sword cut. A young girl with a wound on her arm that would not heal unless she got better food, and more of it. An infant with a mass in its liver that would kill it before the new moon. She told its mother so, and saw that she was only confirming what the woman had already suspected. She talked, through Leo, to a Choctaw healer who lived in a tiny room with three other women and five children. She gave her name as Yellow-Sapling, and she looked Hannah directly in the eye in the way of a strong woman who knew her worth, and was not afraid of other strong women.

In French she told Hannah that she had no space to store the herbs and plants she saw growing around her.

Without hesitation Hannah said, "You can store what you find here. There is room enough, and you are welcome to work alongside me."

Leo said, "She will not come. She was just testing you, to see if you are one of the Real People or if you are a white who has conjured a red skin for yourself, in order to poison us all."

Hannah said, "You heard her talk of this?"

Leo's mouth set itself stubbornly. "I have heard talk."

"Then you continue to listen," Hannah said. "And I'll continue to work."

She did just that, right through the dinner hour. Paul Savard himself came, first to insist that she join them and then, later, with a tray of food. Hannah ate two spoonfuls of stew and then saw to it that the children got the rest.

Toward mid-afternoon a man came in and walked up to Hannah directly. He had a blanket wrapped around shoulders that had once been powerful, and his bearing was that of a chief. His body was covered with old scars faded to glimmering pink welts, and his bones seemed to shine through his skin.

There were many masses, the largest in his stomach, other, smaller ones in his lower intestines and liver. She knew without being told that the pain was very bad, that there was blood in his stool and urine, that he could take no food and could keep down only a little warm water. He did not need to hear from her that he would be dead in days.

Leo, subdued, told her his name before she could ask. Rattling-Gourd, a Chickasaw chief.

Hannah said, "What do you want of me, Grandfather?"

He looked at her, the whites of his eyes as yellow as a full moon. His voice was rough and hoarse and still musical as he spoke, pausing now and then while Leo translated.

"Long ago the Maker of All Life took up some mud and made a man and put him to bake in the sun. But that first man turned out underdone and pale, and so the Creator put him aside. The second man he left too long in the sun, and his skin turned black. This man was also put aside. The third man he took more time with, and watched very carefully while he cured in the sun. This man with red skin was the Creator's favorite.

"The Maker of Life said to the three men, choose what tools you will use. The black man stepped forward and the Creator pushed him aside to let the white man choose first, because he felt pity for him. The white man chose paper and pen and a compass and other things that white men value. When the black man came forward again the Maker of Life pushed him aside so that his favorite, the red man, could choose. The red man took up knives and war clubs and traps, bows and arrows, the things the Real People need for hunting and war. Finally the black man was allowed to choose, but all that was left were axes and hoes and buckets for water, and the yokes needed to drive oxen. And the Creator was pleased to have it thus: Forever the black man must serve the white and the red man in the fields."

When he was finished there was a small silence in the room, and then the murmur of voices. Hannah thought of Ben Savard, and what he had told her, standing right here: *Together, black and red, we might have had a chance. The British understood that and did everything in their power to drive a wedge between the two peoples.*

She felt Rattling-Gourd watching her, to see how much she understood, if she could be trusted to see the truth. She looked back at him evenly, and saw the deep black color of his skin, glossy with fever sweat on the high bones of his face, the broad nose and the deep philtrum over a wide, heavy-lipped mouth. She saw that what was left of his hair was tightly kinked. But she understood, too, that it did not matter where his forefathers had been born or how they had come to this place. Nor did the color of his skin matter: He was Chickasaw, a chief in a village that was gone now, wiped out by one army or another. If she showed him his own face in the mirror he would see a red man, and if she walked with him down to the slave market where other men who looked like him waited to be sold, he would accept no claim of kinship with any of them.

She said, "It is so." She said it because she understood Rattling-Gourd's lesson. The truth was this: The people who had come to her for help, every one of them, understood color in the way that Rattling-Gourd had tried to make clear to her. It didn't matter that all of them had had at least one African grandparent, that some had been slaves or owned slaves.

In the north, among her mother's people and the neighboring tribes, it had been no different. Richard Todd, the white doctor who had loved her mother, had spent most of his early childhood among the Kahnyen'kehàka; his brother had never left. Throws-Hard, if he was still alive, would be of an age with Rattling-Gourd, an old white man who looked at his reflection in the water and saw a Kahnyen'kehàka elder and war chief.

Hannah felt a sudden surge of weariness, but she schooled her expression and began to say the words that were expected of her, words due an elder when he made the gift of a story.

The door opened, and this time the men who stood there were white, and in uniform. All through the room the small sounds—coughs and sighs and scuffling, the murmur of mother to child—stopped. At that moment Hannah felt another presence, just behind her. A welcome presence, at this moment, familiar and trusted.

A white man, in the uniform of an army captain. A man of medium height, with the bowlegs of someone who has spent most of his life on horseback. His dark hair was tied into a queue, and in a face burned dark by the sun his eyes were a pale gray. Those eyes fixed Ben, who came forward to stand beside Hannah.

"Jean-Benoît," the soldier said. His tone friendly, but guarded. "A word?"

Hannah would have preferred to stay out of the conversation, but Ben put a hand on her shoulder and asked her to step out with them into the courtyard. To refuse him in front of these people would hurt him in more ways than she could count. She went with the two men, stepping out into the courtyard and closing the door behind herself.

He introduced her by her American name, which irritated Hannah for no good reason. She was Hannah Bonner;

she would always be Hannah Bonner. The impulse to use her Kahnyen'kehàka name, to identify herself as a daughter of the Longhouse of the Wolf, would bring her no advantage. In this place where no one knew of the Mohawk, her pride was out of place.

And then the surprise: Captain Pierre Gabriel de Juzan offered her his hand. Hannah tried to remember the last time a white man other than Paul Savard had showed any willingness to acknowledge her at all. His hand was hard and calloused and firm. He met her eye, and smiled.

The captain told his news in the Spanish-influenced French Hannah had first heard in Florida. "You should know that some of the Creole ladies are trying to get you shut down."

If this news surprised Ben, he was hiding it well. He inclined his head for a moment. "I'll talk to Dr. Kerr," he said finally. "His word will count for a lot, and he owes me a favor."

That made Juzan grin. "I shouldn't be surprised that you are owed favors, I suppose. And I should have known you'd have a plan."

"I have many plans," Ben said dryly.

"Then add another to your list," said Juzan. "When Jackson gets here I'm going to approach him about putting together a company of Choctaw. Can I count on you?"

"You can," said Ben, without hesitation.

Hannah's mouth shut with an audible snap.

Juzan bowed from the shoulders and touched his brow in her direction, and then he disappeared through the alleyway.

Ben said, "Juzan is married to my cousin. In case you were wondering."

That explained some things, but not the most important ones. Hannah, flushed with anger she could neither explain nor justify, started to turn back toward the clinic when Ben put out a hand to stop her.

"You looked surprised when I said I'd join Juzan's company."

"Why should anything you do surprise me?" said Hannah, trying and failing to keep the tremor from her voice. "You are a stranger to me, after all."

"Something that would change over time," Ben said.

Hannah took a very deep breath. "I will confess that I am confused. I thought you were an admirer of Quaker beliefs?"

"I'm an American first," he said. "And then a Choctaw. If the British try to take this city, I will defend it. Would your father not fight to defend his home?"

Hannah thought of the things she might say to him, the pictures she could draw with words, the battlefields she had seen. In Ben's face she saw that he knew what she was thinking, and that he knew as much as she did about what was to come. A wave of exhaustion moved through her, but she forced it away, pushed it away, and straightened her back. Men went to war, and died.

"What about the clinic?" she said. "Will it have to close?"

"No," Ben said. "I don't think Mme. Girot will get her way this time."

"An old enemy," Hannah said.

He shrugged. "She's not known for her generosity or open-mindedness. Last year she had two slaves whipped to death."

"Ah." Hannah closed her eyes and then looked at him directly. "This is the government you are willing to defend. To die defending." She heard herself laugh, a shallow sound. "That is something I can never understand, not in a thousand years."

• • •

In the evening, the women and the children sat together in the Savards' small parlor. Jennet had the almost irresistible urge to look out the window, which she must not: The sun had set long ago, and there were enough candles burning to show her face clearly to anyone on the street who cared to look up. Mme. Poiterin, who did not bow to defeat gracefully, had recently increased the reward for the return of her great-grandson to five hundred dollars.

The truth was that to be kept here, even for her own good and her son's welfare, had grown tiresome. Jennet could not keep such thoughts at bay, though she knew herself to be the most ungrateful of creatures. The Savards had offered her safety and friendship and comfort, and she repaid them with melancholy and moods.

She looked at Hannah, who sat, straight-backed, an unread newspaper on her lap. Hannah was too thin and often distracted, but she seemed to have her health back, and for all her doubts about this new clinic, Jennet had the sense that the work today had given her a sense of purpose and satisfaction. Jennet thought of Jean-Benoît and Paul Savard, who were off right now talking to the men who would decide if the clinic might stay, or should be closed down for reasons that would be small-minded and mean-spirited, if they bothered with reasons at all.

The real question was what Hannah was hoping for. If she wanted to continue as she had begun today, or if she would be relieved to hear that the whole venture must be put aside.

Julia, who was usually so attentive to everybody's moods, was lost in the contents of a packet that had reached her today by means of a flatboat that had begun its journey months ago. The package had come from Manhattan, through New Jersey and Pennsylvania and into the western territories until it reached the twist of rivers that emptied into the Mississippi; this morning it had been carried off the flatboat and brought here by a breathless boy. For his troubles he had been given a coin and a bowl of soup, drunk under Clémentine's watchful eye in the kitchen.

Julia held the bundle of letters from her family and friends, newspapers and magazines and books, on her lap like a much-loved child. Rachel had her own letters, all of which she had read many times already, and would no doubt continue to read until she had committed them to memory. With the exception of one letter that she tucked away with a blush, Rachel shared her news with the family. Not all the reports from Manhattan were to her liking.

"I cannot believe that my cousin Matthew really is going to marry that—that—that *harridan* Catherine Astor." She shot her mother a defiant look. "What is he thinking?"

Julia said, "Most likely they are already married, Rachel. These letters were written some two months ago..." She looked at the open letter in her hand. "We must write back and wish them every happiness." Her tone was as mild as ever, but she gave her daughter a pointed look.

The tarot cards sat in a neat pile on the table while Jennet leafed through one of the newly arrived, but sadly out-of-date, newspapers. "Bonaparte, Bonaparte, Bonaparte. I know the wee mannie was a great deal of trouble, but why is there no other news? What of Scotland?" She looked in Hannah's direction, but her cousin's attention was unfocused, her mind busy elsewhere.

Jennet touched the deck of cards with one finger and then withdrew it.

"Oh, what rot," Rachel said with all the contempt a young woman of sixteen could muster. She flapped the bit of paper in her hand. "I don't know why my uncle sends these clippings. I don't care if I never read another word of the *London Courier*. They insult President Madison in every possible way, and very rude they are as well. 'A compound of canting and hypocrisy, of exaggeration and falsehood, of coarseness with strength, of malignant passions; of undisguised hatred of Great Britain, and of ill-concealed partiality and servility toward France.' "

She huffed to herself. "And if I adored everything about England, I should hate it now, after reading such drivel."

"Impassioned polemic is the province of newspapers," Julia said evenly. "They are concerned first and foremost with selling papers."

Hannah managed a smile. "I think you and my stepmother could have some very interesting discussions. She writes for the Manhattan papers."

"I would enjoy that," Julia said. "But at the moment I think we should have a look at the books my father has sent." She put down the letter to look through the box on the table next to her. "Here. *Travels to the Source of the Missouri River and across the American Continent to the Pacific Ocean*—imagine, Rachel, how excited Henry will be—*Performed by the Government of the United States, in the years 1804, 1805, and 1806. By Captains Lewis and Clark.*"

Hannah's face turned toward Julia. "I met Captain Lewis, in Manhattan. I vaccinated him against smallpox. Or maybe I just checked his vaccination site. It seems a long time ago." A smile moved across her face. "I was very young. I lectured him."

"Captain Lewis was murdered," Rachel said, her eyes sparking.

"There is no evidence to support that claim," Julia said calmly. "And I'm sure he'd prefer people to be reading about his travels rather than gossiping about his death."

Jennet said, "Is that the first copy of his book to reach New Orleans?"

Rachel's face brightened. "Most likely it is. Oh, think how in demand we shall be!" She saw her mother's expression, and dropped her head, regretful if not penitent. Then she said, "The gentlemen will be very curious." Her tone was not quite so light as she might have wanted it to be. "We mustn't be selfish, Mama."

"You may offer it to your uncle Livingston when we have finished with it," her mother said. "But not before. We could read the first chapter out loud this evening, if Paul and Ben aren't much longer."

And they were not long; in fact, Jennet heard their step on the stair before Julia had quite finished her thought.

"They will want tea," Julia said. "Please go ask Clémentine to bring some up, Rachel."

The news was brief and, it seemed to Jennet, ambiguous. "Is the clinic to stay open, or no?" she asked. And, "What is this talk of Redbones? I haven't heard that word before, have I?"

She looked at Ben quite deliberately, but it was Paul who answered her.

"It's what some call mixed-blood Indians."

"Ah," said Jennet. "As the English call us Scots sheep shaggers."

"To get on with the story," said Dr. Savard, who was having a hard time hiding his impatience, "Mme. Girot made her complaint directly to the governor."

"And?" Julia said.

"The clinic can stay open," Paul said. "But only because Bernard Marigny and Dr. Kerr took our side, and Edward Livingston spoke up in its defense. And with the understanding that if there is fighting near or in the city, it will be converted into a hospital for soldiers."

"Well, then," Julia said, smiling. "Is that not good news, Hannah?"

"Yes," Hannah said. "Of course it is."

There was a small, tight silence. Paul and Ben were looking at Hannah, and Hannah was looking at a spot on the wall, her expression revealing nothing. Jennet, who knew her best of all the people in the room, did not know what to make of this. Neither did Julia, but she was not content to wonder. She had folded her hands in front of herself, a posture that Jennet recognized, one that Elizabeth Bonner favored when she wanted to share something she considered very important.

"There are unsaid things in this room," Julia began. "Those things must be brought into the light."

Paul Savard closed his eyes briefly and dropped his chin to his chest. "Must we, Julia?"

"There is nothing to fear from the truth, husband," Julia said.

"It's not the truth that worries me," Paul said with a small smile, "but where the conversation is going when you start thee-ing and thou-ing."

"Hannah," Julia said, ignoring her husband. "If thou cannot take on the work of the clinic, it is best to say so without apology. We have no wish to coerce thee. The work is hard, and thou has every reason to guard thy strength. It is enough if thou should say, 'I cannot.' "

Dr. Savard let out a soft sigh but said no word of protest. As if his wife, when she reverted to her Quaker ways, was a force he did not wish to challenge.

"Jean-Benoît?" Julia Savard asked.

"It is for Hannah to decide," he said, his tone easy.

Jennet wondered if Ben would be able to hide his disappointment if Hannah were to walk away from the clinic he so clearly held dear, and if that disappointment would really be about the loss of her help and skills. She asked herself, as she often did, about the nature of Ben Savard's true feelings for Hannah. She suspected that he was becoming more attached to her every day.

She saw that Hannah was uneasy, and she felt the pull of what her cousin might want, the things she needed, and what she could not bring herself to say.

"Of course it is for Hannah to decide," Jennet said, speaking up suddenly, and with considerable energy. "But ye've saved her life, and mine and my son's...how can she refuse ye anything?"

She closed her mouth with an audible click and color flooded her face. "Please pardon me," she said. "I apologize for my temper, and my manners. My mither would box my ears."

"There is no need to apologize for plain speaking," Julia said. "But Hannah, we should really like to hear from thee."

Hannah looked at Julia's face, the steady brown eyes under a low brow, the dimpled cheek, the fan of lines at the corners of her mouth. She thought of saying that she would not, could not do what they seemed to think she must want to do. She thought of the long afternoons in these small rooms, and Jennet's unhappiness and growing desperation. She thought of Rattling-Gourd, his black eyes fixed on her, the things he expected of her.

Choose.

"What I would like most of all," Hannah said, "is to go home. All of us, the four of us, my brother and his wife and their child, too. I'd like to leave for home today. I miss my father and my stepmother and my brothers and sisters, and my friends. I miss the village where I grew up. I miss Curiosity, who is more to me than a grandmother. She is very old, and she may not live out this winter. I hate the idea that she may be gone when I come home again. Those are the things that I want.

"But I am here, and I will stay here until my brother comes back, or we know for certain he will not." She paused.

"Go on," said Jennet, her voice wavering.

"I don't know how I feel about the clinic, whatever it is called. I know that the work there is important. I know that I can help the people who come to me. It feels right to be putting the things that were taught to good use. But the truth is, I would rather not. I would like to tell you that I cannot, but the truth is, I must."

She looked at Jennet, who had tears in her eyes. "I am sorry to leave you here all day long, cousin, but I must."

Ben looked at Hannah directly for the first time since she began to speak. His expression was fraught with things she could not name, or did not care to understand.

"You asked me once how you could thank me," he said. "I think you have found a way." His tone was easy and even, but the way he looked at her, even here in this room where they were not alone, was unmistakable. The pulse in Hannah's wrists and throat jumped, and she was suffused with a girlish pleasure she had forgotten.

When Ben had left the room she still felt it, warm and liquid and heavy, in the hollow space below her heart.

CHAPTER 24

At first light, Luke found the nearest livery stable and hired a sturdy mare with a placid disposition. The blacksmith gave him directions and he set out, skirting the city until he found the canal that joined the city to the Bayou St. John and the narrow shell road that ran along beside it.

In less than an hour he found himself on the bayou, a sluggish, sinuous tongue of gray-green water. It was raining in earnest now and Luke passed the reins from one hand to the other and tucked the free one, fire red with cold and wet, into his cloak to warm it. He should have taken the time to find gloves, and better boots, and a decent cloak. Another hour wouldn't have made any difference.

Where the bayou emptied into the lake, an old Spanish fort squatted in the rain. He looked at it for a few minutes and turned the horse back toward the canal, passing one house after another closed up tight against the driving rain. At the arched bridge he pulled up to stand in its very center. As far as he could see in the driving rain, not one living creature was brave enough to venture out.

The world was water and the sound of water. Even the noise of the horse's hooves on the crushed white shell of the roadway was muffled. And then the bang of a nearby door, and a small boy shot out into the roadway and ran flat-out toward the bridge, a covered basket clutched tightly to his chest and his round face creased in concentration. When he saw Luke he stopped so suddenly that his bare feet skidded on the wet wood, and for a moment it seemed as though he must go off the bridge into the bayou.

He raised his face when Luke called to him, blinked rain out of his eyes, and produced an expansive frown that contorted his whole face and said very clearly that whatever kind of French Luke was speaking, it was both comical and unfamiliar.

In the end the boy answered the questions put to him, almost hopping in place with the cold. Then he snatched the coin Luke tossed out of the air, and ran off again.

Wet, chilled to the bone, and no wiser than he had been the day before, Luke came back to the city. He had lost the list of contacts that Lacoeur had given him before they left Port Royal, but he did remember three. The first two men, one a French furrier and another an exporter of spices, were not at home, and in fact seemed to have left New Orleans altogether. Luke asked for directions once more, and in the last light of day he found himself in front of the offices of Fitch & Jerome, textile merchants.

Luke couldn't remember any details his stepfather had provided about Cornelius Fitch. Whatever the connection, it was clear that it was not strong enough to be of any use to Luke. Fitch was uneasy and abrupt and defensive, a man who had something to hide or, at least, thought he did. Almost more disturbing was the fact that he seemed not at all surprised to see Luke or hear who he was looking for.

"I remember your half sister," Fitch admitted. "She was here, yes, and asked for assistance. Which I provided."

Behind his spectacles his eyes were small and too close together, and his gaze slid away across the counter, as if the most important thing in the world at this moment was to count the bolts of cloth piled there.

"Do you have any idea where she might be now?" Luke asked, keeping his tone light.

"No," said Fitch. "I gave her directions to an old black woman who I thought would take her in as a lodger. She seemed to be satisfied with that. She never came back to ask for more help."

"I see," Luke said, and under the sparse beard Fitch's hollow cheeks went a splotchy red.

"I'll write down the directions for you," said Fitch. "And then I must excuse myself. Business matters to attend to, you understand. I hope you will give your stepfather my best regards when next you write to him."

Luke let his silence do its work as Fitch scribbled out a few lines on a piece of paper. When he scattered sand over the wet ink, his hand was trembling.

It took an hour to find the place, a shack on the far side of the city on the edge of the ciprière, in a huddle with a dozen other shacks like it. Luke stood at the opening that served as a door, and put away all hope that there might be someone here who would help him find Hannah.

A half dozen young children tumbled across the dirt floor around a tired-looking woman no more than thirty. It was her grandmother Luke wanted, she told him in the patois, made a few degrees more challenging by the fact that she had only a few teeth. The grandmother who had rented a pallet to Hannah for a single night was gone herself, many weeks in her grave.

"Do you remember the Indian woman?" Luke asked. He held coins in his open hand and felt her gaze latch on to them.

She did remember, new energy and conviction coming

into her tone. A younger woman, very pretty but tired looking. Where she had gone, what had become of her, that she could not say. But she could ask, she told Luke. By day she worked as a laundress and she came across many people who would have noticed such a woman on her own in this city. She would ask, if he cared to come again to find out what she had learned.

One of the older children, a boy with sores on his face and beautiful green eyes and skin the color of old honey, came up and said something to his mother. She put a hand on his head as he spoke, her fingers spread wide to cup his skull, her expression patient and sad at the same time. When he had finished she spoke a few words and he darted out of the shack, sidling by Luke as if he feared to be struck.

"Maybe I can find out something quick," she said. "If you can wait for a moment."

Five minutes passed and then ten. Luke was thinking of leaving when the boy came back and went straight to his mother. What he had to tell her took longer this time, and she stopped him twice to ask a question.

"Monsieur," she said, lowering her head, "there was an Indian woman boarding with Mme. Soileau some time ago. She isn't there anymore, but maybe Madame can tell you more."

Luke said, "And how do I find Mme. Soileau?"

"Her establishment is on Decatur Street near Esplanade across from the old fort. If you inquire of any man you see on the street he will be able to point out the house."

She lowered her gaze to the floor, and Luke understood what kind of business this Mme. Soileau ran. He left her with the coins in his hand, and walked back to the city.

From the street the house seemed like nothing out of the ordinary. The building was recently whitewashed, the banquette was swept clear of trash, there were lace curtains and heavier drapes of some rich material, all prettily lit by candlelight.

The woman who answered his knock was not the wife of a banker or merchant, but exactly what he had supposed she must be. She was dressed in the latest fashion, with a décolletage that left little to the imagination. Her smile lasted only as long as it took Luke to make clear that he was not a customer, and had come only in search of information. For which, he made clear, he would pay handsomely.

He was shown to a small office at the back of the house. A neat room, where someone who understood something of business kept books and records. The woman who joined him there might have once been a prostitute; she might still be the kind of woman who appealed to men who liked to be dealt with harshly. She sized Luke up in a moment and decided, it seemed, that it would not do to antagonize him unduly. He had the air of a successful man.

"Yes," she said, in a heavily accented English. "The Indian squaw was here. When her money was gone she was put out."

Luke felt his face stiffen at her tone and choice of words, but he could control his temper when to do otherwise would be foolish. "You have no idea where she went?"

"To her grave, I expect," said Mme. Soileau. "If I had known how sick she was I never would have taken her in the first place, money or no. I run a respectable establishment, and a clean one."

Luke set his face in an expression that was as blank as he could make it.

"How was she sick? Was she seen by a doctor?"

The woman looked genuinely surprised. "I don't know what things are like up north," she said. "But down here no white doctor would have a Redbone as a patient." Her mouth pursed with distaste at the idea.

"Who nursed her? Would that person have any information?"

"She's not here any longer. You might be able to interview her if Freeman still has her." And then, in response to Luke's expression: "Freeman is a slave trader. He bought the girl from me. His place is right around the corner. Follow the stink, you'll find it."

"And the person I'm looking for is called—"

"Just ask for the Chinese girl, they'll know who you mean. Freeman will want to sell her to you. That's the only way you'll get near her." She cocked her head to one side, and took his measure. "I can't offer you a squaw but I've got good girls here, clean, Christian girls who know their business."

Luke managed a smile that was exactly as sincere as the one she had given him. He put a few coins on the table, and took his leave.

He found the place easily, not because of the smell but because it was all too big to overlook. A series of businesses, each with a complex of buildings and enclosed yards surrounded by fences fifteen feet high. Signs in bright colors hung over office doors: Theophilus Freeman, Slaves; Charles LaMarque & Co., Negroes. Paper bills fluttered on every wall, lists of slaves, bank notices. EASY CREDIT TERMS in letters three inches high. Tucked in between businesses were taverns, a barbershop, a doss-house of the kind that catered to sailors and dockworkers.

Luke, caught up for a moment in the scene in front of him, paused to make sense of it all. The street was crowded with men who dressed and comported themselves as merchants, but there were also others strolling along as tourists do, looking at the slaves who had been brought outside as they would have studied hats in a milliner's window.

There were dozens of slaves, all the women standing on stools. Younger men, all wearing what amounted to a uniform of cheap blue fabric pantaloons and jackets, were paraded up and down.

Salesmen strutted up and down the banquette, so alike in dress, bearing, and tone of voice that they could have been brothers. Each seemed determined to outdo the next in the expansiveness of gesture and speech, singing out the virtues of one slave or another, calling out to passersby.

In front of the office where Theophilus Freeman's sign hung, a salesman had gathered a small group of men around him. He was a strongly built man with heavy jowls and a mustache like a dirty waterfall. Behind him four slaves stood on stepstools, two men and two women. Each of them stared into the middle distance, as if they had left their bodies behind and wanted nothing more to do with their physical selves.

"I tell you," the salesman was saying, in a clipped English that had its genesis north of Pennsylvania. "And I'll tell you true. This is a rare opportunity, four skilled, loyal niggers, well fed as you can see, niggers of the very best kind, all trained to work together. A carpenter, a cooper, a blacksmith, a cook and housekeeper. Their master died on them, a month ago it was, and I bought them from the estate. Because I said to myself, I said, Jack, these four niggers are more than the sum of their parts. Some man who knows his business is going to snap them up and be thankful for the opportunity."

Luke found it impossible to move or even look away. The salesman's patter held him right where he was, struck for the first time with a full understanding of what it meant to buy and sell human beings.

Slavery was a topic that didn't concern Luke greatly in the normal course of his life. There had been no slaves in Canada for so long that he had no memories of them, even as a boy, and there had been even less mention of them when he lived in Scotland. He took note of the debates in the newspapers the same way he took note of political campaigns, as a problem that existed in another part of the world and had nothing to do with him. That his stepmother and many others in the village where his father lived were committed abolitionists was known to him, as he knew what kind of corn they grew and which banks they dealt with in Albany.

But this. He could never have imagined something like this. People lined up like cattle at market, prodded and turned, directed to lift a foot or open the mouth. There was a knot in his throat, hard and sour.

One of the onlookers was asking questions. Prices and bank loans and how was a man to pay for anything with his cotton sitting on the docks for close to a year, and no money coming in?

The talk turned to the war and trade, and the salesman had a hard time steering them back to the subject at hand. Luke left them to it and went into the office, a long, shallow room bisected by a counter. It smelled of tobacco and sweat. A man standing over a ledger glanced up at him.

"I'm looking for Mr. Freeman."

The clerk turned his head to spit on the floor and then jerked a thumb toward one of the doors.

"In the showroom."

Luke hesitated at the door, trying to remember why he was here. The Chinese girl sold by her mistress to a slave trader, a girl who might be able to tell him something about Hannah. He steadied himself with a deeply drawn breath and went into the showroom.

It was very large, and here was the odor Luke had been warned about. Sawdust and lye and woodsmoke, sweat and wet wool and above all else, fear that hung like a mist in the dank air. A double line of slaves snaked around the perimeter of the showroom, two hundred or more, men and women and children in the same uniform of blue suit or calico dress. They seemed, at first glance, to be healthy. No one obviously ill or starving or mad with fear. The older slaves stood quietly, contained within themselves; the youngest, six or seven years old, had not learned to hide their fear, and many of them trembled.

The purchasers and onlookers moved around the room, stopping now and then to examine a slave, to give directions and ask questions.

Luke was trying to gather his wits when a slender man approached him. His neck linen was soiled and there was a sour smell about him, but he presented himself without hesitation. Theophilus Freeman, owner of the establishment, and in what way might he be helpful?

"I've got too much stock, sir, as you can see—" He gestured around the room. "Cotton and cane aren't the only goods piling up while this war drags on. Of course this works to your advantage, I can't deny it. Make me any reasonable offer—"

"I was told you purchased a young Chinese woman from the establishment around the corner."

Freeman tilted his head and pressed a knuckle to his lip, as if such transactions were so common he could hardly remember one in particular. Luke bit back his impatience and schooled his expression. If he could convince himself this was nothing more than a business transaction, he could manage Freeman well enough.

"I see I'm mistaken," Luke said. "If you'll excuse me then."

Freeman's expression sharpened. "No, sir, no indeed. You're not mistaken. I believe that Chinese gal is still here. Business is slow, as I've said, and the novelty items even slower. If you'll come with me—"

Luke followed the man out of a door that led into an

enclosed yard, twice again as big as the showroom had been, and twice again as crowded. He heard himself draw in a sharp breath, and Freeman glanced at him over his shoulder.

"You see my problem."

"Yes," Luke said. "I do."

"Every slave-pen in New Orleans looks like this," said Freeman. "It is truly a buyer's market, Mr.—"

Luke said, "Where is the girl?"

Freeman's mouth quirked. "I understand you are a busy man. I'll waste no more of your time. She's in the gaol here."

They came to a stop before the building that spanned the entire width of the lot. It was three stories high, each story connected by external staircases and balconies. Doors led from the balconies into the building, and a guard stood outside of each door. Freeman stopped to speak a few low words to one of the guards.

The man's already florid complexion flushed a shade deeper as Freeman took a key from the bunch at his belt and opened the door. A fetid odor welled out, unwashed bodies, waste, vomit. Freeman backed out immediately and shut the door. The conversation that followed with the guard was short and violent in tone. Then the trader visibly straightened his shoulders and turned back toward Luke.

"She will be brought to you in my office within the half hour. If you will wait?"

Luke wanted nothing more than to be gone, but he had come this far and he couldn't take the chance that the girl might know something of Hannah. He agreed to wait in the office, and then wished that he had offered to find his way there alone.

Freeman said, "Every color comes through here, you understand. Black as coal and quadroons with skin like milk. Redbones now and then, though there's not much market. Incorrigible, most of them."

"Redbone," Luke prompted.

"Mixed blood, mostly Indian," said Freeman. "Brings out the worst traits from every side. Surely you must see such things in the north?"

He was still trying to get more information, and Luke was more determined than ever to deny him. He said nothing at all, for fear of saying too much. It would be foolish to draw attention to himself.

Luke sat in Freeman's private office for a half hour, listening to conversations between clerks and customers. He had no choice; the walls were thin, and business was conducted in this part of the world in a vigorous and declamatory way, in a half dozen languages.

Soon he found himself trying to make sense of the bits of information that came to him. It seemed that the slaves in the showroom had been bought over the course of the summer months, from as far away as Tennessee. A steady stream of slaves made its way to New Orleans to fill the needs of planters who grew sugarcane and cotton. In the half hour that Luke sat in the dim office, a man bought a hundred and fifty human beings, to be delivered to his plantation the very same day.

But most of the business was between private citizens who were selling or buying slaves. Freeman's primary role seemed to be in brokering those sales and the long, wordy negotiations that preceded them. Luke heard talk of health and attitude and history, where slaves had been born and raised, what kind of work they had done, if they had husbands or wives or children nearby. A good part of the talk was dedicated to buyers and sellers reassuring each other that they were treating their chattels well.

I did promise Little Joe I wouldn't sell him away from his wife, but in such difficult times . . . Marcy went and hid her three oldest children in the ciprière and refused to cook another meal until I swore to her that I wouldn't sell them away from her . . . Can you imagine, a letter came a few months back from a slave woman I sold two years ago, wanting to know could I buy her back so she could be with her husband.

An uncomfortable ripple of laughter, and another voice asking who would be silly enough to take dictation from a nigger and then actually send it off. And if she really expected an answer from a busy man with a business to run.

Luke thought of the other establishments like this one, here and across the south. Thousands and thousands of people being bartered like meat. A whole economy based on buying and selling human beings. He was thinking about Freeman's casual tone when he spoke of Redbones when the man himself brought the Chinese girl to the door.

"She speaks French," Freeman told Luke. "And a little English. She will answer your questions, so she assures me."

Freeman was standing in the door behind the young woman. She might have been deaf for all the indication she gave that she heard him. Even after he was gone, she stood just where she was and made no eye contact.

She was so thin that it was hard to estimate her age. Her complexion was sallow and there was perspiration on her upper lip and brow, as if she might have a fever. Her hair was wet, and it was clear to Luke that she had been hastily cleaned up for his sake.

Luke said, "Do you want to sit down?" And when she didn't answer: "I need to ask you about the Indian woman who you nursed through an illness. Do you know who I mean?"

"*Oui.*" The voice was low and melodious and slightly rough. "I know."

"Can you tell me what happened to her? I need to find her."

For the first time the girl blinked.

The Indian woman had rented a room at Mme. Soileau's establishment, she told him. *Une femme de couleur libre*—a free woman of color—had paid for the room for a full week and then gone away and never came again. When the rent was gone, the Indian woman had been put out on the street at dawn on the same day, as Madame directed. An hour later when Girl took the slop jars out, she had disappeared. Picked up by the street cleaners and taken to a pauper's grave, perhaps. She had been very ill, with marsh fever.

Luke hadn't really expected any other report, but still he could hardly swallow down his disappointment.

"And no one else came to ask after her? Did she ask you to go see anyone on her behalf?"

The girl shook her head. "She spoke sometimes in her fever, but in a language I didn't know. Sometimes she cried aloud. But mostly she was quiet." The oval face lifted suddenly. "She offered to buy me if I would help her get away."

Luke managed a small smile. "That sounds like her." He stood. "I will of course fulfill my sister's promise to you."

The black eyes met his for a moment.

"You are her brother?"

"Yes."

The sleek head ducked. She said, "I didn't help her."

"Nevertheless," Luke said.

She shook her head. "It would be a waste of your money. I will be dead in a day or two."

She said this with such calm assurance that Luke was

momentarily unsure how to respond. He cleared his throat. "I can see that you're ill. I will pay for a doctor."

For the first time she smiled. "That's how I ended up here in the first place. When Madame realized I was failing she sold me quick."

Luke said, "I am not made of the same stuff as Mme. Soileau. If your illness is so far advanced that there is no hope, you could at least have a comfortable bed, and food."

"No," said the Chinese girl. "I want nothing now but death itself."

It was early evening and the rain had stopped, so Luke walked the streets of the city as one of a crowd. People were eager to be out-of-doors finally after rain that lasted days.

"It's like living inside the Book of Revelations," he heard an elderly American woman say to her companion. The two ladies sat in a carriage with gold-painted trim and an elaborate and meaningless crest on the door.

When his stomach reminded him that he must eat, Luke thought of the ride back to the inn and decided it would be best to stay in the city. To leave now would be to admit defeat, and he was far from that point. Nowhere near giving up, not on his sister or his wife or the boy.

He found what he wanted on Rampart Street. The inn stood across from a graveyard that looked like a child's model of an ancient city.

The landlord was a Frenchman, whippet thin, who spoke the local French so quickly that Luke had to concentrate to follow the patter. The man showed Luke a room on the top floor, small and spare, but it had been aired and the blanket on the bed looked clean. The room looked out over the street, the graveyard, and a large open

square. There was a stable behind the inn. Luke paid to
have a boy fetch the horse from the blacksmith where he
had left it; he paid for clean water and for a week's lodging. He asked for a bottle of brandy and had to settle for
one of rye whisky, to be brought to the room. Then he
went down to eat.

In the common room Luke found a spot close enough
to the hearth to make steam rise off his damp clothes and
he settled himself. He ordered food and ale and applied
himself to it.

The table next to him was crowded with tankards and
bowls of stew. The men around the table were in uniform.
Mostly Americans, by the sound of them, and from the
south. They had the look of men who knew how to live
rough and would think nothing of it, but to Luke's eye
there was something a little off about them. Soldiers hardened to battle had a way of treating their weapons, keeping
them near and ready. These men shunted their weapons off
in a pile, and never even glanced in that direction.

Luke thought of his father in this place, or tried to.
Nathaniel Bonner of Lake in the Clouds would have rejected out of hand the idea that his eldest daughter could
be brought low by swamp fever. He would have a dozen
ideas on where to start looking for two missing women
and an infant. Luke would have given a great deal to talk
to his father. To any trustworthy man who might have an
idea on where to go and what to try next.

A servingwoman brought him his food: venison, corn
bread, stewed greens. She had a quick smile and she leaned
in close so that Luke caught the scent of her: woodsmoke
and roasting meat and the sweet smell of a generous and
willing woman. Her cleavage was deep and very dark.
Luke buried his face in his tankard and thought of Jennet.

When he looked up she said, "You speak good French
for an American."

In French he said, "And you speak good American for a Creole."

The men at the next table broke out into rough laughter. The servingwoman winked at them and then turned her attention back to Luke.

"*Tabernac!*" she said. "You know how to laugh, you. Where you from, *chèr*?"

"New-York State, near the Mohawk River."

"Far from home."

"Too far," Luke agreed.

"Louie tell you about the drums when he show you that room upstairs?"

"Drums?"

"I thought not. Tomorrow is Sunday, *oui*? Half of Africa will be out there——" She jerked her chin in the direction of the street. "Congo Square. Dancing and pipes and drums until late in the night. A deaf man couldn't sleep through that. I'd look for another room tomorrow, if I were you. Unless it ain't sleeping you got on your mind."

With her thumb she rubbed a glistening damp spot between her breasts just where the cleavage began, and winked at him.

When she was out of earshot one of the men at the next table turned toward Luke. He was trim and neat and looked like a schoolteacher, though his clothes and his hands showed him to be a man who spent his days working out-of-doors, and working hard.

He said, "I do not usually mix in another man's business, but if I may offer a word of caution? Anne-Marie will entertain you very ably, but she would leave you with more than fond memories." He lifted one shoulder in a Gallic shrug that matched his accent exactly. "One of my colleagues learned this lesson at significant personal cost."

"He's talking about Cal here," said another of the men,

this one American. "He's still suffering the aftereffects of Anne-Marie."

Luke said, "Thank you for the tip." And: "You men been in town long enough to know your way around?"

"Seems like we been here for goddamned ever," said the second man.

"If I may—" the Frenchman offered a hand that was fire red with a recent scrubbing. "Major Arsène Lacarrière-Latour, at your service. We are engineers with the Seventh Military District."

Luke thought of the miles of riverfront, acres of swamp cut by winding bayous, about the forests that crowded right up to the city. "You've got a big job in front of you, if it's your job to keep the British out of New Orleans."

That observation earned him an invitation to join them at their table. He introduced himself as Luke Bonner, and was relieved to find out that all the men aside from Latour were from Kentucky and Virginia. A man from New-York was more likely than not to have heard the name Bonner, and to know something about the family.

Melchior Langpole was a Kentuckian. He had a big voice and a bigger way about him, and nobody seemed surprised or put out when he took it upon himself to introduce each of the men at the table: Calvin Cook, Moses Blakeslee, Monty MacIntyre.

"And this pretty one here is my little brother, Quentin."

"Quentin's the one can steer you in the direction of a woman who won't give you a dose," Cal Cook volunteered. "It's those red cheeks and the curls. He looks like an angel in your grandma's Bible, don't he?"

Quentin Langpole was clearly used to being teased, because the only response he offered was a soft belch.

"And there's his God-given gift for stimulating conversation," Blakeslee said dryly.

"Drunk or sober I can still outcipher any of you in my

head," Quentin said, belching with more force. "That's all you need to know."

MacIntyre had been studying Luke with open distrust. He was a sour-faced man with a shock of gray-streaked hair, vaguely cross-eyed, with a nose that was the shape and approximate color of a ripening strawberry. He claimed to be from Virginia but Luke would have wagered quite a lot that he was less than one generation out of Scotland. Luke had lived in Annandale long enough to recognize a certain type of Scot, one he didn't come across often: suspicious to the bone, meaner still, and stupid enough to think himself quick.

When MacIntyre leaned forward and shot a question in Luke's direction, he was ready for it.

"What brings you down to New Orleans all the way from New-York State?"

"Let the man tell his story in his own time," said Langpole.

Luke raised a conciliatory hand. "I'll tell you how I got here, though it's a story you're like to have heard before. I signed onto a schooner on a run from Pensacola to Barataria. This was back in September. Two days out of port the *Puma* ran us down—"

Every man at the table sat up straight at the mention of the *Puma*.

"—boarded us, and the next thing I knew I was humping sugar barrels on the São Paulo docks."

"That was bad luck of the first order, running into Ten-Pint. Unless you found privateering to your tastes."

Luke looked MacIntyre directly in the eye and raised one brow, and the older man cleared his throat and looked away from the challenge.

Latour said, "If I may inquire, how did you remove yourself from Ten-Pint's ship?"

Luke shrugged. "First day in port I knocked the watch on the head, took off, and signed onto the *Cartagena,* and here I am."

The men looked at each other. Luke said, "I've heard all the stories about Ten-Pint, and I'm not worried. I can take care of myself, on land or sea."

"The whole damn city is crawling with idle sailors," grunted MacIntyre. "And here's one more, with naught to do but get in the way."

"Major General Jackson will put us to work," Luke said easily. "If he ever gets here."

Latour stiffened slightly, and Luke shot him a questioning glance. "He's here?"

"He's on his way from Mobile. He'll be here within the week."

"And high time," said Langpole. "If we're going to dance with the Tories, well, I'd just as soon get to it. Where did Anne-Marie get to? I'm dry as a bone."

When the conversation finally turned in the direction of the subjects that interested Luke, he found that the engineers knew less about New Orleans than he'd hoped. Latour had been moving around the city and the countryside making maps, but it was hard work. The local landowners were suspicious and unwilling to answer questions.

"They don't like us," Cook said. "Want nothing to do with Americans, though I guarantee you they'll scream loud enough for us when the Tories start running off with their slaves."

There was more to say about the city's fortifications— or lack of them. Langpole cleared off the table and brought over an armful of kindling so they could build a model of the city. As the engineers talked, Luke began to fully comprehend the impossibility of keeping the British out.

Latour ran his finger through the long puddle poured in a serpentine shape to represent the Mississippi.

"It's more of a sieve than a city," he said. "And not just any sieve," he said, thumping the table. "How do you say *rouillé?*"

"Rusty," Luke supplied. "*Rouillé comme un vieux ongle.*"

"Like an old nail, *exactement,*" said Latour. He put a hand on Luke's shoulder. "You speak French like a Canadian, my friend."

"I'm from New-York State," Luke said, grinning to hide his discomfort. He poured Latour more ale with a generous hand. "We live cheek and jowl with the damn Canadians. They near killed my little brother in a border skirmish, two years ago now."

He felt MacIntyre's gaze on him, rheumy and suspicious, and was glad that Cook picked up the conversation to take it in another direction.

"Don't know why the bloody Tories want this bloody town. It's a fishy kind of place. Bloody damp all the time."

Latour seemed the only one of the engineers who liked New Orleans. The others ticked off the city's many sins: too crowded, too hot in the summer, pissy with rain in the winter, damp, Langpole asserted, as a baby's ass, all the time. There were bugs the size of small dogs that flew into a man's mouth when he was sleeping, the water tasted like mud and was full of creatures of biblical ferocity.

Most of all the American engineers were scandalized by the sheer numbers of free blacks, some of whom actually owned property and businesses and slaves of their own.

"It ain't right," said MacIntyre. "It's an insult to have them lording it over us, come down here to save their sorry black asses from the Tory bastards."

Luke thought of Jennet, who had no patience with bullies or blustering idiots, and would have cut this one into small pieces with the sharp side of her tongue.

"If it was up to me," MacIntyre went on, "we'd march them all into the sea, black and red."

"And who's going to be out there digging in the mud and blocking up the bayous?" asked Latour. "Major Plauché and the Creole sons of planters and merchants? You?"

"I'm not afraid of hard work," MacIntyre said, leaning forward so that the edge of the table pressed into the soft swell of belly. "And I say we'd be better off without them. Send every man jack of them back to wherever they come from to start with."

Blakeslee said, "MacIntyre, you are talking stupid again. The Indians were here first. It was us who came over from the old country. Your mama and daddy, for instance, on the boat from Scotland."

"I don't believe they were here first," said MacIntyre, thumping his tankard. "What proof have they got?"

There was a short silence, and then Quentin said, "Some good-looking women in this city. Friendly, too." He grinned at Luke. "What's your poison? White, black, or Redbone?"

Luke took a swallow of his ale and made an attempt to pitch his voice just right: interested, but not too.

"Indians in the city? I haven't seen any."

"The army boys been right busy killing 'em off," MacIntyre agreed. "But they're here, and more's the pity. There's a Choctaw camp between the city and the swamp, maybe a half hour due north on foot."

"And the Redbone slaves off in those shacks down at the end of Rampart," volunteered Blakeslee.

"I hear there's a new hospital for the Redbones," said the younger Langpole. "With a medicine woman to sing over 'em when they're feeling poorly."

Luke saw the other men around the table take this news in, measure it, and find it lacking.

Cook said, "What in the name of sonny Jesus and his blessed mama are you talking about?"

"That's the most foolish thing I ever heard," agreed

MacIntyre. "The army boys risk life and limb clearing out the savages. Ain't nobody going to be opening up no clinic to patch 'em up. Clean out your ears, boy. You must have heard wrong."

Quentin looked affronted. "Suit yourself," he said. "If you're so smart you don't need me to tell you nothing."

Luke was still trying to figure out how to get more information from Quentin Langpole about a clinic where an Indian woman looked after her own kind when the young man pushed back from the table and wobbled off.

At the doorway he said, "There's friendlier company to be had in a pigsty."

"You best go find yourself some of that," said Blakeslee with a boisterous wave of the hand. The boy's whole face contorted like a child faced with a particularly difficult puzzle. Then he shrugged and lurched out the door.

CHAPTER 25

At the supper table on Saturday evening Rachel made an announcement: She had a plan, and it had to do with the first Sunday in Advent, an event of great social significance in Catholic New Orleans.

The plan had delighted Jennet to such a degree that the other adults had kept their doubts to themselves, which was no doubt part of the plan itself. Standing at the window on Sunday morning, Hannah acknowledged that the girl had outmaneuvered them all.

People were streaming from all directions toward the great cathedral on the Place d'Armes. They carried evergreen boughs or wreaths of woven myrtle branches, with costly wax candles tied at the four compass points. The smell of the evergreens rose in the chill morning air, sweet and sharp. Tonight, Hannah thought, she would dream of the Endless Forests, of black spruce and white pine, beech and hemlock and cedar.

Jennet was listening closely to Hannah's description of what was going on in the street. There were maids in threadbare winter cloaks that showed flashes of white apron with every step, couples trailing clots of children with faces scrubbed to a shine, army officers and gentlemen with tall hats on horseback, ladies in carriages that seethed with yards of silk and brocade and taffeta, like milk pots coming to the boil. Rich and poor, workingmen and their families and their masters, slaves and free people of color, it seemed that the whole city must press itself into the cathedral for Mass today.

"Has she gone past yet?" Jennet asked. She was walking up and down the room with the baby on her shoulder. He had one fist wrapped in the fabric of her shawl and the other lodged in his mouth, and he looked as content and healthy a child as had ever lived, in spite of his mother's agitation. Young Nathaniel had far more of his father's solid temperament than his mother's more volatile one.

Jennet was dressed in plain linen and a workday cloak like one a shopgirl or lady's maid might wear, and she had a pair of Clémentine's clogs on her feet.

Hannah wished again that she could call the whole ridiculous plan to a halt. Instead she studied the street, and said, "She is coming now."

Jennet drew in a loud breath. "Is he with her?"

"Yes, Honoré is there, too, on horseback behind the carriage."

Though the Poiterins could not see her where she stood—and would not recognize her if they did—Hannah stepped back from the window, but not before she saw Ben Savard fall into the crowd just behind Mme. Poiterin's carriage.

"And there is Ben, too, as he said he would be."

Rachel had enlisted her uncle Ben as a primary player in the morning's scheme. While the Mass was being said, it would be safe for Jennet to be out walking, if she took reasonable care to keep her face hidden. Rachel would guide Jennet through the city streets and point out the most important places. Ben would do his part by keeping an eye on the Poiterins, and intervene if something threatened to go wrong.

"What is he to do?" Hannah had asked Rachel. "Knock

Mme. Poiterin on the head if she decides to leave Mass early?"

"You must give my uncle credit," Rachel said, with all the aplomb of a sixteen-year-old set on getting her way. "He is very inventive."

For the next ten minutes Hannah watched quietly while the crowd trickled down to the perennially late and the last of the stragglers, and then Jennet said, "It will be safe now."

It was not safe at all, but Hannah understood that this was a chance they must take. Jennet handed her son to Hannah, took up her cloak, and went to the door. Rachel was waiting in the hall, hopping with excitement, her round cheeks flushed with color.

"A half hour," Hannah called after them. "And no longer."

With her nephew half asleep on her shoulder Hannah watched Rachel and Jennet skipping down the street, two girls on a lark, and for a moment she wished she had gone with them.

Julia came into the parlor directly from her morning duties in the clinic, with a cloth still bound around her hair, a swipe of near-dried blood on the bib of her apron. She smelled of camphor and quinine and worry.

"How long?"

Hannah looked at her. "Forty minutes."

"Is it very bad of me to want to throttle my own daughter?"

"I think it would be unusual if you didn't feel that way now and then. She is a good girl, at heart."

"But so thoughtless at times," Julia said. And: "There they are now. Rachel is laughing, so perhaps it all went well after all."

Jennet looked up at the window and met Hannah's gaze.

"Perhaps," Hannah said, and sat down to wait.

Rachel felt obliged to recount the whole of their walk, where they had gone, which houses and shops they had passed.

"And when we came across Mrs. Patterson and her party they didn't even look at Jennet," Rachel continued, triumphant. "They took her for the servant she was meant to be, and didn't I say so? Really, we could go out more often."

"And where was it you came across Mrs. Patterson?" Julia asked, her tone deceptively light.

"Don't worry, Mama, I didn't venture onto the Place d'Armes. I did keep my word. We saw Mrs. Patterson and her party on the rue de Chartres near Canal Street. Mrs. Patterson and both her sons and"—she paused for effect—"Christian Renaud was with them. You look surprised, Mama. I was surprised, too; I thought he would be at Mass."

But to Hannah Rachel didn't look at all surprised; she looked content, and a little smug. Like a child who has mastered a magic trick she has been told was beyond her abilities.

"What did you think of him?" Rachel was asking Jennet. "Is he not wonderfully handsome, and so polite?"

"Aye," Jennet said, her smile small and tight. "He seemed to be both things, and more."

Hannah followed Jennet to their chamber a few minutes later, and found that she had already settled into the chair by the window that looked out on the gallery and put the baby to her breast. Her eyes were closed, and the hollows beneath her cheekbones and at the corners of her eyes were blue with shadow.

"I can feel you looking at me," Jennet said.

"Then tell me, whatever it is, so I can stop."

Nathaniel's fist thumped his mother's chest and he mewled, unsettled, while she shifted herself to his satisfaction.

She said, "Kit Wyndham is in New Orleans. He calls himself Christian Reynaud."

The silence between them was punctuated by the rhythm of the baby's swallow and the sound of wooden clogs on the cobblestones of the courtyard. The churchgoers were coming home. In a few minutes' time the platters and plates would come up the gallery stairs and be set out in the family dining room. She and Jennet would go in to dinner, and sit there with the Savards and eat well and fully.

Kit Wyndham was in New Orleans, posing as a merchant.

"He recognized you?"

"Oh, yes," Jennet said.

Hannah said, "He is a spy."

The expression on Jennet's face was closed and tight. She said, "Luke told me that Kit was bound for this part of the world. With everything that's happened, I had completely forgot about it."

Hannah went to the window. Above the kitchen the balcony of Ben's small apartment was empty, though the louvered doors stood open. The room behind them might have been empty. Or someone might be standing there, watching this window.

"You had no idea?" Jennet asked.

"Kit told me he was on his way back to Canada," Hannah said.

She thought of Kit, who had been a friend to her and more. Who had meant to be at home by now, and married. Or so he had told her.

"He risks a great deal," Jennet said. "If he's found out he will hang."

In the next room Julia was scolding Henry for putting his dirty shoes on his bedcover.

"I expect the war office changed his orders," Hannah said. "But really, the question is, what do we do now?"

Jennet said, "I can think of three or four possibilities. The first would be to give him the choice between leaving the city, or turning himself in. Of course he could counter with threats of his own. I am as vulnerable as he is. Do you think he will put friendship above duty?"

Hannah thought of Kit as she had last seen him, on board the *Patience* in the tiny cabin she had had for her own. His hair brightened by the sun and his skin damp and cool to the touch. The expression on his face when he was over her, inside of her, around her. As if he had no other place to be, and could imagine no other world than the one they made between them. And still he had always been, must always be, a stranger to her. She had never lost sight of that one elemental truth: There was no place in the world where they could be together and happy, and so they must be apart.

"Hannah?" Jennet's voice came thin as paper.

Hannah thought of the comforting things she might say, the words that would settle Jennet and buy her rest. Words they could not afford. She said, "Kit will do what duty demands of him."

Jennet stroked her son's cheek. "That is true of all of us," she said. And then: "How will you find him?"

Of course there was only one way, and they both knew it. "I will ask Jean-Benoît for his help." She did not look at her cousin when she said this, but she felt the weight of Jennet's consideration.

CHAPTER 26

In New Orleans, Sunday was divided directly down the middle: In the mornings the churches and chapels demanded their due, and the faithful responded. French, Creole, Spanish, black, and white, most of the city was Catholic, and observant; the primarily Protestant Americans, more recently arrived and less entrenched, found their way to places of worship that were remarkable for their modesty and small size. Rachel sometimes attended services with her uncle and aunt Livingston; Paul Savard had no use for priests of any stripe.

Julia Savard went to a Quaker meeting that numbered eight souls, including, it turned out, her son Henry and her brother-in-law Ben. That revelation had first surprised Hannah, and then it had seemed logical and even oddly satisfying.

"You disliked the idea of me studying for the priesthood," Ben observed. "But a Quaker meeting doesn't shock you?"

"I'm not easily shocked," Hannah said, adopting the light tone she cultivated so carefully to use with him. "And my experiences with Quakers have all been good."

Ben watched her from beneath a lowered brow, and smiled to himself.

Sunday afternoons were so different from the mornings

that the whole city might have been moved in the blink of an eye to another continent. As soon as the church bells had faded away, the drums began on the far side of the city. It was a sound pointedly ignored by most of white New Orleans, which retired to parlors to visit or nap or play cards. It was the people of color—those who had come directly from Africa, or from the islands, or whose mothers and grandmothers had been born in slavery, free and slave alike—who answered the call to come to the large open space at the edge of the city called Congo Square.

Which was what made the drums so enticing, Jennet said. Something forbidden was always far sweeter than what was freely available, and African drums and dancing must engage the interest of any young person. Rachel's curiosity was natural, and unrelenting. Every Sunday she asked for permission to go and watch, and every Sunday Julia refused.

This was another one of the areas where Paul Savard let his wife deal with her teenage daughter, and Hannah had to admire him for his ability to keep his opinion to himself while Rachel asked the same questions from a dozen different angles. Julia always answered quietly, calmly, and without wavering from her position: Sunday afternoons were the one time that slaves were free to meet and socialize with other slaves and free people of color. It was their time and place, and should be respected as such.

"You'll have to stop treating me like a child sooner or later," Rachel would say, unflustered and unmoved by logic.

When she heard that Hannah was to go to Congo Square on the very Sunday she had had her successful outing with Jennet, Rachel's face went very red and then pale, and finally she left the parlor for her chamber, where she shut the door with something just short of a bang.

·   ·   ·   ·

Hannah had no special interest in Congo Square, but neither could she find any reason to refuse Ben's suggestion, which had been couched—whether by chance or design, she could not tell—in terms she could not logically refuse. There were many healers and herbalists among the slaves and free people of color, and there was one woman in particular she should meet. It would be easiest to arrange an introduction in public, on a Sunday afternoon.

She went down to meet Ben in the courtyard with the idea that it would be best to ask his advice about Kit Wyndham straightaway. But she hesitated too long over the question of whether she needed to disclose the full nature of her attachment to Wyndham, and by the time she had an idea of where to start, they had been caught up in a tumbling river of people.

It was late November and the sky, lowering and gray, threatened with rain or sleet or both; the temperature had dropped, but that seemed of no concern to anyone at all. There was an excitement in the crowd that reminded Hannah of market fairs she had visited as a child, in Scotland and nearer home, where jugglers and men on stilts and storytellers made magic. Except she had never been to a fair like this one, where out of fifty faces only one was white.

Ben steered her toward one of these, a priest by his dress. He was introduced as Père Tomaso.

"My sister-in-law has told me about you," Hannah said. She had to raise her voice to be heard above the musicians. "Thank you very much for your assistance in her time of need."

Ben and the priest exchanged quick glances. Tomaso Delgado said, "I was happy to be of help to her and I hope you will call on me again if the need arises."

Hannah wondered what help a Catholic priest might offer them in their current situation, and thought of the Poiterins.

"I hope that will not be necessary," she said. "But I will remember your offer."

When the priest had disappeared back into the crowd she asked Ben about him.

"We grew up together," he said, and seemed to think that was enough of an answer. In fact it was becoming more difficult to talk at all as the crowds grew in size and the noise increased.

The drums were both immediately familiar and completely unlike the drums of her experience among the Kahnyen'kehàka or the Seneca or any of the tribes to the west where she had traveled with her husband. African drums and African rhythms, distinct and unmistakable, though Hannah could not describe the difference to herself. And then the oddest thing of all: The street they walked down was part of the United States of America, but now in the swelling crowds Hannah saw not one white face, not even when they passed out of the funnel of the rue Orleans and into the open area Americans called Congo Square.

The square was uncobbled but the earth had been hard packed, pounded to a smooth surface that stretched right up to a maze of live oak, cypress, and sycamore that would give way to ciprière.

Ben put a hand on Hannah's shoulder and steered her past the vendors who had spread out their goods on blankets. Men and women shouted out to the passersby, joked with them, encouraged them to buy. A woman with a basket of bread called *Qui a faim?* and *Bon pain! Le meilleur pain!*

There was a world of food here, for those who had the means to indulge. Stews of bacon, corn, turnips, sweet potatoes, okra, and peas served in hollow gourds, mounds of oysters, piles of crab, roasted quail and rabbit and squirrel, yams that had been skewered onto sharp sticks and thrust into coals, buttermilk dispensed by the dipperful, sticks of sugar-cane, wedges of pie, and a dozen different kinds of fritters.

The faces and bodies around her were just as various as the food. Hannah had the strange idea that all of Africa had squeezed itself into Congo Square for the afternoon, not to mingle, but to re-create the continent itself and the tribal boundaries, to make that old world new and real again. The men and women who had been born in Africa and come to this country on slave ships were called *bossal,* and they kept themselves separate from the Creoles, some slave, some free, who had been born in the islands or on this continent.

Ben put names to the individual groups for her: Senagalese from the islands off the western coast of Africa, Mandingo from the Gambia River, Foulas from the Niger, the Susu and Bakongo and Ciokwe, Ashanti and Fanti, Boule, Agni, Bete, Malinka. Tall and short, with sharp long noses or broad flat ones, heavy-lipped or thin; those who weren't dancing stood in groups speaking the languages of their homelands.

She thought to ask Ben how he knew the things he shared so easily. Whether he had set out to learn the distinctions, or had been raised understanding them, and why. More and more she wondered about his mother, and what kind of woman had raised a man who could move so easily from group to group, respected by all of them, though he seemed to belong nowhere.

Bossal or Creole, Hannah found everyone simply preferred to ignore her, which suited her very well. It gave her leave to study her surroundings, and to wish that she had some of her younger sister's artistic talent, so that she need not depend on words alone to describe this place to her family, when she was with them again.

Most of the men wore homespun shirts and well-worn, much-mended pantaloons, but a few stood out for dress that must be hidden away for days like this one, the kinds of things they had worn as free people in their homeland, so strange to see here. A group of three elderly men wore lengths of bright cotton wrapped around their bodies so that one shoulder was bare, and they looked as if the cold had nothing to do with them. They were straight of back and proud in bearing. Tomorrow they would return to working in the rice field or driving mules or loading barges, but for these few hours they were chiefs or kings or princes, and they reclaimed their own names and remembered the stories of their forefathers. Each of the three held a long wooden pole, intricately carved, topped by what looked to be birds of prey. None of them looked at Hannah.

Of the many hundreds of people Hannah saw, fewer than half seemed to be of mixed blood. There were men and women with freckled skin the color of weak tea, eyes that were green or gray, and hair that was not so black as her own, but showed a reddish cast. Some of these people would be free, and others slaves, or so it seemed by the cost of their clothes and baubles.

Most of the women wore shawls against the winter air and loose dresses with skirts of many layers; some wore necklaces of beads and seeds and polished and carved stone. Hannah stood out not just for her color, but because she wore a plain gown and shawl and sturdy boots and a plain headcloth to cover her plaited hair. Clémentine had offered her a cotton tignon, yellow with a pattern of flowers in red and blue; she would have folded it for Hannah so that it stood up in points around her head, like a crown. But that would have been as absurd as one of the African women coming here in a Kahnyen'kehàka overdress and leggings. Hannah was curious about these people and well disposed toward them, but she could not pretend to be one of them.

The noise was tremendous—hundreds of voices in dozens of languages, the vendors calling out their wares, and above and through it all, the music.

The musicians squatted in a crescent near the edge of the open square. Some hunkered over drums, others squatted and held them between their knees or in the crook of an arm. The drums were not so different from the ones at home: finely scraped skins stretched tight over hollow gourds or logs. Some were painted with symbols or trimmed with squirrel and deer tail that bounced with every stroke of finger or palm. There were pipes of reed and quill, penny-whistles and tambourines and triangles made of iron, and a stringed instrument that looked like a violin with a body made from half a gourd. A tall man, bare-chested and shiny with sweat, held a horn to his mouth as long as his arms. Scars ran from his temples down his cheeks and neck, not so much tattoos as scars deliberately drawn.

The dancers made music of their own by keeping the movement of their bodies in strict time with the instruments as they leaped and plunged and stamped bare feet into the dirt, the bells at wrist and elbow and ankle jangling. Three or four or five hundred people, Hannah could not get a real sense of how many they were, all moving together in a circle, shuffling forward and then back, forward and back, swaying together as though governed by a knowing wind. Now and then someone would begin to jump and others would follow, and for a while the whole ring would be moving in two directions at once, circles within circles.

Hannah felt herself in two places: standing on the ground with Ben just behind her, in a bubble of sound and smell and color, and at the same time looking down on all of it, this bubble-bright world under the gray cap of winter sky.

Next to her ear Ben shouted, "This way." He took her wrist in his hand and pulled, and she followed him, winding through the crowd, head turned back toward the dancers and the music, her curiosity stronger than her need to be away.

•   •   •

The five old women sat together on makeshift chairs fashioned out of rolled rugs, at a spot far enough away for them to hear each other talk and close enough to make out the faces of the dancers. As Hannah walked toward them next to Ben, she understood that she was being brought to meet these women as someone would be called before the clan mothers of the Kahnyen'kehàka at Good Pasture.

It was hard to tell their ages, though Hannah guessed that none was younger than fifty. The frailest of the women, with skin the color of fresh-turned earth that had been worn down thin over the years, might have been ninety or more. There was no need to tell Hannah what to do; she had been raised among strong women, and knew what they were owed.

Hannah crouched and bowed her head and shoulders. She introduced herself in French and English, and thanked each of them for seeing her. From the corner of her eye she saw two of the younger women exchanging glances.

Ben stepped forward and then went down on one knee to clasp the hands of the oldest woman, who smiled at him widely—her teeth were still strong, though they had yellowed with age—and cupped his cheek in her hand.

"You been too long away, Jean-Benoît," she said to him in the wobbling, creaking voice of the very old. "Set down here and let me look at you. It's like having Amélie back with us, to see you. My but I miss her, your *maman*."

Ben called the oldest woman Maman Antoinette, and he spoke to her with a tone that hovered on an exact point between respect and playfulness. In Hannah's experience few men really knew how to talk to old women, but this one did and they loved him for it. Hannah understood that if Ben had not brought her here, these women would have never deigned to look at her.

Finally Maman Antoinette called Hannah closer and took her hands. She studied them for a long moment, front and then back, though Hannah had the idea she was not so much seeing as she was simply thinking.

"Listen to me now," she said, and she described a set of symptoms. Twice Hannah had to confer with Ben to see if she had understood a French term correctly. When Maman Antoinette had finished, Hannah thought for a minute.

She said, "The whites call this disease you are talking about the bloody flux, or dysentery. It most often strikes in the late summer and fall, where there are too many people living too closely together, and there is too little clean water. It will kill a child in two days, and a grown man in a week, if it is not stopped."

She paused to collect her thoughts, and felt the eyes of all the women on her.

"The whites treat dysentery with aconite and ipecac, and sometimes with magnesia. One of my teachers believed that if the cycle could be broken, and the body given a chance to rest, there was a good chance of quick recovery. He sometimes gave laudanum to enforce bed rest and relief of anxiety. My mother's people treat it with winterbloom."

"And which cure do you prefer?" asked Maman Antoinette.

"I would not know," Hannah said. "Until I examined the patient. There is no one medicine that suits every person."

There was a flicker of a smile at the corner of the old woman's mouth. She said, "Did you come here to take this good man away from his people?"

Hannah was surprised enough to jerk away, or she would have, if Maman Antoinette's hold hadn't been so very firm.

"Maman Antoinette." Ben's voice was low but sharp.

"Hush now," she said. "This Indian woman and me, we understand each other. Let us talk."

Her eyes were a rich dark brown, clear still after so many years of seeing. Hannah looked at her directly, calmed her thoughts, and said the first thing that came to mind.

"I take nothing that isn't given to me out of free will."

Maman Antoinette let Hannah's wrists go. She made a gesture with one hand, braiding her long fingers together and flicking them. "Take her to Zuzu," she said. "Be sure to say I sent her."

The crowd was worse now than it had been, and Hannah followed Ben closely until they broke free of it, suddenly, at the corner of Rampart and Saint Philip. It was as if they had passed through an invisible gate beyond which the negroes dare not go. Even as the idea was forming itself in Hannah's mind, she took in the fact that the street here wasn't really empty at all.

Some fifty men, all white, had gathered at this corner to watch the dancing. They had come on foot or on horse-back; some stood in small groups on the banquette; a few had gathered on balconies. There were middle-class shop-keepers and teenage boys, men in expensively cut coats and tall beaver hats and others in homespun, militia soldiers and—she craned her neck to make sure—two young priests. Some of the men looked bored, as if this were a the-ater piece too often seen; others wore expressions of great excitement, tinged with studied disapproval or outright fas-cination. One man in dusty black worn to fraying at wrist and elbow leaned against a wall, a board propped on his ab-domen while he sketched with a piece of charcoal.

A cluster of fine coaches stood blocking the lane, leather and silver and brass polished to reflect the meager Novem-ber sunlight. Rich men reclined under blue-gray clouds of tobacco smoke from pipes and cigars. Some of them wore the gaudy uniforms of the militia, brilliant blues and scar-lets, plumed hats, silver buttons, heavy epaulettes of gold and silver that caught what little sunlight was to be had, but most were in civilian dress of the finest sort.

When Hannah and Ben had turned into the side street, they stopped in the shadows.

"Did you recognize any of them?" Hannah asked.

Ben gave her a bemused look. "I recognized all of them. I have lived here all my life." He stepped deeper into the shadows beneath a balcony and Hannah followed him.

"Do you see Edward Livingston?"

Hannah did, and said so.

"Those three men opposite him? The whole Committee on Defense. Marigny, Rofignac, Louaillier."

Names familiar to Hannah from Rachel's stories and the newspapers. "They're waiting for word of Major General Jackson's arrival."

Ben nodded. "And did you see Honoré Poiterin? In the carriage with Major Plauché and Captain Morgan and Philogène Favrot."

Hannah had seen Poiterin only a few times and from a distance, and never at rest, as he was now. He lounged against bolsters, overdressed, languid, bored. His complexion was naturally highly colored, but today it seemed especially flushed with the crowd or liquor or thoughts of the women who danced, breasts swaying, in the open square.

Hannah said, "If only I had a rifle."

"He will die," said Ben easily. "Just not today. Unless he goads Philogène Favrot into a duel, then he may well be dead at sunrise."

Hannah could see that the young man sitting opposite Poiterin was pale with anger, and barely in control of his temper.

"I think sometimes that is really what he wants," Ben said quietly.

"If only someone would oblige him." Hannah turned her head away.

She felt Ben's hand on her shoulder, and she resisted the urge to lean toward him, but she couldn't keep herself from saying what came to mind. "I am even less of a Quaker than you are."

When he pressed her shoulder Hannah let herself be turned, and then she looked up into Ben's face. There was no affection, no lust, no longing, nothing but simple curiosity in his expression.

"You look at me like a creature you have never seen before."

"That is exactly what you are," Ben said evenly. Then something passed over his face, uncertainty or distrust.

He said, "Poiterin is looking this way. Don't turn around, just follow me." A few minutes later he said: "It would be best if you told me what it is you're worried about."

Oddly enough, the words came quite easily. Hannah had told the Savards the story of how Jennet had been abducted in Canada and of the search for her that had lasted for more than a year, but she had never mentioned Major Christian Pelham Wyndham of the King's Rangers.

"He was supposed to bring Dégre back for trial, and so we joined forces and traveled together," Hannah finished. "But Dégre was killed outright, and so he started back for Canada empty-handed. Or so I believed."

"I could find him if you like," Ben said. "What do you want me to do? Turn him in as a spy?"

"No," Hannah said firmly. "He has seen Jennet, and he could cause her as much trouble as we cause him. I don't want to see him."

And that was the truth, she realized as the words left her mouth. She didn't care to see Kit Wyndham, because she had nothing to say to him, and only questions that he wouldn't answer.

She said, "Tell me about this woman you are taking me to see."

"She is called Zuzu," Ben said. "Maman Antoinette's only daughter." The two women had come from the islands more than forty years ago, and were the most respected healers in the community of free people of color.

"Why wasn't Zuzu with her mother at Congo Square today?"

"She doesn't go out in public in the day," Ben said. "She'd be arrested if she did. Tonight, very late, she will be there."

"Who has she offended?" Hannah asked. "The Church or the government?"

"Both," said Ben. The blue-green eyes regarded her for a moment and then nodded, satisfied and—Hannah was sure of it—relieved. She could be trusted to understand the most important things without long explanations.

They walked on, out of the city into a neighborhood that Hannah didn't know. The lanes here were barely wide enough for a horse and cart, and dark as night in mid-afternoon. The smell of the river was strong here, and there were other smells: a cypress wood fire, long-standing water, cooking fish, boiling milk, and the faint scent of the herbs Hannah associated with childbirth and its aftermath: blue co-hosh and raspberry leaf, pennyroyal, chamomile and hyssop.

Ben took her arm suddenly and pulled her into the shadows beside a cottage. His whole body was tense, and Hannah had the idea that he was going to kiss her, here and now, in the shadows; he would press her against the rough wall and kiss her and she would let him. More than that: She would kiss him back.

He said, "Is your Kit Wyndham a tall man, and fair?"

Hannah's thoughts would not organize themselves, but she managed a nod.

"Then I think you will have no choice but to speak to him. He's been following us." Ben took the knife from the sheath that hung at the small of his back.

Hannah felt her pulse leap in her throat, in her wrists and in the pit of her belly. She opened her mouth to say the words that would stop what was about to happen, this confrontation that must certainly end badly, when the cottage doors that faced the street swung open and a woman's voice rang out.

"Jean-Benoît Savard!" And again: "Jean-Benoît! Show yourself!"

Hannah pulled her wrist out of Ben's grasp and moved out of the shadows into the narrow street.

"Here," she said. "He is right here." The woman held up a lantern that swung a little, and in the long oval of light that it cast, Hannah saw her own shadow shivering.

The street was empty. No sign of Kit Wyndham or any other man; no one but the older woman in the open door.

Maman Zuzu, sixty years or more, was a small woman with blunt features and wide-set, sharp black eyes. Ben spoke to her in the local patois, his tone respectful. Zuzu seemed to be ignoring him completely, so focused was she on Hannah.

In English she said, "You the Redbone healer I heard about."

Hannah nodded. "I am."

Zuzu finally turned to look at Ben. She said, "Go away from here now, we got no use for men. Come back after dark. And don't be standing out here in plain sight, boy. You draw attention."

Hannah followed Maman Zuzu into the cottage. When she glanced over her shoulder, there was no sign of Ben.

"He won't go far," said Zuzu. "You come now, sit here with me."

Hannah thought to ask about the woman in labor, and then she looked more closely around the small, tidy room and saw the cot in the corner, and the young woman who slept there, a swaddled newborn tucked next to her.

"Girl child come to her easy," said the older woman, lifting her chin in the direction of mother and child. "Hardly nothing for me to do but catch her. Slippery as a fish, that one."

"Your mother said you might need help."

"Did she now. Never mind, me and Marie, we get along just fine. Sit."

Hannah did as she was bid, her curiosity getting the upper hand. She studied the cottage, the simple furnishings, the blue-and-white hangings at the long shuttered windows, the row of jars and jugs that lined the shelves on two walls.

Maman Zuzu sat across the table from Hannah, her hands folded in front of her. The fingers were swollen at the joints and rough with work.

"You tell me," said Maman Zuzu. "Tell me how you got mixed up with Agnès Poiterin and that grandson of hers, that Honoré."

Hannah heard the click of her own jaw dropping in surprise.

Maman Zuzu laughed. "Close your mouth, *chère,* before something fly down your throat."

"How did you—"

The older woman waved the question away with a flutter of her fingers. "This place is black in its bones," she said. "For every white we are two dozen. We are everywhere, *chère.* We hear everything."

Hannah gathered her thoughts. "Why are you interested in our dealings with the Poiterins?"

Maman Zuzu tilted her head so that the candlelight moved over her face. After a moment she said, "We keep an eye on that devil, that Honoré."

"I've heard others call him that."

"We know him. Yes, we do."

Hannah said, "They mean us harm."

Maman Zuzu was looking at her intently, searching for something in Hannah's face. A full minute went by in silence broken only by the hissing of the fire. Hannah felt no alarm, no concern, no need to be anywhere else. She wondered, with one part of her mind, if the old woman had cast some kind of spell over her. Among her mother's people there were women who could do such things.

Then Maman Zuzu reached across the table and touched Hannah's hand, and she woke out of her stupor with a start.

"The only thing to do with that one is put fear in his heart. I can't get close enough to him to do it."

Hannah said, "I don't think he is afraid of anything in this world."

"He is afraid of *voudou*. He is afraid of me." Maman Zuzu said this calmly, without pride, and Hannah believed her.

"And his grandmother? She's just as bad. Together they will take a lot of stopping."

Maman Zuzu smiled suddenly. "You come to me when you're ready. Together we can do it."

From the corner came the mewling of a hungry infant, but Maman Zuzu didn't even look in that direction. Instead she got up and went to a table. She began to pull bottles and jars from the shelves, and from each of them she took what she needed. The smell of dried herbs filled the room, some familiar to Hannah and some strange. Everything went into a small stone bowl while Maman Zuzu muttered to herself in her own language. Finally she poured the contents of the bowl into a square of muslin, pulled the four corners together and used a bit of string to tie it all together.

The bundle was no larger than a walnut, but there was a weight to it in Hannah's palm. She saw now that it had been tied shut not with string, but with hair.

"You keep that in your pocket," said Maman Zuzu. "Keep it near. When the smell go away, you come back to me and I make you another one."

Hannah thought of the small leather bag her grand-mother Falling-Day had given her as a girl, and the things she had put in it over the years. To give her strength and speed and to protect her. She had lost it in the west, with so many other things. This muslin bag on her palm was very different, and still Hannah was comforted by its weight.

"He means you harm, *oui*," said the old woman. "You watch out for him."

Hannah closed her hand around the charm.

The old woman leaned a little closer to Hannah, and the smell of her clothes and skin rose in the warm air: lye soap, mint, tallow, sweat, a dozen different herbs and roots.

She said, "There's another man outside, waiting for you. A good man, him. Mind you don't let the good one get away from you. He's the one you've been waiting for."

Then Maman Zuzu sat back and smiled. "Come now, *chère*," she said. "Come show me how you mix up your fever tea. Marie, she is going to need one—" She pointed with her chin to the cot in the rear of the room. "Let me see what you know."

CHAPTER 27

In the chill dark of an unfamiliar street in an unfamiliar city, Luke knew himself to be at a disadvantage, and beyond that: He wasn't thinking clearly. When he had first seen Hannah weaving through the crowds at Congo Square the flood of relief and simple joy had been so overpowering that the urge to put himself in front of her had been almost more than he could resist.

Hannah was alive and well. No matter that their plans had come to nothing, that he had disappeared without a word all these weeks; somehow or another she had coped. He had trusted her to do just that, but now he realized how deeply worried he had been.

Hannah was here, and Jennet would be nearby, with or without the boy, it didn't matter. As long as she was here and whole, nothing else mattered.

He followed Hannah at a distance. She was thin, but she moved with all her normal grace and energy. Luke studied the man with her. Strong and well built, he walked like an Indian, but it was clear from the color of his skin and his features that he had had both white and black grandparents or great-grandparents. Whoever he was, the way he held himself said two things clearly: He knew his own value and he knew Hannah's. He moved through the crowd the way a good hunter moved through the brush, aware of everything.

And Hannah seemed at ease with him. More than that, she seemed to trust him, to move closer to him when she might have moved away, to turn toward him often and listen attentively when he lowered his head to speak to her.

Luke wondered if what he was feeling was brotherly concern or healthy skepticism. What he did know for sure was simple: It would be the height of stupidity to rush in and upset whatever story Hannah had put together to keep herself—and Jennet—safe here.

In a narrow and darkening lane, Luke had to fall back or risk being seen before he was sure it was safe to do so. Twice he almost lost them, the second time on a narrow street lined with small cottages. An old woman came to a door and spoke to Hannah, and she went inside, casting a look at her companion as she went. Luke settled into the shadows to wait.

"Keep your hands where I can see them."

Luke started out of a doze, and realized that he was chilled to the bone and his muscles were cramped. More than that, the point of a very sharp knife was poised on the underside of his jaw, and the man who held it was behind him.

There was little Luke could make out about the man, beyond the obvious fact that he was three kinds of trouble. They were about the same height, but the stranger outweighed him by more than a little, and he carried that extra weight in heavily muscled shoulders and arms.

"Renaud," he said.

Luke blinked in surprise. "Who?"

"Or I could just call you Wyndham."

"Kit Wyndham?" It was the last name Luke had expected to hear and for a moment he could make no sense of it.

"If you've forgot your own name you must be denser than you look."

Luke let out a startled half-laugh. "I'm not Wyndham, and I'm not Renaud, whoever that is."

"No?" The voice was cold and utterly calm. "Then what do you want with us?"

"Nothing," Luke said. "You don't interest me in the least." Not completely true, but he wasn't about to give away too much at this point. "I don't have any idea who you are."

The stranger made a deep sound in his throat, impatience and distrust. Then the sharp stunning first moment as something hard (a club? a stave?) connected with his skull, and as he began to fall Luke had two last thoughts: In his own eagerness to see his sister, he had underestimated, again, and if he survived this night, it would be dumb luck and more than he deserved.

Full dark, cold, and clear, with enough of a moon to cast a dim shadow, Hannah was surprised but not unhappy to see that Ben was waiting for her with a wagon.

"What's this?"

He pointed with his chin. "Borrowed. It's a long walk home, and it's late." Ben held out a hand and she let herself be lifted up onto the buckboard. He flicked the reins, and they were off.

Hannah's head ached and she was worn down, but more than that, she was satisfied. She had a new ally in Maman Zuzu. A knowing woman, severe, plainspoken. *We may need each other in the weeks to come,* she had said to Hannah. No gesture of friendship, no false gestures at all. A woman with a larder full of herbs and roots and prayers to the gods she had brought with her, from Africa and the islands. A good evening's work.

Hannah straightened and looked around herself. Ben was focused on the street, the shadows between the buildings, the darkness beyond the shadows. As if he expected something to jump out at them. There was a pistol laid ready across his lap.

"Was it Wyndham?" she asked, remembering those tense moments in the shadows before Zuzu had called out.

Ben lifted a shoulder, shook his head. "He didn't have an English accent."

Hannah wondered at herself, that she should feel both relief and disappointment. She had told Ben that she did not want to meet Kit, but now she wasn't sure if she had told the truth, to him or to herself. What good would it do to see him again? What harm?

"Maybe he wasn't following us, then."

"He was following us," Ben said. He flicked a glance over his shoulder. "He still is."

Hannah saw that the wagon bed wasn't empty. Under a tarpaulin she could make out the long shape of a man. A still shape.

"Who is it?"

"No time to find out," Ben said.

"He attacked you."

"Never gave him the chance."

Hannah thought about this. She thought about Père Petit, who had died unexpectedly at exactly the right moment, so that Père Tomaso could get Jennet and the boy away from the Poiterins.

"You didn't kill him outright." She made a statement of it.

"No. At least, I didn't hit him that hard. Maybe when he comes around he'll be more willing to talk about why he was following us."

It was one solution, certainly. Maybe not the one Hannah would have chosen.

"You couldn't just tie him up?"

"I did that, too, for good measure."

Hannah said, "You are no Quaker, Jean-Benoît Savard."

He clucked at the horse, shifted on the buckboard, looked at her.

"I'm no kind of Quaker you've run into before."

"You're no kind of man I've run into before."

His right arm snaked out and around her waist and he pulled her up against him. She had a sense of him, the shape of him and his smells, and then he kissed her. His mouth was warm, soft, and then hard. A short, jarring kiss.

He let her go and she heard herself gasp.

"I've been wanting to do that for a while."

Hannah adjusted her headscarf. "You said you had no interest in me." Trying for dignified, and sounding instead like a girl in a snit.

He glanced at her, surprised. "I never said that."

"You did. On the stairs."

"I said I knew you had no interest in me. I'm hoping maybe you've changed your mind."

"And if I haven't?"

Cool appraisal, calculating, knowing. Hannah looked away. When she looked back again, he was smiling.

She could get down and walk the rest of the way, if she knew where she was.

After a while he said, "You could come to me, tonight."

She laughed out loud, a sharp, not quite surprised sound with something of admiration in it. And not another word was spoken until he turned the horse into the carriageway and brought it to a halt in the courtyard behind the clinic.

Hannah sat where she was for a moment while Ben spoke to Leo, who came from his bed in the stables sleepy-eyed and yawning. He was to turn the wagon around and take it back where it belonged and stay there until morning. Then she collected her wits and jumped down, her skirts gathered up in one hand.

Pulling aside the tarpaulin Ben said, "You want to have a look, see if you recognize him?"

"I want to see how much damage you've done," Hannah said. She waited while Ben lifted the prostrate form out of the wagon bed, shifting it over his shoulders and pausing to adjust to the burden. Hannah moved ahead to open the door into the little clinic. Leo had banked the fire carefully and it took only a moment to coax the embers into life while Ben put the man down on the long examination table.

Hannah took a candle from the mantelpiece and lit it, and then crossed the length of the room, alive with leaping light and shadow. She stopped at the examination table and held the candle high.

The stranger was on his side facing away from her into the shadows, his wrists and ankles bound, a hank of dirty cloth jammed into his mouth and then secured by a rawhide thong tied around his head. A trickle of color from his scalp: dried blood.

She said, "I need fresh water."

"I'm not leaving you alone with him." Ben said this as Hannah pushed on the man's shoulder to bring his face up into the light.

She stopped. Everything stopped. Her breath caught in her throat, and for a moment she was close to swooning. The candle dish in her hand shook so that a splash of hot wax fell onto the crest of a cheekbone. The man twitched and moaned and his eyes opened, unfocused, and closed again.

"Is this Wyndham?" Ben said, stepping closer. "Is it Wyndham after all?"

"No," Hannah said, wiping the rapidly cooling wax away with her fingers. "This is my brother Luke. Bring me that water, will you? Right now."

• • •

Luke said, "Where's Jennet?" And then, wincing with a hand to his head: "Christ almighty damn, that hurts."

Hannah ignored her brother's complaint and continued to probe at the gash on his head. "Hold that light up higher," she said to Ben, her tone curt. "I've got to stop the bleeding."

Luke caught her wrist, and his eyes met hers. "Jennet."

"Upstairs," Hannah said. "Asleep, and your son with her."

"Thank God." Luke let go of her wrist, and his eyes darted toward Ben. "Who are you, and why in the name of God did you hit me so hard?"

"You wouldn't tell me your name," Ben said evenly.

Luke yelped. "That's only half an answer."

Hannah said, "I'll tell you what you need to know if you stop moving and let me work. I can't take you up to Jennet like this. If you won't hold still I could give you enough laudanum to put you to sleep. Or I could hit you in the head again. It's up to you."

At that Luke relaxed, and then he nodded. "Get on with it," he said. "But talk while you're working. Who is he?"

"This is Jean-Benoît Savard," she said. "Before you set your heart on taking revenge on him, you should know that he saved your wife's life, and your son's. And mine, too."

"He's been busy." Luke's breathing came a little easier as Hannah talked. He interrupted her once or twice to ask questions, and she felt his pulse pick up when she recounted the facts of her own illness.

"How did you get from the bordello to the clinic?"

Hannah stopped, her hands in midair, and she let out a short laugh. "I don't know," she said. "I never thought to ask. I was in a delirium." But over Luke's form she saw Ben drop his gaze to the floor. Later she would have to ask him about that expression on his face.

Luke wanted to know about Kit Wyndham, about Poiterin, about Paul Savard and Hannah's connection to him.

She told him what he needed to know, and finished cleaning and binding the wound.

Then he had a request that took her completely by surprise.

She said, "You spoke to Girl at the slave market?"

"I had no way to find you, and I had to track down every possible bit of information."

Hannah considered. Finally she said, "It can be done, with the right amount of money. I'm sure Paul will take her into the clinic and treat her."

"I thought you would approve the plan," Luke said.

"I do." Hannah went to the water barrel and filled a cup. "Of course I do." She glanced at Ben Savard.

"You could arrange it?"

Ben nodded. "If she's still alive."

"I'd appreciate it," Hannah said, and the smile he gave her was so open and clear to read that she had to turn her face away.

To Luke she said, "Tomorrow your head will feel like a well-used drum, but you will survive. Before I take you up to Jennet I need to say something else."

"You're glad to see me, I hope."

"Oh, yes." She cast a glance at her brother. "And so will Jennet be. But she's had a hard time of it. Let her tell what she has to tell at her own pace."

He barked a short laugh as he pushed himself off the table. "That's good advice, Hannah. I'm hoping she'll do the same for me."

The cathedral bells were striking midnight when Hannah let herself out of the chamber she shared with Jennet. The chamber she *had* shared with Jennet. There was no room for her now, and she could hardly disturb Julia to demand new quarters in an already overcrowded apartment.

She would have to go to the night nurse in the clinic and ask for an empty bed or a pallet. Hannah hesitated for a moment and then went out onto the gallery, her candle throwing a small circle of light before her as she went down one flight of stairs, her skirts held up in her free hand.

Hannah thought of Kit Wyndham, sleeping somewhere nearby. She thought of Ben Savard, and turned to look into the courtyard, filled with rustling shadows. The kitchen building was a vague shape, squat and solid. On the floor above it, the French windows weren't dark, as she had expected them to be. As she had hoped they would be. Ben had lit a candle.

Come to me.

She imagined the small apartment. A bed, a stove. A shirt hanging on a hook, a table, a washbasin. A straight-backed chair. Books and papers, a bullet mold, a whetstone, a shaving mug. A picture hanging on the wall, a portrait of his father or a painting of the family plantation. She could close her eyes and see all these things, and Ben there, waiting.

She opened her eyes. He was on the small balcony, outlined in the glow of the candle. Looking at her, as she looked at him. He might have been carved of marble, he stood so very still, watching.

Hannah looked up into the night sky, and tried to recall Kit Wyndham's face the last time they had been together. The shape of his mouth, the rasp of stubble. The sound of his voice.

I have to go back.

Of course, Hannah had said to him. *Of course you must go back to your life, to your bride.*

She had been relieved when he left her, and then, surprisingly, she had missed him. In the last weeks she had thought of him as often as she thought of Strikes-the-Sky, who no longer came to visit her, as he had so often, before he had resigned himself to the shadowlands.

If she went into the clinic and found an empty bed, she had the sense that her husband might come tonight to sit beside her and ask her questions she didn't know how to answer.

Why do you hesitate to take what you want, when it is offered to you? and: *What do you fear?*

Hannah walked down the rest of the stairs into the courtyard and across the cobblestones and then up more stairs. The skin of her face felt too tight, as though she had been weeping for a long time, or floating in a salt sea.

Ben met her at the door, stood aside, and smiled.

Come to me.

Hannah said, "She is so brittle with relief, I fear she might shatter."

They were standing in the soft light, close enough to touch. Not touching. The candle she had brought and the one already here sat side by side on the table. In spite of the fire their breath hung milk white in the cold air.

After a moment Ben said, "Do you want to talk about your sister-in-law?"

Hannah hiccupped a small laugh, shook her head. "I am so tired."

His gaze was steady. "Then sleep."

The bed was as she had imagined it. Hannah folded her shawl, took off her shoes and stockings, drew the tignon from her hair, and unpinned her braids. She felt Ben watching her, silently, solemnly. With steady hands she undid buttons and ties and then she stepped out of her clothes until all that was left was a shift of plain linen.

She went to the bed and drew back the covers, sat, drew her legs up and settled. Heard herself sigh. She knew she should say something, make it clear to him that she would not turn him out of his own bed, call him to her. There were questions to ask, things to say, important things.

This is only for a short time. And: *When I leave, I will go without looking back.*

Christian Wyndham had agreed to her conditions. If he wanted her, Jean-Benoît Savard would do the same. That thought was in her mind as she drifted off to sleep.

At first light Hannah woke, alone in Ben's bed.

She turned on her side. He was asleep on the floor in front of the hearth, wrapped in blankets. Soundly, peacefully asleep.

How courteous of him. How exceedingly polite.

Hannah reached down and picked up one of her sturdy, plain shoes, and she threw it, hard. It struck somewhere in the vicinity of the third and fourth vertebrae with a solid thump.

Ben shot straight up out of the blankets, like a porpoise raising long and sleek from the waves. His eyes flashed at her, angry. Aroused.

"Tabernac!" he barked. "What was that for?"

Hannah said, coming up on her knees, "That was for exactly nothing."

He crossed the small room in three long steps, took her by the elbows, and lifted her until they were face-to-face.

"Is that how a Kahnyen'kehàka woman invites a man to her longhouse?"

"Yes," Hannah said, flustered and angry and embarrassed beyond all experience. "Exactly like that. Unless she's mad, and then she throws a tomahawk instead."

Ben's expression shifted, suddenly, from anger to something fine and bright. He smiled.

"Remind me not to make you angry," he said, and he kissed her.

· · ·

Later, ten minutes or an hour or a day, Hannah broke a kiss, turned her head away to listen, or tried to. She said, "Clémentine."

They could hear every word of the song the older woman was singing as she started the cooking fires in the kitchen below them.

Ben's mouth was swollen, his gaze unfocused, as if he had been drinking. As if she had spoken a language that he could not understand, didn't care to know.

"Clémentine," Ben agreed, and turned her face to kiss her. Hannah, amazed, confounded, forgot why she had stopped him in the first place.

He moved her around the bed like a doll, draped her body to his liking, rearranged limbs, spread flesh, used mouth and tongue and teeth and fingers, used all of himself and every bit of her. Angled her hips, pushed her knees further apart, breathed soft words into her ear. Questions, instructions, praise, in English and French and Choctaw.

He never closed his eyes. Beautiful eyes, like none she had ever known. His hands were so large, his fingers supple and quick and curious. He played with her. He touched, licked, suckled, grinned when he got a sound he liked. He slid the flat of his tongue over her nipple and gooseflesh broke out over her whole body.

She flung out a hand and he caught it, laced his fingers through hers, and stretched her arm over her head to suckle the curve of underarm where it met the swell of a breast. Sweat glued them together at thigh and belly. He lifted her knee and pressed it to her shoulder and she gasped again, louder, to feel him at the very center of her.

He would split her in half, like a peach.

I am greedy, she thought. *For this, for him. For more and more and more.*

He shifted again, lifted her, moved his hips in a grinding motion that sent a wave of shivery small shocks up her spine. She heard herself grunting with every stroke.

"Shhhh. Remember Clémentine."

"Who?"

He pressed his forehead to hers, arched his back, drove harder still. Slid his free hand down and down into the hot wet where he filled her, one blunt fingertip questing, circling, flicking.

Hannah arched, tried to stifle a scream, failed.

"Shhhhhh."

"Not while you're doing—".

"What?"

"That."

"This? Do you want me to—"

"Don't. Don't. Don't stop."

Flushed, satiated, too exhausted for embarrassment, Hannah turned her back to the bed, closed her eyes, took a very deep breath and then another. Willed herself to stop trembling. She fumbled for her clothes, and her hair swung around her and stuck to her skin. She would smell of him, of this, all day if she didn't wash, but to go to Clémentine now and ask for the water was beyond her.

"Why are you running off?"

Ben was splayed across the bed on his stomach. She cast him a quick glance. Intolerable conceit, and so beautiful. He was smiling at her.

"You remember," she said. "My brother?"

Ben said, "It's too early. Come sleep a while. Come talk."

"Which?" Hannah said. "Sleeping or talking?"

"Both." He grinned. "Neither."

She was tempted, if only because her legs were trembling

and it would be good to sit for a moment. He saw her inde-
cision, held out a hand and made a motion with his fingers.

Come to me.

Hannah sat down carefully, smoothed her skirts, and
folded her hands. "I do have a few things to say."

Ben had propped his head up on one hand. He looked
curious, and not at all concerned.

"In a few days I'll be gone from here," Hannah began.
"You must know that I won't hesitate, as soon as it's safe for
us to travel."

He blinked at her. "Is that the speech you gave Wyndham?"

Hannah's jaw dropped; she felt it.

"Why do you assume—What do you—" She had never
said anything to this man—to anyone—about sharing
Wyndham's bed. She forced her voice to steady. "The only
thing that concerns me at this moment is that you and I understand each other."

Ben ran a thumb along his lower lip. "Let me see if I've got
this right. You make the rules, and I follow them. Is that it?"

The sound that came from her throat was something between a cry of protest and a laugh. A dozen different replies
jumbled together in her mind, but only one came out of
her mouth.

"Yes," she said. "That's it exactly. If you want—" She
looked him directly in the eye. "More."

His expression gave nothing away. Not surprise or pique,
no hurt feelings. None of the resignation she had seen in
Kit's expression. In the early morning sun Ben's skin was
like a river after a storm, seething with colors, alive and vibrant with light. A pearl of sweat on the crest of his cheekbone, like a jewel. A well-made man, long-boned, strong.
His short black hair, rough, rumpled by her own hands,
standing up in peaks. Hannah felt a tug in the muscles of her
womb, a trickle of fresh wanting. If he touched her now she
would fall open to him.

He said, "Do you want more?"

"That depends," she said.

The muscle at the corner of his mouth twitched. She was a liar, and they both knew it.

"I amuse you, I see."

"Ah, *chère*," he said, and he reached out for her hand. She let him take it. "You do many things to me."

"I mean what I say."

"I know you do. So do I, so listen: I won't be dictated to, and I won't make promises about how I'm going to feel when the day comes for you to go. So you'll share my bed and take that risk, or you'll find someplace else to sleep."

Hannah started to get up from the bed, but he caught her wrist and held her, pulled her close. Brushed her hair from her face and kissed her cheek, her jaw, the corner of her mouth.

"We were good."

She nodded. "It would have been a waste, you as a priest."

That earned her a laugh.

"I hope you'll come back to me," he said, and let her go.

CHAPTER 28

Pressed into service on the *Puma* among men who routinely killed for tarnished baubles and imagined slights, Luke had gone for days at a time without speaking. As it was, they already knew more about him than was to his taste; they had gone through his things and pocketed everything of worth. It was pure luck that he had kept the most important papers tucked under his shirt.

Now he found that the habit of silence was harder to shake off than he had imagined. Alone with Jennet, all the things he thought to say, had meant to say, were gone. She didn't seem to care, or maybe, Luke realized, she was feeling the same way. They spoke very little that first night. He told her the minimum she needed to know: about being boarded, his escape when the *Puma* docked at São Paulo, the voyage back as a crew member on another ship.

"What about money?" she had asked him. "Didn't the pirates take everything?"

"They did," Luke said. "But I retrieved what I could before I left them."

She didn't require details, and he was glad.

In the morning the Savards were presented with the fact of Luke Bonner's unannounced arrival. They never flinched at the idea of another guest in an already overcrowded apartment, or at least they showed nothing but kindness and hospitality. Paul Savard examined the wound to Luke's head, made a deep sound that seemed to be approving of his condition, and handed him something to drink that Luke swallowed down without a question. Laudanum, he realized too late, and the next time he woke it was mid-afternoon and his headache was much improved.

Hannah had gone to her clinic for the day, Jennet told him, because it would arouse suspicion if she did not. And the young woman Luke had interviewed at the slave market had arrived and was established in one of the two cots, under Hannah's care.

"How is she?"

"Dying," said Jennet. "Hannah says the trouble is in her belly."

"I'm sorry for the girl," Luke said. "But I need to hear about you."

Sitting beside him with the baby on her lap, she told him in more detail about the weeks since they had last seen each other in Pensacola. Luke stopped her now and then to ask a question.

"And Savard's brother, the one who—" he gestured at his own bandaged head. "It was his idea, how to get you away from the Poiterins?"

Jennet said, "It was his doing, from beginning to end." And then she gave him a small smile, one of the few she had been able to produce during the telling of the story. "So you see you will have to forgive him for last night."

"Aye," Luke said. "I suppose I will."

When she was done he understood three things very clearly. The first was that the debt they owed the Savards, most especially Ben Savard, was so large that he would never be able to repay it. The second was that they could not impose on their hospitality much longer, and the last: that they had nowhere to go. He couldn't even go out on the street, for fear that Poiterin might see him. What he needed, he realized, was a lawyer he could trust, one who would tell him whether the Poiterins' claims had any chance of being honored in court. Something to ask Savard about, when they could talk.

The rest of the first afternoon passed in relative solitude. Luke still had his own story to tell, but Jennet didn't seem in a hurry to hear it. It was a relief to simply sit together with the boy between them.

Their son. A vigorous, healthy child of almost eight months. A being with a surfeit of personality. If Jennet put him down on the floor he crawled away at high speed, his mouth set in a determined line. Caught up and tickled, he opened his mouth wide to show four white teeth. He had an infectious belly laugh, and when presented with anything he had never seen before—a quill, a shoe buckle, a stranger's hand, a newspaper—he would turn it over once or twice in his hands, his gaze as serious as any banker's, and then put it in his mouth to see if it might be edible.

In Luke's arms the boy first examined every button, working his way up to the neck of his shirt, where he wound his fingers in a few chest hairs and yanked, crowing with satisfaction at his father's grunt of surprise. Luke captured the offending hands and the boy promptly lifted himself to a standing position and bounced, flexing his knees and stamping like a drunken sailor on a dance floor. He babbled the whole while in a language that rose and fell like English, but contained not one recognizable word.

Luke had never let himself think too much about the fact of his own fatherhood, out of dread, out of superstitious worry. That they would never find the boy; that they would, and he would have Dégre's dark hair and eyes. These were things he would never say aloud. Jennet, who had borne so much by herself, should not have to carry the weight of doubts that had lasted only until she put the boy in his arms.

She had named him for Luke's father. A gesture of hope,

certainly, but not without a certain amount of irony. Luke had grown up without knowing his father, had not even seen him until he was on the brink of manhood himself. For the first time, Luke began to understand what it must have been like for Nathaniel Bonner to learn that he had a son who had been kept from him. A new kind of anger, one he hadn't been able to imagine.

He helped Jennet bathe the baby, handing her the things she needed, letting himself be splashed, obediently lifting the rosy pink boy with his perfectly round belly and the evidence of his sex below it, and wrapping him in toweling. Deposited on the bed he attempted escape by rolling away, and then, resigned to being dressed, kicked his legs with vigor, flung out his arms, contorted his face and mouth elaborately, as if he were reciting an epic poem and required their full attention.

Almost shyly Jennet said, "Dr. Savard says he shows no ill effects from his—from the early separation. He seems healthy, does he no?"

Luke looked Jennet directly in the face and smiled. "He is perfect."

For the moment that seemed to be enough for all of them.

When Hannah came in the evening, looking very tired, even ill, Jennet came suddenly fully awake. The disquiet and tension that had drained away from her over the course of the day were back.

"Hannah," she said. "Are ye fevered?"

"Just very tired," Hannah said. "Clémentine has had a cot put in Rachel's room for me. Will you forgive me if I go straight to sleep?"

It was not really a question; she had already turned away before the last word left her mouth.

"We have things to talk about," Jennet said, and Hannah paused.

"Tomorrow is soon enough," Luke said, and he saw an

expression flit across Jennet's face. Disagreement, frustration, and something that looked like panic.

Later, when the boy was asleep and they lay down together, as nervously as twenty-year-olds newly married, Luke smoothed the curls away from Jennet's face and kissed her. He kissed her gently, though he was thinking of the last time they had been together: the heat and strength of how she had come to him. Now she felt limp in his arms, empty of desire of any kind, drugged.

She trembled a little, pressed her face to his, sighed. She said, "I want to go home."

"I'll take you home," he said.

"Tomorrow? Can we set off tomorrow?"

He put a thumb to the corner of her mouth, smoothed it over her cheek. "If it's in my power," he said. "We'll set off tomorrow."

She nodded, her eyes fluttering closed. "Don't leave me again."

"Never," Luke agreed.

And then she was asleep. He pulled her closer so that her head was bedded on the hollow of his shoulder, and listened to the sound of her breathing.

To Hannah's great relief, she found that Rachel had already retired and was deeply asleep. In the light of a small candle she undressed down to her chemise and slipped between the sheets of the cot Clémentine had made up for her. Clémentine, who had looked at Hannah with her piercing dark eyes when she had made the request.

"Rachel's chamber?" she had repeated twice, and Hannah, thinking of the early morning hours she had spent in a bed over Clémentine's kitchen, nodded resolutely and willed herself not to blink.

There was no help for it. If she never went back to Ben's

bed again, the damage was done. She hadn't seen him all day, something that at first had seemed a kindness on his part, and then, as the hours passed, began to feel like something else. Not so much a threat as a demonstration, and a challenge: *I can stay away. Can you?*

Hannah was so weary that the room seemed to tilt and spin even in the dark. Eyes open or closed, nothing changed except that she had lost her balance and had not the first idea how to get it back again.

CHAPTER 29

Julia Savard had left the Society of Friends when she married her first husband, but she would always be a Quaker at heart. Luke came to this conclusion on his second morning, when Mrs. Savard met them in the family parlor. Her arms were full of clothing for him, and her expression was without apology or embarrassment, though she laid out linen underdrawers and shirts and stockings along with a variety of vests, fashionable pantaloons, and threadbare breeches. A hodgepodge of clothing, no doubt collected to be distributed among the poorer patients.

Jennet had warned him that Julia Savard would handle the practical matters associated with this extended stay like a benevolent general, and so it was. He was to try on the things she had available until he had a suitable wardrobe, or, if nothing fit or was appropriate, she would make the necessary purchases later in the day. So he appeared at the dinner table at midday feeling more himself: rested, washed, shaved, and in plain, well-fitting clothing. Julia only nodded at his thanks and offered him a plate of ham.

They crowded around the table in the small dining room, Hannah arriving last from her clinic. There was no sign of Ben Savard, but Luke asked no questions and contented himself with answering them, telling his own story for the first time to this attentive audience, leaving out the bits that the youngest Savard, with his huge brown eyes and eager expression, was hoping for. He was actually glad to have the boy there, because it gave him permission to skirt the things he wasn't ready to share.

"And no sign of the *Jackdaw*," Jennet said, showing some of her old playfulness. "I thought by now Mac Stoker would have shown himself."

For her sake and his own, Luke did what he could to divert the talk in another direction and would have thought he had managed very well, if not for the way his sister looked at him out of the corner of her eye.

When the meal was finished, Paul Savard said, "I think that's Ben on the stair. He's bringing the maps you'll want to see."

Luke was looking at Hannah at that moment and he saw her start and straighten very suddenly in her chair. His calm sister, unflappable, folded her hands in her lap and pressed her fingers together, and would not meet his eye. Jennet would, however, and she gave him a look whose significance he couldn't be sure of, except it had something to do with Ben Savard and his sister.

"I do like maps," Rachel Livingston announced. It was clear she was anticipating being sent away, but didn't care to go. Her mother saw through this ruse and Rachel left, but not without first looking very pointedly at her uncle and then at Hannah.

Ben Savard spread out a large map on the cleared table, and all of them bent their heads over it. The Savard brothers on one side of the table, the Bonners on the other. Hannah was directly across from Ben Savard but she kept her gaze fixed firmly on the map and listened without speaking while the men talked.

What they had to say was important and interesting enough to distract Luke from the idea that had been put in his head. Ben Savard traced all the roads that led away from the city of New Orleans, the larger well-traveled ones, the minor tracks and trails and footpaths, the waterways. Ben spoke of troop movements and camps, and Paul of the reports from the paper and the rumors that ran through the city like fire. It seemed that every passable byway was crowded with troops on their way to New Orleans.

"Back roads?" Luke asked. "Through the swamps?"

"Dozens of them," said Paul Savard.

"Guides?"

Ben Savard glanced up at him. "If that's what you want, I can guide you."

What he meant, Luke understood immediately, was that of the many competent men who might be hired to guide them from New Orleans to Mobile and beyond, Ben Savard was the only one they could be sure of. The reward the Poiterins were offering for news of Jennet and the boy had been tripled.

"The safest thing," Paul Savard ventured, "would be to travel south to Barataria, and get a ship from there. You would have to go far out of your way, all the way to Gibraltar most probably, but by the time you turned back for New-York the war is likely to be over and you'd be safe."

"No," Luke and Jennet said in one voice. Luke cleared his throat. "I'm afraid it's not a good idea for me to be seen in Barataria."

Ben Savard looked at him for a long moment. "Something we should know?"

Luke raised a shoulder, wondering how best to begin. The men waited, looking vaguely interested. Jennet looked worried, and Hannah's expression was purposefully blank.

"Let's say that when we parted ways in São Paulo I didn't go empty-handed," Luke said. "I paid myself for services rendered. Generously."

"Ah," said Paul Savard. "I'm remembering some of the

stories about the Bonner family." And: "What is your objection, Jennet?"

She said, "I want as little to do with ships as possible. I am not eager to see the Gulf again."

Luke was surprised to hear something so plainly nonsensical from Jennet spoken in so resolute a tone.

Hannah said, "Do you want to walk overland from here to Lake in the Clouds? That would take many months, Jennet."

"How far do we need to go to stop worrying about Poiterin? How far could you take us?" she asked Ben. "As far as Kentucky? Or perhaps the Ohio, where Kentucky borders Virginia?" She flushed a little. "I've been studying the maps in the newspapers."

Luke couldn't hide his unease, but Ben Savard understood something about the questions and the reasons behind them. His expression gave nothing away except a kind of quiet and indulgent compassion.

He said, "I have responsibilities here. I can't leave the city just now."

"What responsibilities?" Jennet asked, her tone sharper, and when Luke put a hand on her arm, she shook it off. "Surely you know that we would pay you for your help."

Luke heard Hannah draw in a sharp breath, but Ben Savard was refusing to take offense. He said, "I would help you if I could, without payment."

"What my brother isn't telling you," Paul Savard said, "is that he joined the militia yesterday. He can't leave New Orleans until the fighting is over and he's released."

Jennet's face drained of color. To the man who had saved her life at considerable peril to himself and his family, she spoke with a chilly undertone.

"So we are to stay here. The whole force of the British navy and army are massing to overrun this city, and yet there is no safer place for us to be."

Savard had a calm way, but there was nothing soft about him. He met Jennet's gaze without apology or excuse.

"There is no safe place," he said. "Anywhere. The safest is right where you are."

Luke had his hand on Jennet's shoulder, and he could feel how close she was to breaking. He said, "Thank you for your help. If we could have a few minutes—"

Ben Savard paused before leaving the room, and looked directly at Hannah for what seemed to Luke the first time. His brother hesitated a little longer.

He said, "How is your head?"

"Much better," Luke said.

"I should like to look at it again," Savard said.

Hannah said, "You cannot resist the urge to check my work. Once a teacher, always a teacher."

Savard's mouth twitched but he didn't rise to the bait. To Luke he said, "It is a serious wound. You never did say how you got it."

Luke would have kept that information to himself, but Hannah spoke up. She said, "Your brother took him for somebody else."

There was something of satisfaction in her voice, like a girl tattling about a brother's poor behavior.

Luke glanced at Hannah. "It's nothing. I'm thankful to Ben for all he's done for me and mine."

"Any double vision?" Savard said, ignoring that part of the information he didn't want to deal with. "Forgetfulness?"

Luke started to say no, when a thought came to him. "I have forgot something," he said. "A letter, for my sister."

Very few material things could have survived the last few months with Luke, and so the battered condition of the letter he produced and put on the table in front of Hannah was not surprising in and of itself. The surprise was the handwriting, faded and water-stained. Even so it was immediately familiar. Hannah could no more forget the look of her stepmother's handwriting than she could her own son's face.

Mistress Hannah Bonner or Master Luke Bonner
in the company of Madame Giselle Lacoeur
D'Evereux Plantation
Port-au-Prince
Saint-Domingue

"It was delivered to my mother the day after we left for Pensacola," Luke said. "She sent it straight on, and I received it just before I set sail. The day after you left, Hannah."

"It's very odd, isn't it," Hannah said in a voice that trembled. "To be afraid of a piece of paper."

"Open it," Jennet said. "Or I'll scream."

" 'To my children,' " Hannah read aloud, and then she cleared her throat. "It was written last November. Only the first part is in Elizabeth's hand. The rest is in our father's."

"Go on," Luke said. He was standing behind Jennet with his hands on her shoulders. "Please."

I take up pen so that you may see these words come from me most directly. Yesterday was I delivered of a daughter, who came whole and healthy into this world. The birth was a long and difficult one but I will recover. Indeed I am already well on the way to full good health, and my joy in this new daughter is in no small part responsible. When you return home—all three of you—I will take great pleasure in introducing you to her.

Your father and I have named her, this last child we will have, for our dear friend, our most beloved

Curiosity Freeman, who attended me, along with
your aunt Many-Doves.

Many-Doves says the spirit of your grandmother
Cora shines in this little girl and that she will be a
strong woman and a great healer.

Your father thinks that is all very well but insists
that I turn this letter over to him and go to sleep. I
think he worries far too much, but I will indulge
him and thus must close with the wish that you
will do everything in your power to come home to
us as quickly as you may.

Your loving stepmother,
Elizabeth Middleton Bonner

Postscript. Though she would not like me to share
this news with you, Curiosity is not well of late. She
consults with Many-Doves, in privacy.

Hannah paused to press the back of her hand to her
face, damp with tears and hot to the touch. She handed the
letter to Luke, because she did not trust her voice.

He took it and began, his tone easy and confident, and
Hannah was struck by the similarity in their voices: the
man who had written the letter and the one who read it
aloud.

You will worry that your stepmother has not been
truthful with you on the matter of her health, but let
me make it clear. The child was big and the birth
hard, but Many-Doves says Elizabeth will be up and
about and taking on too much within a month's
time. If you could see the way she scowls at me now,
having handed over pen and paper only to find that I

will not take dictation, you would have no doubt that she will soon be up to her usual tricks.

Gabriel and Daniel were invited to an audience with their new sister this morning. As soon as Gabriel took young Carrie in his arms she struck out with one small fist and hit his nose a sounding good thump. Though his eyes watered he laughed and declared her a Bonner of the first rank. She got up to no such mischief with Daniel, but studied his face with great interest as if planning how she might get the best of him at their next meeting. She is indeed a fine strong girl with her mother's coloring and—if today's episode is any indication—disposition. Many-Doves sees my mother in this child and I hope she is right.

It is true also that Curiosity is not well. She says there is nothing that ails her but old age, and she is determined to be here when you return. You know well enough what it means when Curiosity sets herself a goal.

As to the rest of the family. Your brother Daniel is not with us in the village but stays in the house at Lake in the Clouds, where he says the quiet and solitude allow him to sleep. He makes no complaint but it is clear that his arm and shoulder are not much improved, either in his ability to use them or in the pain they cause. Thus far he declines your uncle Spencer's invitation to Manhattan, where he could be seen by surgeons. I cannot say I think him wrong in this. Manhattan is a fine enough place for some— young Martha Quick, or Martha Kirby, as she is now known, has gone there to live with the Spencers, and we receive regular letters with long accounts of lectures and concerts and new gowns and lessons. Martha will receive an education there that will better prepare her to deal with the estate and fortune left to her by Liam. We have had no word of Martha's mother. We can only hope Jemima stays away for good. In any case, Martha thrives in Manhattan, as Daniel could not.

You may be surprised to learn that this fall Daniel took over the school from your mother, and that he shows affinity for the work and a native understanding of the minds of the students. Your mother believes that the demands that teaching place on him allow him to forget his pain for short periods of time. My view of things is that thirty children aged five to fifteen in a single classroom would be enough to distract the moon from her course across the sky.

After hearing this last paragraph read aloud, your stepmother reminds me that you cannot know that there are ten new families in Paradise, which accounts for the thirty children in Daniel's classroom. The new residents are the work of your cousin Ethan, who seems to spend all his time in Manhattan arranging improvements for Paradise. Every week there is some new plan from him or from your uncle Spencer, and packets arrive with instructions and bank drafts. The bridge has been rebuilt and improvements made to the public buildings, the main road, the doctor's place, and many of the cabins. Two new public wells have been dug. The result of all this industry is that even those men who are not much worried about money and generally content to earn enough from trapping to buy ale and cornmeal have all been pressed into profitable employment by Tobias Mayfair, one of the new men here who acts as Ethan's factor.

McGarrity's trading post now bears a fine painted

sign with the word Emporium on it. I believe Anna's pleasure in the sign is sorely tried by the fact that few people seem to know what the word means, and continue to ask impertinent questions. Anna's poor mood is made some better by the fact that there is so much new business in the village and money to spend in her place, no matter what folks want to call it. Your mother's position is that all these changes are long overdue and welcome, but none of the improvements has had such positive effect as Ethan's ability to seek out tenants who will fit in here for the vacant farms. She reminds me that I have forgot to say that every one of the families newly come to Paradise is Quaker, which will explain why they are willing to put up with our strange and scandalous ways.

For my part, I'm not sure what I think about it all. It's true that the village is more settled than I ever imagined it would be when Richard Todd was alive and seemed set on letting it all fade back into the endless forests. All the new families farm, but every one of the men also has some other trade. We've got a cobbler, a couple of joiners, a cabinetmaker, a cooper, and a millwright who has bought Charlie LeBlanc out and set the millworks to rights. Charlie has gone back to his particular brand of making do. He has shown himself capable at well digging.

Gabriel sends his good wishes and the news that he has a rifle of his own. While he is not so very pleased to have his brother as a teacher, he is otherwise content because Annie is in the classroom, too. Runs-from-Bears and Many-Doves are at Lake in the Clouds for the winter, as are Blue-Jay and Teres. Runs-from-Bears sends his good wishes for your safe return and Many-Doves dreams of you, all

three of you, on a ship. I have every confidence in
her dreams, and in your persistence. As do we all.

Lily and Simon are returned to Montreal. We had a
letter from them last week and learned that everyone
at Carryck is in good health though they continue to
be concerned about Jennet, as is right. Simon writes
that Carryck's business concerns are all in good order.
Lily tells us that she is pleased with her surroundings
and her husband both. Your mother wonders aloud if
there is not some other good man who could take
over the direction of Forbes & Sons in Montreal so
that Lily and Simon could come back here to stay, and
that Luke and Jennet might do the same. She imagines
the next years with all the children and their families
nearby, in peace and good health.

We trust that Giselle will find a way to get this
letter to you, if such a thing is possible at all. That we
may not have word of you for a long time, given the
state of the war and the shipping lanes, is also clear to
us. If it should be a day or a year, know that we trust
that your determination will be rewarded in the end,
and you will come home to us as soon as you may.

And now I must quit, for my hand aches with
writing.

Your devoted father,
Nathaniel Bonner

Jennet's color was very high, it seemed to Luke more
with anger than with sorrow or frustration. She had always
been easy to rouse, passionate about many things, and unable to hide her feelings. Jennet had never been retiring, but
she had always been kindhearted and fair. Sometime in the
last year she had lost that balance, because she was looking
at Hannah with a narrow expression that bordered on re-

sentiment. Luke realized that Jennet was still thinking about the maps, and the options—or the lack of options—that had been laid before them.

Now she said, "It has been more than a year. Curiosity may be dead."

Hannah jerked as though she had been slapped.

"Three miles an hour does not seem such a bad idea at this moment, does it, cousin?" Jennet went on. "If we could set off today, we might be back with them in eight weeks' time."

Luke said, "Three miles an hour?" But Hannah's whole attention was on Jennet.

"That is not a course that is open to us, and you know it," Hannah said. "There are no steamboats traveling up the Mississippi."

"There will be, very soon." Jennet's chin came up; ready, even eager for an argument.

"Not before this war is over," Hannah said calmly. And: "I want to be away as much as you do, Jennet. It is unfair of you to hint otherwise."

Jennet made a small sound that might have been disagreement, or amusement. Luke put a hand on her shoulder and for a moment—a very short moment, but he felt it clearly—it seemed as though she would turn on him, too.

He said, "Jennet, why do you—"

Hannah interrupted him. She said, "Jennet believes I am too cautious. She thinks we should leave here now, regardless of the risks."

"Regardless," Jennet added in sharp tones, "of the new connections made here that will be broken."

And then bright tears came to her eyes and welled over as she put a hand to her cheek. She opened her mouth to say something—to apologize, Luke thought—and then she hiccupped a small sob. Under his hand her whole body was humming with tension.

Luke met Hannah's gaze, and she shook her head ever so slightly. Her message was clear: No more. Push her no further.

Though Hannah was the one who had been pushed, as far as Luke could see. Jennet had accused her of something—what, he could only guess—but she seemed determined not to take offense.

"I'm going down to the clinic," she said. She had closed long enough for this discussion, but Luke didn't point that out and Jennet, who had turned her face away to the wall and seemed unable to move, said nothing.

"I won't be long," Hannah said, though she didn't meet his gaze when she left them.

Alone in their chamber, Jennet said, "I must apologize to her."

Luke kept his silence, and let it draw out while Jennet settled herself and put the baby to her breast. She was pale, and her hands trembled a little, but he watched as she made the effort to calm her tone and soften her touch, speaking encouraging words to the baby, who seemed as unsettled as she was.

Luke lay on the bed and closed his eyes. His head ached in spite of the tea that Hannah had given him; he had a bitter taste in his mouth, and he was tired. They were all tired. He had just decided that sleep would be a better idea than an involved discussion that might end badly, when Jennet cleared her throat.

"I dinna begrudge her joy in the man."

Luke pushed himself up and rested his head on his hand. "Savard?"

"Where do ye think she spent the night?" Jennet's tone sharpened a little, and then she sighed. "I only wonder that it took so long. They are weel suited, the twa of them."

"You're speaking Scots," Luke said.

"Aye, weel." Jennet adjusted the baby and began to rock. "I am a Scot. Hardheided and harder hearted. I should be glad for Hannah, but I can think of naught but getting away."

The thought of Hannah with Ben Savard filled Luke with worry, and an odd sense of having somehow shirked his duty toward his sister. In those first hours after he had come into this room to find Jennet asleep with the boy on her chest, he had been so filled with relief and joy that he had no energy for coherent thought at all beyond the simplest facts: Hannah and Jennet and the boy were here, and safe.

Jennet had thought him dead; he had thought her lost; and they had both been wrong. He would have liked a week to do nothing but convince himself of that fact, but Jennet was hurt in ways that he could hardly imagine but must now learn to understand.

The late afternoon light lay on her face and hair like a layer of gold dust, outlining the arch of her eyebrows and the loose curls that fell across her brow. Her eyes were very large, and bluer than he had remembered. During this last separation he had often called her image up in his mind, and still over the weeks it had begun to fade.

And now here she was, his wife, the mother of his son. Seeing them together, he was overwhelmed by feelings he could hardly put words to, but he understood, too, that he must at least try.

He said what came to mind first, and hoped it would calm at least some part of what was bothering her.

"The boy is safe because of you. Whatever the journey has cost us—whatever cost there is still to be paid—I have no regrets, not when I see him there in your arms."

Her expression went very still, but color flooded up from her throat over her face, and her eyes brightened with tears that caught the light. Very carefully she got up from the chair, and she came to the bed, where she sat down next to Luke and then reclined so that the boy was between them. He was almost asleep, his cheeks working lazily.

"Thank you," she said.

"You did the right thing, Jennet. Now I need you to do one more thing. For all of us."

She waited, her eyes fixed on his face.

"It may not happen as quick as you like, but I'll get all of us away from here, and home in one piece. I swear to you I will, but you've got to trust me. Do you think you can do that?"

She blinked at him. Swallowed, and swallowed again. "I am so afraid, Luke."

"I know," he said, and touched her face. "I know you are. But I'm here, and Hannah's here, and we have strong allies and friends."

"It's Poiterin," she said. "I dream of him. Not what he did—not what he could do to me, but . . ." Her voice trailed away and she looked down at the boy, who had drifted away to sleep. When she looked up again, something new was in her expression. An anger so complete that for that first moment she looked like a stranger, a woman he had never imagined.

"I think of killing him," she said. "I think of killing him with a knife, of slitting his throat. I want him dead. And if it means an eternity in hell, I want to kill him with my own hands. I thought I understood what my father meant when he spoke of blood feuds, but I had no idea. I do now."

Luke held his breath, afraid that even the smallest sound or movement might stop the flow of words. He was no doctor; he knew nothing of fever teas or broken bones, but he did understand that some deep wound in Jennet had come to the bursting point. The best he could do for her right now was to listen while she rid herself of the black heart of it.

She said, "He made me lie down with him. It was the cost of getting the boy away from Dégre. And all the time he was using me——" Her voice cracked and she paused. "He kept whispering that if I didn't please him, he would throw my child overboard before the ship was out of the cove, so that I could watch him die. He wanted me to do things—he wanted me to beg him to do things to me and smile the whole time."

Luke had closed his eyes, but her voice went on.

"He put a child in me, and I willed it dead. I willed it dead every day and then it died, and I was glad. God help me, but I was glad to see the blood running down my legs. What kind of woman am I, to hate my own child?"

She shuddered. The baby made a mewling sound in his sleep. Luke stroked the boy's head, taking in the fact of him: feather-soft hair, warm skin, the curve of his skull. Jennet was waiting for him to say something, but Luke understood that there were no words that could fix what was wrong. His throat worked, swollen with anger and sorrow, until he could force himself to swallow it all down.

He said, "Did you think I'd be angry, or disappointed? That I'd think less of you?"

She closed her eyes.

"Jennet, listen to me now and I'll tell you what I think of you. You're the strongest woman I know, and I count myself a fortunate man to call you my wife."

She opened her eyes and looked at him. The uncertainty and hope he saw in her face were almost harder to bear than her tears.

"I killed Dégre for you," Luke said. "I'll kill Poiterin, too, if that's what you need."

Jennet drew in a deep breath, as though some terrible

pain she had been living with for a very long time had left
her suddenly.

She said, "Can ye stand tae touch me, now?"

"Let me put the boy in his cot," Luke said. "And you'll
see I can't stand not to."

CHAPTER 30

Hannah stood for a moment on the gallery with her shawl wrapped around her head and shoulders and considered. She had spent last night in Rachel's room, and though she had been bone tired she had slept very little. Out of anxiety and worry for Jennet, she told herself, but also because she wasn't sure she was where she should be. She wanted to go back to Ben—about that she must be honest, with herself at least—but the idea also frightened her. He frightened her, in a way Kit Wyndham never had.

Because I could control Kit, she reminded herself, and winced.

Hannah went down the stairs, out into the open courtyard. There was a cold sleet coming down but she went slowly, wondering if Ben might be at his window, and watching her. When she finally allowed herself to look, she saw that the room was dark and the window had been shuttered closed.

Which was just as well, she told herself. What she needed now most of all was rest, and there were two cots in the little clinic. She imagined them, freshly made, on either side of the hearth. It was that picture she had in her mind when she opened the door and found Leo sweeping the floor.

Hannah turned as she took off her cloak and shook it. A shower of sleet hit the floor with a hissing sound.

"I'll be done here soon," Leo said. "Or I can leave this until tomorrow."

He was calculating something for himself, she could see it in his face. Hannah said, "As you like, Leo. I have work to do." Which was true enough.

She went to the table where her daybook—so new that she had filled only one page—had its home. She read over the last entry:

Ltilakna. 6-year-old Choctaw girl with a rash of small open, infected blisters at the right corner of the mouth. Cleaned area thoroughly and applied a distillation of dock root. Asked mother to bring the child back in two days' time.

Thomas. 54-year-old Catawba seized with colic. Severely undernourished, probably eating refuse. Gave him a decoction of snakeroot & saffron and a bowl of bread soaked in beef broth.

She had notes for another six entries to be made, and so Hannah brought the candle on its saucer closer to the daybook and reached for the stoppered ink bottle. The long room was clean and dry and there was a good fire in the hearth. Hannah took a moment to close her eyes and be thankful for the fact that she was—that they all were—alive and safe, for the tasks she had to keep her mind occupied, for the good black ink and the smooth paper of the daybook. And then she asked herself how long it would be before she fell asleep over her work.

"Ben came in earlier," Leo said, startling her out of her thoughts.

"Did he?" Hannah took up a penknife to trim her quill, observing Leo from the corner of her eye.

She was very aware of how gossip moved through the household, and had no doubt that everyone, including Leo, knew where she had spent Sunday night. The part of her that was Kahnyen'kehàka was not bothered by this; it was every woman's right to choose, and that she had done. She would not pretend otherwise, though the other part of her—the O'seronni half, raised by a Scots grandmother and an English stepmother—stumbled a little at this lack of privacy.

Leo would know where she spent Sunday night. He would know, too, that Ben Savard had joined the militia.

"He left you a note, under that bottle on the corner of your table. I didn't read it."

"Can you read?" Hannah asked, surprised.

He smiled proudly. "The priests will teach anybody who wants to learn."

"As long as they convert."

He gave a shrug worthy of an old man. "It's a small enough price."

Hannah took the note, feeling her pulse jump as she opened it. She spread it flat on the open daybook and saw that Ben Savard's handwriting was even and schooled and still was distinctly his own. He had written only two words: the name she had been given by her husband's people.

Walking-Woman

She touched the letters on the page and then she folded it and tucked it into her bodice.

Leo was saying, "A stranger came by as well. A white man. He said he'd call again."

"An American?"

Leo's lip curled. *"Pas du tout."*

"I understand you don't like Americans," Hannah said. "But you should remember that Dr. Savard's wife is one. I hope you don't make a face like that at her."

"Mrs. Savard is no American," he said, indignant. "Mrs. Savard is a Quaker."

That brought Hannah up short. "That is her religion, not her nationality. Some Quakers are Americans. Mrs. Savard is both."

Leo seemed to take this as a personal affront. "I don't believe you."

"Well, then, what about her children? What of Rachel?"

"Oh, she's an American," Leo said.

"Very well," Hannah said, irritated and amused at the same time. "But I suggest that you talk to Mrs. Savard and see what she says. So this stranger was not American. What did he look like?"

Leo shot her a sidelong glance that said very clearly what an odd question this was. "I couldn't say. I know better than to look white men in the face when they speak to me." He raised his head with a sudden movement. "Why do you speak French like a white?"

Hannah paused and considered the question. "I learned French from a teacher. A white woman. Do people have trouble understanding me?"

Leo said, "We understand you well enough, but it's hard to trust somebody who talks like you. Who doesn't talk like us."

Hannah understood very well what he was trying to tell her: Many people, including Leo himself, had not yet made up their minds about her.

A timid knock at the door made them both turn in that direction. Leo was across the room before Hannah could move a step. He opened the door and Hannah saw a young boy, his dark face wet with rain. He caught Hannah's eye and then looked down at his own feet while he said a few hushed words to Leo. There were some questions and answers, and then Leo closed the door in the boy's face.

Hannah said, "What is it?"

"Do you know somebody named Titine? A free woman of color?" His expression was uneasy.

"Yes," Hannah said. She gathered her thoughts, or tried to. She realized, with some disquiet, that she hadn't given Titine a thought in days. Titine, who had disappeared, and possibly died, trying to be of help to the Bonners.

"The boy says that this Titine's aunt has got word of her. The aunt is the housekeeper at the Maison Verde on the Bayou St. John, and she's wondering if you'd come. And bring your doctor's bag."

"Now?"

"He's waiting to show you the way. But you can't go. It'll be dark soon, and Ben isn't here."

Very calmly Hannah said, "Was the message for Ben?"

Leo scowled at her. "You can't go alone. You don't know the way."

"I'll ride," Hannah said. "I can take the boy up on the saddle with me."

"You have no boots."

"Boots?" Hannah looked down at the clogs on her feet, and thought of her stepmother, Elizabeth Middleton Bonner, who had earned the name Bone-in-her-Back from the Kahnyen'kehàka, for her strong will and sense of justice, and for her bravery. Hannah's father had given her another name, Boots. For her one indulgence, the love of pretty footwear. Leo could not know it, but to remind Hannah of her stepmother at this moment was only to steel her resolve. She said, "Will you go to the stable for me, or should I do that myself?"

Leo's usual obstinate expression faded. Hannah could almost read his mind, and in some small way she understood and even liked the boy for his caution and the way he assumed responsibility for her welfare. But there was no time to shepherd him through his doubt, and so she went back to the long table where she prepared medications and hurriedly gathered the things she might need, medicines and salves and instruments she had once carried in a leather bag, but now tied into a large square of linen that she could tear into bandages if the need arose.

"Your cloak is still wet."

That was certainly true. For a moment Hannah considered going up to the apartment to get more suitable clothes, and then she remembered Jennet and Luke as she had last seen them. Jennet, who was already on the verge of falling apart. Luke must find a way to calm Jennet, though he had a bump on his head. Luke would feel obliged to come with her, though the Poiterins lived on the Bayou St. John and for him to come face-to-face with Honoré at this point would be a disaster.

She would not be put off, but neither could she go out unprepared. She needed warmer clothes, boots, money, a weapon.

As she went out Leo said, "I have to go to the clinic to see Dr. Savard."

Hannah gave him a grim smile. "I'm on my way to see him myself. Come along, if you like."

Paul Savard did not much like her plan, but he didn't try to stop her, either, and for that Hannah was thankful. Instead he gave her a pistol and a knife in a beaded sheath, a small leather bag of ammunition, another of powder, and the last, the heaviest, of coin. Leo watched all this, at first surprised and then barely able to contain his disapproval. He made a number of pointed comments under his breath, dire predictions and promises, dark certainties.

Paul finally said to him, "A smart man knows when it is time to stand out of the way of a strong woman. I could tell you stories about Hannah—" He broke off with a smile, and turned around to pick up a book. Its stained leather binding and sprung spine said that it had seen hard use and a number of mishaps in the apothecary, and even before she could read the words embossed she guessed what they would say: *Seats and Causes of Disease Investigated by Means of Anatomy.* The doctor began to leaf through the pages, not reading so much as looking for familiar landmarks.

Paul Savard was known to quote Morgagni in all kinds of professional discussions, but what bearing he could have on the present situation was beyond Hannah. She was about to say as much when he found what he was looking for and pulled out something that had been lodged between the pages.

He held up a small piece of discolored paper. The handwriting was clean and strong but the ink had faded with time, and still Hannah recognized it immediately. She sent Paul Savard a startled look and he returned a Gallic, one-shouldered shrug as he handed the note to Leo.

"My wife tells me you are an excellent reader," he said. "Read it aloud."

Leo began, stumbling a little with the English. "A man needs medical help. If you will attend to him, be outside the almshouse kitchen door at three this afternoon."

"How did you come by that?" Hannah asked, unsettled and moved by the vivid memories those few words could pull forth.

"What does it mean?" Leo asked.

To Hannah, Paul Savard said: "That's a long story."

Hannah met his gaze directly and when she saw that she could not move him, she said, "I must go, the boy is waiting."

The doctor inclined his head. "Of course. Leo, see that Hannah sets off and then come back here and I'll tell you the story. Unless she would like to tell you herself, tomorrow?"

She took the time to wonder what Paul Savard was trying to accomplish, and then she shook her head. "You must suit yourself," she said. "As you always do."

•   •   •

The messenger seemed greatly relieved to see Hannah come out of the courtyard on horseback, and he took her hand and climbed up behind her without a moment's hesitation. Through chattering teeth he told her his name was Michel. Hannah sent Leo back into the little clinic to get a dry blanket to wrap around the boy, and then with his arms around her waist they set off. She was aware of Leo watching from the window, his expression disapproving and wistful both.

Now and then Michel gave directions in short sentences, taking them down one street and then another, until finally they were on the path that paralleled Marigny's canal. This was the lesser-used road, the longer way to the Bayou St. John, but Hannah could think of many reasons to avoid the main byway, and so she urged the mare to a jolting trot at the same moment that the sky split open. The sleet turned into an icy deluge, and the mare whinnied her disapproval.

The temptation was to break into a canter, but the road was unknown to her and the combination of the dusk and fog called for caution. Beyond that, Hannah had been raised by men who spent a good amount of time traveling through the endless forests, and she knew the importance of paying attention in strange territory.

The path ran between the canal on one side and the beginnings of the swamp on the other. The smell of the canal was strong in the air despite the rain. Rotting fish and waterweeds and dung. A half dozen mules stood at the open half door of a stable, waiting to be let in after a day of treading the towpath, oblivious to the rain. Shacks and small cabins straggled along the way, weathered board walls festooned with fishing nets and lines. The tools of men who made their living on the swamp were everywhere: crates and barrels and wooden tubs, flat-bottomed boats dragged onto land and turned over to show scarred underbellies, piles of fish bone. A pack of dogs watched them passing from a shadowy corner, and Hannah was glad of the pistol she had tucked into her belt.

In the open door of a cabin that seemed filled with smoke, a man with a pinched face was skinning an alligator carcass that looked to be twice his own length. Inside her deep hood Hannah was glad that he didn't try to talk to her. If he knew the boy who rode behind her there was nothing of recognition to see in his face.

The land changed suddenly from swamp to the cultivated fields of a large plantation, acres of cut sugarcane and, just visble in the distance, a cluster of cabins around a larger house. Michel saw her looking.

"Michie Fauchier's place," he said, pointing in one direction, and then in the other: "Michie Dejan."

The swamp closed in again and then opened suddenly where the canal joined the bayou. The rain had faded away to a despondent drizzle by the time they turned west to follow the waterway to the settlement. There was no one to be seen out-of-doors, which was a great relief. Hannah was just about to ask Michel to point out Maison Verde when the boy gave a great wiggle and slid off the saddle. He looked up at her and pointed to the nearest house, and then ran off.

Uneasy now, and thinking of Leo's warnings, Hannah hesitated. She remembered that a stranger had come by the little clinic to see her today, a white man; she wondered now which of the houses on the bayou belonged to the Poiterins. She had two choices: to trust the boy, or to turn the horse around and go back to the city.

She walked the mare around the main house to a small cluster of buildings: stable, barn, kitchen, others she could not put a name to. The door of the kitchen building opened and a woman beckoned to her. She was strongly built and tall, wrapped in a white apron that seemed to glow in the growing dark. She gestured again, and called a word over her shoulder. Michel came running, his mouth still full of food.

"Amazilie says to come right in, you shouldn't be out here where anybody could see you. I'll look after the horse."

Hannah had understood that for herself, but still she hesitated. There was a tingling in her hands, and her mouth had gone dry. Something was about to change; she knew that without a doubt. Whether it would be for the good or bad was unclear, but what she did know, with certain dread, was that it would start here and now. She slid off the horse and started toward the woman in the doorway.

Luke woke early in the evening from a deep sleep and sat up, disoriented and sweat drenched.

The dream was gone. Nothing to hold on to beyond a sense of something very wrong, someone in trouble. It was a familiar dream, one he had been living with since the day Jennet had been taken away from him. He rubbed his eyes and drew a deep and shuddering breath.

Beside him she was deeply asleep. Beneath the covers she was naked, a thought that made his flesh stir. He would have liked to look at her while she was quiet like this, but the room was chilly and he was not a boy, after all. He didn't have to indulge every urge. He was repeating this to himself when he realized that he was not the only one who was awake.

The baby was lying on his side in his cot, his wide eyes fixed on Luke. He looked content, his round cheeks flushed with color. Luke wondered if the boy was capable of curiosity about this man who had appeared out of nowhere. A man who took liberties with his person and, no doubt more troubling, with his mother's. But there was nothing of fear in the small face, and so Luke got out of bed as quietly as he could manage, and dressed.

Then he stood over the cot and considered. He had little experience with infants, and remembered only vaguely things he had heard over the years. Luke remembered that his grandmother had had great success in quieting unsettled infants by wrapping them firmly in warm flannel and then rocking them, but this boy stood, sturdy and curious, and wanted something other than quiet cuddling.

Luke leaned over and picked up the boy, gingerly, carefully, and tucked him into the crook of his arm. He smelled of his mother's milk and his own soggy linen, and of something that was unfamiliar to Luke and was most likely simply himself.

"Let's go find some tea, you and me." He glanced at Jennet, who had not moved an inch. "Leave your mother to catch her breath."

The boy lifted his fist to his mouth and began to mouth it.

"At least until you can't wait any longer," Luke amended.

Luke knocked lightly on the parlor door, where he found Julia and Paul Savard sitting alone at the table over a simple supper of bread and cold pork and tea. Julia would have got up from her place to see to the baby had not Clémentine come in with more water. She scooped him up like a gold coin found on the street, and bore her prize off to his bath and clean linen.

Luke decided to dispense with social niceties and put his concerns out plain. He said, "After the scene we had this morning I don't know what I should do first, thank you or apologize. Jennet is—" He paused, not quite sure what to say, beyond the fact that he needed help.

Julia Savard seemed to have been expecting this. "Jennet has been through a great deal. For a very long time her

survival depended on her ability to dispense with all emotion, and now that you are reunited—she is awash. You must
take her behavior now as what it is: evidence that she loves
and trusts you above all others."

Paul said, "You must forgive my wife. She hasn't lost the
habit of plain speech."

"And I never shall," Julia said. "Though I hope I haven't
distressed you."

"No," said Luke. "I think surprise is closer to the truth. I
hadn't seen it that way, but it makes sense." He cleared his
throat. "Since we're talking plain, I've got something else to
say. We can't set off for home just yet, but maybe we can get
out of your way, at least. If you knew of a small house we
could rent for the next few weeks."

Paul Savard glanced at his wife and raised an eyebrow; his
expression said clearly that they had been discussing something, and that Paul had been proved right. Julia's mouth set
itself in a resolute line, and that line turned into a smile that
could only be called grim.

Julia said, "Could we please put the subject of your lodging aside for the moment? We have an idea to share with
you. One that may solve most of your problem."

Paul leaned toward his wife. "Julia, you must leave him
room to disagree with you."

"Of course he may disagree with me," Julia said, though
her tone said he would not.

"Now I'm curious," Luke said. "What is it?"

Paul said, "You know of Edward Livingston?"

That was a name well known in New-York as well as New
Orleans, and Luke said so. "Prominent family, successful
lawyer. There was some kind of scandal before he left
Manhattan. He's been here for a good while."

"He came in '04. As a lawyer he's without equal, and few
can match him for his business sense."

"Or aggressiveness," Julia added.

Paul nodded his agreement. "He's the most prominent figure in the American community. His influence reaches as far as Washington and London and Paris, and he's connected to everybody and everything here, starting with the governor and the leading Creole families."

"And the Baratarians," said Julia.

"He's connected to your family as well," Luke said. "Your daughter gave me the family history this morning."

Julia looked a little embarrassed, but before she could say anything Luke went on.

"I like Rachel," he said, with complete sincerity. "She reminds me a little of Jennet at sixteen. Eager to fling herself out into the world, no worries about the cost."

"That is our Rachel," Julia agreed.

Paul made a small humming noise in his throat. "The point is, we're connected to Livingston through Julia's first marriage, and he's connected to everybody else. And here's another point: His secretary has resigned suddenly due to ill health." And then: "I see you understand my thinking. I'd like to introduce you to Livingston and recommend you as a replacement. A temporary replacement, of course, though we needn't mention that to start with. You have all the business experience and skills, you speak English and French fluently, and you're American. Or at least you're enough of an American to satisfy him."

Luke tried to sort through the questions that had presented themselves. "I'm not sure what advantage there'd be in the arrangement, but I can see one problem. I'm bound to run across Poiterin if I'm out in the city day by day."

"Yes, you are," Julia said. "But if Edward Livingston takes your part, and you are presented as his trusted colleague and employee, Poiterin won't be able to touch you."

"Not in public he won't," Paul added.

Julia went on. "You'll be free to act on your own behalf while you're working for Livingston."

"And what of Jennet?" Luke said. "What do I say if Poiterin approaches me about Jennet and the boy?"

"We have talked that through," Paul Savard said. "And it seems to us that you have to turn the tables on him. Produce papers to prove your marriage—you do have your marriage lines? We'll introduce you and Jennet to Livingston and his wife at the same time."

"With your son," said Julia. "Louisa will be besotted with him."

"Tell them the story of Jennet's abduction, and then Poiterin must back off," Paul Savard said. "He can't afford to have his name linked to the men who were responsible. His reputation here is shady as it is, and he must tread carefully if he doesn't want to be exposed completely."

"Though by rights he should be arrested and tried," Julia said. No doubt she knew that Poiterin was involved with the illegal importation of slaves, something that would be anathema to any Quaker.

"And his grandmother?" Luke said.

"She hates Americans," Paul said. "But I don't believe she'd be willing to take on Livingston, though that's something we have to ask him about."

"Nor will she put Honoré at risk," Julia said. "She'll forfeit claim to your son rather than do that."

Luke was struck by how simple and elegant this plan was, but he also knew more of Honoré Poiterin than these two good people did. He said, "I have seen Poiterin's work firsthand. He has no conscience. He has killed innocent men out of nothing more than the desire to demonstrate that he can do as he likes. He will strike out at us if the opportunity presents itself. You'll be a target, too, even after we're gone. We've already put you in enough danger."

Savard leaned back in his chair. "You are thinking that a doctor with a Quaker wife is no match for Poiterin with revenge on his mind."

Luke inclined his head. "Something like that."

"You're forgetting my brother," Savard said. "But let me assure you—Poiterin won't forget Jean-Benoît."

Julia was studying her folded hands, her cheeks flushed with anger or discomfort, her jaw set hard. Luke tried to make sense of what he had stumbled across. A family argument with deep roots, and none of his business, except insofar as his own actions might cause any of these people difficulty.

"I don't want any part of this plan if Julia cannot endorse all of it," he said. "I'd rather we took our chances in the city than cause you any more trouble."

"You would gamble with your son's life?" Julia asked him. And: "Of course you would not. I admit that some elements of this plan concern me, but those are matters between my brother-in-law and his conscience."

"So you think we should do this thing?" Luke asked her.

She nodded. "I think it is the best chance you have. If Jennet approves, we will call on the Livingstons this evening, the four of us. Might I—" She hesitated. "Might I go to her now and tell her about all of this? I think I can present it in the best light."

It was as close as she would come to telling Luke he would make a mess of it.

He said, "I'd be thankful."

Ben Savard came into the parlor while they were waiting for Jennet and Julia. When Paul nodded at him, Luke understood that he had had a part in putting the plan together, but had stayed away while it was being explained. He would have tried to acknowledge the debt he owed the Savards, but Jennet came flying into the parlor flushed with color, her eyes and expression as bright as Luke had ever seen them.

She came to him directly, her hands held out before her

for him to take. Her eyes were wet, but this time she seemed to have been weeping not out of fear and frustration, but joy.

"You like the plan?"

"I do," she said. "It is a very good plan, I think." She glanced around the room. "Where is Hannah? What does she say to all this?"

Luke said, "We haven't talked to her about it yet." And to Savard: "Is she still down in the little clinic?"

"Hannah isn't here," Paul said. "She was called out to the Maison Verde, late this afternoon."

Jennet's expression clouded over immediately. "Hannah is gone to the Bayou St. John? By herself? Why would you allow such a thing?"

Savard's head tilted to one side, as if he were imagining what it would mean to deny Hannah Bonner some task she had set herself.

Jennet said, "It's not safe. We have to go after her."

Just that simply her high spirits and hopefulness were gone, replaced by something very like terror.

"I don't like this at all," she said. "Honoré is behind it, I'm sure of it. Luke, you'll have to go after her if nobody else will." She threw Ben Savard a look that was plain in its meaning.

He met her gaze with a steady one of his own. "I'll go. I'm on my way out to the old Spanish fort tonight to join my company."

"You'll look in on her?" Jennet said. "You'll bring her back here safely?"

"I will make sure she gets back safely," Ben Savard said. "You can count on me."

Suddenly presented with the solution to the problems that worried her so deeply, Jennet was filled with new energy.

Her hands trembled as she got ready to leave the house on rue Dauphine in the company of her husband and friends. They continued to tremble while she let Rachel fix her hair and she got her son ready. Nathaniel was uneasy, too; he flexed and turned in her arms, as if he wanted to swim away through the air. Julia had a rare talent for quieting unsettled infants, but it took her an unusually long time to convince him that all was well and that it was safe to leave the business at hand to the adults.

Setting out for the short walk to the Livingstons', Jennet was struck with the absurdity of the situation. She had what she wanted, and she was terrified.

If only, she told herself, there had been some time to sit quietly with Luke and talk it all through. If only Hannah were here. Jennet felt that absence with every forward step, but just as strongly she felt the responsibility that had been given to her. When Hannah came back to the rue Dauphine, Jennet hoped she would find that their situation had much improved. It would be a gift to her, and Jennet was willing to suffer this hour of uncertainty and fear to that end. Others had been bearing the burden long enough.

But it was strange to walk the street with Luke on one side and Paul Savard on the other, as if it were nothing out of the ordinary for them to be going to pay a call. As if there were no chance of Honoré Poiterin coming around a corner. The image of him leaning against a wall, his legs crossed at the ankles, was easily conjured. Any one of the people they passed on the street might recognize her and, remembering the reward, shout out to the world who she was: a madwoman, unfit to care for her own child.

When they finally stood in front of the Livingstons' fine house—carved wooden lintels and gleaming brass, beveled glass in tall windows aglow with candlelight, so that the whole gleamed like a treasure box—Jennet stopped to catch her breath.

Luke waited patiently beside her. He looked at ease, though she knew he was not; he had that knack, of hiding his feelings. She wished she had more of it. The borrowed clothes might not fit him exactly as they should, but no one would take note of that. They would see the blond hair smoothed back to a queue, and the strong nose and jaw and high brow, his suntanned face solemn above the stark white linen at his throat.

He smiled back, scar high on his cheekbone. It was small and white and curved like a quarter-moon.

The inconstant moon.

Jennet shook her head to dislodge that unwelcome echo. This was her husband, who would protect her and their son with his life. She squeezed his arm, and gave him a sincere smile.

He said, "All will be well, girl. I promise you that. Can you trust me?"

Jennet remembered, quite suddenly but very clearly, the day she had realized she loved him. She had been fifteen and furious because he had refused to let her ride out with the men.

When will you stop seeing a little girl when you look at me? she had asked him, and he had paused at the door and glanced at her over his shoulder. The look in his eyes had given her a very clear answer: He did see her as she wished to be seen.

He knows me, she had thought. *And he loves me for who I am.* It had been that simple.

"Let them do their worst," Jennet said now. "I'm not afraid so long as we're together."

CHAPTER 31

Hannah had never before met Titine's aunt, but she recognized her from Jennet's stories. Amazilie stood there looking uncertain, as if she regretted sending for an Indian woman she didn't know, but now could not think how to send her away.

"Amazilie?"

The woman in the doorway nodded, and her hands twisted together.

"Jennet has told me about your many kindnesses. I am her sister-in-law, Hannah Bonner."

"*Oui*," Amazilie said. Everything about her posture said she was fearful. Hannah's own sense of disquiet had risen to the point that she felt a little dizzy.

"Titine?"

The lined face sagged a little. "No. But there's a man here who can tell us about her, if he doesn't die first." And with that odd statement, she stepped back to let Hannah into the kitchen.

The kitchen was much like the one on the rue Dauphine, small and crowded, with whitewashed walls stained by woodsmoke, a brick hearth and baking oven built into its wall, pots and pans hanging from nails, and plates and platters on a wall rack. On the big table that took up the middle of the room lay a man.

There was a thin blanket that reached to his chest, and then a gauze dressing that did little to hide the swelling near his right shoulder. He was a small man but roped with muscle; a slave, without a doubt. It was not just the deep blue-black of his skin, but the scars that told the story.

Even before she lifted the gauze Hannah knew that he was close to death. He was breathing rapidly, and the muscles in his face were trembling in a way that said his nervous system had been compromised. There were great swellings beneath his jaw, as though the lymph nodes had been stuffed with pebbles, and he groaned constantly, the reluctant sound of a man who had always been strong and now found himself mastered by pain.

"Snakebit," said a man standing in the corner.

"My son Tibère," Amazilie said.

Hannah nodded her acknowledgment of the introduction and turned her attention back to the dying man. *Snake.* Such a small word to explain the disaster that had befallen him.

"Who is he?"

Amazilie said, "His name is Caspar. He was born and raised right here on the bayou—" Her voice dropped to a whisper. "He ran off from the Poiterins five years past."

"Didn't run away." His voice was deep and hoarse and came in a whisper that hitched and broke as he struggled to breathe.

Hannah made a soft sound to quiet him, and shook her head sharply at Amazilie. Then she pulled the gauze away.

The snake had struck on the heavy pad of pectoral muscles, and the poison had gone to work immediately. The flesh around the bite was so swollen that it looked as though a mountain had erupted out of his chest, the crater at its middle full of blood and pus and black with dying tissue. In spite of the open windows the smell of putrefaction was so bad that Hannah took short, shallow breaths while she considered.

This man, slave or free, would be dead before morning.

There was nothing she or any healer alive could do for him, and yet Amazilie had sent for her. Because he was a runaway slave and they could not trust anyone else, or because he had asked for her. What this man had to do with Titine she could not imagine.

Hannah retrieved a bottle of laudanum from her bundle, aware all the time that he was watching her. The truth was sometimes the only thing of real value she could offer, and she did that now.

She said, "If the pain is very bad, this will ease it. You will fall asleep and most likely you won't wake again."

The whites of Caspar's eyes had gone the color of egg yolks, but there was still a sharpness there and no small amount of intelligence, and more than that, an abiding sense of the absurd. When he tried to smile Hannah saw that he was closer to forty than the fifty-some years she had at first assumed for him.

"No wonder Titine likes you," he said. "You and her, you just alike."

Amazilie leaned closer to Caspar. "You've seen her? You've seen Titine?"

"That's why I'm here," he said. "Though I didn't count on that big old cottonmouth that got in my way."

"You shouldn't tire yourself out," Hannah said, though what she wanted to do was ask this man a hundred different questions. "The more you expend yourself—"

"The faster I'll die," Caspar finished for her, wheezing. "So put that sleep potion away now and let me give you a message from Titine."

She could not say exactly how such a thing should be, but even in her sleep Hannah knew when Caspar's soul left his body.

It had taken more than an hour of stops and starts for him

to get his story out, and when he was finally done he had had a convulsion that Hannah thought would end it. But he had recovered long enough to take leave of Amazilie and Tibère, and to thank Hannah for her help. Then she had held up his head while he drank the glass of water and laudanum, as peacefully as a sleepy child at the breast.

As Caspar fell into a deeper and deeper sleep, Hannah had slipped away, too, in the straight-back chair that stood at the head of the table. She was only vaguely aware of Amazilie leaving the kitchen, and far too weary to ask her where she was going, or how long she would be away.

They would be worried about her in town. This thought came to Hannah very clearly, but could not survive the pull of sleep. On the straight chair with her arms folded against her waist she gave in to it.

Still asleep, minutes or hours later, she heard the low rattle of a man's last breath and a click, like the snapping of fingers. Then a flickering in the dark like the wings of a bird, and cool fingers on her skin.

Some part of Hannah's mind occupied itself with the idea of going to the pallet in front of the fire, and then let the idea go. Even when she heard the door open and felt the cold night air on her skin she could not force her eyes open. Whether it was Amazilie come to check on Caspar or Honoré Poiterin himself, she seemed powerless to rouse herself. Then she realized that someone was bent over her.

"Jean-Benoît Savard," she said finally, recognizing the smell of him and the very shape his body made in the world.

"Your people are worried about you," he said, his voice low and easy.

She opened her eyes. "And you? Were you worried about me?"

"No," he said, his expression very serious.

She closed her eyes again, satisfied. "Good." And then, "Did you know Caspar? He was Titine's husband."

"I knew him," Ben said. "He was old Michie Poiterin's

valet. He disappeared one day, maybe a week after he married Titine. That must be five years ago now." And then: "Go ahead, and tell the story."

What Hannah wanted to do was to find a bed somewhere, a warm bed with clean sheets and pillows. A bed she could climb into, and sleep. Ben Savard would be welcome in that bed, if it could be found.

"It would be easier to tell," she said, aware that she was trusting him to follow her thoughts without any help, "someplace else."

"I will sit with him," said Tibère's voice from the other side of the room. Hannah had forgot Tibère, but it was good to know he was there.

"I will sit with him until first light, and then I'll dig his grave," Tibère went on. "You can have my room, upstairs."

Hannah's clothes were still damp from the ride through the rain. She stood in front of Tibère's neatly made bed, aware that her breath hung white in the cold air, aware of Ben nearby and the fact that he was watching her.

She stripped to her shift and sat down on the edge of the bed.

Ben sat down next to her. "What Caspar came to say made you angry."

"What Caspar came to say made me tired," Hannah corrected, and then, after a moment: "And angry. Tired of being angry." She reached down to strip off her stockings. "Tell me about Caspar and Titine."

He considered this request for what seemed like a long time, and then he pushed out a sigh and rubbed his palm over his face.

"Old Mr. Poiterin liked him. Everybody liked Caspar, really, except Honoré. He had a singing voice people came from miles around to hear.

"So back then, Titine was still living right here——" He looked out the window toward the main house, where the Widow Preston must be soundly asleep. "And they fell in love. Poiterin gave Caspar permission to marry off the property, mostly because Titine was his own blood, I think, and he liked the match. A week later Caspar was gone, run away, or so they claimed."

"You doubted it."

"Many did. Do you want to tell me what really happened?"

"No," Hannah said. "You tell me first what you suspected."

Ben lay down, dressed as he was, and waited for her to stretch out next to him. He gave off warmth like a stove; he smelled of horse and wet leather and damp cloth and of his own sweat. He smelled of comfort, and Hannah was glad to have him next to her.

He said, "A slave runs off from the Poiterin place twice, maybe three times a year. I can't think of another big planter with a worse record. But I will bet that the Poiterins are most likely to lose a slave when Honoré's gambling debts get out of hand."

"You think Honoré takes them and sells them and lies to his grandmother?"

Ben nodded. "But I haven't ever been able to figure out where he takes them. For a long time I thought he must put them on a ship, but now, with the blockade——" His voice trailed away. "So tell me."

Hannah drew in a breath. "He sells them to a sugar-cane planter three days' ride away. A man he calls Michie Christophe."

"Cedar Grove," Ben said. "That explains it, then."

"Explains what?" Hannah moved a little closer to him.

"Christophe Jardin goes through more slaves than any other planter, and he's always looking for more. If the price was right he wouldn't bother asking about papers or owner-ship." He turned on his side. "Titine?"

"Yes," Hannah said, and she drew in a sharp breath. "I can't stop thinking about her."

She is on her way back to the room where she left Hannah, with medicine and instructions for the girl who looks after her. Titine walks quickly, but she is very aware of where she is. These are the streets she grew up on. This is where she was born to Valerie Maurepas, the most beautiful mulatto woman of her generation, and Archange Poiterin. When Titine's father died and they were put out of the cottage, it was as if a part of her own body had been taken away.

Titine is willing to help Jennet, to do what she can for this woman who has had her child stolen away. She is a kind woman, and Titine believes that these northerners might help her, once they have their son back. They might help her come home to New Orleans for good, to bring her mother home.

She is passing the very cottage that had been her mother's when she sees him. He has been standing in the shadows, leaning against a wall with his hands in his pockets. Looking like nothing more than a rich young man at leisure. His eyes tell another story. Titine thinks of bolting, but he moves very quickly to take her arm.

What good will struggling do? None at all. Her mind races and races but gets nowhere as he pulls her into the cottage.

It is stifling hot inside. The air is heavy and unmoving, rife with dust and the smell of dead mice. Her mother's beautiful furniture is still here, but the brocade cushions are ripped and there is hardly a surface that hasn't been scratched and gouged.

"What do you want?" Titine asks him.

He pushes her down to sit. "Answers."

If she knew the things he asks her—about Luke Scott, his where-abouts, his plans—she would tell him. Sooner or later, she would tell him. Honoré will have what he wants in the end. Titine is both glad that she doesn't know and terrified.

After an hour, when he has broken into a sweat and his fists are as bloody as her face, he steps away to the window. Leans his forearm

against the wall and his head on his forearm, the picture of a desper-
ate man. He turns his head just enough to look at her, and then he
smiles.

The smell of urine rises in the close air. Titine lowers her head
and begins to shake.

Later she will remember very little of the journey out of the city.
Bound and gagged, tied to the saddle of a horse, she slips in and out
of consciousness for what could have been hours or days. In the brief
times she is aware, the pain in her head and face hardly allows her to
open her eyes. By the sound the horses' hooves make, by the smells in
the air, she knows that they are on a shell road or passing alongside
the c-iprière or crossing fields. Sometimes in the distance she hears the
sounds of slaves singing. La roulaison has started, the sugarcane har-
vest. There is sweet in the air, and ash. Somewhere nearby bagasse is
being burned.

Titine remembers where she was going when Honoré took her. To
the Indian woman, to Hannah, to bring her medicine for her fever.
Swamp fever. What will become of the Indian woman? The question
buzzes around her head like a fly. Another question, louder and more
persistent, comes to drive everything else away: What will become of
my mother?

When they stop, Titine rouses out of her stupor to see a small
camp, tucked into a field surrounded by rushes on one side and
ciprière on the other. A few tents, some horses, a cook fire. It is near
dark. Honoré pulls her from the horse and drops her to the ground.
Titine cannot stop herself from groaning.

"Did you say something?" he asks her in a tone that is all polite-
ness.

She squints up at him. "My mother was kind to you. Always."

"Your mother," says Titine's half brother, "is a whore." He leans
down to speak directly into her face. "You are the daughter of a
whore. Speak to me again without being spoken to first and I will cut
off an ear and send it to your mother the whore. Try to run away and

I will ride straight to Pensacola and I will cut off both her ears and her nose and feed them to my dogs. Do you understand?"

Titine closes her eyes, and nods.

The night passes in a blur. The sounds of crickets and cicadas and birds from the ciprière *rising and falling in her ears, the horses shifting in their sleep nearby. Pain of many kinds. Sharp and aching and burning.*

At some point a young white man comes and holds up her head so that she can drink from the dipper he puts to her mouth. He comes again later with corn bread soaked in broth. She turns her head away, gagging at the smell.

"You had best eat," says the young man. He's English, by the sound of him, or Irish. Titine isn't good at those accents.

"You had best eat," he says again. "I don't like to think what Poiterin will do to you otherwise. He's been drinking for hours, and he's a mean one when he's drunk. Mean sober, too, but you know what I'm trying to say."

She does know, and she's thankful for this young man's kindness. He unties her hands so she can eat, and he allows her to go behind a tree to relieve herself, and he brings more water for her to wash her face.

"Thank you," she says.

The young man's smile is open and friendly. "Let's see how thankful you really are," he says. When she struggles he shakes his head in disappointment, as if she is a student who has failed to learn her lesson.

"If you make noise," he says, "the others will hear and they'll want a turn, too. Unless you like the idea?"

Titine goes still, makes her mind as blank as it can be. When he is done, she rolls into a ball, her knees to her chin, and swallows down disgust and anger until they fill her belly like a misbegotten child.

She wakes to the sound of voices, men around the fire. Honoré is with them, speaking English, or trying to. The others ask him questions, three men who sound sober, and very intent. And all of them British. They ask questions and Honoré answers, sometimes at great length, sometimes stopping to tell a story in which he conquers his enemies. He is drunk, very drunk, but he is also sure of his audience, of their attention. He doesn't bother to hide his scorn for them. He is rude and overly familiar; he calls them by name, and laughs.

But they don't send him away. They seem intent on talking, and the conversation goes on and on. Titine finds herself listening, with growing amazement and, finally, understanding.

Two days later, her headache has receded enough that she is awake for most of the day. She is awake on the morning that they ride onto a plantation. It is at first like other plantations they've passed. Slaves are cutting sugarcane, bundling it, piling it in wagons so it can be hauled off to the grinders. There is a house, smaller than most with peeling paint and a sagging porch. There is no wife here, no one to care about things like clean windows. The usual outbuildings, the cabins where the slaves sleep, each with a small garden beside it, and in the distance, the sugarhouse with its long roof and open walls. The smell of cooking cane juice hangs in the air, coats the tongue.

A man comes out on the veranda of the main house. He is not old and not young, with a flowing beard that is red and gold and a bald head. The master. He is grinning broadly.

"Honoré, you sly dog," he shouts. "Can't stay away from Cedar Grove, can you."

It is at this moment that Titine fully understands where she is, and what her half brother intends. The shock of it robs her of human speech.

"You brought me something, I see," the master of Cedar Grove is saying. "She looks a little simple but strong enough to lift a hoe, I reckon."

"Not this one," says Honoré Poiterin. "This one you put on the Jamaica train. The sugarhouse is the place for her."

The master puts back his head and laughs with his mouth wide open. He has beautiful teeth, white and even. Titine is reminded of Grand Nez. She would be better off in the ciprière with Grand Nez than she is here at Cedar Grove.

In the dark Hannah could only make out the vaguest outlines of Ben's face. She wished suddenly for a candle, so she could read his expression.

"You're not surprised."

"Nothing Poiterin does could surprise me," he says. "Not even this."

"He sold a free woman of color into slavery."

"His half sister," Ben said. "Yes. And he's spying for the British."

Hannah waited for the questions that must logically come: *Did Titine recognize any other voices?* and *Is there any real proof? Did she hear any names?* And Hannah would answer him truthfully, because she must:

Lieutenant Colonel Anderson, Captain Geiger, Major Wyndham.

Titine had marked those names into her memory for safekeeping. She had passed them on to Caspar, and he had said them out loud in the company of three people. Hannah remembered the look on Amazilie's face exactly, the dismay and fear and anger. Caspar had died leaving them with a burden they could neither carry alone nor put down safely.

Even in time of war, when fears ran high and rumors of invasion seemed to rise up out of the very ground, a colored man who took it upon himself to accuse a white man of treason and espionage was putting his life on the line. And all they had by way of proof was names.

Lieutenant Colonel Anderson. Captain Geiger. Major Christian Pelham Wyndham.

Hannah could share this information with Ben, who would know what to do, who to talk to. Tomorrow Poiterin would be arrested, and as soon as Kit Wyndham showed his face in the city, he would be executed. What he might say before he died couldn't be predicted.

"Go on," Ben said. "Tell the rest of it."

A woman comes, a slave who might be forty or sixty years old, worn down and transparent as a sliver of soap. She takes Titine to a well where she is permitted to drink. There will be no food until all the slaves eat at seven, the woman explains. She is near toothless and hard to understand, but Titine is hardly listening anyway.

It simply cannot be the case that Honoré has sold her into slavery. She is a free woman of color, born to a free woman of color. There are laws in place, not to protect her so much as to protect men who might unknowingly become party to such a transaction.

There have been rumors over the years. How Honoré manages to meet his gambling debts without his grand-mère's help, how he affords the luxuries he buys himself. She had chosen not to believe them. It was much better to imagine that the disappeared had gone north, were living their lives in places where slavery had been outlawed altogether. That is where her husband is, her Caspar. She has been telling herself this for years.

That night she sleeps in a shack with five other women who have come in from the fields to eat and then collapse into sleep, too exhausted to even take note of Titine or ask her name. Titine sleeps, too, and dreams of her father. She asks Archange Poiterin about his son, if he is capable of such a thing as this.

I taught him everything I know, says Titine's father. I did my best to make a man of him.

In the morning Titine is turned out with the rest of them in a steady cold rain. The slaves gather in the clearing in front of the main house while they are counted by the overseers. There are four of them, and one seems to be the leader. He is a middle-aged man with soft features but hard eyes. He is on horseback. He carries a whip and there is a musket at his waist. His gaze fixes on Titine and he takes her in, as a man might study an insect.

She is about to speak up, to tell this man that she doesn't belong here, that she is a free woman of color, when a hand grips her elbow so hard that she gasps and tries to turn, but the hold on her arm cinches tighter and keeps her in her place. At her ear a man's voice says, "Don't do it."

Titine is taking short breaths. Bile rises in her throat.

"Don't do it," the voice whispers again. "He'll whip you til you would rather die, but he'll stop just short of killing you."

The grip on her arm relaxes, and Titine's knees almost give way. The hand is back, far gentler now, supporting her.

She says, "Caspar?"

"Right here. Don't turn around, Titine. Don't move your mouth when you talk."

She feels her husband's warm breath on the nape of her neck. Caspar. They had been married a week when he disappeared. One of Agnès Poiterin's house slaves, born and raised on her plantation and then brought to the Bayou St. John to be trained, chosen for his size and light color. Then one day he was gone, and his name and description showed up in the paper along with the other runaways. Reward for the return of.

"How?" she says, her eyes fixed on the ground, her mouth barely moving.

Caspar says, "The same way you got here, chère. The exact same way."

The overseers are calling out commands, and the mass of slaves begins to shift, some in one direction, some in the other. Titine watches as Caspar walks away without a backward glance.

A door opens onto the veranda of the main house and Honoré Poiterin comes out to lean his hands on the railing and watch. M. Jardin follows him, holds out a box of cigars. Honoré takes one absentmindedly. He is looking at Titine, and she is looking back at him. She can't help herself.

"You! Girl, what are you gawking at?"

The overseer's horse is suddenly beside her, and he is leaning down over Titine so that she can smell his sweat.

"She's looking at me," calls Honoré. "Isn't that so, Titine? Are you looking at me?"

She hesitates and the overseer prods her with his whip.

"Answer when you are spoken to, girl."

"Yes," Titine says, her voice cracking.

The slaves around her are drifting away. She sees this and understands what it means, but she is unable to stop herself.

"Yes, brother, I am looking at you. I am a free woman of color. You can't sell me."

M. Jardin is smiling broadly, but Honoré simply tilts his head to study her.

Titine raises her voice. "I am a free woman of color and by law you cannot sell me into slavery."

She is being pushed by the horse now, step by step.

She shouts. "You burned my papers, Honoré, but you can't burn up the truth. You know the truth."

Caspar is right. The whipping is almost, but not quite, enough to kill her.

It is a week before she is well enough to work, and by that time Honoré is long gone. On that first morning she is sent to the sugarhouse to work the Jamaica train.

When Caspar came to this part in his story Amazilie had moaned out loud, and now Ben shuddered. Hannah felt it, the way the words moved through him, like a fever chill.

"It doesn't mean anything to me," Hannah told him. "Sugarhouse, Jamaica train. I don't know what those words mean. It must be very bad."

"There's hardly anything worse," Ben said, "than standing in a sugarhouse for eighteen hours at a time with a ladle in your hand, scooping boiling hot cane juice from one kettle to the next at a breakneck pace. The heat is enough to kill you, if you're not used to the work, and the fires—" He paused. "You can tell those slaves who have worked the Jamaica train by the burn scars on their hands and arms. The only time it stops is so they can clean out the fireboxes." Ben looked away for a moment.

"I know where this story is going," he said. There was a

new tightness in his voice, as if he had reached inside her head and scooped out some of her anger for himself.

To everyone's surprise except her own, Titine lasts a week in the sugarhouse. Her anger keeps her alive, and Caspar. Caspar works the sugarhouse alongside her, and they find time to exchange a few words, now and then, when the overseer is busy elsewhere.

It takes a week of stolen moments for them to exchange their stories. On the seventh day Titine is whipped again, this time because she is too slow in her work. When she comes back to the sugarhouse a few days later, there's a fire burning inside her to match the ones that burn, day and night, in the sugarhouse.

The first time she has the chance to speak to Caspar, Titine tells him what she is going to do. She extracts a promise from him. He memorizes the names she recites to him without protest, keeps them in the forefront of his mind, touches them as he would touch a charm, for strength and courage and luck.

Anderson. Geiger. Wyndham.

Late in the night, when the overseer is looking the other way, Titine pours out the contents of a spirit lamp down the middle of the sugarhouse, and then she reaches under one of the kettles into the fire. She pulls out a coal with her bare hand.

Caspar is outside of the sugarhouse when this happens. He hears the soft punch of sound, like a fist in a feather pillow, as the coal ignites the spirits. He watches the fire blossom and then jump from one huge kettle to the next. In a matter of seconds the building has been turned into a torch. Another kind of fire has been lit, too. This one more volatile and louder, rising up in a hundred voices. From one moment to the next the slaves have freed themselves.

The alarm bell is tolling. There is no more time to stand and watch Cedar Grove burn. If Caspar is to fulfill the promise he made to his wife, he must turn his back on the sugarhouse, on Cedar Grove, on her.

With dozens of others he disappears into the ciprière as the alarm bell tolls.

"But he's the only one to get this far, I'll bet."

Except that he hadn't, Hannah could have pointed out. Caspar was dead. Just before she had given him the laudanum he had taken her hand with his own, hot and dry, and squeezed with all the strength he had left.

"Don't let *Michie* Honoré get away with it," he had whispered, unable to deny Honoré Poiterin the title Michie, even now, close to death as he was. "Don't let him get away."

They were quiet for a long moment, while Hannah remembered the way the dying man had looked at her. He was asking something of her, and she gave it to him. For his own sake and for Titine's, for the old women Poiterin had put out of their homes, for the terror and sorrow he had inflicted on Jennet. And for herself, too, because now the taste of blood was in her mouth and wouldn't be satisfied until Poiterin was dead.

"I promised him," Hannah told Ben. "I promised him I would take revenge on Poiterin."

"Unless I get to him first," Ben said grimly. He turned his head to look at the night sky through the window, weighing the passing of time and the hours until dawn.

"How would you do that?" Hannah heard herself ask.

Ben's voice was cool. "Things happen in the middle of battle," he said. "Afterwards the crows can argue among themselves about it."

It was something her own father might have said, and it both chilled her and made her glad that she had told him the story. Or as much of the story as she could tell him, until she had had the chance to talk to Luke.

For a long time they were so quiet that Hannah began to think that Ben had fallen asleep. She herself was no longer tired, but she was content to lie with him, warm and safe for this moment at least. Then she realized that Ben was looking at her, and his breath was warm on her skin.

"I should go back to the rue Dauphine. They'll be wondering about me."

"I doubt they're even home yet," said Ben. His hand came to rest on her belly, the fingers spread. "They went out to meet the Livingstons."

Hannah sat up suddenly. "Luke and Jennet went out—"

"To meet the Livingstons," Ben finished. He took her arm and began to draw her back down to him. "I've got a story to tell, too."

She put her hands on his upper arms to hold him off. "Tell me, then. Tell me now, or I won't be able to—"

"You won't be able to what?"

"Concentrate."

A finger worked its way under her shift and traced the outline of her breast. Then he leaned forward and kissed her, a soft kiss, full and warm and open.

"I might take that as a dare," he said against her mouth. "Now that you've finally invited me back into your bed."

Hannah turned her face away. "This is not my bed, or yours."

"True." He let her go and sat up suddenly. There was an awkward pause, and then he pushed out a sigh. "And I have to report to Hughes before morning."

A pang of regret flexed in Hannah's belly, and she was glad of the dark because she was sure she must be flushed. "So tell me about Luke and Jennet," she said. "What are they doing at the Livingstons'?"

"Telling the truth," Ben said. "Looking for allies."

CHAPTER 32

In Montreal Luke lived in the house his mother had gifted to him, the house she had grown up in, originally built by her father, who had been lieutenant governor of Lower Canada. It was a large, fine house, one of the most beautiful in the city, with furniture imported from France and England, and artwork from all over Europe. It had always seemed a little too much of a house to Luke, but then again it was the kind of place a successful merchant had. In Montreal he had been—he was still, Luke reminded himself—a merchant of the first rank, on an equal footing with men such as Livingston. He expected that the Livingstons would live in a similar setting, adjusted for the heat and humidity of New Orleans.

Later, when he confessed this to Jennet, she had pointed out the flaws in his reasoning: a much younger, very fashionable wife, and a husband who took satisfaction in indulging her.

And in truth the Livingstons' home worked something like a doll's house on a grand scale. Every room glimmered with candlelight reflected in mirrors and silver and polished wood. The draperies and furnishings of silk and damask and double-cut velvet were as colorful as jewels—gleaming ruby, emerald, sapphire. There were Turkey carpets on every floor, Chinese porcelain figurines crowded along the mantelpieces, heavy gold-framed oil paintings, expensively bound books piled on a long table of inlaid rosewood and ivory next to a dish of sugared almonds. The air itself smelled of money.

The part of Luke's mind that could not stop being a merchant catalogued all this, but only until Jennet, fully aware of what he was doing, pinched him hard enough to make him mind his manners. Paul was in the middle of the introductions, which he carried out in a sharply efficient, almost curt manner. Luke had noted before that physicians were allowed to dispense with certain social niceties, the only thing about the profession that had ever appealed to him. But even Paul Savard could not do much to shorten an introduction to Edward Livingston, originally of Clermont, New-York. One-time attorney general of that state, three times elected to Congress.

"The legislature has appointed Mr. Livingston to make sense out of the mess of laws the French and Spanish left us," said Paul. "He's writing a code of judicial procedure."

"Which is just as boring as it sounds," Livingston said. "Let's have no more talk of the legislature tonight."

Rachel had prepared Luke for Mrs. Livingston's elegant self, though she hadn't mentioned what a small, slender person she was. Nor had Rachel told them that Mrs. Livingston would sweep down on Jennet and appropriate the drowsy baby, overflowing with praise for everything from the way his eyebrows were formed to the dimples on his feet. Julia took Jennet's arm and they followed Mrs. Livingston into the parlor, leaving the men to find their own way.

For the first half hour, so many people came and went that even Luke's superior memory for names and faces was put to the test. It seemed that much of Mrs. Livingston's family had fled to New Orleans after the revolution in Saint-Domingue. They were introduced to Madame D'Avezac de Castera, Mrs. Livingston's mother, a sister, two brothers—one of whom was an attorney in practice with Louisa's husband—and an uncle, Jules D'Avezac. The Livingstons' young daughter came in with her nurse to curtsey and smile, a quiet, pretty girl who was most clearly her father's special pet.

Edward Livingston was a type immediately familiar to Luke. A man close to fifty, broad across the shoulders but tending toward corpulence, a softness around the jawline, a puffiness of the flesh of the neck beneath the carefully barbered whiskers. Soft hands, too, with faint ink stains, as Luke's hands had once been permanently stained with ink. A successful lawyer and merchant, his intelligence always infused with a good amount of skepticism and a thorough understanding of man's basic venality. Luke felt himself closely observed, and could almost see Livingston come to some preliminary conclusions after no more than five minutes of ordinary conversation. At that point he seemed to settle back in his chair and let his wife take over the ritual of a formal evening visit.

There were platters of *calas,* a sugary cake the locals liked to take with their coffee, pralines filled with pecans and pistachios and fruit preserves, thick slices of cake, candied orange peel and ginger, porcelain pots of hot chocolate and tea and coffee, all in such profusion that a casual observer would never guess at the rarity of such delicacies in the middle of war. Ben Savard had mentioned that Livingston represented the interests of the Baratarians; no doubt it would take more than a war to deprive this household of luxuries.

"You must have more of this fine seedcake," Mrs. Livingston was saying to Jennet. "It is my husband's favorite. Very plain for Creole tastes, but I have come to appreciate it." She herself was busy dandling Nathaniel on her knee and had eaten nothing at all. "You are so thin, my dear, and it is full of the things that will nourish you. Eggs and milk and butter. Julia, encourage her, please."

Outwardly Jennet seemed to be holding her own, and there was even some color in her complexion, a hint of the younger Jennet who would have been the center point of such a meeting, full of laughter and odd observations that would delight and disturb her hosts.

Later Livingston invited Luke and Paul Savard to his study. He lit a cigar and then sat quietly, both hands on his knees, his eyes resting thoughtfully on Luke.

He said, "I need a secretary, Mr. Bonner, as you know. My question is why you'd be interested in work that is so far beneath you."

Luke appreciated the directness, and repaid it in kind. "I'll tell you," he said. "With the understanding that what information I share with you now must remain in this room."

Livingston listened to it all, his head cocked slightly to one side, an elbow propped on a knee. His expression gave away little surprise or unease, though he grunted once to himself when Luke recounted what had happened to his ship and crew in Pensacola. Twice he asked short questions for clarification and then nodded for Luke to continue.

When Luke had finished, Livingston got up and went to the hearth, where he lit a spill from the fire and then took a long, fumbling moment to light his pipe. From a cloud of smoke he said, "I have one question to begin with, and the answer to that question will decide whether we proceed with this conversation or carry on as if it never happened."

Paul caught Luke's eye and gave him a half smile.

"You have anticipated the question," Livingston said. "Which is half an answer unto itself. But let me proceed. Mr. Bonner, have you aided or do you intend to aid the British in this war? I am speaking of any kind of aid, direct or indirect, active or passive. If your allegiances are to the

British, I can have nothing to do with you, no matter how intrinsically sound your reasoning or dire your cause."

Luke took a deep breath. He said, "I am Canadian by birth, but my father and grandfather were born and raised in New-York State. My wife, as you know, is the daughter of a Scottish earl. My mother lives on Saint-Domingue. When we can leave this place we will most likely go back to Montreal until we can decide where to settle. At this moment I am thinking of Albany, if my business concerns can be addressed. But to answer your question directly: I have no allegiances to the British, and have done nothing to advance their interests on this continent, nor will I. If I were at liberty to share details with you, I could provide evidence that in the year before I left Canada to look for my wife, I acted for the best interests of the United States, though," he added, after a pause, "I was never in uniform."

He kept his gaze on Livingston throughout this speech, and saw what he had hoped for: This was a man who understood what was said, and what could not be said, and how to reconcile the difference.

Livingston said, "If I should find out that you've misrepresented your history or connections, I will not hesitate to see you arrested and tried for sedition."

"I understand," Luke said.

"Very well." Livingston began to pace. "Let us talk about what might be done. The biggest problem you face is not Honoré Poiterin, at least not at the moment. If you are allied to me he will not dare call you out." He stopped and gave Luke a sharp look. "I assume you wouldn't be so foolish as to call him out, either. He's the best shot I've ever seen. But I say this because I know that your grandfather was called Hawkeye."

"I won't call him out," Luke said. "And it's what he's willing to do out of the public eye that has me worried."

Livingston made a gruff sound. "Your family must be

closely guarded, of course. But my real worry is Poiterin's grandmother. She is a powerful force in this town, and it would be a mistake to underestimate her. She has been talking to the governor and to every well-placed Creole about this situation, and she has called in favors."

"For what?" Luke asked. "What is she asking of them? That they produce Jennet and the boy out of thin air?"

Livingston shook his head. "She wants a new law, one that would forbid taking a child out of Louisiana while his custody is being challenged. She's convinced your wife is still here in the city."

Paul sat back and let out a sigh. "She can't expect—"

"She can expect," Livingston said. "That is, under normal circumstances she most likely would get what she is asking for. Men have done far stupider things to silence a troublesome woman of means."

"Other circumstances," Luke prompted.

"The war, of course. A war may well be the only thing that could come between Agnès Poiterin and what she wants."

"Do you have any suggestions?" Paul asked.

"Certainly," Livingston said. "We could simply take her to court. We would most certainly win, but it could take up to a year. Am I correct in assuming that wouldn't suit?"

"It would not suit," Luke said. "There are other considerations I haven't outlined—none of them relevant." He felt Paul's gaze on him, but he didn't turn.

"As it is far too dangerous just now to try to smuggle you out, I see only one other option." He pulled a watch from his pocket and consulted it. "If you are prepared to take up your post as my secretary immediately."

"I am," Luke said.

"Good," said Livingston. "It would be best if you and your lady moved in here straightaway, within the hour. She will be safe here while you are away."

Luke sat up straighter. "Where am I going?"

"Major General Jackson arrived on the Bayou St. John this evening. He's spending the night at the home of an American merchant. You and I will be there at first light. I can't think of a more perfect opportunity to introduce you as my secretary. Kilty-Smith's wife will see to it that word gets back to New Orleans before we do."

Luke couldn't help but grin. "You're saying that Andrew Jackson trumps Agnès Poiterin."

Livingston looked at him sharply. "With the British breathing down our necks? That is exactly what I'm saying." His own smile had gone sharp and cold, the expression of a lawyer who was used to winning, and had no intention of giving any ground once he had joined the battle. "This city is on the brink of full-fledged panic. Andrew Jackson will receive a welcome much like Julius Caesar did when he returned to Rome from Gaul. Once you have made a connection to him, Mme. Poiterin will not be able to touch you."

"And how am I to do that?" Luke asked, curious and somewhat uneasy.

"You won't have to do anything," said Livingston. "Except stay close to me. Jackson and I served together in Congress, and we've been in touch these last weeks. Best of all, he's got no French. You and I will be indispensable to him before the first day is out."

CHAPTER 33

Louisiana Gazette

News reached us late yesterday evening of a short-lived slave uprising in Whitehall County, Mississippi. We report the verified details of this horrible event to forestall rumors and panic.

Cedar Grove Plantation has been burned to the ground. The violence began when the slaves who were at work in the sugarhouse rose up and overpowered an overseer. Cedar Grove's owner, M. Christophe Jardin, died when fire spread to his mansion. M. Jardin was an unmarried man, and to our certain knowledge he and his three overseers were the only casualties of this savagery. No other innocents died in the conflagration.

Some two dozen slaves escaped before neighbors and officials could gain control of the situation. It is our understanding that most of those runaways have already been caught, and those responsible for the uprising summarily executed, as justice demands.

Our local officials take great pains to point out that the rebellion at Cedar Grove is in no way part of a larger, more sinister plot. In this case, rumors that the uprising was incited by British spies are simply false. Officials in Whitehall County have satisfied themselves that what happened at Cedar Grove had other causes, specifically an owner who was too liberal with his slaves, and an overseer who was too trusting.

We are reminded of our responsibilities to those lesser creations who depend on us to instill in them the discipline, self-control, and Christian principles which are foreign to their natures.

CHAPTER 34

"It will be light in an hour," Ben said into the dark. He sounded as sleepy as Hannah felt.

She said, "Do you have to go?"

He turned on his side. "I have to go. Do you have to stay?"

"No, I'm going back to the city." She yawned. "I'll walk out with you."

But neither of them moved. Finally Hannah said, "I have this feeling that everything is changing. The whole world is changing around me, and it's going to be hard to hold on."

"It's the war," Ben said. "And me."

She snorted a surprised laugh. "Such modesty."

"Go on," he said. "Deny it." His voice was low and sure. And then: "I unsettle you. Have you figured out why?"

"Why don't you tell me," Hannah said, and wished she could snatch back the words.

"Because we fit," he said. "And you can't pretend we don't."

"Are you talking about the fact that we're both half white?"

He pushed himself up on an elbow. "That's only part of it."

It was odd, wanting to disagree and unable to find any flaw in his reasoning.

"We fit in some ways," she said. "But not in the most important ones. You belong here, and I don't."

Ben traced a finger along her hairline. He seemed to be picking his words, but then he only shook his head. His smile sometimes made him look almost boyish. He said, "Come. Walk out with me."

The freezing rain of last night might have been a dream, if it weren't for the fact that Hannah's clothes were still vaguely damp. The air was sweet and much warmer than she had expected. By the time they had finished saddling their horses and walked them out to the shell path the sky was full light.

Hannah glanced toward the kitchen and wondered if Tibère was still there with Caspar. He would be buried today, no doubt in secret. To announce to the world that a slave who had run away so many years ago had come back to die would bring a lot of unwanted attention. It would bring Honoré Poiterin, almost certainly, to make sure that his bad habits didn't become public knowledge.

Ben was so quiet that Hannah thought he must be thinking about Caspar, too, or about Honoré.

She said, "How long will your company be stationed here?"

He turned as if he could see through the trees as far as the old Spanish fort, which stood on high ground at the point where the bayou met Lake Pontchartrain.

"I've been assigned to Major Hughes, so I'll be here as long as he has command, or until they figure out which direction the British are going to invade from," he said. He glanced down at her, the color of his eyes particularly strong and strange in the first light. Then he turned his head toward the north, and at that moment Hannah heard it, too: the sound of men on horseback. A lot of them, moving at a fast clip.

Ben took both horses by the bridle and pulled them into the trees that led down to the water. Hannah followed, more curious than alarmed. They stood while the horses thundered by, shoulder to shoulder. Ben leaned over and spoke into her ear so that gooseflesh moved in a wave down her back.

"Hughes and the men. I'll have to catch up."

Hannah said, her voice oddly high and far away: "Try not to get yourself killed, will you?"

The smile he turned on her was so wicked that Hannah should have been alarmed. Before she could step away he bent his head and kissed her as if it were the most natural thing in this strange world, as if she belonged with him and nowhere else. She kissed him back anyway.

He was still holding the reins, and he turned to loop them around a low branch.

Hannah said, "You have to catch up."

"I won't have far to go," Ben said. "They're stopping at the Kilty-Smith place. You could see them if you went down to the water's edge."

There were many good reasons to refuse, but none came out when Hannah opened her mouth to protest. Instead she let him pull her deeper into the trees. She went with him because she was intrigued and flushed and couldn't think of an excuse not to go, at least not an excuse that wouldn't make him laugh at her outright. So she let herself be pressed up against the trunk of a tree—a cypress, she noted with some part of her mind—and be kissed. And she kissed him back, glad of the chance, glad of the feel of him. Things were changing, that was true, but Hannah realized that she didn't want Ben Savard to be one of those things.

One large hand was lifting her skirt and moving up her thigh with a touch as light as feathers.

"Really, Ben—" She shuddered as Ben's tongue traced from the hollow of her throat to the jut of a collarbone.

Against her ear he said, "Send me off to war with a smile on my face."

"You've been smiling for hours," she said, her voice wobbling.

There was no more talking for a while, though Hannah
could not make her mind stop working, couldn't stop the
words tumbling and then disappearing into the long kisses
that shifted and deepened and broke only long enough for
Ben to lift her, her skirts caught up around her waist, her
legs wound around him.

"You see?" he said. "We fit."

She saw, yes. She saw him, the truth of him and of herself. She wanted this. Ben Savard so deep inside her and still
it wasn't enough, couldn't ever be enough. With one part of
her mind she heard more horses on the shell road, and men
on foot marching in formation, and then that sound was
gone, too, lost in the shudder and shift, the heat and commotion and push and pull and the final plunge, like falling
from a great height, heart pounding, to be caught up again
in the tangled web of the world.

"What is going on?" Hannah asked, when she had her
breath back and was trying to put her clothes back in order.
"A hundred men must have gone by here in the last fifteen
minutes."

"Major General Jackson," Ben said. He retrieved the
slouch hat he had dropped from the ground and settled it
on his head. "Come to rescue us from the presumptuous
enemy." He leaned down to kiss Hannah, a hard stamp of his
mouth. "Get back to the rue Dauphine," he said. "You may
not see me for a week or more. Sleep in my bed while I'm
gone."

CHAPTER 35

The ride out to the Bayou St. John was unexpectedly pleasant, though Luke had got little sleep and less rest. Jennet, relieved beyond words at this change in their fortunes, had climbed up onto the great bed in the large, almost opulent chamber they had been given for their use, and fallen asleep while the baby was still nursing. Luke had untangled him and was considering whether or not he should wake Jennet when a maidservant scratched at the door. It turned out to be the Livingstons' wet nurse, who had the care of their young daughter and who had been instructed to take on Nathaniel's needs as well.

And so Jennet had slept on, undisturbed, and Luke had lain next to her, not quite asleep, while the evening's conversation drifted in and out of his mind. He was deeply uneasy for a dozen reasons, and also oddly resigned. They had taken a great risk in approaching Livingston, but it seemed as though the Savards' intuition had been correct.

In the morning, things moved so quickly that there was no time to reconsider. A manservant—a slave, no doubt—appeared with clothes suitable for Livingston's secretary, the jacket a little small, the linen a little large, the boots, thankfully, the right size and well broken in. Then he had been given a bowl of coffee and milk and a roll of soft white bread, and before first light they had ridden out of the city.

The first day of December. In Montreal there would be snow and cold, but here the skies were clear, and the temperature was no more than chilly. Another thing to be thankful for: Luke found he wasn't expected to make any kind of conversation. They were in a larger party of men, among them the mayor and the governor.

Luke was surprised at Claiborne's youth—the man looked to be no more than thirty-five, though he had been appointed to his post by Jefferson some years ago. Worse than his relative youth was the fact—Luke couldn't overlook it after even ten minutes in the man's company—that he was severely limited in terms of intelligence, excessively prideful, and completely unaware of the way he presented himself to the world.

After so many years in business dealing with politicians, Luke knew a bad one when he came across him. A man in Claiborne's high position needed a few basic skills, including the ability to hide his true feelings in the company of rivals, but Claiborne's dislike of the lawyer was palpable. And still he spent the entire seven-mile ride arguing with Livingston about the Baratarian pirates who had volunteered to fight for the American cause. Or better put, Claiborne argued a dozen different reasons that Lafitte's offer be turned emphatically down. Livingston rebutted all of them shortly, almost carelessly, and as each argument failed, Claiborne's mood worsened. He had a face as long and oval and pale as a poached egg, and there were flecks of red on his cheeks and neck, evidence of his irritation with Livingston or of the cold, or both.

It was no less than Luke had been led to expect from talks with the Savards and from the newspapers. The American governor was so far out of his depth that the Creole legislature ignored him with impunity. The whole of the city seemed to take particular pleasure in Claiborne's crusade to shut down Lafitte's well-organized company of thieves, pirates, and slave runners. Clearly the governor's obsession with Lafitte had passed into the realm of the ridiculous, something not entirely unexpected from an American, but nonetheless regrettable. When Claiborne announced a reward of five hundred dollars for the capture of Lafitte, Lafitte retaliated by offering a reward of his own: a thousand dollars for the capture of the governor.

Claiborne was a ridiculous figure and the perfect foil for Lafitte, who was admired for his business sense, his bravery, and his adventures. Most important, Lafitte provided the residents of New Orleans with hard-to-get goods and services—many of which had been in plain view in Livingston's own home.

To Luke it was clear that Claiborne was determined to win Livingston over to his view of how Lafitte was best to be handled, as if another American would have no choice but to see things his way. Luke listened as closely as he could, given the roughness of the road and the wind, and stored away what information might prove to be useful at some point.

Luke noted the exact moment when Livingston's patience gave way. He sent Claiborne a look that Luke recognized, a look he himself used when negotiations had broken down past the point of usefulness, and ended the conversation with a single sentence.

"Major General Jackson will decide what to do about Lafitte, not you." And he used his spurs to put distance between himself and the governor.

They were riding through a wide savannah, brilliant green even now in the first week of December. A great heron, stark white against the flashing blue of a pond, lifted awkwardly into the air as they passed. Luke saw ten different kinds of birds in just as many minutes. This was strange and beautiful country—nothing like Canada, and yet it caused a surge of homesickness to rise in his throat.

"There," said Livingston. They had come to the edge of an expanse of fallow fields where a small city of tents had sprung up. Luke calculated some thousand men, militia and volunteers out of uniform, milling around. They looked as if they had been living rough for a long time.

"Not the most inspiring sight, are they?" one of the other men said.

Luke spoke to him directly for the first time. "They lack spit and polish," he said. "But their reputation as fighting men makes up for that."

Beyond the fields were a line of pecan trees, a scattering of houses, and the Bayou St. John. Livingston pointed to a large, rather run-down house that stood on a rise at the junction of the canal and the bayou. "That's Kilty-Smith's place."

As they picked their way through the camp, Luke studied the landscape until he was able to identify the Maison Verde. He wondered if his sister might still be there, and what had brought her here in the first place.

Even so early in the day the crowds had already begun to gather. They threaded their way through groups of onlookers as cheerful and unruly as children waiting for a play party to begin. Jackson was here. They were safe, they told each other, from the British. Now they were safe. Washington had burned, but New Orleans would stand.

Luke handed his horse over to a young boy and followed Livingston into the merchant's house, which was as overrun as the campground. Soldiers, officers, militiamen, merchants and bankers and plantation owners, all hoping to be admitted into the dining room and the company of Jackson and his officers. The mass of men opened to let the governor and mayor through, and Livingston walked with them as unself-consciously as a prince behind a king. Luke followed, but he felt himself being observed and wondered, too late, if Poiterin himself might be here. Before he could look around to answer that question, he was inside the dining room and the doors had closed behind him.

Andrew Jackson sat at Kilty-Smith's breakfast table over a bowl of boiled hominy. Long weeks of living out-of-doors had deeply tanned his skin, but still his color was vaguely off, a hint of yellow beneath the leathery brown. The tufts of hair that stood up on his head made his already narrow face with its sunken cheeks seem almost absurdly long.

To Luke he looked like a man who had risen from a sickbed far too soon, and would pay for his folly. Then, oddly, that first impression of severe poor health fell away as soon as Jackson raised his head. The deep wrinkles around the eyes might have had something to do with pain, but the eyes themselves could have belonged to a bird of prey. They were sharp and unblinking and unflinching, and Luke had no doubt that in that one sweep of the room Jackson had taken in everything and everyone around him, long before his host had finished with the introductions.

Any secretary worth his salt had to be good with faces and names and so Luke paid attention, marking into his memory the barrel shape of Major Hughes, who commanded Fort St. John; Jackson's secretary Captain Reid, whose face was mostly hidden behind a profusion of sleek beard that reached to his cheekbones; Major Butler, Jackson's adjutant, famous for his ability to assimilate, organize, and retain thousands of details crucial to his superior; Commander Patterson, severe and as inflexible as an iron rod in full naval uniform. A dozen other officers, and then the leading men of the city: Bernard Marigny, the richest and most powerful Creole in New Orleans, and a man dedicated above all things to spending the fortune his father had left him; Ignace de Lino de Chalmette, an elderly Marigny uncle; Magloire Guichard, a dignified old man and speaker of the legislature. When

Livingston was introduced, Jackson's expression opened and became less guarded. For a long minute there was what amounted to a private conversation in the crowded room, Livingston and Jackson renewing their acquaintance. Claiborne looked at first surprised, then disgruntled, and then almost sick to his stomach.

Then Livingston introduced Luke as his new secretary. Jackson's gaze met Luke's. He returned the gaze without flinching, aware that he was being judged not just by Jackson, but by every other man in the room. Aware, for the first time, of a group of militiamen in the far corner, hidden by the men of the legislature. Men in uniforms as gaudy as peacock feathers, and in their middle, Honoré Poiterin.

"Gentlemen," Jackson was saying in a gravelly voice. "The British are at the gate, and they must be stopped. To do that, I will need your assistance. Your full and unquestioning assistance. Whatever quarrels you've got among you, let them go. Until New Orleans is secure, you must forget these distinctions you make between Americans and Creoles. We are all Americans, or we will all be British."

His gaze settled momentarily on certain men in the crowd and then moved on. "If I've made myself understood, we'll start," Jackson said.

For the next hour Luke was aware of two things: Poiterin, who stared at him with open and unwavering hostility, and Jackson, who dispensed judgment and directions with the bare minimum of social nicety and a great deal of sharp commentary. Each man was evaluated for what he had to contribute, and made short work of. Some were passed along to be dealt with by Butler or Patterson; others were told that they would be called on as they were needed. More than once Jackson waved a hand to cut off a speech filled with empty platitudes to ask questions that must be seen as rude.

Little by little the men began to trickle away, orders and

instructions in hand. Through all of this, Livingston only observed, calmly, a man sure of his value and his place in the company. Through all of this, Poiterin stayed exactly where he was until two thirds of the room had gone.

"May I introduce Commander Henri de Ste-Gême," Kilty-Smith was saying. "And some of his Hulans, or Dragons à Pied, as they are called. Pierre—"

"Commander," Jackson interrupted. "We count on your local boys to show us the lay of the land."

"Of course," said Ste-Gême, a man as short and rotund as a cork. His English was so heavily influenced by French that it sounded almost as though he must be joking. "We will lead the charge. As you know, Major General, we are originally sons of France, and we will be pleased to send the English dogs back to their island, as my forefathers did at Agincourt."

Jackson's gaze was hard but his mouth twitched at the corner, out of amusement or pique, Luke couldn't say. "I look forward to seeing you in action," he said, and his gaze flickered toward Major Butler with a message that Luke understood from across the room. Ste-Gême allowed himself to be led away, the handful of men he had brought with him following like ducklings. Poiterin continued to stare at Luke until he was summoned specifically, and then he turned away with obvious reluctance.

"So it begins," said Livingston, who had observed the entire silent exchange. And then: "Stay close."

Jackson had winnowed the crowd of men down to the ones he considered most worthy and potentially useful to him, and Livingston was among that number, a man of like mind and ability. Before they left his company, Livingston had pledged all his time and energy to Major General Jackson and had joined his staff as a voluntary aide. When Jackson and his officers made ready to ride into the city,

Luke found himself among the small party of men invited to join them.

On the way out to the horses, another surprise: Ben Savard stood in the early morning light next to Hughes, who had command of Fort St. John. As he passed the men, Luke said, "Hannah?"

"On her way home."

"What about you?"

Ben shrugged. "Depends on what they have in mind for me. I see you've worked things out."

At that moment Jackson turned his head in their direction. Luke, who had stood his ground with far more imposing men, felt the jolt of that cold blue gaze in his spine.

"Major Hughes," said Jackson. "You are satisfied with your Indian scout?"

"Jean-Benoît Savard," said Hughes. "There is none better in Louisiana. I'm about to lose him to Captain de Juzan's regiment of Choctaw."

Ben's expression was impassive, as if they spoke a language he didn't care to understand.

"Keep him here," Jackson said. "I have a need for such men, and he will be more useful out of uniform, for the moment at least. Savard."

Ben looked at Jackson directly and gave a slight, stiff bow from the shoulders. "At your command, Major General."

Jackson's mouth was like a bloodless cut in a face carved from stone. He turned away and disappeared into the crowd of his officers.

Jennet woke with a gasp and lay frozen with fear until she made out the embroidered bed hangings and remembered where she was, and why.

The Livingstons'. They were safe.

The pillows and covers showed that while Luke was not

here, he had slept beside her. Jennet remembered, now, where he had gone this morning, and why. She wondered if he had tried to wake her. With a sigh of relief, she sank back into the small mountain of pillows, all encased in finest linen and smelling of lavender water.

The house was very quiet, though by the quality of the light, it must be at least nine. Even without the light she would have known the hour; her breasts were full and tender. If they did not bring the baby to her soon, she would have to go look for him. And, she noted with some surprise, she was hungry herself. She sniffed and took in the faint smell of coffee.

Just that simply she was more fully awake and it seemed, looking around the room, that at some point in the last months all the color had drained out of the world in such a slow way that she hadn't even noticed. Now it was as if a hundred candles had been lit at once so that grays gave way to strong color: the sky blue of the coverlet, the crimson and grass-green embroidery on the pillow slip, the crisp gold of sunlight on the polished cypress wood floor, the same warm color as Hannah's skin.

Jennet sat up in the bed, thinking of her sister-in-law. She would ask the butler to send a message. Mrs. Livingston had told her that she was to act here as if she were at home, and that she would do. She would send a half dozen boys out on errands, but the first one would carry a note to Hannah. Just as soon as she found her clothes and took care of the baby.

A soft knock at the door. Jennet jumped back into the bed and pulled the covers up around herself—she was wearing only the simplest muslin shift—and a servant came in carrying a tray covered with a linen cloth the same brilliant white as the tignon wrapped around her head. Behind her was Rachel, carrying a fussy, scowling Nathaniel. His expression shifted just as soon as he saw her, first going blank and then breaking into a smile. He lurched, trying to fling himself out of Rachel's arms.

She handed him over with a laugh. "He's had porridge this morning, but clearly it's not enough. He doesn't like to be kept waiting, does he?"

"I suppose I should wean him," Jennet said, knowing even as she said it that she had no intention of doing any such thing. It would be too cruel, after such a long separation. They would both feel the loss.

In a matter of minutes the servant had set a table with china, silver, a tea service, baskets of toast and rolls, and a plate filled with shirred eggs, ham, and a buttery mound of hominy. Then she disappeared without saying a word. Jennet's mother, who had been the housekeeper at Carryckcastle for all of her adult life, would have approved. For her own part, Jennet was rather sorry, as servants were generally the best source of real information about the way a household worked, and there were things she would have liked to ask.

Jennet climbed out of bed and wrapped a shawl around herself and the baby, who was nursing so enthusiastically that she could barely contain a wince. Settled in a chair, she used her free hand to accept the teacup Rachel had filled for her.

"So," Jennet said. "Is the great man arrived in the city?"

Rachel's excitement was answer enough, but of course she must also describe what Jennet had missed.

"You should have seen it," she said. "The whole city turned out to welcome the general. My uncle Livingston was riding next to him, and your husband just behind, and he looked so very handsome, you would have been proud. It was so thrilling. I'm surprised you could sleep through the noise."

"It has been a long time since I had a proper night's rest," Jennet said. "It would have taken more than a parade to wake me."

Rachel said, "It's so exciting; the major general is only five minutes away. We will be seeing a lot of him, I think."

There was no end to Rachel's enthusiasm for Major General Jackson and his party, which continued while Jennet looked to the boy and ate her own breakfast with her one free hand.

"The troops will be pouring in," Rachel said with a pretty blush. "Corbeau—have you met Corbeau? my uncle's valet—Corbeau says we will be overrun by Americans, and my aunt said—"

"Better than the alternative, to be overrun by the English."

"Yes," Rachel said, sitting back. "Exactly." She pushed out a sigh, and then seemed to really look at Jennet for the first time.

"You think me silly. Well, I suppose I am, a little, but it really was exciting."

"Of course it was," Jennet said. She gave the girl a sincere smile. "And I don't think you silly. I think I was much like you at your age, actually."

This pleased Rachel greatly. She said, "Your color is much improved. You like it here with my uncle and aunt?"

"We are safe," Jennet said. "And your aunt keeps a verra comfortable home, forbye."

"You are feeling better, if you're speaking Scots so early in the day and without provocation," Rachel said with a smile.

"It's good of you to come by so early," Jennet said.

"Aunt Livingston thought you might like to see a familiar face," said Rachel. "And I wanted to tell you about the parade, and oh, I haven't even thought to tell you about the speech the general gave on the Place d'Armes. Even Mme. Derilemont was impressed, and you know what she thinks of Americans."

Jennet's plate was empty before Rachel came to the end of her story of what had transpired on the Place d'Armes.

"And I have messages to deliver. My mother has sent your things, and wants to know what else you might need or want, and Hannah is back from the Bayou St. John and needs to speak to you."

Jennet would have liked to have heard that particular bit of news first, but she couldn't find it in herself to be irritated with the girl. "I was hoping she would come straight here."

Rachel got up suddenly and went to look out on the garden.

"Rachel."

The girl turned back, all her happiness gone, and in its place an expression of supreme discomfort.

"What's wrong?"

"Nothing," Rachel began in a tone that made it clear that there was in fact something amiss. "It's just that my aunt Livingston has very specific ideas about callers."

Jennet swallowed and put down her fork. She took a moment to settle the baby on the floor with a piece of dried toast, and to right her clothes.

"Is it Hannah she objects to, or the hour?"

"I'm not sure," Rachel said. She looked so unhappy that Jennet understood exactly what she hesitated to say. Mrs. Livingston's kind welcome didn't extend to half-breed, half-blood sisters. Rachel could come and go as she pleased, but Hannah could not.

Jennet looked down at her son, who was rubbing his face with the toast as if it were a washcloth. This was all for his sake, after all. It was worth any price to keep this child safe until they could take him home. Hannah of all people knew that.

And still, the relief that Jennet had felt on waking was gone, replaced by resentment and guilt. Hannah, who was worth ten of Mrs. Livingston, was not welcome here. There must be some compromise, and Jennet would find it.

"I will speak to your aunt."

Rachel let out an audible sigh of relief. She said, "I came here straight from the Place d'Armes, but she's still out. I'm sure she'll want to talk to you as soon as she's home again. Now, I'm supposed to ask which gown you want to wear to tea this afternoon, so it can be brushed and pressed." And at Jennet's look of confusion: "You remember, my aunt invited us to tea this afternoon? And she included Hannah in that invitation, at least."

"I had forgot," Jennet said. "I suppose half the ladies will be coming to examine Hannah to see if she wears scalps on a belt around her waist."

Rachel frowned. "I think you do my aunt a disservice—"

"No doubt I do," Jennet said. "She has been the very soul of generosity, and deserves to be treated in the same way. Forgive me."

But Rachel, who was indeed very young and sometimes thoughtless, was also her mother's daughter, and she had a conscience. Jennet wished she had kept her worries to herself.

There was a soft knock at the door and the nursemaid came in for the baby. She was a woman of at least forty, with a round, pleasant face the color of molasses and eyes the exact same shade. With a deep laugh she scooped the baby from the floor and parted him from what was left of the toast. He responded by grabbing onto her nose and launching into a loud and impassioned speech.

"You two are getting along very well," Jennet said. "Thank you very much for your kind attentions, Jeanne."

The nursemaid looked surprised at being thanked, and she ducked her head. "Such a strong boy, so handsome. He demands admiration, and I supply it."

Rachel got up to follow Jeanne out. "What shall I tell the housekeeper about your gown?"

"It's not as though I have a dozen to choose from,"

Jennet said, thinking very briefly of the beautiful gowns that had been made for her at Giselle's insistence, now sitting in a trunk in Mme. Poiterin's house, never to be retrieved. She could feel no real regret for the lost finery. The three simple gowns Julia Savard had found for her were all she needed or wanted.

"The blue?"

"Certainly," Jennet said. "Whatever you think will suit best."

It wasn't until the early afternoon that Mrs. Livingston returned home, and then she disappeared into the back of the house to consult with her housekeeper.

Jennet retired to the lady's small but elegant drawing room to wait. She found it impossible to sit still with a book, and so she went to retrieve her tarot cards from the basket of things that had been delivered from the rue Dauphine, and began to lay them out on a table by the window that looked over the rear garden.

The noise in the hall was the first indication that something was wrong. She heard the butler's alarmed voice, and the unmistakable sound of a cane on the polished wood floors. The door opened abruptly.

The butler's name was William. He had come with Edward Livingston from New-York, a spare, quiet, dignified free man of color with exacting manners. Now he was agitated, and barely in command of his emotions.

Alarmed, Jennet rose, but before she could think to ask what might be wrong, she saw for herself. A pulse began to hammer at her temples and wrists and elbows.

"You will let me pass," said Mme. Poiterin in heavily accented English. "Or I will buy you from your master just to have the pleasure of watching the flesh being whipped from your bones."

"He is no slave," Jennet said, her voice catching in her throat. "William, please fetch your mistress."

"Indeed," said Mme. Poiterin. "Fetch her so that I can tell her what I think of people who hide runaway lunatics and abducted children."

"Fetch Mrs. Livingston now," Jennet said. A great calm had come over her, a detachment so complete that she seemed to be watching the scene from outside her own body.

Jennet held her ground as the old lady thumped across the room. Her face was red with exertion and choler, and one small fist in its black kid glove was pressed against her bosom.

"I've come for my great-grandson," she said, in French. "Produce him immediately and perhaps the law will go gently with you."

"You have no great-grandson here," Jennet said. "My son is none of your blood."

Jennet was not tall, but Mme. Poiterin was shorter still, a small hill of beaded black brocade topped with an elaborate construction of black lace and wool in the shape of a stove-pipe. Jennet thought of it belching smoke, and she found herself smiling. Unadvisedly.

Mme. Poiterin was small, but she was surprisingly strong and very quick. Her slap made Jennet stagger.

"How dare you laugh at me! You should be cowering in shame and fear."

"Madame!" Mrs. Livingston stood in the door of the drawing room with William behind her. "What do you mean, forcing your way into my home and assaulting my guest? Have you taken leave of your good sense?"

"The constables are on their way," said Mme. Poiterin. "They will arrest this—this woman for the assault on my slave and the stealing away of my grandson's child."

"They will do no such thing," said Mrs. Livingston

sharply. "You are not yourself, madame, or you would not intrude into a private home without invitation. You must leave immediately, or I will have you arrested for trespass."

For one moment Mme. Poiterin's mouth made a small, pale circle in her face. "You may forget who you are, madame, but I do not. I remember you on your knees taking up my hem, when you hadn't two coins to rub together. You would not dare have me arrested."

Jennet had to admire Mrs. Livingston's ability to remain calm—to maintain her regal bearing—in the face of such provocation. She merely shook her head, and spoke very quietly. "I would dare that much, and more. What my husband will do, I can only imagine. Do you think the first families will stand behind you when they hear about this outrageous behavior?"

The old lady's hand tightened its grip on her cane, and it seemed to Jennet that her color climbed even higher. "You are hardly the person to judge what the first families will do, as you have never belonged and will never belong. I tire of this. Give me the boy, and I will go."

Jennet pulled herself up to her full height and walked to the middle of the room, where she was positioned between Mrs. Livingston and Mme. Poiterin. "I never bore your grandson a child. The boy is mine and my husband's."

The whole of Mme. Poiterin's face, powder white and round as a penny, trembled. "That is a lie."

Anger was an odd thing, Jennet realized. It could come like a flare, throwing everything into stark relief. Now she felt a click in her mind, like the snapping of fingers. Blood rushed up her neck and down her arms to her hands and immediately ebbed, leaving her trembling in a white anger. The image of her father came to her, and his voice: It is better to dwell in the wilderness than with a contentious and angry woman.

"Get out," Jennet said. She felt the anger gathering in her

throat, pushing up and up, but her voice sounded oddly calm to her own ears.

In the soft folds of the old lady's cheek, a muscle twitched. "You ill-bred slut," she said. "I know all about you. You dare to deny me?"

"Madame," said Mrs. Livingston. "I suggest you spare yourself further embarrassment—"

"I have recourse," Mme. Poiterin said. Her mouth jerked as if she might spit in Jennet's direction. "I can report to the authorities what I know to be true. She"—she pointed at Jennet—"and the whoremaster she calls a husband are spies. They are spies, do you hear me? My grandson has proof. They will hang, and then the boy will be returned to his rightful place with me."

Jennet's skin felt too tight on her face, as if it would suddenly split and a new Jennet—one capable of terrible things, her father's daughter—would push out into the light. She bore down on her anger, for her son's sake.

"Madame," she said slowly. "My husband and I are not spies, and never have been. But if they hang men for piracy and theft and murder, then your grandson will hang, when I give evidence against him. Shall I tell you what I know about his dealings? Then you can decide if you care to go to the authorities with your stories."

The old lady pressed a hand to her chest. "I don't have to listen to this."

"No?" Jennet said. There was a knock at the door, and men's voices raised in concern. "Then let me tell the constables what I have seen with my own eyes. Mrs. Livingston, please, open the door."

CHAPTER 36

In the almost unbearable sun and heat of the late summer, New Orleans had at least been free of crowds, and Kit Wyndham had found things to like about the town tucked into a fold in the great Mississippi River. By November the weather had turned cool but not unpleasantly so, and all the rich merchants and bankers had brought their families back from summer houses perched on Lake Pontchartrain or the Gulf. As New Orleans roused from her summer-heat stupor her streets began to fill, and Kit Wyndham—known in this town as Christian Reynaud—had been drawn into the social season.

He had expected to dislike it, and found himself again taken in against his inclinations. The wealthy of New Orleans were as self-important and self-indulgent as their counterparts everywhere, but they also knew how to play.

Now things had changed again, and the city was bursting at the seams. Any other time he would have turned on his heel and fled the crowds, but it was only by losing himself in the masses of people coming into the city to catch a glimpse of the newly arrived Major General Jackson that he had dared even this much.

Pure idiocy, to be here at all.

He had left New Orleans within hours of coming face-to-face with Lady Jennet of Carryck on an otherwise unremarkable Sunday morning stroll. That encounter had left him no choice but to get out of the city immediately. If he returned at all, it would be after the British forces were established here. That had been his plan, and now here he was, risking everything. He was a spy, a British officer out of uniform. An idiot, he told himself firmly, without peer. If they hanged him, it would be for good reason.

His first month in this place he had spent observing, listening, cultivating connections, supervising, and passing on information that would make its way to the men who were planning the invasion. He had not welcomed the assignment. When it had been explained to him in Saint-Domingue, he had stood attentively, asked the right questions, made the right responses. First and foremost he was Major Christian Pelham Wyndham of the King's Rangers in British North America. He signed his communications with his superiors *Yours to command*. He rarely thought about Margaret, and when she came to mind his memory of her was of someone he had never really known, a pretty girl who had died too young, but had nothing to do with him.

Yours to command. It was the cornerstone of his life, inviolate, and so he found himself in New Orleans.

Once he was settled he found that it suited him. Apparently, a year of chasing Dégre across the Antilles had had more of an effect on him than he had realized. Sometimes, at night, he examined his conscience for signs of guilt or remorse, and found none. New Orleans had changed hands many times and survived. Once more would make no difference.

In the first days he had sometimes been afraid of very specific things. That he would not be up to the sensitive work that he had been assigned; that he would send insufficient or useless information; that he would not be able to sustain the façade of himself as a merchant. Never once had

QUEEN OF SWORDS 383

he ever feared being recognized and called out as a spy. He
had no connections to anyone in this part of the world, or
so he believed until that unexpected, unexplained Sunday-
morning encounter with Lady Jennet.

The last he had seen of her was on Saint-Domingue, the
morning he had taken leave of Luke Scott and his party.
They had been bound for Pensacola to retrieve the child
Lady Jennet had sent there for safekeeping, and then they
were to sail north, for home. They were long gone. Or so he
believed.

But there she had stood, dressed like a lady's maid in at-
tendance to Miss Rachel Livingston, one of the flock of
pretty, silly girls who had been fluttering around him since
he first arrived. Miss Livingston got more attention than
some of the others because her uncle was so well placed, but
not enough to engage a close examination by her family. As
it was, she had never had any useful information to share
and Kit had dismissed her until she came into sight with the
daughter and sister of the Earl of Carryck in tow.

It made no sense, none at all. Why was Jennet Huntar
Scott here, and where was her husband? Where was her
sister-in-law?

Kit hadn't allowed himself to think of Hannah very often,
but now that barrier came down. The questions had multi-
plied themselves in his head like rabbits even as he rode
away from the city. He shifted his base of operations to the
north, exchanged the fine clothes of a successful merchant
for rougher wear. But the questions couldn't be dropped so
easily.

If Jennet was in New Orleans, Hannah would be nearby.
Unless she was dead. Perhaps, he reasoned, Lady Jennet was
stranded here, separated again from her husband and sister-
in-law, unable to identify herself for fear of being called a
spy. Which she most certainly was not. One of his own responsibilities was to oversee the men who worked for the

Crown, in hopes of significant reward once the city had passed into British hands. For the most part they were an unsavory and untrustworthy lot. Most probably those very characteristics made them good at what he required of them. To Kit's certain knowledge, none of them had yet to be compromised.

Except himself, of course. For reasons he couldn't articulate even to himself, Kit had neglected to tell his superiors about his encounter with Lady Jennet. Who must know him for a spy, but perhaps—he shied from this thought, though it came to him often—would look the other way, out of gratitude for the part he had played in her rescue.

In a city that seethed with rumors, she would hear every day about spies and the dangers they posed. Spies fomenting the slaves to uprising, skulking in the woods, massing in the ciprière. These rumors were always laid at the doorstep of Creole passion and love of drama, but the fright was real and a man taken to the Cabildo for questioning would have a hard time of it.

If Lady Jennet was passing herself off as a servant for fear of such treatment, he would do best to leave her be. When the British took the city she could declare herself and she would be taken care of. If she was alone.

Now he found himself back in New Orleans. Of the dozen or so men who could be called on, he was the one most likely to get close to Jackson's people. As Christian Reynaud he had connections to the men who could make that possible.

And so here he was. Most likely Jennet—and whoever else was with her—was already gone. Why she had been here in the first place, posing as a lady's maid, he might never know.

Moving along with the jostling crowd, Kit tried to recall where Miss Rachel Livingston lived. Not with her uncle and aunt Livingston, or he would have called on her there, in the hope of making a connection to the most prominent American in New Orleans. As he remembered, her own parents were in the city as well, but her mother had remarried, and what was her new name? The biggest challenge in this new line of work was remembering hundreds of details that might someday prove to be useful.

Kit cursed softly to himself. The old woman in front of him hunched her shoulders as though she expected to be struck. Even dressed like a smallholding farmer, these people knew him for what he was: not one of them. Born to money and privilege. As Reynaud nobody questioned his identity; merchants and bankers and their pretty daughters accepted him immediately.

Before he could reestablish himself as Reynaud, he must first know whether Lady Jennet was still in the city, and whether she was alone. And if she was here, and wasn't alone—he would deal with that if and when the need arose.

The noise of the crowd was tremendous, shouting and singing at odds with the band that played in the open square. People crowded onto balconies and roofs, waving banners and flags. Kit knew himself to be taller than average, but he could make out nothing but a seething mass of bodies.

Hannah could be in this crowd, or standing on one of the crowded balconies that overhung the street. He could imagine her expression as Jackson passed by. Interested, observant, unswayed by the crowd's enthusiasm. A hint of distaste in the set of her mouth. They had avoided political topics for the most part, but when the subject of the Indian wars came up in her presence, her whole demeanor changed. She drew into herself, like a man with a wound that would not heal and must be protected from random blows.

He found himself regretting that he wouldn't be able to talk to her about Jackson. It had been hard to surprise her, and harder still to impress her, and she did not hesitate to say what she saw clearly. It was the thing that had drawn his attention first, her clarity of intellect.

Another lie, of course. Kit made a conscious effort to ban Hannah Scott from his mind, and to deal with the problem at hand.

The people of New Orleans believed that their savior had arrived. An uncouth backwoods American, sure to be snubbed by anyone of standing in the city in any other circumstances, would be carried on upraised hands. Kit heard the rumors seething around him already. Nothing of use to his superiors, who were not interested in the hopes or fears of people like these.

The crowd inched past a set of wrought-iron pillars that supported a balcony. Kit hesitated only for a moment before he climbed up one of them and lifted himself over the edge. He was counting on general high spirits to save him from being pitched back down onto the street, and realized his mistake too late. A large man with a face as broad and highly colored as a pumpkin grasped him by both shoulders and dragged him over the banister. His breath reeked of brandy.

"M. Reynaud!"

Kit composed his face. This was Mr. Huber, a German tailor with a reputation for his skill with a needle, his sense of fashion—so odd for a German, the Creoles often told him openly—and a temper that was slow to flare but then could hardly be put out without a brawl in the street.

"Mr. Huber, pardon my imposition—"

"Never mind! Never mind. How good to see you back with us, and on such a happy day. But, monsieur, how is it you are dressed like a drover of pigs?"

Kit let himself be drawn into the Hubers' parlor, out of the noise of a crowd given over to jubilation.

CHAPTER 37

Julia Savard said, "Jennet has been asking for you all day, Hannah. There was an unpleasant scene with Madame Poiterin earlier today."

Hannah stopped. "Tell me."

"Everyone is safe. Madame made threats, but then she left before the constables came. I truly believe the Livingstons are committed to keeping Jennet and her son safe."

Hannah studied Julia's face and wondered if she was hiding something crucial. But it wasn't in the woman's nature, and so she allowed herself to relax.

"If there's any more trouble, it will most likely come through the courts," Julia offered. "And few men would go up against Edward Livingston in such a matter."

"Yes," Hannah said. "I see that."

"Will you come to tea? For Jennet."

They were standing in the courtyard under the shelter of the stair. Julia had already changed for the visit with Mrs. Livingston, another simple gray gown, but this one scrupulously clean and with a bit of lace at the throat and cuffs. Hannah looked down at the work gown and apron she had been wearing all day, grimy and spattered with all manner of gore. What she wanted to do was fill the hip bath with water as hot as she could stand it and then crawl into bed—crawl into Ben's bed, where she could be alone and sleep.

It had been a difficult day for all of them, in both clinics. It seemed that at least half of the hundreds of people who had come into the city to welcome Major General Jackson had decided that while they were here they might as well take advantage of the free cowpox vaccination at the new clinic on the rue Dauphine, and why not see the doctor at the same time about that carbuncle, a crippling pain that radiated down the leg, a child who seemed to be going deaf. The other, healthier half of the people coming into New Orleans were already roaring drunk in celebration of what was now declared to be an automatic victory over the British. In the distance there was a volley of gunfire and raucous laughter.

But Julia was right: She did need to see Jennet and Luke. To assure herself that this new situation suited them both, and to pass on the information she had about Honoré Poiterin and Kit Wyndham. Instead of the hip bath she made do with cold water and a rough washing, changed quickly, and set off a quarter hour later with Julia. Rachel had gone ahead, and in fact it looked as though they would be the last to arrive at the grand house on the rue de Conde.

"You and I will look like missionaries among heathens," Julia said, glancing through the parlor windows where a dozen young ladies in bright silks and muslins were sitting and talking. "I should have done better for you than plain gray."

Hannah said, "Gray suits me perfectly. I hope to sit quietly in the corner and be overlooked." As she said the words she knew that such a thing would be impossible. It was not the first time Hannah found herself in this kind of situation. She was irresistible to the well-to-do, an oddity to be examined and exclaimed over, as intriguing as a two-headed cat. A red Indian with more education than most of the men, better manners than many of their daughters, an exotic beauty they could not openly admire, and a bearing they would call haughty after she had gone. *Her father is white,* they would explain to each other. *And she was raised by a white stepmother, a lady of some standing in England.*

And so it was, exactly. Hannah, exhausted after the night she had spent on the Bayou St. John and the day's work, let it flow over her as best she could. She allowed herself to be seated directly next to Mrs. Livingston, depending on the trick she had first cultivated in a parlor just like this one: She pretended she was her stepmother, and conducted herself as Elizabeth would. She answered questions that seemed well meant and ignored the impertinent ones.

Soon after she sat down, Pere Tomaso joined and was immediately surrounded by attentive young ladies. Hannah studied him with some interest. He had been such a great help to them, and he seemed as unassuming a man as she had ever known, but Hannah's experience with Catholic priests had taught her to be cautious. Maybe he understood that instinctively, because he took steps to earn her trust. He did this by diverting the questions of a young lady who was very curious about the savages of the northern tribes, and whether Hannah had ever taken a scalp.

Père Tomaso ended that line of questioning and steered the conversation in another direction, while Hannah focused her attention on her teacup and attempted to regain her composure. Then Julia Savard and Jennet were drawn into the conversation, and soon enough interest turned to Jennet's history, which was just as bad, and harder to ignore.

"Is it true," a young lady draped in yards of peach watered-silk wanted to know, "that you were held captive on an island of *pirates* for a year?"

Jennet said, "Och, weel. If you want to talk of pirates, I can tell you about the time Hannah and I came face-to-face with Mac Stoker."

"We have our own stories of Mac Stoker in New Orleans,"

Père Tomaso said. "Why don't you start, and we'll match you one for one."

Hannah found herself laughing at Jennet's story, which was true in its bones but dressed in a great deal of frippery. In a storytelling mood Jennet was a natural wonder, and none of the young ladies seemed to notice that she wasn't answering the questions they found most interesting. Girls were easily distracted, and it was primarily girls who had come to this tea. Hannah doubted their mothers would have been so easily satisfied, but then Père Tomaso seemed to have a deft touch when it came to such matters.

The sound of new arrivals in the hall brought the storytelling to a sudden stop. Rachel got up and went to peek through the lace at the French doors.

"It is my uncle Livingston and Mr. Bonner," she said. "And *Major General Jackson* is with them."

From the expression on Mrs. Livingston's face it seemed to Hannah that this was no surprise, but the young ladies could hardly contain themselves. They squeaked and fluttered and patted skirts and adjusted curls and sat and stood and moved toward the door and back again.

Jennet caught Hannah's eye and then Père Tomaso's, a questionable move as they might have all three broken down and laughed if Mrs. Livingston hadn't risen just then to move forward and greet her husband and his guests. Hannah caught her brother's gaze right away, and he closed his eyes briefly as if to say *All is well*.

She had never before seen Major General Andrew Jackson, but she identified him by his bearing alone. He moved through the room being introduced, bending over white hands and smiling and saying those things gentlemen said to young ladies. He spent a long minute talking to Julia Savard, his posture radiating deference and respect. With Père Tomaso he was much less expansive and far more formal, and moved as soon as he could to Rachel.

To Hannah, Jennet said, "What do you think?"

She watched the major general talking to Rachel. His head was too large for his frame, and his frame was frail, thin unto the point of starvation. His color was very bad. This was a man who was barely out of sickbed, and who should be there still. She said as much to Jennet.

"Aye, but it would take a good deal of rope to tie him down," Jennet said. "He reminds me of my faither. Hard as ironwood, but see how charming he can be to the ladies."

Charming. The word stuck in Hannah's throat, because it was true. This man who had been responsible for the death of so many of her own people smiled winningly, and girls chittered and giggled and blushed.

"Here he comes," Jennet said. "Do ye think he'd like tae hear aboot the pirate Stoker, too?"

She was nervous, and Hannah understood why. Mrs. Livingston would certainly have to introduce the general to the wife of her own husband's secretary, but then there was the matter of the Indian in the parlor.

Hannah sat very still and straight of back and conjured up the image of her stepmother, Elizabeth Middleton Bonner, who never hesitated to stand up to men who made the mistake of underestimating her. It was a lesson Hannah had learned well, but in this particular situation she would have to tread carefully. She took in Jennet's complexion, still too pale, and the way Luke's mouth had clamped down into a line. Their son was asleep somewhere in this house, and out in the city Honoré Poiterin was waiting for the opportunity to take revenge. Of that she had no doubt. There was a great deal at stake.

Jennet's playfulness disappeared when it came her turn to be introduced to the general, and to Hannah it was clear that her cousin had taken a dislike to the man.

"And this," Mrs. Livingston was saying, "is Hannah Bonner of New-York State, Mr. Bonner's half sister, and a healer of great renown. She attends the needs of our local Indians in a small clinic."

"The Redbone Clinic?" said Major General Jackson. "Dr. Kerr mentioned it to me."

Hannah did not offer her hand, but she lifted her eyes to the general's and saw the fierce intelligence in his eyes, along with a cool reserve that came as no surprise. And there was disapproval there, or maybe, Hannah corrected herself, simple discomfort. As well there should be, given his reputation as a man who had no equal when it came to putting down Indian resistance to O'seronni greed.

"Some call it the Redbone Clinic," Hannah agreed.

He inclined his shoulders in an almost imperceptible bow.

"My sister-in-law is a fully trained doctor and surgeon," Jennet volunteered. "Schooled in the traditions of her mother's people and mine. She studied with Dr. Valentine Simon in New-York City—Mrs. Savard's father, you might not realize—and with Hakim Ibrahim Dehlavi ibn Abdul Rahman Balkhi."

"Do you say so, Mrs. Bonner." The general's tone made it clear that he would not challenge a lady's word, and worse: that he found Jennet amusing. It was a mistake, but he couldn't know that. He was about to turn away when Jennet said, "She was just telling me that you look as though you are not fully recovered from some serious illness."

Hannah flicked Jennet a warning gaze, but got in return only one of Jennet's innocent, wide-eyed looks. As a girl, that look had been a sure sign that she had some complicated scheme. Hannah took a deep breath.

". . . did she," Jackson said, his tone cooler. "My own doctor is less than pleased with my recovery. Perhaps you have some suggestion to offer him, Miss Bonner."

He was insulted and affronted. Behind his back Mrs. Livingston had blanched, and the room had gone very quiet. Luke closed his eyes, but Père Tomaso, Julia Savard, and Mr. Livingston seemed more intrigued than concerned.

Jennet would take up the challenge if Hannah did not. Hannah had no interest in sparring with Major General Jackson, but she would not leave Jennet stranded.

She said, "Without an examination I can only give you my impressions. I should guess that you have an amoebic dysentery, as is common in any army. Whatever cures your doctors have prescribed for you, they have failed to kill the parasites in your intestines."

There was a sharp intake of breath from the young ladies, who had most probably never heard the word *intestines* at all, or certainly not in mixed company.

"You continue to lose weight," Hannah went on, keeping her gaze firmly on the general. "You can eat only very small amounts of the blandest food, and you still suffer symptoms on a daily basis. I wonder how you traveled so far on horseback. Strength of will accounts for something, but I assume you have been dosed with laudanum, which will quiet the symptoms for a short while but not address the underlying cause. If you do not get the better of it soon, you will become dehydrated past the point of recovery."

Jackson's gaze was icy, but Hannah went on, her tone as confident and sure as she could make it.

"I would prescribe wormwood, gentian, and agrimony, along with rhubarb and garlic, which are strongly antiparasitic. Also rosehip and slippery elm to soothe intestinal distress. To those I would add dandelion for your liver. You will need a six-week course, three times a day. If you like, I can prepare all of this and have it sent to your headquarters."

The first faint glimmer of surprise showed in the way the general looked away, briefly. When he looked back again the line of his mouth had softened a bit. He cleared his throat. Hannah had the sense that it was not very often he was at a loss for words, and that the lack did not sit well with him.

Hannah got up. She said, "If you will pardon me, Mr. Livingston, Mrs. Livingston, Père Tomaso, Major General, I'll go see to it now. Jennet, could I have a word with you before I go, please?"

Walking out of the room with Jennet just behind her, Hannah felt the young ladies watching her. By tomorrow morning the whole city would know about what had happened in this room, or at least, they would hear some version of it. For a moment Hannah wondered what price she might end up paying for indulging Jennet's temper and her own pride, but then Luke took her arm to steer her toward the staircase, and other worries crowded this newest one out of her head.

"I leave you alone for one night, and see what trouble you get into," Hannah said a half hour later. And then, in response to Jennet's concerned expression: "I can see how it all came about so quickly, and it seems to have worked out well. You trust Livingston?"

Luke nodded. "We pose no competition or threat to him or his business interests, and so yes, I think we can trust him. I am far more concerned about the Poiterins, after this afternoon's episode."

They were sitting in the chamber Luke and Jennet had for their own use. The nurse had brought the boy in, who was busy dragging himself up to a standing position by means of his mother's skirts. Once on two wobbly feet, he collapsed to the comfort of the thick carpet and crawled to his father to try his luck there.

Jennet pushed out a weary sigh. "It wasn't pleasant, but neither were we ever in any real danger. She left as soon as the constables were called, and I doubt she'd try anything so rash again."

"That's what worries me," Hannah said. "That she's off in

some dark corner with her grandson, planning their next move."

There was a short silence while each of them thought through the situation. Hannah looked down at her nephew, who had arrived in front of her and was winding his hands in her skirts. She leaned over and nuzzled the top of his head.

"You are suddenly very calm," Luke said to Jennet. "I fear you are making plans of your own."

"Contingency plans only," said Jennet. "You needn't worry that I'll fly off and do something unwise."

"You mean like the way you introduced Hannah to Major General Jackson?" Luke said.

"All right, yes. My temper got the best of me. But you did show him up, didn't you, Hannah? He turned the most delicate shade of puce. How did you diagnose him by looking at him?"

"I didn't," Hannah said, handing the child a rattle and pulling him into her lap. "This morning Jackson's physician came by to see Paul, a courtesy visit, I think he called it. Paul told me about it later, and we talked about how we would treat him."

Jennet gave a hiccup of a laugh. Luke said, "I hope this doesn't come back to haunt us."

The baby threw the rattle down and then tried to plunge after it. Hannah put him down, glad of the chance to gather her thoughts.

She said, "Speaking of haunting, I have news to share that may help us with Mme. Poiterin. It is a sad story. Jennet, Titine is dead. I'm sorry."

Jennet went very still. "Tell me," she said. "I must know it all."

By the time Hannah had finished the story, Jennet's face was wet with silent weeping. She struck the tears from her face with the edge of her hand, and straightened her shoulders.

"And this is the man I handed my son to," she said. "I put a child into his power."

Luke turned to her. "Stop it," he said. "Don't."

"But it's true," Jennet said. "I handed your son to Honoré Poiterin for safekeeping."

"Did you have any way to know he was capable of such acts?" Luke asked. "Did you have any other choice?"

Jennet stilled. "No."

"And here he is," Hannah said. "Healthy and well. I have never seen a more vigorous child, Jennet. Save your anger for Poiterin, where it may do some good."

Luke caught her eye and Hannah shook her head. *We cannot help her with this,* she wanted to say. *She must come to terms with it on her own.*

Jennet wiped her face again and closed her eyes for a moment. When she opened them she was in control of her emotions.

She said, "What can we do? How can we make amends?" She turned to Luke. "I will write to Titine's mother. Perhaps we can buy her a cottage here. She would never have left New Orleans if Honoré hadn't turned her out of her home."

"Of course," Luke said. "We can do that for her, and more. You will write to her today, and offer whatever you think may help her through the loss of her daughter."

Jennet said, "What I should like to send her most of all is Honoré Poiterin's head on a platter. Maybe Ben Savard can arrange that for us."

Hannah dropped her gaze for a moment and then raised it again. "Maybe he can."

That earned her a real smile from Jennet and a concerned look from Luke.

"You disapprove, brother?"

"Hell, no," Luke said. "Not if Ben gets to Poiterin first. But I hope he treads carefully. They'd hang him without a trial if he kills a white man, I don't care how many friends he's got in the city. No, the best way to deal with Poiterin is to let somebody else do it."

"You want to call him out as a spy?" Jennet said. "What if he turns the same accusation on you? On us?"

"I wasn't thinking of going to the New Orleans authorities," Luke said.

Jennet glanced at Hannah, raising a shoulder as if to ask for help.

"Wyndham," Hannah said. "You want Wyndham to take care of him."

"No," Jennet said. "Absolutely not. You cannot seek out a man we know to be a British spy and ask him for help. If that should come out—and you know that Honoré or his grandmother would make sure that it did—you would hang with them. I think we must turn both of them in, Wyndham and Poiterin both. We must go to Mr. Livingston with this immediately, tonight. There would be no better way to make our allegiance to the American cause clear."

Hannah felt the weight of Luke's gaze on her, asking her to say things he could not say himself.

"Jennet," she began slowly, "before we decide on such a course of action, I want to remind you that without Wyndham's help we never would have found you, and you would still be on that island with Dégre."

"I don't care!" Jennet cried. She stood up, wrapped her arms around herself, sat down again. "I can't afford to care. If he had gone home to Canada as he said he was going to, he wouldn't be in any danger now. My allegiance is to this country, and to you and our family. It must be so. It must."

Luke closed his eyes for a moment. Then he nodded and pushed out a sigh. "Yes, you're right. It must be so." He glanced at Hannah. "Do you want me to talk to the authorities about

Wyndham? If I go through Livingston, things will have a better chance of going our way."

Hannah thought of Kit Wyndham. She tried to recall his face, his smile, the way he stood, but all she could summon was the sound of his voice. The things he had told her about his family, the woman he was engaged to marry, the life he led in Canada, his driving need to advance himself in his career. She had lain down with him a dozen times, two dozen, more, and there had been real affection between them.

And now he was here, and his very presence was a threat to the well-being of her people.

She said, "I would like to try to locate him first. Can you give me a day, a single day? Jennet?"

Her cousin's small face contorted in misery, but she nodded. "One day. Then Luke will speak to Livingston."

Luke rubbed a hand over his face. "If word gets out that you warned him, you'll hang. You know that."

"Yes," Hannah said. "I know that. I may not even be able to find him, but I must try."

CHAPTER 38

It was dark by the time Hannah made ready to leave. Luke only relented on his intention to walk her back to the rue Dauphine when he saw that Leo was waiting with a lantern.

"Julia must have sent him back for me," Hannah said. "She went ahead home with Rachel a good while ago."

Luke said, "We'll never be able to repay them."

It was what he always said when they spoke of the Savards. Hannah knew that their dependency on people who were as good as strangers to Luke was a trial to him. But Leo was waiting, not bothering to hide his impatience, and Hannah was tired. A sensible conversation that would put her brother's mind at ease would have to wait.

Leo, never cheerful, always suspicious, was more dour than usual this evening. Hannah wondered if he might really be worried about their safety, given the fact that the streets were full of men who had been drinking Major General Jackson's health all day long, shopkeepers and clerks and fishermen intermingling with Kentucky riflemen and the militia. But the rue Royale was well lit, and there were constables on most corners, and she and Leo didn't have very far to go.

She pulled the hood of her cape so that her face was more hidden, out of simple good sense and also to calm Leo. She said, "You were a great help to me in the clinic today. Thank you."

He threw her a sidelong glance and nodded. Hannah, over-come with the full force of the last twenty-four hours, couldn't find the energy to work any harder for Leo's smile, and so they walked along in silence. At the gate that led into the courtyard behind the little clinic, Leo paused. He said, "I'm going to see my mother."

Surprised, Hannah turned. He held the lantern so that his face was in the dark, but she still had the sense of his eyes, very large and overly bright. He had never before mentioned his family.

"Is she unwell? Does she need help?"

"That's why I'm going," Leo said. "To find out." He thrust the lantern at Hannah and ran off, disappearing into the dark so quickly and completely that he seemed to have simply melted away.

There was something wrong. That thought was still form-ing itself in her head when she felt a sharp prodding at the small of her back. The muzzle of a gun.

"Don't turn around," said the voice behind her. "It is only a musket, but still, it would make short work of your back-bone."

Hannah took a very deep breath and let it out. "What do you want?"

The musket prodded again, more forcefully. "To start with, some privacy. Your Redbone Clinic will serve, I think."

The thoughts tumbling through Hannah's mind were too bright and quick to grab. A question presented itself: Am I going to die? Is he going to kill me? And the answer: Very likely yes.

Strikes-the-Sky had talked sometimes about what it was like to go into battle. How the world seemed to shrink down and vision to expand, so that there was no room for thought or words of any kind, no sense of mortality beyond a calm understanding that he was walking into the shadow-lands and might never turn back. Now Hannah understood what he meant when he said that to go into battle was to stop feeling.

The shutters were closed tight, so that the little clinic looked like a long, dark cave lit only by the lantern. The few things that would serve as weapons were out of her reach: at one end of the room, in a box on a shelf, the simple surgical tools lent to her by Paul Savard; at the other end, a neat pile of firewood.

She could throw the lantern down and start a fire, but the idea of being in this closed space while it burned brought back memories long buried, and she hesitated too long.

"Put the lantern on the table there, and sit on the stool."

Hannah did as she was directed. The urge to ask questions was strong, but stronger still was the sense of her father, who would volunteer nothing in a situation like this. Not a word, not a tremor.

Honoré Poiterin came into the lantern light to look into her face, and found nothing there at all. At her shoulder she sensed her father, and his approval.

Poiterin wore a long, dark cloak and a hat pulled down low on his brow. There was a deep shadow of beard on his cheeks, and a crusting scab at the corner of his mouth. He vibrated with tension, but it did not feel like anger to Hannah. She would have preferred anger to the cold appraisal and eyes empty of everything that would have made him human.

She understood that he had used Leo, hurt Leo's mother or threatened to hurt her, laid this trap. That meant that he knew where she had been, where Jennet was. Maybe he had followed Luke after they saw each other early in the day; maybe his grandmother had got word to him. He wasn't in uniform, which must mean something, but what?

Poiterin pulled off his gloves one finger at a time, watching her closely, his eyes narrowed. He had tucked the musket into a wide belt at his waist, just next to a knife sheath of tooled leather.

"So," he said in a conversational tone.

Hannah caught the flicker of intent in his eyes but too late. The blow knocked her from the stool. In the part of her mind that remained detached she analyzed the pain in her cheekbone and left shoulder, noted that nothing had broken. She rolled herself into a ball as the first kick came, and it connected with her hip.

Poiterin leaned down and grabbed her by the hair, pulled her upright, and levered her onto the stool, where she sat holding her nerveless arm.

"So," he said again. He was looking at her intently. "You are Luke Scott's half-breed sister, is that right?"

Hannah's voice creaked. She struggled to control her breathing. "Yes."

He nodded. "You were with him on the Isle of the Manatees, when he rescued the slut he calls his wife from Dégre?"

Hannah nodded. "Yes."

"You call yourself a doctor."

It wasn't a question, and Hannah didn't answer it. She watched him pace back and forth, in and out of the lantern light.

"I've seen you before," he said. "But I never made the connection. She was hiding here with the Savards the whole time, waiting for Scott."

Hannah kept still.

He stopped. "And now they're both under Livingston's protection."

She was braced for the next blow, curling around herself as she was hurled to the floor. With her head tucked in the kicks fell on her back and legs. There was a sound a rib made as it cracked, like a walnut shell stepped on by a heavy man's boot.

This time he dragged her to the cot nearest the cold

hearth. Near enough to grab a piece of wood, one she could use to cave in his head. But his grip on her right arm was crippling, and her left arm was still numb and useless.

Poiterin stood over her. "They aren't looking for you," he said. "Savard thinks you're still at the Livingstons', so there will be no rescue for you this night."

Hannah heard herself cough. Pain flared in her ribs, along her spine, in her pelvis. She coughed again, and then she forced herself to look at Poiterin, who stood over her.

He said, "Say something or I'll cut out your tongue."

Hannah tasted blood as she tried to work her mouth. Her voice came finally, in a whisper. "What do you want?"

"What do you think I want?" He leaned over to speak into her face, his words sharp and wet. "What would any man want in my position? Satisfaction. Revenge. Vengeance. The slut made a fool of me in front of the whole city. In front of my grandmother. Someone must pay. You, I think." He smiled and brushed Hannah's hair away from her face. It took every bit of strength she had to allow his touch without stiffening or shuddering.

"Tomorrow," he said, fisting his hand in her hair. "Tomorrow they will look at you and understand that it isn't wise to cross me. A lesson Scott should have learned long ago."

Hannah thought of Ben Savard, of his smile as he bent over her, the smell of him. The look in his eyes when he spoke of killing Poiterin, the plain fact of his intention, and the satisfaction it would afford. As Poiterin used his knife to cut her clothes from her body, as he ripped strips from her skirt and used them to tie her wrists to the frame of the cot, Hannah focused on that image of Ben Savard. A terrible sadness came over her, a sense of loss and her own stupidity.

Poiterin talked. Through the hours of the night, he spoke to her, sometimes in English, more often in French.

"I don't intend to kill you," he told her again and again in a conversational tone. There was a swipe of blood on his face, not his own. "I want you to tell them about this. I want you to tell everybody." And, breathing hard: "Of course, things get away from me sometimes."

Sometimes her mind simply shut him out, refused to allow his words meaning beyond an inhuman hiss.

He seemed to be at ease, sure of himself, unworried about time or interruption. He would pace back and forth across the room, and in the light of the failing lantern Honoré Poiterin looked to Hannah like the devil the O'seronni priests talked about when they came to her grandmother's village. Wild-haired, bloodied, ranting.

Sometimes he used his fists, and when he tired of that, he found other ways to amuse himself.

Hannah turned her mind inward and sang.

I am Walks-Ahead of the Wolf Clan of the Kahnyen'kehàka, the Keepers of the Eastern Door of the Haudenosaunee Nation. We are the People of the Longhouse.

I am the daughter of Sings-from-Books, whose voice I still hear. I am the granddaughter of Falling-Day, whose touch I still feel. I am the great-granddaughter of Made-of-Bones, who was clan mother of the Wolf for five hundred moons. I am the great-great-granddaughter of Hawk-Woman, who killed an O'seronni chief with her own hands and fed his heart to her sons, in the time when we were still many, and strong.

She sang her death song to herself, and when she paused, she heard her ancestors speaking back to her.

You are strong, Hawk-Woman told her. *You are stronger than the O'seronni devil.* And: *You don't belong here with us. Not yet. Not yet.*

At first light Hannah opened her eyes and understood that she was still alive, and alone.

•   •   •

Time drifted. There were faces: her father, her grandfather, her grandmothers, her stepmother, beloved Curiosity, who might be waiting for her in the shadowlands.

Strikes-the-Sky came and sat beside her. There was white in his hair that hadn't been there when she last saw him.

It's not three years since you died, she said to him. *Does time pass so quickly in the shadowlands?*

He touched the jagged wound left in his throat by a Potawatomi arrow and frowned, as if she made too much of it; as if it were no more concern to him than a blackfly bite.

She said, *It was an honorable death.* She did not say: *It was a quick death* or *It was an easy death.* Both of those things were true, but they meant nothing to him. He had died in battle with the Potawatomi, men he had hoped to win over to Tecumseh's cause. He had failed, and then he had died. As Tecumseh failed, in the end. As they had all failed.

He touched her forehead with two fingers. He said: *It is not your time.*

A river of pain coursed through her bones and forced her up out of her body. She looked down at herself, and saw a woman who had been beaten. Her face so swollen and washed in blood that her own father would not know her. Bruises on her throat, and the impression of teeth like a half-moon on the slope of her shoulder. More bite marks on her breasts. A circle of cut rope on each wrist, so sunken into the flesh that it couldn't fall away. Blood in a pool under the skin over the left ribs, blood on her belly and on her legs, like a skirt of red feathers. A bruise in the exact shape of a boot on her thigh.

It is not my time. She said the words aloud.

When she next opened her eyes—five minutes, five hours, five days later—a woman was standing over her. Yellow-Sapling, the Choctaw healer who came in the very early morning to sort through the herbs and medicines she kept in the little clinic, where it was warm and dry, and where it was meant to be safe. Hannah could not speak her name or even raise a hand, but she could be thankful that it was this strong woman who had come to her first. This Indian woman who had survived war and stayed behind to see to the others who had not. There were tears on her own cheeks, but Yellow-Sapling's face was dry.

She studied Hannah for a long moment, her expression placid but her eyes full of fire. Then she went away and came back with water. She dipped a clean rag into the water and then squeezed it so that the cool wet spread over Hannah's lips and tongue and down her swollen throat. Yellow-Sapling chanted under her breath in her own language as she worked, her touch light and sure. There was a fire in the hearth—Hannah had no memory of it being lit—and the smell of herbs burning, and of tobacco thrown into the flames to honor the Great Spirit and ask his help.

The rhythm of the song Yellow-Sapling was singing lulled Hannah to sleep, and when she woke again she was lying between clean sheets someplace else, someplace she recognized but couldn't name. Paul and Julia Savard were bent over her, their mouths moving as they talked. Hannah wondered why her hearing had left her, and then she realized that the pounding of her own blood in her ears was deafening, and worse: She was full of fever, her body a vessel filled to the bursting with steam. A fever bigger than her broken bones and torn skin.

The malaria had come to claim her again, and it bore her off before she could answer even one of their questions.

They gathered in the small apartment on the topmost floor: Julia and Paul Savard, Jennet and Luke, and a man who was a stranger to all of them. He introduced himself as Captain

Aloysius Urquhart of the U.S. Army, the liaison between the armed forces and the New Orleans constabulary.

Jennet wanted nothing to do with Urquhart. She wanted Ben Savard, but he had been sent off on some mission to the west, and could not be reached. Ben Savard would not be satisfied with talk, as these men—her own husband, Hannah's brother—seemed to be. Luke was as angry as Jennet had ever seen him, but still he stood here.

With Julia sitting beside her, Jennet was able to control her own temper while the men talked of the law, and of customs, and what might be done. Urquhart was treating the attack on Hannah like a prank, as if Honoré Poiterin were a rude boy who had taken another man's horse out for a run. The sound of his voice slid down her throat and filled her belly and festered there like a cancer.

"...nothing much to be done without witnesses," Urquhart was saying. When he spoke a mouthful of perfectly straight and white teeth flashed like knives between lips the incongruous red of strawberries. He was hatless, with long greasy hair and a mass of curling dull blond beard stained tobacco brown. One broad thumb, its nail the color of pitch, was curled loosely around the upright barrel of a long rifle in the casual way of a man who never put his gun away from him. He was from Kentucky, and Jennet had to pay attention to follow the unfamiliar rhythm of his English.

Now she stood. Urquhart didn't turn toward her, but she would not be silenced by his disapproval. She said, "We know who assaulted my sister-in-law, Captain. There is no doubt about that, not after his grandmother forced her way into Mrs. Livingston's parlor yesterday afternoon."

Urquhart's look was impatient. "Pardon me, ma'am, but I don't see the connection there at all. If your sister-in-law were to wake up out of her fever sleep and give a positive identification, maybe we could do something—"

Jennet interrupted him. "Then what about Leo? He came

back here with Hannah last night, he might have seen Poiterin. Somebody must have seen him."

"If it was Poiterin," said Urquhart again. "There were a lot of drunk men in the streets last night."

Jennet turned to Paul Savard. "Why is Leo not here?"

"We can't find him," Paul Savard said. His color was poor, and there were new lines creasing his cheeks.

"You'll pardon me for pointing this out again," Urquhart said, "but nobody was killed here. All we've got so far is an Indian woman who was beat."

Luke stepped between Jennet and the captain. Urquhart's hand tightened on the rifle barrel.

Luke said, "We've got a woman who was beaten within an inch of her life and repeatedly raped. Something will be done, by God."

Urquhart's tone sharpened. "There are bigger problems to be dealt with right now than a Redbone woman being roughly handled."

Jennet pushed forward, jerking her arm free of Luke's grasp. "Then I want Mme. Poiterin arrested for trespass and for her threats against me and my son. Mrs. Livingston was a witness to that; it happened in her own parlor. Will you ignore that, as well?"

"Mrs. Livingston filed no complaint, as far as I know," Urquhart said. "But I'll go there now and see if she wants to make a statement. If she won't, there's nothing I can do."

He put the hat he had been holding in his left hand on his head, nodded, and walked out of the room.

Jennet said, "If I had a gun I would shoot him."

"Good thing you're unarmed then," Luke said. "We've got enough trouble as it is."

Julia put a hand on Jennet's arm. "I'm going back to sit with Hannah. Will you come, too?"

"In a moment," Jennet said. And then: "The only weapon we've got against Poiterin is the news Hannah brought us yesterday. He is spying for the British. If they don't care about what he did to Hannah—" her voice cracked, and Julia's hand on her arm tightened, "—they must care about that."

"Jennet—" Luke began, and she whirled toward him.

"Don't say it."

"I have to say it. We've got no evidence on Poiterin beyond Hannah's word."

"We've got more than that," Jennet said. "We've got Wyndham, who is somewhere in this city right now. Once he's in custody he'll give up Poiterin."

"You can't know that," Luke said. He looked as though he would be sick, with sweat on his brow in spite of the underheated room. He looked miserable, and it struck Jennet that she was punishing him because she could not strike out against Poiterin.

She went to him and put her head against his chest, felt his arms come up around her while she wept out her anger and frustration. The door opened and closed beyond them and they were alone.

When there were no more tears left, she took the handkerchief he offered and wiped her face, taking deep, shuddering breaths.

"I promise you he won't go unpunished," Luke said quietly.

"What are you going to do?" Jennet asked. Her head ached and her throat was raw and she was deeply weary, but she couldn't clear her head of the image of Hannah.

"I'm going to talk to Ben Savard," Luke said. "As soon as I can find him. In the meantime, Livingston has arranged for armed guards, here and at his house. You are not to step out onto the street without them, do you understand me?"

Jennet managed a half smile. "I wish Poiterin would approach me," she said. "I wish he were so rash. I would like to see him die."

Luke's expression tightened. "Do not put yourself at risk,"

he said. "For our son's sake, Jennet, promise me you won't go anywhere alone."

She gave him her promise, but Luke's expression didn't change at all. He didn't trust her, and with good cause.

Jennet moved through the next five days like a woman caught in a maze, unable to stop, always turning the same corners.

The clinic was so overrun that Julia and Rachel both were pressed into full-time duty during the day, and so Jennet became Hannah's nurse. Hannah, in the grip of a fever like a winding-sheet.

Jennet bathed her with cool water laced with vinegar, fed her water and tea and the medicines Dr. Savard supplied, teaspoon by teaspoon. There were different salves for her many scrapes and cuts and seeping bruises. Dr. Savard showed Jennet how to change the dressings. The biggest danger was that there had been some damage to the lungs, and that she was bleeding internally. Jennet held her breath when she checked Hannah's pulse, but by the third day when there was no sign of infection, she allowed herself to hope.

Hannah must be bathed, and dosed with the medicines and teas Dr. Savard brought, and her dressings and soiled bedclothes changed. She must be given boiled water by the teaspoonful every hour, and after the first day, chicken broth as well. All the while she worked or sat next to Hannah, Jennet sang and read and told stories. The work was exhausting, but Jennet was more glad of it with every passing day.

Now she went to fetch water and paused to look out of the courtyard. One of the armed guards on duty turned and bowed from the shoulders. They were simple men but good at their work. Three times a day they escorted her back to the Livingstons' so she could see to her son's needs, and then back to the clinic so she could see to her cousin's. The Indian woman who had first found Hannah came to look after her while Jennet was gone. Yellow-Sapling was a somber woman who seemed to speak neither French nor English, but she was devoted to Hannah and brought medicines of her own with every visit. When Jennet came back the room smelled of herbs burning, and the air itself had taken on a new color.

Jennet saw far more of the guards than she did of her husband, whose every minute was monopolized by Livingston. Luke came by the clinic at midday and again in the late afternoon, stayed long enough to tell Jennet his news and hear hers, to spend a few minutes by his sister's bedside, and then he was gone again. It was eleven or later when he came to bed, and he often fell into an exhausted sleep before he was completely out of his clothes. At sunrise he was gone again, and Jennet was on her way to the clinic.

On the sixth day, Jennet was changing the sweat-soaked bedding when she realized that Hannah's eyes were open. She went very still while she composed her face and her voice.

"Cousin," she said calmly. "It's me, it's Jennet."

"I see you," Hannah said. Her mouth, still swollen and bruised, barely moved, and her voice was hoarse.

Jennet sat down heavily beside the bed. "You've had a—"

"—relapse," Hannah said. She closed her eyes, and drifted away into sleep.

Jennet pressed her face into the damp bed linens and wept.

When Luke came to the clinic on the rue Dauphine in the early evening, he found his sister sitting up in bed supported by bolsters, with young Henry Savard by her side. There was no sign of Jennet.

Luke had been raised by a kind and loving grandmother, but Wee Iona had rarely hugged or coddled. Jennet was made of different stuff, and Luke realized that a great deal of her need for physical touch had rubbed off on him. He crouched down at the side of the bed and took his sister's hand in his own, raised it to his mouth. His voice came rough.

"It took you long enough," he said, trying to smile.

She looked at him somberly, this younger half sister who often seemed as old as Iona. There was nothing of pain or anger or confusion in her eyes. Most of her bruises were fading though there were still scabs on her throat and—Luke did not like to think of it—elsewhere.

Hannah said, "You won't be shut of me so easily."

Luke reached for the chair behind him, taking that moment to remind himself that Hannah would not be helped by displays of emotion. Henry was looking at him, chewing his lip as though the question he wanted to ask had to be kept back by brute force.

"Hello, Henry," said Luke. "Are you keeping my sister company?"

The small head with its high brow bobbed eagerly. "Until Jennet comes back." And in a rush: "Did you see Major General Jackson today?"

"I did."

"Did he kill anybody?"

"Not while I was watching," Luke said. He put a hand over his sister's where it lay on the bedcovers, fingers curled.

"Did you see my uncle?"

"No," Luke said. "He's still away on assignment."

"For Major General Jackson," Henry reminded them.

"Yes," Luke said. "Henry, I need to talk to Hannah alone for a while."

The boy pushed out a resigned sigh. "Not about the war?"

"No," Luke said. "Nothing about the war."

The boy left, casting a glance behind him that was full of suspicion.

Hannah said, "It was good to have him here. I almost feel myself again, listening to him chatter."

"Have you talked to Dr. Savard about your condition?"

Hannah blinked. It was, Luke realized, because she was too stiff to nod.

She said, "There is no permanent damage, and the fever is past. This relapse wouldn't have lasted so long if it weren't for—" The fingers under Luke's hand attempted a flutter.

"Your other injuries."

She blinked.

"Ben Savard is out west, on the Sabine River. Disputed territory, claimed by Mexico and Louisiana both. I can't find out what he was sent to do, but I can guess."

"So can I," Hannah said. Her mouth quirked at the corner, but whether that was meant to be a smile, Luke couldn't tell. He went on before she could respond.

"There's no sign of Wyndham, either, though I've been looking. Poiterin is with his regiment on the Chef Menteur road. He hasn't come back to the city."

"Jennet told me," Hannah said.

There was a moment's awkward silence, and then her hand turned under his and she grasped his fingers with some of her old strength.

"You are not to blame yourself," she said. "It is none of your fault."

"There's only one person at fault here," Luke said. "And he won't go unpunished."

"There are two people at fault," Hannah said. Her voice had begun to fade. "Whatever he is, his grandmother made him. You know that better than most."

"Yes," Luke said. He thought again of his grandmother, who had been all the family he had known until he was fifteen. She was a formidable woman, too, but made from a different mold from Agnès Poiterin.

"If Iona were here she'd know how to deal with Mme. Poiterin," Luke said.

"There are women like Wee Iona here in New Orleans," Hannah said. "I know some of them."

"You're healing fast," Paul Savard said to Hannah the next morning. He smiled at Jennet, who stood on the other side of the bed. "Good nursing."

"A strong constitution," Jennet said. "I can take credit for nothing more than bed baths and clean linen."

Hannah turned her head. The headache that had seemed yesterday like a new and permanent appendage had begun to recede after all.

"You can take credit for a great deal more," she said. "Unless it was somebody else telling stories about MacQuiddy and his wee fairy bride."

Jennet looked drawn and pale, but she also looked satisfied. "I knew ye heard me. I knew it. Once or twice I even thought you were trying to laugh."

"You'll have to write down this story for me," Paul Savard said to Jennet. "It seems to have a strong medicinal value. Are you feeling well enough to get out of bed for a short while?"

"I'd like to walk a bit." Hannah saw Jennet's expression darken. "Five minutes on my feet will do me no harm," she said. "You can hold my elbow if you must."

"It's not that," Jennet said, flustered in a way that was nothing like her. "There's someone here to see you."

Hannah looked between them. "No friend?"

Paul cleared his throat. "I wouldn't call him friend or enemy. His name is Captain Urquhart, with the U.S. Army. We called him in after you were found—"

"I asked Mrs. Livingston to call the authorities. It was an error," Jennet said tightly.

"I'm not sure that it was," said Dr. Savard. "But he's here now and wants to take a statement from you."

"Urquhart is the liaison between the army and the local constables," Jennet added, her tone clipped. "He has no interest in the problems of people like us."

"Like me," Hannah corrected. Jennet nodded curtly.

"Your first interview with him didn't go well, I take it," Hannah said. And to Paul: "I expect he won't just go away. If he must see me, he can come in here. But give me a half hour with Jennet, first."

Jennet sat to one side like a prim and disapproving chaperone while Urquhart took a chair without being invited. He drew a notebook and a stub of a carpenter's pencil from inside his jacket, and looked at Hannah expectantly. Hannah met his gaze and kept her expression blank.

"If you could just relate the events of the night you were attacked."

He had amazingly white and healthy teeth, so perfect that they might have been taken for false, though the lack of clicks and whistles in his speech made that unlikely. Everything about the man seemed many shades too bright: ruddy cheeks, red mouth, the curling blond beard and the green pea stuck in it. His vivid coloring stood in stark contrast to his demeanor, which was sober to the point of severity.

Urquhart was only here, Jennet had told her, because Livingston had showed an interest in the case for Luke's sake. Otherwise an assault on an Indian woman would never have earned any kind of formal inquiry, much less this very unusual second visit.

"I spent the afternoon at the Livingstons'," Hannah said.

"On what errand?"

"I was invited to take tea."

If he was affronted by the idea that she had been a guest

in the Livingstons' parlor, he hid it well. It was a trick that
Hannah knew, too; she would not show this man any weakness, no matter how far he tried her patience. Jennet was another matter, of course.

"And then?"

"Just after dark I walked back here in the company of a
young boy called Leo."

"We haven't been able to locate this Leo," Urquhart said.

Hannah raised an eyebrow in Jennet's direction.

"It's true," Jennet said. "There's no sign of him. I think
Honoré may have scared him off."

"Or worse," Hannah said.

Urquhart frowned. "And then?" he prompted.

"When I came into the smaller courtyard—the one off
the rue Toulouse—Honoré Poiterin was waiting in the dark.
He put a gun to my back and forced me into the clinic."

Urquhart looked up from his notebook, where he had yet
to write down a word. "Clinic?"

"The little clinic, we call it," Hannah said. "You probably
have heard it called the Redbone Clinic. It is attached to the
rue Dauphine kine-pox clinic by adjoining courtyards."

He pursed his lips, and then nodded. "Go on."

Hannah looked at him directly. "For the next ten hours or
so he kept me there, bound by my wrists to a cot. You can
see the extent of my injuries. Or Dr. Savard can provide you
with a written list, if you need one."

Urquhart considered his pencil. Finally he said, "It's your
statement that Honoré Poiterin attacked you, bound you,
beat you, and raped you over a ten-hour period."

Jennet drew in a sharp breath.

"Yes," Hannah said. "That is my statement."

"You want me to arrest the man?"

"Captain Urquhart," Hannah said. "You asked for a statement. I made one. What you do with it is outside my sphere
of influence."

Urquhart scratched the corner of his mouth. His fingers were stained with tobacco and gunpowder and ink, and his nails were rimmed black. He said, "I heard rumors about you, but I didn't believe half of them. Now that I hear you talk I guess a lot of what's being said is true."

Hannah gave Jennet a sharp look that said, *Don't*. Urquhart was looking at her, too. "This was the same day you called the constables into Mrs. Livingston's parlor to remove Mr. Poiterin's grandmother."

"That's so," Jennet said.

"The same Mrs. Poiterin who has filed a lawsuit claiming you're unstable and that you should surrender her great-grandson to her care."

Hannah had not heard this news. She saw that Jennet had not wanted to bother her with it yet.

"Captain Urquhart, that lawsuit was dismissed, as you well know," Jennet said. "She has no claim on my son."

He made a humming sound deep in his throat that might have been disapproval or dissent. "Whatever the facts, it looks to me as if you've got the upper hand in this feud you've got going with the Poiterins," Urquhart said. "Why stir things up again?"

"Clearly you don't know Honoré Poiterin," Jennet said stiffly. "He is capable of things—" She broke off and turned her face away. "He will never stop. This assault on my sister-in-law won't satisfy him. Until we can leave Louisiana we are in danger, all of us."

Urquhart's expression gave nothing away. He might believe Jennet or think her a hysteric; he might pity or despise her. He pushed out a great sigh.

"I'll talk to the man," he said. "And make it clear that if any more bad luck comes your way, he'll have to deal with me. Will that do?"

Jennet hesitated. "No. But I understand it is all we can expect of you."

Urquhart stood, put the unused notebook back into his jacket along with the pencil, and touched his brow with one finger. "Thank you for your time."

"Wait," Jennet said, her tone deceptively even. "Aren't you going to write out the statement for her signature?"

Urquhart's brow creased, but Jennet went on before he could respond.

"You're very busy, of course. We anticipated as much." Jennet took a sheet of paper from the table next to her and held it out. "So Miss Bonner dictated her statement to me, and signed it. It has been witnessed by Dr. Savard and his wife, and by me as well."

"So I see," said Urquhart. Inside his beard, his mouth twitched. He took the paper and folded it carefully before he tucked it into his jacket.

"If you should lose it, don't worry," Jennet said. "I will make copies. One for Mr. Livingston, one for Governor Claiborne, one for the mayor—"

"I take your meaning, Mrs. Bonner," Urquhart said with a stiff smile. "Now if you'll permit me to get back to work."

When he was gone Jennet collapsed onto the chair. She said, "That was a waste of time. Honoré is not afraid of men like Urquhart. He's not afraid of anything."

Hannah closed her eyes and remembered saying those very words. Maman Zuzu had smiled at her as one might smile at a deaf child who denies the possibility of song.

She said, "There's a free woman of color called Maman Zuzu. I'd like to send a message to her. I think probably Clémentine could arrange it."

CHAPTER 39

It was a great relief to Luke to know that Hannah was improving day by day, because as the week progressed he found his own responsibilities expanded to fill every waking hour. Livingston was part of Jackson's personal staff, and thus Luke was also at Jackson's beck and call. The major general continued to look sickly and frail, but he had the energy and drive of ten men, and expected no less from those he kept closest.

Jackson had almost no French and even less understanding of the Creole mind, and it was a small group of men he trusted to translate for him: Livingston, and Mrs. Livingston's brother, August D'Avezac, and, on a few occasions, Luke himself.

And so Luke found himself traveling everywhere the major general went. Visiting the troops while they drilled, riding through the woods to watch Captain Beal's riflemen at target practice, and most often visiting the work parties. Some of these had been set to reinforcing escarpments, ramparts, and breastworks, and others to obstructing bayous, a crucial step in impeding an invasion, but one that was not being done to Jackson's satisfaction.

Too much time was spent dealing with the city's aristocrats, who wanted more of Jackson's attention than they were ever going to get. Worse still was the legislature.

Jackson's casual indifference to the long-established hier-
archies of the local government was greeted with disbelief
that gave way to insult and anger. Worst of all was the way
he bypassed the mayor and a half dozen other Creoles and
gave Livingston a whole range of responsibilities. It was
Edward Livingston, an American who had shown himself
far too clever in business, whom Jackson asked to deal with
the lists of questions and suggestions and outright demands
that were delivered to headquarters at least once a day. For
once, the Creole legislature and the American governor
Claiborne were united in their outrage.

Livingston took on every charge and met it with ruthless
efficiency matched only by his willingness to exploit his position to further his own interests. Luke understood that wars
could make fortunes as well as destroy them, and he observed how Livingston strove—and succeeded—in serving
both the war effort and his own purse.

When they were not required to be with the major general, Luke went with Livingston to meetings with bankers
and merchants and landlords, with men who owned ferries
and warehouses, talking to the city's doctors and priests, examining supplies, negotiating contracts, making Jackson's
wishes known. Livingston saw dissent coming before it
could be voiced, and cut it off without hesitation. Luke began to understand why he was so widely feared.

Every day the city grew more crowded and volatile. The
number of street fights doubled and then tripled. Men lost
their tempers over splashed mud, casual glances, a toss of the
dice. A German tailor and a French supplier of buttons beat
each other bloody in the street over a difference in account-
ing that amounted to sixty-three cents. At a quadroon ball
held in the Théâtre St. Philippe, three duels were called out
within the space of an hour, and the next morning two
gentlemen died and one had to have an arm amputated.

Creole ladies put their heads together in church, compared rumors about atrocities inflicted on the female sex in Virginia when the British burned Washington, and fanned themselves vigorously. Slaves were interrogated by nervous owners: Had they been approached by any strangers asking them if they wanted to fight for their freedom? And what would they say if such a thing were proposed to them?

The leading families, fascinated by the new arrivals, invited them into their homes, where they were alternately appalled and titillated by rough manners and plain speech. Even the more comely, elegant, and unmarried officers presented a problem. Young ladies who spoke no English danced with young men who spoke no French, who then had the temerity to call on them. Ladies got together in the afternoons to roll bandages and mend uniforms and discuss how to handle such delicate social situations. They wondered to each other about the odd habits of the men from Kentucky and Tennessee: the shocking lack of personal hygiene, their love of loud laughter, and whether they ever went anywhere without a bottle of whisky and a pack of cards. If God was good they would live up to their reputation as excellent soldiers and marksmen and drive the British off quickly. Then they could return to their mountain farms, and life in New Orleans would resume at its leisurely, more cultured pace.

Soldiers and militiamen and volunteers drifted by the tens and then by the hundreds, and the bulk of the troops under Generals Coffee and Carroll weren't even expected until later in the month. Already New Orleans had been made to accommodate whole regiments and almost a thousand men of the Louisiana militia from outside the city. All this was in addition to the local volunteers, a battalion of free men of color, and another of Choctaw under Pierre de Juzan.

Tents had sprung up like fungus all over the city. The already overwhelmed sewage system collapsed. In Montreal the stink would have been bearable in the cold of December, but winters in New Orleans hardly deserved to be called winter at all. After three days of temperatures in the seventies, the whole city smelled of sewage. The cost of fresh water doubled and then doubled again, and buckets were as dear as they were scarce. Coopers' shops were kept open around the clock, as were smithies and the back rooms where tailors and seamstresses bent over gilded buttons and epaulettes by the bright and precious light of oil lamps. The men of New Orleans were a vain and fashionable lot, and the ones with money to spend wanted uniforms to display their patriotism.

Rumors showed up on the front page of the papers in letters an inch high. Ladies invited Major General Jackson to supper to thank him personally for his bravery and leadership—and by the way: Was it true that—? Could it truly happen if—? Did the English really mean to—?

Jackson's diplomacy and charm lasted only until the ladies left the gentlemen to their brandy and tobacco. He charged Livingston with making the newspaper editors understand the lay of the land, and immediately. Luke went along from newspaper office to newspaper office as Livingston did exactly that. He applied the power he had been given with enthusiasm, and brooked no challenge.

"What are you thinking?" he asked Luke as they walked back to Jackson's headquarters on the rue Royale after one such interview, in which he had promised to simply seize the entire printing press as necessary to the war effort.

"That rumor doesn't take its sustenance from ink. Stopping the pens of the editors won't stop people from talking, and such measures may cause Jackson trouble down the line."

"I can't be worried about the whining newspaper editors," Livingston said gruffly.

"They have long memories."

Livingston flicked the air with a gloved hand. "Jackson is gearing up to declare martial law. He'll shut the papers down until he's ready to ride out of here. Then he won't care anymore what they have to say about him. If he manages to turn the British from the city, they won't dare criticize him anyway."

A young girl carrying a basket of dirty laundry that looked to weigh as much as she did stepped off the banquette into the street, her clogs kicking up muck. Livingston looked down at the hem of his coat and frowned, but she had already disappeared into the crowd. His long, homely face creased in thought.

He said, "I can't deny it's high time to raise the subject of evacuation."

Luke cast a glance over the street. It was crowded now and would be crowded still late into the night. Three long-haired backwoodsmen in homespun and deerskin, the kind who lived and hunted in the ciprière, stood looking around themselves in the middle of the street. Most likely they had never before set foot in New Orleans, but there they were now with ancient muskets, disoriented, confused about everything except the purpose that had brought them here. They wanted to fight under Jackson.

"For every man who walks for days to join the fighting, there's somebody else who should get out but has nowhere to go," Luke said. He was watching a boy of nine or ten years trying to herd a sow down the crowded street.

Livingston followed the line of his gaze, and coughed a laugh.

"The ladies who want evacuation have places to go. My wife and daughter will go to our plantation downriver. Your lady and son will go with them." He cleared his throat. "If she is not determined to stay to work alongside her husband, Mrs. Savard can join them. Certainly she will want my niece Rachel to leave, and young Henry."

Luke kept his tone unremarkable. "My wife will not leave. Not so long as my sister's injuries keep her here."

"Damn it to hell," said Livingston. "Here comes Brussard, and he has seen us."

Luke ducked his head to hide his smile. Pierre Brussard was one of the few men who could upset Livingston's everlasting calm and condescension, simply because he refused to acknowledge it. He was a nondescript man, still very young, and possibly a little simpleminded. Certainly he considered everyone he came across his closest friend, and now he strode toward them with both arms out, as if they were long-lost and much-loved brothers.

"Have you heard?" he called in English. His round cheeks folded to accommodate his smile. "Have you heard about Major General Jackson and Lafitte?"

He stopped, hands on hips and elbows pointing out, chest thrust forward, like a proud hen.

"What is it we should have heard?" Livingston asked, his brow lowering.

"Why, he's agreed to let them fight! Lafitte stopped the major general on the street and they had it out right there, and now the Baratarians are with us."

"Is that so?" Livingston's expression relaxed. For him this was excellent news, though Luke expected that the governor would suffer an apoplexy the minute he heard that his long-lived feud with the pirate had been finally lost, and for good.

"It's so!" said Brussard. "It is truly so!"

"Excellent news," said Livingston. He clapped Luke on the shoulder. "The best possible news. Let's go home and tell Mrs. Livingston."

Kit Wyndham saw Luke Scott—or Luke Bonner, as he was calling himself now—pass by the window of a tavern on the rue St. Pierre where he sat with a half dozen men over coffee. He pulled back into the shadows and picked up his cup, cursing silently to himself.

Time to leave the city. More than time.

"What I want to know," Michel Grandissime was saying to the others, "is if the English will really free the Africans."

"What you want to know is if you should put them up on the auction block now, before that happens," said Étienne de Flechier. "As do we all."

None of the men around the table had the heart to challenge this gloomy view of their situation. These men were all heavily invested in sugar and cotton, land and slaves, and they all stood to lose their fortunes to the English. None of them seemed to put much faith in Major General Jackson's ability to save New Orleans, though that was something they would admit only to each other across this particular table.

"Mark my word," said the dour Scot called Cruikshank in his atrocious French. "Jackson takes his example from the Russian army. He'd rather see Louisiana razed to the ground than lose and hand even a single stalk of cane over to the English."

"I say we hire our own force of armed men," Henri Le Bruere said, half rising from his seat to put all his weight on his fists. "It is the only hope."

"Even that hope he will take from us," said Grandissime.

"You don't know that," added Jean Blangue, who was banker to most of the men at the table.

"I do know that, and so do you." Grandissime's mouth curled down at the corner. "Jackson will declare martial law at the first opportunity."

Sometimes Kit found himself forgetting he was supposed to be one of them, a glum, cynical French expatriate among Creoles, waiting for the worst to happen. It still surprised him, what a boring business espionage was most of the time, sitting around listening to talk that meant nothing and achieved nothing.

Louaillier slammed his fist down so forcefully that coffee sloshed and spoons clattered. "Martial law. It is no more than his excuse to invade a man's privacy."

"At least Jackson put Claiborne in his place," said Magloire Guichard. "Now that Lafitte's in the fight, I like our chances a good deal more."

There was a more hopeful silence around the table as they all thought of Jean Lafitte.

"You've got precious little to say today, Reynaud." Grandissime frowned at him.

"I've got less to lose." Best to say it before someone else did. Creoles were the most prideful and easily offended race of men Kit had ever come across. If he didn't pay attention he'd find himself choosing a dueling pistol at dawn.

Time to be gone. His superiors would ask hard questions about what had delayed him, and what could he say? He had come into the city to fix a broken link in the long chain of information that reached from Jackson's headquarters on the rue Royale to Cat Island and an impatient invasion force waiting only for the right moment. His work had been done within days, but still he had waited, and why?

Because he had wanted to catch sight of an Indian woman. One who knew his real name and could see him hanged for a spy with a few well-chosen words. An Indian woman he had known intimately, and to whom he could make no promises. He reminded himself who he was and where his loyalties lay, and would have been on his way north by noon, had he not overheard the stableboys talking. Most usually such conversations were nothing more than part of the noise of the city, no more distinctive than the pealing of church bells or the rumble of an oxcart, but one phrase caught Kit's ear:

. . . that Redbone healer from York State . . .

Kit stopped. When it came to color, Louisiana was like no place else in the world. The terms they used to identify themselves and others were meaningful in a variety of ways that were so nuanced it would take years to fully understand. *Redbone* was a term he had not heard often, but he understood it to mean a person of mixed blood who was predominantly of one Indian tribe or another.

A Redbone healer from York State.

Lady Jennet was not here alone, after all. Hannah was still with her. Kit concentrated on following the silvery-quick French patois, catching five words in ten.

They did not mention Hannah by name, but there could be no mistake. An Indian woman from New-York State who called herself a doctor—one of the boys giggled like a girl at this idea—had been looking after her own kind at a new clinic on the rue Toulouse. That woman had been attacked and beaten near to death. The whole city was talking about it.

Kit went out into the city, where he made his way from one café to another. The only talk he heard was about Jackson, who was wasting no time settling in and had already ridden out with the engineers to examine fortifications. What he wanted to know he would never hear from white men, but the idea of stopping a slave on the street struck Kit as impossible and dangerous. And so he did something worse: He walked past the Kine-Pox Institute on the rue Dauphine, and the smaller clinic around the corner on the rue Toulouse, where there was a notice on the door he could not approach to read.

He was considering Dr. Savard, the physician of record at the Kine-Pox Institute. He could ask about vaccination against the smallpox. No one would see anything odd in that, Kit was telling himself, when Lady Jennet came out of the building in the company of a small armed guard. That she had been too deep in her own thoughts to take note of him was a bit of luck Kit knew he didn't deserve.

And so he followed her to the Livingstons' place on the rue de Conde, where a passing washerwoman had answered his questions. Then, greatly shaken, he retired to his rooms to try to sort out what he had learned.

Luke and Lady Jennet were guests of the Livingstons. Where had they been between the time he had first seen Jennet with Rachel Livingston and now? At the clinic, he reasoned. In hiding, it seemed. But why, and from whom? And how did all this fit into the attack on Hannah?

All he wanted to know, he told himself as one day passed and then another, was whether Hannah Bonner was alive or dead. Simple human compassion and fellow feeling required as much.

The boy who brought his wash water became his primary source of information: The Indian woman had lived through the night, but she was not expected to live out another day. He recited a list of her injuries so avidly that Kit might have slapped him.

There was nothing he could do for Hannah, he told himself. Every day he stayed increased the likelihood that he would be found out, arrested, hanged. His mission compromised, and the network of informants he had put into place scattered or caught. He must go.

M. Reynaud sought out his landlady to tell her that his departure for Mobile had been delayed again. A steady stream of small coins continued to find their way into the servant boy's hand. Using the conduit he had established to pass on information about Jackson's movements, fortifications, troop strength and position, he sent a hasty and uninformative excuse for his delay.

This could be the end of your career, for the sake of a woman you cannot have, who would not have you. He repeated those words to himself every day, and found they had little power.

When an innocent man accused of passing information to the English was taken prisoner and put in front of a firing squad, it seemed to have nothing to do with him.

What is it exactly you wish to accomplish by staying here?

He asked himself the question and tried to answer it: *I want to know that she is well.*

Abominable self-deception.

What he wanted, what he listened for when he went out into the city, was talk of who had been responsible for the attack. If it had been random, or if someone had been lying in wait for her. What he would do with that information once he had it, that was a question he never tried to answer.

The reports came daily. The Redbone woman was out of danger. She had relapsed into swamp fever. She had survived the relapse, and was allowed out of bed. An army captain had come to talk to her. The boy had heard no name mentioned in connection with the attack. And if there were such a name, it didn't matter. No one would be arrested. The boy explained what Kit knew already. No white man, nor even a black one, would be arrested for such a crime. The constables could not be bothered.

What is it I want here?

Kit Wyndham, known in New Orleans as Christian Reynaud, merchant, asked himself this question in complete earnestness. He was asking it again when Girot's coachman came stumbling into the café, out of breath, shaking with fear.

"Narcisse!" Girot was on his feet immediately, his eyes bulging with anger. "What do you mean—"

"The British, Michie Girot. The British on Lake Borgne!" His voice cracked and trembled, as if he were a boy of thirteen and not a man of advancing years. *"Koulye a, tanpri, delivre nou anba men lènmi nou yo, n'a sèvi ou!"*

The entire room was on its feet, men rushing for the doors, shouting to each other and bellowing questions after the slave called Narcisse, who had gone back into the street. Kit and Grandissime were the only two men left at their table.

"When a slave out of Saint-Domingue starts babbling Christian prayers, you know he is in terror of his life." Grandissime managed a dry smile.

"His instincts cannot be faulted," Kit said. He leaned across the table and lowered his voice. "A slave may call on God to deliver us from our enemies. For my own part, I put my hopes in Jackson."

CHAPTER 40

"Papa says you are a very bad patient," Henry Savard told Hannah the next morning. "Mama says he is not one to talk, because when he had the influenza she had to pour laudanum down his throat to keep him in his sickbed. Rachel says—"

Hannah cleared her throat, and Henry, unusually attuned to her moods for a boy of his age, stopped expectantly. "Do you want to sleep now?"

In fact Hannah didn't want to sleep. She wanted to be out of bed, because Paul Savard was right: She was a very bad patient, and moreover she considered his directions too extreme. She bit back the things she might have said, and concentrated instead on young Henry's expression. Such a serious boy, so eager to share his stories.

She said, "I have an idea. If your mama says you may, you might bring me the newspaper. Then we can read together about the war."

Henry's eyes widened with pleasure, and then his whole face fell. "I would like that, but Mama will say no. She thinks the newspaper will give me bad dreams. Because we lost the gunships." He leaned forward and whispered, "I'm not supposed to know, but everybody is talking about it."

Hannah's conscience was no match for her concern or her boredom, especially as Henry already knew what his mother wished he did not. She said, "Won't you tell me?"

He wiggled in his eagerness, glanced at the door to make sure there was no adult there to hear, and told her what he knew. The good news, he wanted her to know first of all, was that the pirate Lafitte had stopped Major General Jackson on the street—in broad daylight, in view of a dozen people—and simply talked the Baratarians into the major general's good favor.

"The governor must be very cross," Henry said. "Lafitte is always getting the best of him. Now that Major General Jackson has taken the Baratarians' side, there's no hope of Lafitte hanging. Especially if he keeps New Orleans safe, as Clémentine says he most certainly will."

"You admire the Baratarians?" Hannah asked.

Henry looked very thoughtful for a moment. "No. I can't admire them. Mama says they really are very bad, that they steal and smuggle slaves. Slave smuggling is the worst thing of all. Mama is a Quaker." He glanced at Hannah to see how she would take this.

"I am not a Quaker," Hannah said. "But I agree with your mama, it is the very worst thing. I once knew a very good woman who ran away from her owner because she wanted to raise her child to be free."

Henry said, "What happened to them?"

Hannah hesitated. "The little boy grew up a free man. He's an apprentice cordwainer in Johnstown, near where I was born."

Henry nodded. Hannah could almost see him sorting away this story for further thought.

Then he said, "There is bad news, too."

And it was very bad, so bad that Hannah at first could hardly credit what she was hearing. The entire American fleet—five gunboats and a tender—had been lost to a British invasion force. The British now had control of Lake Borgne.

"You mustn't worry," Henry said, in a voice and tone

that echoed his father exactly. "Major General Jackson has sent Major LaCoste and his battalion and some dragoons and lots of artillery. They will guard the roads into the city."

"I'll do my best to remain calm," Hannah said.

"Mama says she wishes the rest of the city would do the same," Henry said, his color rising perceptibly. "People are very upset. Mme. Grandissime told Rachel's aunt Livingston that a thousand English soldiers are marching up the Chef Menteur road right now, and a battalion of free men of color could no more stop them than a litter of puppies could stop a stampede of horses. Clémentine says we should go away to a safer place, but Mama—" He looked again over his shoulder and lowered his voice.

"Mama says doctors don't run off when people need them most. Clémentine is very grumpy about it. Rachel might go with her aunt Livingston, if things get much worse."

"And what about you, would you like to go away someplace safe?" Hannah asked.

Henry drew up, his small face creased in surprise and insult. "I am not afraid."

"Of course not," Hannah said. "But if your sister goes, she'll need someone to protect her."

That gave the boy pause. He studied Hannah very closely to see if it was some kind of trick, and she returned his gaze with complete calm.

"Go ask Rachel," Hannah said. "See what her plans are."

Henry got up so abruptly that the stool wobbled. At the same time Hannah heard Jennet's voice in the hall. When she opened the door Henry hurried out of the room.

"Did I interrupt something?" Jennet asked. She was carrying a basket, which she put down on the table near the window and began to unpack. A covered bowl, a basket of fresh white rolls still warm from the oven, a small jug. It seemed to Hannah that the Livingstons' cook was in some kind of competition with Clémentine to force-feed her back to good health.

"Henry has been telling me about the loss of the gunboats."

Jennet's face stilled. "I brought the paper for you to read. In case Henry left out any detail."

"Is it true that the entire American fleet is lost?"

Jennet pushed out a soft sigh. "Such as it was in the southern theater. Our five gunboats against a whole flotilla."

"Maybe you should leave with Mrs. Livingston."

Jennet's mouth pursed itself in distaste. "Aye, weel. She's packed, it's true, but not quite ready to leave, and no more am I. I am determined that we should stay together, Hannah. The troubles start when we let circumstances separate us."

Hannah let out a small laugh. She remembered saying something like that to her own father and stepmother many years ago.

"You may be right," she said. And: "What does Luke think?"

"He won't hear of us going anywhere so long as Honoré is—" She paused, and flicked a hand toward the window.

So long as Honoré Poiterin was in the world, Hannah thought, none of them was safe. She took inventory of her injuries. Her wounds were mostly healed, the last of the bruises faded to a dull yellow cast. There was no tenderness in her belly or ribs. It was true that she was weak and prone to headache, but today she was much improved over yesterday, and she expected that trend to continue.

She was more than capable of walking out of this room, this building, this city. If there were a ship to be had, she could board it, and they could go home. She thought of the American gunboats and the British navy.

"It's almost as if this place wants us to stay," Hannah said.

"Oh, aye," Jennet said, following Hannah's line of thought

without hesitation. "Betimes I can almost feel its grip on my ankle."

The slash of memory made Hannah catch her breath. For a moment she could not rid herself of the feel of Honoré Poiterin's hands on her skin. She turned her head to the pillow and fought for her composure.

". . . tomorrow's parade," Jennet was saying. She put a tray on Hannah's lap and sat down beside her.

"Are you unwell?"

"A little nausea, gone already," Hannah said. "There's another parade?"

Jennet studied her for a long moment, and then relented. "Aye. Luke says it was Livingston's idea, taken up eagerly enough by Jackson. A grand review of all the battalions left in the city. They meant to wait until Kentucky and Tennessee troops get here—it won't be more than a few days, Luke says—but this business on the lake made them reconsider. Can you guess what's really on the great major general's mind?"

"Martial law," Hannah said. She picked up her soup spoon.

Jennet hiccuped a laugh. "Did Henry tell you that?"

"No." Hannah gestured with her chin to the newspaper that lay folded on the tray and the bold headline. "But I can still read."

Hannah ladled soup while she gathered her thoughts. She could feel Jennet's gaze on her, insistent in her curiosity.

"You might as well come out and say it," Jennet said finally. "I can almost see it sitting on your tongue."

Hannah hitched a breath. "I need you to help me convince the Savards that I am well enough to leave here."

"Leave here?" Jennet looked around herself at the small, neat room, at the comfortable bedding and the sunlight coming through the window that opened into the courtyard. There were birds singing in the trees and, in counterpoint, the sound of dice being thrown against a brick wall. The armed guard was still in place, and would be until they left New Orleans. Or until they were called to battle.

"Where would you go?" Jennet asked.

"Not very far. I'd like to move into Ben's apartment." And in response to Jennet's confused look: "Above the kitchen."

"I know where it is," Jennet said.

Hannah couldn't help smiling. "Are you worried for my good name, or my safety?"

"Your safety, of course," Jennet said, so huffily that Hannah thought she had struck closer to the mark than she imagined.

"I don't think Poiterin will come after me again," Hannah said. "And I would dearly like some solitude. Surely you can understand that."

"Oh, aye," Jennet said. "The city feels like a beehive to me, and all of us crawling over each other. I do understand." She nodded firmly, as if to convince herself. "I'll speak to them, then, if it's important to you."

Hannah said, "I've got a better idea. Help me over there now, and speak to them later."

"Aye," Jennet said. "It is far easier to ask forgiveness than permission. I should scold ye but it would be dishonest of me, as I've done exactly the same for all my life. Come then, let's see you dressed."

The landlady who had once done everything in her power to keep M. Christian Reynaud as a tenant through the autumn months was no longer so dependent on his custom. In fact, she could hardly disguise the fact that she was glad to see him go.

He stood with her in the narrow parlor of the little hotel, counting coins into her gloved palm. Her small, thin face creased itself in an attempt not to look pleased, and Kit understood exactly why. She would triple the rent on his modest rooms before he was out the door, and find a new tenant before an hour was out. "I hope you will remember us when next you visit New Orleans, M. Reynaud."

Kit inclined head and shoulders to save himself the trouble of lying. When he came back to this city he would have his choice of accommodations, as would all of the English officers and their families, who waited on Cat Island planning victory and Yuletide balls. Of course he must get out of the city first, before Jackson declared martial law. Once that was done—and no doubt it would happen during the grand review scheduled for this very afternoon—every lane and street out of the city would be blocked, and every able-bodied man would be in one kind of uniform or another.

He made his way to the stables across the way, weaving through the crowded street. People were already gathering for the parade. They would provide cover for his departure, as they had when he came back to the city.

Inside the cool, dim stables there was no sign of Stadler or any of his slaves. No doubt the parade explained the quiet in a place of business that was normally very busy. Stadler did a great deal of business because he kept his stables in meticulous order and his horses were healthy and groomed and properly fed.

He called, and got no answer.

Kit swallowed down his irritation and considered. He could find a different public stable, or he could help himself to a horse and saddle here. That would mean going back into the hotel to leave money for Stadler, but he could see no alternative that didn't involve a great waste of time. He walked deeper into the shadows along the stalls, looking for the bay mare he liked best and finding her at the very end.

"There you are," he said. "Come, old girl, we're off."

The mare nickered at the sound of his voice and shifted on her feet.

"Not today," said an unfamiliar voice from the shadows. And: "Leave your hands where I can see them, Captain Wyndham. I have a musket aimed at your back."

Many things went through Kit's mind in a great tumble, but loudest of all was the echo of his name. Captain Wyndham. Captain Wyndham. Captain Wyndham.

"I think you've mistaken me for someone else," he said in his best local French.

"No mistake," said the stranger behind him, keeping to English. "Christian Wyndham, an officer in His Majesty's forces on the North American continent. Turn around."

Kit forced his breathing to calm, and turned. The man who stood there was a stranger to him. Tall and broadly built. Mixed blood, mostly Indian. Shorn black hair, and eyes of a strange light color that looked almost silver against the dark skin. His own age, or a little younger.

"Who are you?"

There was a flicker of a smile that disappeared as soon as it came. "Jean-Benoît Savard."

Savard. Kit tried to make sense of it, to connect this man to the Dr. Savard of the clinic on the rue Dauphine.

"He's my half brother," said the man.

"You're in the habit of reading minds?"

"I can read yours. You're wondering if you can get to that knife in your belt before I shoot. You can't."

"Not at all," lied Kit. "I was wondering why you are so certain you know me."

Savard inclined his head. "For a spy you are a very bad liar."

Kit considered the few options open to him. He said, "Very well, if you are so sure you know me, what are we waiting for? Let's go to the Cabildo so we can resolve this misunderstanding. I have nothing to fear from the authorities."

Odd, how he almost believed himself, but Savard clearly did not. He wondered where the stabler was, if Savard had paid him to stay away.

"Let's get down to business," Savard said. "What's your interest in the Indian woman at the clinic?"

Kit drew in a sharp breath, considered lying, and reconsidered. "She is a—was an acquaintance of mine. I heard that she was unwell."

"Is she one of your spies?"

His tone was unremarkable, as if he had asked about the weather, or which tailor Kit frequented.

"I haven't spoken to Hannah or been in the same room with her for many months. If you've been watching me you know that."

"You still haven't answered me directly. I suppose I will have to take you both to the Cabildo."

Kit felt his pulse leap like a startled bird. "So far as I know she is no spy."

The stern expression didn't relax, but there was a flicker of something in the strange light eyes. "And Honoré Poiterin?"

Kit blinked. "Who?"

"The English are in trouble if you're the best they have. You've broken into a sweat. Tell me about Poiterin."

"I know Poiterin," Kit said.

"He's a friend?"

Kit lifted a shoulder. "A social acquaintance."

"One of your network."

Silence seemed the only possible response. A long moment passed.

"I'm curious," said Savard. "That you seem to know nothing of the connection between Poiterin and the Bonners."

"Connection?" Kit's mind raced, tried to link what he knew of Poiterin to the Scotts, and failed.

"You haven't heard any talk."

"No," Kit said, letting his anger rise to the surface. "I don't listen to women's gossip, and the men I do business with hardly sit around discussing the affairs of an Indian woman. What is it you want, exactly?"

"I want to know if you had any part in Poiterin's attack on Hannah Bonner."

Kit was sure he had misunderstood, but saw by Savard's expression that he hadn't.

"Poiterin? It was Poiterin who beat and raped her and left her for dead?"

The words hung in the air, almost visible.

Savard said, "You know he is capable of it."

Kit closed his eyes. Poiterin was one of the most valuable and volatile of his network, superbly placed and a source of excellent information, but unpredictable and prone to fits of rage. Kit had seen him shoot an expensive horse for nothing more than balking, and according to rumor he was guilty of far worse things. He had heard some of them the last months. Smuggling, piracy, slave running—that Poiterin was a man of no loyalties and no morals was clear, but then Kit supposed that there were few saints who had ever taken up treason.

A vague memory came to him of the journey that had brought him first to Barataria. Men deep in their cups, telling stories. Lafitte's name had come up, and the men who had sworn him allegiance. Stories of Mac Stoker and his son, of Anne Bonnie and the old days, of rich merchantmen taken after hard battles, feuds and vendettas and stolen children.

There had been some story about a child taken from a white woman as a souvenir, Kit remembered now. An infant taken home to a grandmother, as a man might take a string of pearls to a lover who needed to be wooed after too long an absence.

"Was it Poiterin who took the boy to Pensacola?" The question had been asked before Kit could stop himself.

Savard looked grimly satisfied. "Maybe you're not as dumb as you seem at first. I'll ask you straight out one last time. Have you taken any part in Poiterin's campaign against the Bonners?"

"I knew nothing about it." *And if I had known,* Kit asked himself, *what could I have done?*

"You know now. He's a liability to you."

Kit met Savard's sharp eyes. "You have a proposal for me."

Savard nodded.

"And if I don't accept your terms?"

One shoulder lifted and fell. "I'd prefer to handle this myself."

Kit understood the man perfectly. He could agree to whatever he was going to suggest, or he could die right here. Savard wouldn't risk taking him to the Cabildo for questioning, because Kit knew things about the Bonners that could easily be misconstrued in such anxious times.

"Go on," Kit said. "I'm listening."

It was Clémentine who first discovered Hannah's removal to Ben's two small rooms above the kitchen. As soon as the older woman realized that she couldn't bully Hannah into moving back to the Savards' more comfortable apartment above the clinic, she changed direction. Within an hour Ben Savard's apartment had been transformed.

Clémentine's two daughters, silent in their work as their mother required of them, moved through the two small rooms like spirits. They tightened the bed ropes, replaced the mattress, and remade the bed with fresh linen that smelled of lilac water. A new cloth was spread over the table, dishware and a small tea service appeared on the rack on the wall, and new wax candles replaced the tallow ones that had

suited Ben Savard well enough. All of this was done while
Hannah sat near the hearth, half dozing in its warmth.

Then the Savards came too. Julia brought her books and
newspapers and the report that Jennet would be back tomorrow. Paul Savard insisted on examining her. With obvious reluctance he declared her well enough to be out of his
immediate sight.

Hannah said, "All this fuss. Whatever has got into Clémentine,
do you think?"

Dr. Savard looked at her closely. "It's not just Clémentine,"
he said. "They've taken your part."

"Who has taken my part?"

He glanced toward the door. "Before the attack, they
were watching you and keeping their distance. Now you're
one of them. You've got a common enemy."

He hadn't answered Hannah's question, and she said so.
"You're being very mysterious. It's not like you."

"I'm being cautious. That's very like me." After a moment he said, "I believe you've met Clémentine's mother.
She's called Maman Zuzu."

"Oh." Hannah cleared her throat. "I see. I didn't realize."

"Because they weren't ready to trust you. Now they are."

It was hard to imagine that anyone might have suspected
that Hannah was working with Honoré Poiterin, but that
seemed to be what Dr. Savard meant. If that was true, she
had paid a very high price to earn the trust of women like
Clémentine and her mother. She might have asked more
questions, had Luke not come in with news of the grand review on the Place d'Armes.

"More talk," said Dr. Savard. "And crowds. If we don't
have an outbreak of yellow jack it will be a miracle of the
first order. What of the speech? Did he do it, are we under
martial law?"

"Effective immediately." Luke rubbed his eyes. He looked
as though he had slept very little in the past days.

"Will this make things more difficult for us? Should I be doing something?"

"You should concentrate on getting better," Luke said.

In fact Hannah was feeling a little dizzy and very tired, and her eyes both ached and itched. She said, "Don't go quite yet. Tell me what to expect. Dr. Savard, have you ever been in a city under martial law?"

"No," he said. "Though I've heard stories."

Luke studied the floor between his boots. He said, "For you and the clinic, and for us, there won't be many changes. The city is closed off; you can't get in or out without permission from headquarters. Every able-bodied man will be called into one kind of service or another. The courts have shut down, and business has pretty much come to a full stop. There's a curfew for everybody now, as there always has been for the slaves." He drew a piece of paper from his jacket. "Unless you've got a military pass. They'll give you one," he said to the doctor. "All medical people will get them."

Luke turned to Hannah. "Things are coming to a head. The British are on dry land and making advances. I expect we'll see the first real confrontation within days, but with any luck not until after the Kentucky and Tennessee regiments get here."

Dr. Savard said, "Is it as bad as it looks?"

Luke's mouth pursed itself while he thought. "Yes."

Hannah closed her eyes. "I can't get away from this war. It will never end."

"It will end," Luke said quietly. "One way or the other. Listen, Savard, I need to raise the topic of evacuation with you. The women and children——"

"Julia won't have it," said the doctor. "There's no hope of her going. I'll talk to her again about the children. What about your wife and son?"

"Just as stubborn," Luke said.

Hannah said, "You could make her go, you know you could. You don't want her to."

That struck home, she could see the discomfort of it in the way he looked away. Finally he said, "I'm following my instincts."

Hannah sat back. "Then I must trust your decision."

Later, when Hannah had gotten into bed, Clémentine herself appeared in the door with a tray and an expression that brooked no dissent. Clémentine had never been very forthcoming, and Hannah had never pushed, out of respect and also because of what Ben had told her—and she herself had seen—of the animosity between the Africans and the Indians in this part of the world. If Paul Savard said that Clémentine had changed her mind about Hannah, he must be believed, though her long face with its deep-set eyes showed no hint of approval as far as Hannah could see.

And so Hannah ate the soup and the bread and drank the bitter tisane while Clémentine waited by the fire, darning stockings and keeping her thoughts to herself.

At the door she paused. She said, "There's a bell hanging right here. You ring it good and hard if there's any trouble. I'll hear it."

"Thank you," Hannah said.

In the last moments before she fell asleep in the glow of the banked fire, she thought of Ben Savard, who had been away a long time.

CHAPTER 41

At Larivière on the Bayou St. John an old woman sleeps soundly in a cocoon of lace and embroidered linen. It is the dead of night, and the last hour of her life.

She sleeps deeply, unaware of the quick movement of bare feet on polished floorboards and Turkey carpets, of the opening of doors and cabinets and drawers. The women are leaving. Cookie, born on one of the old woman's plantations to the south; Eve, won by the old woman's husband at a poker game thirty years ago; Pink and Calpurnia and Sukey, born at Larivière in the slave cabins behind the house and gardens. The women who lived only to scrub and carry bath water and polish silver, to wash the old woman's sheets and the pale folded flesh of her body, to serve her the beef and pork and chicken raised by their sons and brothers and husbands. Each of them slips away from the house in the dark, none empty-handed. Silverware, a pewter charger, purses full of coin, a statue of the Virgin Mary carved from cool marble, a tablecloth of heavy linen, books, candlesticks, figurines from China, carvings from Italy, old-fashioned jewelry, a cane with an ivory handle.

These treasures are passed to other hands and will disappear in hidey-holes deep in the ciprière. The women go back to their beds, not to sleep, but to wait.

More movement, this time toward the house. In the full dark it is impossible to make out much beyond the fact that this person— or maybe it is two people walking very close together—is carrying *something bulky tucked under an arm. The door opens and closes silently. In the complete dark of the house, robbed of even the faintest starlight by the heavy draperies, the intruders climb the stairs without hesitation, move down the hall, and open the door to the old woman's bedchamber.*

When she wakes it is to her name being spoken. Since her husband died no one has called her by her first name, and at first she thinks this is a waking dream. Then she sees the outline of a face above her, made indistinct through the fine gauze of the curtain that surrounds the bed.

She is very old, but her outrage and fear give her strength; she fights for a full minute, and the sound of her harsh breathing fills the dark room. In the end she is dragged from the bed and down the stairs like a sack of charcoal, her heels in their lace stockings thudding on each of the risers.

In the next house, not quite so grand, a seventy-year-old man doesn't sleep very well at all. Since he handed his business over to his sons, Jacques Rabat finds that real rest eludes him, and there is no satisfaction to be found in old age. The things he takes joy in are few: his granddaughters, who tease and scold him; the garden; his horses.

Horses, he tells his granddaughters, are the most intelligent of creatures, capable of the best and worst of human emotion. Love and hate, forgiveness and implacable resentment. Today one of his favorites, a mare with eyes like a madonna, was out for her daily exercise when she broke her ankle in a rabbit hole and had to be put down. Jacques feels the loss like a cramp in his gut.

In the dark he dresses without calling his manservant. A walk to the stables in the dead of night is something he does often, in every weather. He wants no help or advice or company.

He takes the small lantern to light his way. It bobs and weaves with his hitching step, swinging out to light the empty flower beds covered with straw against the winter cold, a shawl draped over a bench and forgotten, the form of a man slumped against the whipping post, his body canted forward and his shoulders humped under the strain. He may still be alive; he is a big man, still relatively young and very strong. If he is still alive in the morning he will receive the rest of the whipping due him. A careless slave at fault for the loss of a valuable horse deserves no less.

Still five minutes from the stables, Rabat stops and raises his head to the sky. His great nose wrinkles and the nostrils twitch. He knows this place, every nuance of smell from siprière and bayou, fields and pastures, the house and all its outbuildings, the cabins where his slaves sleep. He knows it all as he knows his own smells, and something here is new. Something is wrong.

Smoke. He turns slowly in a circle, studying the dark, and finds at last what he is looking for. There, at Larivière. A flickering of light outlines a window on the upper floor. Not even a hundred candles could throw that much light.

Larivière is on fire.

A stronger gust of wind brings the whisper and hiss of it. Soon embers will begin to float toward his own property, his fields and house and outbuildings. His stables.

Rabat puts back his head and screams for help, and then he runs, thin old legs working like pistons. He vaults up onto the veranda that surrounds Larivière like a boy of twenty, crashes through the main doors. Stops, because the air is so thick with smoke that breathing is impossible. The air shimmers with heat, and the floorboards are hot even through his boots.

Whoever is still upstairs is dead, or will soon be. There is nothing to be done for them. All this has occurred to him in a split second, but then he sees Agnès Poiterin through the open doors to the parlor. She is bound with ropes to a heavy chair that has been dragged into the middle of the room. Her eyes are open, and behind a gag already dark with smoke, her mouth is open, too.

He has no tools, there is nothing in this room to cut the ropes that bind her so securely to the chair. When he was thirty and at the peak of his strength he might have been able to lift this slab of *woman to carry her out of the house, but the chair is wider than the door, heavy wood lavishly carved. In some part of his mind Rabat recalls that it was brought by ship from France at huge expense, and that they had had to remove doors to get it into the house. He is thinking of this as he takes the gag away from her mouth. It has cut into the flesh at the corners and makes her look as though she is smiling, though her mouth snaps open and shut like a fish. She has no breath to scream, but it's there in her eyes.*

She says, "Get help you fool get help."

The roar of the fire is so loud that he must read this from the shapes her mouth makes. There is the huge crack of exploding window glass, and the temperature in the parlor jumps. Rabat runs to the doors that lead out onto the veranda. He will leave her to the flames—he will save his own life—when she screams. He turns, and the picture he sees will stay with him for what is left of his life: the old woman tied to the chair, her white hair floating in the heated air around her head, her face flushed beyond pink and red to purple, mad eyes rolling, chest heaving for breath.

"Rabat!" she screams with the last of her breath. "Tell my grandson I will be waiting for him in hell!"

At that same moment, at the Grand Trianon plantation fifteen miles to the south and Amboise just as far to the north, similar things are happening. Overseers are gagged and blindfolded and bound while houses are ransacked and fires set. Their women and children are bound and gagged, too, but left outside in the cold rain to watch their homes burn.

Main houses, outbuildings, storage sheds filled to bursting with the sugarcane harvest, years of labor gone in a matter of hours. The slaves slip away silently into the *ciprière*.

The élite of the city, the uniformed militia, have been stationed at Fort St. John. This company calls themselves Hulans, or Dragons à

Pied, after the great companies of soldiers who had fought and died in wars fought in France and Spain. They are the sons of planters and bankers and merchants, young men brought up on stories and swordplay. Since this newest war began they have spent a good portion of their time gathered in taverns and cafés, reading about battles, arguing about strategies, wondering when the war would reach them.

And then there were British ships in the Gulf, and Andrew Jackson rode into town. The sons of the first families would fight, but they would not lower themselves to consorting with the common militia, men who came in from the ciprière with tomahawks and ancient muskets tucked into their belts.

The Hulans, the Francs, the Louisiana Blues, the Chasseurs: four uniformed companies, three hundred and fifty men. The captain of the Hulans is Henri de Ste-Gême, a native Frenchman as short as Napoleon, and given like his hero to tall hats and grand gestures. Ste-Gême's Hulans will go into battle armed with lances, pistols, and sabers, and no practical knowledge of warfare.

In the first days of parades and marching, when the uniforms were still new, the inconveniences seemed small and unimportant. To rise at dawn to start the day's drills made it difficult to play cards all night, nor could the men go off on a whim to visit a brothel or the racetrack. But they are sons of New Orleans, and they will suffer whatever necessary to protect their property. And if that means digging ditches that are necessary to fortifications, well. Among them they own many hundred field slaves. The ones who can be spared from the cane harvest could come and dig, all day, every day.

The Hulans' uniform suits Honoré Poiterin's coloring best, and so he finds himself at Fort St. John in a cold December rain. Two days in camp and he understands that things are not as easily arranged as he had assumed would be the case. If Jackson has his way—and it seems he does get his way in all things—Honoré will find himself digging ditches alongside slaves. Of course he must take steps to avoid such an inappropriate use of his talents.

Perhaps, Honoré admits to himself, the uniformed militia was not such a good idea after all. It might be a good cover for his other, more lucrative activities, but a man has limits and Honoré's are met by the requirement that he live in a muddy camp on the shores of Pontchartrain in the worst of the winter.

The tents smell of shit and mold and sweat; worse, he finds himself sharing one with men he owes money. More absurd still: The camp is less than a mile from his grandmother's comfortable home, his own room and bed, well-laid fires, decent wine, fresh linen. Cramped and uncomfortable, Honoré Poiterin resolves that this will be the last night he spends in such circumstances. He can sleep at home and report for duty at a reasonable hour. If Ste-Gême comes looking for him he can deal with his grandmother. Honoré smiles at the idea, Ste-Gême nose to nose with Agnès Poiterin.

Still laughing, Honoré turns over and goes to sleep.

The noise in the middle of the night would not have been enough to rouse him, under normal circumstances. Honoré prides himself on his ability to sleep through anything, even a fire bell, so long as it is far enough away. He would sleep through this one, if it weren't for the fact that someone is bellowing his name.

He cracks an eye and sees Major Plauché himself leaning into the tent, a lantern in his hand that casts dancing light. Honoré is alone, he sees now. The others roused at the first call of the fire bell, which is still sounding.

"Larivière," Plauché shouts. "Larivière is burning." And then he is gone.

Honoré considers, trying to sort through his options, watching the light flickering on canvas walls. His grandmother's house is on fire. His things will burn up, his best clothes and the portrait of his parents and the books his father left him, his maps and letters and his small collection of souvenirs from his various adventures. A pity, but things can be replaced.

Grand-mère Poiterin will have to go back to the house in Pensacola, or to one of the plantations. Maybe this fire is what the priests call a blessing in disguise. To be free of his grandmother,

Honoré would burn up all his clothes himself. They are months out of fashion anyway, the damned war again, getting in the way of a man's relationship with his tailor.

All around him the camp is up in arms, a huge noise, men rushing off on horseback to join the bucket brigade. Fires are serious business, certainly, but there is no wind tonight. Still, he must go; it would look odd, otherwise, and attract attention he does not want called to himself.

That is the exact thought in Honoré's head when he sits up and begins to look for his clothes. When he realizes that there is something odd about the hard-packed earthen floor. First, that he can see it at all; it is still full dark, and Plauché took the lantern with him when he ran off.

He can see the floor because it has been cleared of boots and weapons and discarded clothes. In that small clearing, a candle has been set on a flat rock. A red candle, and around it on the floor, spread out like a lace tablecloth, a complicated pattern drawn in cornmeal: a heart pierced by a dagger. At the bottom of the pierced heart is a hollow gourd filled with dark liquid that glints in the candlelight.

For a moment Honoré is a small boy again, playing at the feet of his nurse as she and the cook talk in the cool under the arbors. The house in Pensacola, with palm trees all around and sand that seems to come out of thin air to collect in corners, shoes, pockets. His nurse is Mama Dounie, a slave like all the other people who live in this house with him and his grand-mère Agnès. She has been his nurse since he was born. Only Cook has been here longer, Cook who has other names that only Mama Dounie calls her when she thinks no one is listening: Domisaine or, sometimes, Mambo.

Now they are speaking of the island called Saint-Domingue and the families they had there. Mama Dounie cries sometimes for the little girls she left behind. Honoré doesn't like her to be sad but *he doesn't like this talk, either. Mama Dounie has no children but him. She has no other reason to exist but to care for him. He could go to his grand-mère and tell, and then Mama Dounie would be whipped for her lie. He is thinking about this, what Grand-mère would say and if he would have to watch the whipping, when he hears the cook says a name he recognizes: Erzulie.*

Honoré goes very still. If he is quiet enough they might not send him away, and he can hear the stories he likes best, of the Saint-Domingue Iwa, the spirits who can bring good luck or bad. Erzulie is the Iwa Mama Dounie loves most. There is a doll that belongs to the spirit Erzulie that Mama Dounie keeps under her pillow. It is made of black cloth and the face has no eyes or nose or mouth, but it is wrapped in a bit of blue silk.

At five Honoré speaks the language he has learned from Mama Dounie, the Saint-Domingue French he took in at her breast. He knows a little bit of the other French, too, the grand-mère French, as he thinks of it. The bit he needs to use when she summons him every Sunday to be inspected before Père Petit comes to say Mass. When he gets a tutor next year, he will be forbidden to speak anything else, but for now he has the freedom to talk to his nurse in the language that binds them.

Honoré is a boy and has no interest in dolls, but he would like to hold this one.

"Whose is that?"

"It is not a doll to play with. It belongs to Erzulie Dantor."

Mama Dounie knows what he thinks, always. Even when he says the exact opposite, she sees the thoughts in his head, and she never laughs at him.

When he is very good Mama Dounie tells him stories about her God, whose name is Bondye, and who looks like Grand-mère's Jesus. She tells him about the Iwa, the spirits who live on earth among the people, like Gran Bwa Ile, the spirit of the ciprière, and the Simbi Iwa who live in rivers and know magic, and La Kwa, Samdi and Simitye, who rule the graveyard. After he sees the doll, she begins to tell him stories about Erzulie.

Honoré first wants to know what Erzulie Dantor looks like, where she lives, what she eats for breakfast, if she has a little boy, whether she is afraid of snakes.

"She looks like me," Mama Dounie tells him, smoothing a hand over her own cheek, velvety black but for the tattoos that ran along her cheekbone. From when she was a young girl in Africa, another story Honoré likes to hear.

Erzulie, Mama Dounie tells him, never speaks but makes a kai kai kai sound when she walks among the people. She is a good mother and looks out for her children, but when she is angered she is dangerous, even to them. She carries a dagger, she likes the color blue, and she has more than one husband, and sometimes, a wife as well.

It is this last idea that Honoré comes back to again and again, and every time Mama Dounie answers his question the same way. The Iwa Erzulie Dantor treasures beauty and love above all things, love big enough for everybody.

Honoré likes this answer. He takes it out and thinks about it sometimes, a treasure like the others in the small box he keeps next to his bed. He is thinking about it one Sunday morning when he is standing in front of his grand-mère Agnès in his best clothes, answering questions about the Catechism taught to him every Wednesday and Friday by Père Petit. He is five years old; he has no memory of his mother, who died when he was a baby, and he sees his father so rarely that the last time he came, Honoré didn't recognize the slight man standing in the doorway. He has only Mama Dounie and his grand-mère Agnès, who is sometimes generous with sweets and praise and other times hisses like a snake until her face turns the color of plums. He would like to love his grand-mère because everyone tells him he should, but mostly he is afraid that he won't answer her questions right.

This Sunday she is unusually cheerful, for some reason that is unclear to Honoré. There are pralines and she allows him a spoonful of coffee in his sweet milk, and she lets him open the miniature she wears on a ribbon around her neck so he can look at the tiny paintings: Jesus on one side and grand-père Poiterin on the other.

"You resemble your grand-père Poiterin exactly," she tells him. Honoré, eager to please her, volunteers some of his own small store of facts. "As much as Mama Dounie looks like the Iwa Erzulie and her God Bondye looks like Jesus."

It will be a long time before he begins to understand what he said to make the whole world change. After Mama Dounie and Cook and three other slaves have disappeared without even saying good-bye; after a new slave, one who is deaf and dumb, is given to him to help him dress and bathe; after M. Delile, his new tutor, arrives. It is all Père Petit's questions about Mama Dounie's stories that make Honoré understand, finally, what he has done.

When he gets the courage to ask his grand-mère, months later, she only looks at him for a long time. Not angry, not sad, not anything. Finally she says, You were entirely too attached to Dounie, and she filled your head with blasphemies. She has gone back to where she came from, and she took her heathen spirits with her.

That is all twenty years ago. Now Honoré looks at the red candle, the bowl of blood, the intricate drawing on the dirt floor. A veve. He recalls the name for this kind of symbol, though he doesn't remember exactly when Mama Dounie told him about it. Each Iwa has one, and this is Erzulie's. The spirit of mothers, who prizes beauty and love above all things, who protects her children. Who carries a dagger, and whose anger is best not aroused.

Hannah wakes suddenly deep in the night. Confused, she sits up and tries to make sense of what has changed.

A burning candle sits on a saucer in the middle of the table where her supper has been set out. She had put out all the lights, and yet there it is: a thick, short, red wax candle that smells of evergreen and something else, vaguely sweet. The scent raises sudden memories of a man who had been her teacher for a short while, and a tall carved-wood cabinet where he kept his medicines and cures. It is a smell from the other side of the world, or another world altogether, a good and comforting smell.

She gets out of bed and goes to the table slowly, unsure of her strength. A likeness has been carved into the candle wax. A face, neither male nor female, and already half gone. Next to the candle is a small muslin charm bag, tied with hair.

Hannah takes it back to bed with her. For a moment she wonders if it is her own charm, filled with treasures. A bear's tooth, a scrap of rawhide, a coin, a bundle of dried herbs, a lock of hair. Each of those things has its own story, and power. All lost on the day Harrison's troops had burned Tippecanoe to the ground.

Who has brought this charm Hannah can only guess. She remembers Maman Zuzu, the deep-set eyes that weighed and judged and then waited, after all, still unsure of Hannah's place in this world.

If Maman Zuzu has sent these things to protect her or warn her, then Hannah has paid dearly for that trust and help.

It is very late and sleep is stealing over her, as persistent as a tide. She falls asleep watching the red candle burn.

When she wakes at first light the candle is gone. She is still alone, no sign of Clémentine or Jennet, or of Ben. Now Hannah can admit to herself that she slept in his bed, as he had asked her to, in the hope that it would draw him back to her.

Ben is still gone, and she has dreamed of a candle carved from red wax. Hannah presses the heels of her hands to her eyes and takes a deep breath, and then another. The room smells of ordinary candles, of woodsmoke and tea and linen dried in the sun.

She reaches under the pillow, and retrieves the charm bag.

Hannah thinks of her aunt Many-Doves, who could tell her what to make of the dream. All dreams are sacred, sent for a reason—sometimes small but always important. She closes her eyes and concentrates on the feel of the bag in her hand, the shapes inside of it, the smell of the candle. She lets her mind go where it will and waits for pictures, faces, words. Nothing.

Hannah gets up and gets dressed. She has had enough of waiting.

•   •   •

The post-rider's route starts in Memphis, Tennessee, and ends in New Orleans, Louisiana. From July of 1799 until this newest war started, he has brought the mail, as steady and reliable as the sun moving across the sky, arriving in the fourth week of the month. The war has twisted the rhythm of his year into a knot, upset the natural and proper order of things.

He comes into New Orleans many days late, first because of the trouble in the Bowling Green post office—the post-rider, born and bred in Tennessee, was not surprised when he heard about the mess Kentucky had made out of something as important as the U.S. mail—and second by the war. Weather has never concerned him, but he has found himself confounded, again and again, by disrupted roads and troop movements and battles. When he finally believes himself to be within a half day of finishing the worst circuit he has ever ridden, the post-rider comes to a full halt on the outskirts of the city, brought up short by the fact that the city is under martial law.

All roads have been barricaded, and soldiers interview everyone wanting to enter or leave. The post-rider waits an hour, and is passed along without comment into the crowded city streets.

Tied to his pommel is the horn he blows to announce the arrival of the United States mail. In the noise and tumult he doubts anyone would take note, and so he leaves it untouched and urges his horses—the one he rides, and the one that carries the mail in leather pouches—into the rue Chartres in the direction of the Place d'Armes. This street and every cross street—Hôpital, Ursulines, St. Phillip, Dumaine—is overrun with traffic as far as he can see, though he stands in his stirrups and his Moll is a full sixteen hands.

The post-rider is a veteran of the war for independence; he has been to Boston and Manhattan and Philadelphia, but he can't recall ever seeing such a mess of oxcarts and wagons, wheelbarrows and artillery caissons, peddlers leading pack donkeys or carrying their goods in great lumps on their backs, servants and slaves, mer-

chants and shopkeepers and men in a dozen different uniforms ranging from homespun and fustian to the finest broadcloth.

I was a soldier once, too, the messenger thinks of telling a passing dragoon. I left a leg at Brandywine back in '77.

Everywhere the peddlers and merchants are busy with the troops, whose demands never end. For food and water and harder drink, for amusement and distraction, for matches and firewood, newspapers and ink—some of them will be lettered enough to send word home, and the post-rider will take what they write with him when he goes. Children sell meat pies, beef jerky, cold sausages and cheese out of boxes strung around their necks; young women stand outside butcher shops and taverns reciting the fare to be had; old women hawk their skills at those things men are not meant to do for themselves: mending, sewing, laundry, barbering. Younger women, negro and red-skinned, offer other services, their breasts swaying under thin fabric. The post-rider turns his face away.

From the door of a small shop the bookseller Gomez gestures insistently, waving short arms in the air like a woman in a fit. The post-rider would like to ignore him, but the crowds in the street conspire to stop him just there.

"I was starting to despair," Gomez says in his foreign accent. "Anything for me from Indiana?"

The post-rider's job is one of great responsibility and dignity, something that people seem to forget in their eagerness for news of family and friends and business ventures. As a plainspoken man he would like to tell Gomez that his familiarity is uncalled-for, but he can't. To his dismay, he has to repeat to this man the same short speech he has been delivering to everyone who asks him for news of the mail. The speech was composed by his superiors and committed to memory. The post-rider knows it as well as he knows the books of the Bible.

He says, "I have with me the regular post as well as some letters as much as a year old, which were delayed in their delivery. This delay is due to malfeasance on the part of an assistant postmaster in the Bowling Green, Kentucky, post office. On October first of this year Thomas McNulty was found guilty of stealing mail that passed through his office. The investigators found over fifty letters, bills of exchange, drafts, checks, and postal orders amounting to more than half a million dollars hidden in McNulty's home. I carry with me the stolen material. Postmaster Rofignac will restore it to the legal recipients with today's delivery."

The post-rider has to shout over the street noise to be heard. He would have shouted the news anyway, not just because it is a serious matter but also because he is sick unto death of repeating it and shouting provides some small pleasure. At least the bookseller seems to be giving him the attention his message deserves. His mouth hangs open under a neat mustache, his eyes as round as pennies. He is hoping that some of the half million dollars will find its way into his pockets.

Before Gomez can collect himself to ask questions—they always have questions, most of which the post-rider can't or won't answer—he puts his spurs to his horse and disappears into the crowd.

The post office is in the Cabildo, which is on the Place d'Armes, the very name of which irritates the post-rider. This whole territory was taken over by the United States more than ten years ago, and it is more than time that they give up French for English. Pushing his way closer to the plaza, he finds that here, everything has changed. The Place d'Armes is gone, replaced by an army camp.

A great sea of tents stretches from the cathedral to the river. The marketplace, the levee, every available square foot has been appropriated for drills, dozens of units of men moving in response to shouted orders in French, Creole, Spanish, English. Officers stride up and down on the line or ride horses trained for battle. The air itself seems to tremble with the noise and stink of war. Unwashed humans packed together into moldering canvas tents, clothing stiff with dirt and sweat, roasting meat and sizzling fat, overburdened latrines, and the bitter tang of gunpowder. A shock of memory moves down the post-rider's spine, a tingle that continues, against all common sense, into the wooden peg where his leg used to be.

He picks his way toward the Cabildo, a great, squat, imposing building. When he has watered his horses and tied them, he takes the four portmanteaus from the packhorse and hobbles into the building, noting still, after all these years, the odd sound he makes as he walks on cobblestones, his wooden peg alternating with a heavy boot.

The New Orleans postmaster, who is a lawyer and a member of the legislature, is now also a militia officer in a brilliant yellow uniform. He looks harried, but as always he is perfectly correct in his address. He gestures for the portmanteaus to be put on his desk, already piled high with ledgers.

The post-rider recites his speech. Postmaster Rofignac is surprised out of his preoccupation. He is a lawyer, after all, and most probably he expects to find post addressed to himself, letters and bank drafts thought lost in the war. He empties the portmanteaus onto a table and considers. Looks at one letter and another. Picks up a third and a fourth, sifts through and finds a letter that is pristine compared to the rest of them, the paper still white and clean, the ink unsmeared.

The post-rider has had it only since yesterday, and the notation in the upper right-hand corner is in his own hand. It says that the sender paid fifteen cents to send two sheets—folded, sealed, and addressed—less than forty miles. It is an odd case, and the post-rider, who as a rule doesn't volunteer information, gives in to the unusual urge to tell the story.

"An old Redbone woman gave me that yesterday," he said. "Fifteen miles north of here, on the road to Mobile. She was waiting for me, and she had the coin ready." The odd part of this, the post-rider doesn't need to point out, is that the letter is addressed in an elegant, educated, male hand to General Andrew Jackson himself.

Lieutenant Etienne Philippe Rofignac is an elected member of the legislature, one of the few members of the Committee on Defense, a lawyer, a planter, the postmaster for the city of New Orleans, and a conscientious, honest, and excitable man whose vanity has been dealt a blow by his current assignment. He should be drilling with the rest of the uniformed militia, but instead he moves paper from one pile to another.

He is also a lawyer with a keen eye, and of all the letters it falls to him to distribute, he believes the one in his hand to be the most important, for reasons he cannot immediately articulate. A tension in his shoulders, a smell in the air: And what does it matter? He knows what he knows, and so he leaves the office. He leaves the post-rider to sort the mail—the man is insulted, but he will do as instructed, in the end—he leaves the ledgers and the headaches associated with provisioning thousands of men, and he walks to General Jackson's headquarters on the rue Royale, hoping he will be permitted to speak to the general's adjutant, Major Butler, and rehearsing what he will say. If he must be secluded away in an office during the most crucial days of the city's history, he would like it to be the general's headquarters, and thus he must impress Butler with his intelligence, astute perception, and quick action.

The headquarters offices occupy the two floors above Caudin's music shop, and they are as crowded as everything else in New Orleans these last weeks. Soldiers and officers, militia and merchants, everyone has business or would like to have business with Jackson's staff. There is a great deal of money to be made in time of war. More than that, it is rumored that the Kentucky and Tennessee regular army brigades will be arriving in the city today—where they are to be put, that is anyone's guess—but there is a great deal of nervous excitement in the air.

The rooms reek of stale tobacco and sweat and charcoal in the braziers. The floorboards are warped, the ceiling water-stained, and the walls peeling. Above a long table piled high with paper hangs a painting as long as the room itself, portraying what might have been a battle or a crucifixion, or some bloody combination of the two. Rofignac studies it with horrified fascination as he waits his turn to speak to the clerk at the desk. When he arrives there finally, the clerk turns out to be the American he has heard about but never seen, Livingston's new clerk. A tall, well-built man, heavy shoulders under a coat that doesn't fit him as it should, a sharp intelligence in the pale eyes.

"How may I help you, Lieutenant Rofignac?" His French is

flawless, but with an unfamiliar accent, and he knows Rofignac's face and name. It is a merchant's trick, to remember names. Rofignac wishes he were better at it himself.

"I have a letter for the general. It arrived this morning."

The gaze sharpens. "A dispatch?"

"No. This came with the regular United States mail."

Reluctantly he takes the letter from his jacket and puts it on the desk. The American casts a casual glance at it that quickly turns to closer inspection. Rofignac notes that there is new color in the American's face. The American is surprised, and more than that, he is so disturbed that he fails to hide his reaction. Rofignac's instincts were correct: This is an important letter.

The American stands abruptly. At the door to the adjoining room, he turns back.

"Wait here, please, Lieutenant."

The men waiting behind Rofignac don't bother to hide their impatience. Five minutes pass and then another five, and the door opens. It is the American again, and he gestures. Rofignac is being summoned into the inner office. He is letting himself hope that Major Butler will want to speak to him when he comes into the room and finds himself in the company not only of Major Butler, but of General Jackson himself, and that rascal of an American lawyer with his fingers in every pie, Edward Livingston.

"Lieutenant Rofignac," says the general. "I want to hear whatever you can tell me about this letter and how it came to you."

While Rofignac relates the post-rider's story, Luke finds himself rereading the letter, his gaze shifting over the familiar handwriting.

Sir,

I am Major Christian Pelham Wyndham of His
Majesty's Rangers, on special assignment to this
theater of the war for the last six months.

I am a spy. I write this letter at gunpoint. There are,
as you well know, a number of British spies operating

in the Louisiana territory. Some of them I have
recruited myself since my arrival in August, under
orders to seek out those sympathetic to our cause.
While in the city I was known as Christian Reynaud,
a merchant. I had rooms on the rue d'Hôpital. I assure
you that the landlady knew nothing of my true
identity or mission in the city, nor did any of the
gentlemen or families I met with socially. Here is the
information I am compelled to supply to you:

There are seven men and one woman actively
spying for the Crown in southern Louisiana. I will
name two. First, a man of some forty years called
James Thomas, a chandler resident on the rue
Bienville. He is originally of England and loyal to the
English cause. Second, Honoré Poiterin, whose
primary residence is Larivière on the Bayou St. John.
Poiterin has joined Ste-Gême's Hulans. In return for
money and promises of land and favors once the
British have taken the city, Poiterin has supplied me
with information which I passed on to my superiors.
I have had little useful information from Thomas, but
Poiterin has been very active on behalf of the Crown.

If, as I suspect, you doubt my identity, my
truthfulness, and my word on these matters, I suggest
you interview Thomas first. It will not require much
to convince him that he should confess, as he has
never been at ease in his role as spy. As further and
more binding proof, I enclose a sheet of paper. You
should be able to verify from independent sources
that the hand is Poiterin's. At my request he drew this
map, marking locations from Barataria to Bayou
d'Arbonne with all the depths of the passes recorded
clearly, along with observations on the woods, their
thickness and composition, and the exact location,
depth, and width of the waterways. In payment he

received cash to settle his considerable gambling debts. His usefulness as a spy was compromised by his lack of common sense, his pride, and not least, his temper. While I would not expose him to you were I not compelled to do so, I am not unhappy to be shut of further dealings with him.

By the time you are in possession of this letter I will have returned to headquarters and be back in uniform. May I suggest you don't waste time trying to ascertain the reasons behind this confession of mine. It is of no importance to the war effort and will not impact your efforts to repel the British army and navy. In fact, I believe that this information will not improve your chances to any real degree, but again I repeat: I am compelled to share it, or lose my life. I have the honour to be, Sir, with respect,

Major C.P. Wyndham
Parish St. Jacques
19 December 1814
General Andrew Jackson

CHAPTER 42

Jackson's office had gone quiet. The post-rider was gone, and the general sat glowering, on the point of one of the bursts of violence he was so famous for. There would be questions first, or at least, Luke hoped there would be. He had things to say, and the sooner the better.

The questions came first. Was the post-rider telling the truth about the origin of the letter? Would it be at all useful to seek out the Indian woman he described? How best to proceed in terms of the two accused men? Might the whole thing be a diversionary tactic of some kind, and if so, to what end? What did they know of the reputations of the accused?

Through it all Luke's mind raced. He had no doubts that the letter was authentic and that the hand was Wyndham's. The things he didn't know were so many that he could hardly keep them straight. Foremost in his mind was the fact that Livingston knew of his own connection to Wyndham, and that Jackson did not. It was crucial that he volunteer the information before Livingston did, but timing was everything. And beyond all that, there was the question of who had held the gun to Wyndham's head and forced him to write this extraordinary letter.

That Ben Savard had something to do with it, he was certain. Why he was so sure of that fact he couldn't articulate to himself, but Hannah was part of the answer. What had happened to Hannah, and what hadn't happened to Poiterin as a result. He was sure, too, that last night's fires were part of the same puzzle.

Livingston's thoughts had gone in that direction, and now he told Jackson some of what he didn't know. He said, "Not only the house on the Bayou St. John, but both of the Poiterin plantations burned to the ground last night. One north of the city and one south."

Jackson's expression went still, as it did, Luke had learned, when he was intrigued.

"Clever," he said. "Very clever. If one man is behind all three fires and the writing of this letter, he must have wings, or a squadron of trusted accomplices. Is this Poiterin family so disliked? Is this a vendetta? In that case, this letter may be just one more tactic."

The question was directed to Livingston, as were all questions that had to do with the Creole population of the city.

"Agnès Poiterin was very rich and of the first rank," Livingston said. "But she was also mean-spirited and cruel. If it weren't for the other fires and this letter, I'd suspect her slaves in her death. She gave them reason enough. She has been fined more than once for the use of excessive force against her negroes."

Luke said, "If it's slaves you're wondering about, they had as much reason to hate her grandson."

"Explain," said Jackson.

"You've met my sister. Through her I hear a lot of news that circulates among the slaves and free people of color. Apparently Honoré Poiterin is in the habit of taking slaves—some who are his property by law, and others who are not—out of state to sell. He is always short of cash."

"As would you be if you had Poiterin's weakness for cards and faro," Livingston said.

"That's a very involved cabal you're suggesting." Jackson was still looking at Luke. "You think the slaves planned and executed these strikes on the Poiterins to avenge insults?"

Insults, Luke thought. An odd word to use in this connection. But he said, "I am not suggesting one thing or another. I'm providing additional information."

Livingston said, "Poiterin has too many enemies to count, and a good number of them are men of the roughest sort. There's an old feud with some of the Baratarians, and unhappy business associates from Pensacola to Port-au-Prince. Given the nature of the claims the writer makes, it seems to me that the first and most crucial step is to interview the men accused of espionage. We can worry about who wrote the letter once we know if Poiterin and Thomas are spies."

Luke said, "Wait."

Jackson's gaze shifted, knife-sharp, toward him.

"I can say with complete certainty that the letter was written by Christian Wyndham of the King's Rangers. I know the man."

Livingston looked relieved, in spite of the fact that Jackson had risen to his feet. Color flooded up his wiry neck and over the stubble on his cheeks and all the way to his eyes, rimmed with a darker red. His body vibrated like a divining rod. "You *know* the man?"

"I knew him," Luke said, utterly calm, because he must be. Jackson was a bully of the first order, and he could not let himself be intimidated. "I last saw him in Port-au-Prince. I had no military or political connection to him, but I did travel with him." He paused. "On a personal matter."

Jackson's color went pale and then red again.

Luke stepped closer and raised his own voice.

"My wife's life was in danger, Major General. The man who abducted her was wanted by the Crown for larceny and murder in Canada, and Wyndham had been sent to bring him back to trial. We traveled together out of expediency, with no other common cause than finding Jennet and bringing her abductor to justice. I am speaking of my wife and infant son, and I won't apologize for doing whatever was necessary to find them and secure their safety. You of all men understand that an insult to a good woman must not be tolerated."

It was a calculated gamble. Jackson's devotion to his own wife was the stuff of legends, and the cause of more than one duel. Rumor had it that he still had a bullet in his ribs from one such confrontation.

Jackson went suddenly still.

"What became of the rascal?"

Luke said, "I put my pistol to his head and pulled the trigger."

A moment passed and then another. Then Jackson turned, raised his hand, and pointed a finger at Livingston. "You should have told me about this earlier. I don't like surprises."

The lawyer's expression gave nothing away. "I see that now, sir."

"Any other British spies hiding in your closet, Bonner?"

"No," Luke said.

"And you believe what he says in this letter."

"I believe him, yes."

"Was it you who put the gun to his head and made him write it?"

The idea took Luke by surprise. "No."

"And if you come face-to-face with the man on the field of battle, what then?"

Luke didn't hesitate. "I'll shoot to kill."

Jackson's jaw worked, and then he nodded. "Major Butler, take your best men and bring Poiterin to me directly."

Butler had been speaking to a cadet, his head lowered to listen as the boy made his report. He straightened and Luke saw there was a sheet of paper, closely written, in his hand. "I fear Poiterin has already fled," he told the major general. "Captain Urquhart just sent this for approval so it can be printed and distributed."

Jackson tossed his head impatiently. "Read it, and be quick about it."

REWARD

For information leading to the apprehension of the person or persons who burned Larivière on the Bayou St. John to the ground last night, and thereby caused the death of Mme. Agnès Poiterin. At approximately the same time, arsonists struck at Grand Trianon and Amboise, also property of the Poiterins. Both plantations burned to the ground, but without loss of life. The overseers were unable to identify the persons who assaulted and bound them before setting the fires.

Major Villeré, Commander of the Louisiana Militia, wishes to assure the citizens of New Orleans that the possibility of an organized slave uprising has already been considered and discarded. All the Poiterin slaves are accounted for, and all have been questioned closely, to our satisfaction. An investigation is being conducted by a joint committee of the local constabulary, the militia, and the army. It will continue until the guilty parties are brought to justice.

In a series of events which may or may not be related to these horrific crimes, Honoré Poiterin, grandson and heir of the murdered lady, has been reported missing from his militia company, Ste-Gême's Hulans. M. Poiterin is being sought for questioning in this and other matters. Anyone with knowledge of his whereabouts must come forward or be charged with withholding information vital to the investigation of multiple crimes.

The Committee for Public Safety and Captain Aloysius Urquhart of the U.S. Army, liaison between the U.S. Army and the New Orleans Guard.

Jackson's high brow flooded with color, and at the same time the rest of his face clamped down into a fist.

"I'll have this Poiterin's heart, by God I will. Send someone else to arrest this chandler, and don't waste any time. Things are coming to a boil."

Butler wasn't even at the door when it flew open. A cadet stood there, red-faced and short of breath, but he straightened his back and snapped a salute.

"Major General," he said. "Major General, sir. General Coffee and his men are here. Five miles northwest, at Avart's plantation."

Jackson was up again, reaching for his cloak and hat. "Thanks be to God. Major Butler, I'll leave this matter to you. John Coffee is here."

Hannah slept until mid-morning and woke disoriented and aggrieved. The worst part about malaria was how persistent it was, and how long the symptoms lingered. She rose finally, dressed, and standing, ate the breakfast Clémentine had left for her, all gone cold with waiting.

She needed some kind of work, some way to keep busy. It would have been a pleasure to her to help in the kitchen or sweep floors, but Hannah knew that Clémentine would try to force her back to bed if she were so foolish as to suggest such a thing.

Which left the little clinic. The only place in this city that felt like her own, or had felt that way. Her first venture back would be a trial, one for which she wanted no witnesses.

Julia had told her, in a matter-of-fact way, about what measures had been taken to keep the little clinic open while Hannah was ill. In spite of the increased work for all doctors since Jackson's arrival, the Savards had found a few hours every day to see Hannah's patients—or, at least, the ones who would come to them. Sometimes Yellow-Sapling spent a morning there as well, treating whoever came to see her.

Every day, Julia told her, her patients asked after her, and every day she answered their questions in the same way. Of course Hannah would come back to her work at the little clinic. As long as she was in New Orleans, she would do what she could for the Indians who lived in the shadows of the city.

Hannah wondered that Julia should have such faith in her ability to carry on. When she said so, Julia only paused and sat down beside her, hands folded while she bowed her head and considered. Julia's Quaker silences were something Hannah liked best about her, because in this at least the Quakers were something like Hannah's mother's people: Unlike most whites, Quakers did not feel the need to fill every silence with words.

When she raised her head again, she looked at Hannah with simple affection and understanding as comforting as any touch. She said, "It is your gift and your work. It would be wrong to let Honoré Poiterin take it from you."

Hannah reminded herself of those words as she pulled a heavy shawl around her shoulders against the chill. She went down the stairs and through the courtyards to the long, low building where she had been attacked, and where she had survived.

Until she stood in front of the door Hannah had been able to turn her thoughts away from Leo, who had not come back since that night. Who was, she had no doubt, dead, at Poiterin's hand. Leo, with his carefully nurtured skeptical view of the world and great ambitions. Her son had been younger by a few years, but she had the idea that the two boys would have been well suited.

She opened the door and went inside.

It had been carefully kept in her absence. The floor and hearth were swept, the stove blackened, the tables dusted. The jars and bottles were carefully lined up on the shelves. The cot that had been near the fire had been moved and was made up with fresh sheets and blankets, and still the sight of it made Hannah's flesh crawl, just as a bugle sounding in the street made her jump.

She stood for a moment with a hand pressed to her chest, waiting for her breath to ease and listening to the sound of men marching, of drums and fife and horses. Finally she went to the door that led out onto the street and opened it.

The city was being overrun, not by the British, but by the American army. All along the banquettes the citizens of New Orleans had turned out to greet the troops that marched down the narrow street three abreast. The noise was overwhelming, but joyous. Hannah was about to retreat when she saw Père Tomaso, who waved at her, and next to him Henry Savard. Henry caught sight of her and ducked and wove his way through the crowd until he stood, breathless and gleaming, looking up at her in the open door.

He bounced on his toes and waved his arms. "It's the Forty-fourth!" he shouted. "Colonel Ross and the Forty-fourth, and Colonel McRea's artillery. Eight hundred regulars!"

Hannah took the boy by the hand and drew him into the little clinic. She said, "You can see much better from here, Henry." *And your mother would prefer to have you out of the crowds,* she thought, but that she kept to herself.

Henry wouldn't have heard her in any case; he was far too lost in the parade of the army regulars. To Hannah's eye the soldiers looked undernourished and worn down, but where she saw threadbare uniforms and hollow cheeks, he saw only guns and adventure.

He had dragged a stool over and climbed up to get a better view. "Look," he said, wobbling so that Hannah had to grab him around the waist or watch him fly. "Look, the dragoons! Those must be the ones from Mississippi."

Wherever they came from, they made a fine show in dark uniform coats with scarlet facings. White saber belts crossed their chests. They wore knee-high boots polished to a gloss, and short capes swung around them. Their horses were just as finely turned out and full of high spirits.

Henry said, "I was hoping General Coffee's men would come this way, too. He has his brigade north of the city. I think this time there really is going to be a battle." Suddenly all the light left his face. "But we won't be here to see it," he said. "Mama says we have to go away until the fighting's done."

Hannah wanted to ask about this newest plan, who was to evacuate and how, as Jackson had commandeered every horse and wagon in the city for the use of the military. These and a dozen other questions came to mind, but the cheering suddenly doubled in volume and intensity.

"The major general," Henry said. "Oh, look. That must be General Coffee. They said he was as big as a giant, but he's not. He's no bigger than my uncle."

A crowd of officers and aides rode past, and Hannah caught sight of Andrew Jackson's hair like raw cotton, his long face with the fissured cheeks. His sallow color and the dark circles under his eyes said that he was still suffering from dysentery, and now she remembered talking to Dr. Savard about the major general's treatment. Whether or not anything had come of that she had never heard, but it was clear that he was no better, and maybe even a little worse.

Luke rode by with Mr. Livingston. Her brother raised his hat to her and winked, to Henry's delight.

Then the parade was over and the crowd began to drift away. Hannah found she could see to the other side of the street, where there were more familiar faces. The baker from the next corner, a charwoman, a girl who sold pralines on the Place d'Armes, a water carrier. Clémentine, and with her Maman Zuzu and Maman Antoinette, all three of them wearing tignons in bright colors that seemed to shine against the buff-colored stucco walls. She thought of crossing the street to them and asking about likenesses carved in candle wax and bound with hair, and about fires in the night. She was ready to step off the banquette when she saw another familiar figure in the crowd. A tall figure, with black hair cropped short under a slouch hat with a broad brim. A strong nose and high cheekbones and eyes the color of the seas.

Henry had been talking all this time, about cannons and carronades and what could be done with them. Now he saw her expression and stopped in mid-sentence. He turned, his eyes scanning the crowd, and then he shot out into the street without warning, weaving and dodging like a boy in a hard game of baggataway.

Ben Savard raised his head and met Hannah's gaze just as Henry hurled himself into his uncle's arms.

Because of Henry, those first moments were not as awkward as they might have been. The boy was so full of questions and stories, all of which he seemed determined to produce in a single gush of words, that Ben and Hannah had to be content with exchanging looks and half smiles.

"You were gone far too long," Henry was saying for the third or fourth time. "You missed so much. Did you know about mister law?"

"Martial law," Hannah corrected him.

"Did you know?" Henry pressed on, nodding vigorously.

"Did you know about the gunboats the British sank? Did you know," he paused to pull himself up to his full height, "that Mr. Bonner sees Major General Jackson every single day, and then he comes here?"

"Jackson comes here?" Ben asked.

Henry's expression went scarlet with surprise. "No, not Major General Jackson. Mr. Bonner, Hannah's brother. When Hannah was sick sometimes he came twice a day and he always stopped to tell me what the general was doing."

Hannah was watching Ben's face when he received this last bit of news, but she saw no surprise in his expression, nor even any curiosity. Which might mean that he had heard about what had happened, or it might mean that he wasn't really listening to Henry. She got up and went to the water barrel, filled a cup, and drank. Then she filled it again and brought it to Ben. He took it from her and his fingers touched hers. She felt the shock of that touch in the pit of her stomach, and he smiled, and she felt it again.

She hoped he had heard the story. The idea of telling it made the bile rise in her throat.

Ben was talking to Henry in his usual way, as though the boy were a very small adult. He said, "Will you go tell your father and mother I'm here, and on my way up?"

Henry was delighted to be given any task at all by this uncle. He shot up and out the door, pausing only to look back at his uncle.

"We don't need to go stay with those nuns now, do we? Now that you're here to look after us."

But he left without waiting for an answer.

There was a moment of echoing silence. Hannah tucked her chin to her chest and rocked on her heels, as unsure of herself as a little girl. Her gaze on the floorboards, she heard Ben Savard stand up, and she felt the weight of his step vibrating underfoot, and then he was standing right in front of her. Solid and real, smelling of horse and leather and hard work.

He said, "I know."

Her shoulders rolled forward, her whole body would have rolled forward if he hadn't caught her, his hands sliding down her back to bring her in close. Hannah let her head rest against him. She let him take her weight; she let herself go. A single sigh escaped her but there were no tears, not now. Maybe later, but at this moment all she could find in herself was the kind of echoing relief that came with the cessation of a persistent pain.

Finally she raised her face to look at him and found emotions there she hadn't anticipated, foremost among them anger.

He said, "You did the right thing, sending word to Maman Zuzu."

Hannah pushed out a long breath, drew in another, held it for a moment. "My father taught me to use the weapons at hand."

Ben was silent for a moment.

She said, "What's wrong?"

And so he told her about the events of the last night, things she hadn't heard yet because she hadn't sought out the people who might have told her. In twenty-four hours Honoré Poiterin had lost everything to fire, and been denounced as a traitor and a spy, and that by Kit Wyndham. For a moment she wondered how Ben knew of some of what he was telling her, how long he had been back in the city before he showed himself. But she put that question away for the moment.

"Poiterin has been arrested?"

Ben's hands rubbed her back in a circular motion, as though he meant to coddle her to sleep.

"Ben?"

"Butler sent men to Fort St. John to bring him back

here, but they'll find him long gone. They'll assume he's joined the English."

"But you don't believe that." Hannah stepped away, pulled away so she could look at him from a better distance. "I can hear it in your voice—you don't believe any such thing. Is he dead?"

"I don't know. I doubt it."

She sat down on a stool, folded her hands in her lap. Hannah felt a trembling move through her, and then suddenly stop. So many questions, but she found she had neither the energy to ask them nor the peace of mind to hear the answers.

"Go on," she said. "Finish it. I can see it in your face, some new trouble."

Ben came over and crouched down next to her to bring them face-to-face. He said, "I came to ask for your help, but I'm afraid you aren't well enough."

Hannah scanned his face. "If it's in my power I will do what I can."

He gave her a half grin. "My brother will flay me alive if I drag you off and you collapse again."

"I can deal with your brother," Hannah said. "And I can decide for myself what I'm capable of."

Ben nodded. "Do you remember Captain Juzan? The white man married to a Choctaw cousin of mine. Pierre Juzan."

Hannah pulled up in surprise. She did remember Captain Juzan, who had stood in the courtyard just outside the door and asked Ben Savard for his pledge, one he had given without hesitation.

"You're joining his company of Choctaw warriors."

Ben nodded.

Hannah stood abruptly, folded her hands together and pressed them to her side. "You're headed into battle."

"Maybe today, maybe tomorrow. And we have no doctor."

In her surprise Hannah let out a sharp laugh, but Ben went on talking.

"None of the battlefield surgeons will bother with us, you know that."

"Why would you fight for the sake of men who won't bother with you?"

Ben shook his head, not so much at her as at himself. He said, "We have been allied to the Americans for fifty years."

It wasn't enough of an answer, but it was all he would give her right now.

Hannah turned and walked the few steps to the small shuttered window. If she were to open it she would see the city in turmoil, on the eve of a battle that might bring them yet another flag and king. Or it might simply be the first in a long series of battles that would be the end of New Orleans altogether. Now that they could leave this place without Poiterin trying to stop them, they were pinned down by a war. The same never-ending O'seronni war that had begun with the French and British fighting over furs and land. When they stopped, it was only long enough to change their excuses and for women to bear more sons and raise them. She was so tired of it all.

Ben Savard was watching her. Her pulse leaped at the very sight of him because he was right, because they fit in ways she could hardly explain to herself, but could not deny.

Sometimes she tried to remember what it had been like when she first met Strikes-the-Sky, how that had felt. It seemed such a long time ago, but some things were clear still in her mind, and one of them was how hard it had been. Hannah had wanted and respected the man she took as husband, but he had frightened her, too, in ways she hadn't understood then, as young as she had been. Now, looking back, she saw more clearly. She understood the anger that had shaped him and his view of the world, the anger that drove him.

There was none of that particular kind of anger in Jean-Benoît Savard. His mind worked in ways that surprised and disquieted her, but he didn't frighten her. And now he was asking for her help.

She said, "The last time I was near a battlefield they brought my uncle to me in pieces. Harrison's men hacked off his arms. He was a Red Stick. We were all Red Sticks. Not allied to Americans or British or French, but to each other. It was a just cause, a good cause."

Ben made no sound of protest. "The Red Sticks fought with great courage at Horseshoe Bend."

"How many of them did you kill?"

A tremor ran through him, anger or shame. He said, "I didn't fight in that battle."

"But you stood against them. You stand against us, what we wanted. What we fought for."

"When Tecumseh came here, I listened to him talk," Ben said. "Will you believe me if I say that I wanted to believe him, but couldn't?"

Hannah's breath left her with a hushed sound. She said, "I don't want to believe you now, but I must. I know the truth when I hear it."

Ben said, "It was a good dream, but it was just that and no more. There never was any real hope that we could join together against the whites."

"Once there was," Hannah said. "Once there was such hope. If you could have been there in the beginning—" Her voice trailed away and broke.

"Hannah—"

"Let me finish. The Red Sticks were crushed, but did your side win? What did you take away from Horseshoe Bend and all the other battles but another treaty that favored the O'seronni? How many acres?"

"More than twenty million." He looked her directly in the eye, admitting the worst of it without flinching.

"Twenty million more acres for the whites. That was Jackson's doing. And do you think that will be enough? You know it won't. It will never be enough, not until we are gone, all of us, out of their sight, further west and further until we fall off the edge of the world."

Ben cleared his throat. "There's more of a chance for us in the west than there is here."

She wrapped her arms around herself and dropped her head to her chest. How many times had she listened to her uncle and husband and all the other men at Prophet's Town arguing about this? And every one of them had gone on to die on one battlefield or another.

Very quietly Ben said, "Do you think we'd be better off under the English?"

"No. They would go about it differently, but the ending would be the same."

Ben said, "I respect your decision, Walks-Ahead. We don't need to talk about it any more."

She managed a small smile, and he gave her one in return.

"How soon do you have to leave?"

"That depends," he said. "On whether or not I have a bed to sleep in tonight."

Hannah bit back a smile. "You do."

"Then I'll stay until I have to go. Or you throw me out. Now I have to go see my brother."

At the door Paul Savard said, "I'm right here, Ben. By God, it's good to see you."

Jennet, who had had a chaotic and disturbing morning, was very late for her visit with Hannah. The city was in turmoil, and progress through the streets was slow, especially with the baby on one hip and a basket on the other. The men who had been guarding her had gone off to their companies, but Luke and Mr. Livingston agreed that she was safe in the city. Honoré Poiterin would be arrested on sight on suspicion of espionage, and so he would stay away.

Jennet shifted her son on her hip so he rode more squarely, and touched the small dagger she wore on a belt.

It seemed everyone was running somewhere, carrying something. Mme. Grandissime marched passed Jennet, her lapdog tucked under her arm like a rolled newspaper, a maid trailing behind with a basket of puppies and a pained expression. A shopkeeper with arms full of ledgers, a slave balancing what looked to be an entire side of veal on one shoulder. Old men stood in a semicircle reading broadsides nailed to the wall outside a newspaper office, talking about the city Guard and curfew and patrols.

People acting as if they could protect themselves from artillery fire with clean linen and brave words and soup and raw boards to nail over their windows.

Then Jennet came into the rue Dauphine courtyard and learned that Ben Savard had finally returned home. She heard this news from Clémentine, who was trotting through the courtyard with a basket piled high with freshly washed and folded dressings.

"Where is he now? With Hannah?"

Clémentine's broad lower lip curled down in disapproval. "No. She's in the apothecary, he's off somewhere with his brother."

"Really?" Jennet started to ask an indiscreet question and then stopped herself.

"Lovers' quarrel, it look like to me."

Lovers' quarrel. That brought Jennet to a complete standstill for a long moment. It was something she had surmised long ago, and still it was a shock to hear stated so openly that Hannah and Ben were lovers. The many days Hannah had spent on the brink of death had put all of that out of her mind. When Jennet had thought of Ben Savard, it had not been as Hannah's lover, but as someone who could take revenge on Poiterin in her name.

Which he might have done.

Luke had come by briefly, before he left the city with Jackson to meet General Coffee. He had stopped to bring her news, news so shocking that Jennet could not even make sense of it all until long after he had left again. And all of his news—the fires, the murder of Agnès Poiterin, Wyndham's letter, the disappearance of Honoré—came on top of the fact that the long-awaited Kentucky and Tennessee militias were finally arrived, along with news that the British were on American land. The fighting would start today or tomorrow, and Luke would be a part of it.

There was no argument, there were no words that could keep him away from the battle. He was strong and able-bodied and skilled with weapons; he had declared himself for the American cause. He might protest to her, but she knew him well, and Luke would be as excited as a boy promised a day's hunting. And she would weep in frustration and fear, she would want to beat him and kiss him, but in the end she would wave good-bye and smile bravely, as she was required to do.

So she was here to tell Hannah all this news, of fires and letters, of disappearances and battles, things she would have heard now from Ben. But she had another errand, one that had been pressed on her by her husband. Luke had arranged for Jennet and the boy to go stay with the Ursulines at the first sign of artillery fire targeted on the city, and he wanted Hannah to join them.

Jennet knew—as Luke must know—that Hannah was unlikely to comply with his wishes. She simply couldn't imagine Hannah sitting with a lot of wailing rich women while cloistered nuns prayed on the other side of a screen. She couldn't imagine herself there, either, but she would go, if it meant the boy would be safe.

The baby began to sputter his discontent, his usually placid mood disrupted by the noise and tumult of the city and no doubt by her own frayed nerves. Jennet jiggled him and sang under her breath and then went off to nurse him in the quiet of the little clinic, where they could both have time to calm down.

But the little clinic wasn't empty. Ben Savard sat there, alone. He looked thinner, with new lines in his face and some gray sprinkled in the short shock of hair that fell over his brow, and a preoccupied expression that didn't leave him even while they spoke.

"Paul had to go," he told her. "An emergency in the clinic."

"And where's Hannah?"

He lifted a shoulder. "I think right now she doesn't want to be near me."

"Don't be daft," Jennet said. "Right now is when she needs ye, man."

The baby began to fuss. Jennet sat down with her back to Ben Savard and adjusted her clothes until she could settle the boy to the breast. The whole while Ben Savard was silent.

She said, "Ye willnae find her stood here, man. Gae."

"Hannah told me you speak Scots when you're angry."

"Aye, I am full angry. On your way to battle and ye waste time snattering."

She heard him turn toward the door and stop.

"I wanted to ask you, if she's—how she's—"

"She'll mend," Jennet said. "It will take a long time and much patience, but she will mend. She's made of stern stuff, is our Hannah."

"Do I need to stay away from her?"

There it was, the real question. Jennet considered, and then she looked at him over her shoulder. He looked back at her steadily with his beautiful, oddly colored eyes.

"You must follow her lead," Jennet said. "That's the best advice I can give you."

With so many troops in or near the city and not enough doctors to see to their needs, Dr. Savard told Hannah, he had given in to the inevitable and shut down vaccinations until the battle for the city was decided.

"We've got twenty-seven here and another twenty downstairs," Paul Savard went on. "I've cordoned off the far end of this floor for the infectious cases, mostly measles. Malaria over there, and dysentery." He jerked a thumb over his shoulder to indicate the men he meant. They were all listening, their expressions ranging from stony to curious about this open conversation between a white doctor and an Indian woman he was asking for help.

They were mostly militia out of Kentucky and Tennessee, men who had marched three days straight to answer Jackson's call for help. They were tough men, accustomed to bivouac and hard walking, but the push had taken its toll. Almost certainly the other hospitals were just as overwhelmed, and every private physician and apothecary and healer of any standing was caught up in getting this army on its feet.

A woman Hannah didn't know went by with a tray, soup and bread and milky coffee. Dr. Savard followed her gaze.

"Clémentine has brought in her relatives to help with the cooking and washing."

"Surgical cases?"

He lifted a shoulder. "The usual. Wounds gone bad, gangrenous toes, bullets that need removing. Would you rather work in the surgery or the clinic?"

"I thought you'd want me in the apothecary."

Dr. Savard made a grunting sound deep in his throat. "That would be a waste. Let me worry about the apothecary. You've got more experience than I do with battle wounds, so if you've got no objections I'll have you in the surgery."

She felt his gaze on her. He had been her teacher, once, when she was very young, and now he was treating her as an equal, and in full view and hearing of men who were watching, not bothering to hide their curiosity or disquiet.

She said, "I had no idea you were so devious."

Dr. Savard winked at her as he turned away. "Of course you did, Dr. Bonner. It just slipped your mind."

CHAPTER 43

The room that served as a surgery was across the hall from the apothecary. Until now it had seldom been used; this was, in the first line, a kine-pox clinic, and only secondarily a charity hospital. Surgical cases were mostly referred elsewhere.

There was a short row of chairs outside the surgery, all of them occupied. Some of the men talked quietly, some slept with their heads propped on the wall. A few were playing cards, and one was dictating a letter to Rachel. In this setting, the lighthearted girl who took such pleasure in parties and dinners was unrecognizable. Here she was her mother's daughter, quiet, attentive, efficient. She glanced up at Hannah as she passed and gave her a grim smile.

Julia was waiting inside the surgery. It was the lightest room in the house, with a bank of windows that looked out on the street, but the day was overcast and the lamps had been lit. In the middle of the room was a large table that might have once been in a kitchen. Julia had just finished scrubbing it, and her face was pink with exertion. She wore an apron that covered her from throat to toe, and her hair was tied with a large handkerchief.

"I was hoping you'd be able to assist," Hannah said.

"We can call on Rachel, too, if we need her." Julia used the back of her hand to wipe a stray hair from her cheek.

Hannah took an apron for herself from a hook on the wall. She rolled up her sleeves and tied a large square of linen over her plaited hair, and then she stood for a long minute and studied the row of surgical instruments laid out neatly on a tray. A variety of surgical knives with down-turned points and wide spines, lancets, scissors, bone saws small and large, needle holders and needles. All well used and lovingly maintained so that the blades shone.

Hannah had had her first lessons in surgery from a Muslim doctor called Hakim Ibrahim, and she had never forgot the things he had taught her. His had been the first microscope she had ever seen, and from him she had learned the importance of cleanliness. She examined her nails now, and then scrubbed her hands and arms with water and lye soap at the washstand. Next to the basin Julia had put out a bottle of thirty-percent alcohol solution, as well as one that was marked Dist. *Hamamelis Virginiana*. She glanced at her over her shoulder.

"What's this?"

"Paul insists," Julia said. "It's your doing, I think. You treated his hand when he cut it, and there was a wager?"

"Oh," Hannah said, remembering. "Yes."

With a tone that was a little shy, Julia said, "When there is time, you might ask him about his experiments. He would like to show you his microscope."

Hannah said, "I'd like to see it." And oddly, it was true. Her interest in medicine and science, which had been slumbering for so long, had sparked to life again. She thought of the laboratory she had inherited from another one of her teachers, empty and neglected these many long months. It was odd to think that they would be going home soon, really going home, to take up their lives. She found herself thinking of her father, and wondering if the letters she and Luke had sent off with Lieutenant Hodge on the *Grasshopper* had found their way home, of the letter Luke had sent from Pensacola. She thought of the last letter they had had, and Curiosity.

"Hannah?" Julia said.

"I'm ready."

There was a knock at the door and it opened.

Jennet said, "Shall I bring in the first patient? A great hulk of a man from Kentucky, he tells me his name is Abraham and he's got a bullet stuck in the meat of his shoulder that he'd like to be rid of."

Hannah couldn't help but laugh. It was amazing, the way Jennet could bring light and warmth into the worst situation.

"What have you done with the boy?"

"Och, dinnae worry about wee Nathaniel. Clémentine fairly ripped him out of my arms when I said I wanted to come help." Jennet took an apron as she spoke. "I'll fetch Abraham, shall I? And we can get to work."

By the time the afternoon had slipped into dusk, it was clear to Hannah that she would never again operate so efficiently or well. With Julia and Jennet to assist they made short work of Abraham Finley's bullet, and then went on to amputate toes, clean and drain an abscessed knife wound, and dig a dozen pieces of shrapnel out of a hand so horny with callus that it was like cutting through leather. Now the newest patient on the table had taken off his leggings to reveal an ulcer the size of a saucer that had eaten through muscle to the bone.

Watching Julia handle instruments, Hannah had the idea that she could have done any of the surgeries on her own without hesitation. In contrast, Jennet had had only a few months of training, and cases like this one still caused her difficulty. Now she turned away momentarily. Hannah wouldn't have blamed her if she had brought up her breakfast, the stench was that bad.

When she turned back, Jennet fixed the patient with a stern gaze. "Mr. Corbin," she said to him sharply. "Mr. Corbin, explain to me exactly how it is that you let yersel come to sic a pass. The Almichtie gave ye twa guid legs, man, and look what ye've done with the left one. Guid God, but that must pang ye."

Julia and Hannah exchanged glances, but didn't try to intervene. When it came to dealing with the varied personalities of patients who happened to be soldiers, Jennet had no equal. Her instincts never failed; she knew when to be sympathetic, when to be distant, when a man needed most to be calmed or bullied, pacified or chided.

Mr. Corbin had come into the surgery with a mutinous expression that at first seemed impervious to Jennet's outrage. She went on anyway with her lecture, and Hannah, busy as she was with the mess that had once been the man's calf muscle, had to admire his ability to tolerate more than one kind of pain.

"What baw-heid walks three days on a shank like this?" Jennet demanded. "What use will ye be tae the major general if ye fall doon on yer gizz in the muck?"

Finally Mr. Corbin opened his mouth to respond. Jennet's head snapped up and she fixed him with her most severe expression.

"So noo we'll hear excuses, will we? A sairy tale, nae doot."

A momentary hesitation, and the small pale mouth shut. The two of them glared at each other for a moment and then, with a huff of a sigh, Mr. Corbin seemed to give up the idea of defending himself altogether.

Jennet never lost track of what Hannah required from her, nor did she let up in her lecture. While she brought water and took away basins and handed instruments and bottles and salves she wondered out loud about the idiocy of men who hadn't the sense that God gave a midge.

It wasn't until they were almost finished that Hannah realized that the unfortunate Mr. Corbin had lost consciousness, but that he had done so with a vague smile on his face.

Julia, who was not easily amazed, openly wondered what exactly had just happened.

"Sometimes a harangue-maker is more use than a surgeon," said Jennet, who was just now beginning to get her color back. "At least when it's a Scot ye've got to cut on."

Hannah realized she hadn't heard Mr. Corbin say even a single word. She said, "He's a Scot?"

"Och, aye," said Jennet. "Were he anything else, I wadnae have spoke half so sweet."

The day's work was almost—but not quite—enough to make Hannah put aside all thought of Ben Savard. But when Jennet had gone back to the Livingstons' and Hannah was climbing the stairs to eat her supper with the family, she felt her pulse pick up. Unless he had gone back to the front, he would be there at the table.

According to Paul he hadn't gone back to his company yet, but neither was he at supper. Hannah felt Rachel watching her, but resisted the inclination to meet the girl's gaze. At this moment she could hardly hide what she was feeling.

Rachel said, "Mama, Hannah hasn't heard my news."

"That's true," Julia said. Her smile was a little sad. "Would you like to tell her?"

"I'll tell it," said Dr. Savard, throwing a look at his stepdaughter that was partial amusement and a greater part pride. "Rachel has had an invitation to spend a season in Manhattan in her uncle's household."

The girl's face shone to hear those words spoken out loud. Her joy was so overwhelming that Hannah could hardly look at her.

Henry, who had been scowling at his plate, looked at Hannah. "She'll find somebody to marry there and never come back home again."

"Nothing in this world is certain," said his mother in a calm tone. "But at this moment we are all in good health, and your sister is very happy. Won't you be pleased for her?"

"No," said Henry shortly. "Not if she's going away."

"You'll go to your room to think about that," said Henry's father. "And come back when you're prepared to be kind to your sister, and conduct yourself reasonably at table."

"*Reasonable,*" Henry said, with all the dignity he could muster, "is a word grown-ups use when they can't make you agree with them."

Later, alone in Ben's apartment, Hannah sat down heavily on the bed in the empty room.

Reasonable is the word you use when you can't get somebody to agree with you.

Laughing, she lay down and fell asleep watching her breath make white clouds in the air.

Late in the night Ben came, and leaning over her where she slept, said her name.

Hannah woke immediately. In the light of the candle he carried his expression was severe, his eyes shadowed.

"Have you changed your mind? I can find a bed elsewhere."

"I haven't changed my mind."

She moved to the far side of the narrow bed and then watched as he undressed. He seemed far away in his thoughts, almost unaware of her. Certainly unconcerned that she watched him as his clothes fell to the floor. He pulled his hunting shirt over his head, arms crossed and elbows pointed at the ceiling so that his muscles jumped into stark relief. His skin was the color of old honey, the hair that feathered across his chest and abdomen dark. There was a new scar on his right side, short but wide, and new enough to still be bright pink.

Hannah said, "Did you stitch that yourself?"

He looked down in surprise, as if he had forgot about a wound that might have killed him. With the flat of his hand he covered it briefly and then glanced at her with a grin.

"Surprised I know how to use a needle?"

"Not in the least," Hannah said. "I'm sure you are very handy. But you didn't stitch that yourself; the angle is all wrong."

"Is it?" He came and sat down on the edge of the bed. The air was very cold and his skin had risen in bumps all over his arms and back. Hannah could have held up the covers for him, but somehow it seemed too much work just at this moment.

He said, "A woman on the Sabine River did it for me." And then, when it was clear she wouldn't ask, he said: "I want to tell you about where I was. Do you want to hear?"

Hannah held out the blanket. "Come," she said. "Tell your story."

Jennet was one kind of storyteller, and Ben was another. Jennet used her hands and body and voice, like the actors in the play Hannah had seen at the Park Place theater in Manhattan. Ben went still while he talked, and let his voice create a bubble, and inside the bubble, a world.

He told her about a place called the Disputed Lands, a day's ride to the west. Five thousand square miles, the Calcasieu River on the east, the Sabine on the west. An old Caddo Indian village on the north, and the Gulf on the south. Niprière, canebrake, savannahs, a hundred kinds of water, a thousand kinds of birds and game. Hills covered with yellow pine as far as the eye could see. White oak in the river bottoms, cypress trees five hundred years old.

Mexico claimed it and so did the Americans, but both countries were wound up in other, bigger wars. They agreed to disagree. They called those five thousand square miles neutral territory, but there was nothing neutral about them. Both sides retreated: no troops, no law, and so the lawless moved in.

"The worst of the worst," Ben said. "Men with no footing in the world."

Men who robbed and murdered and raped. Slaverunners determined to ply their trade even after the laws were passed to stop them. And runaway slaves who banded together, determined to survive.

Hannah sat up so suddenly that the room swam a little. Ben was looking at her, cautious, waiting.

She said, "Red Rock."

His hands grasped her forearms and he brought her back down. Ben held her like that, calmly, until her heart regained its normal rhythm.

"Red Rock."

"Yes, Red Rock. Before slavery was outlawed in New-York State, the runaways would go north to Canada, but some of them stayed in the endless forests. Friends of ours—" Her voice wobbled, thinking of Curiosity Freeman, of her son Almanzo. Here they would be called free people of color.

"It ended badly," she said. "The whites won't let them be, you know. It always ends badly."

He was lying on his side, his hands still on her forearms. There was nothing sexual about the way he touched her, which was right and good, and still it made her ache in an unexpected way.

Ben said, "Does that mean they shouldn't try?"

There was something in his tone of disappointment. He had expected a different reaction.

"I couldn't bear it," Hannah said. "I couldn't bear to see it happen again."

There was a long silence, and then Hannah said, "That's what you wanted to ask me, isn't it? You want me to go west with you, to live in that place with the lawless and the runaways. To be a doctor and your woman and anything else that's needed."

He didn't make excuses, or try to hide his feelings. "Yes. I thought—I think it could be a good place. For us. For you, and me."

"No," Hannah said, pulling her hands from his. "I'm not strong enough to go west again, not like that. Not even for you. And you don't need to go, either."

He was silent for a long moment. "They need my help."

Hannah choked out a little cough. "They will die with or without you. Sooner or later the Americans will remember those thousands of acres and the timber and the game, and then they'll come and they'll show no mercy. You know that. You know it."

"And between now and then," Ben said. "They have a chance. We would have a chance."

"I can't," Hannah almost moaned. "I can't watch it all happen again. It would kill me this time. Please, don't ask me."

He held her gaze for a long moment, and then he nodded.

In the morning Hannah was stiff from sleeping perched on the edge of the narrow bed. Her joints ached and her face felt swollen, as though she been crying all night, though the pillow slip was dry.

Ben was dressing with his back to her, and the silence in the room was heavy. Hannah's throat felt tight and hot, incapable of words. And what was there to say, really: He had asked her to go west, and she had given him the only possible answer.

Ben came to sit on the edge of the bed. He leaned over and kissed her, a soft kiss full of longing and affection. Against her mouth he said, "You are a wonder to me, Walks-Ahead."

He got up and went to the table where he had laid out his weapons. Tomahawk and war club, a knife and a long rifle. Ammunition pouches, a patch box, a powder horn. Today or tomorrow or the day after he would find himself on a battlefield. While Hannah worked in the surgery, putting O'seronni soldiers to rights, he would be fighting with a company of Choctaw.

Hannah sat up, and held the blanket to her chest. The sun wasn't up yet, but the sky outside the windows was lighter. There had been a frost; she could smell it in the air.

She said, "I'll come with you, when you go into battle. To tend to the Choctaw under Juzan, and anyone else who asks me."

He stopped and looked at her, his eyes moving over her face as if he might find some answer written there. She watched him consider, and then decide.

Ben nodded. "It may be later today, or early tomorrow." He studied the floor for a moment. "I brought clothes for you." With a swing of his head he indicated one of the two chairs in the room. There was a bundle there, tied with string.

"Thank you," Hannah said.

"I'll try to give you as much notice as possible, but you may not see me until it's time to go."

Hannah pushed out a sound that was meant to be an acknowledgment, or a question, or a request for help. She didn't quite know herself what she hoped for. Even when Ben had gone and her heartbeat had quieted, she couldn't put words to the ache in her belly.

· · ·

The day passed, far more quickly than Hannah thought it would. She spent the morning in the surgery, again assisted by Julia and Jennet, and the afternoon in the little clinic.

She had expected that the afternoon would be as busy as or busier than the morning, and learned that she was wrong. There were only three people waiting for her. The first was Rattling-Gourd, the old Chickasaw chief who had explained to her the difference between white and black and red. She was surprised to see that he was still alive, and even more surprised that he had managed to get here at all.

He came into the clinic still wrapped in his blanket, now gaunt and stripped down to the bone by pain, hardly able to walk. With him he brought a granddaughter, whose swollen abdomen and sticklike arms and legs made a lengthy examination unnecessary. When Hannah asked her name, the girl looked at her as if she had never heard human language before.

The third patient was the young pregnant woman she had treated for swollen legs and ankles. She was pregnant still, but Hannah could see without being told that the child was dead in her belly.

"Make it come," said the young woman, who gave her name as Helen. "Make it come out of me before I die. I have four other children; they will starve."

Without Leo to run errands, Hannah had to leave the clinic to get what she needed, but first she put Rattling-Gourd in one cot and Helen in the other, and set out a pallet for the little girl. Then she went to the kitchen to ask Clémentine to send bread and soup. Finally she went to the apothecary, where she found Julia hard at work.

Hannah took down what she needed from the shelves: roots of black cohosh and goldenseal, borage, flaxseed. Julia, busy with the mortar and pestle, watched for a while as

Hannah tied everything into a square of gauze that she would steep in hot water.

She said, "Overdue?"

"Dead in the womb."

Julia nodded. "Will you need help?"

"I'm going to get Yellow-Sapling," Hannah said. "If Rachel could sit with her while I'm gone—"

Julia nodded. "How long do you need?"

Hannah considered. "Send her in a half hour."

Though it had been weeks since Hannah had visited the Indian village at the edge of the city, she remembered the way. She slipped through the crowds, staying clear of troop movements, keeping her head down and the hood of her boiled-wool cloak pulled low.

Luke would be angry if he knew what she was doing, but Luke was not here, and she had no one but herself to call on.

She turned into the narrow street, and stopped short. Where the Redbone village had been was now a sea of army tents. The militia were turning out to be mustered under the hectoring cries of their officers.

Hannah slipped back into the shadows and away, and didn't stop until she was out of breath.

How stupid she had been, not to realize. Of course her patients hadn't come to the little clinic. The Redbones were gone; there was no room or tolerance for them with the English so close. The three who had come to her were here only because they were too sick to go. She wondered fleetingly where Helen had hidden her other children. She thought of the labor to come. Even with Yellow-Sapling it would be difficult and dangerous, but without her— Hannah forced herself to breathe deeply and think. After a moment, she set off again for a different part of the city.

• • •

She found Maman Zuzu and Maman Antoinette together, drinking coffee. Hannah had time to think about that, as coffee was precious now and expensive, but she didn't ask. Nor did they ask her questions, once they understood she needed help with a difficult delivery. Both of them got up and put things in baskets, pulled shawls around themselves, and waited for her to show the way.

When they got to the little clinic, Rachel met them at the door. She was very pale and her face was damp with sweat, which must mean something; it was hard to upset this girl, for all her youth.

"What is it? Has the labor started?" She had dosed Helen before leaving, because the effect of the tea would take a little while to be felt. Sometimes things moved more quickly than expected, and Hannah had been longer on her errand than she meant to be.

"Step aside, missy," said Maman Antoinette in a creaking English, no hint of deference or apology. "Let us see to her."

Rachel stood aside.

Things were as Hannah had left them. Rattling-Gourd on one cot, staring at the ceiling. His granddaughter on a pallet beside him, asleep now that she had eaten, with a thick rug folded over her thin frame. Helen on the other cot, the great mound of her belly with her hands crossed over it. If she was in labor, she was hiding it well.

Then Hannah saw that there was someone else. She sat on a stool near the hearth, a slight form wrapped in a blanket that was more holes than wool. She raised her head to look at Hannah. A brand on her cheek, so new that it was still mostly blister. How beautiful she had been.

"Rachel," Hannah said. "Who is this?"

"She won't give me a name."

"Jacinthe," said Zuzu. "She's called Jacinthe, her. Belonged once to Poiterin. They sold her because she let the white baby get stole away."

Hannah knew that she had heard the young woman's name, and now she remembered. The young woman who had nursed Jennet's son. What Ben had done for them wasn't without cost.

"She's asking for Jennet," Rachel said. "I wasn't sure what to do."

"You leave her to us," said Maman Antoinette. "We care for our own."

"Jacinthe," Maman Zuzu said.

She said the name aloud, and the girl rose from her stool. She was unsteady on her feet, which were bare and filthy with dirt and dried blood. And in her arms was a bundle that flexed and squirmed.

Hannah and Maman Zuzu reached her at the same moment. Zuzu helped her to sit back down, and Hannah found herself holding the child that Jacinthe had almost dropped. It was no more than a few hours old. Still streaked with the evidence of the womb, its head lopsided from the birth canal. Too small, but it breathed and mewled and flexed, a living child.

"Poiterin's?" She asked the question though she already knew the answer.

"Who else?" said Zuzu.

The two old ladies spoke to Jacinthe in a low singsong, their tone comforting but firm. They asked questions in quick patois. Hannah caught only one word in five, but she understood what they wanted to know, because the same question was foremost in her mind.

Where had Jacinthe been, and how did she get here?

But the young woman only looked at them, dry-eyed, uncomprehending. Blank. When they pressed a cup of water on her she took it and drank, and then she took the bread and chewed it slowly and swallowed.

Hannah had passed the baby to Rachel, and now it let out a thin cry. Jacinthe didn't even blink at the sound.

In the local French Rachel said, "Your baby needs you. Do you have milk?"

Jacinthe turned her face to Rachel. "I have no baby," she said. "I have no milk."

"Jacinthe," said Maman Zuzu in a sharper tone. "Wake up, now. We got no time for such foolishness."

Jacinthe looked at her finally, some life coming back into her expression. "I am looking for Honoré." As if it should be obvious, as if it were Zuzu who were not in command of her senses.

"You don't need that man," said Zuzu. "You don't need that devil."

"His grand-mère is dead," Jacinthe went on, and then she smiled. It was a young girl's smile, simple and pure and frightening. "The woman who carries fire came, and now his grand-mère is dead. He will need me."

Hannah thought, *the woman who carries fire,* but she asked a different question. She said, "What can we do for her?"

"You can't do anything," said Zuzu. "Maman will take her home. We can hide her until we can send her west."

She would go to the Disputed Territories, of course. The memories that came to Hannah were so strong that it was hard to push them aside. Another young woman, heavy with child, fleeing for her life.

Hannah said, "What about the baby?"

Maman Antoinette shook her head. "She would let it starve. If you can't find a wet nurse, feed it goat's milk from a rag. If it lives out the night."

From the near cot, Helen's voice came thin and high. "Let it go," she said. "Let it go." And then she groaned, a sound that came up from her belly.

Rachel said to Hannah, "I'll take the baby to Jennet. Jennet will know what to do."

• • •

Jennet had no idea what to do. She looked at the newborn, red of face and squalling, and she looked at Rachel.

"Even if you don't want to keep him—"

"Keep him?"

"—you could nurse him. He's so hungry, Jennet."

He was hungry, no doubt. Jacinthe's son was hungry, as Jennet's son had once been hungry and needed nourishment. That this was also Honoré Poiterin's child was something she must ignore for the moment. She sat down and held out her arms for the baby, who began to root against her breast even before she had uncovered it.

When the small red mouth snapped down on her nipple, she let out a sharp sound. Pain, and surrender. The round cheeks worked at her breast with such need, Jennet wondered if any woman in the world could refuse it.

Rachel said, "I'll bring warm water and clean towels."

Jennet should have stopped her. There were so many questions: How Jacinthe had come here, if she had run away, where she was now. Why she had not nursed him. If she was alive at all. But the simple fact of the child, the heat and damp weight of him, the dark eyelashes and feathering curls, those things were more powerful than any questions.

When his gulping slowed and then stopped, when he was asleep, Jennet used the tip of her finger to loosen the small mouth from her breast.

Rachel came back with a basin of water and a pile of clean linen. Together they washed him and tied a long strip of gauze around his belly to protect the umbilicus until it was ready to fall away. Jennet fashioned a clout out of linen and finally they wrapped and swaddled him. In an hour or two he would be hungry again, and the whole process must be reversed and repeated, and then again, and again, through the nights and days to come.

"Jacinthe?"

Rachel shook her head. "She repudiates him. And she's—" The young woman hesitated, looking for a word.

"A runaway?"

"Out of her senses," Rachel said. "And a runaway. But she will be all right. Clémentine's people will see to it that she gets away."

Jennet stroked the baby's head with its fine black curls. He was very pale of complexion, his eyes the muddy color of all newborns.

"The sins of the fathers," she murmured.

"What?" Rachel said, almost sharply. Jennet glanced at her.

"A Greek writer said it. The gods visit the sins of the fathers upon the children."

"Not any God of mine," said Rachel stiffly.

"Nor of mine," said Jennet with a sigh. And then: "Tell Hannah I'll be down to help as soon as I've got him settled."

"You mean to keep him, then?"

"She saved my son's life," Jennet said. "She showed him kindness and love. I can do no less for her."

Long after dark, Jennet returned to the Livingstons' simply because there was no bed for her anywhere at the Savards'. In the clinic patients slept two to a cot, on pallets in the hall, on chairs. The Savards' apartment was just as crowded, and the servants' quarters.

There might be room in Ben Savard's small apartment above the kitchen, but Jennet was not so tired that she would intrude there. Instead, two soldiers who were well enough to be sent back to their companies walked her to the rue de Conde, one carrying her basket and the other Jacinthe's infant son. They were both militiamen from Tennessee, capable, quiet men and exceedingly shy. As she was too tired to try to draw them out, they made the trip in silence.

In her arms Nathaniel, sleeping, felt very heavy. He was a healthy child, well fed, round of limb and cheek, flushed with color. His personality was more pronounced every day, a cheerful boy who exchanged periods of contemplation for bursts of activity that ended in crowing laughter or tears of frustration. When Jennet came to take the boy from Clémentine, she found him in earnest study of a darning egg, entranced by its shape and smoothness. She knew without a doubt that, left to his own devices, her son would have tried to fit the whole thing into his mouth.

Jacinthe's son was less than a day old, and there was nothing to read of his personality. If he was to stay with them— and Jennet could think of no alternative—she would watch his mind come alive to the world, and his spirit. He would grow to look like his mother, or his father. By that time, she told herself, she would love him for his own sake. That would make the difference. It must make the difference.

They would call him Adam, she decided, trudging along the street. It was a name that marked him as a man who would be the start of his own line. When he was old enough to ask about his people, she would tell him stories of Scotland and the Carrycks, of Dan'l Bonner, called Hawkeye for his skill with a rifle, whose adoptive father was Chingachgook. He would hear stories of Chingachgook, a Mahican sachem who had taken in a child who was not of his blood and raised him as a son.

She would send away for books on Africa, and together she and Adam would read those stories, too.

Jennet resolved that she would do everything in her power for this boy, who had been sent, she had no doubt, to take the place of the child she had conceived on the night Honoré Poiterin agreed to take her own son away to safety.

The child she had wished dead, and who had died, but was now given back to her.

Jacinthe had brought him into the world alone, crouched in some alley in her travail. That he had survived at all was a miracle. He might have come dead to the world, as Helen's child had. A dead daughter born of a dead mother.

It was always a surprise, how much blood the human body could hold. Hannah and Maman Zuzu had worked hard to stop the bleeding, and then Dr. Savard had come, fetched by Julia, and together they had failed. Helen was gone, and somewhere in this overcrowded city the four children she had hidden away were waiting for her to return.

To Maman Zuzu, Hannah had said, "Will you ask? Will you see if you can find out where they are? I will pay to have them brought here."

The old woman hadn't been cruel, but neither had she offered any comfort. The chances were slim, but she would ask.

Then Dr. Savard had put a hand on Hannah's shoulder. He said, "She has her own to worry about now, but ask Ben. Ben will find them, if they are anywhere to be found."

He could do more for the young Chickasaw girl, who would be alone when her grandfather died, as must happen within hours or days. She would be brought into the household, Julia told Jennet. There were so many orphans, they would do what they could for her.

Jennet should have fallen directly to sleep, once she had washed and changed and nursed both babies. When the nursemaid came to fetch Nathaniel and found two children where there had been one, she hadn't even blinked, nor had she asked any questions. Jennet was thankful. Tomorrow was soon enough to cope with Mrs. Livingston.

The maids had done their work, so that if she had wanted

occupation, there was precious little to do. Her few gowns were clean and carefully pressed, as were all of Luke's things. This household, overseen by Mrs. Livingston and her formidable mother, was ordered enough to please even the housekeeper at Carryckcastle; everything smelled of freshly aired linen, lavender water, starch, beeswax.

She had been far more comfortable in the crowded apartment above the kine-pox clinic, with Hannah sleeping beside her and the smell of damp swaddling clothes in the air.

On the table that stood between the windows was a porcelain vase that held a long spray of ivy, and Jennet's tarot cards. Mrs. Livingston had got into the habit of coming by to ask Jennet to read the cards for her. A small secret, she whispered to Jennet. A diversion in difficult times. Her mother would not understand, of course, but she and Jennet were women of broader experience in the world.

Now Jennet took the cards in hand and sat for a moment concentrating on the weight and shape of them. The softened edges, slightly rough against her palm. She tried to recall the first deck she had had, which she had left behind her in Canada, the shapes and colors. No more could she remember the face of the lady who had given them to her, on her way to Canada for the first time, excited beyond measure. Mme. Rojas had told her she would travel, and Jennet had laughed in delight at this new game. She had understood very little, but she had learned. She had come to understand how the cards worked, how they could open the mind to possibility. One card was sometimes enough.

She turned it, and setting her hands on the table, Jennet let her weariness and imagination lead the way.

PART III

The Chariot: Strength, bravery, vigilance, endurance, discipline. In troubled times the efforts of one extraordinary person can turn the tide.

CHAPTER 44

Jennet found the letter on her pillow, along with a note in Mrs. Livingston's delicate hand.

> Mrs. Bonner, this letter came with the post-rider some days ago, and was waiting at the post office to be claimed. My brother August D'Avezac saw it there today and took it in your name. I pray that the news it brings you in these difficult days is welcome.
>
> Louisa Livingston

The letter, stained and creased from a long journey, had first gone to the care of Mrs. Preston on the Bayou St. John, and then been returned to the post office because no one had been at home at the Maison Verde.

Elizabeth Bonner had written the address.

She should wait for Luke, or go to Hannah; she could rise and dress and ask for an escort to walk with her back to the clinic.

Jennet opened the seal, and unfolded the two sheets of paper, closely written.

Dearest Children,

We are in possession of the letters you wrote to us in late August from the Island of the Manatees in the

French Antilles, as well as Luke's letter from Pensacola
written almost two weeks later.

To say that we were relieved to hear your initial
report of Jennet's safe recovery would be an
understatement of the first order. Indeed, we talked of
little else for three days, all of us gathered together
either here in our kitchen or in Mrs. Freeman's. The
letter from Pensacola arrived yesterday, and has
brought us back together to discuss your difficult
situation.

You must understand that we are full of gratitude
that Jennet has been safely returned to the care of her
family. Once young Nathaniel has been restored to
you, and she has had sufficient time and peace of
mind, I believe she will recover. We hope that you
will come to us for that purpose.

No doubt you can imagine that there has been
considerable debate here on how best to help you.
Uncharacteristically we came to a common resolve
very quickly: None of us can bear to sit by and wait
for word. In the end we have come to a conclusion
that may not surprise you.

Your father and your uncle Runs-from-Bears are
on the way to New Orleans. As war has rendered
travel by sea and overland both exceedingly
unreliable, they are resolved to start the journey by
traveling west to Pittsburgh. From there they will set
out southwest by means of the Ohio River. They
have with them enough money to lease a keelboat
and hire a crew that will take them all the way down
the Mississippi. If all goes according to plan they
should arrive within a week or ten days of this letter
depending on the postal service, the state of the roads,
and, of course, the war.

You know your father and uncle well enough to

believe that they are capable of this, and more. And to tell the whole truth, I believe that they look forward to this journey with great eagerness and anticipation, first and foremost for the chance that they might be of service to you, but also because it is a very long time since they have had any kind of adventure. In truth, I envy them the opportunity to act on your behalf. If it weren't for the baby (who thrives, and is a joy to us all) I think I would be easily talked into making the journey myself.

This letter must go out with the post-rider this afternoon if it is to have any chance of reaching you before our men do. Thus I close in haste, sending you my best wishes and prayers for your continued health of mind and body and quick success in your search. When you are safe home we will have much to celebrate. Your loving mother and stepmother,

Elizabeth Middleton Bonner
Paradise, on the west branch of the Sacandaga
New-York State, the 20th October, 1814

Dear brother & sisters,

Da and Runs-from-Bears are coming to save you, because Da says he will go simpleminded sitting idle while you are fighting alligators and redcoats, and Many-Doves says she will go simpleminded watching Runs-from-Bears pace, and anyway, who better to help you in your time of need?

I think I could, as I have a rifle of my own now and am reckoned a good shot, but no one listens. I have to stay here and go to school, with my own brother Daniel as the teacher. It was hard enough to have my mother as teacher, but this is worse still, I promise you. When you come home with the new baby who is my nephew, I am sure I will be far kinder to him than Daniel is to me, and never scold him for his penmanship, which as you see is perfectly easy to read.

Ma says that I am unfair, and that Daniel is an excellent teacher, which indeed everyone who doesn't sit in his classroom agrees to be the case. He has endless patience with everybody but me, and I forgive him that only because I think that has to do with his arm, which is still not healed and causes him pain in spite of all the medicines Many-Doves and Curiosity and the new doctor give him. I hope his arm is better soon and that his mood gets better with it. Ma and Da are very worried about you. I am not but I think you should come home quickly all the same.

Your brother
Gabriel Bonner, aged ten full years

Dear Brother and Sisters,

I am sending along my rifle for Luke's use or Hannah's. If I were able, I would carry it to you myself to repay some part of the debt I owe you. The newspapers say there will be a battle for New Orleans that will make what has come up to this point look like child's play, but for me this war and every war is over. As it is I stay behind to look after my mother and the children, and to carry on teaching school, but my thoughts and good wishes are with you every step of the journey you must make, home to safety.

Your brother, Daniel Bonner

The morning was overcast and wet and very cold, but Jennet could hardly contain her eagerness to be on her way to Hannah. Good news was rare, and Jennet didn't want to hold it back from her one minute more than necessary. She was busy getting both babies ready to go when there was a knock at her door.

Mrs. Livingston had heard of the new child brought into her house and must have the opportunity to examine him. Jennet stopped what she was doing and made every effort to sound pleased at the delay.

"But, Mrs. Bonner," Mrs. Livingston said, pulling up her skirts so that she could sit on the edge of the bed where Jacinthe's son—Jennet told herself she must start thinking of him as Adam—lay swaddled and asleep. "You will adopt this child?"

"Yes," Jennet said, and flashed a quick, tight smile. "I owe—rather, I owed his mother a debt, and she is gone. He has no one else in the world."

Mrs. Livingston's pretty mouth pursed thoughtfully as she reached for Nathaniel, who was crawling across the wide plain of the bed with the obvious intent of crawling off into space. "You must pardon me, Mrs. Bonner," she said. "But is this a colored child?"

Jennet had believed herself ready to answer questions, and found that she was not. Righteous indignation would do no good, nor would it be possible to distract Mrs. Livingston from this topic. She glanced down at the baby's fragile skull with its dusting of dark hair over a high brow. His skin was lighter than Jennet's own after a summer in the sun. No doubt if she declared the boy to be white, Mrs. Livingston would take her word. But she could not make herself say the words.

"Of course." The lie came so easily to Jennet, she found she could look Mrs. Livingston directly in the eye and say the words with complete composure: "His mother was a free woman of color."

Mrs. Livingston sat back and pulled Nathaniel into her lap. He wiggled and twisted, full of energy and determined to be on his way, but all her attention was on Jennet. Her thoughtful, charitable attention.

Finally she said, "If you like, I can ask Marie to help you with him. She is nursing a daughter, and has enough milk for two. You know I've got enough willing hands to look after both these boys. That way you could return to help at the clinic, if you care to."

Jennet agreed that it would be a great relief to her to have competent help, and they did expect her at the clinic.

Mrs. Livingston said, "You have fallen into our ways very quickly. Here it is common to bring a colored child into the nursery when a new child is born in the family. Our Susan's daughter Pauline has been with Cora since she was a few weeks old. This kind of companion is an excellent thing."

What Jennet wanted to say was that Adam would not be Nathaniel's companion, but his brother. She looked at Mrs. Livingston directly, determined to say this, and then knew that she could not. She was a guest in this woman's home; her husband had rescued them from the need to hide from Honoré Poiterin. They owed the Livingstons as much as they owed the Savards, and she could not repay them in harsh words.

Instead she said, "I would like to get to the clinic. Hannah should see this letter that came yesterday as soon as possible."

"Ah." Mrs. Livingston got up and smoothed her skirts. "On today of all days, a distraction will be very welcome. Things have reached a critical point. Mr. Livingston did not come home before three last night, and he says the major general has not slept at all in two days. He thinks the fighting will begin tonight."

At the door, she cast a last long look over her shoulder. "I will send Marie to you immediately. Mrs. Bonner, promise me you will take two of our grooms when you go out into the streets. These two little boys need you."

She did not say: *because your husband may not come back from this battle,* but Jennet heard the words nonetheless.

Jennet dropped a letter in Hannah's lap. Her expression, her coloring, everything about the way she held herself said that the letter brought good news. Hannah was almost afraid to touch it.

"Go on," Jennet said.

Hannah observed. Her cousin's mood was high, but there were circles under her eyes, a weariness that couldn't be disguised. Yesterday she had left with Jacinthe's newborn son, gone with him back to the Livingstons'.

She said, "Tell me about the baby first."

Jennet's expression sobered immediately. She pressed a fist to her cheekbone and then she pushed out a long and heavy sigh. "He is healthy," Jennet said. "He took to the breast, suckled like a wee demon, and slept."

She looked away for a moment. "I intend to keep him and raise him as our own."

It was the thing Hannah had expected. "You're sure?"

"Aye," Jennet said. "There's naught else for it."

"A child isn't a penance," Hannah said, and Jennet jerked as if she had been slapped. It seemed as if she would lash out in return; the old Jennet would have, but this one, who had been through so much, caught herself.

"For his mother's sake," Jennet said. "For his own, and for mine, too. Aye, I willnae deny it."

"Good," Hannah said. "Where are the boys now?"

"Mrs. Livingston produced a nurse out of thin air to look after the both of them while I'm helping here. A young woman. Her milk is sweet, I'm told, and in that household no baby goes without noodling for so much as an hour. Now will ye please read the letter? There's news you must hear."

Hannah's hands were shaking by the time she finished.

Jennet said, "Can ye believe it? Your faither and uncle on their way to us now."

"Oh, yes," Hannah said. "I can."

For one moment she thought herself in danger of fainting out of sheer joy and relief. Her father, her uncle. On a keelboat on the Mississippi, on their way here. The image filled her with an old energy that she had forgot about.

Jennet was still talking, holding out another letter, this one unopened. "The direction is to you alone. Is that no Curiosity's hand? Open it, Hannah, before I bust every button for wondering."

Hannah did as she was bid.

Dearest Girl, our Hannah,

I have been thinking of you & praying for you every day & every night since you left here with your brother to bring Jennet home where she belongs. Mark me well, I do not say that I have feared for you, for I know no other woman as strong as you, Hannah, and never for one moment have I doubted your resolve nor your ability. When Lily and Simon brought your letters to us your good news was no surprise, but I am thankful & I do praise God. His wisdom is great & His tender mercy is over all His works.

No doubt they told you in their last letter that I am sickly or even on my deathbed. Don't you believe it. It was nothing but a bitty cold that settled in my lights, but Many-Doves made me onion compresses and her special tisane and within a week I was right

as rain, Praise the Lord our God for His Mercy. I was
seventy-eight years old this last spring and on that
morning I was up at dawn baking, a dozen loaves of
good bread and six pies and then I scrubbed my own
floor. How many women my age can say half as
much? You hear me now: I intend to live long
enough to see this new Bonner grandson and more
than that, to see you bring a daughter into this world.
You & I have stories to share before the Lord (Great
& Marvelous are His Mercies) calls me home to join
my good husband and daughter.

One last word before they pull this bit of paper
right out from under my nose, and that is this: You
cannot save the whole world, child. No doubt you
have seen terrible things in this newest war and will
see worse before you find your way back home, but
don't get caught up in trying to fix every broken
sorry creature you come across. Some things must be
left to God.

You get yourself home to us who love you best,
though there be mountains and lyons in the way.

Your loving true friend, Curiosity Freeman

writ by her own hand, the first day of December in
the Year of Our Lord Eighteen Hundred and
Fourteen.

When she had finished reading, Hannah dropped the letter to her lap and put both hands on her face. As if to hide
tears, or a smile, or both.

"Oh, I am so glad," Jennet said, hugging her. "What a
good omen. The best omen."

Hannah nodded, unable to speak for a moment. She
stood, and took a deep breath to clear her head. They were

in the apothecary with the door closed, but all around them the building seethed with noise and movement.

"Luke should hear this news, too. It will mean so much to him to know our father is coming."

"Aye," Jennet said. "But there's no time to go running about looking for him. I'm expected in the clinic this last half hour."

"He's still being kept busy translating, then?"

Jennet drew in a deep breath. "At the moment he's most probably still at headquarters, but they'll assign him to a company today," Jennet said. "Commander Patterson took a liking to him, apparently. Luke expects to be put aboard the *Carolina*."

"I'd rather see him on the *Carolina* than in the infantry," Hannah said.

Jennet's mouth quirked. "Aye, weel. We've been unco unlucky when it comes to ships. I'd prefer—" She paused, and when Hannah gave her an encouraging nod, she went on. "I was wondering if perhaps there wad be a place for him in the same company as Ben."

Hannah saw how very uncomfortable Jennet was making this unusual request, and how much it meant to her. She said, "I can ask."

She folded the letters carefully. "At any rate, Luke needs to see the letter; it's excuse enough to send for him."

"And where will you be?" Jennet asked. Her tone had shifted: sudden awareness, and suspicion, too. And with good cause.

"I'm going to the field hospital," Hannah said. "They need experienced surgeons."

"Oh, no," Jennet said. "Not that. Haven't you done enough?"

"I haven't even started," Hannah said. She would have turned away but Jennet took her by the wrist, her grip hard.

"Who sent for you? The army doctors?"

Hannah laughed. "Of course not. It was Ben's idea."

For a moment they looked at each other, and Hannah was struck by an odd mixture of emotions. Affection, impatience, sadness.

"I can't stay behind," Hannah said, "knowing I could be of help."

Jennet flushed with irritation. She said, "And did ye no just read the wise words of a woman as dear to ye as a grandmither? Ye cannae help every puir soul that comes your way, Hannah Bonner."

"But those that I can help, I will," Hannah said. "As long as we are here, I will."

Jennet blinked, resigned. "I don't like it," she said. "Not one bit. But at least I've got an argument that must swing Luke to my way of seeing things. He'll want to be near you, and that's enough to keep him off the *Carolina*."

She looked about herself as if she were suddenly aware of how late it was in the day. "I'll have to go find him straightaway."

CHAPTER 45

In fine weather, on good roads with a fresh horse, sixty miles was not much of a distance, not to Kit Wyndham, who had been born and raised on the broad expanse of the North American continent. In England and Europe, where land was far more precious, sixty miles was a different proposition altogether. Kit had learned that lesson in his three years on the Iberian Peninsula.

Now he was learning to measure miles again. Sixty miles from New Orleans to Pea Island, where the British troops were massing for the invasion. Every step of the way through the soggy, freezing wet. More than fourteen hours after Kit left New Orleans the fisherman's boat set him ashore on Pea Island, where he was greeted at bayonet point.

He identified himself to the marine on watch, offered the right password. Kit allowed himself one question. "Any word of General Pakenham?"

The marine sent him a sidelong glance, and then shrugged. "Expected any day. Couldn't be too soon, if you was to ask me, sir."

Trudging through the miserable encampment in ankle-deep mud and muck, Kit considered. Spirits must be abysmally low if the men were talking to strangers about their unhappiness with command. Kit thought longingly of hot water and dry clothes and food, things that he would be doing without for a long time to come. As the thousands of men bivouacking on these five barren acres had been doing without. Over the last week Admiral Cochrane's sailors had been ferrying men from the fleet to this island in a frenzy that did not spare space for tents or even sufficient rations.

He made his way toward the command tent, passing company after company: riflemen, infantry, artillery, the Highlanders who made it a point of pride to scoff at the weather. The West Indies troops who suffered more than the rest in the freezing rain. It seemed to his eye that their numbers were already much reduced. The wretches had another twelve hours or more in open boats to look forward to. The navy would dump them on solid ground within reach of New Orleans, but whether they would be in condition to bear arms, that was the question.

For the first time Kit felt real doubt about the outcome of the operation. They had the advantage in numbers of experienced soldiers and sailors, but it seemed a very long way from Pea Island to New Orleans, through bayou and ciprière, and then back again. Not only men, but power and ammunition and artillery guns had to be carried every step of the way.

A week ago he would have been able to share his concerns with his superiors, but now he had a report to deliver that would not lend to his credibility. Just the opposite, in fact. When he finished, his career would most likely be as compromised as his reputation.

The command tent was so crowded that one man had to leave before another could enter. Kit worked his way to the table in the middle, where a dozen officers were gathered around a map, each and every one of them intent on appearing unmoved by the blustering argument in their midst.

To someone less familiar with Admiral Cochrane and

General Keane it might indeed seem that the two men were on the point of blows. The unfortunate truth was that they brought out the worst in each other: Cochrane's conceit and pride, Keane's impulsiveness and temper.

Keane had caught sight of Kit. With a few words the tent emptied out, until he was alone with the two senior officers.

"Not a moment too soon," Keane said. "Now, what can you tell us about Jackson's numbers, Major?"

Kit gave his report. His very dissatisfactory report, its deficiencies laid out clearly. He would not offer excuses. He could save that much pride at least. Getting it all out was something of a relief. Kit wondered if he had spent so much time with Roman Catholics that he had been infected with an inclination toward confession. He wondered if priests were ever truly shocked by what they heard, and if they got angry, as General Keane and Admiral Cochrane were now obviously angry. A humming tension, as high-pitched as a bow drawn across a violin, filled the room.

"If I understand you correctly, Major," General Keane began, "you are telling us that you were forced out of the city before you could get any certain information on the number and quality of troops arriving from the north. The exact information you were sent to gather."

"That is true, sir," Kit said. "The Kentucky and Tennessee troops will have arrived since I left New Orleans."

"And your network of informants is defunct."

"Yes, sir," Kit said. He was able to keep his voice steady.

"So you have nothing to show for your months of work except your life."

"I have nothing useful to show since my last report."

Cochrane could contain himself no longer. He said, "And this is the famous Exploring Officer who gave the French such a run for their money. Wellington's pet, they called you, is that right?"

Kit felt a flush of anger making its way up his face. He met Cochrane's gaze directly. "Not in my hearing, sir."

"Have you lost your mind, man?"

"I think perhaps I did, for a while," Kit said.

Keane held up a hand to ask for patience, and Cochrane sputtered to silence.

"I take it you still haven't found out the location of Lafitte's secret store of ammunition and powder, either."

"On the contrary, sir," Kit said. "That I can tell you, with certainty."

It was his one bit of currency, and it didn't go as far as he had hoped. Not once he told them the rest. Lafitte's stash was on the river, almost directly opposite the city.

"You're saying we can't get to it until we've taken the city and don't need it anymore," said Keane.

"Not at all, sir," said Kit Wyndham. "I'm saying it will require a small party of men, the right kind of transport, and a diversion of the first order."

Cochrane said, "You want to lead this mission, do you, Wyndham?"

"I am yours to command, sir," Wyndham said.

"Looking to redeem yourself, eh?" Cochrane squawked like a gander in a temper.

"Just so, sir."

There was a moment's silence in the tent.

Keane seemed to come to a conclusion. "Not straightaway," he said. "Let's see first how things go tonight. We may not have need of any more powder."

"Is it to be tonight, then, sir?" Kit tried not to let his disquiet show.

"In three brigades," said Keane. "You know the lay of the land between Fisherman's Village and the plantations—" he cast a glance at the map, "belonging to de la Ronde and Villeré?"

"Yes, sir, I know both plantations well."

"You'll join the advance," said Keane. "Under Colonel Thornton. We start at nine."

The next twelve hours did nothing to lessen Kit's doubts. The logistics of moving thousands of soldiers and artillery to the mainland would have been daunting under any circumstances, but Keane and Cochrane seemed to believe that by pure force of will and timing they could overcome what might prove to be a fatal flaw: They had too few boats of the right kind. And then, of course, there was the weather, which was turning from bad to worse.

The troops had been ferried to Pea Island from the fleet by the sailors who rowed sixty miles, back and forth, without pause. This next stage in the invasion would proceed in much the same way. Moving the army in installments was always tricky, as the advance could easily be overrun and dispatched before the next detachment arrived. And so Cochrane and Keane had come up with an alternate plan which did not bode well: The vanguard would sail first in the lighter vessels best able to navigate the shallow waters of the Bayou Catalan. The larger boats, sure to get stuck at some point, would follow. When they could go no further, the lighter vessels could be used to ferry the troops from the larger ones.

There was nothing to do but take on this flawed plan as his own and do everything in his power to make it work.

Kit worked with Thornton, a dour man who was well respected and equally feared by the troops he commanded. They had to move almost two thousand men from the 85th, the 95th Rifles, and the King's Own, along with artillery, engineers, and marines, which meant first that they had to be divided up among the available barges. Plans were made, discussed, changed, and finally set in place late in the night.

With less than three hours until first light, Kit rolled himself—back in uniform, finally—into a piece of waterproof canvas that smelled of mold and urine, and fell into an uneasy sleep.

And of course the plans fell apart immediately. Ten o'clock came and went as men were directed into and out of barges, artillery was reassigned, kits went lost and were found again. It was almost noon by the time the advance pushed off, men packed in so tightly that there was no possibility of movement, not even to adjust a hat when the rain started in earnest. Kit found himself revisiting the calculations that had so plagued him the day before: from the fleet to Pea Island, from Pea Island to Bayou Catalan, through the ciprière and along the canals to the de la Ronde plantation, the site chosen by scouts. And then back again, mile by mile. If they should fail, if they should lose this battle, retreat would be almost impossible. Clearly Cochrane and Keane had simply refused to contemplate such an event. That in itself made Kit uneasy.

Around him men tried to keep their spirits up by telling stories and singing, and for a while it seemed to work. Then the rain turned to sleet and the charcoal fire that was too little to give off real heat went cold, taking with it most of the forced good cheer and leaving every one of them to fold into himself, silent. To conserve what energy and heat they could, while the sailors rowed and rowed toward an unseen shore.

At dusk they reached the fishing village, quiet but for the barking of dogs and apparently deserted.

The troops, wet and dispirited, came back to life by the discovery that there was indeed a guarded camp, and the *piquets* were all sound asleep in the shacks. In a matter of minutes they were surrounded and taken prisoner.

"So much for the fabled American militia." Thornton

allowed himself a small laugh as the prisoners were marched off for questioning.

Kit said, "The ones in blue belong to a company called the Chasseurs."

Thornton grunted. "Chasseurs, indeed. An insult to good fighting men."

"I doubt Jackson realized that the rich sons of New Orleans bankers had been assigned this duty," said Kit.

"Let's hope there's a great deal he doesn't know," said Thornton with a rare grin.

With renewed energy the sailors shoved off and the barges began to work their way laboriously through the shallow waters of Catalan and then, narrower, the Bayou Mazant. None of the men around Kit had seen the ciprière before, and they looked about themselves with interest and some disquiet, thinking, Kit could imagine it well, that they would not like to fight a battle in such a place, neither land nor lake, but a combination of the two. Full of strange trees dripping moss, as welcoming as a graveyard. A Scot asked in a low voice about alligators, as if he believed they might hear him and come to introduce themselves.

"They don't like the cold," Kit told him. "In the summer months you'd see dozens of them sunning themselves, but now they're asleep on the bottom."

His answer seemed to quiet some unspoken fear but also stoked general curiosity, and a half dozen whispered questions came his way. The order for silence was welcome, coming as it did just before they reached the de la Ronde canal, which turned out to be blocked with branches and whole dead trees. Something Kit had tried to tell Keane about, but the general had more faith in his advance party than he did in Kit Wyndham.

The engineers consulted briefly, and pronounced the situation impossible. They moved on, through acres of rushes tall enough to hide a thousand men. Kit was wondering what they might do when they found that Jackson had ordered every one of these canals blocked, when they arrived at the next one and found it completely clear. Thornton issued orders, and the first of thousands of British soldiers put foot on American soil.

They came out of the rushes onto a large plantation that reached all the way to the high embankment of the Mississippi, into recently harvested cane fields, dry and firm underfoot, divided here and there by fences. In the middle distance stood the planter's house, surrounded by mature trees and gardens and outbuildings. Some cows and sheep grazed near the far border of the property, but there was not a soldier in sight, nor even a slave at work.

The Americans had known for many days about the invasion force, its size and location. Jackson had had more good information about the British than they had about him, but now the advance spread out, unseen, unchallenged, to cross the fields that led, like stepping-stones, a mere seven miles to the city of New Orleans.

Kit, glad he had kept his doubts to himself, went with them.

Gabriel Villeré had a favorite chair in his father's parlor, where he settled with a cigar after a solid breakfast. Around him were his hunting dogs, his younger brother Jules, and many of his best friends. An altogether agreeable morning, as the sun had finally come out after a cold and rainy night.

Villeré tugged at his uniform, which was pretty enough to parade in but damn uncomfortable otherwise. It pinched his neck and made him cross, and he wondered if his friends felt

the same but were afraid to say so for fear of sounding soft. A
few weeks ago they had sat in this very room, eager to join
the militia, to get in on the fighting. Some of them out of patriotism, or curiosity, or just simply for the excitement of it.
Gabriel had joined because he couldn't think of an excuse
not to that would satisfy either his father—General Jacques
Villeré, commander of the entire Louisiana militia—or his
father-in-law, who was also in uniform and talked a good deal
about the honor of shedding blood to protect one's home and
land. His father was a good man, but not a particularly in-
sightful one when it came to his own children. His father-in-
law was not quite so enamored and saw Gabriel more clearly.

But he had put on the uniform, and accepted the rank of
major and the assignment that came with it. His responsibilities were few and minor: block the bayous, protect
Fisherman's Village, and keep watch for the British. In return
he could sleep comfortably and eat well. The ladies had been
sent to Grand Terre, but his closest friends were close by.
Really, things could be much worse. He could be with the rest
of the uniformed militia on the Bayou St. John in moldy tents,
suffering the December night winds off of Pontchartrain.

Here all he had to do was dispatch a few men to tramp
along the canal and bayou as far as the fishing village where
Catalan joined Bayou Mazant. The fact that those men
hadn't returned yet seemed nothing to worry about. There
had been freezing rain in the night, and they were smart
enough to take cover out of the weather. No doubt they
would come strolling in before noon complaining of poor
food and wet feet.

What the heir to the Villeré plantation could not put out
of his head, though he tried, was the fact that he had not yet
sent the slaves to obstruct the canal. Jackson's reasoning was
that the man-made waterways that connected the Mississippi
to the bayous and then the Gulf were too tempting for
the British to resist. The planters to either side—including

Gabriel's father-in-law to the north—had made a great production out of the whole silly venture. Gabriel had hesitated, though Jackson's engineer had been by more than once to remind him what the major general expected. What he ordered.

It grated, to have such a man as a commander. Jackson was a Yankee, after all, and really knew nothing of Louisiana or the way things worked here. To obstruct a canal would be the work of a few days, but to clear it again would take much longer, and as owners of a working plantation, the Villerés depended on the canal. Gabriel most especially depended on it, as he kept busy for most of the year running goods for the Lafittes.

As if the British would choose such a route into the city to start with, through swamp and bog. They would come in by way of Pontchartrain and the Chef Menteur road. It was the obvious choice.

"I don't believe it," one of his companions was saying in a heated tone. "I won't believe it until I hear his confession for myself."

Gabriel looked down at his younger brother Jules, who had been playing with the dogs while he listened to the conversation.

"They're still arguing about Poiterin," Jules said. "Whether he really is a spy."

Gabriel shrugged. "I myself find it hard to believe," he said, using his elbows to lift himself out of his chair. He opened the lid of a carved walnut box and hesitated over the selection of cigars as he thought of Honoré Poiterin, who was a good man to have at a dinner party. To be seen with someone so daring was to borrow some of his shine, for a short while at least.

"They say he's gone to fight for the British," said Jules, his voice still low.

"He's signed his death warrant if that's true," said Gabriel.

Moll ambled over and pushed her nose into his hand. He rubbed her head and started for the door. If he smoked in here, he would have both his wife and his mother to deal with, and it simply wasn't worth the trouble.

At the door, Moll went suddenly still. Later Gabriel would remember that one moment as the last peaceful minute of his life, because it was followed by an explosion of wood and glass as the door was kicked open and a company of English soldiers came crashing in.

It had been a quiet morning, and now it was full of English riflemen in dark green jackets and infantry in dull red. They poured in every door, herding the rest of Gabriel's men before them until every one of them stood, some still in short clothes, in a huddle in the middle of the parlor.

Through it all, one thought repeated itself in Gabriel Villeré's mind: Now it's done. Now he'll know.

One of the younger dogs snapped at a soldier and got a kick in the ribs for his trouble. Jules let out a furious cry and would have rushed forward, but was caught up by a more cautious hand: Pierre Solet, whose sharpest look wasn't for any of the men who had invaded this house, but for Gabriel himself.

They were all looking at him, waiting for him to do something. They didn't understand that Gabriel was incapable of doing anything at all. He had lost the power of speech and locomotion and coherent thought, all replaced by the image of his father's face.

Then out of the confusion an officer stepped forward and addressed Gabriel directly. He was Colonel Thornton of the 95th of Foot. His manner was all that was correct and courteous, but his tone was as hard as ironwood. "You are our prisoners, Major—"

"Villeré," Gabriel supplied. "Of the New Orleans Militia." His English was not very good, but he caught the gist of the commands that Thornton spit out, rapid-fire, to men who peeled away to do his bidding. They were all in high good spirits. They had taken the Villeré plantation without firing a shot, and now it would serve as the British headquarters during the battle for New Orleans.

From the window, Gabriel saw that the entire plantation was crawling with British soldiers. Who had come, no doubt, by way of Lake Borgne, the bayous, and finally an unobstructed Villeré canal. What had happened to the men he had dispatched to Fisherman's Village? He could not ask, but he could imagine. He hoped they had put up more of a defense than he had.

As they were herded together against the wall, searched, and stripped of weapons, Jules found Gabriel's side and stayed close. His eyes, as round and bright as pennies, fixed on Gabriel's.

"Do something," Jules said. And it was clear to Gabriel that he must do something, the one and only thing there was to do.

Major Gabriel Villeré offered the officers wine and cigars and a seat by the fire. And while he played host, struggling to maintain a polite, deferential tone, his mind, shocked for once out of lethargy, went to work.

From the veranda, Kit Wyndham watched a feckless Gabriel Villeré move like a puppet from one side of the parlor to another. He looked stunned, as well he should be.

Kit turned away, glad that Thornton had not asked him to take part in the actual capture of the house. Instead he had been assigned responsibility for dealing with the civilians, most specifically the slaves. It was his job to make them comfortable with this rather drastic change in their circumstances. He was to get any information they could provide, and convince them that while they were now free, their services would be greatly appreciated. The quartermaster would have to see to feeding the thousands of men who were coming, and for that he would need the locals. Thornton would expect a proper dinner tonight, and wine, and a fire. He would call the women who served the table servants instead of slaves, but beyond that they would be invisible to him.

There were a dozen slaves, young and old, about half of them the ones who worked in the house and kitchen. None of them, men or women, would meet his eye. Fear, disorientation, confusion. Kit spoke to them in a tone he hoped would strike them as friendly without being coercive. Most probably they wouldn't trust him anyway, and in that they were right. They had been hearing for a long time about what good things the British would do for them, but what reason did they have to believe those rumors? And if things went badly here after all, they would find themselves returned to their owners, and in worse shape than they had been yesterday.

But he did his best. Kit spoke to the slaves in his own approximation of the local French. He offered them a fair wage for their work, pointed out the quartermaster who would pay them, answered the few subdued questions they asked.

A younger man, heavily muscled and as broad through the chest as a barrel, was the one to ask the inevitable.

"And if you British lose? What happens to us then? Will you take all of us to England and give us places to live and work?"

There was only one possible answer, and Kit gave it. "The Americans can't stand up to the full force of the British army and navy. You have nothing to worry about."

Walking away later, Kit hoped the cook and kitchen helpers would not be among the ones who ran off. A dragoon ran up to him, dismayed to find that the slaves had already dispersed.

"I wanted you to ask them where the rest of the horses

have been hid." The invasion forces had only enough horses for the officers; the dragoons, for whom a horse was as basic a piece of equipment as a right arm, had had to come on foot like the infantry. They had been hoping to find mounts on the plantations, but if Villeré was any indication, the dragoons would not be mounted at all for the duration of this campaign.

The dragoons were disappointed, but the rest of the troops were in good spirits. The weather was dry and unusually warm, and there was no sign of resistance.

"Easy pickings," he heard one man say to another. "By tonight they'll have finished with the transport and we can march on New Orleans tomorrow."

After the misery of the journey, it all seemed too easy. A dozen of the Highlanders got the quartermaster's permission to have a look at the levee, where they promptly stripped down and dove into the Mississippi, muddy and cold as it was.

"Yesterday they couldn't wait to get out of the wet," said Quartermaster Surtees to Kit. "Soldiers." And he shook his head with all the exasperated affection of a father.

Standing on the levee, Kit surveyed the river and the bordering properties. To the north was Denis de la Ronde's plantation, with a mansion that had no equal in five hundred miles for beauty or graciousness. De la Ronde intended to transform all of southern Louisiana into a new France, and so he had called his home Versailles. Kit had been invited to an evening party there a few weeks ago, and he had danced with de la Ronde's daughter, Gabriel Villeré's young wife. A pretty but easily confused young lady, who had been sent away with the other ladies to safety.

He was thinking of that pleasant evening, of the wine and card games and conversation, when Kit heard the commotion from the house. He turned in time to see Gabriel Villeré leaping a fence to tear across the fields, one of his dogs running at his heels. Muskets had already come up and began to fire, but it seemed that Villeré could move when the need was on him. He disappeared into a swampy area of trees and bushes that separated this property from de la Ronde's, and a half dozen of the 95th gave chase, only to come back a quarter hour later empty-handed.

"And so he'll carry the tale to Jackson," said the quartermaster, who still stood beside Kit. "You've seen the man. What will he do? Jump up from his dinner to come wave his sword in our faces?"

And the quartermaster laughed uproariously at the idea of the American military on the offensive. Americans had never been known to attack, not in all the years they had been fighting wars on this continent.

Kit looked out over the troops making themselves at home in the expanse of land between the river and the swamp, and some of the disquiet of the last day came back to him. But he said nothing to the quartermaster, who was still laughing at his own joke as Kit walked away.

At mid-afternoon, Jennet showed up at headquarters. Luke heard her voice in the main office and braced himself for some kind of disturbing news; his wife disliked the army headquarters and would never come here unless truly compelled.

And as it turned out the news was both good and bad. The letter she brought was a shock and a pleasure. And then she told him about Hannah.

He took a moment to think it all through: His sister was going to help at a field hospital. Not the main field hospital—Luke realized this immediately though Jennet seemed not to; the army surgeons and the doctors from the city would hardly admit her to their number—but some other, smaller affair with no official standing. It made sense, and it made him uneasy, but he could no more forbid Hannah than he could shoot her.

"And so it's clear," Jennet was saying. "If ye must join a company, you should join the Choctaws. That way ye can keep an eye on your sister."

"And Ben Savard can keep an eye on me, isn't that what you're thinking?"

Jennet's mouth tightened. He knew her expression, and it was one that did not bode well. She would have her way, even should it be necessary to spill blood.

She said, "It is the logical thing to do, and weel ye ken it."

Luke thought of the *Carolina,* where he was expected to report. The ship would be manned mostly by the Baratarians, who were experts in artillery and had supplied their own cannons, guns, ammunition, and black powder. He was uneasy still about this idea, as there were some men from Barataria that he would rather not run into just now.

He said, "If the Choctaw will have me—"

Jennet interrupted him. "Ben Savard will see to it."

"Then I'll talk to Butler."

And Jennet's face blossomed into an unsteady smile that told him just how worried she had been at the idea of his joining a gun crew. She came and put her hands on his chest, went up on tiptoe, and kissed him soundly.

"Thank you," she said. "I'll rest much easier."

Luke took a moment he could ill afford to pull her closer and kiss her again.

"You'll come back to us," Jennet said, nipping at his lower lip to underscore her command. "You'll come back whole."

Before he could go find Major Butler, the man appeared before him with an agitated Creole in tow. A planter by the name of Leroux, who had no English but nevertheless wanted to convey something of importance.

Luke listened for a moment and asked a question, and then reported.

"Another sighting of British sloops," he said. "Almost word for word like the last report."

Major Butler nodded. "Thank him, will you? And send him on his way."

"He also wants to know if the American government will reimburse him for the slaves who run away with the British," Luke went on. He put this question to Butler without any particular intonation, as if he were asking about the weather. In fact it was nothing new; the wealthy landowners were all worried about this particular point. It went hand in hand with the rumor that Jackson would burn New Orleans before he let it fall to the British, something that the major general roundly denied, but which Luke held was highly probable.

Butler's mouth contorted. He said, "Tell him that all reasonable claims will be considered, when the time comes."

Luke translated, and then held up a hand to keep Butler from leaving. He said, "A small matter," and then requested the change in assignment, which Butler agreed to without hesitation. There were far larger things to worry about, after all, such as the shouting from the main office: Major General Jackson in a fit of temper. Butler ran, and Luke followed.

Jackson stood in the middle of the main office with two men. One was a gentleman planter Luke recognized as de la Ronde. The second man was twenty years or so younger. They were both officers in the uniformed militia, and both men were disheveled. In part most probably because they had rushed here—de la Ronde still held his riding crop in one hand—but also because no man living could face Andrew Jackson in a temper and remain unaffected.

The younger man looked as if he might faint. His complexion was the color of cheese, his mouth opening and closing in spasms as the elder one talked, a jumble of French and heavily accented English.

Jackson caught sight of Luke and he made a sharp cutting gesture with his hand in de la Ronde's direction.

"I'll have my own translator." And to Luke: "This is Major Gabriel Villeré and his father-in-law de la Ronde. I want you to ask Villeré to tell the story of what happened since yesterday at his father's plantation, and I want to hear your translation sentence by sentence."

Luke began by introducing himself, trying for a tone that might provide Villeré with the courage to forge ahead. Then the young officer began to speak, at first slowly and in short sentences.

There was nothing complicated about the story, and Luke translated it almost automatically. He was able to keep first his surprise and then his alarm out of his voice as he recounted Villeré's actions: the company dispatched to Fisherman's Village, the orders they had been given, the fact that Villeré had retired early to his bed and not risen until well past first light.

The sudden attack and capture by British soldiers.

"Stop there," Jackson said. "I want you to translate my questions word for word."

Luke nodded his understanding.

"Major Villeré, by what path did the British troops gain access to your property?"

Villeré answered, and Luke translated: "By means of the canal that runs from theciprière across the fields and stops short of the levee."

Jackson's face was very still. "The canal that you were ordered to obstruct two weeks ago?"

Villeré listened to the question. "*Oui.* Yes."

Jackson paused. "You escaped from the British by jumping through a window and running to de la Ronde's plantation?"

"*Oui.*"

"And then you rode here directly."

Another pause, while de la Ronde and Villeré exchanged glances.

"I will have an answer," Jackson said, his voice deceptively calm.

Luke listened to Villeré's halting narrative and then translated.

"First we rowed across the river, and then we found horses and rode north, and crossed the river again."

Jackson's expression was thunderous. "You crossed the river? For what purpose?"

Villeré began to stammer. De la Ronde's expression was as stiff and fragile as glass.

"Let me suggest to you," Jackson said, "exactly what happened. You ran to your father-in-law and told him what had happened in the hope that he would ride here directly and alert us. Then you intended to run away rather than face court-martial for dereliction of duty, and you ran to find a boat. Your father-in-law refused to let you go alone, and spent the crossing convincing you that to add desertion to your crimes would mean certain death. He succeeded, and so you then rode north and crossed the river again and came here. This whole additional episode costing us at least another hour. M. de la Ronde, have I come close?"

When Luke had relayed the entire speech, de la Ronde bowed from the shoulders and clicked his heels. In halting English he said, "In the essentials, yes, Major General."

"You are a wise man, but your daughter married an idiot," said Jackson. Mostly to himself he said, "The British infiltrated and made camp without firing a single shot. That's the short and long of it, would you say, Villeré?"

The sound of Villeré's breathing was very loud as Luke translated.

"*Oui.* Yes."

The movement, when it came, was sudden. Jackson raised both fists and crashed them onto the table before him so violently that the glass in the windowpanes shivered.

"By God," he shouted, the blood rushing into his face. "They will not sleep on American soil. I swear it."

There was a moment of absolute silence, in which none of them even breathed. Then Jackson's gaze fell on Gabriel Villeré, and he walked around the table to stand in front of him.

"Your sword."

Villeré looked at Luke. He meant to be stoic, but the blood had drained from his face leaving only high color on his cheekbones, as if he were in the grip of a fever. He drew his sword and held it out to the major general, who took it.

"Mr. Bonner," said Jackson. "Call on the guard and see to it that this man is escorted to the garrison gaol. Send word to his father as well. The court-martial will have to wait until we've driven the British back to the sea. Major Butler, send word to Fort St. Charles. Three volleys, if you please. We march south today."

CHAPTER 46

New Orleans was a Catholic town full of churches and chapels, and in each church there was a bell tower. Bells told the hour, summoned the faithful to Mass, reminded them when it was time to say their prayers, announced births and deaths, called citizens to fight fires and floods. Now the bells were tolling wildly while the echo of the triple cannon blast from Fort St. Charles still hung in the air.

Jackson was calling all men to arms. The American troops were on their way to meet the British.

Since the moment Hannah had agreed to join the company of Choctaw, a knot had been tightening in the pit of her belly. She felt her whole self being stretched thin, as fragile as a bubble. She tried to recall why she had agreed, what had compelled her to go against her instincts.

Then the signal guns sounded, and just that suddenly all tension left her in a rush, as hot as blood.

With complete calm she finished what she was doing. She folded a blanket and spread it over the hospital cot, shook out the pillow, looked around the clinic—now empty but for an old man too sick to get out of his bed—and left to get ready. Ben Savard would be coming for her.

She passed through the main clinic, where Julia and Rachel were working with Clémentine and a half dozen other women to get ready for the influx of wounded.

Through the windows that looked out on the rue Royale, Hannah caught sight of crowds in the street, driven by panic and excitement both.

It was a kind of madness that came over people; Hannah could see it in their faces, like a fever. Once she had been infected with it, too, but she had passed beyond such things. She would go to tend to the wounded and comfort the dying; she would bring all her skill and knowledge to that work. But she felt no thrill at the sound of drums and bugles, nor any anger or fear or joy. Those were things she could not afford to take with her onto a battlefield.

Jennet was in the little clinic when the triple cannon volley sounded. She startled so thoroughly that the basin of dirty water she was carrying slopped over and soaked her apron, which was none too clean to start with.

The little girl lying on the cot beside her didn't startle, or even blink. Since her grandfather had died she hadn't spoken a word, and it was an hour's work to coax a few spoonfuls of broth into her.

Dr. Savard had asked her to take on the responsibility for the little clinic, and she had been glad to be given work. Once the fighting began and the first wounded were carried back to the city, some of them—the ones with wounds that would not kill them outright—would end up here.

With her, Jennet had two of Mrs. Livingston's servants, older negro women she hardly knew, whose names were Susan and Martha. Though they looked nothing like the women who had run the kitchen at Carryckcastle for all of Jennet's girlhood, she sensed that these two were cut from the same mold: opinionated, steadfast, unflinching in an emergency, and able to exert their will almost effortlessly when it came to dealing with children or the infirm. Together the three of them would look after the lesser wounds, provide food and drink and a place to dry clothes and boots. Then the men they had cared for would go back to battle to be shot at again.

Jennet was stringing a rope across the room so they would have someplace out of the rain to hang wet clothes when she saw Martha, the younger and taller of the two servants, put down the brush she was using to scrub the table and look to the window, where Ben Savard could be seen speaking to a neighbor.

"Jean-Benoît," Martha said, and her dark face split into an affectionate smile.

"My," said Susan. "Look at the man." And she clucked her tongue in admiration.

"Come to fetch the Redbone doctor," said Martha.

Jennet took a deep breath, but before she could think of what to say, or if she should say anything, Ben Savard had come into the room. She got down from her stool to greet him, and realized that the door from the courtyard had opened, too. Henry Savard came in, with Hannah just behind him.

Since they had been in the city Hannah had worn the simple gray gown and sturdy shoes Julia provided, but today she had put those clothes aside. Now she wore a hunting shirt of felted wool dyed a deep red. The shirt was so long that it reached to her knees, and so wide that it hung in folds that had been cinched tight to her waist by means of a long red scarf. Two more scarves of the same color were looped loosely around her neck.

The fringed hem of the shirt touched the embroidered and beaded bands of high winter moccasins dyed a true deep red. Like the hunting shirt and the short cape that hung down Hannah's back, the moccasins had been heavily embroidered. Across her chest she had strapped a leather bandolier with silver fittings; from it, a beaded sheath hung down over her left hip. The grip of a long knife faced forward so she could reach across and draw it easily.

In her hands she carried a wide-brimmed felt hat with a low crown, and slung on her back was a canvas pack.

Jennet knew exactly what was in that pack: an instrument case with scalpels and saws, the tools Hannah would need to amputate an arm or close a wound or draw out an arrowhead or shrapnel. There would be bandages and gauze, lint and plasters. A variety of needles in a flannel roll, heavy thread, laudanum, camphor, and alum to be used as a styptic. In a wooden case lined with felt were stoppered bottles of rectified spirits and brandy and Jesuits' bark tea.

If Hannah must go to war, she would be prepared.

Jennet turned to Ben, who looked far too pleased with himself.

She said, "The clothes?"

"My mother's."

Henry provided the crucial detail. "Grand-mère Amélie," he said. "She was a Seminole princess."

"Of my eight great-grandparents, one was a Seminole princess," said Ben.

"Oh, Amélie was a princess all right," said Martha, who had never stopped smiling. "And don't you look like one, too, in her things."

Hannah managed only a short, tight smile. She said, "If we're done discussing my wardrobe, I'm ready to go."

"I wish I were ready to watch you go," Jennet said dryly.

"It's only six miles south of the city," Hannah said. "I'll be far from the fighting."

"You'll be right in the middle of it all," Jennet said, her voice catching. "As you always are." She turned to Ben Savard.

"If anything happens to her—"

There was a glittering in Ben's eyes that made the color spark like turquoise. No tears, but pride and hope and love, and Jennet understood that those things would have to be promise enough.

It was half past three when they left the clinic. The first thing that struck Hannah was how empty the streets were. After so many weeks of crowds, it was unsettling.

"Jackson is reviewing the troops," Ben said, reading the question from her face. "That's where we're headed."

They trotted at an easy pace through the streets, catching sight now and then of a figure behind a window or on a balcony. There were no children to be seen anywhere, no young women walking, nobody in the cafés. But Hannah sensed them, the women with their children, the men too old to take part in this newest war. Waiting for the fighting to begin, so they could wait for it to end. Sitting in darkened parlors clutching carving knives, having handed even the most antique muskets over to the hundreds of men who had walked into the city to volunteer without weapons of any kind.

The air was cold on Hannah's skin, and it felt good. The smell of rain was in the air, along with a faint tinge of gunpowder that settled on the tongue, a taste as familiar as salt. She felt no tension, but neither could she stop the jumble of questions her mind produced. She hoped that there would be some kind of shelter—a barn, a shed—any place with a roof and walls to cut out the winds and the worst of the wet. She didn't like the idea of treating battle wounds out in the open in such weather, though she had done it more than once before.

"What are you thinking?"

She glanced at Ben. "How strange that it all comes back to me so easily. How it never gets easy."

He made a sound deep in his throat that said he understood.

Ben turned into a narrow street and Hannah followed him, drawing up short when he made a gesture that asked her to wait while he went into a small cottage with shuttered windows. A tabby cat sat on the porch blinking at Hannah until Ben came back. He had a man with him, by his dress and bearing a free man of color, someone of considerable standing in his community. He was wearing strong boots and a traveling cloak and he carried a battered portmanteau.

"Hannah Bonner," Ben said. "May I introduce Hyacinth Rousseau. You are both doctors and surgeons."

In her surprise Hannah stumbled a little. "Dr. Rousseau. My pleasure."

He was smiling at her, a man of at least sixty, with a bald head like a speckled brown egg. The doctor took the hand Hannah offered and his grasp was firm and dry and cool. His eyes were sharp, but not unkind in their appraisal. He spoke English to her, with the local French accent.

"Dr. Bonner. I've heard good things about you. You've won the approbation of Maman Zuzu, which is something I have not managed in more than fifty years."

Hannah said, "It would have happened sooner if you were a woman, no doubt."

His whole face contorted around his smile. The doctor took the hat from under his arm and fit it carefully to his head. "Shall we go?"

There were many questions Hannah would have liked to ask, and she might have even made the attempt, if not for the noise of the bugles and drums.

They came to the levee and climbed it by means of the stairs hacked into the turf. The wide brown river, pockmarked with rain, was higher than the land around it, like a pulsing artery pushing up to run along ridges of muscle. The river was full of boats of every type and size. Hannah saw a large schooner, a good hundred feet in length and heavily armed. Its decks crawled with men out of uniform, the kind of rough sailors she had become familiar with in the year that they had been searching for Jennet. Among them were a few sailors in the dark blue jackets of the American navy.

"The *Carolina,*" Ben said.

They trotted along the levee until they came in sight of an open field to find what must be, it seemed to Hannah, every soldier, militiaman, marine, and sailor in the entire southern United States. Army regulars, backwoodsmen, pirates, farmers, shopkeepers, cabinetmakers, bankers, and lawyers. Two dozen Choctaw, a battalion of free men of color. A total of some two thousand men, many with no experience in battle at all. Some still without weapons.

Downriver, the very best of the British empire—the military force that had defeated Napoleon—waited.

Beside her Dr. Rousseau said, "May the good Lord keep them, every one."

On the far side of the field Hannah picked out General Jackson, surrounded by staff and officers, on the Levee Road that overlooked the field. The troops had begun to march, one company at a time, in formation. The officers were mounted, and the sun glinted on epaulettes and bridles and the telescope that Major General Jackson was using to study the river.

"Where are we going?" she asked Ben.

"The DuPré plantation."

"We had best get moving," said Dr. Rousseau. "It will be dark in another hour."

He was not young, but the doctor proved himself capable enough when speed was called for. It seemed he also had questions, and wouldn't wait to ask them. Ben told what he knew, and none of it was good. The British had got a foothold on a plantation just south of the city, and that without a battle.

"A poor start," said Dr. Rousseau. "But not yet time to despair."

Conversation slowed and then stopped as the road became clogged with men, on foot and on horseback, wagons and caissons, handcarts and wheelbarrows. Hannah let herself be swept along, and kept her eyes on Ben.

She thought of the men she didn't know yet, the Choctaw warriors who would be in her care, and how little she would be able to do for a serious wound to the head or gut. She could bind gashes and extract bullets if they hadn't penetrated the abdomen. She could amputate. She had good instruments, perfectly honed; she had medicines. There was even laudanum, though there might not be time to use it. She had the power of her mind and the sustaining memory of all her teachers over the years, who stood behind her. And she wasn't alone. She was comforted by the presence of Dr. Rousseau.

An hour out of the city, they left the main Levee Road and cut down through the fields, and Hannah realized that they had caught up with Juzan's company of Choctaw warriors. When they came to a stand of trees, they were waiting. Among them was her brother.

Luke grinned as he came to her. His face was smeared with mud and his hair was hidden under a turban, so that at first glance he might have been another Choctaw.

He said, "Jennet insisted."

"Of course she did," said Hannah. "I have this idea that together Jennet and Ben could set even the government to rights."

Luke looked first surprised, and then pleased. "You're right, they are alike in some ways." And then: "I'll have his back, as much as I'm able."

Hannah didn't know what to say to this, and so she only squeezed her brother's arm and turned back to the other men.

One of the warriors, older than the rest, was talking to
Ben. Most probably this was some relative of his, but she
would have to wait for an explanation: In many ways the
southern tribes were no different from her own people; it
would be rude to interrupt the exchange of information
that was part of such a reunion.

And so she took the opportunity to study the older man,
taking in the graying hair that hung down from the rough
linen turban he wore wrapped around his head like many of
the others in the company. Juzan might be the man Jackson
had appointed to lead these men into battle, but Hannah
knew she was looking at a Choctaw war chief, the only
man whose word would count with the warriors who
waited quietly, watching the growing shadows and keeping
track of every living being within hearing.

Finally he turned away from Ben and went directly to Dr.
Rousseau. The two men were clearly acquainted but formal
with each other, each reserved and respectful. They spoke a
language that was mostly the local French but studded with
words in other languages, Spanish and the Indian tongues.
She had been favorably disposed toward Dr. Rousseau, and
she saw that her instincts had been right. This was a man who
could work side by side with Indians and Redbones.

When he finally turned to her, Hannah learned that the
chief's name was David Fairweather. He had a name in his
own language as well, but that was not offered to her. Later
she would have to ask Ben Savard what it meant that the
war chief denied her his name. She feared it couldn't be
anything good, but then she saw no evidence of disapproval
in his face, nor could she hear it in his voice.

David Fairweather was a full-blood Choctaw who wore
tribal tattoos on his cheeks and forehead. His brow had been
purposely flattened by means of a board pressed to his head
when he was an infant, but his clothing was the usual mixture
of native and white: doeskin and homespun. He wore a long,

dull blue shirt without a collar, a scarf knotted around his neck, loose leggings and winter moccasins, everything embroidered and beaded. Across his chest was a broad wampum string with a pattern Hannah didn't recognize, and he carried so many weapons—including war club, long rifle, and bow and arrows—that he might have been setting out to turn back the whole English army single-handed.

No doubt the Choctaw were divided, as was every other tribe, on the matter of traditions. There would still be Choctaw women who bound boards against the soft foreheads of their newborns to force their skulls into this particular version of beauty, just as there would be others who despised those mothers for their inability to leave the old ways behind.

The men talked among themselves for a while, Juzan explaining the orders they had been given. At one point she felt gazes shift toward her and away again, and she realized that they were talking about her. She heard *healer* and *woman* and *friend*. When Ben came over she saw relief and satisfaction in his expression.

She said, "They didn't know you asked me to come?"

"Juzan knew."

Later, Hannah told herself, she would ask more questions. There would be a lot of them.

Ben was saying, "Dr. Rousseau, you know the DuPré slave alley? Mose is waiting for you there; he'll get you what you need."

"I know it," said Dr. Rousseau.

Hannah's throat was very dry, but she made herself speak. "Watch out for yourself, Jean-Benoît Savard. And for my brother."

He grinned at her, sure of himself. Sure of her. His easy smile was more comfort than any empty promise.

· · ·

In the gathering dusk, Hannah studied the countryside and the plantations stacked along the river like layers of a cake. As large farms went, the plantations were not much different from their counterparts in the north. Main houses, some simple and single-storied, others ornate and sprawling; barns and stables, warehouses and outbuildings. Sugar-works. Chicken pens, cattle and sheep grazing, hayricks and cotton bales stacked in pyramids and covered over with tarpaulin. Ditches, fences, canals, and in the distance, the ciprière, a wall of shadows. Bats danced overhead, quick shapes against the darkening sky, and the smell of night rose out of the stubble in the fields as the color seeped out of the world.

They passed through a marshy half acre of reeds and cypress and came out on another plantation, this time directly among the cabins that housed the slaves. They were screened from the main house by a grove of pecan trees so that they seemed almost like a small and isolated village.

The cabins were arranged in two long lanes that intersected at a right angle. Between the cabins, small gardens had been dug under for the winter. A flock of geese waddled by, followed by two boys who looked more surprised than alarmed to see the strangers.

Women were coming to their doors to call to children and nod to Dr. Rousseau, though most of them did not meet his eye. Out of respect or fear it was impossible to say, and, Hannah told herself, unimportant.

"Where are the men?"

The doctor glanced at her. "Jackson's engineers have put every male slave over the age of ten to work for the last three weeks, mostly digging ditches and blocking bayous."

It had been a naïve question, just as it would be naïve to ask why these women and children had not been sent away to safety.

There was one older man left, at least. Mose met them at the door of the cabin they were to have as their field hospi-

tal. And with him was Père Tomaso. Hannah had last seen
him at her bedside in the long days of her last illness, when
she had been so badly beaten that she could hardly breathe
for pain. He had come to sit beside her every afternoon for
two weeks or more, often to tell her stories about Ben that
made her laugh in spite of the pain. Sometimes he read to her
aloud. What he had been reading—a newspaper or the
Bible or poetry—that Hannah could not recall, but his voice
had steadied her, something calm and soothing to focus on in
the worst time.

Hannah wondered what other surprises Ben had waiting
for them, even while she greeted the man. She was glad to
see him; another pair of hands were always welcome in a
field hospital.

He saw the question on her face and answered it. "The
man who owns this plantation is my brother-in-law. My sister offered us the use of the cabin."

"You are good to come and help," Hannah said. "I don't
know why Ben didn't mention it to me."

"Ben likes to set plans in motion, but rarely talks about
them until he sees how they work out," the priest said.

"I'm learning that about him," Hannah said dryly.

Dr. Rousseau ducked his head, too old and wise to make
any comment.

They went inside together. The cabin was small, with
walls that had been recently whitewashed, and a swept hard-
packed earth floor. There was a hearth with firewood
stacked beside it, and two water buckets. The only furniture
was a table, three stools, and two pallets on the ground, each
covered with a clean blanket. An unlit lantern stood on the
table.

Hannah had the sense that these things were the best the
people had to offer, gathered from each of the cabins for
their use. She was thinking this as she saw Père Tomaso take
a dozen fat candles out of the sack he had with him.

"From the church," he said. "I thought you'd need them."

Dr. Rousseau was unpacking his own bag. He said to Hannah, "Tomaso is half a doctor himself. He'll be a big help." He glanced at her over his shoulder, a smile cutting a sickle through his close-cropped beard.

"Now there's nothing to do but wait," said Hannah.

"I've got another idea," said Dr. Rousseau. "There's still enough light; let's go to the levee, have a look and see what the English are up to."

Père Tomaso declined to join them, for reasons that were unclear to Hannah. But she followed Dr. Rousseau readily to the levee and up to the road that ran along it. And there was the river, as always, bending one way and then another like a fat old serpent, the water fast-moving and muddy.

The doctor pointed out the main house on the McCarty plantation, where Jackson had his headquarters.

"And the field hospital," Hannah guessed aloud.

"Oh, yes," said Dr. Rousseau. "Three or four doctors from the city and Jackson's own surgeons, all set up there."

He talked about the plantations that lined the river, who owned them and what they grew, which owners had joined the militia, which had gone away to safety and left the protection of their private property to the army.

"And just down there, you should be able to see the *Carolina*," said the doctor.

"It's two and a half miles," Hannah said. "You give my eyesight far too much credit."

It was full dark now, and the shapes of trees and bushes and wide expanses of empty field had melded together into the shadowy expanse of the ciprière. She thought of what it would be like to have to travel through an unfamiliar ciprière in the dark. There was no reason to worry about the Choctaws, who were more at home in these watery backwoods than any white man, but the English were another matter entirely. She wondered what they made of it all. This place was as different from the battlefields of Spain and France as fire was from water. The Choctaw would move through the ciprière without hesitation, as hard to pin down as smoke, and just as disabling. Kit Wyndham and his like, for all their strength and bravery and battle experience, could not hope to match them. She was confident of that much, at least.

Out here, on the fields between the ciprière and the river, there was far more to worry about. The American troops were there, advancing on the canal that separated the Villeré and LaCoste plantations and marked the British line. No doubt Jackson had sent his best, most seasoned men, but still: The British advance had had a day of good weather to situate themselves and dig in.

Hannah gave in to her curiosity. Paul Savard had lent her a telescope, and now she took it from the loop on her belt. At first it showed her nothing but the darkened fields, and that was a good thing. If the American troops could not approach the British silently in such optimal conditions, there was little hope they might prevail.

What Hannah could see with her telescope was so unexpected that it took a moment to make sense of it. The British encampment was lit up by a half dozen bonfires, as if the troops were trying to advertise their position and strength. She began to doubt her own eyesight, and so Hannah handed the telescope over to Dr. Rousseau.

For a long moment the telescope moved back and forth as he studied the encampment.

He said, "They've settled in like long-lost cousins sure of a warm welcome." He handed her back the telescope.

"They are very sure of themselves," Hannah agreed. "But then, they defeated Napoleon."

Hannah observed men walking from the main house to the outbuildings, from the levee back to the fires.

"They'll have slaughtered most of the Villerés' livestock for their cook pots," the doctor said. And then, in a rougher tone: "They are in for a rude surprise."

"You think there's a chance, then," Hannah said.

But instead of answering her, the doctor turned his face toward the river where he had supposed the *Carolina* must sit in darkness. At that same moment, a rocket shot into the sky from the fields about a half mile farther on, trailing white and red and blue. Before the last of it had sputtered out, a world of sound and light erupted from the dark on the far side of the river. Long tracers of light followed the first volleys as grapeshot arced over the water and tore directly into the very center of the British camp.

Through the telescope, Hannah watched the British camp seethe and roil like an anthill kicked in by a bad-tempered boy. There was a mad rushing, frantic action; fires were doused, and then she could catch only glimpses of what was happening when powder flashed from muzzles and shell after shell crashed into the camp. Even from so far away she could smell the black powder smoke. And added to all this, a misting rain and a fog rising off the river.

And then the shelling stopped as suddenly as it had started. Another signal rocket, and following it, the bugles called out to the troops waiting in the dark, from the ciprière to the levee.

"Here now," said Dr. Rousseau. "Here it starts." He was as calm as an elder telling a story of a battle fought generations before. Hannah was not surprised. She thought of her father, who might be here tomorrow or the day after, of her uncle, who had come to take them home, but who would first fling themselves into this cauldron in the blind faith that they could climb out again whole. She thought of Ben

Savard, who had taken up arms for the O'seronni without
hesitation.

Men liked battle, that was the truth of it. And another
truth: She could do no less than offer her help, once they
had purged themselves of the need to draw blood.

The doctor had turned again, this time toward the fields,
where sputterings of light and sound, gunfire and wild
shouting, made it clear that the infantry had engaged the
British. And then the *Carolina* began again with her bombardment of the British camp.

He said, "We had best get out of the open."

When Hannah thought of battle, it was the noise she remembered most clearly, the pounding that made the
eardrums ache and the whole world tremble. And still it took
her by surprise. The relentless battering of sound that shook
the ground and the walls and made it impossible to speak.
The *Carolina* gave no quarter. As long as she had munitions,
she would give none.

In the makeshift field hospital, they waited in the dark
for their work to begin, reluctant to waste lantern or candlelight until it was most needed. Now and then Père
Tomaso would go out and speak a few words to Mose, or
someone else out of Hannah's line of sight. He would come
in again, and in the next pause in the shelling he would give
them what news he had heard: The British three-pounders
were not of a caliber to reach the *Carolina,* moored as she
was on the far side of the river. They seemed not to have
any bigger guns, which was good luck that could not last;
no doubt the artillery was on its way, and unless the supply
lines could be cut, the one-sided nature of the battle would
not last long.

"The infantry?" Hannah asked.

"The fog is worse, and they are hampered for it."

"Wounded?"

"A handful. At the other field hospital."

Hannah could make out shouts now and then, in the pauses between shells, a shout for ammunition, a muffled scream. A child wailed nearby, and was hushed. Horses thundered by on the Levee Road from the city and then back again.

She sat with her back to the wall and her forehead pressed to her knees, and reached for calm. Memories of other battles rose and fell or were pushed away. She felt Strikes-the-Sky close by, the shape and scent of him. He rarely spoke to her anymore and she found it harder, now, to know what he was thinking. How he felt about her being here, looking after men who fought for Jackson and the O'seronni. If he would understand, if he would forgive her.

If he would disapprove of Ben Savard as he had disapproved of Kit Wyndham.

She remembered the new wound on Ben's side, neatly stitched by some woman who lived in the Disputed Territories, a woman he called a friend.

He hadn't come to her bed last night, and she had slept badly, and now he was out in the night and the fog, killing men who had stepped onto American land in the hope of claiming it for themselves. Something he would never be able to do, even if he lived through this battle, and the next one, and the one after that. Ben Savard might be among the dead already. He might die before her father and uncle arrived, an idea that struck her like a fist. He could die fighting this white man's war, and then all the things she wanted to ask him, all the things unsettled between them, would stay that way forever.

She had asked him one question, in the moment before he went off with Juzan and the Choctaw.

"Why are you fighting this war, really?"

Maybe he knew her better than she believed, because he

seemed to have been waiting for the question. He said, "Because when the dust settles, this place will be American. In another fifty or a hundred years the whole damn continent will be American. There won't be anywhere to hide."

Hannah said, "So your plan is to become your enemy."

"Do you see any alternative?"

"No," Hannah had said. "None at all."

The air heavy and wet, cold hanging gauzy white in the night sky. The stink of gunpowder and blood.

Dr. Rousseau stood at the open door, his mouth drawn down at the corners while he watched two Choctaw carry in the wounded man and put him on the scrubbed table. Père Tomaso was speaking to them in their own language, asking questions and getting short answers in response. Then they slipped away, back into the night.

"This one is no stranger to battle," Dr. Rousseau said.

"His name is Nittakechi, he's the son of Pushmataha. A chief closely allied to Jackson." Père Tomaso said the name as if he believed they must be familiar with it.

"We'll do what we can for him," said Hannah. "No matter who he is allied to."

"Of course," said the priest, inclining his head in apology.

The chief's son was no more than seventeen years old, but his nose and cheeks were a mass of fading scars, and there was an indentation in his skull that made it clear he had survived a blow with a war club sometime in the last year or so. Spider legs of blood ran over his forehead and eyelids from a bullet wound that had plowed through his scalp and along the skull. He was concussed and would not fight again this night, but he would most likely survive.

His eyes fluttered open. Hannah leaned over him with a candle to look at his pupils, and was glad to see that they were equal in size and that they reacted to the light.

He muttered something she couldn't make out, and she dredged up the bit of his language that she had.

"Ak akostinincho." *I don't understand.* The priest was waiting to be asked to translate, but she didn't look at him.

The boy's throat worked. "Water."

She gave him what he wanted, helping him take small sips from the tin cup. Then he closed his eyes.

"Yokoke." *Thank you.*

The doorway filled again, a tall militiaman in the nut-brown homespun coat of the Battalion of Free Men of Color. Another limp form hung over his shoulder.

To Dr. Rousseau he said, *"Pris un dans l'estomac."*

"Mousquet?" Hannah asked. *"Carabine?"*

The soldier looked at her for the first time. *"Baïonnette."*

In a firm voice, one she had not had to use now for a very long time, Hannah replied, "We will take care of him now. You can go."

"You understand soldiers," Dr. Rousseau said to her later. "All they want are clear orders."

When the buglers called retreat some three or four hours later, Hannah went out into the night to lean against a rough wall and clear her head. She stayed there for a half hour, watching the troops pulling back, gathering what information she could by listening to scraps of conversation.

Jackson's offensive had taken the British completely by surprise, and he had pressed his advantage. Now, with the fog so heavy, the fighting had been suspended and he withdrew his men to the Rodriquez Canal—Hannah tried to remember if Dr. Rousseau had pointed that landmark out to her—and would dig in there for the next battle.

Some of the troops were going back to the city. They drifted down the Levee Road, their voices warping and weaving together in the fog, loud and soft. Now and then a bit of rough laughter, or a shout as friends caught sight of each other. The men were exhausted but too satisfied to give in to it, in the way of men who had won a battle they had been expected to lose. Telling each other jokes at the expense of the British, who had been caught looking the other way and pounded to dust by the *Carolina*.

If not for the fog, Hannah heard more than once. *If not for the fog we would have sent the Rosbeefs back to the Gulf once and for all.*

Dr. Rousseau had gone back to the city with one of the wounded, and in the cabin Père Tomaso sat beside a still form, the young man who had taken a bayonet to his belly and bled to death before they could do anything for him. Giles Hermange, the son of a barber, twenty-one years old. Père Tomaso knew the family well, and he would take the boy home to them.

Of the six men they had treated, three had been able to walk away once their wounds were cleaned and bound. To Hannah's relief and surprise, they had not done a single amputation, and the only serious wound left was the young Choctaw. She wondered about the other troops, if they had come away so easily.

There had been no word of Luke or Ben.

Hannah went to the water barrel in the corner and drank from her cupped hands, splashed her face and rubbed her eyes. She offered the dipper to Père Tomaso and watched him drink, thinking that she could go back to the city now, and sleep in her own bed. In Ben Savard's bed. She wondered how much Ben had told the priest, and found the idea irritated her more than it should have.

She turned at a sound. Juzan and the Choctaws crowded into the cabin, all of them at once, to stand around the table. The war chief looked at Hannah.

"He will live?"

Hannah believed he would, and said so. If the Choctaw

could carry their brother to the little clinic, she would look after him there tonight. Tomorrow he would likely be well enough to rejoin them.

Two of the warriors picked him up at a flick of the war chief's finger. They filed out, one by one, leaving Captain Juzan behind for a moment. He studied Hannah for a moment, as if he wasn't sure what to say.

"You're taking him back to your camp," volunteered the priest.

Juzan gave a weary grin, and nodded.

Hannah said, "I thought you might. Bring him to me if he gets worse." And: "What of Ben and Luke?"

Juzan looked over his shoulder. "They'll be along," he said. "Soon. Père Tomaso, Dr. Bonner. Thank you." He touched his cap and disappeared into the fog.

The jangling of a harness announced the arrival of a mule cart. The priest went out to greet the driver, and together they moved Giles Hermange to the wagon bed.

Père Tomaso gave Hannah a kind smile. "I fear we'll see each other again." Because of course this had only been the beginning. There would be another battle, and another, until one side or the other surrendered. He had been an excellent assistant, quick to understand, nimble in his reactions, and able to stay out of the way.

She said, "You were a great help. Thank you."

"I go where I'm needed," he said. "Of course that's not always where I'm wanted."

Hannah felt herself flush. She turned her face away and then back again. "I would be glad to have you assist at any time."

He studied her for a moment, and nodded. Then Hannah stood in the doorway and watched the mule cart go. When the sound of its wheels on the gravel path had faded away, she found the fur-lined cape that she had cast aside when she had been hard at work and hot, and pulled it around herself. She thought of Ben's mother, who had worn these clothes. Spattered with dirt and blood, the fine beadwork on the moccasins obscured by mud. She would scrape the fine doeskin clean, dry and brush the moccasins, and then she would fold all of it neatly and return everything to Ben Savard.

Unless he didn't come. In that case she could sleep right here on the pallet, if the slaves had no objection to her staying the rest of the night. She wondered where Mose had gone, if he was asleep somewhere.

Hannah went to the door and then out into the night, still heavy with fog.

She walked first down the slave row to the point where the fields started. The lantern that hung from a nail on the wall of the last cabin still burned, casting a solid oval of light sharply defined at its edges by the fog. The fields rolled away from where she stood, like waves from a ship. Hannah turned and walked in the other direction until she came to the levee, where she stood in the shadows and watched the troops withdrawing.

These men were quieter, and moved with a certain weariness that made little sense until Hannah realized that these were prisoners being marched back to the city under guard. The guard that walked with them held weapons at the ready, and more soldiers on horseback before and after. A half dozen men carried torches to light the way. In that flickering light she caught a flash of color now and then, a faded red coat or an epaulette that sparked in the firelight, half torn from a shoulder. A bloody cloth pressed to a cheek, muddy boots, forage caps. She stood and watched for a quarter hour until the last of the men had disappeared from sight, and caught not one glimpse of a blond head.

When she turned, Ben Savard and her brother were

coming toward her, moving out of the fog into the feeble
light of the lantern she had left outside the cabin as a guide.
They moved easily, long strides, heads swiveling as they
went, still alert and aware and, above all, alive.

Ben was looking at her, his eyes tracing her shape as if
she were the one who had just fought a battle and might be
injured. As if she were his to worry about. The way she was
looking at him, taking his measure: no obvious wounds, his
face and hands blackened by gunpowder, his smile all the
brighter by contrast.

No blood shed. A man back from battle full of life.

They stopped in front of her.

"I see you managed to keep out of trouble," she said. Her
voice trembled a little.

Luke said, "I'm off away home, or Jennet will have my
skin for letting her worry. Do you have your things?"

Hannah glanced at the cabin. "Not quite—"

"I'll go ahead, then," Luke said, casting a quick sidelong
glance at Ben. "You two take your time."

And he disappeared into the fog and dark at a trot.
Hannah had the sense he would run all the way back to the
city and Jennet.

To Ben she said, "How—" and stopped, because he
caught her up against him with one strong movement, his
arm curling around her waist as hard and certain as a grap-
pling hook. She was pressed against his chest and Ben had
lowered his head to hers, his mouth so close to her own that
when he spoke she felt the shape of the words on her lips.

"I was hoping you'd wait."

He kissed her then, both arms closing around her, pulling
her up against his chest, lifting her off the ground. Hannah
kissed him back, drawing in his smells, gunpowder and
grease and riprière, a faint tinge of blood, and the oils on his
skin. She had forgot how it was, how a man came off the

battlefield smelling like this, as if in the rush and tumult he must sweat out his very essence. *I am alive.*

In the cabin, with the door closed, she said, "Let me see your shoulder," and he laughed at her. There was some blood and a tear in his shirt, but he laughed like a boy without worries or responsibilities. What he wanted from her had nothing to do with medicine.

She could stop him with a word, but could not think of what that word might be. Hannah let herself be drawn down to the pallet, where she might have been frightened or anxious, but she could only laugh herself, caught up in this surplus of energy, the promise of relief.

He was so alive, so full of motion, so intent, as if she were a lesson he had set himself to learn. The texture of the skin below her ear, the taste of her sweat. Her blood ran cold and hot and cold again, fear getting the upper hand.

Ben took her head between his palms and pressed his forehead to hers and whispered.

"We're here together, Hannah. Walks-Ahead. You and me and nobody else. You," his mouth moved against her skin. "You and me and nobody else. You take what you want, and leave the rest."

That made her laugh out loud. "And if I want nothing at all?" He was hugely aroused, as hard as hickory, bursting with need.

"Then we sleep," he said. He kissed her on the cheek, the kiss of a solicitous friend, a proper older brother. But he was not her brother, and Hannah could not pretend he was, had no wish to force that role on him or on herself. She turned her head so that their mouths met, and she kissed him the way she wanted to be kissed. He was a man who could take direction and turn it to his advantage.

Her body responded, and her mind followed along. Ben

Savard had come from a battle where he had fought for his life, where he had killed in order to come back to her. And hadn't she done the same, the very same thing, come back from a place where she might have died, from that night when a different man had tried to break her.

The kiss deepened, turned, flexed, flowed back and forth between them. She had missed kisses like this, she had missed this man's touch.

Ben pulled away, his gaze sharpening as he examined her face. Then he kissed her again, the kiss she didn't want, brotherly, chaste. He rolled over onto his back so that only their hands touched.

He said, "I felt the memory come back to you. Your whole body went cold."

Hannah tried to gather the words that might make him understand. In the end she gave him the simplest truth.

"I am glad," she said. "I'm glad that he never kissed me."

Ben was very silent, his gaze fixed on the ceiling. Then he turned on his side toward her, and cupped her face with his hand.

"I'm glad, too," he said. He let one hand rest on the plane of her belly, his fingers lightly curled. And: "When you are ready," he said. "I am here. I will be here until you send me away."

In the minutes it took her to fall asleep Hannah thought about that, about the idea of sending Ben Savard away. How such a thing might be done, and what the world would be without him.

CHAPTER 47

Dear Mother, dear Brother,

I write this letter on the evening of the twenty-third
of December from New Orleans. Know first that I
am well in body and mind, as are all I love who are
here with me: my husband Luke, my guid-sister
Hannah, and my son Nathaniel.

There are no preparations for the Yule this
evening. Instead I sit in comfort and relative safety in
the home of good friends who have provided for us
these last months as though we were blood kin. Dr.
Paul Savard, a surgeon and his guid-wife Julia, their
daughter Rachel and their son Henry, who reminds
me of Alasdair at that age, though perhaps not quite
so prone to mischief. The Savards moved here from
New-York a year ago. And the babes are here, too. My
Nathaniel, and another boy just a few days old, called
Adam. I was advised to send them away to someplace
safer, and find I am not able to let them go. And so we
will endure, together.

We sit here trembling in the dark, speaking very
little, for a few miles south of the city the English are
locked in battle with the American forces under
Major General Andrew Jackson. The largest ship of

the American line is called the *Carolina,* and it is the artillery fire from that *Carolina* that fills the world with noise and makes the timbers shake. Like a thousand thunderbolts cast down at once, even at seven miles remove.

Luke, who was in guid health and spirits this morning when last I saw him, has been assigned to a company of foot. All able-bodied men have been called to defend this city from the English invaders. He went gladly, half Scott that he is. And he is a man, forbye, and infected as all men are with the need to tear down the world now and then so that they may play at building it up again afterward.

Hannah is somewhere near the front lines in a field hospital, one where the free men of color and the Indians who have joined the fight might find a capable doctor to see to their wounds. Hannah has been ill, but I believe her now on the road to recovery. She has paid dearly for her kindnesses to me, and sacrificed more than should be asked of any woman. And should I live another hundred years I could never repay her, who is more than a sister to me.

You see in some ways I am no changed at all. I still own what is in my heart, without regard for what a lady may properly say.

This is a strange place, my dears. Beautiful in its exotic way, as green and lush as a kingdom in a faery tale with flowers blossoming through a warm winter and birds as colorful as rainbows filling trees hung with moss. For all its beauty I could never make a home here. The people are a mystery to me. Most especially I can make no sense of the Creoles, for so call themselves the class of citizens who are descended from the first French settlers. They can be

so generous and kind to a stranger in need—as they
have been to us—and so very cruel to those who live
among them.

Hannah resides here at the Savards' clinic, but Luke
and I are staying with a Creole family, Mr. and Mrs.
Edward Livingston, important people in New
Orleans and well respected. Their home is always full
of family and friends who crowd the common rooms
and eat well and warm themselves before the fire and
laugh and sing and talk. I don't think it too much to
say when I tell you that Mr. Livingston saved our lives
by interceding on our behalf in a legal matter I won't
trouble to relate now, for simple fear of boring you.
Like her husband, Mrs. Livingston has shown us every
kindness. And still I don't know them at all.

Last week I saw Mr. Livingston on the street, and
behind him walked three men chained together,
wrists and ankles. He had just bought the men from
the slave market, and at a good price, I heard him tell
his lady that evening. New Orleans is under martial
law and all business has suffered, but the slave traders
most especially, who cannot move their goods (so
they call them) but must still see that they are kept fed
and warm lest their value decrease. Mr. Livingston's
concern was all for the strains the war is putting on
the city's businesses, and no a thought for the human
chattel. Luke calculates that the whole economic
welfare of this city and state rests at its heart on the
buying and selling of human beings.

You'll be wondering if there are slaves in the
Livingstons' household. There are seven, two who
came from the islands with Mrs. Livingston's family
when they fled the revolution, though they might
have stayed behind free women. The slaves are treated
well as far as I can see. And yet they are still slaves.

The artillery fire is so relentless that my head has begun to throb in time with the explosions.

You will note I have written nothing of the year I lost to Anselme Dégre, and perhaps you are disappointed. But I will not put that story down on paper. Unless I were to then burn the pages and watch the embers climb into the sky. The Savards' housekeeper is a wise woman called Clémentine, and she believes that fire cleanses and heals.

It is commonly known that Major General Jackson will burn New Orleans to the ground before he allows the English to take it. The citizens of New Orleans are frightened. Most especially the planters who have filled the storehouses along the river with their cotton and sugar are in a state of high agitation. I am frightened, for myself, for my husband and guid-sister, for these friends. For the babes, who greet at the noise and look to us for comfort. My son, my beautiful son, who was taken from me but is now restored, he looks at me with tears on his cheeks, so unsettled is he by the noise. And there is naught I can do for him. And were he old enough to understand, what words of comfort could I offer?

If the city does burn, they will rebuild it. The fine houses and the slave market, and the cottages where the free people of color raise their families. We will not be here to see it happen. By then we will be safe away, and long settled.

I fear this letter is aye melancholy, and so perhaps it is no bad thing that post to Europe must be held until the war is over.

It was my purpose, when I sat down to write, to distract myself. We sit here in Dr. Savard's clinic, waiting for the first of the wounded. You will find it odd, but I have learned a great deal of medicine and assist now wherever I am needed. Most often I work with Hannah in the surgery. Tonight she had to go without me. May God guide her hand and keep her safe.

Finally I am writing to tell you that we have adopted an infant, a few days old. The boy Adam I mentioned earlier in this letter. His father and mother are both missing, and are perhaps dead. It will come as a surprise to Luke, when he returns from battle, to find two babes where yesterday there was only one, but I know his generous and open nature, and I trust he will love this new son with all his heart.

And now I will close until tomorrow, and put this letter away carefully so that I may write more when the battle is done.

Yours aye,
Jennet

CHAPTER 48

At first light, Hannah and Ben walked back to the city to be greeted at the clinic door with the news that Luke was in the little clinic.

"He left the battlefield without a scratch," Hannah said, her alarm making her voice rise.

Paul Savard said, "Someone took a shot at him just as he was coming into the city. He never saw who it was."

He exchanged a glance with his brother, one that wasn't lost on Hannah but would have to be examined later.

"Tell me," she said.

"He was lucky," the doctor told her. "Either the gun misfired or it was poorly loaded, and the bullet deflected off a wagon before it struck him. He's got a back full of splinters. Nothing life-threatening." And: "Unless Jennet's temper gets the best of her."

Hannah took leave of Ben with a flutter of her hand and went to the surgery, where Luke lay prone on the table, his back bared for treatment. Julia stood at one side with tweezers and a scalpel, and Jennet on the other with a bowl of water. Julia said, "This isn't as bad as it looks."

Luke grunted.

"Or as it feels," Julia added. "Would you like to take over?"

"Please no," said Luke. "She'll torture me to death."

Jennet snorted. "Listen to him whinging like a babe in arms. For splinters and a wee bit of blood."

Hannah cast Jennet a sidelong glance. Her fright had given way to anger, and now Luke must bear the brunt of it.

It took Hannah a moment to take full measure of the wounds, but when she was satisfied that Paul Savard hadn't been minimizing the damage, she went to Jennet directly and put a hand on her shoulder.

"There will be scarring, but nothing here is very deep. If there's another battle tomorrow he'll probably insist on rushing off to join it. I will take over if you like, Julia."

Julia left to see to other patients, and Hannah settled at Luke's side with the tray of instruments.

"One of you should just hit me on the head with the hammer," Luke said. "Get it over with."

"What would be the fun in that?" Jennet asked.

There was silence while Hannah worked. A clink as a bit of shot was deposited in a basin, and then Jennet washed away the blood. Luke drew in a hissing breath, and the process repeated itself. Hannah pulled a half dozen long splinters that had dug into the muscle, and a few bits of shot. When she was almost finished, Luke roused himself.

"Not tomorrow." His voice came muffled, because he had buried his head in his arms. "No battle tomorrow."

"Is that so?" Jennet said dryly. "You made your wishes clear to both sides, then?"

He turned his head very slightly and shot her an aggravated look. "The English are still bringing in troops and artillery—"

"By all means, let's wait for the Sassenach to get themselves organized," Jennet said.

"—and our fortifications are weak. Jackson's got every slave in a hundred-mile radius and most of the free men, too, militia and regular army, out there on the Rodriquez Canal."

Jennet made a humming noise deep in her throat. Hannah dug for a splinter and Luke jerked.

To distract Jennet, Hannah asked her about the rest of the wounded. It turned out that there had been twenty-four killed in battle and just over a hundred wounded, only half of those seriously, and that the army surgeons and the city hospital had absorbed them all. Even the captured British—and there were many—had been easily accommodated, the officers taken in by the first families.

"There are many hundreds dead on the other side," Jennet said. "The *Carolina* did serious damage. And then there are those who managed to survive the battles and come home wounded nonetheless."

Luke pushed out a sigh that gave way to a low yip as Hannah got hold of the splinter and pulled. When she had finished he turned his head toward Jennet, reached out, and grabbed her by the wrist.

"Oi," said Jennet, but she let herself be drawn down so she was face-to-face with her husband. Luke looked her directly in the eye for a long moment.

"Now listen to me," he said in a soft and dangerous voice. "I am not badly wounded. I will not die. I'm not going to recount every step I took in battle so you can torture yourself with what might have happened, but didn't. So stop asking."

Then he darted forward to kiss her firmly before he let her go.

He turned his upper body so he could see Hannah more directly, and he gave her a grim smile.

Hannah said, "The worst is over."

"Good," Luke said, and turned onto his stomach again.

Hannah said, "I need some water, Jennet, if you would."

"Of course." She took the ewer and paused at the door. "Would you care for tea?" Her tone had turned conciliatory, and a bit shy.

"I'd prefer whisky, but tea will do," Luke said.

"Well, then," Jennet said. "I'll see to it." And she closed the door after herself quietly.

After a moment Hannah said, "She's been coping with a lot, Luke. She's terrified at the idea of you going back into battle."

He gave a soft grunt. "It's not so easy for me, either. For all I know she'll go out and find another infant to adopt while I'm gone."

Hannah paused. She hadn't been in the room when Jennet told Luke about Jacinthe and the child, and this was the first mention he made of it to her.

"You don't want the boy?"

He jerked impatiently. "I didn't say that."

"But?"

"I'm uneasy about it."

Hannah sat down next to him on a low stool so she could look him in the face. "Why?"

"Because," Luke said, "I intend to kill the boy's father just as soon as I can track him down."

Hannah kept losing sight of the fact that it was Christmas Eve, but Clémentine did not. There was a goose for dinner, and potatoes and peppered turnips mashed with cream, and greens cooked with bacon and onions, and bread warm from the oven.

She found she had an appetite. They all did, crowded around the Savards' table. Everyone was here but Ben, who had gone back to his company after seeing Hannah to the clinic.

"He didn't like to go," Rachel said, looking directly at Hannah. "He had no choice."

Hannah tried to look as if this news were of no particular importance to her. She was not so sure of Ben Savard or her own feelings and loath to have the subject raised, even in the company of such good friends and family.

"I could come with you next time," young Henry was saying. "I would be a great help in the field hospital."

"Of course you would," said Hannah, and: "Of course you cannot," said Henry's mother and father in unison.

"I don't understand what went wrong," Rachel said. "The British seemed so formidable."

"They are formidable," said her stepfather. "But they also suffered from the sin of hubris."

Henry's face contorted as he tried to make sense of the word. "Do you mean they're too big for their britches?"

"Yes," said Paul Savard. "That's exactly what I mean. They underestimated an enemy, which is the height of foolishness. I only hope they go on as they started."

"That would serve us well," Luke agreed. "But they're waiting for a new commanding officer."

"Let's hope he's no more competent than the one he's replacing," said Rachel.

"Do you know who it is?" asked Julia.

Luke paused, and then he answered. "The information that we have from the prisoners of war isn't reliable."

"And?" said Paul Savard. "What name have they given?"

"Pakenham," Luke said.

Hannah saw Dr. Savard's surprise give way to disquiet. "Wellington's brother-in-law? Salamanca?"

"Yes," said Luke. Now everyone was paying attention, looking from Paul to Luke and back again, waiting for some explanation. After a moment's hesitation Luke said, "Most of the regulars and the dragoons are still at de la Ronde's to keep an eye on the enemy."

That was little comfort, but it seemed enough to soothe Rachel, who went back to her food with a sigh.

Her stepfather exchanged a long look with Luke. "Well, then," he said. "I expect there's no joy in the British camp today, after such a pitiful showing as they provided last night."

Hannah caught Luke's eye, and wasn't much comforted by the doubt she saw there.

·   ·   ·

The weather was fine, and so after dinner they went for a walk, Hannah and Jennet and Luke. Rachel and Henry joined them, the boy hopping like a flea in his excitement, ever hopeful for more news of last night's battle, now that his mother wasn't there to interfere. They left Adam with Julia and Paul, who intended a quiet afternoon of reading between visits to the clinic, and took Nathaniel, who sat tucked into the crook of his father's arm, surveying the world like a small emperor wrapped in shawls, his cheeks pink with cold.

Jennet was glad to be out-of-doors, glad of the sun and the clear cool air and the fact that they were together and healthy. For the moment, at least, she could pretend there was no war and nothing wrong in the world.

She thought of the letter she had been writing to her mother and brother, and resolved to add more to it this evening: the good news there was to share, and what it was like to be in New Orleans on Christmas Eve less than twenty-four hours since Jackson had led them to victory in their first battle with the British.

The street vendors were out in full force among the crowds, selling pralines and gingerbread and cake, pickled peppers and eggs. An elderly man with no teeth at all fed the fire beneath a great pot of simmering punch, while a younger man with eyes the exact same shade of green filled a tin cup which could be emptied for a coin.

Henry said, "Oh, I remember that punch."

"As if Mother would let you near it." Rachel laughed.

Luke bought a cupful and drank it down. He flushed a deep red as he handed the cup back and the vendor winked at him.

"Two more of those and you'd have to carry me home," he said.

News of Jackson's activity was to be had on every corner

where militiamen stood together. Apparently most of their number had been held back at the Rodriguez Canal to strengthen entrenchments along its line from the river to the ciprière and to assist the engineers, who were to cut the levee in front of Chalmette's plantation and flood the plain between the two armies.

"Little good it will do with the river so low," she heard one man say to another.

"It can't hurt," said his companion.

Generally the militia seemed to be in good spirits and determined to make the most of the free afternoon before they returned to the Chalmette plantation to take up the backbreaking work that would keep them busy through Christmas Day.

"I plan to report back this evening," Luke said, as though Jennet had asked the question aloud.

There was a set to his jaw that she recognized. She could argue with him now in public and lose, or argue with him later in private and lose. She decided that she didn't care to ruin their walk, and kept her thoughts to herself.

They stopped to watch a pantomime done by men in colorful papier-mâché half masks in a rapid Creole French that had the crowd howling with laughter. Rachel listened only for a moment before dragging a disappointed Henry away, and then consoled him by buying him a piece of candied ginger.

By the time they had worked their way to the river, young Nathaniel's good mood had begun to sour. Jennet judged that in another half hour he would be howling for the breast, and was about to announce the need to start back when they were overtaken by a river of men streaming down from the Levee Road.

"More militia," said Luke. "Just arrived, and look, half of them don't even have a musket."

In the last hour Jennet had managed to banish the idea of

the war to some point far away, much further than the seven miles to the British encampment. But here it was again, come to claim her attention: men newly arrived and ready to fight. Most of them, it looked to Jennet, more in need of a meal and clothing than they were of weapons. They wore ragged hunting shirts and deerskin leggings and a variety of hats, from old tricornes to fur caps. Rough men who would not complain about the hard conditions at the Rodriquez Canal. In passing, she wondered how they would like being handed shovels and set to work alongside slaves.

Henry said, "Look, that man is wearing a whole raccoon on his head," and Jennet laughed out loud because she must. The baby produced a deep belly laugh out of simple camaraderie.

The river of men flowed by and past them, and they continued up onto the Levee Road where they could see the traffic on the river, crowded even now with every kind of boat. The keelboats that had brought the militiamen down the long length of the river rocked and fought against their mooring ropes. They would be broken up for firewood or building lumber. To Jennet's Scots sensibilities it seemed a sinful waste of wood, but in the United States trees were as plentiful and everlasting as the clouds in the sky.

Jennet was standing between Hannah and Luke and she felt them both tense at the same moment that she caught sight of two last men jumping from a keelboat to the dock. Then Hannah bolted, running like a girl, and Luke's face split into a smile.

He turned the baby in the direction of the keelboat and pointed. "There," he said. "There comes the grandfather you were named for, and your great-uncle Runs-from-Bears."

Nathaniel Bonner had been born in the endless forests of New-York State in the fourth year of the nine-year war between the French and the British for possession of the North American continent. Which made him, to Jennet's reckoning, fifty-six years old. Though she had never asked Runs-from-Bears how old he was—he was far too imposing a figure to bother with such things—she believed the two men to be of an age. Though it was true that one was a full-blood Kahnyen'kehàka of the Turtle Clan and the other of pure Scots extraction, the two men had been cast from the same mold. They looked nothing like the men of Carryck in their dress or even in the way they held their weapons, but the sight of them gave her a sense of homecoming.

Henry made a small, choked sound. Jennet had forgot about the boy and his sister for a long moment, but turned now to see their expressions. For once Henry was stunned into silence. Rachel was trying harder to look nonchalant, and failing completely. No one had thought to tell them about Runs-from-Bears, and now Jennet remembered what she had felt on first seeing him. He had very black eyes that never seemed to blink; the dark skin stretched tight over heavy cheekbones was pox-scarred, and a line of tattoos stretched over the bridge of his nose to his temples. Silver earrings dangled from his ears, and there were feathers braided into his hair, which was still full black. He looked nothing like the Indians Jennet had seen in New Orleans or Pensacola. And then there was the matter of his weapons. Both men were armed with rifles, pistols, knives, tomahawks, and war clubs.

"No cause for concern," Jennet said to Henry. "You'll see, they're the kindest men ever put on earth."

Henry said, "Will he let me touch his tomahawk?"

Rachel started to answer him, but Jennet shook her head at the girl. She said, "You'll have to ask him."

Henry glanced up at her, his eyes wide. "He speaks English?"

"He does," Jennet said. "Now I must go say hello, and then I'll introduce you."

As a girl Hannah had been given to tears, a weakness she had disliked and schooled out of herself as she grew into womanhood. She had done such a thorough job of it that even at times tears would have been a blessing she found she could not call them forth. She had buried her son with dry eyes and steady hands, kissed his cold cheek one last time and turned away for the long walk home.

But with her father, here on the Levee Road in New Orleans on a chill Christmas afternoon, she found she was a daughter first. She stood in front of her father, trembling, and when he put his arms around her she collapsed against him as though she were not more than thirty years, hardened by loss and desperation and pain.

Against her hair he said, "Daughter, it is good to see you."

Hannah had no words of her own, and so she stood and listened as he spoke to her in her own language, the language of the Wolf Longhouse of the Kahnyen'kehàka, the language that bound them together as surely as blood. She came to realize that her uncle was standing very close, his hand on her shoulder, and Hannah turned a little from her father to look into his face, this uncle she had loved all her life. As a young girl she had hoped to marry him, and then he had married her aunt and that was almost as good, because it meant he would live with them at Lake in the Clouds. Runs-from-Bears, who understood when other adults did not, who took her out tracking and listened to her stories and who now was here, because she was in need. He had come to help, they had both come to help. Hannah realized that her cheeks were wet, and that her eyes stung, and that she had remembered, finally, how to weep.

CHAPTER 49

The holidays were good for business, but war was even better: Every room in Noelle Soileau's establishment was occupied. She herself had given up her room and was sleeping on the divan in her office; the slaves had been turned out to sleep in the stable with the animals.

Mme. Soileau made the rounds of the parlor, filled to bursting with men who waited their turn to climb the stairs. At home wives and children would be waiting to start the Christmas Eve festivities. She knew many of those women by name and reputation, and they knew her, too, though they did not meet her eye when they passed on the street.

Most of her clients had been coming here for years and many of those had a favorite girl, and were willing to wait until she was available. They waited in comfort, drinking smuggled brandy and talking among themselves. About the war, of course. Always about the war.

There were half a dozen officers in uniform scattered throughout the room. A young man in navy blue held up a hand to get her attention and she went to him, leaning over to give him a view of her cleavage and jewels and the full effect of her perfume. A man of this age, denied release for many days, needed little encouragement to wait his turn, but it did no harm to remind him why he was here.

His mouth worked as if he had lost the habit of language.

"How much longer, do you think, madame?" He was speaking French, or trying to, with horrid results.

Noelle considered. The young man was on the verge of passing out, which would mean she had wasted precious space on him. She glanced up at Peter, an able assistant who could read her thoughts quite easily after twenty years. Peter nodded.

This particular officer would find that the next available girl considered him the most intriguing and irresistible of men. His money would find its way into Peter's palm before he climbed the stairs. If he collapsed before he could take what it had bought him, that would be his loss.

Really, she needed more girls. She needed more of everything, from brandy—difficult to get now that Lafitte and his kind had joined the fighting and were neglecting their usual clients' needs—to beds.

She glanced up the stairs to the landing, where Nicole was taking leave of a regular client. Her gown hung open at the front to reveal the shadowy lines of breast and belly and thigh. Nicole saw herself observed, and retreated back into the room that she called her own. Each of the regular girls had a room, outfitted with good furniture and bed linen that was changed often. It was these niceties that kept regular clients like the elderly judge now descending the stairs coming back.

He stopped in front of her and bowed from the shoulders.

"Mme. Soileau. How good to see you again."

As if they met at church every week. Some of the older men liked to keep up the charade.

"Sir, shall we have the pleasure of seeing you again this week?" With all formality and condescension, as he required for his own peace of mind.

Behind their spectacles, the bright brown eyes moved through the parlor, took note of men standing because they had nowhere to sit.

"Perhaps," he said. "When you are not quite so busy."

Noelle inclined her head in acknowledgment of the gentle rebuke.

She must have more space. If she could not renegotiate rental terms with her one permanent guest, she would have to put him out. It was the opportunity she had been anticipating for years, and now she felt her heartbeat quicken. The exchange would require a certain kind of cunning, a good deal of luck, and brandy.

She cast a glance at Peter, who would supervise in her absence, and went up the stairs.

Honoré Poiterin lay on the brocade-covered divan before the hearth in Noelle Soileau's best room—her own room, though few realized that fact—a bottle of brandy in one hand, a glass in the other, and his gaze fixed on the bit of the street he could see through the windows.

The door of the tavern called the Cock and Hen opened and disgorged three men, all in uniform, all unsteady on their feet from drink. Celebrating Christmas in the time-honored fashion by escaping the family for more genial company. One of the men was Philippe Espinoza, a planter with a passion for dice but no head for arithmetic. Honoré had spent many happy evenings with Espinoza, and would have gladly joined him tonight. But Wyndham had sold him out to Jackson, and it would mean hanging if he showed his face in New Orleans.

He would have to stay just where he was until the British took the city.

The only time he ever ventured out was very late at night, in a hooded cape. A calculated risk he took, for fear of simply losing his mind from boredom.

Now he was tempted to sleep, warmed by the fire and the brandy and the meal he had been served by Noelle

Soileau herself. No one else was allowed in this room. There were spies everywhere, as he knew very well. Noelle Soileau herself was a gamble, but a fairly safe one. She knew the value of a bird in the hand, especially one who had just inherited a large family fortune that included two plantations, numerous houses and other real estate, warehouses of cane and cotton stuffed to the rafters, and investments in every lucrative business in a five-hundred-mile radius. After the British took the city there would be more land, and perhaps even enough money to settle his gambling debts.

Unless, of course, the Americans prevailed. It was a thought he did not often entertain. In that case he would have to flee, and once he was safely away he would have to liquidate everything through his lawyers. He could live a comfortable life in the islands, but the arrangements were complex enough to give a man a headache.

He still had the ship he had taken from Bonner in Pensacola, hidden away in a safe harbor thirty miles away. It would be easy enough to pick up a crew, then sail to the Antilles. Now that Dégre was gone from Priest's Town, he could imagine making it his headquarters. There was a fortune to be made in slave running, and the life suited him.

But of course none of this would be necessary. The Americans had no chance against Wellington's army, and New Orleans would change hands again. Better the English than the Americans.

Honoré didn't realize he had dozed off until he heard the door open. He sprang up from the divan as he grabbed for his pistol.

Noelle went very still, one brow raised in censure.

"'Stie d'tabernac," he said. "You gave me a fright."

Noelle inclined her head, as close as she would come to an apology.

Honoré reached for the glass which had rolled off, dribbling brandy over the fine carpet, and picked up the brandy bottle to fill it again. When he had taken a swallow he looked at Noelle, who still stood near the door.

She was an unappetizing sight, far too thin and with a hard mouth and harder eyes, her hair dyed a deep and objectionable red. He preferred darker complexions, and younger women. Honoré had gone without release for too long, but he was not so desperate as to contemplate using Noelle Soileau.

He said, "News of the war?"

"No." She went to the windows and looked out to the street. "I need this room," she said. "I have to ask you to go."

His laughter gave way to a cough. "If you want to raise the rent I won't refuse you."

"I want the room," she said, glancing at him over her shoulder.

Honoré rubbed his mouth with the back of his hand. "Or what?"

She lifted a shoulder and let it drop. He waited for what would come next, her real demand. She delivered it in the same cool tone.

"You will need a widow," she said. "To see to your family's holdings once they hang you."

Honoré coughed for a full minute. When he had regained his breath he found she was studying him as she might study a bug caught in a web.

"You want me to marry you," he said.

"I want to be your legal heir."

"And how do you suppose to find a priest who will marry us?"

A quirk of the mouth. "I have someone in mind. He owes me a favor."

"I'm sure he does," Honoré said darkly. He said, "You are proposing a business arrangement."

"It's not the pleasure of your company I yearn for," said Noelle.

"So we marry," Honoré said. "And then you report me to the authorities and weep prettily at my hanging."

"Think, Poiterin," Noelle said in the voice of an irritated and put-upon teacher. "If I turned you in, I would hang next to you."

That was true. Honoré turned his head away and tried to gather his thoughts. In the worst case—if the British gave up and retreated, and he had to flee—Noelle would try to sell everything and run off with the money. But in some things the law served a man's best interest, and a wife couldn't sell property without her husband's consent and signature. Once he was dead, it wouldn't matter to him who got the Poiterin family fortune, and in the meantime it would secure his position here while he finalized his plans.

He said, "I find the idea of a Christmas-morning wedding in a whorehouse amusing. Call in your priest." And yawning, he turned his attention back to the street.

CHAPTER 50

It was Henry who made the point, and with great insistence, that the new arrivals must come straightaway to meet the rest of the Savard family, and so they started back. A tangle of conversations trailed along behind them, talk of the long journey by keelboat, the war in the north, yesterday's battle, the city, the living arrangements, the clinic, the Livingstons, Jackson, the British. Other subjects hung in the air, too sensitive to be raised on a public street: Kit Wyndham, the Poiterins.

Henry commanded everyone's attention by telling the story of how his uncle Ben had rescued young Nathaniel and saved Hannah's life.

Hannah saw her father and brother exchange glances, and the communication that passed between them. *Who is this Ben Savard?* her father's glance said, and her brother's: *The boy is telling the truth.*

But Ben was away, Hannah reminded herself, with his company. He might be back tonight or tomorrow or next week, and that would be time enough for him to meet Nathaniel Bonner and Runs-from-Bears. By that time perhaps she would even have figured out for herself what there was to tell.

And then they came into the courtyard and found Clémentine in a temper, her whole body bent forward from the waist as she poked Ben Savard in the chest with a long, hard finger and scolded him in Creole.

Ben glanced over at them, his expression torn between resignation and indulgent good humor and then giving way immediately to surprise. Clémentine's gaze followed his a moment later and her lecture cut off abruptly.

"Nobody gets the best of Clémentine," Henry said in the sudden silence, his tone matter-of-fact. "Not even Uncle Ben."

"Friends," Julia said a half hour later, looking back and forth between Nathaniel and Runs-from-Bears. "Of course you must stay here with us. We are honored to have you in our home and at our table."

Hannah could have cleared up the confusion with a few words: Her father and uncle were not used to cities and would much prefer to sleep rough someplace in the open; it had nothing to do with social niceties. To Julia, who was plainspoken, she might even have been able to say such a thing and not be misunderstood.

"We don't want to intrude on your family Christmas," said Nathaniel, and Rachel sighed audibly, which earned her a glance from her mother.

Paul Savard said, "My wife is a Quaker, and we follow her custom in the matter of Christmas."

"One day is no more holy than another," added Julia.

"But we still have to eat," Henry said. "And Clémentine—"

"Henry," Paul and Julia said in one voice.

The boy hung his head, scowling.

"I'm a little late this year going out to get the turkey," Ben said to Nathaniel. His tone was easy and straightforward, a man still unsure of another but inclined to friendliness. "With the war and all."

"Is that so?" said Nathaniel. "You have turkeys in these parts?"

The question surprised and outraged Henry. "Great big ones," he said. "Bigger than anywhere else in the whole world."

"Well, now. I'd like to see what a Louisiana turkey looks like," said Nathaniel. "What about you, Bears?"

Runs-from-Bears said, "Been a while since we had fresh meat. And I'd like to get out, stretch my legs. If it wouldn't be an imposition, us coming along." He looked directly at Ben when he said this, and Ben did what was called for. He invited Hannah's father and uncle and brother to join him. It would be a matter of three hours at the most.

On her way out of the room, Jennet put a soothing hand on Hannah's shoulder. "If you weren't sure of his bravery before," she said, "you must know now that Ben Savard is not a man to run from a challenge."

Reluctantly, Jennet went back to the Livingstons', though what she would have liked best was to join the men. Luke had seen the longing in her expression when he kissed her good-bye.

"It's about more than Christmas turkeys," he said, casting a glance at Ben Savard.

That her father-in-law wanted some time to examine Ben was understandable, and even, Jennet had to admit at least to herself, her own fault. She had not exactly said anything about Hannah and Ben. Or at least, she had not meant to say anything.

And so she went back to the Livingstons' with Rachel, who was to help with the preparations for the Christmas party. The babies were swept away immediately for baths, and Jennet found herself cornered by the Livingstons, who had heard about the newcomers.

"I don't know why I didn't make the connection before," said Mr. Livingston with some amazement. "I grew up listening to stories about the elder Mr. Bonner—he was called Hawkeye, I believe."

"My father-in-law's father," Jennet said.

Suddenly Mr. Livingston's smile reminded her of Henry's, it was so open and boyish.

"And you met this Hawk-Eye?" asked Mrs. Livingston. She handled the name gingerly, and in two distinct parts, as though such measures might protect her from it biting.

"Och, aye," said Jennet. "They came to Scotland when I was a lass. Hawkeye and my father were first cousins."

"You married a cousin," said Mrs. Livingston.

"A second cousin, once removed," Jennet agreed.

"Now that I didn't know," said the lawyer. "That Hawkeye was first cousin to a Scots earl."

"I am sure there are many things you don't know about this Hawk-Eye," said Mrs. Livingston. "For myself I am more interested in his son. The report we heard this afternoon is that he is traveling with an Indian."

"Hannah's uncle," Jennet said. "He's a Mohawk called Runs-from-Bears. The two families have lived next to each other for more than fifty years."

"Mohawk?" Mrs. Livingston glanced at her husband.

"Defunct, for the most part," he said with a shrug that irritated Jennet to the point of saying more than she should.

"Runs-from-Bears is anything but defunct, Mr. Livingston. Ye'd be hard-pressed tae find a better man, or a more capable one. If General Jackson had a hundred like him, the battle for this city wad be ower the morrow."

The lawyer blinked at her. "I meant no offense," he said, a little stiffly.

"Of course you did not," said his wife. "Mrs. Bonner has had a very long and trying day, is that not so, my dear? I'll have something to eat and some tea brought to you in your room."

Jennet left them feeling awkward, and defiant, too. At the door she turned and looked at the Livingstons. She said, "They are my family, all of them. Hannah and Runs-from-Bears and the rest of the Mohawk. I ask only that you respect my feelings about them, no matter how distasteful it may be to you."

Mrs. Livingston herself brought the tray less than a half hour later. The nursemaid had just brought the boys to Jennet, newly bathed and swaddled in sweet-smelling linen, and she had Adam at her breast.

"I am not disturbing?" Mrs. Livingston asked as she put down the tray.

"Please," said Jennet. "Please come in."

There was a moment's awkward silence, punctuated by the steady rhythm of the baby's swallows. Young Nathaniel was alternately mouthing the rattle Runs-from-Bears had made for him and shaking it.

Mrs. Livingston said, "I fear we have been insensitive, and I come to ask your forgiveness."

To that Jennet could think of nothing to say, but Mrs. Livingston went on nonetheless. "You know that we hold you and your husband in great regard."

"You have been more than kind," Jennet said. "You have been the soul of generosity."

Mrs. Livingston stood abruptly. "To be truly generous one must give when giving is most difficult," she said. "Would you be so kind as to give this to your sister-in-law?" She took an envelope from her pocket and put it on the table next to the tray. "It's an invitation to the party tomorrow evening. For all of your family, including the formidable Runs-from-Bears."

"I will deliver it," Jennet said. "And thank you kindly for your thoughtfulness."

She was still thinking about this exchange when Luke came in a half hour later, soaked to the skin, his face bright with color. He looked as alive and happy as she had ever seen him, and she realized now how the troubles of the last months had weighed on him, and that he had never complained.

He said, "By God, I'm hungry. Are you finished with this tray?"

The babies were both asleep in the middle of the bed and so Jennet went to sit across from Luke. She poured him tea while he worked his way through the plate of delicate little sandwiches and told her, in snatches, of the birds they had got. Even Clémentine would be satisfied.

"Ben knows this country," Luke said. It was a typical understated Bonner compliment.

"That surprises you?"

Luke frowned at her. "Of course not. I know what I owe the man. So does my father."

Jennet waited for a moment, feeling Luke's gaze on her. Finally she said, "Will you out with it?"

And he inclined his head. "If it was a test, he passed it. He's got their attention, and they've got his." He gave her a sharp look. "You don't approve?"

"Of Hannah being disappointed again? No, I don't approve. You men may go out into the bush and swear oaths of brotherhood and undying fealty, but the fact remains that she will go home to Lake in the Clouds, and he'll stay behind."

Luke swallowed the last of his tea and held out the cup to her. After a moment he said, "You're sure of that, that he won't leave here?"

"Hannah is sure of it," Jennet said. "Should I not trust her word on it?"

"A woman in love?" Luke said. "I wouldn't trust her to know right from left."

When she had seen her father and uncle settled for the night, Hannah retired not to the cot in the little clinic, but to Ben's apartment. It was cold and damp, and it took many minutes until she could manage to set fire to the kindling. Then she laid the splits of oak, and when she was satisfied with her handiwork, Hannah wrapped herself in a blanket and sat before the hearth, half dozing in its warmth, waiting for something she couldn't bring herself to put into words.

Hannah dreamed of home, of snowdrifts that reached the eaves, and a full moon as bright as the sun. She dreamed of the Christmas party by the shores of Half Moon Lake, and bonfires that reflected in the ice and on the faces of children who chased each other in circles. In her sleep she could smell the fires, and the hot punch, and the gunpowder that sent the firework rockets up into the sky where they sputtered and blossomed in colors too bright for nature, but close enough to touch.

She woke to the sound of rain on the roof. She had no sense of how late it might be, and no wish to move, even to the comfort of the bed. It seemed clear now that Ben would not come to her this night, not even to take leave. It was not a habit she liked especially, his slipping away so quietly.

The cathedral bells chimed and she counted the number of strikes: ten o'clock. And as the sound faded away, she heard the step on the stair, and then the door opened.

Ben held a saucer with a candle stub that smoked and sputtered, casting shadows over his face.

"I thought you were gone again," Hannah said.

He came in and put the saucer on the table, folded his long frame onto the stool next to it, and leaned forward, his elbows on his knees and his hands dangling.

She said, "Did my father and uncle scare you off?"

At that he gave her a wide smile. "They tried in their own way. Hard as they come, those two."

For a moment they looked at each other across the room. Hannah felt herself flushing with irritation and impatience.

"You came to say good-bye?" Sharper than she meant it to sound, but he wasn't put off.

"I agitate you."

"You irritate me."

"Imagine what I could do if I came any closer."

Hannah turned her face away but couldn't help smiling. "You dissemble. You should go, if you are going."

"You want me to go?"

She shot him a look over her shoulder. "Why do you put words in my mouth?"

"Because you won't say what you're thinking." He came closer, crouching down so they were face-to-face, and she found herself turning, almost as by magic, back to face him. He leaned against her knees, brought his face so close she could feel the warmth of his breath on her face.

"What are you saying, Hannah? Tell me what you want."

"Right at this moment," Hannah said, and she hated the tremble in her voice, "right at this moment I want to slap you."

She wanted to raise her hand to him, it was true. Her whole body shook with the need.

He said, "I'll take what I can get."

It seemed to her later that her arm had come up of its own accord. Her palm struck his cheek with a sound like a door slamming and his head jerked hard to the side. At the same moment his own hand came up and caught her wrist in a grasp that was gentle but unyielding.

He was looking at her so steadily, his strange blue-green

eyes full of things she couldn't name, was afraid to acknowledge.

She said, "I am so weary of leaving people behind."

He drew her forward and kissed the corner of her mouth. "Tell me what you want," he said. "Hannah love, tell me what you want."

"I want to go home," Hannah said, each word hard as a pebble in her mouth. "I want to go home with my people. I want to be safe again, and away from this place."

She meant to hurt him, but what she saw in his expression was understanding.

Hannah said, "I want to feel whole again." And for the second time that day she began to weep. Terrible great sobs that tore her throat and made every muscle cramp. She bowed forward with the pain of it, fell forward out of her chair and let herself be caught up by Ben, cradled in his arms. Hannah pressed her face against his shoulder and shuddered with weeping, wave after wave that poured out of her and into him, and he took it all without hesitation.

When the worst had passed and she had nothing left but small, sharp breaths, other things came to her attention. His hand cupping her head, the fingers threaded through her hair, the muscled shoulder under his shirt, the curve of his arm around her. The warmth of his breath, and the intensity of his regard. Like a doctor keeping watch over a patient poised on the cusp, facing the shadowlands.

She wanted to say things to him. She wanted to thank him, but she could not think why. Most of all she wanted to ask him to stay with her, now and through the night and beyond. Instead she felt herself slipping away into sleep.

Ben picked her up and carried her to the bed, where he covered her and smoothed her hair and murmured words in a language she didn't know. Maybe he was praying over her, or telling her things he feared she wouldn't like to hear. Half asleep, she found no energy to ask. Not even when he stripped down and got into bed with her, his skin warm against hers, could she remember how to make words into questions.

When she woke, minutes or hours later, they were lying face-to-face and Ben Savard was asleep. In the low glow from the dying fire his expression was relaxed, a man who had earned his sleep and had nothing to fear about the day to come. Hannah studied him, the curve of his jaw and cheekbone, the strong brows over deep-set eyes, the line of his nose, and beneath it, the shape of his mouth. There was a small sickle-shaped scar on his chin she had never noticed before, and his lips were dry, as though he had had a fever, or spent many hours in deep cold.

He was beautiful. She could see that and admit it to herself in this moment, in the warmth of a shared bed. He was everything, and she could not stay here with him. But at this moment they were together.

Hannah touched his lower lip with her finger, very lightly.

He opened his eyes and smiled at her.

A world of dark and warm wet, of sliding slick skin and leaping nerves. Deep kisses, a gentle suckling, the touch of tongues. She took it all in as if she had never before lain with a man, learning tastes and textures. The rasp of new beard, the smooth surface of a tooth, the inner lining of his lip.

Like silk, she told him. *Like butter on the tongue.*

His hand slid low, curious fingers parting her flesh.

Like the core of you.

She put her nose to his throat and tasted sweat, salty sweet. Ran her tongue up to his ear and nipped.

She bites. Talking to himself. A deep note of laughter, rumbling up through his torso. A growling, like a cat at play. She pressed her teeth against his skin to feel the thrumming flow of blood, the beat of his heart.

On her tongue his skin tasted of colors beloved above all others: goldenrod, sienna, ocher. The dark ruffle of his hair. A lion of a man. He wound around her purring deep in his chest, and she opened to him, drew him in and in until she was filled to overflowing, and whole.

Afterwards she began to shake. In fear or relief or both, her whole body trembled, wrapped as she was in his arms. His chin on her shoulder, his chest pressed to her back. At her ear he said, "Hannah."

"It's all right," she whispered. "I'm all right."

And she was, for the moment, though she could already feel the sadness seeping back into her bones. Less of it now, but with the same chill that settled in the marrow and sent out small sharp pains, like the onset of labor. Battlefields, a belly laid open by a bayonet, a head cracked like an egg, the flash from a hundred muskets firing at once. Men's ruined bodies piled like cordwood.

Ben said, "You're thinking about the war."

"I wish I could stop."

He pushed out a deep sigh and pulled her closer. "If I had the energy I'd find a way to distract you."

She turned in his arms, put a palm on the cheek she had slapped.

"I know that look," he said. "You have something to say."

"You can read my mind?"

"You're an open book. You're thinking about leaving."

It made no sense to argue with him. Instead she said, "You remember I told you about Curiosity?"

"The woman who helped raise you."

"Yes. She sent a message and my father gave it to me, word for word. She wrote it, too, in her letter: *Though there be mountains and lyons in the way.*"

Ben thought for a moment. "Your people miss you as much as you miss them."

She pressed her mouth to his arm to keep herself from adding the rest of the sentence: *as much as I will miss you, one day soon.*

"Hannah."

"You don't have to say anything," she told him. "We don't have to put words to everything."

"But you want the words. I can see it in your face, how you feel about me. You want to know if I feel the same."

She jerked away from him, affronted, laughing. "You conceited—"

"I see what I see," he said. "You break into gooseflesh when I brush against you, and your whole body trembles."

"I have marsh fever," said Hannah, biting down on a hysterical laugh. "The symptoms return at odd moments."

His mouth flexed at the corner. "I know what you feel, because I feel it, too," he said.

"A tisane would set you right." Her voice came a little breathless, very frightened, almost frantic with the need to run away and the equally pressing need to hold on to him with all her strength.

"Why are you afraid of the thing you desire the most?"

Desire. The word struck a chord that made her pause. She had forgot about desire, had thought never to feel it again. And here it was, as real as the man she held in her arms. She could not deny him; he was right.

"You want me to say I love you," Hannah said.

"Don't you?"

Hannah took a deep breath. "I suppose I do." She put her forehead against his mouth, and felt him say the words she was afraid to hear.

• • •

In the first light of Christmas Day, Hannah watched him dress. He told her about his plans, where he was going, what duties he had to dispatch, when he thought he might be back.

"You don't have to stay with your company at the Choctaw camp?"

He shook his head. "I never did have to. You needed this place to yourself."

The cathedral bells were ringing the Christmas Mass. The sound was crisp and sweet and Ben was going away for the day, but he would be back. Maybe late in the night, but he would come back to her. Something had changed between them.

He finished and came to sit beside her. With his fingers he smoothed out the curtain of her hair on the pillow, his face very solemn suddenly and full of things he thought he needed to say.

Hannah caught his hand, suddenly nervous beyond all reason. She said, "Why have you never married? And don't talk to me of priesthood."

His brow creased in surprise and then smoothed. "Your father asked me that, too."

She said, "My father asked about—the two of us?"

His expression was almost grim. He said, "I like your menfolk, Hannah. We'll work things out between us, but there's something you should know." He leaned forward and kissed her, a brief, firm stamp of his mouth. "I hope I'll win your father's respect, but in the end it's not his opinion that matters to me."

It was, Hannah thought, exactly the right thing to say. A dangerous talent in a man like Ben Savard, who understood her needs and fears so well.

Though there be mountains and lyons in the way.

CHAPTER 51

The mood in headquarters was very bad, tempers so high and so easily sparked that Kit took the only reasonable course of action: He excused himself to see to other duties, unspecified and in part fictitious.

On the veranda he passed one of the surgeons, come to give his report to Keane. Kit found he was interested in what the man had to say, but not interested enough to go back inside. And the blood-spattered clothes told him what he wanted to know well enough. The American artillery had been accurate to the point of devastation. The evidence was impossible to overlook.

Most of the outbuildings were gone, heaps of rubble and wood, dead animals, shattered casks of sugarcane, overturned kettles dribbling the sticky remnants of the men's experiment with oranges and unrefined sugar. The quartermaster had put the soldiers to work at first light, salvaging what they could, burning what could not be fixed. Kit passed a Highlander who was dismembering a dead cow with an axe, and doing what seemed like a creditable job of it. Soldiers learned all kinds of skills in the course of a career. This one sang in a beautiful tenor as he worked.

Troops kept coming in from the bayou route, draggled and filthy and expecting an ordered camp and a hot meal.

Kit saw faces go blank with surprise and then crease with
disappointment, anger, frustration.

Things were worse on the river. The *Carolina* had been
joined by the *Louisiana* and two gunboats, and they jock-
eyed for position like bullies with slingshots. There was no
rhyme or rhythm to the bombardment, which made it all
the more taxing on the nerves. If an American happened to
stumble into camp just now, Kit had the idea that the foot
soldiers would gladly tear him to pieces with their hands, so
filled were they with frustration and humiliation. And to all
of this came the snipe-shooters who hid out of sight and
moved as fast as they aimed and shot. Between the constant
bombardment from the river and the stinging aim of the
sharpshooters, the camp roiled like a nest of fire ants.

It was almost noon when Kit heard the rustle and commotion, and the news came shouted down the fields.

Pakenham was arrived. Pakenham had come, and now,
surely, things would improve. And he did come, his uniform
cape flapping behind him as he strode up the muddy path
from the canal, his posture erect and his head swiveling back
and forth as he took it all in. Behind him a half dozen aides
and officers, a few of whom Kit recognized from his own
time on the Peninsula. Gibbs, Swain, Dickson. Excellent
men.

Keane came out of the house with his own aides behind
him. His expression was stark and blank, and well it should
be, thought Kit. No doubt Pakenham had heard the worst
of the news from Cochrane, who had retreated to his headquarters at the mouth of the Bayou Bienvenu and showed
no interest in coming forward to join in the mess he had
helped create.

Cannons fired in a triple salute. They would hear it in
New Orleans, Kit knew. Jackson would hear it, and the
damned Baratarians and the sailors on the river. They would

all realize that Pakenham had come, and that the battle for New Orleans was about to start in earnest.

Kit had last seen Pakenham in Spain, in the spring of the year '11. As an Exploring Officer he had moved about freely and met dozens of men senior to himself, but few had made as much of an impression as Ned Pakenham.

After the battle of Fuentes de Onoro, Pakenham had offered him a spot on his staff, one that Kit would have taken if news had not come of his father's death. As an only son with dependent mother and sisters—and more importantly, as the godson and potential son-in-law of Sir George Prevost—Kit had been sent back to Canada and reassigned to the King's Rangers. And fate had put in her hand as well, dealing him a fairly serious wound on the day before he was to leave his company.

Once home again, he had been satisfied enough to leave the bloody Peninsular campaign to other men. Spain had taken a heavy toll, and he liked Canada. If there was little for an Exploring Officer to do along the New-York border, His Excellency Sir George Prevost told his godson, the assignment would serve nicely for a man recently invalided home. And then Anselme Dégre had done his worst, and Prevost had decided that only Kit could be entrusted with the important charge of pursuing the blackguard and bringing him back to face the charges against him.

And now Kit must go before Pakenham and admit yet again that he had failed in his assignment, and that the fault was entirely his own.

The call came quicker than he had imagined; within a quarter hour of Pakenham's arrival, Kit stood in the same room with the commander of the British North American army,

General Keane, and both men's staffs. The subject, he realized straightaway, was not his own transgressions but those of Keane and Cochrane.

In the most jovial of moods, Pakenham was an imposing figure. Tall, strongly built, and handsome enough to engage the interest of any and every young lady who crossed his path, he was further blessed with good teeth and an excellent smile, which he used to good effect. In the grip of barely controlled anger, as he was now, even strong men cowered.

"If I understand the situation correctly," he said, his tone clipped and low, "we are camped here between an almost impassable river and an impassable swamp, with a supply line some sixty miles long through the worst possible conditions, insufficient guns, powder, and ammunition, and already down a full tenth of our forces. Do I have the particulars?"

"We are but six miles from our objective," Keane said with all the dignity he could muster.

"It might as well be a thousand," said Pakenham. "So poorly have things been arranged."

For the next hour Kit listened to a discussion of options, which were few and mostly unappealing, from complete withdrawal in order to regroup, to an immediate march on the city. It was an odd relief to hear the realities of their situation laid out so plainly and without prevarication, and even more of a relief not to be drawn into the discussion.

But that came to an end, as Kit knew it must. Pakenham pivoted on his heel and gave him a long look from across the room.

"Kit Wyndham," he said, as if the name had come to him suddenly and from far away. He crossed the room and offered his hand, which Kit took.

"I had heard you were here. May I say how sorry I was

to hear about Margaret? A terrible blow. I know it struck George very hard, to lose such a daughter."

Kit could hardly recall what his fiancée had looked like, but he said the things that were expected of him and received the condolences with the appropriate expression.

"Now tell me," Pakenham said finally. "What think you of our position?"

Kit had been expecting a different question, and so he answered this one after a pause. He said, "We are outgunned on every side. Until we can dispatch the *Carolina,* we will never be able to move about freely, and the infantry is stuck here like a cork in a bottle."

"As good as all that?" Pakenham dropped his chin to his chest and pressed a knuckle to his upper lip. When he raised his head again he said, "I understand your usefulness as an Exploring Officer has been compromised."

Kit agreed that this was true, and braced himself for what was to come.

"Colonel Thornton tells me you wasted no time joining the infantry and proving your worth."

Kit gave a quick bow to hide his surprise. "I am happy to serve, sir, in whatever capacity I am needed."

"That's the spirit," said Pakenham. "Now let's talk about how to dispense with the *Carolina* before another day is passed. Hot shot, I think. Hot shot will do the job."

CHAPTER 52

He is, even by his own standards, very drunk. After the business
with the priest—for a moment Honoré wonders if he imagined the
whole thing, but on further consideration he notes the ink on his
fingers, which corresponds to the vague memory of signing the marriage lines—Noelle made him a gift of a whole bottle of brandy.
His thoughtful wife. His bride.

Two inches left in the bottle. With the first he toasts his grand-
mère, who would have fallen down in an apoplexy to see him wed
a whore. He burps gently, thoughtfully. All her plans for naught, the
family name in disgrace, whispered behind fans in parlors. Very satisfactory, in many ways, to have finally bested the old bitch. If only
his own neck weren't on the line.

Christmas Day. Honoré thinks idly of dinner, contemplates the
last inch of brandy in the bottle, turns over in his solitary bed, and
sleeps.

When he wakes he knows by the quality of the light that it is
dusk. The room is cold, the fire neglected, no sign of his dinner. He
remembers the complaints of married men, and the absurdity of the
whole undertaking makes him laugh.

He is still drunk enough to make the business of flint and
striker a challenge, but eventually the candle on the nightstand is
burning brightly enough for him to locate the pisspot. Sitting on

the bed with his feet on the polished floorboards, he empties his bladder.

Voices in the hall, the usual back-and-forth: Get my hands on you *and* Is that a promise *and* Oh, Captain Urquhart, you are too much man for me.

Honoré blinks, trying to remember where he has heard that name. It comes to him with a click like the snapping of fingers. The army officer working with the local gendarmes while the city is under martial law. A man with a reputation, one to stay clear of. There is a story in the city that he likes to use his pistol, and doesn't usually bother with the courts in the case of spies.

Urquhart's voice is almost enough to render Honoré sober. He contemplates the last inch in the brandy bottle while he listens to the creaking of the bed in the next room. It goes on forever, slow and easy, a man who takes satisfaction at his own pace.

The very least Honoré should do is put on his boots in case he has to run. He picks up the candle and holds it high while he looks around the mess that is his temporary home. He has no memory of a rampage that would cause this kind of clutter, but then he was spectacularly drunk. He ignores skittering in the darkest corner; the mice are worse every day, but what is he to do about it? Complaints to Noelle are met with a pursed mouth and narrowed eyes.

Clothes are scattered everywhere, a shirt spread out on the floor like the torso of a dead man. On the other side of the bed the small carpet has been rolled up and shoved against the wall, and his boots are on top of the roll.

On the wooden planks of the floor between the wall and the bed there is a new veve. Honoré startles so that he nearly drops the candle; hot wax splashes on his hand.

It is perfectly rendered, exactly as it had been in the tent on the Bayou St. John, but this time the sand is blood red. As are the un-lit candles that circle the loa, one at each compass point.

In the next room Urquhart is talking to the girl. He is telling a story about the battle, about Highlanders walking into an American trap in the fog.

Honoré stumbles back, bumps into the divan, and finally steadies himself. When his breathing has settled he gets up to study the veve, forcing himself to look at it from all sides. It is carefully drawn, the thin lines of sand even, the symmetries from side to side perfect.

When his heart stops racing he begins to walk the room, talking to himself in a stern voice. He is no longer a boy to be frightened by stories of a vengeful Erzulie Dantor. A bit of sand, a few candles: There is no power in such things. He kicks the veve and the sand rises into the air in a cloud. The feel of it on his skin is like wasps, and he shudders with disgust, backs away striking at himself to be rid of it.

He drinks the last of the brandy and tries to order his thoughts. To his knowledge, the only person with a key to this room is Noelle. Noelle who disdains everything to do with religion, who would laugh in his face if he were to tell her about Erzulie Dantor, a mother who takes revenge on those who hurt her children.

Staring at the wall he tries to think who might be able to draw Erzulie's veve. There are enough old black women from the islands in this city. They gather on Sundays at Congo Square and whisper to each other. He has seen them watching him. The one called Zuzu, and her mother. And Titine, of course. His half sister.

When Noelle comes in a few minutes later she is dismissive, unbelieving, mocking. All day long she has been out of the house, visiting her mother on the other side of the city. When exactly did he believe someone came into the room, and where is this drawing done in red sand?

His anger cannot stand up to her contempt. It runs away down his leg and leaves him feeling dizzy. He wants his dinner, he wants more brandy, he wants a fuck. This last wish he keeps to himself, for fear she might offer to oblige him. Suddenly he is angry again, so angry that the blood drains away from his face. Noelle steps away. Her instincts are excellent.

Within a quarter hour he has food and brandy. The sand crunches underfoot when he moves from the bed to the divan.

* * *

By ten he is drunk again, his mind shuddering and jerking from one thought to the next, images piled on top of each other. He imagined the veve, of course. He has seen odd things before in the grips of drink. A snake climbing a wall, a child with no eyes. What he needs now is to get out of this room, out of this house. There are women he could call on, places where he might be able to sit in a dark corner and drink without being recognized. He thinks briefly of Jacinthe, and tries to remember who bought her from his grand-mère. A butcher? A farmer? Someone who worked with beasts, who knew how to use a knife. He would have liked to see Jacinthe again, but no matter. The city is full of women, and it is very dark out tonight, the streets empty for rain. And it is Christmas. When the rich give parties, and the night watch looks the other way after curfew.

CHAPTER 53

To my dearest Wife Elizabeth and our children

Yesterday afternoon on the 24th December Runs-from-Bears and me arrived safe in New Orleans. Finding our Young proved easier than we feared. They are all in good enough Health and though they have each taken some blows to Body and Mind I am satisfied that there is no damage that won't heal with time.

The grandson they named for me shows no ill effects of his early adventures, and is a likely boy. My ma would have called him braw. I am reminded of Daniel as a newborn, such a life force as to put shame to the sunrise. They have taken to calling him Nathan for fear of confusing the two of us, and nobody seems to find this idea in the least comical. On the long trip down the Mississippi Runs-from-Bears carved him a rattle which the boy approved straight away and used to bang me firmly on the chin. He is indeed a Bonner, and promises well. There's a second child here, too, a boy that Luke and Jennet have adopted. I expect you will like having babies to raise up with Carrie, if the Noise and Commotion don't bring us low before our time. They call him Adam.

The British are camped on American soil about eight miles south of here. You will be glad to hear that we missed the first battle by less than a day and it looks like neither side is in a hurry to take up arms again. The Americans won that first Skirmish against the odds, mostly it seems because as is usual in war Providence is on the side of the Bold, and Jackson is that and more.

So today the city is celebrating a Victory along with the Yule. We et a good dinner of Roast Turkey with Oysters and Bread Pudding and Onion Gravy, birds we shot yesterday at dusk. The Savards are kindly and generous folks. Bears and me have put down our bedrolls in the main clinic which is mostly empty just now, and they somehow fit us all around their table, our five plus the two Infants and their four, not counting a lively young Boy called Henry. Tales were told and it was a fine time but I would have liked to have you and the rest of the Children here. Runs-from-Bears was quieter than usual. He would be sore offended if I told him he wears his Homesickness on his face.

This evening we are invited to a Christmas Party given by an Edward Livingston and his lady. You will remember the man from Manhattan where he was Mayor for a short while. While you would find his Politics as questionable as ever I know you would be the first to thank the man and his Lady Wife for the kindnesses they have shown Luke and Jennet in difficult times. They claim the invitation is for us all but whether they will actually let such Rough Types as me and Bears in their parlor remains to be seen. I expect they will want to be entertained with stories of Scalpings and such, and I might could oblige them just to see the looks on the Faces of the fine French

Ladies. Though I expect my Guid-Daughter Jennet
will put a stop to such Amusements before they get
started.

You will be muttering under your breath now that
I take so long to come to the subject of Hannah. It is
hard to know what to write. She has been ill with
Swamp Fever and has had other Trials that I do not
like to write about in a letter. She has been tested and
come through whole. Hear me now clearly, Boots:
She is not in Danger of her Life, and her mind is
sound. But I fear there is no Girl left in her anymore,
which is a sorrow to me.

Dr. Savard has a little clinic here attached to his
hospital. It has been made over to see to the needs of
Indians and Colored and Hannah has found
satisfaction in that Work. And there's a man called Ben
Savard. He is Dr. Savard's half brother by a part Indian
woman, about Thirty Five years of age. Yesterday late
in the day we went out Hunting with him, Luke and
Bears and me, and he strikes me as a good man.
Quick and smart and sharp of Eye. He answered
questions put to him without hesitation or apology,
and made no excuses. And he is an Excellent Shot.

Our Hannah has formed an Attachment to this
Savard and he to her, but she will not stay here and so
she is bound to suffer another loss. Young Children
bump heads and sprain limbs and weep over lost toys,
but the Heartbreak of a grown Child draws Blood.
And the truth be told, if she wanted to stay with Ben
and make a Home here I would do everything in my
Power to talk her out of it. She needs her family and
we need her, and this part of the World is no place for
a half-breed woman with an Education and a sense of
her own Value. They will grind her down in time and
I won't have that.

I wish you were here to talk to her the way you do, putting things out so Plain and Reasonable so that a body has no choice but to calm down and think. As it is I can only sit with her and listen to the things she can't quite bring herself to say.

I suppose all these years of watching you scratch away at your writing has infected me as this letter is already far too long and I haven't even told you yet about the Neighborhood or the City or even the War. So I'll say this much at least: Jackson has the city under Martial Law in order to quiet the discontents and leave him free to fight without interference from men who prefer talk to action. All that makes posting Letters some difficult, and harder still to say when we can be away. The biggest Problem, and one we never thought of, is the way the Army swallows up everything. There is not a Wagon or Horse to hire or buy, and so we will have to wait. I would guess that the business with the British will be finished within ten days or two weeks, one way or the other, and then we will be able to set out.

I wish you were here with me, Boots. You'd be a Comfort to Hannah and Jennet especially but I need you, too. Without you to argue with, how am I to know what I think? It's right odd, the way my Mind refuses to go about its business without consulting you. Not to mention the fact that you're not next to me when I wake up.

Gabriel will Complain that I send no news of the battle, shots fired and men buried. No doubt you would like to hear more of this City, which is as odd a place as I have ever seen. I don't think I ever understood the Nature of Slavery until I came south, and now I hope never to see the like again. But I am storing away all these Stories to tell you when we sit

together in the evenings. In the meantime Bears and I
will look after our Young, who have had a hard time
of it and are glad of our help, and trust that Daniel
and Gabriel do the same for you and Carrie.

Please give Curiosity my Regards and tell her I
have delivered her Message to Hannah, word for
word.

Your loving Husband these many years,
Nathaniel Bonner

writ Christmas Day in the year 1814

CHAPTER 54

In the days following Christmas it sometimes seemed to Hannah that she might have dreamed her father and Runs-from-Bears, so little did she see them. The fault, she determined, was not just the war, but also Mrs. Livingston, whose annual Christmas party had turned her father and uncle into objects of curiosity.

Hannah had not been pleased to receive the invitation to start with and had no intention of attending. "I'm surprised at your aunt's change of heart," she said to Rachel, and then was sorry to have embarrassed the girl, who was more aware of her aunt's failings than it might at first appear.

When it became clear that her father and uncle did intend to accept the invitation, she spoke more openly. "Until you and Bears came Mrs. Livingston didn't like to have Indians in her parlor. Or even in her kitchen," she told her father.

"You don't like the woman," Nathaniel Bonner said. "But I'm curious; I'd like to get a look at her after hearing Jennet's stories."

"I'm not going," Hannah said. "I won't be trotted out like a pet."

"I doubt anybody ever took your uncle for a lapdog," Nathaniel Bonner said. "And if they tried to, he'd set them straight. As I'd expect you to do, daughter."

Hannah said, "It's a battle I choose not to fight just now."

He came to sit next to her at that, and let a comfortable silence spin out between them.

"You follow your best instincts," he said finally. "And I'll do the same."

His own instincts had taken him and Runs-from-Bears to the Livingstons', where the élite citizens of New Orleans, already agitated by the presence of a captured British officer, had given up all pretense of calm detachment. But even the most forward of the gentlemen might not have approached directly if it weren't for what happened when Nathaniel Bonner came face-to-face with none other than Major General Jackson.

The general stopped in his tracks, his eyes widening. "If you're not the son of a man called Hawkeye out of the New-York frontier, then I'm seeing ghosts."

"Your eyesight's right good," said Nathaniel. "And as I spring a leak if you stick me, I can own in good conscience that I'm no ghost."

"It was something to see," Paul Savard told Hannah later. "Old Hickory was as delighted as a boy to run into your father and uncle. They spent an hour talking common history and battles and politics, and every Creole in the room was listening. Even the ones who don't have any English."

The story moved through the city on long legs and was everywhere by noon on the twenty-sixth. It seemed another version of it came to Hannah's ears every hour, embellished and polished to a high gloss. It came to the point that she was more likely to hear some tall tale concerning her father than any news of the war. Even Henry had less to relate than usual, and she had to be satisfied with the general report that the whole of the American force had been put to work either building fortifications at Rodriquez Canal, harassing the British, or spying on them.

A neighbor who had never spoken to Hannah stopped her on the street. "I had no idea your father and General Jackson fought together in the Revolution."

"They didn't," Hannah said.

"But I heard—"

"The major general met my father once," Hannah said. "It was during the Revolution, but not in battle. I believe the general was no more than fourteen at the time. My father is some ten years older."

It didn't matter what she said; the citizens of New Orleans loved a good story and weren't about to give up on this one. Two men from the far north had come to New Orleans to join the fighting under their old friend Andrew Jackson. Ferocious in battle, both of them, men to be taken seriously. One was white, but raised by the Mohawk. The other was Mohawk, raised by whites.

Hannah said, "My father was raised by his own parents. My grandmother Cora was born and raised in Scotland, and my grandfather—the one called Hawkeye—was born to Scots immigrants. He was orphaned and raised by a sachem of the Mahican tribe."

The request for a family history was put to her by a lady who had come to bring bandages for the clinic and tarried in the hope of getting a glimpse of Nathaniel and Runs-from-Bears.

"Mahican? Mohawk? Is there a difference?" she asked, wide-eyed.

"My uncle was born in the longhouse of the Turtle Clan at Good Pasture," Hannah went on. "He is a full-blood Mohawk and was raised among his own people."

"Who would have ever imagined a full-blood Indian on Major General Jackson's own staff?"

"My father and uncle have joined Captain Juzan's company," Hannah said. "That's where they can do the most good."

She supposed it was unreasonable of her to be so irritated by stories, especially when there was real trouble to deal with. On the twenty-seventh the British gunners used heated shot to sink the *Carolina* and almost got the *Louisiana* as well, but for quick-witted sailors who warped her up the shore out of range. Then, forced back from his line, Jackson took the precaution of having all the buildings on the Chalmette plantation blown up. None of this was good news, but the loss of the *Carolina* struck an especially hard note, and the city's attention shifted away from the Bonners. Hannah was torn between relief and guilt, both of which gave way quickly to worry.

Her father and uncle had decided to attach themselves to the Choctaw under Pierre de Juzan, and they saw no reason to delay, going out on their first full day to survey the land. Hannah did not try to explain to her father why she disliked this idea, or what struck her as wrong about fighting under Andrew Jackson, because it would have done no good. Nathaniel Bonner made up his own mind, and once he had, the only person who ever swayed him was his wife. Who was not here, to Hannah's great distress.

This informal assignment to Juzan's company turned out to please Major General Jackson. He had distinct favorites among the various companies, and he liked Juzan's Choctaws for their independence and their efficiency and, most of all, for their lack of fuss. Because, Luke concluded, Jackson was fed up with the Creole legislators who continued to plague him with their worries and their presumption on his time and attention. The Tennesseans, who bivouacked in ankle-deep mud and never complained about any duty, were more to his liking.

Juzan was the most reliable source Jackson had for information about the enemy's actions, and he also had some of the best riflemen. Working in tandem with the Tennessee rifles, they picked off the sentries the British sent out to patrol the perimeters, and more than one careless officer. After two days of this, the British withdrew all their men and put a redoubt in their place. At that point, the Choctaws were happy to leave the matter to the Baratarians, who turned their attention and their artillery to putting the forward British guns out of commission.

"You may call those Baratarians pirates and banditti," Nathaniel told his daughter. "But by God, they've got a feel for the big guns."

Hannah said, "Elizabeth will never forgive me if you get killed fighting this war. No matter how much fun you have while you do it."

Her father gave her a grim smile. "Elizabeth knew when we set out where we were headed and what the dangers were. We cain't leave here until this whole mess is settled anyway, so we might as well help it along."

Of course everyone was caught up in the war. Everyone she cared about, everyone precious to her in a five-hundred-mile radius. At night she dreamed all those people were marching past her, and usually Kit Wyndham was among them. She had no idea where he was, if he was even alive. And sometimes, she found herself wondering about Kit Wyndham, and if someday he would find himself on the wrong end of Nathaniel Bonner's rifle.

CHAPTER 55

When their line had been cut in half and the batteries destroyed, when it was clear that the attempt to turn Jackson's flank had failed, the order came. What remained of General Keane's column was to fall back, out of reach of the guns of the *Louisiana* and the batteries. Away from the Chalmette buildings fired by Jackson himself, which had burned so hot and bright that for those few minutes it was possible to forget the damp cold of this place.

As Kit Wyndham prepared to run, a single volley from the direction of the river knocked more than a dozen men to the ground and he was spattered, once again, with blood and bone and shrapnel. Ears ringing, he blinked sweat out of his eyes and headed toward the canals. There was no choice available to them but to go through the swamp.

Ciprière, Kit reminded himself; they called this hellish confusion of water and mud and slime the ciprière. Submerged to his waist in the icy muck, fighting to stay on his feet and keep his weapons dry, Wyndham passed a sergeant who had died leaning on a cypress trunk. There was a gash to his cheek that exposed one yellow tooth. Kit took the man's weapons—powder was as precious as blood—and moved on.

Men straggled along, three or four dozen, many wounded, all breathing like overworked bellows. Faces blackened by powder, eyes red-rimmed, grim of expression, Wellington's veterans waded into an acre of reeds and there they stopped, ducking down to conceal themselves like boys playing hide-go-seek. Their caution was well grounded: The ciprière was where the snipe-shooters were most active. Dirty-shirts, they called the riflemen from Kentucky and Tennessee, hunters of men.

Crouched in the chilly water, shivering so that his teeth clattered, Kit discovered, with little surprise, a bullet fragment in the meat of his upper left arm. No pain yet, and only a little blood.

The man beside him, small and wiry with a pendulous lower lip, watched as Kit pried it out with the tip of his knife.

He said, "Tha were one of Wellington's Exploring Officers, aye? I've heard tell of thee. Tha mun have done summat far wrong, to be out here with us rough ones. What was it?"

"I volunteered," Kit said.

"Och," said the old soldier with a grin. "Art tha seekin' redemption by fire, or art tha pure daft?"

"A little of both," said Kit, and found himself laughing.

Hungry, cold, in pain, covered with scratches and cuts, Kit came into camp at Villeré in the late afternoon and found a grim satisfaction in the fact of his own survival.

There was a thin stew of some unidentifiable meat and beans and chunks of slimy vegetable he recognized as okra. Kit sat with his bowl in his hands in front of a low and smoky fire, waiting for his feet to come back to life. The men around him talked freely of their frustration and anger and dissatisfaction. Affronted by Jackson's tactics, they begrudged his men everything, from better food to more cannons and, most of all, another victory.

"Those bloody dirty-shirts," said the Yorkshire man who had spoken to Kit in the ciprière. "But worse still are the pirates with the cannons."

"Have you ever seen the like?" Another man shook his head in wonder.

"Damn them one and all to hell," muttered someone from the shadows. "Of course they know how to use big guns. What are they but a band of thieves and slave-runners and smugglers?"

The Yorkshire man elbowed Kit. "Did tha meet any of yon pirates while tha were exploring on the other side?"

All eyes turned to Kit. He took a moment to finish his food, wiped his mouth with his hand.

"I did," he said. "I sat and drank with Dominique You more than once, and with Lafitte and his brother. I've watched them argue among themselves, and I've been nearby when worse has happened. They aren't men to cross. No doubt it was one of them who fired on the field hospital from the *Carolina*. The naval commander is a competent man, and wouldn't have ordered such a thing."

"It's our bad fortune that they threw in their lot with Jackson," said one of the older soldiers. "If anybody can keep us out of the city and drive us back to the sea, it will be the fookin' Baratarians."

There was a morose silence as the fire spat and flared. The men needed a victory, but the best Kit could offer them was diversion.

He said, "There's a story about one of them—"

All eyes turned to him as if he were offering heavenly salvation and a pint of ale for the journey.

"A renegade even by their standards. You understand that the Baratarians have their own rules, and Lafitte is the commanding officer. He tells them what ships they can attack and board, what prizes they may take and which they should leave in peace. But there's a captain of a morphidite schooner called the *Puma*—I've never seen her, but I've heard tell that under sail she's all wings and no feet."

"And her captain?"

"He's called Ten-Pint. I don't know his real name, but he's a Frenchman like most of Lafitte's men."

"Fond of the drink, is he?" A soldier with a nose as round and red as a strawberry asked this question, out of what was clearly fellow feeling.

Kit cleared his throat. "I'm sure he is, but that's not where his name comes from.

"The stories about him are legion. He goes his own way and does as he pleases, damn Lafitte. Once he threw a cabin boy overboard with a flick of his wrists for nothing worse than spilling a bucket of water. And that's the very least. A man who steals from him may get away, but sooner or later, Ten-Pint will take his revenge. And when he finds his prey he always says the same thing: 'I've no interest in a pound of your reeking flesh, but I'll take ten pints of your blood.'"

"And he's over there, with the rest of the Baratarians?" asked the younger man, glancing to the north.

"I assume so," said Kit Wyndham. "I hope never to find out directly."

"Aye, weel," said the deep voice from a soldier sitting in the shadows. "If Pakenham don't get the guns we need, you may yet shake Ten-Pint's hand."

The mood shifted immediately.

"It's not Pakenham's fault," said the older soldier. "It's Keane, who set us here in the muck in the first place, sixty miles from provisions."

"Colonel Rennie is worth three of Keane," said one soldier. "That was clear enough today."

"And Thornton," offered another man. "Ten times Keane's worth."

"Rennie might have saved the column, if not for Keane yanking at him, like a dog on a chain."

"More than a hundred dead this day. And not one step have we took over that damn Rodriquez Canal."

There was a grim silence from the circle of men, under-cut only by occasional screams. Raw opium wouldn't be enough to dull the pain of losing a leg to a surgeon's saw.

An ensign was moving down the field, calling out a name. Before he was in hailing distance, Kit knew the boy was looking for him. He was tempted to walk away and sleep in a hay barn where he couldn't be found, but years of training weren't so easily discarded. Kit stood and identified himself.

"Who sent for me?"

"The general, sir." The boy's arm was in a sling and he limped. Kit wondered in passing how many men were whole and uninjured.

Junior officers were milling about on the veranda, talking in low voices. As Kit climbed the stairs, a single shell came whistling over the trees and exploded in what had once been a garden. One of the men on the porch fell to his knees belching blood, and another dragged him away.

"This way, sir," said the ensign. His eyes were glazed, and his tone unremarkable.

Pakenham was pacing the main room, his chin lowered to his chest and his hands clasped at the small of his back. His color was bad; deep lines had dug themselves into his cheeks and along his mouth.

Keane sat on the other side of the room, his whole body turned away, a man who desperately wanted to be alone but could not leave. The rest of the staff moved about restlessly.

Pakenham stopped and turned on his heel to Kit. His mood was black with self-recrimination, which Kit found somehow comforting. He was an honorable man, an excellent officer, and his hands were tied by fate and the decisions made before he arrived.

"Gunpowder," said Pakenham.

"Sir?"

"Lafitte's secret store of gunpowder. You know where it is. Show me." He jerked his head toward the map spread out on the table.

After a moment's study, Kit's finger traced the curve of the river. It was a very good map, but not a perfect one.

"Here," he said, putting his finger on a spot in the ciprière south of the city, on the opposite side of the river.

"You are familiar with the lay of the land?"

Kit agreed that he was.

"Good," said Pakenham. "Take what men you need, and go seize it."

Kit hesitated for only a second, but Keane took the opportunity. "He's afraid of being taken prisoner. Of being shot as a spy."

Pakenham seemed not to hear Keane at all. "You performed a miracle or two for us in Spain, Kit. Are you willing to try again?"

It was in the very bones of a man like Pakenham, the ability to instill courage and purpose.

"Yes, sir," said Kit.

"We need that powder."

"Then I will bring it, sir. Or I will die in the attempt."

CHAPTER 56

To her father, Hannah said, "I'm tired of ladies coming by trying to catch a glimpse of you. Silly hens, all of them."

He was cleaning his rifle in the courtyard, and she was pretending to help him. It was that or go back into the clinic, and the sight of her father was too new and precious to pass up.

Her father laughed to hear her complain. "Now you've gone and hurt my vanity."

"But it makes no sense."

"Folks need distraction with the English hunkered down so close by, and they'll take it where they can get it. Later on they won't even remember our names, and all the war stories will be about their own sons and husbands. It's the way of things."

"You sound like Elizabeth," Hannah told him.

He cocked his head. "Does that surprise you? Cain't live with a woman all these years without some of her ways rubbing off. Someday you'll find that out for yourself."

It was as close as he came to raising the topic of Ben Savard. Of course it hadn't escaped him that Hannah shared Ben's apartment, but he wouldn't push for her confidence and she wasn't ready to talk about Ben yet. She didn't think she'd ever be ready. The day she would have to leave Ben was coming, but to hear her father tell her that was more than she could bear.

• • •

That night he came in past midnight, but she woke immediately. Hannah looked forward to these long conversations in the dark. During the day she imagined telling him about the things people said to her, and what he would say in response. Often he responded with questions instead of answers, another way that he reminded her of Runs-from-Bears.

"Today," Hannah told Ben, "a Mrs. Turner asked me if it was true that my father was President Washington's godson."

"Well, that's just funny," Ben said. "You have to see it that way."

They were in bed, his arm draped across her belly. "Why do you let it get under your skin? Do you even know?"

She did know, at least in part, but that was another subject she didn't want to raise. Instead she caught sight of the rifle leaning against the wall where Ben had left it. Her brother Daniel's rifle. Nathaniel Bonner had given it to Ben for his use.

"My father thinks a lot of you," she said.

"Hannah, the bed's hardly big enough for the two of us. Let's leave your father out of it."

She raised up on one elbow and grinned at him. "You do like my father."

"I do," Ben said, running a hand up her belly. "But I don't particularly want the man looking over my shoulder just now."

"Because you're going to—"

"Yes," Ben said, flipping her over. "Because I am going to."

The next morning, well before sunrise, Ben paused at the door on the way out. The air was chill enough to make his breath hang in clouds.

He said, "There may be some real fighting today. The English have been gearing up for something big."

Hannah sat up in bed and wrapped her arms around herself. "Do you think you'll need me?" She hadn't been called back to the little field hospital yet, and she had begun to wonder why.

He glanced over his shoulder as if there might be an answer in the shadows. Finally he said, "I'm hoping not, but I'll come by if things go bad." And still he didn't go.

Hannah waited for him to come out and say what it was that was sticking in his throat. The light from the candle danced on his face, caught the color of his eyes and the curve of a cheekbone.

"I want you to tell me about your brother Daniel," he said finally. "If I'm going to be using his rifle, I want to know why, how he came to give it up."

It was something she never spoke about, but she found she was pleased to be asked.

"Tonight," she said. "I'll tell you his story tonight."

Ben's mouth curled up at one corner. "I'll look forward to it."

Though there had been few serious wounds thus far in the on-again, off-again war being fought on the plantations to the south, there were enough visitors to the main clinic to keep everyone busy throughout the day.

At one point Hannah found herself examining a young lady of some nineteen years, a friend of Rachel's, who had fallen from her pony on the Levee Road, wrenching her knee and tearing her silk stockings.

"I was visiting my fiancé at the army camp," Mlle. Girot explained to Hannah. "But the fighting started again and we had to leave, all of us."

"You make a habit of calling in at the army camp?"

Hannah was amused by the idea of ladies making social calls to a battlefield. "You bring a picnic supper, and table linen?"

The young woman had the good sense not to be offended by this light teasing. "It seemed safe enough," she said. "And the gentlemen were so glad to see us. The food in the camp is disgusting."

"And your family doctor—"

Mlle. Girot ducked her head. "Dr. Kerr is engaged by Major General Jackson, and has no time to see his usual patients. And Rachel has spoken so highly of you." She managed a shaky smile.

"I take it your parents don't know you're here."

"I was hoping—"

"To hide the injury, I see."

"They would forbid me to go again. Is my leg very bad?" She winced as Hannah removed gravel from the long graze on her shin.

"Your stockings are beyond repair," Hannah said dryly. "But the rest of you will recover. You will have to stay off your feet with your knee elevated for at least a week, until the swelling goes down. What you tell your family about how you came to hurt yourself is your own affair."

Mlle. Girot was so relieved that she hardly twitched while Hannah cleaned and bound her injuries. Throughout the entire operation she told what she knew of the battle.

"The British underestimate our soldiers time and again," said Mlle. Girot in a tone that Hannah suspected echoed her father's. "They push forward into the face of the artillery and then seem surprised when they drop by the dozens. Soon they will give up and go away."

"Or bring in bigger guns," Hannah said.

Mlle. Girot's head tilted to one side as she considered this idea. She seemed to be looking for a counterargument, and when she could produce none, she subsided into uneasy silence that lasted until Hannah was almost finished.

Finally she said, "You have attended soldiers in other battles?"

Hannah glanced at her. "Yes. Many times."

"It is hard to imagine, the things you must see and do. Do you think it is harder for you than it is for a man?"

"There's nothing easy about it," Hannah said. "For anyone."

CHAPTER 57

It was almost eleven before the men came home. They were tired and subdued, but among them they had only minor wounds: a powder burn, a cut on the back of the hand, a broken toe.

And they were hungry, the best of signs, in Hannah's experience.

The adults sat together around the Savards' table and talked. It fell mostly to Luke to tell the day's story, with comments now and then from Nathaniel. Ben was unusually quiet, and Hannah watched him with growing unease.

"They're still hauling guns," said Luke. "Sixty miles over water and through swamp. Pakenham won't really make a move until he's satisfied with his artillery."

"They are taking a long time," Julia said.

"That's the English," Nathaniel said. "They stop and ruminate on the smallest details when it's time to jump—"

"—and rush ahead when they'd do better to stop and think," finished Luke for him.

"Aye," said Nathaniel. "It's bred in the bone."

"And you, married to an English lady," Jennet said, trying to strike a lighter tone and not quite succeeding.

"There are exceptions to every rule," observed Julia.

"The English have been fighting the same way since they first came to this continent," Runs-from-Bears said. There was no disapproval in his tone, nothing of disgust; it was an observation that a man made of his enemy and then put to good use.

"It worked for them with Napoleon," said Paul Savard.

"That's the problem," Nathaniel said. "They can't adapt, and worse still, they've got too many war chiefs. The one that got here on Christmas Day, that Pakenham, he's afraid to stand up to the others, what are they called? Keane, and Cochrane."

Hannah saw Paul and Julia exchange glances. They were wondering how Nathaniel Bonner would have such detailed information. Hannah hoped they wouldn't ask, because she didn't particularly want to hear the details of the risks the men took day by day.

She was sitting next to Ben, and his hand settled on her knee. No doubt her expression was as easy to read as Julia's.

Ben said, "Kit Wyndham is in the fighting."

Jennet dropped her fork with a clatter. "You saw him?"

"We did," said Luke.

"Could have shot him right between the eyes," said Nathaniel. "But it would have made things mighty hot for us."

"That would have been distinctly unsporting," Jennet said. "Wyndham may be fighting for the other side, but he was a help to us. Why do you look at me like that, Luke; you have said so yourself."

Luke shrugged. "A man takes a stand, and lives with the consequences."

Jennet was looking at Hannah as if she wanted her support in this argument, but Hannah could not contradict her brother, for the simple reason that he was right.

"What I'd like to do," Luke said, "is ask the man a few questions. Such as, how he came to write that confession. Any thoughts on that, Ben?"

Every face turned to Ben Savard, whose expression gave

nothing away. It was a question that Hannah had been wanting to ask him, but thus far she hadn't found the right combination of words and courage.

Ben speared a piece of fish out of the stew, and turned his steady gaze to Luke.

"What is it you think I did?"

Luke shrugged. "I expect you caught him unawares and held a gun to his head, and he wrote down what you told him to write."

"Every word of it true," Jennet interjected.

Luke went on without acknowledging the interruption. "What I don't know, is whether it worked out the way you had in mind."

Hannah watched her father following this conversation, his interest so keen that she could almost hear it humming.

Ben said, "Poiterin taking off before they could arrest him, is that what you mean?"

"I figured that's what you were aiming for," Luke said.

"Not exactly," said Ben. His left hand tightened on Hannah's knee and then relaxed. He said, "You'll have to wait a little longer to see how things go with Poiterin."

"How things go?" Jennet said, a little sharply. "You think he'll be back?" Her color rose quickly, anger like a fever in the blood.

Ben turned all his attention to her. He said, "No. You'll never have to deal with the man again. I can promise you that."

Runs-from-Bears made a sound deep in his throat, one of approval.

In Ben's apartment that evening Hannah stripped down to her chemise and took a brush to her hair, but she was so tired that she found it hard to lift her arm. Ben sat on a stool, pulling off his moccasins.

"I want you to know," Ben said, "that if Wyndham dies, it won't be by my hand."

Any response that Hannah gave to this declaration would have been the start of a long conversation, and she was far too weary for anything of the kind.

Ben said, "You want to know about Poiterin?"

She had been hoping that he wouldn't offer to tell her. "I am doing my best not to think about Poiterin."

Ben got up and came to stand behind her. He radiated heat like a hearth.

"You spend a lot of time trying not to think about things," he said. His hands settled on her shoulders and then slid down her back to close around her waist. She shivered at the touch of his mouth on her neck.

"Is that wrong?" she asked, a little breathless.

"It makes it hard sometimes," Ben said. "I don't know how much to tell you."

She turned to look at him.

"Tell me, then, if you must."

His expression was so serious that she could hardly bear to look at him. The urge to run away from whatever it was he had to say was so strong that she shook with it.

Ben cleared his throat. "If you really want to know, here it is: Your uncle has replaced me in Henry's affections."

She struck him with the flat of her hand and tried to pull away, but his embrace was unyielding, and she didn't really want him to let go anyway.

"Jealous?" Hannah said.

"It won't last long," Ben said. He pulled her across the room and tucked her under the blankets, but still Hannah shivered. Whether it was the cold or those words *won't last long,* she wasn't sure. What she did know was that Ben was taking every opportunity to remind her that this was all temporary. The battle for the city would end, and the Bonners would go back to the endless forests. She would go back to Paradise and Lake in the Clouds, and take up the practice of medicine, resume her life. Her good life, among her family and friends. There would be babies to deliver and sore ears to treat, swollen joints and fevers and the aches and pains of the elderly. Her brother, who had still not healed from his wounds and was in constant pain. The new baby, and Gabriel, and Lily in Montreal with her new husband. Curiosity, who had stories to tell her.

Within days or weeks they would be on their way, and she could feel nothing but fear.

It would be nonsensical to be angry at Ben for speaking the truth, and stupider still to let it ruin the time they had. And still it ate at her, his need to raise the subject. In fact it seemed that it was on everybody's mind. The water man stopped her to ask when they were leaving for home, and Mrs. Livingston bemoaned the fact that the end of the war would mean the departure of the fascinating Nathaniel Bonner and his remarkable friends and family.

Rachel especially could hardly keep her excitement to herself, because her parents had arranged for her to travel with the Bonners, who would take her to her family in Manhattan.

In Henry, at least, Hannah had an ally.

He had come to her in the little clinic, his lower lip pooched out as though he were still a baby, and in need of comfort. Everyone was going to New-York, and he had to stay behind, and really, it was unfair.

"Your mother and father and your uncle Ben will still be here," Hannah had pointed out to him. She felt the boy's sharp gaze on her.

"You could stay, too," Henry said. "You could marry my uncle."

"I have family in the north," Hannah said, striving to make her tone neutral. "They miss me as much as your mother and father would miss you if you went away."

"But you sleep in the same bed as my uncle," Henry had persisted. "And that means you're married." His thin face was pinched with worry.

"We are not married," Hannah had said, and refused to be drawn further into the conversation.

Now she said, "Henry is just as jealous as you are of him. He doesn't like the fact that we share a bed."

"Your uncle disapproves?"

Hannah bit him on the shoulder and he yelped. "Henry," she said. "Henry doesn't like"—she shrugged as if to take in the whole apartment—"this."

"Someday Henry will understand," said Ben, his fingers working her buttons.

"He understands too much as it is," Hannah muttered, and then she gave up, as Ben meant her to do.

CHAPTER 58

Brandy is the only thing that makes the long days in Noelle Soileau's establishment bearable, but Honoré Poiterin soon discovers that brandy has its drawbacks. The hallucinations began with the veve, and they are more common every day. Worse still, in his drunkenness he finds that he can't stop himself from trying to draw Noelle Soileau into conversation.

The first day of the new year she brings him a breakfast of coffee and toast and busies herself putting the room to rights. For a moment he watches her while he fights with the urge to ask her a question, and then he gives in.

"Do you know anything about voudou?"

He thinks he sees a tremor run up her spine. Then she turns and her expression is all irritation.

"What would I know about that nonsense? Do I look like a mambo witchy woman to you? You see a tignon on my nappy head?"

She is proud of her silky long hair. It is her one beauty, though she ruins it with dye.

"I knew a mambo once," he says. "She was called Mama Dounie."

"What does that have to do with anything?"

"Nothing." He turns away. "Nothing."

"Come and eat," she tells him. A wiser man would be satisfied with the simple things Noelle offers him, but Honoré has never been very wise, and he has seldom been more drunk.

"I saw Mama Dounie on the street—" He waves his hand toward the windows. "Yesterday. Walking down the street. She had a basket on her arm, with a live eel in it."

Noelle gives him a sharp look. It seems as though she wants to say something, and then changes her mind.

"I've seen others," Honoré says. "Last night just at dusk I saw an English spy. The one who gave my name to Jackson, that one. He was standing on the corner talking to you. If I had a rifle I could have shot him between the eyes."

And as she swings around to him: "It's nothing. Nothing. The brandy makes me—" He burps. "See things that aren't there."

"Then maybe you should stop drinking," says Noelle. "Because the next time you accuse me of meeting with spies on a public street I'll have your itchy tongue cut right out of your head."

She says it so calmly, he knows she means it exactly. For a long moment Honoré thinks about what it would be like. He has seen it done more than once; he has taken a tongue himself in a particularly nasty encounter in Hayti. And his own tongue does itch, he realizes. The brandy, almost certainly.

At the door, Noelle says, "When that bottle is empty I won't give you more. I want you out of here as soon as you're sober. Time for you to be gone."

It is indeed time to get away, but Honoré finds himself unable even to rise from the divan. He sits there with his half bottle of brandy and runs his tongue along the bottom of his teeth. The itch is worse.

The day passes and Noelle comes and goes, saying nothing to him of his uneaten food. She might be a spirit moving through the room, her feet never touching the floor. When he looks out the window now and then he sees her on the street in a long dark cape, sometimes alone, sometimes talking to an old black woman, sometimes pressing herself against a man.

The difference between day and night melts away, and he startles awake with a full bottle of brandy clasped to his chest.

She has changed her mind, his good wife. He is almost weepy

with thankfulness, but then the itch in his tongue is worse, and it has spread to the back of his eyes. He needs to piss, which requires that he get up or wet himself.

Honoré struggles up from the divan and stands for a moment watching red sand as it shifts from every crease in his clothing and falls in a cloud to the floor. Sitting on the pillow on his bed is a doll made of rough black fabric, wrapped in blue silk.

With what is left of his thinking mind, he tries to sort it all out, and comes to a single conclusion: Noelle is poisoning him. He feels himself filling with anger, like a bellows. Breathes it in and holds it, takes strength and purpose from it, the rage that has saved his life so many times before. And then she comes again, and he stands and faces her. Points the bottle like the finger of God.

She laughs at him.

"If I wanted to kill you I'd use a knife," she says. "Poison takes too long." She snatches the bottle away from him, pulls the cork, and takes two long swallows. There is something foreign and hard in her eyes, some understanding that eludes him.

"And what of this?" He grabs the doll and realizes that what he has in his hand is nothing more his own hat and a silk handkerchief.

"You would like a doll?" Noelle says. "I never had them as a girl, but I suppose I could find you one."

It occurs to him that Noelle knows far more of his history than he does of hers.

Honoré says, "Who is your mother?"

It surprises her, the first time he has ever seen that expression on her face.

"You said you went to spend the day with your mother. I thought you came here from Florida."

"Many people do," she says. "My mother included. You want to know about my mother, tell me first about your sister."

His breath catches. "I don't have a sister."

She raises a brow, her mouth purses. "You talk about her in your sleep."

"Once I had a sister," he says, when it is clear she will wait for an answer. "A half sister. My father's by-blow by a mulatto. No more." And then, his voice creaking: "Erzulie Dantor."

She doesn't even blink. "That's what she was called, your sister?"

"No," says Honoré. "That's somebody else entirely."

"Entirely," Noelle says. She stares at him for a moment, her eyes narrowed. "You have a rash." She reaches out and touches his brow, the pads of her fingers like ice. "On your face, a rash."

She takes the brandy with her when she leaves.

Honoré Poiterin studies his face in the mirror that hangs on the wall. His eyes are red and his lips pale. A week's worth of beard, and above it, the ovals of his cheeks, perfectly white. White as a July sky at midday. No sign of rash, not on his face, not on his tongue, where the itch is deep and persistent as a toothache.

He watches as the first faint spots rise on his brow, like tiny seeds under the skin. At the corners of his eyes, in the creases of his nose, spreading across his cheekbones. White and then a delicate pink and then red.

His shirt is suddenly drenched with sweat, and he wishes for the brandy Noelle took away from him.

Sober, his dreams are brighter, longer, far more disturbing; sometimes he cannot tell whether he is awake or asleep.

Is this typhoid?

The women in his dream laugh at him: Too good a death for you.

His grand-mère, Mama Dounie, Jacinthe, others whose names he can't recall. There is no sign of Titine, for which he should thank God. In life he had no fear of her, but now—

No more. No more.

He asks Mama Dounie: Is she the woman who carries fire? She ignores him and his questions and pats the doll she holds to her breast.

Yellow jack. He offers the words to the women. Am I dying of yellow jack?

Even in sleep the itch in his tongue and eyes is unbearable. He wakes, his skin crawling, and shoots up to his feet.

Artillery fire from the south. The city shakes with it, glass rattles in the window frames, the mirror falls from its nail on the wall and breaks into a thousand pieces.

Aside from the itch and the rash, aside from a headache, Honoré feels more himself than he has in many days. A faint hunger in his belly, a restlessness. The whole city will be watching the artillery battle, he thinks. He might be able to slip away for an hour, undetected.

And it is as he expects. From the window the street seems deserted, but for a man who stands on the corner as if he is waiting for someone. A man young enough to be in uniform, but dressed for a formal Sunday visit. Suddenly he turns and looks up at the window where Honoré stands. His expression shifts from anticipation to surprise and then, clearly, delight. Kit Wyndham bows from the waist, sweeping the hat from his head so that his blond hair catches the sun and turns to gold.

In her office bent over her ledgers, Noelle Soileau hears the pounding as soon as it starts, even above the continuous roaring of the artillery. By the time she is on her feet Margot is at her door, breathless.

"Your room, your—guest." The girls have been whispering among themselves for days, trying to guess the name of the man in Noelle's room.

"I am not deaf," Noelle says. "Get back to work."

"But there are no men," says Margot. "The battle, the home guard—"

"Then go look to yourself," Noelle snaps. She comes up to the girl and examines her hands, her face, her clothes. "Your hands and nails are a disgrace, and you've got cock breath. If you want to keep your place here, you'll do better."

Margot is not one to pout; she is more the kind to store up insults until she can do nothing else but lash out. She will bear watching, but right now there are more important things to worry about.

Honoré is pounding with both fists on his door. There is already a crack in the wood. She uses her key and all her strength to push the door open.

He is wild-eyed, his skin like raw meat, hair standing on end. Blood at the corners of his mouth, as if he has bitten his lip. He grabs her arms and pulls her to the window.

"Wyndham," he says. "Wyndham. Wyndham. Right there, on that corner. The bastard. Right there."

There is no one on the corner.

"I'm going to kill him," Honoré says. His voice comes thick and blurred, as if his mouth is swollen. "I need a rifle."

Very calmly Noelle says, "There is not a rifle to be had in the city, you know that. The army has them all."

"Then I'm going to follow him and put a knife in his throat."

Noelle considers telling Honoré the truth, but now isn't the time. She says, "Not in broad daylight. You'll be seen. If he's in the city you can find him after dark."

This catches his attention. His eyes, bloodshot, fix on her.

"Did you think I didn't know you go out? There's nothing that happens in this house that I don't know."

He nods, distracted, and his gaze moves back to the street.

"You need to sleep," Noelle says. "You need your strength. And something for this rash. Really, it is very bad. How it must itch."

He blinks at her, coming back from his daydream of revenge. His voice catches. "You don't think—" He pauses. "It's not yellow jack?"

"Oh, no," Noelle says, and gives him her smile. "Of that much I am absolutely sure."

CHAPTER 59

"Of course it is very foolish of me," Mrs. Livingston said to Jennet, her voice trembling. "But I find my nerves—the artillery—"

"It is very unsettling, even for the most sanguine of temperaments," Jennet agreed.

Around them, the sound of glass breaking as dishes and mirrors and paintings fell with every percussion that shook the house. The worst so far, Jennet thought. Maybe not the worst to come.

Mrs. Livingston pressed a half-gloved hand to her mouth. From down the hall came the sound of her mother weeping piteously.

"She won't calm unless I take her to the nuns," Mrs. Livingston said. "We are all going. Won't you come, too? You and your little ones? With the men away—"

Jennet knew what she was thinking, where her imagination went. If the British won this battle and took the city, she expected the same kind of rape and pillage she had seen as a young woman during a different revolution. It was unlikely, but Jennet could not promise Mrs. Livingston anything. Neither could she go cower in the Ursuline convent and pray the rosary while there was work to do at the clinic.

"At least let me take the babies." Mrs. Livingston grasped Jennet's hands so firmly that she winced. "The nurses will be with us, they will lack for nothing. You can come see them there, when your work is done. And if the worst should happen, I believe that even the English will respect the sanctity of the convent."

Jennet, the daughter of a Scots earl well versed in the history of Englishmen and their way of making war, managed a brief smile.

"Thank you," she said. "It will be a relief to know them well looked after."

Later, making up cots in the main clinic with Hannah, Jennet found that she was angry at herself for letting the boys go.

"Luke won't like it," she told Hannah. "No more do I."

"Luke wasn't there," Hannah told her. "For my part, I would have done the same thing."

Jennet didn't know if that was a lie meant to calm her, but she was thankful nonetheless.

For the next hour they worked without trying to talk over the noise of the battle, and Jennet studied Hannah's face. She looked far more healthy and rested than she had in many months, which most certainly had something to do with the fact that her father and uncle had come. At least in large part.

Three hours after the first shots were fired, something changed. The timing or rhythm of the battle had shifted. Hannah straightened and turned toward the windows, her head tilted to one side as she listened.

Finally she said, "One side or the other has stopped firing."

"The Americans?" Jennet could barely say the word.

"Most probably the British," Hannah said calmly. "Apparently they are very low on powder and ammunition."

Jennet heard herself squeak. "How do you know such

things?" And then: "I hope you do more than talk of war all night."

At that Hannah flushed so completely that Jennet was reminded of her as a young girl, before she had known anything of men. When they had played together at Carryck, and climbed trees, and shared secrets.

She said, "He is a good man, is he no?"

Hannah nodded. "Yes, he is that." Her gaze flickered toward Jennet and then away again.

"Do you regret Wyndham?"

The question took Hannah by surprise. She paused, a pillow in her hands, and seemed to be trying to recall something specific. She leaned against the wall with one shoulder, her head lowered, and when she raised it again there was a distance in her expression, the look that came over her when she was contemplating a patient, and the nature of whatever illness had brought that person to her.

She said, "When I think of Kit, I can see him in my mind doing simple things—looking at a chart, talking to the sailors, eating an apple—but I can't recall his face, or the sound of his voice. But I do remember the things he told me, his own stories. He had a need to hear them told, I think. I don't think he heard himself, it was more in the way of praying that some folks have, repeating words for the sound. Kit was always reminding himself what others expected of him, and why those things were good and necessary. So when I think of him, I wonder if he'll ever find his way and I wish him well, but he feels far away from me. As he always did, even when he slept beside me. A man away from himself."

She stood straight and flexed her shoulders as if her muscles were cramped. "I was glad to know him, but I have no regrets. And now if you have any love for me at all, Jennet, you'll stop there and ask me no questions about Ben Savard."

Jennet opened her mouth, but Hannah stopped her words with a severe look. "I mean what I say, cousin. Every word."

If she had stopped to think about it, Hannah would have known that this conversation with Jennet would be shared with Luke, and from there would make its way to Nathaniel Bonner and Runs-from-Bears. What did surprise her, though, was the speed with which it all happened. Less than twenty-four hours after she had forbade Jennet questions about Ben Savard, her father and uncle sought her out.

She had already retired for the evening, taking with her one of Paul Savard's books on anatomy and a brace of good candles. Ben was likely to be out on patrol all night, and she worried she wouldn't be able to sleep. The greater implications of that worry only made things worse, and the solution, she decided, was to focus on facts and medical histories and diagrams.

So lost was she in a drawing of the nerves of the arm and shoulder that she didn't hear the steps on the stair until the last moment. And then her father's voice.

A wave of panic flooded up from her gut, spread over her breast and throat and down her arms until her fingers jerked with it. As though she were a little girl who had misbehaved and must now face the consequences.

The fact that Runs-from-Bears was with her father made things a little easier in one way, and much worse in another. Together there was no escaping them.

She said, "News of the battle?"

Her father said, "Nobody's hurt, if that's what you're worried about. After yesterday's drubbing it'll take a few days for the Tories to work themselves up to another run at Rodriquez."

"And in the meantime?"

Runs-from-Bears huffed a short laugh. "Every man jack is out there shoring up the fortifications. Except for the rifles, of course. They're not so reckless as to put a shovel in your father's hands."

"Hey, now."

"Nathaniel, if they need somebody to shoot the eye out of a squirrel at a hundred yards you're their man, but a shovel just ain't your kind of weapon. You'd likely take off a toe out of pure boredom."

Many white people were so intimidated by Runs-from-Bears that they never imagined that he might have a sense of humor, but in fact he had always laughed easily and as a young man, the stories went, he had been prone to play tricks on everyone. Now his smile was friendly and easy, which thoroughly alarmed Hannah. Something was coming, and she had an idea it wouldn't be a pleasant conversation.

"You're as jumpy as a flea," her father said to her. "Settle down, daughter."

And so she did. She sat straight of back and let herself be engaged in conversation, listened to the things they had to tell her, stories about the things they had seen that day, including their first sighting of an alligator. They had been sitting up in a cypress tree with a view to picking off a few British officers when the creature came up out of the depths. A hard-shelled overgrown lizard, said Runs-from-Bears. With too many teeth.

Now he was determined to get an alligator skin to take to the Kahnyen'kehàka at Good Pasture; otherwise, they would never believe his descriptions. The subject, Hannah realized finally, was about going home.

"I figure this business with the redcoats will be finished in a week or so, and then we can head out," her father said.

"We'll have to wait that long just to get the horses we'll need and a wagon or two. You think you'll be ready?"

Hannah drew in a sharp breath. "Of course I'll be ready," she said, and she heard the sharpness in her tone. "I can't wait to get home."

"Good," said her father. "That's as it should be. I'm thinking I'll take your stepmother a few saplings. A pecan tree, maybe, and I hear the magnolias are pretty in the spring. She's got into the habit of planting trees, or better said she keeps Gabriel busy digging holes. She's been talking about that greenhouse we saw in Scotland back when you were a girl, and you know what that means. Traveling in caravan like we will be, I expect I can get a few saplings back to Paradise for her to coddle through the winter. Young Rachel will have more than a few trunks with finery and such, and then our Jennet has taken to collecting infants."

Hannah said, "Da, will you get on with it and say what you came to say?"

He tilted his head at her. "I'm talking about the journey home, getting ready to go."

"Packing," added Runs-from-Bears, helpfully.

"I don't have anything to pack," Hannah said. "I lost everything when I fell sick, even the knife you gave me when I was a girl."

"That's right," said her father. "I recall, now that you mention it. I've been keeping an eye out, and I picked this up for you."

He unbuckled a scabbard Hannah had never seen before and handed it over to her. It was a short sword, the kind that officers carried. A very fine weapon with an inlaid grip, double-bladed, well balanced. A beautiful weapon, of little real use to her, but beautiful nonetheless.

Hannah said, "Why, thank you."

"It's pretty to look at, ain't it? When we get home I'll see to it you get a proper knife, but I don't like the idea of you depending on borrowed weapons when you're near the fighting out at the field hospital."

"And now you've got something to pack," said Runs-from-Bears.

Hannah looked back and forth between her father and her uncle. "I'm still waiting for you to get to your real point."

Bears grinned at her, and her father cleared his throat and looked away.

"You were always bright," her father said. "My ma was teaching you your letters when you was no more than four. Learning come easier to you than it does to any of your brothers and sisters, even Daniel. That book there in your lap, I doubt I could make any sense of the title, and were you to take the time to explain it to me. But in some things you're plain slow, girl, and I suppose it falls to me to tell you so. If Elizabeth were here she'd do it without stumbling all over herself, but she ain't."

Hannah felt her color rising. She opened her mouth as if to protest but her father held up a hand to stop her.

"You've been torn up inside since before we got here, and it's worse every day. Now I'm not talking about the wrong done to you, that's something different. That calls for a certain kind of healing, and maybe it won't ever find an end. What I'm talking about is the pain you cause yourself."

The first flush of embarrassment was giving way to anger, but her father wasn't finished yet.

He said, "We like the man, Hannah. He's quick, and he'll do what needs to be done without shirking or excuse. Everybody who knows him—white or black or red—likes and respects him, and the few who don't have reason to fear him. And here's something I cain't often say: He's smarter than you."

"Is he." Hannah's voice sounded strained to her own ear.

"Some smarter," agreed Runs-from-Bears. "He's got you tied up in knots, and you never even saw the rope coming."

Hannah got up and walked across the room and back again. Sat down and stood, crossed her arms and then sat again. Her father and uncle watched her impassively. They would wait all night if she made them.

"So you're saying I should marry Ben Savard."

"That would be the sensible thing to do," said Nathaniel. "As attached as you are to the man, and he to you."

"You don't want me to come home with you. You want me to live here."

"Hell, no," Nathaniel Bonner said. "That's not the idea at all. We'd hog-tie you and cart you home on a mule if need be."

"Gag you, too, if it came to that," said Runs-from-Bears.

"Then I don't understand," Hannah said. Her hands were trembling, and she wound them together.

"You see?" her father said to her uncle. "It's a wonder how a smart woman can be pure blind at times." He turned back to her. "You cain't stay here, and he doesn't have to, either. You bring him on home with you to Paradise."

Hannah took a deep breath. "This is his home. This is everything he knows. What makes you think he would leave here?"

Bears said, "What makes you think he wouldn't?"

Her father said, "Have you ever asked the man?"

Hannah drew in a sharp breath and held it.

"She's never asked him," Bears said to no one in particular. He shook his head in disbelief.

Nathaniel Bonner stood. "Time to get some sleep. You think about asking Ben Savard to come north, will you?"

"You want me to ask Ben to marry me."

Her father raised a brow. "You're a Kahnyen'kehàka of the Wolf Longhouse. You pick your own husband and do the asking."

"This is Louisiana," said Hannah. And: "I wouldn't know how to ask."

"You'll figure it out," her father said. "Your stepmother managed when she asked me, and she had more than a little to do with raising you."

Before he went through the door, Hannah put a hand on her uncle's arm. She said, "He might say no."

That earned her a gruff laugh. "I guess you don't see what you do to the man."

"But he might," Hannah insisted. "He might say no."

Her father winked at her. "We got plenty of rope," he said. "And I'm right good at knots myself."

CHAPTER 60

Honoré Poiterin wakes gasping in the cold night air, fumbling for flint and striker and candle.

The small light hauls him from the dream world back into the realm of the living. Slowly his breathing comes back to normal, sweat dries on his brow, and he becomes aware of his physical self: the itch in his eyes, his tongue, the palms of his hands. The misery of the rash that covers his face and neck.

Every day he is more reluctant to move from the bed, terrified of dreams, afraid to look out the window for fear of whom he'll see there, staring up at him. The boundary between the living and the dead has thinned to the consistency of gauze.

When he mentions this to Noelle she doesn't laugh or call him names. Instead she looks thoughtful, and stands staring out the window herself for a long minute. Honoré's throat constricts in fear. She'll turn now and tell him that he's absolutely right: The dead do walk the streets.

He thinks now and then about the priest who came into this room to marry them. His friends would convulse with laughter if they knew that Honoré Poiterin is longing for a priest. But he imagines that a priest might be able to set his world right again. He would gladly pray a hundred rosaries, if it rid him of the dead. Certainly it seems that Noelle doesn't know what to do for him.

She says, "You'll be better once you can get out in the daylight. It's the drink, and too much thinking."

It's true that his mind never seems to shut off. If he drinks himself into oblivion, the memories fill his dreams and mix together with the visits from the dead. There is simply no escape.

On the seventh of January something changes. He wakes to the smell of good coffee, burnt sugar and cinnamon, a fire of seasoned wood. The air is as sweet as his mouth is sour. Honoré opens his eyes and watches as Noelle picks up the room, her movements quick and efficient. There is a fresh white linen cloth on the table where she has laid out his breakfast.

She says, "There is water beside you."

He drinks until his throat stops hurting and his tongue unglues itself from the roof of his mouth. Then he allows himself to be helped out of bed and into the hip bath, where she cares for him as if he were an infant. Finally she shaves him, and helps him into clean clothes, and then there is breakfast.

Honoré considers asking about his brandy bottle, but he is unsettled by Noelle's easy smile, her odd mood. *What have you done with the harridan, my wife?* He keeps himself from asking the question aloud. Instead he lets her pour him more coffee and hot milk.

While she makes the bed and moves around the room, he tries to sort it all out.

"Is the war over?" he asks finally. "Have the British taken the city?"

She pauses in folding a blanket and then comes to sit across from him.

"No," she says. "I am afraid that things don't look good for the English."

Honoré huffs a laugh. "I don't believe you."

"It's true," Noelle says. "I know it's hard to believe, but they are at a great disadvantage, and Jackson has been both clever and lucky."

"But Pakenham hasn't surrendered," Honoré says.

"No. The rumor is that the last battle will be fought tonight or tomorrow. What did they call it—the big push."

"Then it's not time to panic yet."

She shrugs. It is the kind of shrug that requires close analysis, so full is it of meaning.

"You should consider," she says finally. "What you will do if the worst happens."

Honoré laughs, his voice hoarse. "In that case I have two options," he says. "I can give myself up and hang, or I can flee to the islands."

Another shrug, and now his irritation has the upper hand. "What is it you're trying to say?"

"Nothing. Except there is a third possibility."

He makes an impatient gesture and she spills it all out before him. What if he were to join the British? Fight in this last battle on the other side. If they do take the city, so much the better; he has proved his allegiance. If they lose, he will have a better chance of escape when they retreat to the ships waiting off Pea Island.

"Your concern for my well-being is touching," says Honoré. "Worried that I'll give you up if I'm caught?"

"Of course," Noelle admits without hesitation. There is a flicker of her real self in her eyes, hard as obsidian. "And about the possibility that the courts will seize all your property. All our property."

It is something that has occurred to him before, an idea he has always dismissed without close thought. He finds the missing brandy bottle a real trial.

"With my luck," he says, "Pakenham would shoot me for a double spy, and on sight."

"Then you must bring him some evidence of your loyalty," says Noelle. "Something he needs very badly."

"Jackson's head on a platter." Honoré coughs a laugh.

"The word," says Noelle, "is that they are very short of powder and ammunition."

"Oh, well," says Honoré. "I'll just load up a wagon and drive it down to them."

"You could name your own reward."

"That's easy. Wyndham's head on a platter."

Noelle rises, her mood finally as sour as his own. "Have it your *own way," she tells him. "Sit here and wait for the gendarmerie to find you."*

She is gone before he remembers to ask about the brandy.

Honoré reclines on the divan and finds himself thinking through Noelle's suggestion that he make himself useful to the British. To Pakenham, the hero of Salamanca.

It isn't often he is in the position of having to win over another man. His habit has always been to dispose of men who stood in his way, and negotiation does not come easily to him. That is part of the reason that he has never run with the Baratarians. Lafitte requires loyalty of the men who work with him, a concept which has never meant very much to Honoré. There is something unnatural in Lafitte's ability to bind other men to him, to have them do his bidding in order to earn a place in his kingdom.

Whatever it is that brings him so many loyal men, it is profitable. Lafitte's auctions of smuggled slaves draw buyers from hundreds of miles around. He supplies the city with everything from soap milled in France to firearms.

Honoré sits up. So that is what Noelle was trying to get at: Lafitte's hidden supply of black powder and ammunition kept at Le Tonneau. The rumor is that there is enough stockpiled in Lafitte's secret armory to blow up a thousand ships.

Wyndham had been keenly interested in Le Tonneau, now that Honoré remembers. Once, Honoré had even taken him there.

CHAPTER 61

Rumors blew through the city, a windstorm of conjecture, wild fears and hopes. As the first week of the new year trudged by, tempers were strained to the breaking point and beyond. Funeral processions for fallen soldiers, no matter how humble, grew into huge ungainly affairs attended by hundreds, and the lamentations of the mourners rose up like a cloud over the city. An hour later, the rumor that Jackson was in the city would send those same people into a frenzy of cheers outside his headquarters.

Hannah's menfolk were gone more, and for longer periods. She saw her father and uncle every day for at least a short while; Ben she saw very little, and Luke even less. Men who had been out in the ciprière in the cold rain had little time for long discussions, Hannah explained to herself. Clémentine must shovel great amounts of hot food into him, and he needed fresh clothes and water to wash. He must spend time with Paul and Julia and the children, and then of course he needed his sleep. Her question for him would have to wait.

When he was away she buried herself in work. The clinic suspended vaccinations until the battle for the city was decided, and dealt instead with a steady flow of patients. Soldiers with wounds small and large, broken bones, burns, infections, and the illnesses that were the burden of any army: dysentery, typhoid, measles, malaria. Hannah looked after men too sick to take note of the color of her skin; she worked in the surgery and apothecary; twice she was called to deliver babies for ladies who were normally attended by one of the medical doctors who had gone to the main field hospital for the duration.

There was no sign of Honoré Poiterin or word about him. She saw Maman Zuzu a few times, and learned from her that Jacinthe was safe and would most likely recover. Once she went out to the Bayou St. John to visit with Amazilie, who had grown thinner and very drawn. It was not just the loss of Titine that weighed on her, but also the fact that her son had gone off to join the fighting. Tibère was serving with the Battalion of Free Men of Color, and she had not seen him since Christmas Day.

Where there was so much misery and pain, Hannah told herself, it was truly the height of self-indulgence to be worried about something as trivial as a marriage proposal.

She spent a good amount of time composing a letter to her stepmother in her head. Elizabeth would know what to do. If she had been here during Hannah's very odd, very disturbing discussion with her father and uncle, Elizabeth would have taken control and . . . what? What would she have said?

Here Hannah's imagination refused to cooperate. A very bad sign indeed.

In the late afternoon of the fifth of January, the richest men in the city evacuated their wives and children by means of Henry Shreve's steamboat. Julia Savard would not go, but Rachel and Henry were entrusted to the care of Mrs. Livingston, who left New Orleans with her mother and daughter.

Jennet came back to stay with the Savards, and brought

the babies with her, much to Clémentine's satisfaction. To Hannah's relief Jennet seemed to have forgot entirely about Ben Savard, or at least, she had been warned away from the subject by Luke or more likely, to Hannah's mind, her father-in-law.

The mood in the city was more somber by the hour, and by the evening of the seventh, Hannah had begun to believe the rumors about the coming battle. She left the clinic and climbed the stairs to Ben's apartment, trying not to hope that she would see him this evening. It had been almost two days, and she wanted the opportunity to talk to him before he went into battle. She knew too much of the possibilities to pretend to herself that there was no danger.

No book could hold her attention, and so she lay sleepless, staring at the ceiling and trying to ignore the sound of artillery fire in the distance.

At first she didn't hear the scratching at the door. The people who sought her out here were more likely to knock or call out, and so she went to answer the door already alert and uncertain.

Her visitor was a stranger, a young woman who had painted her face in a manner that left no question as to her chosen work. She wore a pink-and-brown paisley shawl over a low-cut gown, and what was either a fake mole on one breast or the beginning of a fearsome cancer.

And her brow creased in confusion and no small amount of unhappiness at the sight of Hannah. She said, "Where's Ben?"

Hannah's voice came rough with sleeplessness. "On patrol, with his company."

"I have a letter for him."

Hannah stepped aside. "Would you like to wait?"

And then had to bite hard on the lining of her cheek to keep from laughing at the look on the younger woman's face. Affront, surprise, uneasiness.

"I've got to get back," she said. And, with sudden energy: "I know you. I've seen you before."

"Is that so?" Hannah managed a small smile. "Have you come to the clinic to be vaccinated?"

This suggestion was greeted with a hoot of laughter. "As if I'd let the likes of you stick me with a needle full of cow piss."

There was a moment's silence in which the unapologetic examination of Hannah's face continued. She was about to protest when the woman's eyes widened.

"I know," she said, her tone triumphant. "You was the one who spent a week in Girl's room, sick with the marsh fever. I saw you once or twice when I passed by. You look healthy enough now."

"I am healthy now," Hannah said, disoriented. "Who is it who sent you?"

"My mistress," said the girl. "Mme. Soileau. She's got a house on the other side of town." She jerked a thumb over her shoulder. "You don't remember that week at all? My face don't strike you familiar? I'm Nicole."

"I don't recall you," Hannah said. "But I remember Girl."

The woman's expression sobered. "I miss Girl. The mistress sold her when she got sick."

"I know that," Hannah said. She lifted her chin in the direction of the clinic. "She died here, of an obstruction in her bowel."

"Is that so?" Nicole had gone pale beneath her rouge. "Could be she's better off. You hear stories about the planters who buy their slaves from the auction houses."

I've heard those stories, too, Hannah thought, but kept it to herself.

"You said you have a letter—"

"For Ben. I'm supposed to give it to him direct, but she didn't say nothing about waiting half the night."

"I can give it to him," Hannah offered.

The girl gave an uneasy and doubtful shrug. "It's important, the mistress says. You won't read it?"

"I won't read it." And then, against her better judgment: "How is it Ben knows your mistress?"

"Oh, everybody knows Mme. Soileau," Nicole said. "Every man, at least." And she winked. She handed Hannah the letter, heavy paper folded and secured with a solid wax seal.

"I'm trusting you, now," she said.

"I will deliver it," said Hannah. "You can depend upon it."

Nicole's perfume was still hanging in the air when Ben came through the door a half hour later, just as the cathedral bells were chiming eight o'clock. Hannah had lit candles and stoked the fire and she sat in the best chair near the hearth, an unread book in her lap and, on top of the book, the letter.

Hannah stayed just where she was while he took off his weapons and set them carefully aside. Then he came to her directly and leaning over, kissed her on the forehead.

"You've been a long while," Hannah said.

"I have," he agreed. "Long enough that I was hoping for more of a greeting."

Hannah studied his face, and felt her resolve crumbling away. This was Ben Savard, who had given her every reason to trust him, who had saved her life. She loved him, that was clear to her now, and the oddest thing was that love made it all the harder to be fair.

She said, "You had a visitor just a little while ago."

Ben shrugged off his wet cape and spread it out before the hearth. "A visitor."

"Yes. A young woman called Nicole. She brought you a letter from Mme. Soileau."

"Ah." He sat down on a stool and took his time pulling off his moccasins. "So what does it say?"

"It's your letter," Hannah said, her temper flaring. "I wouldn't open it."

"But you look mad enough to throw it into the fire."

"I am not mad."

"No?" He held her gaze.

"How is it you know Mme. Soileau?"

"I don't know her, the way you mean." He grinned. "In the biblical sense. Don't know any of her young women that way, either."

"You do business with her of another kind?"

"I wouldn't call it business," Ben said. "Is this about Girl?"

"Yes," Hannah said. "Your Mme. Soileau—"

"She's not mine."

"—as much as murdered that young woman. Why would you have anything to do with her?"

"You're jumping to conclusions, *chère*. Open it up, read it to me before you decide I need tarring."

Hannah paused, trying to make sense of the things she was feeling. She held out the letter to him.

"This is your business and none of mine. I needn't involve myself."

Ben took the letter, letting his fingers trail over hers. His skin was still cold, and the shock of it ran up her arm. He looked irritated and Hannah thought: *Good. At least we're both mad.*

The wax seal gave a soft crack and he unfolded the single sheet. His eyes moved over the page, and then he handed it to her.

"It's your business, too," he said. "But you're right, you needn't involve yourself."

The hand was firm and straight, the ink very black.

He goes to Le Tonneau after midnight.

Hannah looked at Ben. He was studying the fire, his face set in hard lines. He spoke without turning toward her.

"Poiterin has been hiding out at Noelle Soileau's place since the night his grand-mère died in the fire."

Hannah tried to make sense of the words. "And you knew where he was? Why didn't—how could—" She broke off.

"I didn't tell you and I didn't turn him in for a couple reasons," said Ben. "Mostly because Noelle asked me to hold off. She had her own plans for the man."

Hannah took a deep breath. "We are talking about Honoré Poiterin, who put Jennet through such torture for so many months, who took Titine and sold her, who raped me."

"You think I could ever forget about that?" Ben gave her a long and very sober look.

"No," Hannah said. "But I don't understand."

After a moment Ben said, "As much as he's done to you, he's done that and more to Noelle and her family." He ran a hand over his eyes. "You met Valerie Maurepas in Pensacola?"

It took a moment for Hannah to collect her thoughts. "Titine's mother. Yes, I met her."

"When Noelle was sixteen or so—about Rachel's age—she was taken off the street. By one of the slave traders of the sort who isn't fussy about where his stock comes from, or how legal it is. Noelle was free, born to free parents, but that didn't matter to him. He took her north and sold her to a planter in Virginia, and she'd be a slave to this day if she hadn't got word to Valerie. Valerie hired a lawyer and got the papers together and they sued, and eventually Noelle got her freedom back. She was nineteen by that time, and those three years—they took a toll."

"I can see that they would," Hannah said, her tone

milder now. "You're saying Noelle Soileau is connected somehow to Valerie Maurepas."

"Noelle may be without mercy when it comes to business, and if you're waiting for me to explain how somebody with her history would hold slaves, well, then I have to disappoint you. I don't understand it myself, but she's not alone. There's more than one dark-skinned slave holder in this part of the country. But I can tell you this about Noelle: To her own people she's loyal unto death, and her great-aunt Valerie Maurepas and her cousin Titine are two of those people she counts as her own." And to Hannah's blank look: "You didn't realize that Noelle is colored, did you? Most folks don't, but she signs herself that way: Noelle Soileau, FWC."

Hannah said, "I should have thought to ask why Titine took me to that house, but I was too sick, and later I just—" She paused.

"It was the one place in the city she knew you'd be safe, because she asked Noelle to take you in as a personal favor to her."

"My recollection," Hannah said slowly, "is that rent was paid. And when the money was used up, I was thrown out."

"*Mais* yeah, rent was paid. She's a businesswoman first and foremost. And then Titine got snatched up and stole away—"

Hannah closed her eyes and opened them again. Of course. Of course that would send someone with Noelle Soileau's history into a frenzy. "She must have been out of her mind with grief."

"Mostly it's anger that moves Noelle," Ben said. "But now you'll see where it comes from. Titine got snatched up by Poiterin because of you and Jennet coming to New Orleans. Noelle put part of the blame on you. Maybe that seems unreasonable to you—"

"But we are partly to blame," Hannah said.

"Even so, Noelle didn't throw you out to die, not the way you think. She sent word to me, and I came to get you."

Hannah let the silence spin out while she thought it all through.

She said, "There's still Girl."

"Yes," Ben said. "There's Girl. I can't make any excuses for that, and I won't. But I can tell you that whatever ill you wished on Honoré Poiterin, it's nothing compared to what Noelle has put him through."

"What did she do?" Hannah asked.

"She called in Maman Zuzu."

Hannah stood and walked to the window. There was nothing to see in the courtyard except the darkened shape of the fountain. Without turning she said, "Tell me about this place he's going tonight—"

"Le Tonneau. On the other side of the river, a half mile or so south. Pretty well hid."

"Noelle arranged this."

"She's been working on getting him out of the city, yes. It took some handling, from what I hear."

"And now it's up to you to waylay him."

"I'm not going alone."

It all fit together, quite suddenly and with clarity. "My father."

"And your uncle and your brother," said Ben. "Between the four of us, we'll put paid to the whole business."

He was taking dry clothes down from the pegs on the wall. For a moment, Hannah watched him.

"Why does he need to be out of the city? Why couldn't you go take him out of her place?"

Ben cast her a sidelong glance. "Because it can't look like Noelle had anything to do with it. If there's any suspicion of foul play on her part, the court will stop her from inheriting."

"Inheriting?" The word caught in Hannah's throat.

"Honoré Poiterin is as good as dead," Ben said. "And Noelle Soileau is his wife." He drew in a deep breath and let it go.

"His legal wife." It wasn't a question, but Ben nodded. For a moment he seemed to be ready to tell her more, and then he shook his head. "I was hoping to spend the night, but I've got to go straightaway. Are you going to give me a kiss good-bye, or will I have to make do with a few fond words?"

Hannah went to him then. She put her hands on his chest and went up on tiptoe to kiss him.

"Is it true about tomorrow, about the battle that's coming?"

"It's true," Ben said. He ran a hand over her hair. "I may not have time to come back here tonight. If that's the case I'll send somebody to fetch you to the field hospital. If you're still willing."

"I'm willing," Hannah said. There were other things she wanted and needed to say, but she couldn't bear the idea of raising the questions she had for him and then having him leave before they had time to talk it all through.

Instead she said, "You take care, Jean-Benoît Savard. You take good care. Don't turn your back on Honoré Poiterin, or on the English army, either."

Jennet showed up at her door shortly after Ben had left.

She said, "Can ye take Adam, please, afore I drop the puir wee thing on his heid."

"I was about to come find you," Hannah said. "I didn't want to wait for word alone."

The babies were quickly settled, side by side on Ben's bed. Hannah stood for a moment considering the two of them, strong and healthy, full of promise. Adam, who had

had such a difficult start, had been coddled and nursed to rounded surplus. His black hair curled prettily at his temples, and his skin glowed the shade of aged oak. He had a cleft in his chin that marked him as Honoré Poiterin's child.

Beside her Jennet said, "I will do right by this boy, I swear it."

Hannah thought of her brother, of her father and uncle and all the family at Lake in the Clouds who would have a hand in his raising and education. "We all will," she said.

"Weel now," Jennet said, as if coming out of a trance. "We'll no be sleeping this night, so here's my plan. I'm going to brave Clémentine's kitchen and bring back tea and whatever else I can find, and then we'll sit together, the twa of us, and I'll read the cards. And I've got a question or two that Ben couldna take the time to answer when he came to fetch Luke. Will ye tell me what ye ken?"

"You get the tea," Hannah said. "And I'll provide what answers I can."

CHAPTER 62

"For my part," Nathaniel Bonner said to nobody in particular, "I'd prefer six or seven feet of solid snow to this damp cold."

He expected no response, and got none. The three other men in the canoe were thinking the same thing, with the exception of Ben Savard, who most probably had never seen a proper snowfall in his life.

The Mississippi was a fearsome river, muscular and stubborn, and no doubt many a less experienced party had found themselves dragged along until she spit them into the Gulf. But they were all at home in a canoe and familiar with the river, and they worked their paddles in rhythm and made the other side in good time.

They made landfall at the foot of a good-sized garrison that surrounded the city's main powder magazine. There was no lack of guards, but all of them were men seventy or older, armed with ancient muskets. If the British got this far, it went without saying, the city had already fallen.

A few of the guards greeted Savard as they passed, and then the four of them broke into an easy trot and left the brightly lit camp behind.

For all the cold damp, it wasn't so overcast that they couldn't make their way. Savard had proved time and again that he knew this whole territory, stick and stone, and so they followed the shape of him along canals and through orchards, keeping off pathways.

The plan was to settle in at this secret armory of Lafitte's, the one called Le Tonneau, and wait for Poiterin to show up. According to Savard, Lafitte's place was a well-kept secret, something easy to believe as they followed him deeper into the swamp. Nathaniel was curious to see what such a place looked like. Rumor had it that Lafitte had provided most of the big guns and ammunition for the *Carolina* and the *Louisiana*. He had seen for himself that the Baratarians had brought their own guns to man the Rodriquez Canal. Bears had watched them at work for a while and pointed out in his casual way that Lafitte was better armed than the United States navy and army combined.

Savard paused now and then to listen. The night was full of sounds, many unfamiliar to a backwoodsman from the New-York frontier, though Nathaniel had learned a bit in the last week. Then the ground underfoot went from soggy to pure water, and Savard was pulling out a canoe hidden away in the brush.

They set to paddling again, this time through still black waters. What moonlight there was fell on cypress trees, some no more than stumps, others great in their age and size. A half hour later Savard held up a hand and they floated for a moment while he listened. He spoke to them in a low voice, his head turned so they could hear him.

"There's something wrong," he said. "Lafitte most usually has guards all along here, but there's not a single man on patrol."

"You sure Poiterin is by himself?" Luke asked.

Savard nodded. "He's good, but he's not good enough to lay all of Lafitte's men low."

"You got a plan?" Bears asked.

It turned out that Savard did indeed have a plan.

• • •

A half hour later they had taken their spots. The armory was on an island no more than a half acre in size, but solid underfoot. Le Tonneau turned out to be a low building constructed out of cypress logs and without windows of any kind. A big double door was set into the front under the eaves, and a lantern hung to either side of it. Around the building itself was a clearing that gave way to cypress trees. Nathaniel, hunkered down with Savard in the shadows, studied the situation as a hollow feeling rose from his gut into his throat.

Not one guard, but standing in front of the door were two caissons, each hitched to a pair of dray horses. Lying on his back, half in the shadows, was a man who had lost a good part of his head to a hatchet blow. Nathaniel liked to deal with one thing at a time.

"Horses in this part of the country swim through swamp, do they?"

Savard pointed with his chin. "There's a road leads south and then forks. One spur goes right to the big river."

"So who's inside? The British?"

Savard glanced at Nathaniel. "Most likely. That's one of Lafitte's men dead on the ground. There must be another five or so like him around here."

The situation required some thought. Somehow or another the British, short on powder and ammunition, had found this place, hid away as it was deep in the swamp. Nathaniel recalled what he had been told about Wyndham, but then there had to be more than one spy still at work for the British. It was a complication, and no small one. If they moved on this little raiding party—and they would have to—they'd lose their chance at Poiterin.

"I'm going to go talk to Bears and Luke." Savard slipped away into the shadows and was back in five minutes.

"They don't see things much different," he said. "We'll wait a while longer, see who comes out those doors." And he swung his rifle up and reached for his powder horn.

Waiting was a skill learned in boyhood or never learned at all. Nathaniel was pleased to see that Savard had the knack of it, his whole frame relaxing against the tree trunk to the point that he seemed to melt right into the bark. The primed rifle rested in his arms, and his eyes moved over the clearing as steady as a new-wound clock.

He found himself wishing, as he did every waking hour, for Elizabeth. He had the idea that she would like Ben Savard, but then sometimes she still surprised him, seeing things tucked away in a man's mind that he never would have guessed. He was thinking about what it would be like, that first conversation between Savard and Elizabeth, when the double door opened up.

British. Four redcoats, two Indian scouts of a tribe Nathaniel couldn't identify, and an officer in dark green. Another four redcoats. Both the Indian scouts and two of the redcoats immediately fanned out, weapons at the ready. The rest of them were humping barrels and boxes.

From the other side of the clearing came an owl hoot, Runs-from-Bears making his intentions known.

"I've got the tall one." Nathaniel brought up his rifle and fired. Savard did the same, and from the other side of the clearing came two more reports. Then they were moving into the chaos in front of the armory. All four armed men were down, one of them screaming. Barrels and boxes were dropped as men reached for weapons, and then Luke stepped out of the shadows and put a musket to the officer's neck.

"Kit," Luke said in a conversational tone. "You're just about the last person I expected to see here."

"Luke."

"Tell your men to stand down," called Ben Savard. "Or I'll fire a bullet into one of those casks and we can watch them burn."

There was a moment of silence, and then Wyndham did as he was bid.

In short order they stripped the prisoners of their weapons and stood guard while they returned the powder and shot to the armory. Nathaniel stayed close to Wyndham, not talking to the man but watching and wondering at the odd turn of fate. They had come here for Poiterin and were ending up instead with a man who had proved himself a friend and ally over a long and difficult year. They'd have to march him back to the city, where he'd be tried and hanged as a spy.

"We could tie them all up and leave them back in the trees while we deal with Poiterin," Luke said.

"Best move those wagons around back then," Bears said. "Nathaniel?"

"I'd say it's worth a try, if it gets us Poiterin."

Nathaniel caught Savard's gaze. The younger man nodded. "Lots of rope in those caissons," he said. "But we'll have to work quick."

They left Wyndham until last. As an officer he would get better treatment than enlisted men, had he been captured by regular army. As it was, Nathaniel was in no mood to take chances. He tied the man's wrists, taking the time to study him. He looked battle weary and worn down, but he was tough. Nathaniel said, "This shouldn't take long. We've just got some business to settle with an old friend of yours."

"Poiterin is no friend of mine."

"Call him a colleague, then. He's on his way here, hoping to buy Pakenham's forgiveness the same way you had in mind."

Wyndham looked him straight in the eye. "I require no one's forgiveness," he said. "I am proud to be an officer of His Majesty's army. I only wish I were a better one."

Nathaniel said, "Do I have to gag you, or will you go quiet to stand with the rest of your men?"

Wyndham looked at Luke. He started to say something and then just shook his head. "I promise not to do anything to warn Poiterin. In return, I'd just as soon you'd shoot me here and now."

"I can see how that might appeal," Nathaniel said to him. "But I fear you'll have to take your chances with the court."

The last word was barely out of his mouth when the gunshot sounded, and in that same second Nathaniel felt the rush of a bullet skimming by. Wyndham sagged and then fell to the ground.

Runs-from-Bears and Savard went into the brush after Poiterin, and came back a half hour later. Empty-handed.

Hannah, rolled into blankets before the hearth, was dreaming of home, and resisted the hand that settled on her shoulder to shake her awake.

"Daughter," came her father's voice in Kahnyen'kehàka. "Squirrel."

It was his use of her girl-name that woke her. Hannah sat up.

Nathaniel Bonner crouched before her. He was damp with sweat and his color was high. He had been running, hard and long.

"You're needed at the field hospital," he said. "I've come to fetch you."

Hannah dressed quickly and quietly. For once it was a blessing that Jennet was so hard to rouse, because at this moment they could afford no delay. Her father's expression told her that something was very wrong.

At the door he was waiting with her medical pack slung over his shoulder.

"Who?"

He looked her direct in the eye and said, "It's not your brother or Savard or Bears."

Hannah's breath hitched and caught. With relief, and with a new kind of worry. "Who?"

"Kit Wyndham," he said. "Poiterin shot him."

The six miles to the field hospital on the DuPré plantation gave Hannah time to think of many questions, but to ask only a few. The answers were sobering. Kit Wyndham was both badly injured and a prisoner of war, and Poiterin had disappeared again. He wouldn't go back to Noelle Soileau's, unless it was to kill her for her part in the trap that he had managed to escape. When Hannah said as much to her father, it turned out that Ben had already thought of this possibility. On his way through the city Nathaniel Bonner had stopped and delivered a message.

Hannah had seen her father deal with all kinds of people over the course of her life, but she could not see him in a room with Noelle Soileau.

"She's safe?"

"If she does as she's told."

It would have to serve. There were other matters to worry about just now. One wounded man and more to come. Even in the full dark, evidence of the coming battle was everywhere on the Levee Road, supply wagons and caissons and men. Hannah was hungry and she was thirsty, but that would have to wait. Something occurred to her.

"Dr. Rousseau?"

"Already there," said her father. "Since yesterday, according to Savard."

Hannah was glad to know that Kit was not lying alone in his own blood.

They cut through the fields on a path that was already familiar, moving at a fast trot. For as long as she could remember she had followed her father like this, on one kind of trail or another. It felt right and proper and was a comfort to her.

At the beginning of the row of slave cabins her father took his leave.

"I wish you could stay here with me," she said, and was embarrassed. But he grinned at her.

"And miss all the fun?"

His hand, hard and rough, settled on her shoulder. "Do what you can for him, daughter, but be prepared. He won't last the day."

"Da." She grasped at his hand as he pulled it away. "Where's Ben?"

Nathaniel looked over his shoulder, his eyes narrowed as if he could see the battlefields just to the south. "He's gone to work," he said finally.

"I need to talk to him," Hannah said, her voice catching.

"I'll send him back to you," her father said. "Soon as we have a free minute."

Then he winked at her, and turning on his heel disappeared into the first featherings of a rising fog.

Dr. Rousseau's hands and lower arms were bloody, and his expression said everything Hannah needed to know. She stood beside the table where Kit Wyndham lay.

The bullet had lodged in his upper abdomen and was there still. Dr. Rousseau had done what little could be done, but a bullet that pierced the peritoneum meant only one thing. Unless they were to open his torso there was no way to know exactly what damage it had done, but it was damage no man would survive.

He was heavily bandaged in linen that matched the pallor of his skin. He had lost so much blood, Hannah wondered how he could still be alive. If he still was alive, or if she was imagining the rise and fall of his chest. Then he opened his eyes and looked at her.

"Walks-Ahead." His voice was easy and his tone light. As if she had come to tea.

She sat down on the stool beside him and touched his face. His fever was climbing, but it wouldn't last long. Soon his body would recognize a battle lost.

"Stomach wounds," Kit said. "You told me once how it's the hardest way to die."

"Not this time," Hannah said, struggling to match his tone. "It looks as though the bullet did damage to an artery."

"What good news." Kit managed a smile.

It was still at least an hour to sunrise, but from far off came the sound of bugles calling men from sleep. Kit turned his head and listened. He said, "Their haversacks will be soaked with dew and rain. Fires forbidden. Cold breakfast."

"You're sorry to miss the battle."

"I would have liked to fight under Thornton," Kit said. "If Pakenham had a dozen more like him, Jackson would have no chance."

"Then I'm glad there's only one Thornton," Hannah said.

He turned his face toward her. There were darkening shadows under his eyes. "If we take the city, no harm will come to you."

It was an empty promise, and they both knew it.

Hannah said, "Would you like me to write to your family?"

His brow creased in confusion, as if he had forgot that he ever had a mother or sisters or a fiancée.

He said, "I failed him." And: "Make no excuses for me."

Hannah took Kit Wyndham's hand and held it until he had gone.

When she went out of the cabin there was no sign of Dr. Rousseau, but there were soldiers milling about in the fog and dark, cooking breakfast over small fires. She hadn't realized that the slaves had been turned out so that the militia could be housed here, and even stranger was the mood among the men as they fried bacon and ate it between slabs of corn bread. Her own stomach was grumbling but she moved on, thinking that she would find Dr. Rousseau somewhere close by.

Then Hannah realized what was so very odd about these men. They were unarmed. Many of the volunteers who had come from the north had expected to be supplied with weapons by the army, and had found themselves disappointed. They had been assigned to the rearmost lines, where they served as nothing more than window dressing.

As she passed she heard them speaking among themselves in tones that ranged from disappointment and agitation to outright indignation. Having put aside their farms and families and traveled so far, they were being denied the release of battle. No wonder, Hannah thought, that Dr. Rousseau didn't show himself.

She passed a small group of men who stopped to look her over, openly suspicious. One of them, a man with few teeth and missing one ear, challenged her directly, and Hannah found herself lying without hesitation. This outlying field hospital had been established on Jackson's direct order, and she and Dr. Rousseau were here at his command.

She left the idle men behind her and walked to the embankment. In the dark she climbed up to the Levee Road, but there was nothing to see in the fog, not the river itself or the ships on the river, not a flicker of fire anywhere. But in the darkened fields to the south, men were massing. One

QUEEN OF SWORDS

673

army ready to march forward and take by force, the other determined to stop them.

A drumming of hooves, and a patrol swept by on horseback, a half dozen men with cloaks fluttering behind them. Hannah stepped back, but not before she was seen. The lead rider pulled up abruptly and the others followed his lead, their horses dancing in place and kicking up mud. One of them held up a lantern, and Hannah found herself in the middle of a puddle of light.

"Mistress Bonner," called Major General Jackson. "I wish I had a hundred more like your father and uncle."

"So do I," Hannah said.

His leathery face folded into a smile. "That's a fine weapon you've got. Do you know how to use it?"

Hannah touched the sword her father had given her, hanging from her belt in its leather scabbard. "I do," she called back. "But I'm far better with a scalpel."

The smile widened. "Best you stay here then," he said. "And see to our brave lads."

And he put spurs to his horse, and galloped off with his staff close behind him.

CHAPTER 63

The next hours went by so slowly that Hannah thought at times she must scream or lose her mind. As the noise of the battle filled the world, they waited for wounded, but none came.

"Of course we must be glad," Dr. Rousseau said. He sounded not glad, but as tense as Hannah felt.

The idle militiamen had gone up onto the Levee Road to watch as much of the battle as they could see through billowing smoke: the stuttering flash of rifles firing ten or twenty or fifty at a time, and the jagged light of cannon fire, never ending, relentless.

One particularly dour Kentuckian crept forward far enough to get real news. He came back torn between glee—the British were being pounded to shreds—and resentment that he had had no part in any of it. Hannah heard this reported by Dr. Rousseau, whom the militiamen did not like but found more tolerable than Hannah. They had heard of educated negroes, even if most of them had never before seen such a creature. An educated Indian woman was a different matter entirely.

"He says," Dr. Rousseau reported, "that it's turning into a bloodbath. A sea of redcoats on the field, and more keep coming, marching right over their dead, only to be mowed down in turn."

"What does that have to do with war?" Hannah asked.

Dr. Rousseau lifted a shoulder in helpless agreement.

At midday a boy came from the city with provisions, one of the doctor's grandsons still too young to join the Battalion of Free Men of Color. He brought them bread and cold meat and a leek-and-potato pie, and more news.

"They say Pakenham is shot dead," he reported. "And some of the other generals, too."

"Who says this?" his grandfather inquired, his tone reminding Hannah of her stepmother in the classroom.

The boy looked sheepish. "I shouldn't spread unfounded rumors?"

Hannah would have asked for more details on the origin of the boy's news, but at that moment the door flew open and thudded into the wall with such force that the cabin shook.

Luke and her father stood there, with Ben Savard propped up between them.

For a moment Hannah wondered if she'd ever be able to draw another breath, and then she saw her father's grim smile and Luke's, an exact duplicate.

Ben said, "I've already got one bullet in me—you going to shoot me again?"

"If only I had a musket," Hannah said, relief flooding through her. "I would gladly oblige you."

Her father and brother stayed only long enough to eat what was left of the food, and then they went back to Juzan's company.

"How bad is it?" Hannah asked her father, and his hooded gaze told her that everything she heard had been true.

"Won't last much longer," he said. "It's like shooting fish in a barrel."

Over her shoulder he glanced at Kit Wyndham's still

form on the far cot. "There wasn't much anybody could have done with him, gut-shot."

"You could find Poiterin," Hannah said. "And do the same to him."

"I plan on it," said her father, and touched his cap as he left.

"An awkward place for a bullet," Dr. Rousseau said. Ben was lying on the table on his stomach, his left leg lifted so that they could examine his foot. The bullet had entered his heel and failed to exit.

"It's got to come out," Hannah said.

"I hear Jackson has still got a bullet or two in him," Ben said. "He seems to do all right."

"This will cripple you," said Dr. Rousseau. "If it doesn't cost you your foot, first."

Thus far Hannah had avoided looking directly at Ben, but now she met his eye. She said, very clearly, "It has to come out, now."

His muscles in his jaw rolled and clenched, and he nodded.

"So," she said a few minutes later when the instruments had been assembled. "Tell me how it is you got a bullet in your heel."

"Ricochet," said Ben gruffly. "And I was sitting in a tree at the time, trying to get a bead on an officer. Your father beat me to it, and then I caught this—" He waved his leg in the air. "Damned unlucky."

To that Hannah only made a deep sound in her throat. She said, "What happened last night with Poiterin?"

For the most part it was Jennet who could draw a patient out while Hannah worked, but here she was alone with Ben

Savard. Even Dr. Rousseau had left, walking out with Hannah's father and brother to ask more questions.

Ben said, "Are you trying to distract me? Because I know this is bound to hurt."

"It will hurt," Hannah said, picking up a probe. "And I am trying to distract you, but I also want to know how Kit Wyndham died."

And so he told her, in short quick sentences that came between longer, tense moments while she worked.

She said, "I'm starting to think that Poiterin is a ghost himself, one who can't be killed." And then: "I have to make an incision to get to the bullet and see what damage it's done."

"I don't think it's hit the bone, if that's what you're worried about."

A fracture of the os calcis was a definite possibility, and one that brought real dangers with it—but even so, Hannah told him, he was strong and young and generally healthy, and most likely he would keep his foot and walk again.

He pushed himself up on an elbow to look at her.

"I intend to walk today," he said. "As soon as you've dug that bullet out, I'm going back to my company."

"No," Hannah said. "You're not. You won't be able to bear any weight on this heel for some time. For a long time, if the bone's broken."

He stared at her for a long moment and then turned his face away, but what he meant to say was clear: *We'll just see about that.*

Hannah concentrated on the task before her, aware as she worked that the pain she was causing him was considerable and that he was fighting the urge to cry out. She made her voice as neutral as she could when she spoke to him.

"Bite down on that pillow if you have to," she said. "But don't move this foot while I'm cutting."

He said, "Remind me never to make you angry when you've got a knife in your hand."

Hannah held up the surgical tweezers between her bloody fingers and studied the bullet fragment, smaller than a pea. Then she dropped it into a basin.

"No fracture," she said. "If no infection sets in, you'll be walking again in a few days."

"How likely is no infection?" Ben asked her.

She shrugged. "I'll do what I can, but I expect there will be some draining and pus. You'll have to stay off of it."

"You keep saying that."

"And you keep ignoring me."

When she was finished washing out the wound and had bandaged it, Ben flipped over on his back and took her by the wrist.

"Hannah Bonner," he said. "I want you to answer me plain. Are you telling me this wound is worse than it is to keep me out of the fighting?"

His expression was so stern that she had to bite back a smile. She said, "Go ahead, walk out of here."

He blinked at her, his mouth pursed as he thought. Then he sat up and after a moment's hesitation, stood.

"Christ Jesus," he said, sitting down again.

"You believe me now?"

He put back his head and yipped. When he had his breath back he said, "I'm sorry I doubted you."

"Remember that," Hannah said. "For next time."

Standing next to him, Hannah felt less than steady on her own feet. Gooseflesh rose on her arms and legs and thighs and ran up her back, and she turned away from him before he could read any of that in her expression.

"Are the rumors true?" she said. "Is it as bad as it sounds for the British?"

"Worse," said Ben. "I hope never to see the like again.

There are men on the line out there who can hardly stand it. They load and fire with tears running down their faces."

"Why doesn't Pakenham call a retreat?"

"Pakenham is dead," said Ben. "He rode in, trying to rally the Forty-fourth, and got shot off his horse. I hear the Kentucky rifles are taking credit for it, but it may have been the Tennesseans."

Hannah had seen such things before, men so frantic that they forgot everything they knew of practical value, lost all ability to think and fear; borne along by reckless courage alone, they plunged into chaos, sure that it must be possible to call forth victory by pure force of will. Such men did not last long, and often caused great harm to their own causes. Certainly such a man should never have been made a war chief.

Ben was saying, "He was well loved by his men, but today he failed them."

Hannah busied herself with arranging Ben's bandaged foot on its cushion, checking the dressing for seepage. The question she must ask was one she feared, but she could not hide from it.

"What now?"

He looked at her down the long length of his body. "I hope to God they put up a white flag. Then there'll be a truce, long enough to collect the dead and injured. I expect that's when your work will start in earnest."

She knew very well what was coming, and preferred not to dwell on it. Ben was watching her closely, as if trying to guess which way she might jump if he were to reach out to touch her.

He said, "The city is safe for the moment at least. Most probably for good. I don't think the British can recoup from this to try again."

A long silence drew out between them. The artillery fire

filled it, and the sound of men talking in the long alley between the slave cabins.

"I expect you'll be able to start for home in a day or two," Ben said. "Your father has already got some wagons and horses, taken from the British we captured at Le Tonneau."

"He's got a keen eye for an opportunity," said Hannah.

She forced herself to raise her head and meet Ben's gaze. He was looking back at her with great seriousness. A man hoping for a single word, or a man who feared that word. Hannah's stomach clenched and a sour taste rose into her throat.

She said, "Right before we set off on the search for Jennet, the man who was with Strikes-the-Sky when he died came back to Paradise. Strikes-the-Sky was my husband."

"I recall the name," Ben said quietly.

"This friend wrote the story of that day down and sent it to me in a letter, but I couldn't stand the idea of the words on the page, and so I threw it in the fire. I thought at the time I didn't need to know the details, that they would only give me worse dreams than I had already.

"But Almanzo—you remember I've talked about Curiosity; Almanzo is her son—needed to tell me more than I needed not to hear it, and when I finally understood that, we sat down together. Manny had been with my husband's people for so long that he spoke their language as well as his own, and listening to him that afternoon was like hearing Strikes-the-Sky himself.

"Manny told me about the day that they came to the Bad Axe River in Mesquakie territory. Have you ever heard of it?"

Ben nodded. "I have."

"They were sent west with the specific task of seeking out as many Asakiwaki and Mesquakie chiefs as they could find, to tell them Tecumseh's plan and to ask them to join us. You know that these messengers from Tecumseh were not always welcome." She paused for a moment, but Ben's expression encouraged her.

"And worse still, there is a history of bloodshed between the Mesquakie and the Seven Nations. Strikes-the-Sky was everything they feared and hated, and they ambushed him before he ever had a chance to speak a word of Tecumseh's message. Manny told me every moment of it, every detail. The number of warriors, and how they were dressed, the way they had painted the ponies they rode, and the exact angle of the arrow that struck Strikes-the-Sky in the throat. How long it took him to bleed to death. Of what came later, Manny had nothing to say. There are scars, but he never spoke to me of his own trials. He only wanted to talk about Strikes-the-Sky and the way he died. He spoke to me as Catholics speak to their confessors, as if I could absolve him of some sin he believed he had committed.

"So I told him that I didn't hold him responsible for Strikes-the-Sky's death, and that's when he said something that I had never expected. It wasn't guilt that was eating at him, but anger. He was angry at Strikes-the-Sky for getting himself killed and leaving Manny behind. For leaving me and our son without a husband and father and protection.

"I remember how he said it, because it struck me so forcibly. He said, every day the anger grew in him until sometimes he was afraid it would start to bleed from his eyes and ears. And he was telling me about it in the hope that bringing it out into the open would loosen the grip his anger had on him."

"And what did you tell him?"

Hannah took a breath and held it for a long moment. "I told him that if his anger was a sin, then I needed forgiveness as much as he did. There wasn't enough space in the world to hold all my anger. Most of it was for my husband, but I was so angry then at all of them, at Tecumseh and The

Prophet and all the men who had dared to think they might be able to stop the whites from taking everything.

"I don't think Manny expected to hear me say such a thing. He was shocked, and silent for so long that I wondered if he would ever speak to me again. But then he took my hands and kissed them and thanked me. So he came to me for forgiveness and left with something else, but it seemed to be what he needed."

Ben Savard said, "Why do you tell me this story now?"

"Because," Hannah said slowly. "Because I want to ask you a question, but before I do I want you to understand. I had come to believe that I would never be strong enough to take another husband. That I could not control my anger. Anger like that would poison a marriage. I believed I could live my life alone, as long as I had my family with me and my work."

"Go on," Ben said.

"I would like you to come home with me," Hannah said. She met his gaze. "I would like to live with you as your wife, if you can leave this place and come with me to Hidden Wolf. But if you will come, you have to know what I am capable of. If you leave me to go to war, I will not forgive you. I will leave you and never look back. I have had enough of war, and I want no more. Never again."

She was standing now at the end of the table, afraid to move for fear of what he might say or do. When she looked at him there was nothing of surprise or anger or joy in his expression. Then he held out his hand and she took a step forward and took it.

His fingers curled around her own, and he drew her closer as he sat up. His hunting shirt was torn and dirty from battle, and he smelled of sweat and gunpowder and the ciprière. There was a bruise on his temple and another on his jaw, and a deep calm.

"I never make a promise unless I believe I can keep it. I

know nothing of your endless forests. How can I know what will be required of me to keep you safe?"

"If you leave me I am lost," Hannah said.

"And if one day there is a threat to our home, to the children we will have? If you say to me, it is time to take up your weapons?"

Hannah shook her head. "I will not. I could not."

Ben said, "Then if you will promise me never to ask, I will promise never to go to war."

Hannah held his gaze. "I will promise."

"And so do I."

"You are willing to leave this place?" Her free hand fluttered, and he caught it up, took both her hands, and pressed them to his chest just over his heart.

"I've been waiting for you to ask," said Ben Savard. "Someday you'll have to explain to me what took you so long."

Hannah leaned forward and let her forehead rest against his shoulder. She was trembling with love and fear and joy, trembling like a woman in the grip of a fever. His hand smoothed her hair and then suddenly stopped. Hannah pulled away and saw his expression, wary and focused.

Outside the cabin voices were raised, men quarreling among themselves. A curse, a cry of pain. Dr. Rousseau's shouted instructions.

Ben said, "Stand back."

"But—" Hannah began. Ben came off the table in one fluid motion. His face contorted in pain as he stepped toward his weapons, and then he stopped where he was because the door opened and a crowd of militiamen came in carrying a limp body.

Just behind them Dr. Rousseau said, "Quick, on the table. He will bleed to death."

Hannah tried to pass, but Ben held her back. She said, "What—" and he held up a hand to quiet her.

The injured man was on the table now; Hannah could see nothing of him but one trailing arm, dripping blood. There was a scattering of pinfeathers on the hand, goose feathers, it looked to Hannah, and how odd, it made no sense. Dr. Rousseau was on the far side of the table.

"Clear out now," he shouted. "Away so that we can see to him. Away."

"He's a white man," said one of the men in a surly tone. "He needs a white doctor."

"He'll bleed to death before you could get him to the army surgeons," barked Dr. Rousseau. The militiamen were backing toward the door and his gaze followed them. "If you want his death on your hands, take him."

And then the world lurched. Later Hannah would think about it and it would come back to her, the strong sense of the floor collapsing beneath her feet, of the world spinning off in a new direction just as she stepped around Ben to reach the wounded man. In the same moment she saw three things very clearly: that he was drenched with blood but that there was no clear wound anywhere on his person, that his eyes were open and aware and filled with purpose, and that she knew him. Knew his face and the terrible strength of his hands and the warp and weave of his mind.

He sat up as lithe and quick as a cat, and pulled a short-barreled musket from his belt.

"I take it that's Wyndham lying cold in the corner," he said to her. "So I can use this bullet on you."

Hannah's thoughts came in a jumble all wound around with sadness. To have wasted so much time, to never see her father again or the people she loved, the home she missed. As she braced for the bullet she sent her thoughts out to all of them, a burst of sorrow and regret. She was aware of Ben just beside and behind her and she was glad to have him there, and filled with a dark satisfaction. She was the one leaving; she would disappear into the shadowlands and he would not be able to follow her.

She never registered the tug, which must have come while Poiterin was speaking to her, Ben reaching for the leather scabbard that hung from her belt. She only saw the flash of steel and a blur of movement as Ben lunged forward and ran Honoré Poiterin through the heart. Poiterin's arm jerked up and the gun went off, the bullet burying itself in the wall.

His eyes were open and aware, the look there more of puzzlement than fear, and then all emotion was gone. He was gone. Ben pulled the sword from Poiterin's chest and stood looking down at his body.

"By God," said a voice at the door. "That red nigger killed a white man in cold blood, right in front of us."

Dr. Rousseau seemed to wake up then. He turned and drew himself up to his full height. His voice, Hannah thought in a distant way, must have sounded to the militiamen like the voice of God himself, it was so deep and resonant.

"The authorities," he said. "In a case such as this there can be no delay. You must fetch the authorities from the city so they can arrest this man for murder."

Hannah might have said something then, but Ben's hand clamped down hard on her wrist.

"We can string him up ourselves," said the smallest of the men. His gaze was fixed on the bloody sword, still in Ben's hand.

"There is no need for that," said Dr. Rousseau. "Two of you can go to the city to alert the authorities, and the rest will guard this cabin so he's here waiting when they come to arrest him. He's not running anywhere with that foot, you can be sure of that."

There was muttering and whispering, but in the end the militiamen, unarmed as they were, withdrew. The small one was the last to go. He said, "Do you think you can get that sword away from him without getting stuck yourself?"

"Leave that to me," said Dr. Rousseau. "Organize a guard, and send to the city."

When the door closed there was a moment in which they looked at each other without speaking. Between them on the table, Honoré Poiterin lay with his back arched as if he had risen up to meet death.

Ben put his hands on her shoulders and turned her to him.

He said, "You've got to go get your father and brother. They're the only ones who can get me out of this cabin alive."

"But he was a spy," Hannah said, unable to look away from Poiterin. "There's a warrant for his arrest."

"Do you think that will matter?" Dr. Rousseau said. "Do you think that will make even the slightest difference, when a mixed-blood Indian kills a Creole of one of the first families?"

"You have to hurry," Ben said. "Those men are out there right now trying to work up the courage to come in here after me."

"I don't know where to go," Hannah said. "I don't know where to look for them."

Ben took her face between his hands and touched his forehead to hers. He said, "Listen. Listen to me now, and pay heed."

As a girl Hannah had taken great joy in running. She never felt more alive or free. Now, running toward a raging battle, she wanted nothing more than to fall to the ground and close her eyes.

To give in to her fear would be like putting a gun to Ben's head and pulling the trigger, she knew that. And so Hannah picked up her pace, searching for landmarks in the

haze of gunsmoke, dodging men who seemed to take no
note of her, occupied as they were with moving ammunition and water and a dozen other things to the frontmost
lines. In the distance she could see the flash and flare of
hundreds of guns. The Rodriquez Canal, where the
Americans were dug in and fully occupied with mowing
down the waves of British soldiers that came and came and
came without pause.

A quarter hour brought her to the edge of the viprière.
Mud sucked at her feet and slowed her down, and she heard
herself gasping for breath. The taste of gunpowder on her
tongue, and of panic and fear.

She plunged into the dark of the viprière, and a hand
closed over her face.

The urge to struggle, to fight was almost more than she
could resist. It took tremendous effort to make herself relax,
to let her muscles go. The man behind her relaxed, too,
though his hand stayed clamped over her mouth.

He said, "Easy now, missy. Easy. Where you headed in the
middle of a firefight?"

When he let her go, she took a moment to draw in a
deep breath. Without turning she said, "I have a message
for Captain Juzan. Do you know where I can find him and
the Choctaws?"

"A message, you say. You wouldn't be trying to get over
to the British side with your message, would you?"

"My father and brother are fighting under Juzan,"
Hannah said. "I need to get this message to him."

She felt the man's thoughts as he spun through them,
weighing his options. Then a half dozen or more rifle shots
echoed through the viprière.

"Sounds like Juzan's boys to me," he said. "But watch
yourself—it's more water than dirt underfoot, and there are
still a couple Britishers hiding out, waiting for the chance to
strike back."

Hannah felt her eyes filling with tears. Of relief, of aggravation. As soon as the stranger had taken his hands off her, she broke into a run, and a moment later the ciprière had closed around her. Dark even in the light of day, shadows on shadows. She waited for her eyesight to adjust, tried to sort out what she was hearing.

Sound bounced and echoed between water and sky. She remembered what Ben had told her, and paid attention to the way light moved on water as she picked her way forward. Listening for familiar voices, for some sign of the Choctaw. A warbling birdsong, one unfamiliar to her, rose and then repeated itself.

A fluttering of scarlet wings, and Hannah stopped where she was, remembering.

She gave a call of her own, one from home, one that her own people would recognize. She had learned this call from her uncle Runs-from-Bears, and she gave it now with all the strength she could pull from her lungs.

The call came back, faintly at first, and then louder. Hannah called and called again, and then they were there, her father and uncle and brother, filthy and wet and beautiful beyond all imagination.

"What the hell," her brother said.

The words exploded out of her, a long garbled sentence that could hardly make sense, but that they understood, nonetheless. Poiterin had followed them when they brought Wyndham to the cabin, and hid himself away to wait. When it was clear that the British were losing and his last chance was slipping away with them, his rage took over, and he found a way into the cabin.

"He was covered with blood," Hannah said. "But it wasn't his."

"Best get a move on," said Hannah's father with his usual dry common sense. "Before that man of yours gets himself strung up in the nearest tree."

"Ben can't walk," Hannah said. "Not for more than a few steps."

"Then he'll have to ride," said Bears. "Leave that to me."

Hannah stood back in the shadows and watched it all happen. Her father and brother, tall and well made and white-skinned, walking through the crowd of militiamen with all the confidence of conquering generals.

"Make way," Hannah heard her father bark. "Get out the way, you damn useless puppies. Go throw rocks at the lobsterbacks if that's the best you can manage."

Voices rose and fell. Luke followed the lead he had been given.

"We're here on official business. You feel the need to interfere with us, we'll find room for you in the Cabildo."

The crowd began to drift away, breaking up as it went. A few men stood at a distance watching as the strangers went into the cabin and then came out, moments later, with Ben Savard between them. He was limping heavily.

Nathaniel said, "We'll send a wagon for the bodies." And Hannah saw Dr. Rousseau standing in the open door.

The crowd of men had come drifting back. Hannah's father turned and scanned their faces. He said, "Maybe they didn't feel you boys was worthy of a rifle, but I got one here, and a musket, too, and a tomahawk for good measure. You interfere with us and you'll find out how good I am with them."

And that was all it took. Hannah watched the three of them move off. The urge to follow was almost more than she could stand.

When she came back into the cabin Poiterin's body had gone, and Dr. Rousseau was bent over a young man on the table. This one most definitely alive, and moaning in pain.

To Hannah the doctor said, "This is Alex Guzman, a

nephew of mine. He's got some metal in his leg that needs to come out."

Work was the only thing that could take her mind off of the last hour. Hannah went to the basin to wash her hands, and stayed there until they had stopped shaking.

CHAPTER 64

For the rest of the day they were occupied with minor wounds and injuries, nothing out of the ordinary for men in battle, and none of it life-threatening. When her thoughts drifted back to Ben, Hannah took on some task that required her full attention.

But he was persistent. He followed her when she went to fetch water, the image of him lying on the table with one leg in the air, grinning at her. Of the muscles in his arm flexing as he lunged and put a blade through Honoré Poiterin, as easily as another man would spit a bird.

Poiterin was dead; she had seen that for herself. Jennet could put away her nightmares, and Titine's mother and aunt would know some measure of relief. For her own part, any satisfaction Poiterin's death might have brought her was gone, lost in new fears for Ben's safety.

Because he had been drawn into the affair, Hannah told Dr. Rousseau some of their history with Poiterin. He had listened, his expression impassive, and when she finished it was a long while before he spoke.

He said, "We know what Honoré Poiterin is. What he was. May he rot in hell."

It was spoken with a hissing vehemence that worked like a balm to Hannah. She said, "What about Ben, do you think—"

"His life here is over," said the doctor. "The Creoles will never tolerate a free man of color who has killed one of their own. It's best he goes north with you."

"He told you?"

The other doctor nodded. "It's a loss for us."

"Yes," Hannah said. "I understand that it is."

It was sunset by the time word came to them that the battle was won. Jackson was not about to release his troops until he had convinced himself that the British weren't secretly preparing for another assault, but the general sense of things was that formal surrender would come within a day.

If Hannah had been disinclined to believe the reports, what came next convinced her. A steady stream of wagons left the battlefield filled with the wounded, hundreds and hundreds of them, and all British. The American casualties had been so minor that the army surgeons had been quite capable of keeping pace, but the British were overwhelmed.

There were troops from the West Indies among the wounded, dark-skinned men who would need care. Dr. Rousseau climbed up onto a wagon filled with them and lifted a hand in farewell. A few minutes later Hannah did the same. The mule driver paused long enough for her to lift her medical kit into the wagon bed, and then with a chirrup the wagon lurched and began the slow, rough ride back to the city. In the space of the journey Hannah watched three men die of wounds no doctor could have fixed, two of them never regaining consciousness and another who wept without pause. There was no water to give any of them, but she could break open her kit and what was left of her supplies: some tea, a little brandy, and for the worst of them, the rest of the laudanum.

The Levee Road curved hard to the right and the wagon creaked and groaned. Hannah looked up for a moment and was struck by the sight of so many wagons, dozens of all kinds and shapes, moving in convoy toward the city. On the far side of the river the sky was darkening, blue and gold giving way to pewter gray. The last of the sunlight moved and flexed, touching the bayonet of one of the guards who walked along beside the wagons, a brass button, an open and sightless eye.

As they came into the city, the citizens of New Orleans hurried forward to meet them. There was little of jubilation in the faces that pressed close to the wagons, but then they had seen what destruction Jackson's men had wrought, and it was enough. More than enough. Wounded men were sent off to the hospitals, to the Savards' clinic, to the homes of gentlewomen who came forward to offer guest rooms and personal care with such open generosity that Hannah must pause and remember that this was New Orleans, too. These same people who would hang Ben Savard if they got the chance wept for wounded soldiers and took them home to sleep on fine linen.

She would spend the rest of her life trying to make sense of it all, but she would do that at home. They would be going home, all of them.

She found Ben in a bed in the clinic, his head cleverly wrapped in gauze so that no one might recognize him as anything more than a wounded soldier. Which he was.

"There's some fever," Paul Savard told her. "But not much. The heel has already begun to seep."

Hannah said, "How long can he stay here safely?"

Paul had no answer to that question and neither did Julia, but Jennet, who sat beside Ben whenever she could be spared from other work, had an opinion.

"We mustn't take chances," she said. "We have to get him

away. After all he's done for us, we have to get him safely away."

Hannah thought these things through in the long hours that she spent in the surgery with Dr. Savard. They took off hands and arms and legs, sutured gashes and tied off arteries, and made lists of the living and the dead for the quartermaster who called for such information.

A young Highlander who had lost part of one foot and would certainly lose an eye stared up at them in his delirium and spoke in long strings that meant nothing to Hannah.

"Gaelic," said the doctor. Hannah was sorry not to be able to listen to the story the boy needed to tell.

Well past midnight, when she had been on her feet for twenty-four hours, Hannah went back to sit beside Ben's cot in the clinic and found another man there instead.

She went to the apartment, but Ben was not there, either, or anywhere else she looked. She did find her father.

"It was best he slip away now," he said. "Before anybody came looking for him."

"He just left?" Hannah asked. "He took no leave of anyone?"

"I cain't say about his brother or his guid-sister," said Hannah's father. "But I know for a fact that he ain't took leave of you."

It was many days before she saw Ben again. Working in the clinic, moving from apothecary to surgery to apartment, Hannah sometimes convinced herself that he was dead, and no one had the heart to tell her so.

Urquhart came again to ask questions, this time about Poiterin's death. If she had seen Savard strike Poiterin down, and if she would testify to such a thing.

"Am I allowed to give evidence in Louisiana?" she asked, trying to sound innocent.

It was not an answer to his question and he wouldn't be put off, so finally Hannah told him what she wanted him to hear. She said, "I tended Ben Savard for a wound in his foot. That's the last time I talked to him. Where he is now, I really have no idea."

In the courtyard, Luke worked on converting the caissons they had taken from the British into something more appropriate for transporting women and children. Hannah's father and uncle went out hunting, and came back with a good-sized alligator, which Clémentine helped them clean, much to Henry's satisfaction.

On the morning they were ready to go, Rachel decided that she'd rather stay in New Orleans after all, and only a long quiet talk with her mother could convince her otherwise. Her trunks loaded, she let Luke hand her up into the wagon, tears streaming down her face.

Henry, red in the face from his determination not to weep, saluted his sister and then called. "I'm coming, too, one day," he said. "Watch and see." But he stayed just where he was, held to this particular patch of earth by the ties to his mother and father.

Hannah was taking one last look around Ben's apartment when she saw that some women had come into the courtyard. All of them elderly, and all wearing colorful tignons on their heads. Standing at the window she recognized Zuzu, and then Titine's aunt Amazilie and finally, after a long moment in which she fought with tears, Valerie Maurepas, leaning on a cane, and Gaetane, her maidservant.

Jennet met her as she came down the stairs. "You'll never guess," she said. "Honoré was married, and his wife wants to make reparations. She has given Valerie Maurepas back her cottage, for a start."

It could not replace the daughter she had lost, that

Hannah knew with certainty. She went to tell Valerie Maurepas what the old woman already knew but would need to hear from her, most especially: that a thousand cottages were not worth a woman like Titine. And to express her sorrow, and her gratitude.

CHAPTER 65

The wagons pulled out into the street under overcast and rainy skies. Nathaniel Bonner drove one team and Runs-from-Bears the other, while Luke rode alongside the wagons on a sturdy horse. Jennet could look up at any time and see him there, his eyes narrowed as he kept watch.

"The war is over for us," she told him, and tried to believe that it was true. Jennet glanced at Hannah, who sat next to her father with young Nathan in her lap. Her complexion was drawn and stark with worry, and Jennet thought her own face must look much the same.

"Where is he?" she asked Luke, for the tenth or fiftieth time.

"Patience," said her husband, and moved his horse out of the reach of her pinching fingers. To Jennet's eye he looked more concerned than he would admit, and this kept her awake that first night, when they made camp under a clear and cold night sky.

On the second day they made camp after crossing into Mississippi. The women and children slept in the covered beds of the wagons; the men put bedrolls on the ground when they weren't on watch. Jennet felt safe, but unsettled. Her mood subdued, watchful, reluctantly hopeful. She saw those same things in Hannah's face.

By the light of the cook fire Jennet thought of the things

she would say to Ben Savard if she ever saw him again. And if it meant digging him up to say those things, she would have that satisfaction.

When next Jennet looked up, he was there, standing behind Hannah.

Hannah saw Jennet's expression and understood before she even got to her feet that everything had changed. It was in her smile as she turned and Ben Savard's arms came up to draw her in to him. It was in their faces, full of light and promise.

EPILOGUE

Dear Paul and Julia,

Do you recall my promise that, as soon as we reached
Paradise, I would write to tell you of our journey?
My good intentions were all for naught, as we have
been here three days full, and it is just this morning
that I sit down with pen in hand. To tell the whole
truth, I should not have recalled but for the sight of
my guid-brother Ben, who sits opposite me writing a
letter to young Henry.

It is my hope that you will forgive my
muddleheaded ways when I tell you that while the
journey was long and hard at times—no doubt Ben is
writing the story of the bear and the wildcat in his
letter to Henry at this very moment—we survived
and we are here, healthy and whole. I trust, too, that
you've had a long letter from Rachel with the tale of
the two brothers in Kentucky who proposed to her
on first sight, tripping over their own feet in the rush
to be the first. And how after she had given her polite
refusal, they fell to pummeling each other when they
could not agree on which of them she had rejected
more reluctantly. One day soon I will write down the
whole story of the journey, and bind it up in a book.

Gabriel claims it's far more interesting a story than the bits his mother reads aloud from the newspapers.

The babies are in good fettle. Young Nathan took his first steps one evening in Pennsylvania, and landed on his bottom in a puddle of spring mud, which suited him so well that for the rest of the journey he took every opportunity to repeat the performance. Adam crows and coos when he catches sight of his older brother, and truth be told, a soothing word from Nathan does far more to settle Adam when he's out of sorts than anything I might think to do.

Luke and I talk evenings of what we shall do next, and how hard it will be to leave Lake in the Clouds. And should we decide to make our home here, we must still return to Montreal so that Luke can see to the disposition of Forbes & Sons, which after all belongs to my brother, and canna simply be tossed aside. For my part I should be glad to stay here and raise up the boys in Paradise, but where Luke goes, so shall I, as the tail must follow the dog.

Of your brother and my guid-sister there is little to say that you canna imagine for yourselves. Ben is determined to make a good start here, and to that end he has spent our first three days with Elizabeth and Curiosity, answering their questions and telling his own story. Strangely enough most of what Curiosity wants to know of him has naught to do with Ben himself or what kind of husband he'll make. She's far more interested in his opinion on Mr. Shakespeare's plays, and politics, and they often fall into intense discussion.

These days Hannah rises every morning smiling, and sometimes she sings, when there's nobody nearby to hear her. She's got a lovely voice, deep and true, but truth be told, it would please me were she to honk like an angry goose. The sound of her singing says to me that Hannah is happy, truly happy as she hasnae been for far too long.

As for Ben, I can tell you that he is full of questions and observations and that he has already learned enough Mohawk to understand a simple conversation and take his part in it. He swims in the lake under the waterfalls at sunrise with the other men, and goes out with Gabriel to explore the mountain, and has visited Daniel in the schoolhouse and the little cabin where he lives alone close by the strawberry fields. But mostly he spends his time with Hannah, and he takes great pleasure in teasing her, almost as much pleasure as she takes in being teased. In short they are both as happy as is right and pleasing for those newly wed. It fills us all with joy to see them together, and while it will be hard for you to have him so far removed, I trust you will be as glad for them as are we all.

Your good friend and true,
Jennet Bonner
Lake in the Clouds
April 20, 1815

To our dearest girl Lily and her Simon,

The war is done, your father and uncle and sisters and brothers are home safe and whole, and all is well in our universe but for the fact that you and Simon are so far away and cannot join in our celebration.

I have great good news for you, but let me say first that Luke and Jennet have brought us not one but two healthy grandsons. The younger one is a war orphan they adopted, and he is called Adam. A bright

and happy child indeed. The elder boy is the exact
image of the grandfather he is named for, and I fear
he will be as energetic as Daniel and Gabriel rolled
together into a single wriggling boy. We call him
Nathan. Many-Doves will give both boys their
Kahnyen'kehàka boy-names just as soon as she
knows them.

I simply cannot wait any longer to give you our
most surprising and happy news: Your sister Hannah
has come home with a new husband. He is called
Ben, though his full name is Jean-Benoît Savard,
originally of New Orleans. The first and most
important thing to say about Ben Savard is the simple
fact that Hannah loves him, and he is devoted to her.
He was raised by strong women of the Choctaw
tribe, and is descended from others like them among
the Seminole, as well as from those who were
brought to this continent in chains. He is a man who
has no illusions about controlling Hannah, which
bodes well for their marriage.

After the first afternoon she spent in his company
Curiosity remarked that Ben reminded her of
Galileo, a compliment of the highest order, as well
you know. And in fact there is something of Galileo's
calm and sharp intelligence and wry good humor in
Ben Savard. Beyond that, in the course of the long
journey home he earned your father's and your
uncle's respect and regard, things they do not bestow
lightly.

You will have a hundred questions, but I cannot
spend all day at my desk, and so I suggest simply that
you come for a long visit. I would like to have all the
children around me for a while at least. Ben and
Hannah are to live with Curiosity, as she will hear
of no other plan, and Luke and Jennet intend to stay

through the spring at least, when they will come to
Canada to see to business affairs.

All I require for perfect happiness is to have you
and Simon join us, so that you may hear the many
stories there are to tell, and tell your own in turn.

Your loving mother,
Elizabeth Middleton Bonner
Lake in the Clouds
on the west branch of the Sacandaga
in the village of Paradise

Author's Notes

The War of 1812 is not widely studied or known, something which has always struck me as odd. My interest in that war is part of the reason this story exists. I have tried to tell a little of what happened here and in the novel that precedes this one in the Wilderness series (*Fire Along the Sky*) but it is only a very little. It would require many novels told from many different perspectives to give a reader any real sense of the importance of what some still call the Second Revolution.

In the process of writing these two novels I have consulted the work of dozens of historians. A list of reference works is available on my Web site, but in all fairness I must make two things clear: While I have tried to stay true to the facts, the demands of the story sometimes outweighed the dictates of the historical record, and thus a student of the period will find infelicities. Those I claim as my own. The stuff I get right I owe to the historians and librarians, such as the good people at the Historic New Orleans Collection, who dug out piles of old books and microfilm for me and answered endless questions.

I owe thanks to so many people who have been helpful and supportive along the way. These include Wendy McCurdy, who originally acquired the Wilderness books for Bantam; Shauna Summers, who has picked up where Wendy had to leave off; my agent, Jill Grinberg; my husband and daughter; and the readers who have been so faithful and vocal.

You will be wondering now about unfinished business. About Daniel and Gabriel and Carrie, about Jemima and Martha and all the others whose stories have not come to a conclusion. I fully intend to finish the tale, if you want to hear it, and if you can be patient.

Sara Donati
aka Rosina Lippi
www.rosinalippi.com

About the Author

SARA DONATI is the pen name of Rosina Lippi. She lives with her husband, daughter, and various pets in an area between the Cascade Mountains and the Pacific Northwest Coast. Visit her weblog at www.rosinalippi.com for news about her next novel.